THE GLASS PALACE

Rajkumar is only a boy, helping out on a market stall in the dusty square outside the royal palace in Mandalay, when the British force the Burmese King, Queen and court into exile.

Thus begins *The Glass Palace*, a novel that not only grasps the reach and fall of empires across the twentieth century, but also maps with unerring skill the rival geography of the human heart.

In the upheaval that follows the British arrival in Mandalay and the shattering of the kingdom of the Glass Palace, Rajkumar, a stateless orphan in a tattered lunghi, is lifted on the tides of chaos deep into the teak forests of upper Burma. There, with the help of an itinerant merchant from Malacca, he will make his fortune. Yet he is haunted by the vision of Dolly, a child attendant of the royal entourage being escorted under armed guard into exile in India. So, now adult and wealthy, he leaves Burma to find her.

Through the intertwining stories of Dolly and Rajkumar, the history of the twentieth century is told across three generations, spread over three interlinked parts of the British Empire: Burma, with its conflicting undercurrents of discontent; Malaya, with its vast rubber plantations, and India, amid growing opposition to British rule. Here, too, is the story of Dolly, bound to the magisterial Queen Supayalat, and her ill-fated struggle to maintain the standard of a vanished court while living in exile in the small Indian district town of Ratnagiri. Through Arjun, an Indian officer and soldier of the Empire, the story moves into another generation, one caught in the crossfire between old loyalties and new aspirations. With World War II and the terrifying arrival of the Japanese juggernaut, Rajkumar is again set adrift. In an ocean of refugees fleeing war and devastation, he and his family make a treacherous one thousand-mile trek across the border to India. The door to Burma closes behind them and the glittering light of an extraordinary civilisation is at last extinguished.

In *The Glass Palace*, Amitav Ghosh, the highly praised author of *The Calcutta Chromosome* and *The Shadow Lines*, has conceived a shimmering and monumental epic.

Amitav Ghosh was born in Calcutta and spent his childhood in Bangladesh, Sri Lanka and northern India. He studied in Delhi, Oxford and Egypt and has taught in various Indian and American universities. He is the author of a travel book and two novels. He has written for *Granta*, the *New Yorker*, the *New York Times* and the *Observer*. He is married and lives in New York with his two children

By the same author

THE CIRCLE OF REASON
THE CALCUTTA CHROMOSOME
IN AN ANTIQUE LAND
THE SHADOW LINES

THE GLASS PALACE

AMITAV GHOSH

HarperCollins *Publishers*

First published by HarperCollins Publishers UK 2000

First published in India by
HarperCollins *Publishers* India 2000

First impression 2011

ISBN 13: 978-0-00-742746-8

This novel is entirely a work of fiction. The names, characters and incidents portrayed in it are the work of the author's imagination. Any resemblance to actual persons, living or dead, events or localities is entirely coincidental.

A catalogue record for this book is available
from the British Library.

Cover Photography © Nigel Amies/Impact Photos

HarperCollins *Publishers*
A-53, Sector 57, NOIDA, Uttar Pradesh - 201301, India
77-85 Fulham Palace Road, London W6 8JB, United Kingdom
Hazelton Lanes, 55 Avenue Road, Suite 2900, Toronto, Ontario M5R 3L2
and 1995 Markham Road, Scarborough, Ontario M1B 5M8, Canada
25 Ryde Road, Pymble, Sydney, NSW 2073, Australia
31 View Road, Glenfield, Auckland 10, New Zealand
10 East 53rd Street, New York NY 10022, USA

Printed and bound at
Thomson Press (India) Ltd.

To my father's memory

CONTENTS

Acknowledgments

pp. 15–16: adapted from W. S. Desai: *Deposed King Thebaw of Burma in India, 1885–1916*, Bharatiya Vidya Series, Vol 25, Bharatiya Vidya Bhavan, Bombay, 1967 (appendix VII, p. 119)

p. 89: adapted from, Patricia Herbert, *The Hsaya San Rebellion (1930–1932) reappraised*, Monash Univ., Melbourne, 1982 (p. 5)

p. 349: from Majjhima Nikaya [adapted from *The Buddhist Tradition in India, China and Japan*, ed. W. T. de Bary, Vintage, New York, 1972; p. 27]

p. 350: from Samyutta Nikaya [adapted from *The Buddhist Tradition in India, China and Japan*, ed. W. T. de Bary, Vintage, New York, 1972; p. 16]

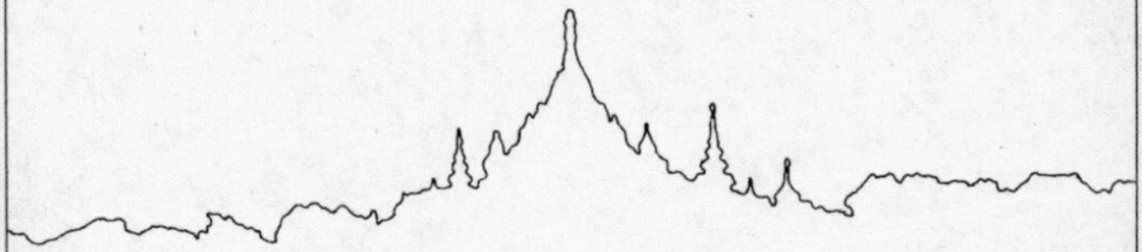

PART ONE

Mandalay

One

There was only one person in the food-stall who knew exactly what that sound was that was rolling in across the plain, along the silver curve of the Irrawaddy, to the western wall of Mandalay's fort. His name was Rajkumar and he was an Indian, a boy of eleven – not an authority to be relied upon.

The noise was unfamiliar and unsettling, a distant booming followed by low, stuttering growls. At times it was like the snapping of dry twigs, sudden and unexpected. And then, abruptly, it would change to a deep rumble, shaking the food-stall and rattling its steaming pot of soup. The stall had only two benches, and they were both packed with people, sitting pressed up against each other. It was cold, the start of central Burma's brief but chilly winter, and the sun had not risen high enough yet to burn off the damp mist that had drifted in at dawn from the river. When the first booms reached the stall there was a silence, followed by a flurry of questions and whispered answers. People looked around in bewilderment: What is it? *Ba le?* What can it be? And then Rajkumar's sharp, excited voice cut through the buzz of speculation. 'English cannon,' he said in his fluent but heavily accented Burmese. 'They're shooting somewhere up the river. Heading in this direction.'

Frowns appeared on some customers' faces as they noted that it was the serving-boy who had spoken and that he was a *kalaa* from across the sea – an Indian, with teeth as white as his eyes and skin the colour of polished hardwood. He was standing in the centre of the stall, holding a pile of chipped ceramic bowls. He was grinning a little sheepishly, as though embarrassed to parade his precocious knowingness.

His name meant Prince, but he was anything but princely in appearance, with his oil-splashed vest, his untidily knotted *longyi* and his bare feet with their thick slippers of callused skin. When people asked how old he was he said fifteen, or sometimes eighteen or nineteen, for it gave him a sense of strength and power to be able to exaggerate so wildly, to pass himself off as grown and strong, in body and judgement, when he was, in fact, not much more than a child. But he could have said he was twenty and people would still have believed him, for he was a big, burly boy, taller and broader in the shoulder than many men. And because he was very dark it was hard to tell that his chin was as smooth as the palms of his hands, innocent of all but the faintest trace of fuzz.

It was chance alone that was responsible for Rajkumar's presence in Mandalay that November morning. His boat – the sampan on which he worked as a helper and errand-boy – had been found to need repairs after sailing up the Irrawaddy from the Bay of Bengal. The boatowner had taken fright on being told that the work might take as long as a month, possibly even longer. He couldn't afford to feed his crew that long, he'd decided: some of them would have to find other jobs. Rajkumar was told to walk to the city, a couple of miles inland. At a bazaar, opposite the west wall of the fort, he was to ask for a woman called Ma Cho. She was half-Indian and she ran a small food-stall; she might have some work for him.

And so it happened that at the age of eleven, walking into the city of Mandalay, Rajkumar saw, for the first time, a straight road. By the sides of the road there were bamboo-walled shacks and palm-thatched shanties, pats of dung and piles of refuse. But the straight course of the road's journey was unsmudged by the clutter that flanked it: it was like a causeway, cutting across a choppy sea. Its lines led the eye right through the city, past the bright red walls of the fort to the distant pagodas of Mandalay hill, shining like a string of white bells upon the slope.

For his age, Rajkumar was well-travelled. The boat he worked on was a coastal craft that generally kept to open waters, plying the long length of shore that joined Burma to Bengal. Rajkumar had been to Chittagong and Bassein and any number of towns and villages in between. But in all his travels he had never come across thoroughfares like those in Mandalay. He was accustomed to lanes and alleys that curled endlessly around themselves so that you could never see beyond the next curve. Here was something new: a road that followed a straight, unvarying course, bringing the horizon right into the middle of habitation.

When the fort's full immensity revealed itself, Rajkumar came to a halt in the middle of the road. The citadel was a miracle to behold, with its mile-long walls and its immense moat. The crenellated ramparts were almost three storeys high, but of a soaring lightness, red in colour, and topped by ornamented gateways with seven-tiered roofs. I ong straight roads radiated outwards from the walls, forming a neat geometrical grid. So intriguing was the ordered pattern of these streets that Rajkumar wandered far afield, exploring. It was almost dark by the time he remembered why he'd been sent to the city. He made his way back to the the fort's western wall and asked for Ma Cho.

'Ma Cho?'

'She has a stall where she sells food – *baya-gyaw* and other things. She's half-Indian.'

'Ah, Ma Cho.' It made sense that this ragged-looking Indian boy was looking for Ma Cho: she often had Indian strays working at her stall. 'There she is, the thin one.'

Ma Cho was small and harried-looking, with spirals of wiry hair hanging over her forehead, like a fringed awning. She was in her mid-thirties, more Burmese than Indian in appearance. She was busy frying vegetables, squinting at the smoking oil from the shelter of an upthrust arm. She glared at Rajkumar suspiciously: 'What do you want?'

He had just begun to explain about the boat and the repairs and wanting a job for a few weeks, when she interrupted him. She began to shout at the top of her voice, with her eyes closed: 'What do you think – I have jobs under my armpits, to pluck out and hand to you? Last week a boy ran away with two of my pots. Who's to tell me you won't do the same?' And so on.

Rajkumar understood that this outburst was not aimed directly at him: that it had more to do with the dust, the splattering oil and the price of vegetables than with his own presence or with anything he had said. He lowered his eyes and stood there stoically, kicking the dust until she was done.

She paused, panting, and looked him over. 'Who are your parents?' she said at last, wiping her streaming forehead on the sleeve of her sweat-stained *aingyi*.

'I don't have any. They died.'

She thought this over, biting her lip. 'All right. Get to work, but remember you're not going to get much more than three meals and a place to sleep.'

He grinned. 'That's all I need.'

Ma Cho's stall consisted of a couple of benches, sheltered beneath the stilts of a bamboo-walled hut. She did her cooking sitting by an open fire, perched on a small stool. Apart from fried baya-gyaw, she also served noodles and soup. It was Rajkumar's job to carry bowls of soup and noodles to the customers. In his spare moments he cleared away the utensils, tended the fire and shredded vegetables for the soup pot. Ma Cho didn't trust him with fish or meat and chopped them herself with a grinning short-handled *da*. In the evenings he did the washing-up, carrying bucketfuls of utensils over to the fort's moat.

Between Ma Cho's stall and the moat there lay a wide, dusty roadway that ran all the way around the fort, forming an immense square. Rajkumar had only to cross this apron of open space to get to the moat. Directly across from Ma Cho's stall lay a bridge that led to one of the fort's smaller entrances, the funeral gate. He had cleared a pool under the bridge by pushing away the lotus pads that covered the surface of the water. This had become his spot: it was there that he usually did his washing and bathing – under the bridge, with the wooden planks above serving as his ceiling and shelter.

On the far side of the bridge lay the walls of the fort. All that could be seen of its interior was a nine-roofed spire that ended in a glittering gilded umbrella – this was the great golden *hti* of Burma's kings. Under the spire lay the throne room of the palace, where Thebaw, King of Burma, held court with his chief consort, Queen Supayalat.

Rajkumar was curious about the fort but he knew that for those such as himself its precincts were forbidden ground. 'Have you ever been inside?' he asked Ma Cho one day. 'The fort, I mean?'

'Oh yes.' Ma Cho nodded importantly. 'Three times, at the very least.'

'What is it like in there?'

'It's very large, much larger than it looks. It's a city in itself, with long roads and canals and gardens. First you come to the houses of officials and noblemen. And then you find yourself in front of a stockade, made of huge teakwood posts. Beyond lie the apartments of the Royal Family and their servants – hundreds and hundreds of rooms, with gilded pillars and polished floors. And right at the centre there is a vast hall that is like a great shaft of light, with shining crystal walls and mirrored ceilings. People call it the Glass Palace.'

'Does the King ever leave the fort?

'Not in the last seven years. But the Queen and her maids sometimes walk along the walls. People who've seen them say that her maids are the most beautiful women in the land.'

'Who are they, these maids?'

'Young girls, orphans, many of them just children. They say that the girls are brought to the palace from the far mountains. The Queen adopts them and brings them up and they serve as her handmaids. They say that she will not trust anyone but them to wait on her and her children.'

'When do these girls visit the gateposts?' said Rajkumar. 'How can one catch sight of them?'

His eyes were shining, his face full of eagerness. Ma Cho laughed at him. 'Why, are you thinking of trying to get in there, you fool of an Indian, you coal-black kalaa? They'll know you from a mile off and cut off your head.'

That night, lying flat on his mat, Rajkumar looked through the gap between his feet and caught sight of the gilded hti that marked the palace: it glowed like a beacon in the moonlight. No matter what Ma Cho said, he decided, he would cross the moat – before he left Mandalay, he would find a way in.

* * *

Ma Cho lived above the stall in a bamboo-walled room that was held up by stilts. A flimsy splinter-studded ladder connected the room to the stall below. Rajkumar's nights were spent under Ma Cho's dwelling, between the stilts, in the space that served to seat customers during the day. Ma Cho's floor was roughly put together, from planks of wood that didn't quite fit. When Ma Cho lit her lamp to change her clothes, Rajkumar could see her clearly through the cracks in the floor. Lying on his back, with his fingers knotted behind his head, he would look up unblinking, as she untied the aingyi that was knotted loosely round her breasts.

During the day Ma Cho was a harried and frantic termagant, racing from one job to another, shouting shrilly at everyone who came her way. But at night, with the day's work done, a certain languor entered her movements. She would cup her breasts and air them, fanning herself with her hands; she would run her fingers slowly through the cleft of her chest, past the pout of her belly, down to her legs and thighs. Watching her from below, Rajkumar's hand would snake slowly past the knot of his longyi, down to his groin.

One night Rajkumar woke suddenly to the sound of a rhythmic creaking in the planks above, along with moans and gasps and urgent drawings of breath. But who could be up there with her? He had seen no one going in.

The next morning, Rajkumar saw a small, bespectacled, owl-like man climbing down the ladder that led to Ma Cho's room. The stranger was dressed in European clothes: a shirt, trousers, and a pith hat. Subjecting Rajkumar to a grave and prolonged regard, the stranger ceremoniously raised his hat. 'How are you?' he said. *'Kaisa hai? Sub kuchh theek-thaak?'*

Rajkumar understood the words perfectly well – they were what he might have expected an Indian to say – but his mouth still dropped open in surprise. Since coming to Mandalay he had encountered many different kinds of people, but this stranger belonged with none of them. His clothes were those of a European and he seemed to know Hindustani – and yet the cast of his face was neither that of a white man nor an Indian. He looked, in fact, to be Chinese.

Smiling at Rajkumar's astonishment, the man doffed his hat again, before disappearing into the bazaar.

'Who was that?' Rajkumar said to Ma Cho when she came down the ladder.

The question evidently annoyed her and she glared at him to make it clear that she would prefer not to answer. But Rajkumar's curiosity was aroused now, and he persisted. 'Who was that, Ma Cho? Tell me.'

'That is . . .' Ma Cho began to speak in small, explosive bursts, as though her words were being produced by upheavals in her belly. 'That is . . . my teacher . . . my Sayagyi.'

'Your teacher?'

'Yes . . . He teaches me . . . He knows about many things . . .'

'What things?'

'Never mind.'

'Where did he learn to speak Hindustani?'

'Abroad, but not in India . . . he's from somewhere in Malaya. Malacca I think. You should ask him.'

'What's his name?'

'It doesn't matter. You will call him Saya, just as I do.'

'Just Saya?'

'Saya John.' She turned on him in exasperation. 'That's what we all call him. If you want to know any more, ask him yourself.'

Reaching into her cold cooking fire, she drew out a handful of ash and threw it at Rajkumar. 'Who said you could sit here talking all morning, you half-wit kalaa? Now you get busy with your work.'

There was no sign of Saya John that night or the next.

'Ma Cho,' said Rajkumar, 'what's happened to your teacher? Why hasn't he come again?'

Ma Cho was sitting at her fire, frying baya-gyaw. Peering into the hot oil, she said shortly, 'He's away.'

'Where?'

'In the jungle . . .'

'The jungle? Why?'

'He's a contractor. He delivers supplies to teak camps. He's away most of the time.' Suddenly the ladle dropped from her grasp and she buried her face in her hands.

Hesitantly Rajkumar went to her side. 'Why are you crying, Ma Cho?' He ran a hand over her head in an awkward gesture of sympathy. 'Do you want to marry him?'

She reached for the folds of his frayed longyi and dabbed at her tears with the bunched cloth. 'His wife died a year or two ago. She was Chinese, from Singapore. He has a son, a little boy. He says he'll never marry again.'

'Maybe he'll change his mind.'

She pushed him away with one of her sudden gestures of exasperation. 'You don't understand, you thick-headed kalaa. He's a Christian. Every time he comes to visit me, he has to go to his church next morning to pray and ask forgiveness. Do you think I would want to marry a man like that?' She snatched her ladle off the ground and shook it at him. 'Now you get back to work or I'll fry your black face in hot oil . . .'

A few days later Saya John was back. Once again he greeted Rajkumar in his broken Hindustani: '*Kaisa hai? Sub kuchh theek-thaak?*'

Rajkumar fetched him a bowl of noodles and stood watching as he ate. 'Saya,' he asked at last, in Burmese, 'how did you learn to speak an Indian language?'

Saya John looked up at him and smiled. 'I learnt as a child,' he said, 'for I am, like you, an orphan, a foundling. I was brought up by Catholic priests, in a town called Malacca. These men were from everywhere – Portugal, Macao, Goa. They gave me my name – John Martins, which was not what it has become. They used to call me João, but I changed this later to John. They spoke many many languages, those priests, and from the Goans I learnt a few Indian words. When I was old enough to work I went to Singapore, where I was for a while an orderly in a military hospital. The soldiers there were mainly Indians and they asked me this very question: how is it that you, who look Chinese and carry a Christian name, can speak our language? When I told them how this had come about, they would laugh and say, you are a *dhobi ka kutta* – a washerman's dog – *na ghar ka na ghat ka* – you don't belong anywhere, either by the water or on land, and I'd say, yes, that is exactly what I am.' He laughed, with an infectious hilarity, and Rajkumar joined in.

One day Saya John brought his son to the stall. The boy's name was Matthew and he was seven, a handsome, bright-eyed child, with an air of precocious self-possession. He had just arrived from Singapore, where he lived with his mother's family and studied at a well-known missionary school. A couple of times each year, Saya John arranged for him to come over to Burma for a holiday.

It was early evening, usually a busy time at the stall, but in honour of her visitors, Ma Cho decided to close down for the day. Drawing Rajkumar aside, she told him to take Matthew for a walk, just for an hour or so. There was a *pwe* on at the other end of the fort; the boy would enjoy the fairground bustle.

'And remember –' here her gesticulations became fiercely incoherent – 'not a word about . . .'

'Don't worry,' Rajkumar gave her an innocent smile. 'I won't say anything about your lessons.'

'Idiot kalaa.' Bunching her fists, she rained blows upon his back. 'Get out – out of here.'

Rajkumar changed into his one good longyi and put on a frayed *pinni* vest that Ma Cho had given him. Saya John pressed a few coins into his palm. 'Buy something – for the both of you, treat yourselves.'

On the way to the pwe, they were distracted by a peanut-seller. Matthew was hungry and he insisted that Rajkumar buy them both armloads of peanuts. They went to sit by the moat, with their feet dangling in the water, spreading the nuts around them, in their wrappers of dried leaf.

Matthew pulled a piece of paper out of his pocket. There was a picture on it – of a cart with three wire-spoked wheels, two large ones at the back and a single small one in front. Rajkumar stared at it, frowning: it appeared to be a light carriage, but there were no shafts for a horse or an ox.

'What is it?'

'A motorwagon.' Matthew pointed out the details – the small internal-combustion engine, the vertical crankshaft, the horizontal flywheel. He explained that the machine could generate almost as much power as a horse, running at speeds of up to eight miles an hour. It had been unveiled that very year, 1885, in Germany, by Karl Benz.

'One day,' Matthew said quietly, 'I am going to own one of these.' His tone was not boastful and Rajkumar did not doubt him for a minute. He was hugely impressed that a child of that age could know his mind so well on such a strange subject.

Then Matthew said: 'How did you come to be here, in Mandalay?'

'I was working on a boat, a sampan, like those you see on the river.'

'And where are your parents? Your family?'

'I don't have any.' Rajkumar paused. 'I lost them.'

Matthew cracked a nut between his teeth. 'How?'

'There was a fever, a sickness. In our town, Akyab, many people died.'

'But you lived?'

'Yes. I was sick, but I lived. In my family I was the only one. I had a father, a sister, brothers . . .'

'And a mother?'

'And a mother.'

Rajkumar's mother had died on a sampan that was tethered in a mangrove-lined estuary. He remembered the tunnel-like shape of the boat's galley and its roof of hooped cane and thatch; there was an oil lamp beside his mother's head, on one of the crosswise planks of the hull. Its flickering yellow flame was dulled by a halo of night-time insects. The night was still and airless, with the mangroves and their dripping roots standing thick against the breeze, cradling the boat between deep banks of mud. Yet there was a kind of restlessness in the moist darkness around the boat. Every now and again, he'd hear the splash of seed pods arrowing into the water, and the slippery sound of fish, stirring in the mud. It was hot in the sampan's burrow-like galley, but his mother was shivering. Rajkumar had scoured the boat, covering her with every piece of cloth that he could find.

Rajkumar knew the fever well by that time. It had come to their house through his father, who worked every day at a warehouse, near the port. He was a quiet man, who made his living as a *dubash* and a *munshi* – a translator and clerk – working for a succession of merchants along the eastern shore of the Bay of Bengal. Their family home was in the port of Chittagong, but his father had quarrelled with their relatives and moved the family away, drifting slowly down the coast, peddling his knowledge of figures and languages, settling eventually in Akyab, the principal port of the Arakan – that tidewater stretch of coast where Burma and Bengal collide in a whirlpool of unease. There he'd remained for some dozen years, fathering three children – of these the oldest was Rajkumar. Their home was on an inlet that smelt of drying fish. Their family name was Raha, and when their neighbours asked who they were and where they came from they would say they were Hindus from Chittagong. That was all Rajkumar knew about his family's past.

Rajkumar was the next to fall sick, after his father. He had returned to consciousness to find himself recovering at sea, with his mother. They were on their way back to their native Chittagong, she told him, and there were just the two of them now – the others were gone.

The sailing had been slow because the currents were against them. The square-sailed sampan and her crew of *khalasis* had fought their way up the coast, hugging the shore. Rajkumar had recovered quickly, but then it was his mother's turn to sicken. With Chittagong just a couple of days away she had begun to shiver. The shore was thick with mangrove forests; one evening, the boatowner had pulled the sampan into a creek and settled down to wait.

Rajkumar had covered his mother with all the saris in her cloth bundle, with longyis borrowed from the boatmen, even a folded sail. But he'd no sooner finished than her teeth began to chatter again, softly, like dice. She called him to her side, beckoning with a forefinger. When he lowered his ear to her lips, he could feel her body glowing like hot charcoal against his cheek.

She showed him a knot on the tail end of her sari. There was a gold bangle wrapped in it. She pulled it out and gave it to him to hide in the waist knot of his sarong. The *nakhoda*, the boat's owner, was a trustworthy old man, she told him; Rajkumar was to give him the bangle when they reached Chittagong – only then, not before.

She folded his fingers around the bangle: warmed by the fiery heat of her body, the metal seemed to singe its shape into his palm. 'Stay alive,' she whispered. '*Beche thako*, Rajkumar. Live, my Prince; hold on to your life.'

When her voice faded away Rajkumar became suddenly aware of the faint flip-flop sound of catfish burrowing in the mud. He looked up to see the boatowner, the nakhoda, squatting in the prow of the sampan, puffing on his coconut-shell hookah, fingering his thin, white beard. His crewmen were sitting clustered round him, watching Rajkumar. They were hugging their sarong-draped knees. The boy could not tell whether it was pity or impatience that lay behind the blankness in their eyes.

He had only the bangle now: his mother had wanted him to use it to pay for his passage back to Chittagong. But his mother was dead and what purpose would it serve to go back to a place that his father had abandoned? No, better instead to strike a bargain with the nakhoda. Rajkumar took the old man aside and asked to join the crew, offering the bangle as a gift of apprenticeship.

The old man looked him over. The boy was strong and willing, and, what was more, he had survived the killer fever that had emptied so many of the towns and villages of the coast. That alone spoke of certain useful qualities of body and spirit. He gave the boy a nod and took the bangle – yes, stay.

At daybreak the sampan stopped at a sand bar and the crew helped Rajkumar build a pyre for his mother's cremation. Rajkumar's hands began to shake when he put the fire in her mouth. He, who had been so rich in family, was alone now, with a khalasi's apprenticeship for his inheritance. But he was not afraid, not for a moment. His was the sadness of regret – that they had left him so soon, so early, without tasting the wealth or the rewards that he knew, with utter certainty, would one day be his.

It was a long time since Rajkumar had spoken about his family. Among his shipmates this was a subject that was rarely discussed. There were many among them who were from families that had fallen victim to the catastrophes that were so often visited upon that stretch of coast. They preferred not to speak of these things.

It was odd that this child, Matthew, with his educated speech and formal manners, should have drawn him out. Rajkumar could not help being touched. On the way back to Ma Cho's, he put an arm round the boy's shoulders. 'So how long are you going to be here?'

'I'm leaving tomorrow.'

'Tomorrow? But you've just arrived.'

'I know. I was meant to stay for two weeks, but Father thinks there's going to be trouble.'

'Trouble!' Rajkumar turned to stare at him. 'What trouble?'

'The English are preparing to send a fleet up the Irrawaddy. There's going to be a war. Father says they want all the teak in Burma. The King won't let them have it so they're going to do away with him.'

Rajkumar gave a shout of laughter. 'A war over wood? Who's ever heard of such a thing?' He gave Matthew's head a disbelieving pat: the boy was a child, after all, despite his grown-up ways and his knowledge of unlikely things; he'd probably had a bad dream the night before.

But this proved to be the first of many occasions when Matthew showed himself to be wiser and more prescient than Rajkumar. Two days later the whole city was gripped by rumours of war. A large detachment of troops came marching out of the fort and went off downriver, towards the encampment of Myingan. There was an uproar in the bazaar; fishwives emptied their wares into the refuse heap and went hurrying home. A dishevelled Saya John came running to Ma Cho's stall. He had a sheet of paper in his hands. 'A Royal Proclamation,' he announced, 'issued under the King's signature.'

Everybody in the stall fell silent as he began to read:

> To all Royal subjects and inhabitants of the Royal Empire: those heretics, the barbarian English kalaas having most harshly made demands calculated to bring about the impairment and destruction of our religion, the violation of our national traditions and customs, and the degradation of our race, are making a show and preparation as if about to wage war with our state.

> They have been replied to in conformity with the usages of great nations and in words which are just and regular. If, notwithstanding, these heretic foreigners should come, and in any way attempt to molest or disturb the state, His Majesty, who is watchful that the interest of our religion and our state shall not suffer, will himself march forth with his generals, captains and lieutenants with large forces of infantry, artillery, elephanterie and cavalry, by land and by water, and with the might of his army will efface these heretics and conquer and annex their country. To uphold the religion, to uphold the national honour, to uphold the country's interests will bring about threefold good – good of our religion, good of our master and good of ourselves and will gain for us the important result of placing us on the path to the celestial regions and to Nirvana.

Saya John pulled a face. 'Brave words,' he said. 'Let's see what happens next.'

After the initial panic, the streets quickly quietened. The bazaar reopened and the fishwives came back to rummage through the refuse heap, looking for their lost goods. Over the next few days people went about their business just as they had before. The one most noticeable change was that foreign faces were no longer to be seen on the streets. The number of foreigners living in Mandalay was not insubstantial – there were envoys and missionaries from Europe; traders and merchants of Greek, Armenian, Chinese and Indian origin; labourers and boatmen from Bengal, Malaya and the Coromandel coast; white-clothed astrologers from Manipur; businessmen from Gujarat – an assortment of people such as Rajkumar had never seen before he came here. But now suddenly the foreigners disappeared. It was rumoured that the Europeans had left and gone downriver while the others had barricaded themselves into their houses.

A few days later the palace issued another proclamation, a joyful one, this time: it was announced that the royal troops had dealt the invaders a signal defeat, near the fortress of Minhla. The English troops had been repulsed and sent fleeing across the border.

The royal barge was to be dispatched downriver, bearing decorations for the troops and their officers. There was to be a ceremony of thanksgiving at the palace.

There were shouts of joy on the streets, and the fog of anxiety that had hung over the city for the last few days dissipated quickly. To everyone's relief things went quickly back to normal: shoppers and shopkeepers came crowding back and Ma Cho's stall was busier than ever before.

Then, one evening, racing into the bazaar to replenish Ma Cho's stock of fish, Rajkumar came across the familiar, white-bearded face of his boatowner, the nakhoda.

'Is our boat going to leave soon now?' Rajkumar asked. 'Now that the war is over?'

The old man gave him a secret, tight-lipped smile. 'The war isn't over. Not yet.'

'But we heard . . .'

'What we hear on the waterfront is quite different from what's said in the city.'

'What have you heard?' said Rajkumar.

Although they were using their own dialect the nakhoda lowered his voice. 'The English are going to be here in a day or two,' he answered. 'They've been seen by boatmen. They are bringing the biggest fleet that's ever sailed on a river. They have cannon that can blow away the stone walls of a fort; they have boats so fast that they can outrun a tidal bore; their guns can shoot quicker than you can talk. They are coming like the tide: nothing can stand in their way. Today we heard that their ships are taking up positions around Myingan. You'll probably hear the fireworks tomorrow . . .'

Sure enough, the next morning, a distant booming sound came rolling across the plain, all the way to Ma Cho's food-stall, near the western wall of the fort. When the opening salvoes sounded, the market was thronged with people. Farm wives from the outskirts of the city had come in early and set their mats out in rows, arranging their vegetables in neat little bunches. Fishermen had stopped by too, with their night-time catches fresh from the river. In an hour or two the vegetables would wilt and the fish eyes would begin to cloud over. But for the moment everything was crisp and fresh.

The first booms of the guns caused nothing more than a brief interruption in the morning's shopping. People looked up at the clear blue sky in puzzlement and shopkeepers leant sidewise over their wares to ask each other questions. Ma Cho and Rajkumar had been hard at work since dawn. As always on chilly mornings, many people had stopped off for a little something to eat before making their way home. Now the hungry, mealtime hush was interrupted by a sudden buzz. People looked at each other nervously: what was that noise?

This was when Rajkumar broke in. 'English cannon,' he said. 'They're heading in this direction.'

Ma Cho gave a yelp of annoyance. 'How do you know what they are, you fool of a boy?'

'Boatmen have seen them,' Rajkumar answered. 'A whole English fleet is coming this way.'

Ma Cho had a roomful of people to feed and she was in no mood to allow her only helper to be distracted by a distant noise. 'Enough of that now,' she said. 'Get back to work.'

In the distance the firing intensified, rattling the bowls on the benches. The customers began to stir in alarm. In the adjoining marketplace a coolie had dropped a sack of rice and the spilt grain was spreading like a white stain across the dusty path as people pushed past each other to get away. Shopkeepers were clearing their counters, stuffing their goods into bags; farm wives were tipping their baskets into refuse heaps.

Suddenly Ma Cho's customers started to their feet, knocking over their bowls and pushing the benches apart. In dismay, Ma Cho turned on Rajkumar. 'Didn't I tell you to keep quiet, you idiot of a kalaa? Look, you've scared my customers away.'

'It's not my fault . . .'

'Then whose? What am I going to do with all this food? What's going to become of that fish I bought yesterday?' Ma Cho collapsed on her stool.

Behind them, in the now-deserted marketplace, dogs were fighting over scraps of discarded meat, circling in packs around the refuse heaps.

Two

At the palace, a little less than a mile from Ma Cho's stall, the King's chief consort, Queen Supayalat, was seen mounting a steep flight of stairs to listen more closely to the guns.

The palace lay at the exact centre of Mandalay, deep within the walled city, a sprawling complex of pavilions, gardens and corridors, all grouped around the nine-roofed hti of Burma's kings. The complex was walled off from the surrounding streets by a stockade of tall, teak posts. At each of the four corners of the stockade was a guard-post, manned by sentries from the King's personal bodyguard. It was to one of these that Queen Supayalat had decided to climb.

The Queen was a small, fine-boned woman with porcelain skin and tiny hands and feet. Her face was small and angular, the regularity of its features being marred only by a slight blemish in the alignment of the right eye. The Queen's waist, famously of a wisp-like slimness, was swollen by her third pregnancy, now in its eighth month.

The Queen was not alone: some half-dozen maidservants followed close behind, carrying her two young daughters, the First and Second Princesses, Ashin Hteik Su Myat Phaya Gyi and Ashin Hteik Su Myat Phaya Lat. The advanced condition of her pregnancy had made the Queen anxious about her children's whereabouts. For the last several days she had been unwilling to allow her two daughters even momentarily out of her sight.

The First Princess was three and bore a striking resemblance to her father, Thebaw, King of Burma. She was a good-natured, obedient girl, with a round face and ready smile. The Second

Princess was two years younger, not quite one yet, and she was an altogether different kind of child, very much her mother's daughter. She'd been born with the colic and would cry for hours at a stretch. Several times a day she would fly into paroxysms of rage. Her body would go rigid and she would clench her little fists; her chest would start pumping, with her mouth wide open but not a sound issuing from her throat. Even experienced nurses quailed when the little Princess was seized by one of her fits.

To deal with the baby, the Queen insisted on having several of her most trusted attendants at hand at all times – Evelyn, Hemau, Augusta, Nan Pau. These girls were very young, mostly in their early teens, and they were almost all orphans. They'd been purchased by the Queen's agents in small Kachin, Wa and Shan villages along the kingdom's northern frontiers. Some of them were from Christian families, some from Buddhist – once they came to Mandalay it didn't matter. They were reared under the tutelage of palace retainers, under the Queen's personal supervision.

It was the youngest of these maids who had had the most success in dealing with the Second Princess. She was a slender ten-year-old called Dolly, a timid, undemonstrative child, with enormous eyes and a dancer's pliable body and supple limbs. Dolly had been brought to Mandalay at a very early age from the frontier town of Lashio: she had no memory of her parents or family. She was thought to be of Shan extraction, but this was a matter of conjecture, based on her slender fine-boned appearance and her smooth, silken complexion.

On this particular morning Dolly had had very little success with the Second Princess. The guns had jolted the little girl out of her sleep and she had been crying ever since. Dolly, who was easily startled, had been badly scared herself. When the guns had started up she'd covered her ears and gone into a corner, gritting her teeth and shaking her head. But then the Queen had sent for her and after that Dolly had been so busy trying to distract the little Princess that she'd had no time to be frightened.

Dolly wasn't strong enough yet to take the Princess up the steep stairs that led to the top of the stockade: Evelyn, who was sixteen and strong for her age, was given the job of carrying her. Dolly followed after the others and she was the last to step into the guard-post – a wooden platform, fenced in with heavy, timber rails.

Four uniformed soldiers were standing grouped in a corner. The Queen was firing questions at them, but none of them would answer nor even meet her eyes. They hung their heads, fingering the long barrels of their flintlocks.

'How far away is the fighting?' the Queen asked. 'And what sort of cannon are they using?'

The soldiers shook their heads; the truth was that they knew no more than she did. When the noise started they'd speculated excitedly about its cause. At first they'd refused to believe that the roar could be of human making. Guns of such power had never before been heard in this part of Burma, nor was it easy to conceive of an order of fire so rapid as to produce an indistinguishable merging of sound.

The Queen saw that there was nothing to be learnt from these hapless men. She turned to rest her weight against the wooden rails of the guard-post. If only her body were less heavy, if only she were not so tired and slow.

The strange thing was that these last ten days, ever since the English crossed the border, she'd heard nothing but good news. A week ago a garrison commander had sent a telegram to say that the foreigners had been stopped at Minhla, two hundred miles downriver. The palace had celebrated the victory, and the King had even sent the general a decoration. How was it possible that the invaders were now close enough to make their guns heard in the capital?

Things had happened so quickly: a few months ago there'd been a dispute with a British timber company – a technical matter concerning some logs of teak. It was clear that the company was in the wrong; they were side-stepping the kingdom's customs regulations, cutting up logs to avoid paying duties. The royal customs officers had slapped a fine on the company, demanding arrears of payment for some fifty thousand logs. The Englishmen had protested and refused to pay; they'd carried their complaints to the British Governor in Rangoon. Humiliating ultimatums had followed. One of the King's senior ministers, the Kinwun Mingyi, had suggested discreetly that it might be best to accept the terms; that the British might allow the Royal Family to remain in the palace in Mandalay, on terms similar to those of the Indian princes – like farmyard pigs in other words, to be fed and fattened by their masters; swine, housed in sties that had been tricked out with a few little bits of finery.

The Kings of Burma were not princes, the Queen had told the Kinwun Mingyi; they were kings, sovereigns, they'd defeated the Emperor of China, conquered Thailand, Assam, Manipur. And she herself, Supayalat, she had risked everything to secure the throne for Thebaw, her husband and step-brother. Was it even imaginable that she would consent to give it all away now? And what if the child in her belly were a boy (and this time she was sure it was): how would she explain to him that she had surrendered his patrimony because of a quarrel over some logs of wood? The Queen had prevailed and the Burmese court had refused to yield to the British ultimatum.

Now, gripping the guard-post rail the Queen listened carefully to the distant gunfire. She'd hoped at first that the barrage was an exercise of some kind. The most reliable general in the army, the Hlethin Atwinwun, was stationed at the fort of Myingan, thirty miles away, with a force of eight thousand soldiers.

Just yesterday the King had asked, in passing, how things were going on the war front. She could tell that he thought of the war as a faraway matter, a distant campaign, like the expeditions that had been sent into the Shan highlands in years past, to deal with bandits and dacoits.

Everything was going as it should, she'd told him; there was nothing to worry about. And so far as she knew, this was no less than the truth. She'd met with the seniormost officials every day, the Kinwun Mingyi, the Taingda Mingyi, even the *wungyis* and *wundauks* and *myowuns*. None of them had so much as hinted that anything was amiss. But there was no mistaking the sound of those guns. What was she going to tell the King now?

The courtyard beneath the stockade filled suddenly with voices.

Dolly stole a glance down the staircase. There were soldiers milling around below, dozens of them, wearing the colours of the palace guard. One of them spotted her and began to shout – 'the Queen? Is the Queen up there?

Dolly stepped quickly back, out of his line of sight. Who were these soldiers? What did they want? She could hear their feet on the stairs now. Somewhere close by, the Princess began to cry, in short, breathless gasps. Augusta thrust the baby into her arms – here, Dolly, here, take her, she won't stop. The baby was screaming, flailing her fists. Dolly had to turn her face away to keep from being struck.

An officer had stepped into the guard-post; he was holding his sheathed sword in front of him, in both hands, like a sceptre. He was saying something to the Queen, motioning to her to leave the cabin, to go down the stairs into the palace.

'Are we prisoners then?' The Queen's face was twisted with fury. 'Who has sent you here?'

'Our orders came from the Taingda Mingyi,' the officer said. 'For your safety Mebya.'

'Our safety?'

The guard-post was full of soldiers and they were herding the girls towards the steps. Dolly glanced down: the flight of stairs was very steep. Her head began to spin.

'I can't,' she cried. 'I can't.' She would fall, she knew it. The Princess was too heavy for her; the stairs were too high; she would need a free hand to hold on, to keep her balance.

'Move.'

'I can't.' She could hardly hear herself over the child's cries. She stood still, refusing to budge.

'Quickly, quickly.' There was a soldier behind her; he was prodding her with the cold hilt of his sword. She felt her eyes brimming over, tears flooding down her face. Couldn't they see she would fall, that the Princess would tumble out of her grip? Why would no one help?

'Quick.'

She turned to look into the soldier's unsmiling face. 'I can't. I have the Princess in my arms and she's too heavy for me. Can't you see?' No one seemed to be able to hear her above the Princess's wails.

'What's the matter with you, girl? Why're you standing there? Move.'

She shut her eyes and took a step. And then, just as her legs were starting to give way she heard the Queen's voice. 'Dolly! Stop!'

'It's not my fault.' She began to sob, her eyes pressed tightly shut. Someone snatched the Princess from her arms. 'It's not my fault. I tried to tell them; they wouldn't listen.'

'It's all right.' The Queen's voice was sharp but not unkind. 'Come on down now. Be careful.'

Weeping in relief, Dolly stumbled down the steps and across the courtyard. She felt the other girls' hands on her back, leading her down a corridor.

Most of the buildings in the palace complex were low, wooden structures, linked by long corridors. The palace was of relatively recent construction, just thirty years old. It was closely modelled on the royal residences of earlier Burmese capitals, at Ava and Amarapura. Parts of the royal apartments had been transported whole after the founding of Mandalay, but many of the smaller outlying buildings were unfinished and still unknown, even to the palace's inhabitants. Dolly had never before been in the room she was led to now. It was dark, with damp, plastered walls and heavy doors.

'Bring the Taingda Mingyi to me,' the Queen was screaming at the guards. 'I will not be kept prisoner. Bring him to me. Right now.'

An hour or two went slowly by; the girls could tell from the direction of the shadows under the door that morning had changed into afternoon. The little Princess cried herself out and fell asleep across Dolly's crossed legs.

The doors were thrown open and the Taingda Mingyi came puffing in.

'Where is the King?'

'He is safe, Mebya.'

He was a stout man with oily skin. In the past, he'd always been ready with advice but now the Queen could not get a single clear answer out of him.

'The King is safe. You should not worry.' The long, drooping hairs that sprouted from his moles shook gently as he smiled and showed his teeth.

He produced a telegram. 'The Hlethin Atwinwun has won a famous victory at Myingan.'

'But those were not our guns I heard this morning.'

'The foreigners have been halted. The King has dispatched a medal, and decorations for the men.' He handed her a sheet of paper.

She didn't bother to look at it. She had seen many telegrams over the last ten days, all filled with news of famous victories. But the guns she'd heard that morning were not Burmese, of this she had no doubt. 'Those were English guns,' she said. 'I know they were. Don't lie to me. How close are they? When do you think they will reach Mandalay?'

He wouldn't look at her. 'Mebya's condition is delicate. She should rest now. I will return later.'

'Rest?' The Queen pointed to her maids, sitting on the floor. 'The girls are exhausted. Look.' She pointed to Dolly's red eyes and tear-streaked face. 'Where are my other servants? Send them to me. I need them.'

The Taingda Mingyi hesitated, and then bowed. 'Mebya. They will be here.'

The other maids arrived an hour later. Their faces were sombre. The Queen said nothing until the guards had shut the doors. Then everyone clustered tightly around the new arrivals. Dolly had to crane her head to catch what they were saying.

This was what they said: the British had destroyed the fort at Myingan with immaculate precision, using their cannon, without losing a single soldier of their own. The Hlethin Atwinwun had surrendered. The army had disintegrated; the soldiers had fled into the mountains with their guns. The Kinwun Mingyi and the Taingda Mingyi had dispatched emissaries to the British. The two ministers were now competing with one another to keep the Royal Family under guard. They knew the British would be grateful to whoever handed over the royal couple; there would be rich rewards. The foreigners were expected to come to Mandalay very soon to take the King and Queen into captivity.

The invasion proceeded so smoothly as to surprise even its planners. The imperial fleet crossed the border on 14 November, 1885.

Two days later, after a few hours of shelling, British soldiers took possession of the Burmese outposts of Nyaungbinmaw and Singbaungwe. The next day, at Minhla, the fleet came under heavy fire. The Burmese garrison at Minhla was a small one, but it resisted with unexpected tenacity.

The British forces were armed with the latest breech-loading rifles. Their artillery support consisted of twenty-seven rapid-firing machine guns, more than had ever before been assembled on the continent of Asia. The Burmese could not match this firepower. After an exchange of fire that lasted several hours, the British infantry was sent ashore.

There were some ten thousand soldiers in the British invasion force and of these the great majority – about two-thirds – were Indian sepoys. Among the units deployed at Minhla there were three battalions of sepoys. They were from the Hazara Regiment and the 1st Madras Pioneers. The Indians were seasoned, battle-hardened troops. The Hazaras, recruited from the Afghan border, had proved their worth to the British over decades of warfare, in India and abroad. The 1st Madras Pioneers were among the most loyal of Britain's foot soldiers. They had stood steadfastly by their masters even through the uprising of 1857, when most of northern India had risen against the British. The Burmese defenders of Minhla stood little chance against these sepoys, with their newly manufactured British equipment and their vastly superior numbers. The dogged little defence force dissolved when the redoubt was charged.

The aftershock of the collapse at Minhla was felt a long way upriver. At Pakokku the garrison melted away; at Nyaungu, near the great, pagoda-covered plain of Pagan, Burmese gunners spiked their own cannon after firing a few shots. At Mygingan, which was under the command of the Hlethin Atwinwun, the defenders were forced to abandon their positions after a bombardment that lasted several hours. A few days later, without informing King Thebaw, the Burmese army surrendered.

The war lasted just fourteen days.

Three

For two days after the bombardment of Myingan, Mandalay was strangely, almost eerily quiet. Then the rumours started. One morning a man went running through the marketplace, past Ma Cho's stall. He was shouting at the top of his voice: foreign ships had anchored off the shore; English soldiers were marching towards the city.

Panic struck the market. People began to run and jostle. Rajkumar managed to push his way through the crowd to the adjoining road. He could not see far: a cloud of dust hung over the road, drummed up by hundreds of racing feet. People were running in every direction, slamming against each other and pushing blindly at anything that came their way. Rajkumar was swept along in the direction of the river. As he ran, he became aware of a ripple in the ground beneath him, a kind of drumbeat in the earth, a rhythmic tremor that travelled up his spine through the soles of his feet.

The people in front of him scattered and parted, pushing up against the sides of the road. Suddenly he was in the front rank of the crowd, looking directly at two English soldiers mounted on brown horses. The cavalrymen were waving people away with drawn swords, clearing the road. The dust had made patterns on their polished boots. Looming behind them was a solid mass of uniforms, advancing like a tidal wave.

Rajkumar darted to the side of the road and pressed himself against a wall. The crowd's initial nervousness melted as the first squad of soldiers marched past with their shouldered rifles. There was no rancour on the soldiers' faces, no emotion at all. None of them so much as glanced at the crowd.

'The English!' someone said, and the words went quickly from mouth to mouth, growing louder and louder until they became a kind of murmured cheer. But as the vanguard passed and the next squad came into view, an amazed silence descended on the spectators: these soldiers were not English – they were Indians. The people around Rajkumar stirred, as though moved to curiosity by the sight of an Indian in their midst.

'Who are these soldiers?' someone said.

'I don't know.'

It struck Rajkumar suddenly that he hadn't seen any of the usual Indian faces in the bazaar all day: none of the coolies and cobblers and shopkeepers who always came there every day. For a moment this seemed odd, but then he forgot about it and was once again absorbed in the spectacle of the marching sepoys.

People began to ask Rajkumar questions. 'What are these soldiers doing here?'

Rajkumar shrugged. How was he to know? He had no more connection with the soldiers than did they. A group of men gathered around him, crowding in, so that he had to take a few backward steps. 'Where do the soldiers come from? Why are they here?'

'I don't know where they come from. I don't know who they are.'

Glancing over his shoulder, Rajkumar saw that he had backed himself into a blind alley. There were some seven or eight men around him. They had pulled up their longyis, tucking them purposefully up at the waist. The sepoys were just a short distance away, hundreds, perhaps thousands of them. But he was alone in the alley – the only Indian – out of earshot, surrounded by these men who were clearly intent on making him answer for the soldiers' presence.

A hand flashed out of the shadows. Taking a grip on his hair, a man pulled him off the ground. Rajkumar swung up a leg and dug it back, aiming his heel at his assailant's groin. The man saw the kick coming and blocked it with one hand. Twisting Rajkumar's head around, he struck him across the face with the back of his fist. A spurt of blood shot out of Rajkumar's nose. The shock of the blow slowed the moment to a standstill. The arc of blood seemed to stop in its trajectory, hanging suspended in the air, brilliantly translucent, like a string of garnets. Then the crook of an elbow took Rajkumar in the stomach, pumping the breath out of him and throwing him against a wall. He slid down, clutching his stomach, as though he were trying to push his insides back in.

Then, suddenly, help arrived. A voice rang through the lane. 'Stop.' The men turned round, startled.

'Let him be.'

It was Saya John, advancing towards them with one arm in the air, looking oddly authoritative in a hat and coat. Tucked snugly into the palm of his upraised hand was a small, blunt-nosed pistol. The men backed away slowly and once they'd gone, Saya John slipped the pistol into his coat pocket. 'You're lucky I saw you,' he said to Rajkumar. 'Didn't you know better than to be out on the streets today? The other Indians have all barricaded themselves into Hajji Ismail's compound, at the foot of Mandalay hill.'

He held out a hand and helped Rajkumar to his feet. Rajkumar stood up and wiped the blood off his throbbing face. They walked out of the alley together. On the main road soldiers were still marching past. Rajkumar and Saya John stood side by side and watched the triumphal parade.

Presently Saya John said: 'I used to know soldiers like these.'

'Saya?'

'In Singapore, as a young man I worked for a time as a hospital orderly. The patients were mainly sepoys like these – Indians, back from fighting wars for their English masters. I still remember the smell of gangrenous bandages on amputated limbs; the night-time screams of twenty-year-old boys, sitting upright in their beds. They were peasants, those men, from small countryside villages: their clothes and turbans still smelt of woodsmoke and dung fires. "What makes you fight," I would ask them, "when you should be planting your fields at home?" "Money," they'd say, and yet all they earned was a few annas a day, not much more than a dockyard coolie. For a few coins they would allow their masters to use them as they wished, to destroy every trace of resistance to the power of the English. It always amazed me: Chinese peasants would never do this – allow themselves to be used to fight other people's wars with so little profit for themselves. I would look into those faces and I would ask myself: what would it be like if I had something to defend – a home, a country, a family – and I found myself attacked by these ghostly men, these trusting boys? How do you fight an enemy who fights from neither enmity nor anger, but in submission to orders from superiors, without protest and without conscience?

'In English they use a word – it comes from the Bible – *evil.* I used to think of it when I talked to those soldiers. What other word could you use to describe their willingness to kill for their masters, to follow any command, no matter what it entailed? And yet, in the hospital, these sepoys would give me gifts, tokens of their gratitude – a carved flute, an orange. I would look into their eyes and see also a kind of innocence, a simplicity. These men who would think nothing of setting fire to whole villages if their officers ordered, they too had a certain kind of innocence. An innocent evil. I could think of nothing more dangerous.'

'Saya,' Rajkumar shrugged offhandedly, 'they're just tools. Without minds of their own. They count for nothing.'

Saya John glanced at him, startled. There was something unusual about the boy – a kind of watchful determination. No excess of gratitude here, no gifts or offerings, no talk of honour, with murder in the heart. There was no simplicity in his face, no innocence: his eyes were filled with worldliness, curiosity, hunger. That was as it should be.

'If you ever need a job,' Saya John said, 'come and talk to me.'

Just before sunset the occupying troops withdrew from the fort. They carried away cartloads of booty from the palace. To the astonishment of the townsfolk, they left without posting pickets around the fort. For the first time that anyone could remember the gateways of the citadel stood open and unguarded.

The soldiers marched back the way they had come but through streets that were now empty. As the tramp of their feet faded away an uneasy quiet descended on the city. Then, with the suddenness of a night-time eruption in a chicken-coop, a group of women burst out of the fort and came racing over the funeral bridge, their feet pounding a drum roll on its wooden surface.

Ma Cho recognised some of the women. They were palace servants; she had seen them going in and out of the fort for years, stepping haughtily down the road in their slippered feet, their longyis plucked daintily above their ankles. They were running now, stumbling through the dust without a thought for their clothes. They were carrying bundles of cloth, sacks, even furniture; some were bent over like washerwomen on their way to the river. Ma Cho ran out into the street and stopped one of the women. 'What are you doing? What's happened?'

'The soldiers – they've been looting the palace. We're trying to save a few things for ourselves.' The women disappeared and all was quiet again. Presently the shadows around the fort began to stir. There were ripples of activity in the darkness, like the fluttering of moths in the recesses of a musty cupboard. People crept slowly out of the dwellings that surrounded the citadel. Advancing to the walls they peered distrustfully at the empty guard-posts. There were no soldiers anywhere in sight, nor even any sentries from the palace guard. Was it really possible that the gates had been left unguarded? A few people stepped on the bridges, testing the silence. Slowly, walking on the balls of their feet, they began to advance towards the far bank of the eighty-foot moat. They reached the other side and went creeping to the gates, holding themselves ready to run back at the slightest check.

It was true: the guards and sentries were all gone. The palace was unguarded. The intruders slipped through the gates and vanished into the fort.

Ma Cho had been watching undecided, scratching her chin. Now she picked up her sharp-bladed da. Tucking the wooden handle into her waist she started towards the funeral bridge. The fort's walls were a blood-red smear in the darkness ahead.

Rajkumar ran after her, reaching the bridge abreast of a charging crowd. This was the flimsiest of the fort's bridges, too narrow for the mass that was trying to funnel through. A frenzy of jostling broke out. The man beside Rajkumar found himself stepping on air and dropped over the side; a wooden plank flipped up, tipping two women screaming into the moat. Rajkumar was younger than the people around him and lighter on his feet. Slipping through the press of bodies, he went sprinting into the fort.

Rajkumar had imagined the fort to be filled with gardens and palaces, richly painted and sumptuously gilded. But the street he now found himself on was a straight and narrow dirt path, lined with wooden houses, not much different from any other part of the city. Directly ahead lay the palace and its nine-roofed spire – he could see the gilded hti flashing in the darkness. People were pouring down the street now, some carrying flaming torches. Rajkumar caught a glimpse of Ma Cho rounding a corner in the distance. He sprinted after her, his longyi tucked tight around his waist. The palace stockade had several entrances, including doorways reserved for the use of servants and tradespeople. These were set low in the walls, like mouseholes, so that no one could pass through them without bowing. At one of these small doorways Rajkumar caught up again with Ma Cho. The gate was quickly forced. People began to tumble through, like water over the lip of a spout.

Rajkumar stayed close behind Ma Cho as she elbowed her way to the entrance. She heaved him in and then squeezed through herself. Rajkumar had the impression of having fallen upon a perfumed sheet. Then he rolled over and found that he was lying on a bed of soft grass. He was in a garden, within reach of a sparkling canal: the air was suddenly clear and cool, free of dust. The orientation of the palace's gateways was towards the east: it was from that direction that ceremonial visitors approached, walking down the formal pathway that led to the great glass-tiled pavilion where the King held court. On the western side of the stockade – the side that was closest to the funeral gate – lay the women's quarters. These were the halls and apartments that now lay ahead of Ma Cho and Rajkumar. Ma Cho picked herself up and hurried, panting, in the direction of a stone archway. The doors of the main chamber of the women's palace lay just beyond, yawning open. People stopped to run their fingers over the doors' jade-studded panels. A man fell on his knees and began to pound the slats of wood with a rock, trying to knock out the ornaments. Rajkumar ran past, into the building, a couple of steps behind Ma Cho. The chamber was very large and its walls and columns were tiled with thousands of shards of glass. Oil lamps flared in sconces, and the whole room seemed to be aflame, every surface shimmering with sparks of golden light. The hall was filled with a busy noise, a workmanlike hum of cutting and chopping, of breaking wood and shattering glass. Everywhere people were intently at work, men and women, armed with axes and das; they were hacking at gem-studded *Ook* offering boxes; digging patterned gemstones from the marble floor; using fish-hooks to pry the ivory inlays from lacquered sadaik chests. Armed with a rock, a girl was knocking the ornamental frets out of a crocodile-shaped zither; a man was using a meat cleaver to scrape the gilt from the neck of a *saung-gak* harp and a woman was chiselling furiously at the ruby eyes of a bronze *chinthe* lion. They came to a door that led to a candlelit anteroom. There was a woman inside, standing by the latticed window in the far corner.

Ma Cho gasped. 'Queen Supayalat!'

The Queen was screaming, shaking her first. 'Get out of here. Get out.' Her face was red, mottled with rage, her fury caused as much by her own impotence as by the presence of the mob in the palace. A day before, she could have had a commoner imprisoned for so much as looking her directly in the face. Today all the city's scum had come surging into the palace and she was powerless to act against them. But the Queen was neither cowed nor afraid, not in the least. Ma Cho fell to the floor, her hands clasped over her head in a reverential *shiko*.

Rajkumar dropped to his knees, unable to wrench his gaze away. The Queen was dressed in crimson silk, in a loose garment that billowed over her hugely distended stomach. Her hair was piled in lacquered coils on her tiny, delicately shaped head; the ivory mask of her face was scarred by a single dark furrow, carved by a bead of sweat. She was holding her robe plucked above her ankle and Rajkumar noticed that her legs were encased in a garment of pink silk – stockings, an article of clothing he had never seen before. The Queen glared at Ma Cho, lying on the floor in front of her. In one hand, Ma Cho was holding a brass candlestand with a chrysanthemum pedestal.

The Queen lunged at the prostrate woman. 'Give that to me; where did you get it? Give it back.' Leaning stiffly over her swollen stomach, the Queen tried to snatch away the candlestand. Ma Cho eluded her hands, pushing herself backwards, crab-like. The Queen hissed at her: 'Do you know who I am?' Ma Cho offered her yet another respectful genuflection, but she would not part with her candlestand. It was as though her determination to cling to her loot was in no way at odds with her wish to render due homage to the Queen.

Just one day earlier the crime of entering the palace would have resulted in summary execution. This they all knew – the Queen and everyone who had joined the mob. But yesterday had passed: the Queen had fought and been defeated. What purpose was to be served by giving her back what she had lost? None of those things was hers any more: what was to be gained by leaving them to the foreigners to take away?

Through all the years of the Queen's reign the townsfolk had hated her for her cruelty, feared her for her ruthlessness and courage. Now through the alchemy of defeat she was transformed in their eyes. It was as though a bond had been conjured into existence that had never existed before. For the first time in her reign she had become what a sovereign should be, the proxy of her people. Everyone who came through the door fell to the floor in a spontaneous act of homage. Now, when she was powerless to chastise them, they were glad to offer her these tokens of respect; they were glad even to hear her rail at them. It was good that they should shiko and she berate them. Were she meekly to accept her defeat none would be so deeply shamed as they. It was as though they were entrusting her with the burden of their own inarticulate defiance.

Rajkumar's eyes fell on a girl – one of the Queen's maids. She was slender and long-limbed, of a complexion that was exactly the tint of the fine *thanaka* powder she was wearing on her face. She had huge dark eyes and her face was long and perfect in its symmetry. She was by far the most beautiful creature he had ever beheld, of a loveliness beyond imagining.

Rajkumar swallowed to clear his throat, which was suddenly

swollen and dry. She was in the far corner of the room with a group of other girls. He began to work his way towards her along the wall.

She was an attendant, he guessed, perhaps nine or ten years old. He could tell that the bejewelled little girl beside her was a Princess. In the corner behind them lay a heap of richly coloured cloths and objects of brass and ivory. The girls had evidently been busy salvaging the Queen's possessions when they were interrupted by the mob.

Rajkumar looked down at the floor and saw a jewelled ivory box lying forgotten in a corner. The box had a gold clasp and on its sides were two small handles, carved in the shape of leaping dolphins. Rajkumar knew exactly what he had to do. Picking the box off the ground, he ran across the room and offered it to the slender little girl.

'Here.'

She wouldn't look at him. She turned her head away, her lips moving silently as though in a chant.

'Take it,' said one of the other girls. 'He's giving it to you.'

'Here.' He thrust the box at her again. 'Don't be afraid.'

He surprised himself by taking hold of her hand and placing it gently on the box. 'I brought it back for you.'

She let her hand rest on the lid. It was as light as a leaf. Her lowered eyes went first to the jewelled lid and then travelled slowly from the dark knots of his knuckles to his torn and dirt-spattered vest and up to his face. And then her eyes clouded over with apprehension and she dropped her gaze. He could tell that her world was ringed with fear so that every step she took was a venture into darkness.

'What's your name?' Rajkumar said.

She whispered a couple of inaudible syllables.

'Doh-lee?'

'Dolly.'

'Dolly,' repeated Rajkumar. 'Dolly.' He could think of nothing else to say, or as much worth saying, so he said the name again louder and louder, until he was shouting. 'Dolly. Dolly.'

He saw a tiny smile creep on to her face and then Ma Cho's voice was in his ear. 'Soldiers. Run.' At the door, he turned to look back. Dolly was standing just as he'd left her, holding the box between her hands, staring at him.

Ma Cho tugged at his arm. 'For what are you staring at that girl, you half-wit kalaa? Take what you've got and run. The soldiers are coming back. Run.'

The mirrored hall was echoing with shouts. At the door, Rajkumar turned back to make a gesture at Dolly, more a sign than a wave. 'I will see you again.'

Four

The Royal Family spent the night in one of the furthest outbuildings in the palace grounds, the South Garden Palace, a small pavilion surrounded by pools, canals and rustic gardens. The next day, shortly before noon, King Thebaw came out to the balcony and sat down to wait for the British spokesman, Colonel Sladen. The King was wearing his royal sash and a white *gaung-baung*, the turban of mourning.

King Thebaw was of medium height, with a plump face, a thin moustache and finely shaped eyes. As a youth he had been famous for his good looks: it had once been said of him that he was the handsomest Burman in the land (he was in fact half Shan, his mother having come to Mandalay from a small principality on the eastern border). He'd been crowned at the age of twenty and in the seven years of his reign had never once left the palace compound. This long confinement had worked terrible ravages on his appearance. He was only twenty-seven but looked to be well into middle age.

To sit on the throne of Burma had never been Thebaw's personal ambition. Nor had anyone in the kingdom ever imagined that the crown would one day be his. As a child he had entered into the Buddhist boy's customary novitiate in the monkhood with an enthusiasm unusual in one of his birth and lineage. He had spent several years in the palace monastery, leaving it just once, briefly, at the behest of his father, the august King Mindon. The King had enrolled Thebaw and a few of his step-brothers in an English school in Mandalay. Under the tutelage of Anglican missionaries Thebaw had learnt some English and displayed a talent for cricket.

But then King Mindon had changed his mind, withdrawing the princes from the school and eventually expelling the missionary. Thebaw had returned gladly to the monastery on the palace grounds, within sight of the water-clock and the relic house of the Buddha's tooth. He had proceeded to earn distinction in scriptural study, passing the difficult *patama-byan* examination at the age of nineteen.

King Mindon was perhaps the wisest, most prudent ruler ever to sit on the throne of Burma. Appreciative though he was of his son's gifts, he was equally aware of his limitations. 'If Thebaw ever becomes king,' he once remarked, 'the country will pass into the hands of foreigners.' But of this there seemed to be little possibility. There were forty-six other princes in Mandalay whose claims to the throne were as good as Thebaw's. Most of them far exceeded him in ambition and political ability.

But fate intervened in the familiar guise of a mother-in-law: Thebaw's happened to be also his step-mother, the Alenandaw Queen, a senior consort and a wily and ruthless exponent of palace intrigue. She arranged for Thebaw to marry all three of her daughters simultaneously. Then she shouldered him past his forty-six rivals and installed him on the throne. He had no choice but to assent to his accession: to accept was an easier alternative than to refuse, and less potentially lethal. But there was a startling new development, something that threw everybody's calculations off kilter: Thebaw fell in love with one of his wives, his middle Queen, Supayalat.

Of all the princesses in the palace, Supayalat was by far the fiercest and most wilful, the only one who could match her mother in guile and determination. Of such a woman only indifference could have been expected where it concerned a man of scholarly inclination like Thebaw. Yet she too, in defiance of the protocols of palace intrigue, fell headlong in love with her husband, the King. His ineffectual good nature seemed to inspire a maternal ferocity in her. In order to protect him from her family she stripped her mother of her powers and banished her to a corner of the palace, along with her sisters and co-wives. Then she set about ridding Thebaw of his rivals. She ordered the killing of every member of the Royal Family who might ever be considered a threat to her husband. Seventy-nine princes were slaughtered on her orders, some of them new-born infants, and some too old to walk. To prevent the spillage of royal blood she had had them wrapped in carpets and bludgeoned to death. The corpses were thrown into the nearest river.

The war too was largely of Supayalat's making: it was she who had roused the great council of the land, the Hluttdaw, when the British began to issue their ultimatums from Rangoon. The King had been of a mind for appeasement; the Kinwun Mingyi, his most trusted minister, had made an impassioned appeal for peace and he was tempted to give in. Then Supayalat had risen from her place and gone slowly to the centre of the council. It was the fifth month of her pregnancy and she moved with great deliberation, with a slow, shuffling gait, moving her tiny feet no more than a few inches at a time, a small, lonely figure in that assembly of turbaned noblemen.

The chamber was lined with mirrors. As she approached its centre, an army of Supayalats seemed to materialise around her; they were everywhere, on every shard of glass, thousands of tiny women with their hands clasped over their swollen waists. She walked up to the stout old Kinwun Mingyi, sitting sprawled on his stool. Thrusting her swollen belly into his face, she said, 'Why, grandfather, it is you who should wear a skirt and own a stone for grinding face powder.' Her voice was a whisper but it had filled the room.

And now the war was over, and he, the King, was sitting on the balcony of a garden pavilion, waiting for a visit from Colonel Sladen, the spokesman of the conquering British. The evening before, the colonel had called on the King and informed him, in the politest and most discreet language, that the Royal Family was to be transported from Mandalay the next day; that His Majesty would do well to use the remaining time to make his preparations.

The King had not stepped out of the palace in seven years; he had not left the vicinity of Mandalay in all his life. What were his preparations to be? One might as well try to prepare for a journey to the moon. The King knew the colonel well. Sladen had spent years in Mandalay as a British emissary and had often visited the palace. He was fluent in Burmese and had always shown himself to be correct in his manners, at times affable and even friendly. He needed more time, the King had told Sladen, a week, a few days. What could it matter now? The British had won and he had lost: what difference could a day or two make?

The afternoon was well advanced when Colonel Sladen came walking up the path that led to the South Garden Palace, a pebbled trail that meandered between picturesque pools and goldfish-filled streams. The King stayed seated as Colonel Sladen approached.

'How much time?' said the King.

Sladen was in full dress uniform, with a sword hanging at his waist. He bowed regretfully. He had conferred at length with his commanding officer, he explained. The general had expressed his sympathy but he had his orders and was bound by the responsibilities of his position. His Majesty must understand; left to himself he, Sladen, would have been glad to make accommodations, but the matter was not in his hands, nor anyone else's for that matter . . .

'How much time then?'

Sladen reached into his pocket and pulled out a gold watch. 'About one hour.'

'One hour! But . . .'

A guard of honour had already been formed at the palace gates; the King was being waited on.

The news startled the King. 'Which gate?' he enquired in alarm. Every part of the palace was charged with portents. The auspicious, ceremonial entrance faced east. It was through these gates that honoured visitors came and departed. For years British envoys to Mandalay had been consigned to the humble west gate. This was a grievance of long standing. Sladen had waged many battles with the palace over such fine points of protocol. Would he now seek to exact revenge by forcing the King to exit the palace by the west gate? The King directed an apprehensive glance at the colonel and Sladen hastened to reassure the King. He was to be allowed to leave by the east gate. In victory the British had decided to be generous.

Sladen looked at his watch again. There was very little time now and a vitally important matter had yet to be settled: the question of the entourage that was to accompany the Royal Family into exile.

While Sladen was conferring with the King, other British officers had been busy organising a gathering in a nearby garden. A large number of palace functionaries had been summoned, including the Queen's maids and all other servants still remaining on the grounds. King Thebaw and Queen Supayalat looked on as the colonel addressed their servants.

The Royal Family was being sent into exile, the colonel told the assembled notables. They were to go to India, to a location that had yet to be decided on. The British Government wished to provide them with an escort of attendants and advisors. The matter was to be settled by asking for volunteers.

There was a silence when he finished, followed by an outburst of embarrassed coughs, a flurry of awkward throat-clearings. Feet were shuffled, heads lowered, nails examined. Mighty wungyis shot sidelong glances at powerful wundauks; haughty myowuns stared awkwardly at the grass. Many of the assembled courtiers had never had a home other than the palace; never woken to a day whose hours were not ordered by the rising of the King; never known a world that was not centred on the nine-roofed hti of Burma's monarchs. All their lives they had been trained in the service of their master. But their training bound them to the King only so long as he embodied Burma and the sovereignty of the Burmese. They were neither the King's friends nor his confidants and it was not in their power to lighten the weight of his crown. The burdens of kingship were Thebaw's alone, solitude not the least among them.

Sladen's appeal went unanswered: there were no volunteers. The King's gaze, that mark of favour once so eagerly sought, passed unchecked over the heads of his courtiers. Thebaw remained impassive as he watched his most trusted servants averting their faces, awkwardly fingering the golden *tsaloe* sashes that marked their rank.

This is how power is eclipsed: in a moment of vivid realism, between the waning of one fantasy of governance and its replacement by the next; in an instant when the world springs free of its mooring of dreams and reveals itself to be girdled in the pathways of survival and self-preservation.

The King said: 'It does not matter who comes and who does not.' He turned to Sladen: 'But you must come with us, Sladen, as you are an old friend.'

'I regret this is impossible, Your Majesty,' answered Sladen. 'My duties will detain me here.'

The Queen, standing behind the King's chair, directed one of her flinty glances at her husband. It was all very well for him to express fine sentiments, but it was she who was eight months pregnant, and saddled moreover with the care of a colicky and difficult child. How was she to cope without servants and attendants? Who was going to calm the Second Princess when she had one of her raging tantrums? Her eyes scanned the assembly and settled on Dolly, who was sitting on her heels, braiding leaves of grass.

Dolly looked up to see the Queen glaring at her from her place on the pavilion balcony. She gave a cry and dropped the leaves. Had something happened? Was the Princess crying? She jumped to her feet and hurried towards the pavilion, followed by Evelyn, Augusta and several of the others.

Sladen breathed a sigh of relief as the girls came up the steps of the pavilion. Some volunteers at last!

'So you're going?' he said, as the girls hurried past, just to make sure.

The girls stopped to stare; Evelyn smiled and Augusta began to laugh. Of course they were going; they were orphans; they alone of the palace retainers had nowhere else to go, no families, no other means of support. What could they do but go with the King and Queen?

Sladen glanced once again at the assembly of courtiers and palace servants. Was there no one else present who would accompany the King? A single shaky voice answered in the affirmative. It belonged to an official of advanced age, the Padein Wun. He would go if he could bring along his son.

'How much time left?'

Sladen looked at his watch. 'Ten minutes.'

Just ten more minutes.

The King led Sladen into the pavilion and unlocked a door. A wedge of light fanned into the darkened room, igniting a firefly display of gold. The world's richest gem mines lay in Burma and many fine stones had passed into the possession of the ruling family. The King paused to run his hand over the jewelled case that held his most prized possession, the Ngamauk ring, set with the greatest, most valuable ruby ever mined in Burma. His ancestors had collected jewellery and gemstones as an afterthought, a kind of amusement. It was with these trinkets that he would have to provide for himself and his family in exile.

'Colonel Sladen, how is all this to be transported?'

Sladen conferred quickly with his fellow officers. Everything would be taken care of, he reassured the King. The hoard would be transported under guard to the King's ship. But now it was time to leave; the guard of honour was waiting.

The King walked out of the pavilion, flanked by Queen Supayalat and her mother. Halfway down the meandering path the Queen turned to look back. The Princesses were following a few paces behind with the maids. The girls were carrying their belongings in an assortment of boxes and bundles. Some had flowers in their hair, some were dressed in their brightest clothes. Dolly was walking beside Evelyn, who had the Second Princess on her hip. The two girls were giggling, oblivious, as though they were on their way to a festival.

The procession passed slowly through the long corridors of the palace, and across the mirrored walls of the Hall of Audience, past the shouldered guns of the guard of honour and the snapped-off salutes of the English officers.

Two carriages were waiting by the east gate. They were bullock-carts, *yethas*, the commonest vehicles on Mandalay's streets. The first of the carts had been fitted out with a ceremonial canopy. Just as he was about to step in, the King noticed that his canopy had seven tiers, the number allotted to a nobleman, not the nine due to a king.

He paused to draw breath. So the well-spoken English colonels had had their revenge after all, given the knife of victory a final little twist. In his last encounter with his erstwhile subjects he was to be publicly demoted, like an errant schoolchild. Sladen had guessed right: this was, of all the affronts Thebaw could have imagined, the most hurtful, the most egregious.

The ox-carts were small and there was not enough room for the maids. They followed on foot, a ragged little procession of eighteen brightly-dressed orphan girls carrying boxes and bundles.

Several hundred British soldiers fell in beside the ox-carts and the girls. They were heavily armed, prepared for trouble. The people of Mandalay were not expected to sit idly by while their King and Queen were herded into exile. Reports had been heard of planned riots and demonstrations, of desperate attempts to free the Royal Family.

The British high command believed this to be potentially the most dangerous moment of the entire operation. Some of them had served in India and an incident from the recent past weighed heavily on their minds. In the final days of the Indian uprising of 1857, Major Hodson had captured Bahadur Shah Zafar, the last of the Mughals, on the outskirts of Delhi. The blind and infirm old emperor had taken refuge in the tomb of his ancestor, Humayun, with two of his sons. When it came time for the major to escort the emperor and his sons back into the city, people had gathered in large numbers along the roadside. These crowds had grown more and more unruly, increasingly threatening. Finally, to keep the mob under control, the major had ordered the princes' execution. They had been pushed before the crowd and their brains had been blown out in full public view.

These events were no more than twenty-eight years in the past, their memory freshly preserved in the conversation of messes and clubs. It was to be hoped that no such eventuality would present itself now – but if it did it would not find King Thebaw's escort unprepared.

Mandalay had few thoroughfares that could accommodate a procession of this size. The ox-carts rumbled slowly along the broader avenues, banking steeply round the right-angled corners. The city's streets, although straight, were narrow and unpaved.

Their dirt surfaces were rutted with deep furrows, left by the annual tilling of the monsoons. The ox-carts' wheels were solid, carved from single blocks of wood. Their rigid frames seesawed wildly as they ploughed over the troughs. The Queen had to crouch over her swollen stomach to keep herself from being battered against the sides of the cart.

Neither the soldiers nor their royal captives knew the way to the port. The procession soon lost its way in the geometrical maze of Mandalay's streets. It strayed off in the direction of the northern hills and by the time the mistake was discovered it was almost dark. The carts wound their way back by the light of oil-soaked torches.

During the daylight hours the townsfolk had been careful to keep away from the streets: they had watched the ox-carts go by from windows and rooftops, at a safe distance from the soldiers and their bayonets. As dusk gathered, they began to trickle out of their homes. Reassured by the darkness, they attached themselves to the procession, in small and scattered groups.

Dolly looked very small when Rajkumar spotted her. She was walking beside a tall soldier, with a small cloth bundle balanced on her head. Her face was grimy and her *htamein* was caked with dust.

Rajkumar still had a few small things that he had found in the palace the night before. He went hurrying to a shop and exchanged them for a couple of handfuls of palm-sugar sweets. He wrapped the sweets in a banana leaf and tied the packet with string. Sprinting back, he caught up with the procession as it was making its way out of the town.

The British fleet was moored just a mile or so away, but it was dark now and the going was slow along the rough and uneven roads. With nightfall, thousands of Mandalay's residents came pouring out. They walked alongside the procession, keeping well away from the soldiers and their moving pools of torchlight.

Rajkumar sprinted ahead and climbed into a tamarind tree. When the first ox-cart came into view he caught a glimpse of the King, just visible through the tiny window. He was sitting straight-backed, his eyes fixed ahead of him, his body swaying to the cart's lurching motion.

Rajkumar worked his way slowly through the crowd until he was within a few feet of Dolly. He kept pace, watching the soldier who was marching beside her. The man turned his eyes away for a moment, to exchange a word with someone behind him. Rajkumar saw his chance: he darted through to Dolly and pressed his banana leaf packet into her hand.

'Take it,' he hissed. 'It's food.'

She stared at him, in uncomprehending surprise.

'It's the kalaa boy from yesterday.' Evelyn jogged her elbow. 'Take it.'

Rajkumar raced back into the shadows: he was no more than ten feet from Dolly, walking beside her, shrouded by the night. She picked the packet open and stared at the sweets. Then she held the packet up in her hands, offering it to the soldier who was marching beside her. The man smiled and shook his head, in friendly refusal. Someone said something in English, and he laughed. Several of the girls laughed too, Dolly included.

Rajkumar was astonished, even angry. What was Dolly doing? Why was she giving these hard-won tidbits to the very men who were leading her into captivity and exile? But then, slowly, his initial sense of betrayal turned to relief, even gratitude. Yes, of course, this was what one must do; Dolly was doing exactly what had to be done. What purpose would it serve for these girls to make a futile show of resentment? How could they succeed in defiance when the very army of the realm had succumbed? No, better by far to wait, and in the meanwhile to smile. This way Dolly would live.

Half a mile from the port, the soldiers formed a cordon across the road to hold the crowd back. People began to climb trees and gather on rooftops, looking for vantage points. Unexpectedly Rajkumar came upon Ma Cho sitting on a tree-stump. She was weeping, and between sobs, telling anyone who would listen the story of her encounter with the Queen the night before.

Rajkumar tried to console her by running a hand gently over her head. He had never seen an adult cry like this before. What was she weeping for? He glanced up, as though looking for an answer on the faces around him. It was not till then that he noticed that many others were crying too. He had been so intent on keeping pace with Dolly that he had paid little attention to the people around him. Now, looking on either side, he could see that every face was streaked with tears.

Rajkumar recognised several people from the looting of the night before. He recalled how they had hacked at the furniture and dug up the floors. Now those very men and women were lying prostrate with grief, mourning the loss of their King and sobbing in what looked like inconsolable sorrow.

Rajkumar was at a loss to understand this grief. He was, in a way, a feral creature, unaware that in certain places there exist invisible bonds linking people to one another through personifications of their commonality. In the Bengal of his birth those ties had been sundered by a century of conquest and no longer existed even as memory. Beyond the ties of blood, friendship and immediate reciprocity, Rajkumar recognised no loyalties, no obligations and no limits on the compass of his right to provide for himself. He reserved his trust and affection for those who earned it by concrete example and proven goodwill. Once earned, his loyalty was given wholeheartedly, with none of those unspoken provisions with which people usually guard against betrayal. In this too he was not unlike a creature that had returned to the wild. But that there should exist a universe of loyalties that was unrelated to himself and his own immediate needs – this was very nearly incomprehensible.

An anguished murmur ran through the crowd: the captives were moving, alighting from their ox-carts, entering a ship. Rajkumar jumped quickly into the branches of a nearby tree. The river was far away and all he could see was a steamer and a line of tiny figures filing up a gangplank. It was impossible to tell the figures apart. Then the ship's lights went out and it disappeared into the darkness.

Many thousands kept vigil through the night. The steamer's name was *Thooriya*, the sun. At daybreak, when the skies lightened over the hills, it was gone.

Five

After five days on the Irrawaddy the *Thooriya* slipped into the Rangoon river in the near-darkness of late evening. It anchored at mid-river, a good distance from the city's busy dockside.

At first light the next day the King went up on deck, carrying a pair of gilded binoculars. The glasses were of French manufacture, a prized heirloom that had once belonged to King Mindon. The old King had been much attached to the binoculars and had always carried them with him, even into his Audience Hall.

It was a cold morning and an opaque fog had risen off the river. The King waited patiently for the sun to scorch away the mist. When it had thinned a little he raised his glasses. Suddenly, there it was, the sight he had longed to see all his life: the towering mass of the Shwe Dagon pagoda, larger even than he had imagined, its hti thrusting skywards, floating on a bed of mist and fog, shining in the light of the dawn. He had worked on the hti himself, helped with his own hands in the gilding of the spire, layering sheets of gold leaf upon each other. It was King Mindon who had had the hti cast, in Mandalay; it had been sent down to the Shwe Dagon in a royal barge. He, Thebaw, had been a novice in the monastery then, and everybody, even the seniormost monks, had vied with each other for the honour of working on the hti.

The King lowered his binoculars to scan the city's waterfront. The instrument's rims welled over with a busy mass of things: walls, columns, carriages and hurrying people. Thebaw had heard about Rangoon from his half-brother, the Thonzai Prince. The town was founded by their ancestor, Alaungpaya, but few members of their dynasty had ever been able to visit it. The British had seized the town before Thebaw's birth, along with all of Burma's coastal provinces. It was then that the frontiers of the Burmese kingdom were driven back, almost halfway up the Irrawaddy. Since then the only members of the Royal Family who had been able to visit Rangoon were rebels and exiles, princes who had fallen out with the ruling powers in Mandalay.

The Thonzai Prince was one such: he had quarrelled with old King Mindon and had fled downriver, taking refuge in the British-held city. Later the Prince had been forgiven and had returned to Mandalay. In the palace he was besieged with questions: everyone wanted to know about Rangoon. Thebaw was in his teens then and he had listened spellbound as the Prince described the ships that were to be seen on the Rangoon river: the Chinese junks and Arab dhows and Chittagong sampans and American clippers and British ships-of-the-line. He had heard about the Strand and its great pillared mansions and buildings, its banks and hotels; about Godwin's wharf and the warehouses and timber mills that lined Pazundaung Creek; the wide streets and the milling crowds and the foreigners who thronged the public places: Englishmen, Cooringhees, Tamils, Americans, Malays, Bengalis, Chinese.

One of the stories the Thonzai Prince used to tell was about Bahadur Shah Zafar, the last Mughal emperor. After the suppression of the uprising of 1857 the British had exiled the deposed emperor to Rangoon. He'd lived in a small house not far from the Shwe Dagon. One night the Prince had slipped off with a few of his friends and gone to look at the emperor's house. They'd found him sitting on his veranda, fingering his beads. He was blind and very old. The Prince and his friends had meant to approach him but at the last minute they had changed their minds. What could you say to such a man?

There was a street in Rangoon, the Prince had said, that was named after the old emperor – Mughal Street. Many Indians lived there: the Prince had claimed that there were more Indians than Burmese in Rangoon. The British had brought them there, to work in the docks and mills, to pull rickshaws and empty the latrines. Apparently they couldn't find local people to do these jobs. And indeed, why would the Burmese do that kind of work?

In Burma no one ever starved, everyone knew how to read and write, and land was to be had for the asking: why should they pull rickshaws and carry nightsoil?

The King raised his glasses to his eyes and spotted several Indian faces, along the waterfront. What vast, what incomprehensible power, to move people in such huge numbers from one place to another – emperors, kings, farmers, dockworkers, soldiers, coolies, policemen. Why? Why this furious movement – people taken from one place to another, to pull rickshaws, to sit blind in exile?

And where would his own people go, now that they were a part of this empire? It wouldn't suit them, all this moving about. They were not a portable people, the Burmese; he knew this, very well, for himself. He had never wanted to go anywhere. Yet here he was, on his way to India.

He turned to go below deck again: he didn't like to be away from his cabin too long. Several of his valuables had disappeared, some of them on that very first day, when the English officers were transporting them from the palace to the *Thooriya*. He had asked about the lost things and the officers had stiffened and looked offended and talked of setting up a committee of inquiry. He had realised that for all their haughty ways and grand uniforms, they were not above some common thievery.

The strange thing was that if only they'd asked he'd gladly have gifted them some of his baubles; they would probably have received better things than those they'd taken – after all, what did they know about gemstones?

Even his ruby ring was gone. The other things he didn't mind so much – they were just trinkets – but he grieved for the Ngamauk. They should have left him the Ngamauk.

On arriving in Madras, King Thebaw and his entourage were taken to the mansion that had been made over to them for the duration of their stay in the city. The house was large and luxurious but there was something disconcerting about it. Perhaps it was the contingent of fierce-looking British soldiers standing at the gate or perhaps it had something to do with the crowds of curious onlookers who gathered round its walls every day. Whatever it was, none of the girls felt at home there.

Mr Cox often urged the members of the household to step outside, to walk in the spacious, well-kept gardens (Mr Cox was an English policeman who had accompanied them on their journey from Rangoon and he spoke Burmese well). Dolly, Evelyn and Augusta dutifully walked around the house a few times but they were always glad to be back indoors.

Strange things began to happen. There was news from Mandalay that the royal elephant had died. The elephant was white, and so greatly cherished that it was suckled on breast-milk: nursing mothers would stand before it and slip off their blouses. Everyone had known that the elephant would not long survive the fall of the dynasty. But who could have thought that it would die so soon? It seemed like a portent. The house was sunk in gloom.

Unaccountably, the King developed a craving for pork. Soon he was consuming inordinate amounts of bacon and ham. One day he ate too much and fell sick. A doctor arrived with a leather bag and went stomping through the house in his boots. The girls had to follow behind him, swabbing the floor. No one slept that night.

One morning Apodaw Mahta, the elderly woman who supervised the Queen's nurses, ran outside and climbed into a tree. The Queen sent the other nurses to persuade her to climb down. They spent an hour under the tree. Apodaw Mahta paid no attention.

The Queen called the nurses back and sent Dolly and the other girls to talk to Apodaw Mahta. The tree was a *neem* and its foliage was very dense. The girls stood round the trunk and looked up. Apodaw Mahta had wedged herself into a fork between two branches.

'Come down,' said the girls. 'It's going to be dark soon.'

'No.'

'Why not?'

'I was a squirrel in my last birth. I remember this tree. This is where I want to stay.'

Apodaw Mahta had a pot belly and warts on her face. 'She looks more like a toad than a squirrel,' Evelyn whispered. The girls screamed with laughter and ran back inside.

U Maung Gyi, the interpreter, went out and shook his fist at her. The King was going to come down from his room, he said, and he was going to bring a stick to beat her with. At that Apodaw Mahta came scurrying down. She'd lived in the Mandalay palace for a very long time and was terrified of the King.

Anyone could have told her that the last thing in the world the King was likely to do was to run out into the garden and beat her with a stick. He'd never once stepped out of the house in all the time they'd been in Madras. Towards the beginning of their stay he had once asked to visit the Madras Museum. This had taken Mr Cox by surprise and he had said no, quite vehemently. After that, as though in protest, the King had refused to step out of the house.

Sitting in his room, with nothing to do, curious fancies began to enter the King's mind. He decided to have a huge gold plate made in preparation for the birth of his new child. The plate would weigh several pounds and it would be set with one hundred and fifty of his most valuable rubies. To pay for the plate, he began to sell some of his possessions. The household's Tamil employees served as his emissaries.

Some of these employees were spies and Mr Cox soon found out about the sales. He was furious. The King was wasting his wealth, he said, and what was more, he was being cheated. The servants were selling his things for a fraction of their value.

This made the King even more secretive in his dealings. He handed Dolly and Evelyn expensive jewellery and asked them to arrange to have it sold. The result was that he got even lower prices. Inevitably the Englishmen found out through their spies. They declared that the King couldn't be trusted with money and enacted a law appropriating his family's most valuable properties.

A mutinous quiet descended on the mansion. Dolly began to notice odd little changes in Evelyn and Augusta and her other friends. Their shikoes became perfunctory; they began to complain about sore knees and refused to stay on all fours while waiting on the Queen. Sometimes when she shouted at them they would scowl back at her.

One night the Queen woke up thirsty and found all her maids asleep beside her bed. She was so angry she threw a lamp at the wall and slapped Evelyn and Mary.

Evelyn was very upset. She said to Dolly: 'They can't hit us and beat us any more. We don't have to stay if we don't want to.'

'How do you know?' Dolly said.

'Mr Cox told me. He said we were slaves in Mandalay but now we're free.'

'But we're prisoners, aren't we?'

'Not us,' said Evelyn. 'Only Min and Mebya' – meaning the King and Queen.

Dolly thought about this for a while. 'And what about the Princesses?'

Now it was Evelyn's turn to think.

'Yes,' she said at last. 'The Princesses are prisoners too.'

That settled the matter as far as Dolly was concerned. Where the Princesses were, she would be too: she couldn't imagine what they would do without her.

One morning a man arrived at the gate saying he'd come from Burma to take his wife back home. His wife was Taungzin Minthami, one of the Queen's favourite nurses. She had left her children behind in Burma and was terribly homesick. She decided to go back with her husband.

This reminded everyone of the one thing they'd been trying to forget, which was that left to themselves they would all rather have gone home – that none of them was there because he or she wanted to be. The Queen began to worry that all her girls were going to leave so she began to hand out gifts to her favourites. Dolly was one of the lucky ones, but neither Evelyn nor Augusta received anything.

The two girls were furious at being passed over and they began to make sarcastic comments within the Queen's hearing. The Queen spoke to the Padein Wun, and he took them into a locked room and beat them and pulled their hair. But this made the girls even more resentful. Next morning they refused to wait on the Queen.

The Queen decided that the matter had passed beyond resolution. She summoned Mr Cox and told him that she wanted to send seven of the girls back to Burma. She would make do by hiring local servants.

Once the Queen had decided on something there was no

question of persuading her to change her mind. The seven girls left the next week: Evelyn, Augusta, Mary, Wahthau, Nan Pau, Minlwin, and even Hemau, who was, of all of them, the closest to Dolly in age. Dolly had always thought of them as her older sisters, her family. She knew she would never see them again. On the morning of their departure she locked herself into a room and wouldn't come out, even to watch their carriage roll out of the gates. U Maung Gyi, the interpreter, took them to the port. When he came back he said the girls had cried when they'd boarded the ship.

A number of new servants were hired, men and women, all local people. Dolly was now one of last remaining members of the original Mandalay contingent: it fell on her to teach the new staff the ways of the household. The new ayahs and maids came to Dolly when they wanted to know how things were done in the Mandalay palace. It was she who had to teach them how to shiko and how to move about the Queen's bedroom on their hands and knees. It was very hard at first, for she couldn't make herself understood. She would explain everything in the politest way but they wouldn't understand so she would shout louder and louder and they would become more and more frightened. They would start knocking things over, breaking chairs and upsetting tables.

Slowly she learnt a few words of Tamil and Hindustani. It became a little easier to work with them then, but they still seemed strangely clumsy and inept. There were times when she couldn't help laughing – when she saw them trying out their shikoes, for example, wiggling their elbows and straightening their saris. Or when she watched them lumbering around on their knees, huffing and puffing, or getting themselves tangled in their clothes and falling flat on their faces. Dolly could never understand why they found it so hard to move about on their hands and knees. To her it seemed much easier than having to stand up every time you wanted to do something. It was much more restful this way: when you weren't doing anything in particular you could relax with your weight on your heels. But the new ayahs seemed to think it impossibly hard. You could never trust them to carry a tray to the Queen. They would either spill everything as they tried to get across the room, or else they would creep along so slowly that it would take them half an hour to get from the door to her bed. The Queen would get very impatient, lying on her side and watching her glass of water move across the room as though it were being carried by a snail. Sometimes she would shout, and that would be worse still. The terrified ayah would fall over, tray and all, and the whole process would have to be resumed from the start.

It would have been mucn easier of course if the Queen weren't so insistent on observing all the old Mandalay rules – the shikoes, the crawling – but she wouldn't hear of any changes. She was the Queen of Burma, she said, and if she didn't insist on being treated properly how could she expect anyone else to give her her due?

One day U Maung Gyi caused a huge scandal. One of the Queen's nurses went into the nursery and found him on the floor with another nurse, his longyi pulled up over his waist. Instead of scurrying off in shame he turned on his discoverer and began to beat her. He chased her down the corridor and into the King's bedroom.

The King was sitting at a table rolling a cheroot. U Maung Gyi lunged at the nurse as she went running in. She tripped and grabbed at the tablecloth. Everything flew into the air: there was tobacco everywhere. The King sneezed and went on sneezing for what seemed like hours. When he finally stopped he was angrier than anyone had ever seen him before. This meant still more departures.

With the head nurse thinking herself to be a squirrel and another gone home to Burma, the Queen now had very few dependable nurses left. She decided to get an English midwife. Mr Cox found one for her, a Mrs Wright. She seemed pleasant and friendly enough, but her arrival led to other problems. She wouldn't shiko and she wouldn't go down on her hands and knees while waiting on the Queen. The Queen appealed to Mr Cox but the Englishman came out in support of Mrs Wright. She could bow, he said, from the waist, but she needn't shiko and she certainly wouldn't crawl. She was an Englishwoman.

The Queen accepted this ruling but it didn't endear Mrs Wright to her. She began to rely more and more on a Burmese masseur who had somehow attached himself to the royal entourage. He was very good with his hands and was able to make the Queen's pains go away. But the English doctor found out and made a huge fuss. He said that what the masseur was doing was an affront to medical science. He said that the man was touching Her Highness in unhealthy places. The Queen decided he was mad and declared that she would not send the masseur away. The doctor retaliated by refusing to treat her any more.

Fortunately the Queen's labour was very short and the delivery quick and uncomplicated. The child was a girl and she was named Ashin Hteik Su Myat Paya.

Everyone was nervous because they knew how badly the Queen had wanted a boy. But the Queen surprised them. She was glad, she said: a girl would be better able to bear the pain of exile.

For a while Mandalay became a city of ghosts.

After the British invasion, many of the King's soldiers escaped into the countryside with their weapons. They began to act on their own, staging attacks on the occupiers, sometimes materialising inside the city at night. The invaders responded by tightening their grip. There were round-ups, executions, hangings. The sound of rifle-fire echoed through the streets; people locked themselves into their homes and stayed away from the bazaars. Whole days went by when Ma Cho had no call to light her cooking fire.

One night Ma Cho's stall was broken into. Between the two of them, Rajkumar and Ma Cho succeeded in driving the intruders away. But considerable damage had already been caused; lighting a lamp, Ma Cho discovered that most of her pots, pans and utensils had been either stolen or destroyed. She let out a stricken wail. 'What am I to do? Where am I to go?'

Rajkumar squatted beside her. 'Why don't you talk to Saya John?' he suggested. 'Perhaps he'll be able to help.'

Ma Cho snorted in tearful disgust. 'Don't talk to me about Saya John. What's the use of a man who's never there when you need him?' She began to sob, her hands covering her face.

Tenderness welled up in Rajkumar. 'Don't cry, Ma Cho.' He

ran his hands clumsily over her head, combing her curly hair with his nails. 'Stop, Ma Cho. Stop.'

She blew her nose and straightened up. 'It's all right,' she said gruffly. 'It's nothing.' Fumbling in the darkness, she reached for his longyi, leaning forward to wipe the tears from her face.

Often before, Ma Cho's bouts of tears had ended in this way, with her wiping her face on his thin cotton garment. But this time, as her fingers drew together the loose cloth, the chafing of the fabric produced a new effect on Rajkumar. He felt the kindling of a glow of heat deep within his body, and then, involuntarily, his pelvis thrust itself forward, towards her fingers, just as she was closing her grip. Unmindful of the intrusion, Ma Cho drew a fistful of cloth languidly across her face, stroking her cheeks, patting the furrows round her mouth and dabbing the damp hollows of her eyes. Standing close beside her, Rajkumar swayed, swivelling his hips to keep pace with her hand. It was only when she was running the tip of the bunched cloth between her parted lips that the fabric betrayed him. Through the layered folds of cloth, now wet and clinging, she felt an unmistakable hardness touching on the soft corners of her mouth. She tightened her grip, suddenly alert, and gave the gathered cloth a probing pinch. Rajkumar gasped, arching his back.

'Oh?' she grunted. Then, with a startling deftness, one of her hands flew to the knot of his longyi and tugged it open; the other pushed him down on his knees. Parting her legs she drew him, kneeling, towards her stool. Rajkumar's forehead was on her cheek now; the tip of his skinned nose thrust deep into the hollow beneath her jaw. He caught the odour of turmeric and onion welling up through the cleft between her breasts. And then a blinding whiteness flashed before his eyes and his head was pulled as far back as it could go, tugged by convulsions in his spine.

Abruptly, she pushed him away, with a yelp of disgust. 'What am I doing?' she cried. 'What am I doing with this boy, this child, this half-wit kalaa?' Elbowing him aside, she clambered up her ladder and vanished into her room.

It was a while before Rajkumar summoned the courage to say anything. 'Ma Cho,' he called up, in a thin, shaking voice. 'Are you angry?'

'No,' came a bark from above. 'I'm not angry. I want you to forget Ma Cho and go to sleep. You have your own future to think of.'

They never spoke of what happened that night. Over the next few days, Rajkumar saw very little of Ma Cho: she would disappear early in the morning, returning only late at night. Then, one morning, Rajkumar woke up and knew that she was gone for good. Now, for the first time, he climbed the ladder that led up to her room. The only thing he found was a new, blue longyi, lying folded in the middle of the room. He knew that she'd left it for him.

What was he to do now? Where was he to go? He'd assumed all along that he would eventually return to his sampan, to join his shipmates. But now, thinking of his life on the boat, he knew he would not go back. He had seen too much in Mandalay and acquired too many new ambitions.

During the last few weeks he'd thought often of what Saya John's son, Matthew had said – about the British invasion being provoked by teak. No detail could have been more precisely calculated to lodge in a mind like Rajkumar's, both curious and predatory. If the British were willing to go to war over a stand of trees, it could only be because they knew of some hidden wealth, secreted within the forest. What exactly these riches were he didn't know but it was clear that he would never find out except by seeing for himself.

Even while pondering this, he was walking quickly, heading away from the bazaar. Now, looking around to take stock of where he was, he discovered that he had come to the whitewashed facade of a church. He decided to linger, walking past the church once, and then again. He circled and waited, and sure enough, within the hour he spotted Saya John approaching the church, hand in hand with his son.

'Saya.'

'Rajkumar!'

Now, standing face to face with Saya John, Rajkumar found himself hanging his head in confusion. How was he to tell him about Ma Cho, when it was he himself who was responsible for the Saya's cuckolding?

It was Saya John who spoke first: 'Has something happened to Ma Cho?'

Rajkumar nodded.

'What is it? Has she gone?'

'Yes, Saya.'

Saya John gave a long sigh, rolling his eyes heavenwards. 'Perhaps it's for the best,' he said. 'I think it's a sign that the time has come for this sinner to turn celibate.'

'Saya?'

'Never mind. And what will you do now, Rajkumar? Go back to India in your boat?'

'No, Saya.' Rajkumar shook his head. 'I want to stay here, in Burma.'

'And what will you do for a living?'

'You said, Saya, that if I ever wanted a job I was to come to you. Saya?'

One morning the King read in the newspapers that the Viceroy was coming to Madras. In a state of great excitement he sent for Mr Cox.

'Is the Viceroy going to call on us?' he asked.

Mr Cox shook his head. 'Your Highness, I have not been informed of any such plan.'

'But protocol demands it. The Kings of Burma are the peers of such sovereigns as the kings of Siam and Cambodia and of the emperors of China and Japan.'

'I regret, Your Highness, that it is probably too late to effect a change in the Viceroy's itinerary.'

'But we must see him, Mr Cox.'

'The Viceroy's time has already been spoken for. I am sorry.'

'But we wish to find out what the Government plans to do with us. When we came here, we were told that this was not to be our permanent residence. We are eager to know where we are to live and when we are to go there.'

Mr Cox went away and came back a few days later. 'Your Highness,' he said, 'I am glad to be able to inform you that the matter of a permanent residence for you and your family has finally been resolved.'

'Oh?' said the King. 'And where is it to be?'

'A place by the name of Ratnagiri.'

'What?' The King stared at him, nonplussed. 'Where is this place?'

'Some hundred and twenty miles south of Bombay. An excellent place, with fine views of the sea.'

'Fine views?'

The King sent for a map and asked Mr Cox to show him where Ratnagiri was. Mr Cox indicated a point somewhere between Bombay and Goa. The King was thoroughly alarmed to note that the place was too insignificant to be marked on the map.

'But we would rather be in a city, Mr Cox. Here in Madras. Or Bombay. Or Calcutta. What will we do in a small village?'

'Ratnagiri is a district headquarters, Your Highness, not a village by any means.'

'How long are we to remain there? When will we be allowed to return to Burma?'

Now it was Mr Cox's turn to be nonplussed. It had not occurred to him that the King still harboured hopes of returning to Burma.

Mr Cox was a kindly man, in his gruff way. 'Your Highness,' he said, in a quiet and gentle voice, 'you must prepare yourself to be in Ratnagiri for some time, a considerable time I fear. Perhaps . . .

'Perhaps for ever?'

'Those were not my words.' Mr Cox coughed. 'Not at all. Those words were not mine. No, I must insist, they were not . . .'

The King rose to his feet abruptly and went to his room. He did not step out again for several days.

They left Madras a month later on a steamer called the *Clive*. The voyage was very different this time around. They sailed along the coast with the shore rarely out of sight. They went through the Palk Straits, with the northern tip of Ceylon visible on the left, and the southernmost point in India, Cape Comorin, in view on the right.

Four days after leaving Madras the *Clive* nosed into a wide and sunlit bay. There were cliffs at either end of the bay, a sweeping beach and a meandering river. The town was on a hill, above the bay; it was so thickly blanketed with coconut palms that very little could be seen of it.

They spent the night on the steamer and went ashore the next morning. The *Clive* pulled in beside a jetty that reached a long way out into the shallow bay. Carriages were waiting for them at the far end, near a fishing village. The King was greeted with a gun salute and a guard of honour. Then the carriages set off in single file down a narrow, tree-shaded path. There were red-tiled houses on either side, with gardens of mango trees and areca palms. There were policemen everywhere, holding back the people who'd gathered to watch. They passed a bazaar and a grey-walled gaol and a line of police-barracks. The road ended at a large, two-storeyed bungalow set inside a walled garden. It was on a bluff above the town, overlooking the bay. It was called Outram House.

The King went in first and climbed slowly up the stairs. He came to a large bedroom and went inside. The room was furnished with a desk, a bed and three armchairs. It opened on to a small balcony that faced westwards, towards the sea. The King walked very slowly round the room. He toyed with the slatted wooden shutters, scratched at a rosette of candlewax and ran a finger over a half-effaced mark on the wall, crumbling the flaking plaster between finger and thumb. There was a faintly musty smell in the room and a tracing of mildew on the wall. He tried to mark these things in his memory for he knew they would fade in time and a day would come when he would want to remember them – the vividness of his first encounter with the site of his captivity, the sour mildewed smell of it and the roughness of its texture upon the skin.

Downstairs Dolly was running across the garden with the First Princess, chasing a lizard of a bright red colour. This was different from the mansion in Madras, much smaller but more welcoming. Here one could run and play hide-and-seek between the trunks of leaning coconut palms. She came to a mango tree whose branches reached all the way up to a window on the top floor of the bungalow. Perhaps that would be her room, her window, with twigs scratching against the glass.

A bell began to ring in a temple, somewhere in the town below. She stopped to listen, looking down the slope of the garden, across the canopy of coconut fronds, towards the wide sparkling bay. She could smell drying fish and incense. How bright it was, how peaceful. Everything seemed so safe here, behind these high stone walls.

The King heard the bells too. He stepped out on to the balcony of the upstairs bedroom. The whole town lay spread out below, framed by the sweep of the bay and the two steep promontories on either side. The view was magnificent, just as Mr Cox had said. He went back into the bedroom. He sat in one of the armchairs and watched the ghostly shadows of coconut palms swaying on the room's white plaster walls. In this room the hours would accumulate like grains of sand until they buried him.

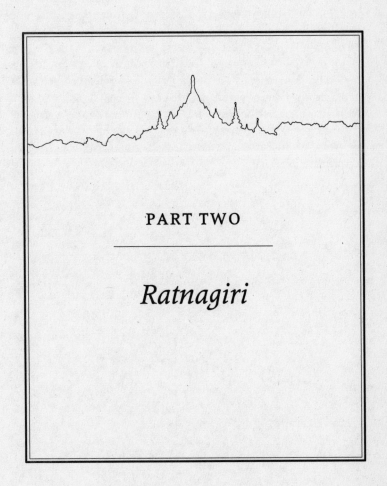

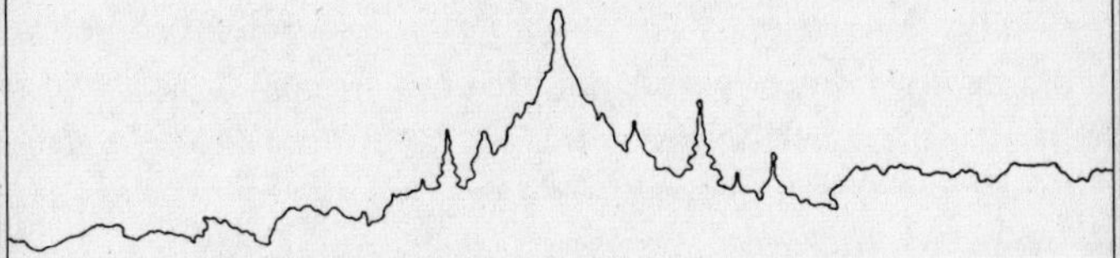

PART TWO

Ratnagiri

Six

For Rajkumar and Saya John the busy time of year was when the rivers rose. Every few weeks they would load a cargo of sacks, crates and boxes on to one of the Irrawaddy Steamship Flotilla's riverboats: shuddering, paddle-wheeled steamers, captained, more often than not, by Scotsmen, and crewed mainly by Chittagong khalasis, such as Rajkumar had himself once sought to be. With the weight of the engorged river behind them, they would go shooting downstream from Mandalay at such speeds as to put the flotilla's itineraries to rout. At sunset, when it was time to pull into shore, they would frequently find themselves anchoring beside some tiny river-bank hamlet that consisted of nothing more than a few thatched huts, clustered around a police station parade ground.

No matter how small the village, a fair would materialise instantly around the anchored steamer: hawkers, food vendors, boat-borne shopkeepers, sellers of fried snacks and distillers of country liquor would come hastening with their wares, delighted by the unexpected netting of this great shoal of customers. Sometimes news of the steamer's arrival would filter through to a travelling troupe of entertainers. At nightfall, to the accompaniment of a concert of rain-bred croaking, puppeteers' screens would come alive above the banks and the gaunt, twitching outlines of the Bodaw and the Bayin, the Minthami and the Minthagyi, the Natkadaw and the Nan Belu would loom out of the darkness, as large and as familiar as the shadows on the moon.

Saya John liked to travel first-class, in a cabin: his business was flourishing and he had money to spare. He had moved into a large house on Mandalay's 33rd Street – a dwelling that housed Rajkumar as well as everyone else who was in any way connected with his business. The British occupation had changed everything: Burma had been quickly integrated into the Empire, forcibly converted into a province of British India. Courtly Mandalay was now a bustling commercial hub; resources were being exploited with an energy and efficiency hitherto undreamt of. The Mandalay palace had been refurbished to serve the conquerors' recondite pleasures: the west wing had been converted into a British Club; the Queen's Hall of Audience had now become a billiard room; the mirrored walls were lined with months-old copies of *Punch* and the *Illustrated London News*; the gardens had been dug up to make room for tennis courts and polo grounds; the exquisite little monastery in which Thebaw had spent his novitiate had become a chapel where Anglican priests administered the sacrament to British trooops. Mandalay, it was confidently predicted, would soon become the Chicago of Asia; prosperity was the natural destiny of a city that guarded the confluence of two of the world's mightiest waterways, the Irrawaddy and the Chindwin.

Saya John was earning rich profits now, ferrying supplies and provisions to teak camps. Although not a man who had a great craving for luxuries, he felt it necessary to grant himself a good night's sleep when he was setting out on one of his supply expeditions. A cabin on the first-class deck of an Irrawaddy steamship was, after all, but a small indulgence.

As for Rajkumar, he spent his shipboard nights on the lower deck. Some of the crew were boys his own age, whose job it was to hang over the bows of the vessel, plumb line in hand, just as he himself had once done, watching for shifting sandbanks and calling out the depths, '*Ek gaz; do gaz, teen gaz* . . .' With them he would slip into his own Chittagong tongue, and when the steamer lay at rest, they would rouse him from his deckside mat and take him over to land, to show him the places where boatmen went at night.

When it came time to go ashore, the next day, Rajkumar would be red-eyed and Saya John fresh, heartily breakfasted and eager to get his cargo unloaded, to be on his way to the camp where he was headed. The first part of the journey was usually by ox-cart.

They would breast rivers of mud as they went creaking towards the distant mountains.

When everything went as planned, these journeys would end at some tiny inland hamlet, with a team of elephants waiting to relieve them of their cargo, leaving them free to turn back. But all too often they would arrive at their roadhead only to learn that the camp ahead could spare no elephants; that they would have to find their own porters to carry their cargo into the mountains. Then Rajkumar too had to yoke a basket to his back, a wickerwork *pah* with a deep cover and a forehead-strap. To his particular charge would fall the small bespoke luxuries that were specially ordered by the forest Assistants who ran the timber camps – cigars, bottles of whisky, tins of canned meat and sardines, once even a crystal decanter sent up by Rowe & Co., the big Rangoon department store.

They would set off at daybreak with Saya John leading a long line of porters and Rajkumar bringing up the rear; they would climb sideways, like mules, along the rain-sodden paths, digging the edges of their feet into the red, purchaseless mud. It was a ritual with Saya John, a kind of superstition, always to start these journeys in European clothes: a sola topee, leather boots, khaki trousers. Rajkumar went barefoot, like the porters, wearing nothing but a vest, a longyi and a farmer's wide-brimmed hat.

But no matter how much care he took, Saya John's costume never survived long intact: the undergrowth would come alive as they passed by, leeches unfurling like tendrils as they awoke to the warmth of the passing bodies. Being the most heavily clothed in the party, it was Saya John who invariably reaped the richest of these bloody harvests. Every hour or two he would call a halt. The trails were lined with thatched bamboo shelters, erected at regular intervals by the timbermen. Sitting huddled beneath the dripping thatch, Saya John would reach into his bags to retrieve the tarpaulin-wrapped packet in which Rajkumar had packed his matches and cheroots. Lighting a cheroot he would draw deep until a long, glowing tip had formed. Then he would go over his body, burning off his leeches, one by one.

The thickest clusters of leeches were gathered always along the fissures of the body, where cloth chafed on skin: the folds and creases would guide the creatures to their favourite destinations – armpits, the groin, the cracks between legs and buttocks. In his shoes Saya John would sometimes find scores of leeches, most of them clinging to the webbed skin between the toes – to a leech the most prized of the human body's offerings. There were always some that had burst under the pressure of the boot, leaving their suckers embedded in the flesh. These were the sites that were most likely to attract fresh attacks, from insects as well as leeches; left unattended they would fester, turn into foul-smelling, deep-rooted jungle sores. To these spots Saya John would apply *kow-yok* – a tar-like touch of red tobacco, smeared on paper or cloth. The poultice would fasten itself so tightly to the skin as to stay attached even when immersed in water, drawing out the infection and protecting the wound. At each stop Saya John would shed an article of clothing, and within the space of a few hours he would be dressed like Rajkumar, in nothing more than a longyi and a vest.

Almost invariably they would find themselves following the course of a *chaung*, a rushing mountain stream. Every few minutes a log would come hurtling through the water, on its way down to the plain. To be caught in mid-stream by one of these hurtling two-ton projectiles was to be crippled or killed. When the path switched from one bank of the chaung to the other, a lookout would be posted to call out the intervals between logs so that the porters would know when it was safe to cross.

Often the logs came not singly but in groups, dozens of tons of hardwood caroming down the stream together: when they hit each other the impact would be felt all the way up the banks. At times a log would snag, in rapids or on the shore, and within minutes a tangled dam would rise out of the water, plugging the stream. One after another logs would go cannoning into one another, adding to the weight of the accumulated hardwood. The weight of the mass would mount until it became an irresistible force. Then at last something would give; a log, nine feet in girth, would snap like a matchstick. With a great detonation the dam would capsize and a tidal wave of wood and water would wash down the slopes of the mountain.

'Chaungs are the tradewinds of teak,' Saya John liked to say.

In the dry season, when the earth cracked and the forests wilted, the streams would dwindle into dribbles upon the slope, barely able to shoulder the weight of a handful of leaves, mere trickles of mud between strings of cloudy riverbed pools. This was the season for the timbermen to comb the forest for teak. The trees, once picked, had to be killed and left to dry, for the density of teak is such that it will not remain afloat while its heartwood is moist. The killing was achieved with a girdle of incisions, thin slits, carved deep into the wood at a height of four feet and six inches off the ground (teak being ruled, despite the wildness of its terrain, by imperial stricture in every tiny detail).

The assassinated trees were left to die where they stood, sometimes for three years or even more. It was only after they had been judged dry enough to float that they were marked for felling. That was when the axemen came, shouldering their weapons, squinting along the blades to judge their victims' angles of descent.

Dead though they were, the trees would sound great tocsins of protest as they fell, unloosing thunderclap explosions that could be heard miles away, bringing down everything in their path, rafts of saplings, looped nets of rattan. Thick stands of bamboo were flattened in moments, thousands of jointed limbs exploding simultaneously in deadly splinter blasts, throwing up mushroom clouds of debris.

Then teams of elephants would go to work, guided by their handlers, their *oo-sis* and *pe-sis*, butting, prodding, levering with their trunks. Belts of wooden rollers would be laid on the ground, and quick-fingered *pa-kyeiks*, specialised in the tying of chains, would dart between the elephants' legs, fastening steel harnesses. When finally the logs began to move such was the friction of their passage that water-carriers would have to run beside them, dousing the smoking rollers with tilted buckets.

Dragged to the banks of chaungs, the logs were piled into stacks and left to await the day when the chaungs would awaken from the hibernation of the hot season. With the first rains, the puddles along the streams' beds would stir and stretch and join hands, rising slowly to the task of clearing away the debris accumulated over the long months of dessication. Then, in a matter of days, with the rains pouring down, they would rear up in their beds, growing hundreds-fold in height: where a week before they had wilted under the weight of twigs and leaves, they would now throw two-ton logs downstream like feathered darts.

Thus would begin the logs' journey to the timberyards of Rangoon: with elephants nudging them over the slopes into the frothing waters of the chaungs below. Following the lie of the land they would make their way from feeder-streams to tributaries, until they debouched finally into the engorged rivers of the plains.

In years of bad rain, when the chaungs were too feeble to heft these great weights, the timber companies' profits plummeted. But even in good years they were jealous, punishing taskmasters – these mountain streams. At the height of the season a single snagged tree could result in a pile-up of five thousand logs or even more. The servicing of these white waters was a science unto itself, with its own cadre of adepts, special teams of oo-sis and elephants who spent the monsoon months ceaselessly patrolling the forest: these were the famed *aunging* herds, skilled in the difficult and dangerous arts of clearing chaungs.

Once, while sheltering beside a dying and girdled trunk of teak, Saya John gave Rajkumar a mint leaf to hold in one hand and a fallen leaf from the tree in the other. Feel them, he said, rub them between your fingers.

Teak is a relative of mint, *tectona grandis*, born of the same genus of flowering plant, but of a distaff branch, presided over by that most soothing of herbs, verbena. It counts among its close kin many other fragrant and familiar herbs – sage, savoury, thyme, lavender, rosemary and most remarkably holy basil, with its many descendants, green and purple, smooth-leaved and coarse, pungent and fragrant, bitter and sweet.

There was a teak tree in Pegu once, with a trunk that measured one hundred and six feet from the ground to its first branch. Imagine what a mint's leaf would be like if it were to grow upon a plant that rose more than a hundred feet into the air, straight up from the ground, without tapering or deviation, its stem as straight as a plumb-line, its first leaves appearing almost at the top, clustered close together and outspread, like the hands of a surfacing diver.

The mint leaf was the size of Rajkumar's thumb while the other would have covered an elephant's footprint; one was a weed that served to flavour soup while the other came from a tree that had felled dynasties, caused invasions, created fortunes, brought a new way of life into being. Yet even Rajkumar, who was in no way inclined to indulge the far-fetched or the fanciful, had to admit that between the faint hairiness of the one and the bristling, coarse-textured fur of the other, there was an unmistakable kinship, a palpably familial link.

It was by the bells of their elephants that teak camps made themselves known. Even when muted by rain or distance, the sound could always be counted on to produce a magical effect on a line of porters, lengthening their pace and freshening their step.

No matter how long he had walked or how tired he was Rajkumar would feel a surging in his heart when a camp loomed suddenly into view – a forest clearing with a few thatch-roofed huts clustered around a *tai*, an elongated wooden house on stilts.

Teak camps were always the same and yet they were all different, no two camps ever being built in the same place, from one season to the next. The initial felling of the forest was done by elephants with the result that the clearings were invariably scarred with upturned trees and ragged pits.

A tai stood at the centre of each campsite and it was occupied always by the forest Assistant, the company officer in charge of the camp. To Rajkumar's eye these tais were structures of incomparable elegance: they were built on wooden platforms, raised some six feet off the ground on teakwood posts. Each was endowed with several large rooms, one leading into another, and ending finally in a wide veranda, always so oriented as to command the best possible view. In a camp where the forest Assistant was served by an industrious *luga-lei*, the veranda of the *tai* would be sheltered by a canopy of flowering vines, with blooms that glowed like embers against the bamboo matting. Here would sit the Assistant of an evening, with a glass of whisky in one hand and a pipe in another, watching the sun go down across the valley and dreaming of his faraway Home.

They were distant, brooding men, these Assistants. Before going to see them Saya John would always change into European clothes, a white shirt, duck trousers. Rajkumar would watch from a distance as Saya John approached the tai to call out a greeting, with one hand resting deferentially on the bottom rung of the ladder. If invited up he would climb the ladder slowly, placing one foot carefully after the other. There would follow a flurry of smiles, bows, greetings. Sometimes he would be back in a matter of minutes; sometimes the Assistant would offer him a whisky and ask him to stay to dinner.

As a rule the Assistants were always very correct in their manner. But there was a time once when an Assistant began to berate Saya John, accusing him of having forgotten something he had ordered. 'Take that grinning face out of here . . . ,' the Englishman shouted, 'I'll see you in hell, Johnny Chinaman.'

At the time Rajkumar knew very little English but there was no mistaking the anger and contempt in the Assistant's voice. For an instant Rajkumar saw Saya John through the Assistant's eyes: small, eccentric and erratically dressed, in his ill-fitting European clothes, his portliness accentuated by the patched duck trousers that hung in thick folds around his ankles, with his scuffed sola topee perched precariously on his head.

Rajkumar had been in Saya John's service three years and had come to look up to him as his guide in all things. He found himself growing hot with indignation on his mentor's behalf. He ran across the clearing to the tai, fully intending to haul himself up the ladder to confront the Assistant on his own veranda.

But just then Saya John came hurrying down, grim-faced and sombre.

'Sayagyi! Shall I go up . . . ?'

'Go up where?'

'To the tai. To show that bastard . . .'

'Don't be a fool, Rajkumar. Go and find something useful to do.' With a snort of annoyance, Saya John turned his back on Rajkumar.

They were staying the night with the *hsin-ouq*, the leader of the camp's oo-sis. The huts where the timbermen lived were well to the rear of the tai, so placed as not to interrupt the Assistant's view. These structures were small, stilt-supported dwellings of one or two rooms, each with a balcony-like platform in front. The oo-sis built the huts with their own hands, and while they were living in a camp, they would tend the site with the greatest diligence, daily repairing rents in the bamboo screens, patching the thatch and building shrines to their *nats*. Often they would plant small, neatly fenced plots of vegetables around their huts, to eke out the dry rations sent up from the plains. Some would rear chickens or pigs between the stilts of their huts; others would dam nearby streams and stock them with fish.

As a result of this husbandry teak camps often had the appearance of small mountain villages, with family dwellings clustered in a semi-circle behind a headman's house. But this was deceptive for these were strictly temporary settlements. It took a team of oo-sis just a day or two to build a camp, using nothing but vines, freshly-cut bamboo and plaited cane. At the end of the season, the camp was abandoned to the jungle, only to be conjured up again the next year, at another location.

At every camp it was the hsin-ouq who was assigned the largest hut, and it was in these that Saya John and Rajkumar usually stayed. Often when they were at camp, Saya John and Rajkumar would sit on the huts' balconies, talking late into the night. Saya John would smoke cheroots and reminisce – about his life in Malaya and Singapore and his dead wife.

The night when Saya John was berated by the Assistant, Rajkumar lay awake a long time, staring at the flickering lights of the tai. Despite Saya John's admonitions, he could not put aside his indignation at the Assistant's behaviour.

Just as he was drifting off to sleep, Rajkumar heard someone crawling out to the balcony. It was Saya John, armed with a box of matches and a cheroot. Rajkumar was suddenly awake again and just as angry as he had been earlier in the evening.

'Sayagyi,' Rajkumar blurted out, 'why didn't you say something when that man was shouting like that? I was so angry that I wanted to go up to the tai to teach him a lesson.'

Saya John glanced across the clearing to the Assistant's tai, where a light was still shining. The Assistant's silhouette was clearly visible, outlined against the thin cane walls; he was seated in a chair, reading a book.

'You have no business to be angry, Rajkumar. In his place you would be no different, perhaps worse. What amazes me is that more of them are not like this one.'

'Why, Sayagyi?'

'Think of the kind of life they lead here, these young Europeans. They have at best two or three years in the jungle before malaria or dengue fever weaken them to the point where they cannot afford to be far from doctors and hospitals. The company knows this very well; it knows that within a few years these men will be prematurely aged, old at twenty-one; and that they will have to be posted off to city offices. It is only when they are freshly arrived, seventeen or eighteen, that they can lead this life, and during those few years the company must derive such profit from them as it can. So they send them from camp to camp for months on end with scarcely a break in between. Look at this one: I am told he has already had a bad bout of dengue fever. That man is not much older than you, Rajkumar – maybe eighteen or nineteen – and here he is, sick and alone, thousands of miles from home, surrounded by people the likes of whom he has never known, deep inside a forest. And look at him: there he is, reading his book, with not a trace of fear on his face.'

'You are far from home too, Sayagyi,' said Rajkumar. 'And so am I.'

'But we are not so far as he is. And left to ourselves none of us would have been here, harvesting the bounty of this forest. Look at the oo-sis in this camp; look at the hsin-ouq, lying on his mat, dazed with opium; look at the false pride they have in their skill as trainers of elephants. They think, because their fathers and their families have all worked with elephants, that no one knows their animals as they do. Yet until the Europeans came none of them had ever thought of using elephants for the purposes of logging. Their elephants were used only in pagodas and palaces, for wars and ceremonies. It was the Europeans who saw that tame elephants could be made to work for human profit. It was they who invented everything we see around us in this logging camp. This entire way of life is their creation. It was they who thought of these methods of girdling trees, these ways of moving logs with elephants, this system of floating them downriver. Even such details as the structure and placement of these huts, the plan of the tai, the use of bamboo thatch and rattan – it was not the oo-sis with their hoary wisdom who thought of these things. All of this came from the minds of men like this one sitting in this tai – this boy who is not much older than you.'

The merchant thrust a finger at the silhouetted figure in the tai. 'You see that man, Rajkumar?' he said. 'That is someone you can learn from. To bend the work of nature to your will; to make the trees of the earth useful to human beings – what could be more admirable, more exciting than this? That is what I would say to any boy who has his life before him.'

Rajkumar could tell that Saya John was thinking not of him, his luga-lei, but of Matthew, his absent son, and the realisation bought a sudden and startling pang of grief. But the pain lasted only an instant and when it had faded Rajkumar felt himself to be very much the stronger, better prepared. He was here, after all, in this camp – while Matthew was far away in Singapore.

Seven

In Ratnagiri there were many who believed that King Thebaw was always the first to know when the sea had claimed a victim. He spent hours on his balcony every day, gazing out to sea with his gold-rimmed glasses. Fishermen had learnt to recognise the distinctive twin flashes of the King's binoculars. Returning to the bay, of an evening, they would look up in the direction of the hilltop balcony, as though for reassurance. Nothing happened in Ratnagiri, people said, but the King was the first to know of it.

Yet, the King himself was never seen after that first day when he rode up from the harbour with his family. The royal coaches were a familiar sight around town, with their teams of dappled horses and their moustachioed coachman. But the King never went out in them, or if he did, it was impossible to tell. The Royal Family had two *gaaris* – one an open trap and the other a brougham with curtained windows. There were rumours that the King was sometimes hidden inside the brougham, but no one could be sure because of the heavy velvet curtains.

The Princesses, on the other hand, were seen around town three or four times every year, driving down to the Mandvi jetty or to the Bhagavati temple, or to the houses of those British officials whom they were permitted to visit. The townsfolk knew them all by sight – the First, Second, Third and Fourth Princesses (the last was born in Ratnagiri, in the second year of the King's exile).

In their early years in India, the Princesses usually dressed in Burmese clothes – aingyis and htameins. But as the years passed their garments changed. One day, no one quite remembered when, they appeared in saris – not expensive or sumptuous saris, but the simple green and red cottons of the district. They began to wear their hair braided and oiled like Ratnagiri schoolgirls; they learned to speak Marathi and Hindustani as fluently as any of the townsfolk – it was only with their parents that they now spoke Burmese. They were pleasant-looking girls and there was something about them that was very direct and unaffected. When they drove through the streets they neither averted their gaze nor looked away. There was a hunger in their eyes, a longing, as though they yearned to know what it was like to walk through the Jhinjhinaka bazaar, to dawdle at the shops and bargain for saris. They sat alert and upright, taking everything in, and occasionally asking questions of the coachman: Whose sari shop is that? What sort of mangoes are those on that tree? What kind of fish is that hanging in that stall over there?

Mohan Sawant, the coachman, was a local boy, from an impoverished hamlet down by the river. He had dozens of relatives in town, working as rickshaw-pullers, coolies and tonga-wallahs: everyone knew him.

When he came down to the bazaar, people would seek him out: 'Give the Second Princess these mangoes. They're alphonsos from our garden.' 'Give the little girl a handful of this dried kokum. I saw her asking you about it.'

The Princesses' eyes touched everyone they lit upon. They were children: what had they done that they should live like this? Why should they be prevented from visiting local families; from forming friendships with Marathi children of good education? Why should they grow to womanhood never knowing any company other than that of their servants?

Once or twice a year the Queen would ride out with her daughters, her face a white mask, stern and unmoving, her lips stained a deep, deathly mauve by her cheroots. People would crowd into the streets to look at her as she rode by, but she never seemed to notice anyone or anything, sitting as straight as a rod, her face stern and unmoving.

And then there was Miss Dolly, with her long, black hair and her chiselled face, as beautiful as a fairytale princess. Over the years, all the others who had accompanied the Royal Family to

Ratnagiri had drifted slowly away – the maidservants and royal relatives and household officials. Only Miss Dolly stayed.

The King knew what people said of him in Ratnagiri, and if he was alarmed by the powers attributed to him, he was also amused and not a little flattered. In small ways he tried to do his duty by the role that had been thrust on him. Sometimes women would stand on their roofs, holding high their newborn children in the hope of attracting the imagined benedictions of his gaze. He would keep his glasses trained on these credulous mothers for several minutes at a time. It seemed a very small thing to ask for and why should he not grant those things that were in his power to give?

And the fact was that not everything that was said about him was untrue. The matter of the boatmen, for example: every day, when he stepped on the balcony at dawn, he would see the square white sails of the fishing fleet pasted across the bay like a string of stamps. The boats were *horis*, deep-hulled catamarans with single outriggers, from the fishing village of Karla at the mouth of the river. In the evenings, with the sun growing ever larger as it dipped towards the horizon, he would see the same boats tacking before the wind as they slipped into the bay. He was never aware of counting the boats that set sail in the morning, but somehow he always knew exactly how many there were. One day, when the catamarans were far out to sea, he saw a sudden squall sweeping down on them. That evening, when the fleet was straggling back, he could tell that the number wasn't right, that one was missing.

The King sent for Sawant: he knew that the fishing village was not far from the hamlet where the boy's family lived. Sawant was not yet a coachman at this time: he was fourteen and still just a syce, a groom.

'Sawant,' said the King, 'there was a storm at sea.' He explained what had happened. Sawant went hurrying down the hillside, and the news reached the fishing village before the boats were home. Thus began the legend of Ratnagiri's watchful king.

From the vantage point of his balcony, the King had the best seaward view of anyone in the district: it was only natural that he should see certain things before others. Down on the bay, not far from the jetty, there stood a small boathouse, a thatched shed adjoining a godown. There was a story attached to the boathouse. It was said that a British general, Lord Lake, had once ridden into Ratnagiri, with a unit of crack troops known as the Royal Battalion. This was after a long campaign in which several native rulers had been put to rout. His Lordship was in high spirits and one night, after a long evening of merry-making, he'd organised a boat-race for his officers. Boats had been commandeered from the local fisherfolk and the officers of the Royal Battalion had gone wallowing across the bay in canoes and dug-outs, paddling furiously, cheered on by their soldiers. According to legend, His Lordship had won by a full length.

Subsequently it had become something of a tradition among the officialdom of Ratnagiri to go sculling on the bay. Other stations in India afforded diversions such as pigsticking and polo: the bay was Ratnagiri's sole offering. Over the years the boathouse had acquired its own small pantheon of rowing heroes and sailing legends. The best-known of these concerned one Mr Gibb, a rowing blue from Cambridge and a district official of great repute. Mr Gibb was so expert an oarsman that he had been known to steer his long, slim racing shell through the bay's narrow and turbulent channel, out into the open sea. It was the King who had observed the first performance of this amazing feat; it was through him that Ratnagiri had come to learn of it.

It was to the King too that the inhabitants of Ratnagiri looked for reliable information on the coming of the monsoons. One morning each year he would wake to see a faint but unmistakable deepening in the colour of the line that bisected his window. That smudge on the horizon, as fine as a line of antimony on an eyelid, would grow quickly into a moving wall of rain. Perched high on the hill, Outram House would mark the monsoon's first landfall; rain would come smashing into the balcony; it would seep under the door and through the cracks in the shuttered windows, gathering inches deep under the King's bed.

'Sawant! The rains are here. Quick. Seal the shutters, put out the buckets and take everything off the floor.'

Within minutes the news would flow down the hillside. 'The

King has seen the rains.' There would be a great stir below; grandmothers would rush to remove their pickles from the sun, and children would run cheering from their houses.

It was the King also who was the first to spot the steamers when they headed into the bay. In Ratnagiri, it was the comings and goings of these vessels that marked the passage of time, much as cannon-shots and clock-towers did in other district towns. On mornings when a steamer was expected people would congregate in large numbers at the Mandvi jetty. Fishing boats would slip into the bay at dawn, with cargoes of dried fish. Traders would ride in on ox-carts that were loaded with pepper and rice.

No one awaited the steamers' arrival more impatiently than King Thebaw. Despite warnings from the doctor he had not been able to curb his craving for pork. Since there was none to be had in Ratnagiri, consignments of bacon and ham were shipped to him every week from Bombay; from Goa came spicy Portuguese *chouriço* sausages, peppered with chillies.

The King tried, as best he could, to battle this unseemly longing. He thought often of his distant predecessor, King Narathihapati of Burma, famously a glutton for pork. For the infamy of abandoning his capital to the armies of Kubilai Khan, Narathihapati had earned the immortally shameful title 'The King who ran away from the Chinese'. His own wife and son had handed him the poison that was to end his life. A love of pork was not a good portent in a king.

The King usually spotted the steamer when it was still far out to sea, an hour or so from the jetty. 'Sawant! The boat!' Within minutes the coachman would be on his way, in the brougham.

The carriage became the steamer's harbinger. No longer did people have to wait all day on the jetty: the brougham's descent gave them ample warning of the steamer's arrival. In this way, the burden of marking the days passed slowly from the steamers to the black coach with the peacock crest: it was as though time itself had passed into Thebaw's keeping. Unseen on his balcony Thebaw became the town's guardian spirit, a king again.

* * *

The year Dolly turned fifteen there was an outbreak of the plague along the coast. Ratnagiri was particularly hard hit. Fires burnt night and day in the crematorium. The streets emptied. Many people left town; others locked themselves into their houses.

Outram House was situated at a good distance from the sites of the outbreak, far enough from the principal centres of population to be safe from the contagion. But as terror spread through the district it became evident that this isolation was not without its own perils: Outram House found itself besieged by neglect. The bungalow had no sewerage and no water supply. The toilets had to be emptied daily of nightsoil, by sweepers; water had to be carried up in buckets, from a nearby stream. But with the outbreak of the plague, the sweepers stopped coming and the coolies' water-buckets lay upturned beside the kitchen.

It was Dolly who usually served as the intermediary between the compound's staff and the Royal Family. By default, over the years, more and more of the household's everyday duties had fallen on her. It was no easy job to deal with the scores of people who worked in the compound – the bearers, grooms, gardeners, ayahs, cooks. Even at the best of times Dolly had trouble finding servants and persuading them to stay. The trouble was that there was never enough money to pay their salaries. The King and Queen had sold almost everything they'd brought over from Mandalay: their treasure was gone, all except for a few keepsakes and mementos.

Now, with the town stilled by the fear of disease, Dolly had a taste of what it would mean to manage the house without help. By the end of the first day, the toilets were giving off an unbearable stench, the tanks were running empty and there was no water with which to wash or bathe.

The only servants who remained were the half-dozen who lived on the estate, Sawant among them. Sawant had risen quickly from the position of syce to that of coachman and his stolidity and cheerfulness had conferred a certain authority on him, despite his youth. In moments of crisis, it was to him that everyone turned.

For the first couple of days, with Sawant's help, Dolly managed to make sure that the tanks in the Queen's bedroom were kept filled. But there was no water for the King and the toilets were very nearly unusable. Dolly appealed to Sawant, 'Do something, Mohanbhai, *kuchh to karo*.'

'Wait.'

Sawant found a solution: if the Queen were to allow the household's workers to build temporary shelters around the walls of the compound, then they too would be safe from the contagion. They would return and, what was more, they would always be on hand to do their jobs. No more would messengers have to run back and forth between the compound and the town, summoning this cook or that ayah; no more would there be any talk of quitting. They would become a self-contained little village, up on the hill.

Dolly gave his arm a grateful squeeze. 'Mohanbhai!' For the first time in days she felt able to breathe again. How dependable he was, always ready with a solution. What would they do without him?

But now, how to get the Queen's consent? She was always complaining about how small the compound was, how cramped, how much like a gaol. What would she say to the prospect of having the entire staff move up from town? But time was running out. Dolly went to the Queen's door. 'Mebya.'

'Yes?'

Dolly raised her head off the floor and sat back on her heels. 'The servants have stopped coming because of the sickness in town. In a day or two they will escape to the countryside. No one will remain in Ratnagiri. Soon there will be no water in the house. The toilets will run over. We will have to carry the filth down the hill ourselves. Mohanbhai says, why not let the others build a few rooms around the compound, beyond the walls? When the fear is past they will leave. This will solve everything.'

The Queen turned away from the kneeling girl to look out of the window. She too was weary of dealing with servants – wretches, ungrateful wretches, what else could you say of them? The more you gave them the more they seemed to want – yes, even the good ones, like this girl Dolly. No matter what they received there was always something else, some other demand – more clothes, another necklace. And as for the rest, the cooks and sweepers and ayahs, why did they seem harder to find with every passing year?

You had only to step outside to see thousands of people standing about, staring, with nothing better to do than loiter by the roadside. And yet when it came to finding servants you would think you were living in a world of ghosts.

And now, with this sickness spreading, they were sure to perish in their thousands. And what then? Those who were willing to work would become even rarer – like white elephants. Better have them move while there was still time. It was true what the girl said: it would be safer to have them on the hill, well away from town. Otherwise they might well carry disease into the compound. And there would be advantages to offset the unsightliness. They would be available to be called upon whenever necessary, night or day.

The Queen turned back to Dolly. 'I have decided. Let them build their shelters on the hill. Tell Sawant to let them know that they can go ahead.'

Within days a *basti* arose around the compound, a settlement of shacks and shanties. In the bathrooms of Outram House, water began to flow; the toilets were clean again. The settlers in the basti daily thanked the Queen. Now it was her turn to be deified: overnight she became a guardian goddess, a protector of the unfortunate, an incarnate *devi* who had rescued hundreds from the ravages of the plague.

After a month the outbreak subsided. There were some fifty families living around the compound now. They showed no signs of returning to their old homes in the congested lanes of the town: it was far nicer on the breezy hill. Dolly talked the matter over with the Queen and they decided to let the settlers stay. 'What if there's another epidemic?' the Queen said. 'After all, we don't know that it's really over yet.'

The Princesses were delighted to have the shacks remain: they had never had playmates their own age before. Now they had dozens. The First Princess was eight, the youngest three. They spent their days running around the compound with their new friends, discovering new games. When they were hungry they would run into their friends' shacks and ask for something to eat; in the afternoons, when it was too hot to play outside, they would fall asleep on the mud floors of the palm-thatched shanties.

Four years later there was another outbreak of the plague. More people moved up the hill. Just as Sawant had predicted, the basti around the compound became a little village in its own right, with winding lanes and corner shops. No longer did the dwellings consist solely of shacks and shanties: tiled houses began to appear, one by one. But the little settlement had no provisions for sewage and no other facilities. When the breeze turned, a smell of excrement and refuse engulfed Outram House, wafting up from the ravines on the far side of the bluff.

An English district official became concerned about the Princesses' education and arranged for the hiring of an English governess. Only one of the Princesses showed any aptitude for study, the youngest. It was she and Dolly who profited the most from the governess's stay. They both became quickly fluent in English and Dolly even began to paint with watercolours. But the governess didn't last long. She was so outraged by the conditions of the Royal Family's captivity, that she fell out with the local British officials. In the end she had to be sent back to England.

The Princesses were older now, and so were their playmates. Sometimes the boys would tweak the girls' pigtails and brush up close against them as they were running around the compound. It fell to Sawant to take on the role of their defender and champion. He would go storming off into the basti, only to return with bruises on his face and cuts on his lip. Dolly and the Princesses would gather round in silent awe: without asking they knew that his wounds had been acquired in their defence.

Sawant was by this time a tall, swarthy young man with a deep chest and a trimmed black moustache. He was not just a coachman now but a gatekeeper as well. In that capacity he had been allotted the guardroom beside the gate to use as his own. The room was small, with just a single window and a string bed, and its only adornment was a picture of the Buddha – a token of Sawant's conversion, under the King's influence.

In the normal course Sawant's room was forbidden to the girls, but they could scarcely stay away when he lay inside, nursing wounds that had been acquired on their behalf. They would find ways of slipping in, unnoticed, with plates of food and packets of sweets.

One hot July afternoon, entering Sawant's room on a household errand, Dolly found him asleep on his string bed. He was naked but for a white loincloth, a cotton *langot*, knotted between his legs. Seating herself beside him she watched his chest, undulating with his breath. Thinking to wake him she reached for his shoulder, but her hand dropped instead to his neck. His skin was slippery, covered with a thin film of moisture. She ran her forefinger down the centre of his chest, through the puddle of sweat that had gathered in the declivity, to the spiral pit of his navel. A line of fine hair snaked downwards, disappearing into the damp folds of his cotton langot. She touched the filaments with the tip of her finger, brushing them backwards, against their grain, pushing them erect. He stirred and opened his eyes. She felt his fingers on her face, tracing the shape of her nose, pushing ajar her lips, grazing the tip of her tongue, following the curve of her chin down to her throat. When he reached her neckline, she stopped his hand.

'No.'

'You touched me first,' he challenged her.

She had no answer. She sat still as he fumbled with her strings and clasps. Her breasts were small, late-developing, tipped with tiny, blooming nipples. There were prickly calluses on his coachman's hands, and the ridges of his palms scraped hard against the soft tips of her breasts. She put her hands on his sides and ran them down the cage of his ribs. A lock of hair came loose at her temple, and drops of sweat went circling down the strands, dripping slowly off the end, on to his lips.

'Dolly, you are the most beautiful girl in the world.'

Neither of them knew what to do. It seemed impossible that their limbs could be made to fit together. Their bodies slipped, fumbled, scraped. And then, suddenly, she felt the kindling of a great flame of pain between her legs. She cried out aloud.

He unrolled his cotton langot and dried her blood with it, swabbing it from her thighs. She took hold of one end of the cloth and wiped the red stains from his empurpled glans. He reached between her legs and patted her pubis clean. They sat back on their heels, facing each other, their knees thrust between each other's legs. He spread the wet, white cloth over their knitted limbs: the sunburst of her blood was flecked with the opacity of his semen. They stared at the vivid cloth in silent amazement: this was their handiwork, the banner of their union.

She returned the next day and for many days afterwards. Her bed was in a dressing room on the upper floor. In the adjoining bedroom slept the First Princess. Beside Dolly's bed there was a window, and outside, within easy reach, stood a mango tree. Dolly took to slipping out at night and climbing back before dawn.

One afternoon, in Sawant's room, they fell asleep, sweating on the damp string of his bed. Then a scream filled the room and they sprang awake. It was the First Princess, standing over them, eyes blazing, hands on hips. In the heat of her anger she was transformed from a twelve-year-old girl into a woman.

'I was wondering, and now I know.'

She ordered Dolly to dress, to leave the room. 'If I ever see you alone again together, I will go to Her Majesty. You are servants. You will be thrown out.'

Sawant, all but naked, fell to his knees, clasping his hands together. 'Princess, it was a mistake, a mistake. My family, they depend on me. Open your heart, Princess. It was a mistake. Never again.'

From that day on, the eyes of the First Princess followed them wherever they went. She told the Queen that she had seen a burglar climbing up the mango tree. The tree was cut down and bars were installed in the window frames.

It came to be decided that the Bombay newspapers would be delivered to Outram House, along with the King's shipments of pork. The first batch was found to carry reports on a subject of absorbing interest: a narrative of the European tour of King Chulalangkorn of Siam. This was the first time an Asian monarch had travelled to Europe on a state visit. The tour lasted several weeks and through that time no other interest existed for King Thebaw.

In London King Chulalangkorn stayed at Buckingham Palace. He was welcomed into Austria by the Emperor Franz Joseph; befriended in Copenhagen by the King of Denmark; feted in Paris by the President of France. In Germany Kaiser Wilhelm stood waiting at a railway station until his train rolled in. King Thebaw read the reports over and over again, until he knew them by heart.

It was not so long ago that Thebaw's great-grandfather, Alaungpaya, and his grandfather, Bagyidaw, invaded Siam, crushed her armies, unseated her rulers, and sacked Ayutthaya, her premier city. In the aftermath, the defeated nobles had chosen a new ruler and Bangkok had become the country's new capital. It was because of the kings of Burma, because of Thebaw's ancestors, because of the Konbaung dynasty, that Siam had its present dynasty and its ruling king.

'When our ancestor, the great Alaungpaya, invaded Siam,' Thebaw said to his daughters one day, 'he sent a letter to the King of Ayutthaya. There was a copy in the Palace archives. This is what it said: "*There is no rival for our glory and our karma; to place you beside us is to compare the great Galon of Vishnu with a swallow; the sun with a firefly; the divine hamadryad of the heavens with an earthworm; Dhatarattha, the Hamsa king with a dung beetle.*" That is what our ancestor said to the King of Siam. But now they sleep in Buckingham Palace while we lie buried in this dungheap.'

There was no denying the truth of this. With the passing of the years Outram House had grown ever more to resemble the surrounding slums. Tiles had blown away and had not been replaced. Plaster had crumbled from the walls, baring great swathes of brick. Branches of peepul had taken root in the cracks and grown quickly into sturdy young saplings. Inside, mildew had crept upwards from the floor until the walls looked as though they had been draped in black velvet. Decay had become the Queen's badge of defiance. 'The responsibility for the upkeep of this house is not ours,' she said. 'They chose this to be our gaol, let them look after it.'

Newly arrived Collectors sometimes talked of razing the basti and moving the servants back to town. The Queen would laugh: how besotted they were, these men, in their arrogance, to imagine that in such a land as India they could hold a family imprisoned in isolation on a hill. Why the very soil would revolt against it!

The rare visitors who were allowed to call were shocked by the sight of the basti, the smell of waste and excrement, by the pall of woodsmoke that hung thick in the air. Often they descended from their carriages with looks of stunned surprise on their faces, unable to believe that the residence of Burma's last King had become the nucleus of a shantytown.

The Queen greeted them with her proud, thin-lipped smile. Yes, look around you, look at how we live. Yes, we who ruled the richest land in Asia are now reduced to this. This is what they have done to us, this is what they will do to all of Burma. They took our kingdom, promising roads and railways and ports, but mark my words, this is how it will end. In a few decades the wealth will be gone – all the gems, the timber and the oil – and then they too will leave. In our golden Burma where no one ever went hungry and no one was too poor to write and read, all that will remain is destitution and ignorance, famine and despair. We were the first to be imprisoned in the name of their progress; millions more will follow. This is what awaits us all: this is how we will all end – as prisoners, in shantytowns born of the plague. A hundred years hence you will read the indictment of Europe's greed in the difference between the kingdom of Siam and the state of our own enslaved realm.

Eight

The Irrawaddy was not the only waterway that Saya John used. His work often took him farther east, down the Sittang river and into the Shan highlands. A day's journey inland from the riverbank town of Pyinmana, there stood a village called Huay Zedi. Many years before, when the teak companies first started to explore this stretch of forest, Huay Zedi was itself a temporary teak camp like any other. But with the passing of the years the annual camps had migrated higher and higher up the slopes so that the business of providing them with supplies had become increasingly difficult. In time, because of the advantages of its location, on the sloping hinge where the mountains joined the plain, Huay Zedi became a kind of roadhead for the highlands. Many of the loggers and elephant trainers who accompanied the company into that previously unpopulated region chose to settle in and around this village.

Very few of the oo-sis, pe-sis and pa-kyeiks who lived in Huay Zedi were Burman by origin: some were Karen, some Karenni, some Pa-O, some Padaung, some Kadu-Kanan; there were even a few families of Indian *mahouts*, elephant trainers from Koraput, in the eastern Ghats. The inhabitants of the village kept to themselves and had little to do with plainspeople; Huay Zedi was a place that was entire unto itself, a part of the new cycle of life that had been brought into being by teak.

The village stood just above a sandy shelf where a chaung had strayed into a broad, meandering curve. The stream was shallow here, spread thin upon a pebbled bed, and through most of the year the water rose only to knee-height – a perfect depth for the villagers' children, who patrolled it through the day with small crossbows. The stream was filled with easy prey, silver-backed fish that circled in the shallows, dazed by the sudden change in the water's speed. The resident population of Huay Zedi was largely female: through most of the year the village's able-bodied males, from the age of twelve onwards, were away at one teak camp or another up on the slopes of the mountain.

The settlement was ringed with immense, straight-limbed trees, growing thickly together to form a towering wall of foliage. Hidden behind this wall were vast flocks of parakeets and troupes of monkeys and apes – white-faced langurs and copper-skinned rhesus. Even commonplace domestic sounds from the village – the scraping of a coconut-shell ladle on a metal pot, the squeaking wheel of a child's toy – were enough to send gales of alarm sweeping through the the dappled darkness: monkeys would flee in chattering retreat and birds would rise from the treetops in an undulating mass, like a wind-blown sheet.

The dwellings of Huay Zedi differed from those of teak camps only in height and size – in form and appearance they were otherwise very alike, being built of identical materials, woven bamboo and cane, each being similarly raised off the ground on shoulder-high teakwood posts. Only a few structures stood out prominently against the surrounding greenery: a timber bridge, a white-walled pagoda and a bamboo-thatched church topped by a painted teakwood cross. This last was used by a fair number of Huay Zedi's residents, many of whom were of Karen and Karenni stock – people whose families had been converted by followers of the American Baptist missionary, the Reverend Adoniram Judson.

When passing through Huay Zedi, Saya John stayed usually with the matronly widow of a former hsin-ouq, a Karenni Christian, who ran a small shop from the vine-covered balcony of her tai. This lady had a son, Doh Say, who became one of Rajkumar's closest friends.

Doh Say was a couple of years older than Rajkumar, a shy, gangling youth with a broad, flat face and a cheroot-stub nose. When Rajkumar first met him, he was employed as a lowly *sin-pa-kyeik*, an assistance to a pa-kyeik, a handler of chains: these were the men who dealt with the harnessing of elephants and the towing of logs. Doh Say was too young and too inexperienced to be allowed to do any fastening himself: his job was simply to heft the heavy chains for his boss. But Doh Say was a hard and earnest worker and when Rajkumar and Saya John next returned they found him a pa-kyeik. A year later he was already a pe-si, or back-rider, working with an aunging herd, specialising in the clearing of streams.

At camp, Rajkumar would attach himself to Doh Say, following on his heels, occasionally making himself useful by lighting a fire or boiling a pot of water. It was from Doh Say that Rajkumar learnt to brew tea the way that oo-sis liked it, thick, bitter and acid, beginning with a pot that was already half stuffed with leaves and then replenishing it with more at every filling. In the evenings he would help Doh Say with the weaving of cane walls, and at night he would sit on the ladder of his hut, chewing betel and listening to the oo-sis' talk. At night the herd needed no tending. The elephants were hobbled with chain-link fetters and let loose to forage for themselves in the surrounding jungle.

It was lonely at the camp, and Doh Say would often talk about his sweetheart, Naw Da, a girl in her early teens, slender and blooming, dressed in a tasselled white tunic and a homespun longyi. They were to be married as soon as Doh Say was promoted to the rank of oo-si.

'And what about you?' Doh Say would ask. 'Is there a girl you're thinking of?'

Rajkumar usually shrugged this off, but once Doh Say persisted and he answered with a nod.

'Who is she?'

'Her name is Dolly.'

This was the first time that Rajkumar had spoken of her and it was so long ago now that he could scarcely recall what she'd looked like. She was just a child, and yet she had touched him like no one else and nothing before. In her wide eyes, saturated with fear, he had seen his own aloneness turned inside out, rendered visible, worn upon the skin.

'And where does she live?'

'In India I think. I don't know for sure.'

Doh Say scratched his chin. 'One day you'll have to go looking for her.'

Rajkumar laughed. 'It's very far.'

'You'll have to go. There is no other way.'

It was from Doh Say that Rajkumar learnt of the many guises in which death stalked the lives of oo-sis: the Russell's viper, the maverick log, the charge of the wild buffalo. Yet the worst of Doh Say's fears had to do not with these recognisable incarnations of death, but rather with one peculiarly vengeful form of it. This was anthrax, the most deadly of elephant diseases.

Anthrax was common in the forests of central Burma and epidemics were hard to prevent. The disease could lie dormant in grasslands for as long as thirty years. A trail or pathway, tranquil in appearance and judged to be safe after lying many years unused, could reveal itself suddenly to be a causeway to death. In its most virulent forms anthrax could kill an elephant in a matter of hours. A gigantic tusker, a full fifteen arms' length off the ground, could be feeding peacefully at dusk and yet be dead at dawn. An entire working herd of a hundred elephants could be lost within a few days. Mature tuskers were valued in many thousands of rupees and the cost of an epidemic was such as to make itself felt on the London Stock Exchange. Few were the insurers who would gamble against a disease such as this.

The word anthrax comes from the same root as anthracite, a variety of coal. When anthrax strikes human beings it shows itself first in small pimple-like inflammations. As these lesions grow little black dots become visible at their centres, tiny pustules, like powdered charcoal: thus the naming of the disease. When anthrax erupts on an elephant's hide the lesions develop a volcanic energy. They appear first on the animal's hindquarters; they are about the size of a human fist, reddish-brown in colour. They swell rapidly and in males, quickly encase the penis sheath.

The carbuncles are most numerous around the hindquarters and as they grow they have the effect of sealing the animal's anus. Elephants consume an enormous amount of fodder and must defecate constantly. The workings of their digestive systems do not stop with the onset of the disease; their intestines continue to produce dung after the excretory passage has been sealed, the unexpurgated fecal matter pushing explosively against the obstructed anal passage.

'The pain is so great,' said Doh Say, 'that a stricken elephant will attack anything in sight. It will uproot trees and batter down walls. The tamest cows will become maddened killers; the gentlest calves will turn upon their mothers.'

They were at a camp together once when an epidemic struck. Saya John and Rajkumar were staying, as was their custom, with the camp's hsin-ouq, a small, stooped man with a shoelace moustache. Late one evening Doh Say burst in to tell the hsin-ouq that an oo-si was missing: it was thought that he had been killed by his own elephant.

The hsin-ouq could make no sense of this. This elephant had been in its oo-si's care for some fifteen years and had not been known to cause trouble before. Yet just before his death the oo-si had led his mount away from the herd and shackled her to a tree. She was now standing guard over his corpse and would not let anyone approach. None of this was as it should have been. What had gone wrong? Late as it was, the hsin-ouq headed into the jungle, with Doh Say and a few others. Saya John and Rajkumar decided to go with them.

It so happened that the Assistant who was in charge of the camp was away for a couple of days, staying in the company's chummery in Prome. In his absence there were no firearms in the camp. The oo-sis were armed only with flaming torches and their customary weapons, spears and das.

Rajkumar heard the elephant from far away. The noise grew very loud as they approached. Often before Rajkumar had been amazed at the sheer volume of sound that a single elephant could produce: the trumpeting, the squeals, the flatulence, the crashing of saplings and undergrowth. But this was something other than the usual feeding-time racket: there was a note of pain that pierced through the other accustomed sounds.

They arrived on the scene to find that the elephant had cleared a large space around itself, flattening everything within reach. The dead oo-si lay under a tree, battered and bloody, just a yard or two from the elephant's chain-shackled feet.

Saya John and Rajkumar watched from a distance as the hsin-ouq and his men circled around the angry cow, trying to determine what had gone wrong. Then the hsin-ouq gave a cry and raised his hand to point at the animal's rump. Dim though the torchlight was, Rajkumar could tell that there were swellings on the elephant's rear, an angry red in colour.

Immediately the hsin-ouq and his men turned around and plunged headlong into the forest, racing back the way they had come.

'Sayagyi, what is it? Why are they running?'

Saya John was hurrying through the undergrowth, trying to keep the oo-sis' torches in sight. 'Because of anthrax, Rajkumar.' Saya John flung the word breathlessly over his shoulder.

'What, Saya?'

'Anthrax.'

'But, Saya, why don't they try to rescue the corpse?'

'No one can approach the creature now for fear of contagion,' said Saya John. 'And in any case they have more pressing things to think of.'

'More pressing than their friend's body?'

'Very much more. They could lose everything – their animals, their jobs, their livelihood. The dead man gave up his life in an effort to keep this elephant from infecting the rest. They owe it to him to get the herd out of harm's way.'

Rajkumar had seen many epidemics come and go – typhoid, smallpox, cholera. He had even survived the outbreak that had killed his family: to him disease was a hazard rather than a danger, a threat that had to be lived with from day to day. He found it impossible to believe that the oo-sis would so easily abandon their comrade's corpse.

Rajkumar laughed. 'They ran as if a tiger was after them.'

At this Saya John, usually so equable and even-tempered, turned on him in a sudden fury. 'Be careful, Rajkumar.' Saya John's voice slowed. 'Anthrax is a plague and it was to punish pride that the Lord sent it down.'

His voice slowed and deepened as it always did when he was

quoting the Bible: *'And the Lord said unto Moses and unto Aaron, Take to you handfuls of ashes of the furnace, and let Moses sprinkle it toward the heaven in the sight of Pharaoh. And it shall become small dust in all the land of Egypt, and shall be a boil breaking forth with blains upon man, and upon beast, throughout all the land of Egypt.'*

Rajkumar could understand only a few words of this but the tone of Saya John's voice was enough to silence him.

They made their way back to camp to find that it had emptied. Doh Say and the others had departed with the evacuated herd. Only the hsin-ouq remained, to wait for the Assistant. Saya John decided to stay on in order to keep him company.

Early next morning they returned to the site of the accident. The infected elephant was quieter now than before, dazed by pain and weakened by its struggle with the disease. The swellings had grown to pineapple size and the elephant's hide had begun to crack and break apart. As the hours passed the lesions grew yet larger and the cracks deepened. Soon the pustules began to leak a whitish ooze. Within a short while the animal's hide was wet with discharge. Rivulets of blood-streaked pus began to drip to the ground. The soil around the animal's feet turned into sludge, churned with blood and ooze. Rajkumar could no longer bear to look. He vomited, bending over at the waist, hitching up his longyi.

'If that is what this sight has done to you, Rajkumar,' Saya John said, 'think of what it must mean to the oo-sis to watch their elephants perish in this way. These men care for these animals as though they were their own kin. But when anthrax reaches this stage the oo-sis can do nothing but look on as these great mountains of flesh dissolve before their eyes.'

The stricken elephant died in the early afternoon. Shortly afterwards the hsin-ouq and his men retrieved their comrade's body. Saya John and Rajkumar watched from a distance as the mangled corpse was carried into the camp.

'And they took ashes of the furnace,' Saya John said, softly, under his breath, *'and stood before Pharaoh; and Moses sprinkled it up toward heaven; and it became a boil breaking forth with blains upon man, and upon beast. And the magicians could not stand before Moses because*

of the boils; for the boil was upon the magicians, and upon all the Egyptians . . .'

Rajkumar was eager to be gone from the camp, sickened by the events of the last few days. But Saya John was proof against his entreaties. The hsin-ouq was an old friend, he said, and he would keep him company until the dead oo-si was buried and the ordeal ended.

In the ordinary course of things, the funeral would have been performed immediately after the body's retrieval. But because of the forest Assistant's absence, there arose an unforeseen hitch. It was the custom for the dead to be formally released from their earthly ties by the signing of a note. Nowhere was this rite more strictly observed than among oo-sis, who lived their lives in daily hazard of death. The dead man's note of release had still to be signed and only the Assistant, as his employer, could sign it. A messenger was dispatched to the Assistant. He was expected to return the next day with the signed note. It only remained to wait out the night.

By sunset the camp was all but deserted. Rajkumar and Saya John were among the few who remained. Rajkumar lay awake a long time on the hsin-ouq's balcony. At the centre of the camp's clearing, the tai was blazing with light. The Assistant's luga-lei had lit all his lamps and in the darkness of the jungle there was an eerie grandeur to the empty tai.

Late at night Saya John came out to the balcony to smoke a cheroot.

'Saya, why did the hsin-ouq have to wait so long for the funeral?' said Rajkumar on a note of complaint. 'What harm would have resulted, Saya, if he had buried the dead man today and kept the note for later?'

Saya John pulled hard on his cheroot, the tip glowing red on his glasses. He was so long silent that Rajkumar began to wonder whether he had heard the question. But just as he was about to repeat himself Saya John began to speak.

'I was at a camp once,' he said, 'when there was an unfortunate accident and an oo-si died. That camp was not far from this one, two days' walk at most, and its herds were in the charge of our host – this very hsin-ouq. The accident happened at the busiest time of year, towards the end of the rains. The season's work was nearing its close. There were just a few stacks left when a very large log fell askew across the banks of the chaung, blocking the chute that was being used to roll the stacked teak down to the stream. The log wedged itself between two stumps, in such a way as to bring everything to a halt: no other logs could be rolled down until this one was moved.

'The Assistant at that camp was a young man, perhaps nineteen or twenty years old, and his name, if I remember right, was McKay – McKay-*thakin* they called him. He had been in Burma only two years and this was his first season of running a camp on his own. The season had been long and hard and the rain had been pouring down for several months. McKay-thakin was proud of his new reponsibility and he had driven himself hard, spending the entire period of the monsoons in the camp, never giving himself any breaks, never going away for so much as one weekend. He had endured several bad bouts of fever. The attacks had so weakened him that on certain days he could not summon the strength to climb down from his tai. Now with the season drawing to a close, he had been promised a month's leave, in the cool comfort of the Maymyo hills. The company had told him that he was free to go as soon as the territory in his charge was cleared of all the logs that had been marked for extraction. With the day of his departure drawing close, McKay-thakin was growing ever more restless, driving his teams harder and harder. The work was very nearly completed when the accident happened.

'The jamming of the chute occurred at about nine in the morning – the time of day when the day's work draws to a close. The hsin-ouq was at hand and he immediately sent his pa-kyeiks down to harness the log with chains so that it could be towed away. But the log was lodged at such an awkward angle that the chains could not be properly attached. The hsin-ouq tried first to move it by harnessing it to a single, powerful bull, and when this did not succeed he brought in a team of two of his most reliable cows. But all these efforts were unavailing: the log would not budge.

Finally, McKay-thakin, growing impatient, ordered the hsin-ouq to send an elephant down the slope to butt free the obstinate log.

'The slope was very steep and after months of pounding from enormous logs, its surface was crumbling into powder. The hsin-ouq knew that it would be very dangerous for an oo-si to lead an elephant into terrain of such uncertain footing. But McKay-thakin was by now in an agony of impatience and, being the officer in charge, he prevailed. Against his will, the hsin-ouq summoned one of his men, a young oo-si who happened to be his nephew, his sister's son. The dangers of the task at hand were perfectly evident and the hsin-ouq knew that none of the other men would obey him if he were to order them to go down that slope. But his nephew was another matter. "Go down," said the hsin-ouq, "but be careful, and do not hesitate to turn back."

'The first part of the operation went well, but just as the log sprang free the young oo-si lost his footing and was stranded directly in the path of the rolling, two-ton log. The inevitable happened: he was crushed. His body was unscarred when it was recovered, but every bone in it was smashed, pulverised.

'This young oo-si, as it happened, was much loved, both by his peers and by his mount, a gentle and good-natured cow by the name of Shwe Doke. She had been trained in the company's aunging herds and had been in his charge for several years.

'Those who know them well claim to be able to detect many shades of emotion in elephants – anger, pleasure, jealousy, sorrow. Shwe Doke was utterly disconsolate at the loss of her handler. No less saddened was the hsin-ouq, who was quite crushed with guilt and self-reproach.

'But worse was still to come. That evening, after the body had been prepared for burial, the hsin-ouq took the customary letter of release to McKay-thakin and asked for his signature.

'By this time McKay-thakin was not in his right mind. He had emptied a bottle of whisky and his fever had returned. The hsin-ouq's entreaties made no impression on him. He was no longer capable of understanding what was being asked of him.

'In vain did the hsin-ouq explain that the interment could not be deferred, that the body would not keep, that the man must have his release before his last rites. He pleaded, he begged, in his desperation he even attempted to climb up the ladder and force his way into the tai. But McKay-thakin saw him coming and came striding out, with a glass in one hand and a heavy-bored hunting rifle in the other. Emptying one barrel into the sky, he shouted: "For pity's sake can you not leave me alone just this one night?"

'The hsin-ouq gave up and decided to go ahead with the burial. The dead man's body was interred as darkness was gathering.

'I was staying the night, as always, in the hsin-ouq's hut. We ate a sparse meal and afterwards I stepped outside to smoke a cheroot. Usually a camp is full and bustling at that time of day: from the kitchen there issues a great banging of tin plates and metal pots and the darkness is everywhere pierced by the glowing tips of cheroots, where the oo-sis sit beside their huts, savouring their last smoke of the day and chewing a final quid of betel. But now I saw, to my astonishment, that there was no one about; I could hear nothing but frogs and owls and the feathery flapping of great jungle moths. Absent also was that most familiar and reassuring of a camp's sounds, the tinkling of elephants' bells. Evidently, no sooner had the soil been tamped down on the dead man's grave than the other oo-sis had begun to flee the camp, taking their elephants with them.

'The only elephant that was still in the camp's vicinity was Shwe Doke, the dead man's mount. The hsin-ouq had taken charge of his nephew's riderless elephant after the accident. She was restless, he said, and nervous, frequently flapping her ears and clawing the air with the tip of her trunk. This was neither uncommon nor unexpected, for the elephant is, above all, a creature of habit and routine. So pronounced an upheaval as the absence of a long-familiar handler can put even the gentlest of elephants out of temper, often dangerously so.

'This being the case, the hsin-ouq had decided not to allow Shwe Doke to forage through the night, as was the rule. Instead he had led her to a clearing, some half-mile's distance from the camp and supplied her with a great pile of succulent treetop branches. Then he had tethered her securely between two immense and immovable trees. To be doubly sure of keeping her bound he had used, not the usual lightweight fetters with which elephants are shackled at night, but the heavy iron towing chains that are employed in the harnessing of logs. This, he said, was a precaution.

'"A precaution against what?" I asked. By this time his eyes were dulled by opium. He gave me a sidelong glance and said, in a soft, slippery voice: "Just a precaution."

'There now remained in the camp only the hsin-ouq and me and of course, McKay-thakin in his tai. The tai was brightly lit, with lamps shining in all its windows, and it seemed very high, perched on its tall, teakwood stilts. The hsin-ouq's hut was small in comparison and much closer to the ground, so that standing on its platform I had to tilt my head back to look up at McKay-thakin's glowing windows. As I sat staring, a low, reedy wail came wafting out of the lamplit windows. It was the sound of a clarinet, an instrument the thakin sometimes played of an evening to while away the time. How strange it was to hear that plaintive, melancholy music issuing forth from those shining windows, the notes hanging in the air until they became indistinguishable from the jungle's nightly noise. Just so, I thought, must a great liner look to the oarsmen of a palm-trunk canoe as it bears down on them out of the night, with the sounds of its ballroom trailing in its wake.

'It had not rained much through the day, but with the approach of evening clouds had begun to mass in the sky, and by the time I blew my lamp out and rolled out my mat there was not a star to be seen. Soon the storm broke. Rain came pouring down and thunder went pealing back and forth across the valleys, echoing between the slopes. I had been asleep perhaps an hour or two when I was woken by a trickle of water, leaking through the bamboo roof. Rising to move my mat to a dry corner of the hut, I happened to glance across the camp. Suddenly the tai sprang out of the darkness, illuminated by a flash of lightning: its lamps had gone out.

'I was almost asleep again when, through the chatter of the rain I heard a tiny, fragile sound, a distant tinkling. It was far away but approaching steadily, and as it drew nearer I recognised the unmistakable ringing of an elephant's bell. Soon, in the subtle tensing of the hut's bamboo beams, I could feel the animal's heavy, hurrying tread.

'"Do you hear that?" I whispered to the hsin-ouq. "What is it?"

'"It is the cow, Shwe Doke."

'An oo-si knows an elephant by its bell: it is by following that sound that he locates his mount every morning after its night-long foraging in the forest. To do his job well a hsin-ouq must know the sound of every animal in his herd; he must, if the need arises, be able to determine the position of all his elephants simply by concentrating on the ringing of their bells. My host was a hsin-ouq of great ability and experience. There was not, I knew, the slightest likelihood of his being mistaken in his identification of the approaching bell.

'"Perhaps," I ventured, "Shwe Doke was panicked by the storm; perhaps she managed to break loose of her fetters."

'"If she had broken loose," the hsin-ouq said, "the chains would still be dragging on her feet." He paused to listen. "But I hear no chains. No. She has been freed by a human hand."

'"But whose could that hand be?" I asked.

'He silenced me abruptly, with a raised hand. The bell was very close now and the hut was shivering to the elephant's tread.

'I started to move towards the ladder but the hsin-ouq pulled me back. "No," he said. "Stay here."

'The next moment the sky was split by lightning. In the momentary glare of that flat sheet of light, I saw Shwe Doke, directly ahead, moving towards the tai, with her head lowered and her trunk curled under her lip.

'I jumped to my feet and began to shout in warning: "Thakin; McKay-thakin . . ."

'McKay-thakin had already heard the bells, felt the tremor of the elephant's approaching weight. A flame flickered in one of the tai's windows and the young man appeared on the veranda, naked, with a lantern in one hand and his hunting rifle in the other.

'Ten feet from the tai Shwe Doke came to a standstill. She lowered her head as though she were examining the structure. She was an old elephant, trained in the ways of the aunging herd. Such animals are skilled in the arts of demolition. It takes them no more than a glance to size up a dam of snagged wood and pick a point of attack.

'McKay-thakin fired just as Shwe Doke began her charge. She was so close now that he could not miss: he hit her exactly where he had aimed, in her most vulnerable spot, between ear and eye.

'But the momentum of Shwe Doke's charge carried her forward even as she was dying on her feet. She too hit the tai exactly where she had aimed, at the junction of the two cross-beams that held it together. The structure appeared to explode, with logs and beams and thatch flying into the air. McKay-thakin was catapulted to the ground, over Shwe Doke's head.

'Such is the footwork of the skilled aunging elephant that it can balance its weight on the lip of a waterfall, perch like a crane upon a small mid-stream boulder, turn in a space that would trip a mule. It was with those small, practised steps that Shwe Doke turned now, until she was facing the Assistant's prone body. Then, very slowly, she allowed her dying weight to go crashing down on him, head first, her weight rolling over in a circular motion, in a technically perfect execution of the butting manoeuvre of the aunging elephant – an application of thrust so precise as to be able to cause a ten-thousand-ton tangle of teak to spring undone like a sailor's knot. McKay-thakin's lantern, which had been sputtering beside him, went out and we could see nothing more.

'I threw myself down the hut's ladder with the hsin-ouq close behind me. Running towards the tai I stumbled in the darkness and fell, face first on the mud. The hsin-ouq was helping me up when a bolt of lightning split the sky. Suddenly he let go of my hand and unloosed a hoarse, stammering shout.

'"What is it?" I cried. "What did you see?"

'"Look! Look down at the ground."

'Lightning flashed again and I saw, directly ahead of me, the huge scalloped mark of Shwe Doke's feet. But beside it was a smaller impression, curiously shapeless, almost oblong.

'"What is it?" I said. "What made that mark?"

'"It is a footprint," he said, "human, although crushed and mangled almost beyond recognition."

'I froze and stayed exactly where I was, praying for another bolt of lightning so that I would be able to ascertain for myself the truth of what he had said. I waited and waited but an age seemed to pass before the heavens lit up again. And in the meanwhile it had rained so hard that the marks on the ground had melted away.'

Nine

In 1905, the nineteenth year of the King's exile, a new District Collector arrived in Ratnagiri. The Collector was the district's administrative head, the official who was ultimately responsible for dealing with the Burmese Royal Family. The job was an important one and the officials who were appointed to this post were almost always members of the Indian Civil Service – the august cadre of officials who administered Britain's Indian possessions. To join the Indian Civil Service candidates had to pass a difficult examination that was held in England. The overwhelming majority of those who qualified were British, but there were also among them a small number of Indians.

The Collector who arrived in 1905 was an Indian, a man by the name of Beni Prasad Dey. He was in his early forties, and an outsider to the Ratnagiri region: he was a Bengali from Calcutta, which lay diagonally across the map of India, at the other end of the country. Collector Dey was slim and aquiline, with a nose that ended in a sharp, beak-like point. He dressed in finely-cut Savile Row suits and wore gold-rimmed eyeglasses. He arrived in Ratnagiri accompanied by his wife, Uma, who was some fifteen years his junior, a tall, vigorous-looking woman, with thick, curly hair.

King Thebaw was watching from his balcony when Ratnagiri's officialdom gathered at the Mandvi jetty to receive the new Collector and his young wife. The first thing he noticed about them was that the new Madame Collector was dressed in an unusual garment. Puzzled, he handed his binoculars to the Queen. 'What's that she's wearing?'

The Queen took a long look. 'It's just a sari,' she said at last.

'But she's wearing it in the new style.' She explained that an Indian official had made up a new way of wearing a sari, with odds and ends borrowed from European costume – a petticoat, a blouse. She'd heard that women all over India were adopting the new style. But of course everything came late to Ratnagiri – she herself had never had an opportunity to look into this new fashion at first hand.

The Queen had seen many Collectors come and go, Indian and English; she thought of them as her enemies and gaolers, upstarts to be held in scant regard. But in this instance she was intrigued. 'I hope he'll bring his wife when he comes to call. It'll be interesting to see how this kind of sari is worn.'

Despite this propitious beginning the Royal Family's first meeting with the new Collector came close to ending in disaster. Collector Dey and his wife had arrived at a time when politics was much on people's minds. Every day there were reports of meetings, marches and petitions: people were being told to boycott British-made goods; women were making bonfires of Lancashire cloth. In the Far East there was the war between Russia and Japan and for the first time it looked as though an Asian country might prevail against a European power. The Indian papers were full of news of this war and what it would mean for colonized countries.

It was generally not the King's custom to meet with officials who came to Outram House. But he had been following the Russo-Japanese war very closely and was keen to know what people thought of it. When the new Collector and his wife came to call, the King's first words were about the war. 'Collector-sahib,' he said abruptly, 'have you seen the news? The Japanese have defeated the Russians in Siberia?'

The Collector bowed stiffly, from the waist. 'I have indeed seen reports, Your Highness,' he said. 'But I must confess that I do not believe this to be an event of any great significance.'

'Oh?' said the King. 'Well, I'm surprised to hear that.' He frowned, in a way that made it clear that he wasn't about to let the subject drop.

The night before Uma and the Collector had been briefed at length on their forthcoming visit to Outram House. They'd been told that the King was never present at these occasions: it was the Queen who would receive them, in the reception room on the ground floor. But they'd entered to find the King very much present: he was dressed in a crumpled longyi and was pacing the floor, smacking his thigh with a rolled-up newspaper. His face was pale and puffy, and his wispy grey hair was straggling unkempt down the back of his neck.

The Queen, on the other hand, was exactly where she was meant to be: sitting rigidly upright on a tall chair, with her back to the door. This, Uma knew, was a part of the set order of battle: visitors were expected to walk in and seat themselves on low chairs around Her Highness, with no words of greeting being uttered on either side. This was the Queen's way of preserving the spirit of Mandalay protocol: since the representatives of the British were adamant in their refusal to perform the shiko, she in turn made a point of not acknowledging their entry into her presence.

Uma had been told to be on her guard in the reception room, to look out for delinquent sacks of rice and stray bags of dal. This room was sometimes used as an auxiliary storeroom and several unwary visitors were known to have come to grief in its hidden pitfalls: it was not unusual to find heaps of chillies hidden under its sofas and jars of pickles stacked on its bookshelves. On one occasion a beefy superintendent of police had sat down heavily on the spiny remains of a dried fish. Another time, ambushed by a powerful whiff of pepper, a venerable old district judge had sneezed his false teeth clear across the room. They had fallen clattering at the Queen's feet.

These reception-room stories had caused Uma much apprehension, prompting her to secure her sari with an extravagant number of clips and safety-pins. But on entering the room she'd found its effects to be not at all as expected. Far from being put out, she felt oddly comforted by the familiar fragrances of rice and mung dal. In any other setting Queen Supayalat, with her mask-like face and mauve lips, would have seemed a spectral and terrifying figure. But the odours of domesticity seemed to soften her edges a little, adding an element of succour to her unyielding presence.

Across the room, the King was smacking his newspaper loudly

on his palm. 'Well, Collector-sahib,' he said, 'did you ever think that we would live to witness the day when an Eastern country would defeat a European power?'

Uma held her breath. Over the last few weeks the Collector had conducted many heated arguments on the implications of a Japanese victory over Russia. Some had ended in angry outbursts. She watched anxiously now as her husband cleared his throat.

'I am aware, Your Highness,' the Collector said evenly, 'that Japan's victory has resulted in widespread rejoicing among nationalists in India and no doubt in Burma too. But the Tsar's defeat comes as no surprise to anyone, and it holds no comfort for enemies of the British Empire. The Empire is today stronger than it has ever been. You have only to glance at a map of the world to see the truth of this.'

'But in time, Collector-sahib, everything changes. Nothing goes on for ever.'

The Collector's voice grew sharper. 'May I remind Your Highness that while Alexander the Great spent no more than a few months in the steppes of central Asia, the satrapies he founded persisted for centuries afterward? Britain's Empire is, by contrast, already more than a century old, and you may be certain, Your Highness, that its influence will persist for centuries more to come. The Empire's power is such as to be proof against all challenges and will remain so into the foreseeable future. I might take the liberty of pointing out, Your Highness, that you would not be here today if this had been pointed out to you twenty years before.'

The King flushed, staring speechlessly at the Collector. It fell to the Queen to answer for him. She leant forward, digging her long, sharp fingernails into the arms of her chair. 'That is enough, Mr Collector,' she said. 'Enough, *bas karo*.' There was a moment of stillness in which the only sound was that of the Queen's nails, raking the polished arms of her chair. The room seemed to shimmer as though the floor had given off a sudden haze of heat.

Uma was seated between Dolly and the Second Princess. She had listened to her husband's exchange with the King in dismayed silence, sitting frozen in her place. On the wall ahead of her was a small watercolour. The painting was a depiction of a landscape at sunrise, a stark red plain dotted with thousands of mist-wreathed pagodas. Suddenly, with a clap of her hands, Uma uttered a loud cry. 'Pagan!'

The word had the effect of an explosion in a confined space. Everyone jumped, turning to look in Uma's direction. She raised a hand to point. 'On the wall – it's a picture of Pagan, isn't it?'

The Second Princess was sitting next to Uma. She seized eagerly on this diversion. 'Yes – that is it. Dolly can tell you – she painted it.'

Uma turned to the slim upright woman on her left. Her name was Dolly Sein, she recalled: they had been introduced on the way in. Uma had noticed that there was something unusual about her, but she'd been too busy concentrating on protocol to give the matter any further thought.

'Did you really paint that?' Uma said. 'Why, it's wonderful.'

'Thank you,' Dolly said quietly. 'I copied it from a book of prints.' Their glances crossed and they exchanged a quick smile. Suddenly Uma knew what it was that she'd been struck by: this Miss Sein was perhaps the loveliest woman she'd ever set eyes on.

'Madame Collector,' the Queen tapped a knuckle on the arm of her chair, 'how did you know that was a picture of Pagan? Have you had occasion to visit Burma?'

'No,' Uma said regretfully. 'I wish I had but I haven't. I have an uncle in Rangoon and he once sent me a picture.'

'Oh?' The Queen nodded; she was impressed by the way the young woman had intervened to save the situation. Self-possession was a quality she'd always admired. There was something attractive about this woman, Uma Dey; the liveliness of her manner was a welcome contrast to her husband's arrogance. If not for her presence of mind she would have had to order the Collector out of the house and that could only have ended badly. No, this Mrs Dey had done well to speak when she did.

'We would like to ask you, Madame Collector,' the Queen said, 'what is your real name? We have never been able to accustom ourselves to your way of naming women after their fathers and husbands. We do not do this in Burma. Perhaps you would not object to telling us your own given name?'

'Uma Debi – but everyone calls me Uma.'

'Uma?' said the Queen. 'That is a name that is familiar to us. I must say, you speak Hindustani well, Uma.' There was a note of unfeigned appreciation in her voice. Both she and the King spoke Hindustani fluently and this was the language she preferred to use in her dealings with officials. She had found that her use of Hindustani usually put the Government's representatives at a disadvantage – especially the Indians. British civil servants often spoke Hindustani well and those who didn't had no qualms about answering in English. The Indians, on the other hand, were frequently Parsis or Bengalis, Mr Chatterjee this or Mr Dorabjee that, and they were rarely fluent in Hindustani. And unlike their British counterparts they were hesitant about switching languages; it seemed to embarrass them that the Queen of Burma could speak Hindustani better than they. They would stumble and stutter and within minutes she would have their tongues tied in knots.

'I learnt Hindustani as a child, Your Highness,' Uma said. 'We lived in Delhi for a while.'

'*Achha?* Well, now we would like to ask something else of you, Uma.' The Queen made a beckoning gesture. 'You may approach us.'

Uma went over to the Queen and lowered her head.

'Uma,' the Queen whispered, 'we would like to examine your garments.'

'Your Highness!'

'As you can see, my daughters wear their saris in the local style. But I prefer this new fashion. It is more elegant – the sari looks more like a htamein. Would it be too great an imposition to ask you to reveal the secrets of this new style to us?'

Uma was startled into laughter. 'I would be glad to, whenever you please.'

The Queen turned stiffly to the Collector. 'You, Collector-sahib, are no doubt impatient to be on your way to the Cutchery and the many pressing tasks that await you. But may I ask if you will permit your wife to remain with us a little longer?'

The Collector left, and in defiance of the initial auguries of disaster, the visit ended very amicably, with Uma spending the rest of the afternoon in Outram House, chatting with Dolly and the Princesses.

The Collector's house was known as the Residency. It was a large bungalow with a colonnaded portico and a steep, red-tiled roof. It stood on the crest of a hill, looking southward over the bay and the valley of the Kajali river. It was surrounded by a walled garden that stretched a long way down the slope, stopping just short of the river's gorge.

One morning Uma discovered a narrow entrance hidden behind a thicket of bamboo at the bottom of her garden. The gate was overgrown with weeds but she was able to open it just wide enough to squeeze through. Twenty feet beyond, a wooded outcrop jutted out over the valley of the Kajali river. There was a peepul at the lip of the gorge, a majestic old tree with a thick beard of aerial roots hanging from its gnarled grey branches. She could tell that goats came to graze there: the earth beneath the tree's canopy had been cropped clean of undergrowth. She could see trails of black droppings leading down the slope. The goatherds had built themselves a platform to sit on by heaping earth and stones around the peepul's trunk.

Uma was amazed by the view: the meandering river, the estuary, the curve of the bay, the windswept cliffs – she could see more of the valley from here than from the Residency on top of the hill. She returned the next day and the day after. The goatherds came only at dawn and for the rest of the day the place was deserted. She took to slipping out of the house every morning, leaving the door of her bedroom shut, so that the servants would think she was still inside. She would sit in the peepul's deep shade for an hour or two with a book.

One morning Dolly surprised her by appearing unexpectedly out of the peepul's beard of hanging roots. She'd called to return some clothes that Uma had sent over to Outram House – petticoats and blouses, for the Princesses to have copied by their tailors. She'd waited in the drawing room of the Residency while the servants went looking for Uma. They'd looked everywhere before giving up: memsahib wasn't at home, they said, she must have slipped out for a walk.

'How did you know I was here?'

'Our coachman is related to yours.'

'Did Kanhoji tell you?' Kanhoji was the elderly coachman who drove Uma around town.

'Yes.'

'I wonder how he knew about my secret tree.'

'He said he'd heard about it from the herdsmen who bring their goats here in the morning. They're from his village.'

'Really?' Uma fell silent. It was odd to think that the goatherds were just as aware of her presence as she was of theirs. 'Well, the view's wonderful, don't you think?'

Dolly gave the valley a perfunctory glance. 'I've grown so used to it I never give it a thought any more.'

'I think it's amazing. I come here almost every day.'

'Every day?'

'Just for a bit.'

'I can see why you would.' She paused to look at Uma. 'It must be lonely for you here, in Ratnagiri.

'Lonely?' Uma was taken aback. It hadn't occurred to her to use that word of herself. It was not as though she never met anyone, or that she was ever at a loss for things to do – the Collector made sure of that. Every Monday his office sent up a memorandum listing her engagements for the week – a municipal function, a sports day at a school, a prize-giving at the vocational college. She usually had only one appointment a day, not so many as to keep her uncomfortably busy nor so few as to make her days seem oppressively long. She went through the list carefully when it arrived at the beginning of the week, and then she put it on her dressing table, with a weight on it, so it wouldn't blow away. The thought of missing an appointment worried her, although there was little chance of that. The Collector's office was very good about sending reminders: a peon came up to the Residency about an hour before each new appointment to tell Kanhoji to bring the gaari round. She'd hear the horses standing under the porch; they'd snort and kick the gravel, and Kanhoji would click his tongue, tuk-tuk-tuk.

The nicest part of these appointments was the journey into town and back. There was a window between the coach and the driver's bench. Every few minutes Kanhoji would stick his tiny, wrinkled face into the window and tell her about the places around them – the Cutchery, the gaol, the college, the bazaars. There were times when she was tempted to get off so she could go into the bazaars and bargain with the fishwives. But she knew there would be a scandal; the Collector would come home and say: 'You should just have let me know so that I could have arranged some *bandobast*.' But the bandobast would have destroyed any pleasure she might have taken in the occasion: half the town would have gathered, with everyone falling over themselves to please the Collector. The shopkeepers would have handed over anything she so much as glanced at, and when she got home the bearers and the *khansama* would have sulked as though she'd dealt them a reproach.

'What about you, Dolly?' Uma said. 'Are you lonely here?'

'Me? I've lived here nearly twenty years, and this is home to me now.'

'Really?' It struck Uma that there was something almost incredible about the thought that a woman of such beauty and poise had spent most of her life in this small provincial district town.

'Do you remember anything of Burma?'

'I remember the Mandalay palace. Especially the walls.'

'Why the walls?'

'Many of them were lined with mirrors. There was a great hall called the Glass Palace. Everything there was of crystal and gold. You could see yourself everywhere if you lay on the floor.'

'And Rangoon? Do you remember Rangoon?'

'Our steamer anchored there for a couple of nights, but we weren't allowed into the city.'

'I have an uncle in Rangoon. He works for a bank. If I'd visited him I'd be able to tell you about it.'

Dolly turned her eyes on Uma's face. 'Do you think I want to know about Burma?'

'Don't you?'

'No. Not at all.'

'But you've been away so long.'

Dolly laughed. 'I think you're feeling a little sorry for me. Aren't you?'

'No,' Uma faltered. 'No.'

'There's no point in being sorry for me. I'm used to living in places with high walls. Mandalay wasn't much different. I don't really expect much else.'

'Do you ever think of going back?'

'Never.' Dolly's voice was emphatic. 'If I went to Burma now I would be a foreigner – they would call me a kalaa like they do Indians – a trespasser, an outsider from across the sea. I'd find that very hard, I think. I'd never be able to rid myself of the idea that I would have to leave again one day, just as I had to before. You would understand if you knew what it was like when we left.'

'Was it very terrible?'

'I don't remember much, which is a kind of mercy, I suppose. I see it in patches sometimes. It's like a scribble on a wall – no matter how many times you paint over it, a bit of it always comes through, but not enough to put together the whole.'

'What do you see?'

'Dust, torchlight, soldiers, crowds of people whose faces are invisible in the darkness . . .' Dolly shivered. 'I try not to think about it too much.'

After this, in what seemed like an impossibly short time, Dolly and Uma became close friends. At least once a week, and sometimes twice and even more, Dolly would come over to the Residency and they would spend the day together. Usually they stayed in, talking and reading, but from time to time Dolly would have an idea for an expedition. Kanhoji would drive them down to the sea or into the countryside. When the Collector was away touring the district, Dolly would stay over to keep Uma company. The Residency had several guest rooms and Uma assigned one of these exclusively to Dolly. They would sit up talking late into the night. Often they would wake up curled on one another's beds, having drifted off to sleep in mid-conversation.

One night, plucking up her courage, Uma remarked: 'One hears some awful things about Queen Supayalat.'

'What?'

'That she had a lot of people killed . . . in Mandalay.'

Dolly made no answer but Uma persisted. 'Doesn't it frighten you,' she said, 'to be living in the same house as someone like that?'

Dolly was quiet for a moment and Uma began to worry that she'd offended her. Then Dolly spoke up. 'You know, Uma,' she said in her softest voice. 'Every time I come to your house, I notice that picture you have, hanging by your front door . . .'

'Of Queen Victoria, you mean?'

'Yes.'

Uma was puzzled. 'What about it?'

'Don't you sometimes wonder how many people have been killed in Queen Victoria's name? It must be millions, wouldn't you say? I think I'd be frightened to live with one of those pictures.'

A few days later Uma took the picture down and sent it to the Cutchery, to be hung in the Collector's office.

Uma was twenty-six and had already been married five years. Dolly was a few years older. Uma began to worry: what was Dolly's future to be? Was she never to marry or have children? And what of the Princesses? The First Princess was twenty-three, the youngest eighteen. Were these girls to have nothing to look forward to but lifetimes of imprisonment?

'Why doesn't someone do something,' Uma said to the Collector, 'about arranging marriages for the girls?'

'It's not that no one's tried,' the Collector replied. 'It's the Queen who won't allow it.'

In his offices at the Cutchery, the Collector had found a thick file of correspondence chronicling his predecessors' attempts to deal with the question of the Princesses' futures. The girls were in the prime of their womanhood. If there were to be a scandal or an accident at Outram House the incumbent Collector would be held responsible: the Bombay secretariat had left no room for doubt on this score. In order to protect themselves, several previous Collectors had tried to find suitable grooms for the Princesses. One had even written to his colleagues in Rangoon, to make enquiries about eligible Burmese bachelors – only to learn that there were only sixteen such men in the whole country.

The custom of the ruling dynasties of Burma was to marry very closely within their houses. Only a man descended of Konbaung blood in both lines was eligible to marry into the Royal Family. It was the Queen who was to blame for the fact that there were now very few such pure-blooded princes left: it was she who had decimated her dynasty by massacring all of Thebaw's potential rivals. As for the few eligible men that there were, none found favour with the Queen. She announced that not a single one of them was a fit match for a true-born Konbaung Princess. She would not allow her daughters to defile their blood by marrying beneath themselves.

'But what about Dolly?' Uma said to the Collector. 'Dolly doesn't have to worry about finding a prince.'

'That's true,' said the Collector, 'but hers is an even stranger circumstance. She's spent her whole life in the company of the four Princesses. But she's also a dependant, a servant, of unknown family and origin. How would you set about finding a husband for her? Where would you start: here or in Burma?'

Uma had no answer for this. Neither she nor Dolly had ever broached the subject of marriage or children. With some of her other friends, Uma could talk of little else but of husbands, marriage, children – and of course, of remedies for her own childlessness. But with Dolly it was different: theirs was not the kind of friendship that was based on intimate disclosure and domesticity – quite the opposite. Both she and Dolly knew instinctively what could not be spoken of – Uma's efforts to conceive, Dolly's spinsterhood – and it was this that lent their meetings such an urgent wakefulness. When she was with Dolly, Uma felt as though a great burden had dropped from her mind, that she could look outside herself, instead of worrying about her own failings as a wife. Driving in the countryside for instance, she would marvel at the way in which people came running out of their houses to talk to Dolly, to hand her little odds and ends, fruits, a few vegetables, lengths of cloth. They would talk for a while, in Konkani, and when they were on their way again, Dolly would smile and say, in explanation, 'That woman's uncle [or brother or aunt] used to work at Outram House.' Despite her shrugs of self-deprecation, Uma could tell that there was a depth to these connections that went far beyond the casual. Often Uma longed to know who exactly these people were and what they and Dolly were speaking of. But in these encounters it was she who was the outsider, the memsahib: to her, for once, fell the silence of exile.

Occasionally, when the crowds around them grew too large, Kanhoji would issue scoldings from his bench, telling the villagers to clear the way for the Collector's gaari, threatening to call the police. The women and children would glance at Uma; on recognizing the Collector's wife, their eyes would widen and they would shrink away.

'You see,' Dolly said once, laughing. 'The people of your country are more at home with prisoners than gaolers.'

'I'm not your gaoler.'

'What are you then?' Dolly said, smiling, but with a note of challenge audible in her voice.

'A friend. Surely?'

'That too, but by accident.'

Despite herself, Uma was glad of the note of scorn in Dolly's voice. It was a tonic restorative to the envy and obsequiousness she met with everywhere else, as the wife of the Collector and the district's pre-eminent memsahib.

One day, while driving out in the coach, Dolly had a sharp exchange of words with Kanhoji through the connecting window. They quickly became absorbed in their argument and Dolly seemed almost to forget Uma's presence. At intervals she made attempts to resume her normal manner, pointing at landmarks, and offering anecdotes about villages. But each time her anger got the better of her so that within moments she was at it again, whipping round to hurl a few more words at the coachman.

Uma was mystified: they were speaking in Konkani and she could understand nothing of what they said. What could they possibly be arguing about with their voices tuned to the intimately violent pitch of a family quarrel?

'Dolly, Dolly,' Uma shook her knee, 'what on earth is the matter?'

'Nothing,' Dolly said, pressing her lips primly together. 'Nothing at all. Everything is all right.'

They were on their way to the Bhagavati temple, which stood on the windswept cliffs above the bay, sheltered by the walls of Ratnagiri's medieval fort. As soon as the gaari came to a halt Uma took hold of Dolly's arm and led her towards the ruined ramparts. They climbed up to the crenellations and looked over: beneath them, the wall fell away in a straight line, dropping sheer into the sea a hundred feet below.

'Dolly, I want to know what the matter is.'

Dolly shook her head distractedly. 'I wish I could tell you but I can't.'

'Dolly, you can't shout at my coachman and then refuse to tell me what you were talking about.'

Dolly hesitated and Uma urged her again: 'You have to tell me, Dolly.'

Dolly bit her lip, looking intently into Uma's eyes. 'If I tell you,' she said, 'will you promise not to tell the Collector?'

'Yes. Of course.'

'You promise?'

'Solemnly. I promise.'

'It's about the First Princess.'

'Yes? Go on.'

'She's pregnant.'

Uma gasped, her hand flying to her mouth in disbelief. 'And the father?'

'Mohan Sawant.'

'Your coachman?'

'Yes. That's why your Kanhoji is so angry. He is Mohanbhai's uncle. Their family want the Queen to agree to a marriage so that the child will not be born a bastard.'

'But, Dolly, how could the Queen allow her daughter to marry a coachman?'

'We don't think of him as a coachman,' Dolly said sharply. 'He's Mohanbhai to us.'

'But what about his family, his background?'

Dolly flicked her wrist in a gesture of disgust. 'Oh, you Indians,' she said. 'You're all the same, all obsessed with your castes and your arranged marriages. In Burma when a woman likes a man, she is free to do what she wants.'

'But, Dolly,' Uma protested, 'I've heard that the Queen is very particular about these things. She thinks there's not a man in Burma who's good enough for her daughters.'

'So you've heard about the list of husbands-to-be?' Dolly began to laugh. 'But you know, those men were just names. The Princesses knew nothing about them. To marry one of them would have been a complicated thing, a matter of state. But what's happened between Mohanbhai and the Princess is not a complicated thing at all. It's very simple: they're just a man and a woman who've spent years together, living behind the same walls.'

'But the Queen? Isn't she angry? The King?'

'No. You see, all of us are very attached to Mohanbhai – Min and Mebya most of all. In our different ways I think we all love him a little. He's been with us through everything, he's the one person who's always stood beside us. In a way it's he who's kept us alive, kept us sane. The only person who's really upset by this is Mohanbhai. He thinks your husband will send him to gaol when he finds out.'

'What about the Princess? How does she feel?'

'It's as though she's been reborn – rescued from a house of death.'

'And what of you, Dolly? We never talk of you or your future. What about your prospects of marriage, of having children of your own? Do you never think of these things?'

Dolly leant over the wall, fixing her eyes on the pounding sea. 'To tell you the truth, Uma, I used to think of children all the time. But once we learnt about the Princess's child – Mohanbhai's child – a strange thing happened. Those thoughts vanished from my mind. Now when I wake up I feel that the child is mine, growing inside me. This morning, I heard the girls asking the First Princess: "Has the child grown?" "Did you feel her move last night?" "Where are her heels this morning?" "Can we touch her head with our hands?" I was the only one who didn't need to ask her anything: I felt that I could answer every one of those questions myself; it was as though it were my own child.'

'But, Dolly,' Uma said gently, 'this is not your child. No matter how much it may seem your own, it is not, and never will be.'

'It must seem very strange to you, Uma. I can understand that it would, to someone like you. But it's different for us. At Outram House we lead very small lives. Every day for the last twenty years we have woken to the same sounds, the same voices, the same sights, the same faces. We have had to be content with what we have, to look for what happiness we can find. For me it does not matter who is bearing this child. In my heart I feel that I am responsible for its conception. It is enough that it is coming into our lives. I will make it mine.'

Glancing at Dolly, Uma saw that her eyes were brimming with tears. 'Dolly,' she said, 'don't you see that nothing will be the same after the birth of this child? The life you've known at Outram House will end. Dolly, you've got to leave while you can. You are free to go: you alone are here of your own will.'

'And where would I go?' Dolly smiled at her. 'This is the only place I know. This is home.'

Ten

When the timber-heavy streams of the monsoons debouched into the Irrawaddy the impact was that of colliding trains. The difference was that this was an accident continuously in the making, a crash that carried on uninterrupted night and day, for weeks on end. The river was by now a swollen, angry torrent, racked by clashing currents and pock-marked with whirlpools. When the feeder streams slammed head-on into the river, two-ton logs were thrown cartwheeling into the air; fifty-foot tree trunks were sent shooting across the water like flat-bottomed pebbles. The noise was that of an artillery barrage, with the sound of the detonations carrying for miles into the hinterland.

It was at these points, where the river intersected with its feeder streams, that the teak companies' profits were at greatest risk. So fast were the Irrawaddy's currents in this season, that the timber was as good as lost unless quickly brought to shore. It was here, of necessity, that the logs passed from their terrestrial handlers to the aquatic, from oo-sis and elephants to river-folk and raftsmen.

The streams' confluences were guarded by retrievers specialised in the capture of river-borne logs: for the sum of three annas per log these swimmers strung a human net across the river, wresting the logs from the currents and guiding them in to shore. At the start of the season whole villages moved location to take up stations along the river. Children kept watch along the banks, while their elders breasted the currents, darting between the giant trunks, treading water around churning whirlpools of teak. Some of these retrievers came back to shore lying prone on their captured logs while others sat astride them, legs dangling. A few rode in standing on their feet, guiding the spinning, moss-covered logs with prehensile toes: these were the monarchs of the river, the acknowledged masters of retrieval.

Once brought to the banks, the logs were anchored and moored. When enough had accumulated, skilled raftsmen bound them together into river-worthy craft. These rafts were all of the same size, the number of their logs being set, by the companies' ordinance, at an exact three hundred and sixty in each, a round sum of thirty dozen. At one ton or more per log this gave each raft the tonnage of a small battleship and a deck space that was many times larger, wide enough to accommodate a fair or a parade ground. At the centre of each of these immense floating platforms, there stood a small hut, built by the raftsmen as housing for the crew. Like the temporary dwellings of teak camps, these raft-borne huts were erected in a matter of hours. They were all exactly the same in plan, and yet always different in execution – one being marked by the trailed shoots of a quick-growing vine, another by a chicken coop or even a shelter for a pig or a goat. Each raft bore a tall mast and a pole with a handful of grass affixed to the top, an offering to the river's nats. Before being cut adrift the rafts were assigned numbers, to be displayed on their masts along with the flags of the companies that owned them. The rafts travelled only between dawn and dusk, covering some ten to fifteen miles a day, powered solely by the flow of the river, and guided only by oars. The journey to Rangoon from upcountry forests could take five weeks or even more.

Each season Rajkumar found one pretext or another to spend a few days on these rafts. There was something hypnotically pleasurable about the variable rhythms of life on these immense, rectangular platforms – in the contrast between the delectable languor of the daytime hours, when there was often nothing more to do than to watch a fish-hook trailing through the water, and the tense excitement of the sunset mooring, when ropes flew hissing between deck and shore, and everyone had to race to douse the smoking logs. Despite their immense size, the rafts were fragile in construction: running afoul of a shoal or sandbank, they could disintegrate in a matter of minutes. Solid in appearance, their surfaces were as deceptive as quicksand. Thousands of gaps constantly opened and closed between the logs, each a small but deadly ankle trap.

Many of the raftsmen were from Chittagong, and for Rajkumar there was a special satisfaction in being able to revert to the dialect of his boyhood; in savouring on his tongue the remembered heat of fish-head dals and fish-tail *jhols*, flecked with nigella seed and mustard; in watching once again, the changing flow of the river, slowing as it spread itself across a flood plain, and then abruptly speeding up again at the approach of a gorge; in observing the unexpected mutations of the landscape, now green and thickly wooded, and now a baked, red desert, dotted with the skeletal trunks of parched toddy palms.

Of all the river's sights the strangest was one that lay a little to the south of the great volcanic hump of Mount Popa. The Irrawaddy here described a wide, sweeping turn, spreading itself to a great width. On the eastern bank of the river, there appeared a range of low, foul-smelling mounds. These hillocks were covered in a thick ooze, a substance that would sometimes ignite spontaneously in the heat of the sun, sending streams of fires into the river. Often at night small, wavering flames could be seen in the distance, carpeting the slopes.

To the people of the area this ooze was known as earth-oil: it was a dark, shimmering green, the colour of bluebottles' wings. It seeped from the rocks like sweat, gathering in shiny green-filmed pools. In places, the puddles joined together to form creeks and rivulets, an oleaginous delta that fanned out along the shores. So strong was the odour of this oil that it carried all the way across the Irrawaddy: boatmen would swing wide when they floated past these slopes, this place-of-stinking-creeks – Yenangyaung.

This was one of the few places in the world where petroleum seeped naturally to the surface of the earth. Long before the discovery of the internal-combustion engine there was already a good market for this oil: it was widely used as an ointment, for the treatment of certain skin conditions. Merchants came to Yenangyaung from as far away as China to avail themselves of this substance. The gathering of the oil was the work of a community endemic to those burning hills, a group of people known as *twin-za*s, a tight-knit, secretive bunch of outcasts, runaways and foreigners.

Over generations twin-za families had attached themselves to individual springs and pools, gathering the oil in buckets and basins, and ferrying it to nearby towns. Many of Yenangyaung's pools had been worked for so long that the level of oil had sunk beneath the surface, forcing their owners to dig down. In this way, some of the pools had gradually become wells, a hundred feet deep or even more – great oil-sodden pits, surrounded by excavated sand and earth. Some of these wells were so heavily worked that they looked like small volcanoes, with steep, conical slopes. At these depths the oil could no longer be collected simply by dipping a weighted bucket: twin-zas were lowered in, on ropes, holding their breath like pearl divers.

Often, when moored within walking distance of Yenangyaung, Rajkumar would go over to watch the twin-zas at their work. Standing on the lip of a well he would look on as a man went down the shaft, rotating slowly on a sling. The rope would be attached, by way of a pulley, to his wife, family and livestock. They would lower him in by walking up the slope of the well, and when they felt his tug they would pull him out again by walking down. The lips of the wells were slippery from spills and it was not uncommon for unwary workers and young children to tumble in. Often these falls went unnoticed: there were no splashes and few ripples. Serenity is one of the properties of this oil: it is not easy to make a mark upon its surface.

After these visits to Yenangyaung, oil-soaked spectres would haunt Rajkumar's imaginings. What would it be like to drown in that ooze? To feel that green sludge, the colour of insects' wings, closing over your head, trickling into your ears and nostrils?

When he was about eighteen, Rajkumar came upon an unfamiliar sight at Yenangyaung. He noticed a couple of foreigners, white men, walking from well to well. From that time on, whenever he returned, there were more and more of these men around the slopes, armed with instruments and surveyors' tripods. They were from France, England and America, and they were said to be offering the twin-zas good money, buying up their pools and wells. Wooden obelisks began to rise on the hillocks, cage-like pyramids inside which huge mechanical beaks hammered ceaselessly on the earth.

On one of these visits to Yenangyaung Rajkumar's raft picked up a passenger. He was called Baburao and he was from Guntur, in India. Hair grew so thick upon his body that even when wearing a cotton vest he seemed to be coated in a fine wire mesh. He had a lot of money and dispensed liquor freely to the raftsmen, late into the night. He was a *maistry*, he said, a labour contractor: he had just transported forty-eight Cooringhees from eastern India to Yenangyaung. There was no quicker money to be made anywhere. Many foreign companies were busy digging for oil and they were desperate for labour. They needed workers and were willing to pay handsomely. It was hard to find workers in Burma: few Burmese were so poor as to put up with conditions like those of Yenangyaung. But back at home in India, Baburao said, there were uncountable thousands of people who were so desparate to leave that they would sign over many years' earnings. A young man like Rajkumar could grow rich quickly in this trade. What easier way to make money? All one needed was a few hundred rupees to pay one-way passages for the recruits.

Rajkumar wandered slowly to the edge of the moored raft and lit a cheroot, lying flat on his chest. His face was inches from the water, and schools of tiny riverbank fish rose to the surface to snap at his flaking ash. The encounter with the maistry had come at a time when the future was much on his mind. For the better part of the last year Saya John had been talking to him of planning ahead: 'Your days as a luga-lei are coming to their end, Rajkumar. The time has come when you have to make your own place in the world.'

What Rajkumar wanted most was to go into the timber business. Of this he was certain, for he knew he would never be so well acquainted with any other trade. But the problem was that he possessed none of the specialised skills that would have let him join a company's workforce as an oo-si or a raftsman. Nor did the prospect of earning a meagre twenty or thirty rupees a month hold any appeal. What then?

The best possible way to enter the teak business, Rajkumar had decided, would be through the acquisition of a timberyard. On his journeys downriver, Rajkumar stopped occasionally at the river port of Henzada. His old friend Doh Say lived there now, with his wife, Naw Da, and their two children. He worked in a small dockside yard, supervising a team of two elephants. Doh Say had suggested to Rajkumar that he set up a timberyard of his own: warehousing was a good way of entering the trade. 'You can start small,' he'd said. 'You can manage with just one elephant. I'll come and work with you, for half the usual salary, in exchange for a share of the business.' All that was needed was an outlay of capital.

It was Rajkumar's practice never to collect more than a part of his salary, banking the rest with Saya John. But after all these years his savings still amounted to no more than some two hundred rupees. The cost of setting up a timberyard amounted to several thousand – too much to ask from Saya John. To go to India with Baburao on the other hand would take not much more than he had already saved. And if he could persuade Saya John to lend him the rest, well then, within a few years he might have enough for his yard.

Back in Mandalay he waited for a good time to approach Saya John. 'All I need is a loan of a few hundred rupees,' he said quietly, taking care not to explain too much. 'And it'll come back to you many times over. Saya?'

Three months later Rajkumar left for India with Baburao. It took four days from Rangoon to Calcutta and another four to travel down the coast in the direction of Madras. Baburao rented two ox-carts at a small market town and had them tricked out in festive cloths. He bought several sacks of parched rice from the bazaar and recruited some half-dozen stick-wielding *lathiyals* to act as guards.

They headed into the countryside accompanied by drummers: it was as though they were a bridal procession, journeying to a wedding. On the way Baburao asked passers-by about the villages ahead. Were they rich or poor? Did the villagers own land or work for shares? What were the castes of the people who lived in them?

They stopped at a small hamlet, a shabby little cluster of huts huddled around an immense banyan tree. Baburao seated himself under the tree and told the drummers to start beating their instruments. At once all other activity came to a halt. Men came running in from the fields, leaving their oxen tethered to their ploughs. Children came floundering across the rice paddies. Women slipped out of their huts with their babies balanced on their hips.

Baburao welcomed everyone to the shade of the tree. Once the crowd was thick and deep he began to talk, his voice slowing to a chant in the reverential manner of a reciter of the *Ramayana*. He spoke of a land of gold, Burma, which the British Sarkar had declared to be a part of India. He pointed to the tasselled shawl that hung round his neck and invited his listeners to touch it with their fingers; he held up his hand so that everyone could see his gold and ruby rings. All of this, said Baburao, had come from Burma, the golden land. Before going there, he had had nothing, not even a goat or cow.

'And all these things can be yours too,' Baburao said to his listeners. 'Not in your next life. Not next year. Now. They can be yours now. All you need is an able-bodied man from your family to put his thumbprint on this sheet of paper.'

He took a handful of silver coins out of a velvet bag and let them fall back again, tinkling. 'Are there any here who have debts? Are there any who owe money to their landlords? You can settle your obligations right now, right here. As soon as your sons and brothers make their marks on these contracts, this money will be yours. In a matter of a few years they will earn back enough to free themselves of debt. Then they will be at liberty to return or stay in Burma as they choose.'

Fifteen men signed on in that village and twenty-three in the next: some rushed eagerly forward, some were pushed on by their relatives and some had their hands held forcibly to the paper by their fathers and brothers. Carrying tin boxes and cloth bundles, the recruits followed Baburao's ox-cart back to town. The lathiyals brought up the rear to make sure they kept in step. They stopped once every few hours, to eat parched rice and salt.

When they reached the coast, Baburao hired a country boat to take them to Calcutta. Many of the men had never been on the sea before. They were frightened by the waves and that night one of the men leapt overboard. Baburao jumped in after him, and pulled him back into the boat. The would-be runaway had swallowed a bellyful of water. He was limp and scrawny, with bones sticking out of his body. Baburao draped the man over the side of the boat, doubling him over the gunwale. Then he climbed on top of him, pinning his torso below with a bent knee. With a thrusting motion of his foot, he pushed the man against the beam, pumping his stomach until the water he had swallowed came dribbling out of his mouth, along with a spongy mass of parched rice and salt.

'Where did you think you were going?' Baburao crooned, almost tenderly, as though he were singing to a lover. 'And what about all the money I gave your father so he could pay off his debts? What use would your corpse be, to him or to me?'

At Calcutta they boarded the S.S. *Dufferin*, which was owned by a British company. Baburao had an arrangement with the steward of the ship: he was a valued customer because of the business he brought. He was given free passage, second class. Pocketing Rajkumar's fare he allowed him to sleep on the floor of his cabin. The thirty-eight men they had brought with them were sent below, to a holding space at the rear of the ship.

Some two thousand other would-be immigrants were there already. Most were men, but there were also some hundred and fifty women. At the back, jutting out over the ship's wake, there was a narrow wooden platform with four holes to serve as toilets. The passage was rough and the floor of the holding area was soon covered with vomit and urine. This foul-smelling layer of slime welled back and forth with the rolling of the ship, rising inches high against the walls. The recruits sat huddled on their tin boxes and cloth bundles. At the first sight of land, off the Arakan coast, several men leapt off the ship. By the third day of the voyage the number of people in the hold had dwindled by a few dozen. The corpses of those who had died on board were carried to the stern and dropped into the ship's churning wake.

On reaching the Rangoon docks, Baburao found that the voyage had cost him two men. He was not displeased. 'Two out of thirty-eight is not bad,' he told Rajkumar. 'On occasion I've lost as many as six.'

They travelled together to Yenangyaung and then Rajkumar told Baburao that he needed to go up to Mandalay. But this was a ruse. Rajkumar set off in a northerly direction, but once he'd put a little distance between himself and Baburao, he doubled back, heading straight for Rangoon. At a small shop on Mogul Street he bought a gold chain and a bright turquoise ring. Then he went down to the docks and boarded the *Dufferin*. During his last crossing, he had taken care to work out his own deal with the stewards of the ship: he was now welcomed as a maistry in his own right.

Rajkumar went back to the same district that he had visited with Baburao. He hired an ox-cart at the same market and employed the same lathiyals. He succeeded in indenturing fifty-five men and three women. On the way back to Calcutta, mindful of what had happened the last time, he sat up all night in his hired country boat, keeping watch over his recruits. Sure enough, one night, he spotted a man trying to slip silently overboard. Rajkumar was bigger and more alert than Baburao and had no need to jump in. He pulled the man out of the water by his hair and held him dangling in front of the others. He succeeded in bringing the whole group intact to Yenangyaung, and there he sold their indenture contracts to a local boss. The money was enough to pay off Saya John's loan.

Three years passed before Doh Say found a promising timberyard. By that time Rajkumar had made eight more trips to India. His accumulated savings now amounted to almost two-thirds of the asking price of the yard. Saya John lent him the rest.

The yard was in Rangoon, off Lower Kemendine Road. There were many sawmills in the area, and the air was always filled with the fragrance of sawdust. There was a Hindu cremation ground nearby, in Sanchaung, and sometimes, when the wind turned, clouds of ash would rise in circles above the funeral pyres. A brick wall ran most of the way round the compound, and at the back there was a narrow jetty, sticking like a tongue into the Rangoon river. At low tide the riverbank expanded into a vast shelf of cottony mud. In the front of the yard there were two small cabins, built of cast-off lumber and bamboo thatch. Rajkumar moved into the smaller of the two; the other went to Doh Say, Naw Da and their children, of whom there were now four.

On his first visit to the yard, Saya John ate a meal in the cabin where Doh Say and Naw Da lived. Saya John had not known that Doh Say was to be a partner in Rajkumar's business, but he was not particularly surprised to find that this was so. Rajkumar had always possessed a dogged kind of consistency – this was a quality quite different from loyalty, but no less enduring. The same shadows seemed to recur over and over again in his life, just as they did on puppet screens.

The following year Saya John went into semi-retirement and moved from Mandalay to Rangoon. The sale of his firm had made him a wealthy man. He set up a small office in Merchant Street, and bought a flat on Blackburn Lane. He bought a lot of furniture for his flat, hoping that his son, Matthew, would soon come home. But the boy was farther away than ever – a relative had taken him to San Francisco and he had written to say that he was studying in a Catholic seminary. There was no telling when he'd come back.

With time on his hands, Saya John began to take long walks, to air his pet birds. Rajkumar's timberyard was just a half-hour's stroll from his home and it became a ritual with him to stop by every morning, with a birdcage in his hand and a newspaper under his arm.

One morning he arrived to find Rajkumar waiting at the gate, hopping with impatience. 'You're late today, Saya.'

'Late? For what?'

'Late with your paper, Saya.' Rajkumar snatched the *Rangoon Gazette* out of Saya John's hands. 'Doh Say heard on the docks that an Indian railway company was going to put out a notice, asking for tenders for the supply of sleepers.'

'Tenders for the supply of sleepers!' The mynah inside Saya John's birdcage chirruped in imitation of its owner's chortling laugh. 'And what of it, Rajkumar? A contract with a railway company would mean the shipping of thousands of tons of teak. To supply timber on that scale you would need teams of oo-sis, pe-sis, raftsmen, agents, Assistants. All you have is Doh Say and one elephant. How do you think you would fulfil this contract?'

'This railway company is small and new, Saya, and it needs cheap supplies. I don't have to start by acquiring the timber: I'll start with the contract. Once I have it, the timber will follow automatically. You will see. There are dozens of yards here that are overstocked. Once they see that I'm offering down payments they'll all come to me.'

'And where will you get the money to make these down payments?'

'Why, Saya,' Rajkumar smiled, a little sheepishly, 'from you, of course. Why would I offer such an opportunity to anyone else?'

'But consider the risk, Rajkumar. The big English companies could destroy you, make you a laughing stock in Rangoon. You could be driven out of business.'

'But, Saya, look at what I have here now.' Rajkumar gestured at his rickety cabin and his half-empty yard. 'Saya, this is no better than a roadside teashop – I might as well still be working for Ma Cho. If I'm ever going to make this business grow, I'll have to take a few risks.'

'Think, Rajkumar, think. You're just starting out. You have no idea of how these deals are struck in Rangoon. All the big people here know each other. They go to the same clubs, eat at the same restaurants, put money on each other's horses . . .'

'It's not just the big people who always know everything, Saya,' Rajkumar said. 'If I could find out exactly how much the other companies are going to quote, then I might be able to put in a winning bid.'

'And how would you find out?'

'I don't know, Saya. But I think I have a way. We'll see.'

'But, Rajkumar, you can't even read English: how do you think you're going to make this bid?'

Rajkumar grinned. 'It's true that I can't read English, Saya, but I've learnt to speak it. And why do I need to read when you can do it for me? Saya?'

And so it fell to Saya John to deal with the paperwork for the bid. It was to him that Rajkumar went with the letter the company sent back.

Breaking open the florid seal, Saya John gave voice to an incredulous shout. 'Rajkumar! You've been asked to meet with the directors of the Chota-Nagpur Railway Company next week. They are coming to Burma to scrutinise the bids. You are to go to the offices of the Chartered Bank on the Strand at ten o' clock on Thursday.'

Saya John clicked his tongue incredulously as he looked up from the crackling sheet of paper in his hands. 'Rajkumar, I really never thought you would get this far.'

'I told you, Saya.' Rajkumar smiled. 'I found out what the other companies were offering and I made a better bid.'

'And how did you find out?'

Rajkumar smiled. 'That will be my secret, Saya.'

'Your secret isn't going to be of any help to you now. It's the meeting that will decide everything. That's what you've got to think about.' Saya John ran his eyes critically over Rajkumar's green longyi and scuffed pinni vest. 'For example: what are you going to wear? The Chartered Bank won't even let you past its doors if you're dressed like that.'

The next day Saya John came to the timberyard with a dapper young man. 'This is U Ba Kyaw,' he said to Rajkumar. 'He was a valet to an English planter in Maymyo. He can teach you many things, like how to eat at a European table with a knife and fork. Buy exactly what he says and do exactly as he tells you.'

On the morning of the meeting Saya John arrived at the timberyard in a hired coach, dressed in his best black suit and equipped with a fine malacca cane and a new hat. He stepped into Rajkumar's cabin to find him already clothed in his new trousers and shirt, standing rigidly still while U Ba Kyaw worked on his tie.

When Rajkumar's costuming had been completed, Saya John looked him over and decided that there was nothing to fault in his appearance: his suit was appropriately plain and black, and his tie neatly tied, the collar turned to just the right angle. It was true that his clothes were not quite as well tailored as they would have been in Singapore or Hong Kong, but for Rangoon they were more than adequate. In any event, no matter how costly Rajkumar's clothes or how well-fitting, it was a certainty that he would never be mistaken for a man who'd been born to wealth or office. There was a roughness to his face that was a surety against that.

'I'm coming with you, Rajkumar,' Saya John said. 'Just to bring you luck.'

At the Chartered Bank Saya John and Rajkumar were shown into an anteroom by a cashier, an Indian. Saya John saw to his surprise that Rajkumar was already acquainted with this man – D. P. Roy was his name. 'Everything is arranged,' Mr Roy said, in an undertone. 'The directors are in the boardroom now. They will call for you soon.'

The cashier left and they were on their own. The room was dark and cavernous, and its deep leather chairs smelt of cigar smoke. After a long wait a turbaned bearer came in to summon Rajkumar. Saya John rose to his feet too, with the intention of uttering a few words of encouragement and reassurance. But just as he was about to speak he stopped, his eyes resting on Rajkumar. It struck him that his one-time luga-lei was now so sure of himself, so confident, that there was nothing he could say that would not be superfluous. Saya John moved back a little, withdrawing a pace or two to observe him better. Suddenly, from that altered angle of vision he had the impression that he was looking at someone he had never seen before, a reinvented being, formidably imposing and of commanding presence. In that instant there flashed before Saya John's eyes a clear vision of that Mandalay morning when he had gone racing down an alley to rescue Rajkumar – he saw him again as a boy, an abandoned kalaa, a rags-clad Indian who had strayed too far from home. Already then, the boy had lived a lifetime, and from the look of him now it was clear that he was embarking on several more.

Then Rajkumar did something he had never done before. Just as he was about to walk through the door, he stooped to touch Saya John's feet, in the Indian way.

'Give me your blessings, Saya.'

Saya John turned his head to hide the tears that had welled into his eyes. 'That which a man takes for himself no one can deny him. The contract will be yours, Rajkumar. I was wrong to doubt it.'

Eleven

The post came twice a week and was delivered directly to the Collector's office in the Cutchery. Uma's letters were usually picked out by the Collector and sent up to the Residency with a peon. Her mail was mostly from her parents but once or twice each month there was also a book or a magazine, posted by a Calcutta bookshop.

On maildays Uma spent hours daydreaming by the peepul tree. If she happened to have one of her official appointments she would be snappish and impatient, eager to get back to her letters. She'd think of her mother, at home in Calcutta, writing in bed, worrying about her inkwell and spills on the sheets.

One mailday morning the Collector's peon delivered a letter with an unusual postmark. The Collector had scrawled a note on the envelope: 'From Rangoon.' Uma turned the envelope over and saw her uncle's name on the back, D. P. Roy. She was surprised: it was years since she'd last heard from him. But after her marriage she'd grown accustomed to receiving letters from long-unseen relatives: the Collector wielded a lot of influence; he was a man who could get things done. She surmised that her uncle needed something.

She took the letter down to the peepul tree. Just as she'd expected, her uncle had written to ask a favour, on behalf of a friend – a Rajkumar Raha who was on his way to Bombay on business. The man had expressed a desire to come down to Ratnagiri for a quick visit. He was keen to pay his respects to the former King and Queen.

'I would be very grateful, Uma, if your husband could arrange for Rajkumar-babu to call on the former King. Having somehow learnt of my connection with the Collector, he expressly sought me out to request my help in this matter. I might add that I am indebted to Rajkumar-babu for several good turns – indeed many members of our Bengali community in Rangoon have benefited from his assistance in one way or another.'

Rajkumar-babu, the letter continued, had lived in Rangoon many years but for much of that time he had had no contact with the other Bengalis of the city. Then suddenly one morning, he had dropped down like a hailstone from the sky, right into the Durga temple on Spark Street, the gathering-place of the city's Hindu Bengalis. He had come perfectly costumed for the occasion, in a starched white dhoti and a gold-buttoned *punjabi*. To ease his entry he had taken the precaution of bringing along a substantial donation for the *purohit*.

It turned out that Mr Raha was in the timber trade. He was planning to make a bid for a major contract and had come to ask the purohit to pray for him. Like all his kind the purohit had the intuition of a famished tiger when it came to the judging of potential prey. He did much more than offer a blessing. At the temple there were several employees of the big European banks and timber companies: the purohit made it his business to introduce Rajkumar-babu to all these men.

Over the next few days messages had flown back and forth between Spark Street and Merchant Street, between the Kalibari and the offices of the timber companies. Finally, when the directors of the Chota-Nagpur Railway Company announced their decision, it was learnt that one Mr Rajkumar Raha, a name then unknown in the world of teak, had succeeded in underbidding all the major companies.

On that contract alone Rajkumar-babu had netted a profit of eight lakh rupees – a fortune. Out of gratitude he'd virtually rebuilt the temple, paving its floors in marble, gilding the walls of the shrine and erecting a beautiful new dwelling for the purohit and his family. Since that time he had had several other successes and had risen to eminence within the business community. And all this at the age of thirty, before he had even had time to marry.

You will understand what I mean, Uma, when I say that our Rajkumar-babu is not the kind of person to whose society you are accustomed. You may well find him somewhat rough and even uncouth in his manner. You will no doubt be astonished to learn that although he speaks several languages fluently, including English and Burmese, he is for all practical purposes, an illiterate, barely able to sign his own name.

At home in India a man like Rajkumar-babu would stand little chance of gaining acceptance in the society of people like ourselves. But here in Burma our standards are a little more lax. Some of the richest people in the city are Indians, and most of them began with nothing more than a bundle of clothes and a tin box.

I fully understand that in India a man of Rajkumar-babu's station could scarcely hope to be entertained – or even received – by a District Collector. But you must consider that he has lived in Burma so long that he is now more Burmese than Indian and may well be counted as a foreigner. I hope you will make allowance for this, recalling that I for one would certainly be very grateful for your condescension in this matter.

Also associated with maildays was a special treat: fresh ice, shipped out from Bombay on the steamer. On mailday evenings the Collector liked to sit out in the garden, on a wicker chair, with an iced drink. Uma waited until the Collector had been served his whisky before she started reading him her uncle's letter. At the end of her recital the Collector took the sheet of paper from her and read it through himself.

He handed the letter back with a gesture of regret. 'If it were within my power,' he said, 'I would have liked to oblige your uncle. But unfortunately it's out of the question. The Government's instructions are quite clear. Their Highnesses are not to have visitors.'

'But why not?' Uma cried. 'You're the Collector. You could let him come if you wanted to. No one needs to know.'

The Collector placed his glass abruptly on the small peg table that stood by his chair. 'It's impossible, Uma. I'd have to forward the request to Bombay and from there it would be sent on to the Colonial Secretary in London. It could take months.'

'Just for a visit to Outram House?'

'Our teachers,' the Collector began – it was a running joke with him to speak of his British colleagues as *amader gurujon* – 'our teachers don't want political trouble in Burma. It's their richest province and they don't want to take any risks. The King is the one person who could bring the country together, against them. There are more than a dozen different tribes and peoples there. The monarchy is the only thing they have in common. Our teachers know this and they want to make sure that the King is forgotten. They don't wish to be cruel; they don't want any martyrs; all they want is that the King should be lost to memory – like an old umbrella in a dusty cupboard.'

'But what difference could a single visitor make?'

'He might get back and talk. Something could get into the newspapers. The Colonial Office won't even allow the King to be photographed for fear that the picture could get back to Burma. The other day I had a letter from a photographer, a Parsee woman. She's out on a picture-taking tour and wanted to stop by to take some photographs at Outram House. I forwarded her request to Bombay and heard back within the week: no pictures of the Royal Family are to be allowed. Government policy.'

'But that's monstrous,' Uma cried.

'Not at all.' The Collector's eyes narrowed. 'It's merely judicious. Do you think Burma would be well served by political trouble? Do you think this man Raha would have been able to get rich if Thebaw were still ruling? Why, if it were not for the British, the Burmese would probably have risen up against these Indian businessmen and driven them out like sheep.'

Uma knew she would not be able to best the Collector in an argument. She lowered her voice and placed a hand on his arm.

'You know,' she said, 'it's not for the King's sake, or even my uncle's that I'm asking you this.'

'Then why?'

Uma hesitated.

'Tell me.'

'It's because of Dolly.'

'Dolly?'

'She's lived here all her life, as a virtual prisoner, and she can't imagine anything other than the life she has. But she'll have to leave Outram House some day, and where is she to go? She's forgotten about Burma and I think she needs to talk to people who can remind her of it.'

'Dolly can go back to Burma whenever she wants.'

'But she doesn't have any family in Burma and she doesn't know anyone there. That's exactly why she needs to meet people who live there.'

The Collector fell silent and Uma sensed that he was beginning to relent. 'It's such a small thing,' she prompted. 'I'm sure there's a solution.'

'All right then,' he said at last, on a note of exasperation. 'Since it means so much to you I suppose there is one thing I could do.'

'What?'

'I could invite this Raha here as my personal guest. I could say he's a relative by marriage. And then, if he were to pay a visit to Outram House, it would be just a private visit – nothing official . . .'

'I'd be so glad . . .'

The very next morning a telegram was dispatched to Uma's uncle in Rangoon, to tell him that his friend, Mr Raha, was welcome to visit Ratnagiri; he would be received as the Collector's personal guest.

Twelve

Within moments of the steamer's arrival, word went out along the waterfront that there was a rich prince on board, one Rajkumar, a foreigner who was very free with his money. An uproar ensued: coolies and porters laid siege to the gangplank; idlers drifted in from the shaded shoreline and gathered on the beach.

Rajkumar was still asleep in his cabin when the steamer docked. It was U Ba Kyaw who woke him. It was Rajkumar's practice to bring a number of his people with him, when he was travelling abroad. This was his way of protecting himself from the pitfalls of his new circumstances. This particular journey had induced apprehensions of a novel kind and as a result his retinue was even larger than usual. Along with a stenographer and an accountant he had also brought U Ba Kyaw, his most trusted employee.

Rajkumar sent U Ba Kyaw ahead to distract the crowd and then slipped quickly off the steamer. There were two carriages waiting at the far end of the jetty: one was from the Residency. The Collector was out of town that morning, but he had left careful instructions on how the visitor was to be received. Kanhoji was to drive him to the Dak Bungalow where he was to stay. In the evening he was to dine at the Residency.

The other carriage at the jetty was the Outram House phaeton. Along with Kanhoji, Sawant was leaning on a rail, watching the uproar on the jetty. Both men were taken by surprise when Rajkumar was pointed out to them. Of all the party he looked the least likely to be the man whom Kanhoji had been sent to meet.

After dropping Rajkumar at the Dak Bungalow, Kanhoji headed

back to the Residency to give Uma a full account of the uproar at the jetty. His report was unsparingly detailed: he told Uma about the half-chewed cheroot in Rajkumar's mouth, the dishevelled untidiness of his attire, his crumpled longyi, his greasy vest and his uncombed hair. Uma was left with a sense of lingering unease. Was it prudent to invite someone like this to dinner? What exactly did he eat?

In a striking departure from custom, the Collector had entrusted the organising of the evening's meal to Uma. Usually it was he who oversaw the Residency's entertaining. Although otherwise uninterested in domestic matters, he was very particular about his dinner parties: he liked to examine the table and the place settings personally, tweaking the flowers and pointing out the plates and glasses that needed another round of polishing. It was to him that the servants went for their instructions on what to serve and which dinner service to use.

That morning when the khansama came to enquire about the menu, Uma had been taken by surprise. Thinking quickly, she told him to serve exactly what he had served the week before, when the Director of Public Education came to dinner. She remembered shepherd's pie and fried fish and blancmange.

'I want all of that tonight,' she'd told the cook, '*ekdum woh hi cheez*.' Then, on an impulse she wrote a note to the Anglo-Indian Superintendent of Police, Mr Wright, asking him to come to dinner, with his wife. She had already asked Mr Justice Naidu and Mrs Naidu – an elderly couple, unfailingly pleasant, undemanding. And of course Dolly was to come too: that had been arranged long before.

As evening approached, Uma tried to recall everything the Collector did before a dinner party. For once, she told herself, she would be a good memsahib. She went to the dining room and fussed with the plates and forks and flowers. But when the Collector came home, she discovered that she might as well have spared herself the effort. The Collector was plainly unimpressed. After stepping into the dining room to inspect her handiwork, he emerged with an unspoken rebuke on his face.

'The fish-knives weren't in the proper place,' he said. 'And there was dust on the wine glasses . . .' He made her go back to rearrange everything. 'I'll come back again later to check.'

Waiting for the guests to arrive, Uma sat by a window, her hands folded in her lap like a chastened schoolgirl. Perhaps it was a mistake, this dinner party, inviting Dolly to meet this stranger. Perhaps even her own presence here was a mistake. This was a thought that had never occurred to her before, but its chill shadow lengthened quickly in her mind. Was this what they called a premonition?

'Madame . . .'

It was the Naidus, grey-haired, tall, brimming with soft-voiced goodwill. 'How nice . . .' And then in came the Wrights, with Dolly following a few minutes later.

Rajkumar was the last to arrive. Rising to greet him, Uma found that her first impressions were unexpectedly favourable. Looking over her folded hands, she noted that he had gone to some trouble to dress neatly and plainly, in 'English' clothes: a sober black suit, a carefully knotted tie. His pumps were polished to a fine sheen and in his hands he was carrying a malacca cane with a handle of delicately carved jade. He looked much older than she'd expected: his face was weathered with hard use and his lips were heavy and richly coloured, very red against his dark skin. Along the line of his jaw there was a fold of flesh that hinted at jowls to come. He was far from good-looking, but there was something arresting about him, a massiveness of construction, allied with an unlikely mobility of expression – as though life had been breathed into a wall of slate.

Glancing over her shoulder, Uma spotted Dolly sitting half-hidden behind the scrolled arm of a chaise-longue. She was wearing a mauve htamein and an aingyi of white silk. A lily glowed like a light against the black sheen of her hair.

'Dolly!' Uma made a gesture of introduction in Rajkumar's direction. 'This is Mr Raha; I don't believe you've met . . .'

He recognized her at once, at first glance, beyond the remotest possibility of doubt. It was not that she looked the same, because she didn't: her face was much longer than he remembered, and around the corners of her eyes and mouth there was a fine, almost invisible, filigree of lines, like the tracings of a goldsmith's awl. What he remembered was something else – an element of her expression, a kind of forlornness in her eyes. It was this that had held him that night at the Glass Palace and now it held him again.

'Mr Raha –' there was a note of concern in Uma's voice – 'is something the matter?'

'No.' He looked down to find that he was holding his cane suspended in midair. 'No. Not at all. Nothing is the matter.'

To prevent himself from leaving the room, he sat down heavily in the nearest chair. It was too soon: he had not expected to see her here. There was nothing he hated more than to be taken unawares. He had expected to prepare himself for this encounter in slow, measured steps. It had been difficult enough to walk into this house. Even now, after two years of dinners and parties, he found it hard to cope with this atmosphere of constrained enactment.

'Did you have a pleasant journey, Mr Raha?'

It was his hostess, the Collector's wife: there was a look on her face that told him that she was trying to draw him out. He nodded and tried to smile. He could feel his gaze straying towards the chaise-longue and he quickly dropped his eyes. There were others approaching, he could feel them hovering at his shoulder. What was he to say to them? He had never so much wanted to be left alone.

'Dinner. Shall we . . . ?'

On the way to the dining room Uma found herself momentarily alone with Dolly. 'What do you think of our guest?' she said quickly, under her breath.

'He's not what I expected: not at all like a big magnate.'

'Because he's so quiet, you mean?'

'He doesn't seem to be much at ease, does he?'

'Have you noticed how he keeps looking at you? It's almost as though he's seen you somewhere before.'

Dolly's eyes widened. 'That's such a strange thing to say, Uma. I wonder what could have made you say that?'

The Residency's dining room was too large to be properly lit. Its long mahogany table floated adrift in an island of darkness.

There were several enormous candlestands on the table but because of the hand-pulled punkah overhead, the candles in the silver branches could not be lit. As a result the diners' faces were half-obscured, never quite visible, even to their neighbours.

Uma had seated Rajkumar on her right and Mr Wright, the Superintendent of Police, on her left. Dolly was at the other end of the table, sitting next to the Collector. Along the walls, at a distance of some half-dozen paces from the table, there stood a line of bearers, one behind each chair. As was the custom, the diners had each brought their own bearer, all except Dolly, who was as good as a member of the household. The Naidus' bearers were local men, Mr Wright's a Sikh. Behind Rajkumar's chair stood U Ba Kyaw, in a pink gaung-baung and a purple longyi: everyone else was drab by comparison.

Presently, the Collector laid down his napkin, and looked across the table at Rajkumar. 'Burma, Mr Raha,' he said in his ironical way. 'You have told us very little about it. What took you there in the first place?'

'Accident,' Rajkumar said shortly.

'What kind of accident carries a man to another country?'

'I was working on a boat and found myself stranded in Mandalay. This was at the start of the British invasion. The river was closed to traffic.'

'An eventful time.'

'A strange time, sir.'

'Indeed? How so?'

Dolly was watching him from across the table. Hers was the only face he could see: the others were all wrapped in shadow.

'The British fleet took two weeks to move up the river,' Rajkumar said. 'And through most of that time Mandalay was very quiet. I was only a boy then, but I was one of the few in the city who seemed to be aware that trouble was on its way.'

At this juncture there occurred an odd little incident. The fish having just been served, Rajkumar glanced impatiently at the knives and forks that surrounded his plate. Then, as though in exasperation at the profusion of cutlery, he held up his right hand and snapped his fingers. Even before he had completed the gesture U Ba Kyaw had appeared at his side, to hand him the appropriate utensil. This took no more than an instant, but everyone in the room took startled notice. Only Rajkumar himself seemed to be unmindful of the interruption. He resumed his narrative as though nothing had happened.

'One morning we heard cannon-shots somewhere in the distance. When the noise stopped, everything went on again, just as usual. It was only when the foreign soldiers marched into the city that people understood what had happened: that the King had been defeated, the city conquered. Towards evening we saw troops marching out of the fort with sacks of loot. Palace workers too. A crowd gathered around the walls of the fort. I had never been past the walls. When I saw people crossing the moat, I went to join them. We went running in. At the walls of the palace we found a breached gateway. We broke through, hundreds of us. I suppose you could say it was a kind of riot. None of us knew what we were doing, everyone was following someone else. We went running into the rear of the palace: the women's section. The most valuable objects were already gone, but to us what was left seemed to be of an unimaginable sumptuousness, precious beyond imagining. People fell upon everything that was within reach, everything in sight, breaking the furniture, digging stones from the floor. After a while I left the main hallway and turned into an anteroom. There was a woman inside. She was small and slight of figure, and even though I had never seen her before I knew at once that she was Queen Supayalat.'

'The Queen?'

'Yes. Her Majesty herself. I imagine she had come there to salvage whatever was left of her possessions. She was without guards, without an escort. She should have been frightened, but she was not. She shouted at us, threatened us. But what was still more remarkable was that everyone who came into the room fell instantly to the floor, to shiko to the Queen. Imagine how strange this was: there they were, looting the palace and at the same time paying homage to their Queen! I was mesmerised: I sat in a corner, watching. And when I had been there a while I realised that the Queen was not alone. She had two children with her, and some attendants, a group of young girls. Of the children the older was perhaps three. I took her to be a Princess, from the style of her clothes. Standing beside the Princess was an attendant, also a child, perhaps a year or two younger than me, perhaps more, I could not be sure, for this was a child like none I had ever seen before – beautiful beyond belief, beyond comprehension. She was like the palace itself, a thing of glass, inside which you could see everything of which your imagination was capable. All around us there was noise, the sound of knives, axes, running feet. It was evident that the girl was frightened, and yet, at the same time, she was perfectly calm. I could not take my eyes off her. I knew I was watching something I would never forget.'

'Who was she?' Uma broke in. 'This girl – who was she? Did you ever find out?'

'To tell you the truth . . .' Rajkumar was about to go on, when Dolly cut him short.

'It would seem,' she said curtly, addressing the Collector, 'it would seem that this was all a great sport for Mr Raha.'

'No.' Rajkumar's voice grew louder. 'Not at all.'

Dolly kept her gaze away from him. 'Mr Raha,' she said, 'appears to have enjoyed himself thoroughly.'

'No. That was not what I meant.'

Glancing at Rajkumar, Uma saw a look of inexpressible dismay cross his face. Suddenly she was sorry for him: Dolly was being needlessly cruel, unfair; anyone could see that the man had not intended any disrespect.

'Mr Raha . . .' Uma put out her hand to tap him on his wrist, to bring him back to the present and remind him that he was in company. But her elbow brushed accidentally against the table as she was reaching out. A fork slipped off her plate and fell tumbling to the floor. The sound was very small, thinly metallic, but within the confines of that space, it achieved the amplitude of an explosion. Two bearers leapt simultaneously from their places at the wall: one snatched the fallen utensil from the floor while the other proffered a napkin-wrapped replacement.

'Ah, Madame . . .'

The Collector's voice was expansive and loud, filled with mirthful irony. At the sound of it she shrank into her chair, in mortification. She had come to dread this note of derision, this inflexion that so often accompanied his comments on her small acts of clumsiness. She knew the incident would be mentioned many times that evening; there would be innumerable jokes, references, arch asides: these would constitute her punishment.

'Ah, Madame,' the Collector continued, 'may I urge you once again to refrain from juggling with the Government's silver?'

She shivered, her eyes fixed on her plate. How was it possible to endure this? She looked at the new fork, lying on her plate, and as though of its own accord her hand began to move. Her wrist snapped up, sending the fork cartwheeling into the air.

Just before the utensil had completed its arc, Rajkumar shot out a hand and snatched it out of the air. 'There,' he said, slapping it down on the tablecloth. 'No harm done.'

Across the table the Collector was watching in astonishment. 'Uma!' he cried, the note of irony gone from his voice. 'Uma! What is the matter with you today?'

There followed an instant of silence in which they heard the sound of a carriage, rumbling up to the Residency's gate. *'Kaun hai?'* came the sentry's shouted challenge. The reply was muffled and indistinct but Dolly started at once to her feet. 'It's Mohanbhai. Something must have happened at Outram House.'

A bearer came in, bowing, and presented the Collector with an envelope. 'Urgent, sir.'

Slitting the envelope the Collector took out a sheet of embossed notepaper. He read the letter through and looked up, smiling gravely. 'I'm afraid I must leave these revels. A summons. Her Highness wants me at Outram House. At once.'

'Then I should go too.' Dolly pushed back her chair.

'By no means.' The Collector gave her hand a pat. 'Stay and enjoy yourself. It's me she wants. Not you. '

Dolly and Uma exchanged glances: they both knew at once that the Queen had summoned the Collector in order to announce the Princess's pregnancy. Dolly could not decide whether it would be better to go back to Outram House or to stay away.

'Stay, Dolly,' Uma urged.

'All right,' Dolly nodded. 'I'll stay.'

The complicity of the two women was not lost on the Collector. He looked from Uma to Dolly and back again. 'What exactly is going on at Outram House?' he said. 'Does either of you have any idea?'

'No.' Uma was quick to answer, her voice a note higher than usual. 'Whatever it is, I'm sure it won't require Dolly's presence.'

'All right then.' The Collector moved quickly around the table, saying his goodbyes. 'I'll be back when Her Highness sees fit. Do keep yourselves amused . . .'

The suddenness of the Collector's departure set the others astir. The Naidus and the Wrights rose whispering to their feet. 'It's very late . . .' 'Ought to be on our way . . .' There was a flurry of leave-taking and handshakes. Following her guests to the door, Uma stopped to whisper to Dolly: 'I'll be back after I see them off. Wait for me . . .'

Dolly went dazedly into the drawing room and opened one of the French windows. Stepping out into the garden, she stopped to listen to the voices of the departing guests. They were saying their goodbyes. 'Thank you . . .' 'So nice . . .' One of the voices was Uma's, but it seemed very far away. She couldn't think clearly right now: everything seemed a little blurred. It struck her that she should shut the French window to keep the insects out of the house. But she let it pass: there was too much to think about.

Right now, at this very moment, at Outram House, the Princesses were probably sitting by their windows looking down the road, waiting for the sound of the Collector's carriage. Downstairs, the reception room was probably open already, the lamps lit, just two, to save on oil. The Queen would soon be on her way down, in her patched crimson htamein; in a moment she would seat herself with her back to the door. And there she would wait until the Collector was shown in.

This was how the accustomed world of Outram House would end: they'd known this, all along, she and the Princesses. This was exactly how it would happen: one day, suddenly, the Queen would decide the time had come. The Collector would be sent for immediately, not a minute to waste. The next day everyone would know: the Governor, the Viceroy, all of Burma. Mohanbhai would be sent away; perhaps the Princesses too. Only she, Dolly, would remain, to bear the blame.

'Miss Dolly.'

She recognised the voice. It was that man, the visitor from Burma.

'Miss Dolly.'

She turned on him, her temper rising. 'How did you know my name?'

'I heard . . .' He stopped to correct himself. 'The truth is that it was you who told me your name.'

'Impossible.'

'You did. Do you not remember? That night, in the Glass Palace. You were the girl with the Princess. You must remember. I spoke to you, asked you your name.'

Dolly clapped her hands over her ears. 'It's a lie. Every word of it. You've made it all up. Everything, every last word. There was not a line of truth in anything you said tonight. Min and Mebya were gods to the people of Mandalay. No one would have dared do the things you described . . . People cried when we were taken away.'

'They did. That is true. But this too is true: the mob, the palace. I was there, and so were you. You must recall – that night in the palace, someone had snatched something from you – a box. I found it and gave it back. That was when you told me your name: Dolly. I can still hear your voice.'

She averted her face. 'And you are here because of this? Because of what you saw that night at the palace?'

'Yes.'

'You've made a mistake, Mr Raha.' Her voice rose to a cry of plaintive denial. 'It wasn't me you saw. It was someone else. Children change as they grow. I have no memory of what you describe. I was not there. There were many of us – girls working in the palace. Perhaps it was someone else. I don't know. It wasn't me. I was not there.'

'I remember what I saw.'

'How can you be sure? I remember nothing of that time. I have never wanted to. And you yourself were a boy, a child.'

'But I still remember.'

'And for that you came here looking for me?'

'Miss Dolly, I have no family, no parents, no brothers, no sisters, no fabric of small memories from which to cut a large cloth. People think this sad and so it is. But it means also that I have no option but to choose my own attachments. This is not easy, as you can see. But it is freedom of a kind, and thus not without value.'

'And what did you expect to find? Did you come here thinking to find me still a child? Someone who could take you back to your boyhood?'

'I came because I could. Expecting nothing.'

Dolly fanned her face with her hands. She could smell the evening's fallen frangipani dying on the grass around her. 'Mr Raha.' She was calmer now, breathing more evenly. 'You are a rich man, I am told – a successful man. You have evidently lived a colourful life. I am at a loss to understand what it is exactly that has brought you here. I should tell you that, as far as I am concerned, this is my home and I have no other. I have spent twenty years here. I lead a very simple, practical life. There is nothing in me or the life I lead that can be of the remotest interest to someone like yourself.'

'I would like to say, with respect, that that is not for you to judge.'

'Mr Raha, it is best that you leave now.'

'I could not bring myself to leave without telling you that you had misunderstood me tonight at the dinner table. That is why I doubled back on my way out. I have come a long way. I could not leave on that note.'

A shadow appeared in the distance, framed against the drawing room's open window. It was Uma, calling out through cupped hands. 'Where are you, Dolly? In the garden?'

Dolly lowered her voice. 'Mr Raha, I am sorry if I said anything unjust or unkind. I am sure you meant no harm. But your coming here was a mistake and you would do best to put it behind you as quickly as possible. It is a pity that you have wasted so much time and effort.'

'It was not a waste.'

'There is nothing more to say Mr Raha.' Dolly joined together the palms of her hands. 'I must go now. I do not think we shall meet again, but I wish you well. *Namaste*.'

* * *

The Queen received the Collector, as always, seated in her ornate black armchair, with her back to the door. Her face was a painted mask, her lips a sunburst of red. Her ivory skin seemed almost translucent in the dim candlelight. She was dressed in a htamein of red silk and her stockinged feet were enclosed in black slippers, embroidered with fraying threads of gold.

Gesturing to the Collector to seat himself, she began without preamble, speaking in Hindustani. 'It is His Majesty the King's wish, Collector-sahib, that you be informed that our eldest daughter, Princess Ashin Hteik Su Myat Phaya Lat, is pregnant and that her confinement is perhaps just a week or two away. We would be grateful if you would convey the good news to your superiors in the Government of India.'

The Collector's first instinct was to correct her. 'But Your Highness this cannot be, for the Princess has no husband.'

'Not to your knowledge perhaps.'

'This is not a matter of opinion,' said the Collector. 'I have not issued a licence for the Princess's marriage. Therefore she cannot be legally married.'

The Queen was silent for a moment and then a slight smile appeared on her face.

'Collector-sahib, you keep yourself so well informed. I'm surprised that none of your spies have ever thought to tell you that children can be born without a licence.'

'So you mean the child . . .'

'Yes. By your laws, the child will be a bastard.'

'And the father?'

'You've met him often.' She fixed him with an unwavering gaze. 'He is our coachman, a fine young man.'

It was only now that the Collector began to grasp the full import of what she had said. 'But what am I to report? What am I to tell the Government?'

'You will convey what you have been told: you will say that our daughter is soon to have a child and that the father is our coachman, Sawant.'

'But, Your Highness,' the Collector said, 'consider the Princess's reputation, consider your standing in society.'

'Our standing? And what exactly is that, Collector-sahib?'

'Your husband is the King of Burma, albeit deposed. Your daughter is a Princess.'

'I assure you, Collector-sahib, that you of all people need not trouble to remind us of this.'

He could feel the sweat breaking out on his forehead. There was still time, he told himself: the matter could be handled discreetly, without any inkling of it reaching the public. The young man could be persuaded to go quietly back to his village and family. If he made trouble, Mr Wright and his policemen would deal with him.

'Your Highness, I beg you to reflect. Is it appropriate that a Princess of Burma should link herself to a household employee, a servant?'

A tiny, trilling laugh escaped the Queen's lips. 'Collector-sahib, Sawant is less a servant than you. At least he has no delusions about his place in the world.'

The Collector stared at her. 'I am frankly amazed,' he said, 'that Your Highness should choose to make light of such a scandal.'

'*Scandal?*' The Queen's eyes hardened as she repeated the English word. 'You have the insolence to come here and speak to us of *scandals*? There is no *scandal* in what my daughter has done. The *scandal* lies in what you have done to us; in the circumstances to which you have reduced us; in our very presence here. What did my daughters ever do, Collector-sahib, that they should have to spend their lives in this prison? Did they commit a crime? Were they tried or sentenced? We have heard so many lectures from you and your colleagues on the subject of the barbarity of the Kings of Burma and the humanity of the Angrez; we were tyrants you said, enemies of freedom, murderers. The English alone understand liberty, we were told; they do not put kings and princes to death; they rule through laws. If that is so, why has King Thebaw never been brought to trial? Where are these laws that we hear of? Is it a crime to defend your country against an invader? Would the English not do the same?'

The Collector knew that the appropriate response was to make a gesture of protest, a show of indignation. But under the Queen's hard-eyed scrutiny he was unable to find the right words.

'Your Highness,' he said at last, 'I am not your enemy. On the contrary I have acknowledged to you many times that I believe your grievances to be well-founded. The matter unfortunately is not in my hands. Please believe me when I say that I have only your best interests at heart. It is solely out of concern for you and your family that I am requesting you to reconsider your decision to accept this man – this coachman – into your family. I implore you, Your Highness, to think of how the public will view this – of the damage to your family's reputation.'

The Queen tilted her head. 'We are not public servants, Collector-sahib. To us the opinions of people at large are a matter of utter indifference.'

'I see your mind is made up.'

'Shame on you, Collector-sahib, that you should presume to judge the conduct of my children; shame on you that you should have the effrontery to come into this house and speak to me of scandal.'

The Collector rose to his feet. 'Your Highness, may I mention one last consideration? I do not expect it to weigh very greatly with you, but I feel that I have the right none the less, to bring it to your attention. You should be aware that if this matter becomes public, as your custodian-in-chief it is I, in all likelihood, who will bear the blame. Indeed it would almost certainly mean the end of my tenure here as Collector.'

'I assure you, Collector-sahib,' – the Queen laughed – 'we are well aware of this.' She laughed again, raising a tiny hand to cover her mouth. 'I am sure you will find a way to preserve yourself. Public officials usually do. If not you'll have only yourself to blame.'

There was nothing more to say. With a few mumbled words of regret the Collector excused himself from the Queen's presence. On his way out, he spotted Sawant coming out of the gatehouse. He could hear a woman's voice, calling out from within. Walking past the door, eyes discreetly averted, he caught a whiff of the hot, damp air inside. He quickened his pace. Was this where they cohabited then, the coachman and the First Princess, in that tiny hutch of a room? A profusion of images welled up before his eyes: Sawant, leaning on the doorpost, stroking his oiled moustache, beckoning to the girl with a smile; the Princess, stealing in through an unlatched door while the rest of the household lay asleep; the rank little room, reeking of sweat and echoing to their muffled cries; the creaking of a *charpai*.

He hurried into his gaari, calling impatiently to Kanhoji, *'Chalo! Jaldi chalo, jaldi*, to the Residency, quickly.' He leant out of the gaari's window, breathing hard, but even the cool night air could not clear his nostrils of the smell of that room. Was this love then: this coupling in the darkness, a princess of Burma and a Marathi coachman; this heedless mingling of sweat?

And the Queen, with her snapping black eyes? He had heard it said once that she had always really loved Thebaw. But what could they possibly know of love, of any of the finer sentiments, these bloodthirsty aristocrats, these semi-illiterates who had never read a book in all their lives, never looked with pleasure upon a painting? What could love mean to this woman, this murderer, responsible for the slaughter of scores of her own relatives? And yet it was a fact that she had chosen captivity over freedom for the sake of her husband, condemned her own daughters to twenty years of exile. Would Uma do the same for him? Would anyone? He shivered, stretching out his arms to steady himself against the sides of the carriage.

At the Residency, Uma was waiting up. She came running to the door to let him in, waving the servants away. 'What happened? What did she say? Tell me.'

'Where's Dolly?' the Collector asked.

'She was tired. She went straight to bed.'

'Come.'

The Collector led her to their bedroom and shut the door.

'You knew. Didn't you?'

'About what?'

'Uma, whatever I am, I'm not a fool. I'm talking about the Princess's pregnancy.'

Uma sat down on the edge of their mosquito-netted bed, averting her gaze.

'So you knew, didn't you?'

'Yes.'

'Dolly told you?'

'Yes.'

'And it never occurred to you to tell me? That this might be a matter of some importance? That it would have consequences for me?'

'How could I tell you? I promised not to.'

He came to stand beside her, looking down at her lowered head.

'And your promise to Dolly meant more than the bond between us, you and me?' He reached for her hands and took them gently into his own. 'Look at me, Uma. Why could you not trust me? Have I ever betrayed you, in any way? Did you think I would not be discreet?'

'I promised.'

He stared at her in bemusement. 'You've known of this for days, perhaps months. We were together all that time. Did you never once feel the desire to talk of this with me? Not as the Collector of Ratnagiri, not even as your husband, but just as a companion, someone in whose company you spend your days?'

She pulled her hands free of his grip. What did he want of her? She did his bidding in all things: she went to the Club when he told her to; she went to all her appointments. What more was there to give?

She began to sob, covering her face with her hands. The wifely virtues she could offer him he had no use for: Cambridge had taught him to want more; to make sure that nothing was held in abeyance, to bargain for a woman's soul with the coin of kindness and patience. The thought of this terrified her. This was a subjection beyond decency, beyond her imagining. She could not bring herself to think of it. Anything would be better than to submit.

Thirteen

It seemed to Uma that she had only just drifted off, after many long hours of sleeplessness, when she heard a voice at her bedside: 'Memsahib! Memsahib!'

She stirred drowsily, pushing her pillows back against the polished headboard. 'Memsahib!' It was an ayah, her face veiled by the cloudy gauze of the mosquito net. 'Get up, memsahib! Get up!' The windows were open and the ceiling was bathed in reflected sunlight. There was a smell of freshly mown grass in the air. She heard scythes hissing in the garden and remembered that she'd told the *malis* to mow the lawn.

'Memsahib, wake up. A gentleman is waiting in the *baithak-khana*.'

'A gentleman? Who?'

'The one who was here for dinner yesterday – the *bahaarka* gentleman.'

'Mr Raha?' Uma sat up with a start. 'What is he doing here?'

'He asked to see you. And Dolly memsahib.'

'Have you told her this?'

'Dolly memsahib isn't here. She left early this morning.'

'When?'

'Very early. Kanhoji took her back to Outram House.'

The mosquito net had somehow worked its coils around Uma: she couldn't get the webbing off her face.

'Why wasn't I told?'

'Collector-sahib said not to wake you.'

She scratched impatiently at the net with clawed fingers. There was a tearing sound and a gap opened suddenly in front of her.

She climbed through the rent, swinging her legs off the bed.

It wasn't like Dolly to leave in such a hurry, without a word.

'Send some tea to the baithak-khana,' she said to the ayah. 'And tell the gentleman I'll be out soon.'

She dressed quickly and went hurrying down the corridor. She took the ayah with her into the drawing room, and left her squatting by the door for propriety.

'Mr Raha?'

He was on the far side of the room, blowing smoke through an open window. At the sound of her voice, he spun round, flicking away his cheroot. He was wearing 'English' clothes – a white linen suit.

'Madame Collector, I am sorry to have disturbed you . . .'

'No. Not at all.' She began to cough. The room was foggy with acrid tobacco smoke.

'I'm sorry.' He dispelled a cloud of smoke with an apologetic wave. 'I came to thank you . . . for last night.' There was a pause in which she heard him swallow as though he were trying to collect himself to say something. 'And I wanted to thank Miss Sein too, if I could.'

'Dolly? But she isn't here. She's gone back to Outram House.'

'Oh.' He fell into a chair, his lips working silently, as though he were saying something to himself. She noticed that his hair was dishevelled and his eyes bleary from lack of sleep.

'May I ask if she is likely to return here today?'

'Mr Raha,' said Uma quietly, 'I have to say that I am a little surprised that you should concern yourself so much with someone you hardly know.'

He looked up at her. 'Madame Collector . . .'

'Yes?'

'There is something I should tell you.'

'Go on.'

'I have not been entirely frank with you. Or your uncle.'

'How so?'

'This was not my first meeting with Miss Sein. The truth is that it is because of her that I am here. I came in search of her.'

'What?' Uma tried to laugh. 'There must be some mistake, Mr Raha. You are surely thinking of someone else. You could not have met Dolly before this. Dolly has lived here all her life. I can assure you of that. She hasn't left Ratnagiri since she was ten years old.'

'The girl I spoke of last night – the girl in the Glass Palace?'

'Yes?'

'That was her – Dolly, Miss Sein.'

Uma felt the breath rushing out of her body. She rose unsteadily to her feet, and stepped through one of the French windows into the garden. 'Come, Mr Raha.' Without waiting for him, she set off across the freshly cut lawn. The malis were busy sweeping the cut grass to take home to their cows and goats; they looked up and salaamed as she swept by.

Rajkumar caught up with her at the bottom of the garden, just as she was opening the wicket gate. 'This must seem very strange to you.'

'Yes. It does.'

She led him to the earthen seat beneath the peepul tree. The Kajali river shone like glass in the valley below. 'Please sit down, Mr Raha.'

'I didn't know I would find her here,' Rajkumar said. 'Not for sure. This was just a place to begin – a way of settling a score with myself. As long as there existed a place where I could make enquiries, I had to come. I had no choice. I was sure that I'd find the matter settled: she would be married, I thought, or carrying someone else's child. Or dead, or turned into something unrecognisable. That would be that, the sight of her would wash the memory from my mind, set me free. Then I walked into your house last night, and there she was. I knew her at once: her face, her expression. And then the matter was indeed out of my hands, but not in the way I expected.'

'And you'd only seen her that one time?'

'Twice. In Mandalay. But if I had met her a thousand times it would have been no different. I know that. I am sure of that. When I was very young, I used to work on a boat, a Chittagong sampan. This was a long time ago, even before I went to Mandalay. One day we were caught in a storm. We were on the open sea and the storm came up very suddenly, as they do off the coast of Bengal. Water began to pour into the boat, over the stern. I was roped to a mast and given a bucket to bale with. Soon the sky grew so dark that my surroundings became invisible, except by lightning. During one of those flashes, I noticed something. It was an animal, a small, green-backed turtle. It had been washed aboard by a wave and had somehow got itself caught in some netting. It was just beyond my reach, and the waves were hitting the boat so hard I didn't dare undo my rope. We were both bound in our places, the turtle and I. At every flash of lightning, I looked up and there he was. And so it went, through that long, long night: the animal and I, watching one another, through the waves and the wind. Towards dawn the storm abated. I undid my ropes and unloosed the turtle from the net. I can see it clearly to this day. If you were to set a thousand turtles in front of me now, they would not be as real to me as that one animal.'

'Why are you telling me this, Mr Raha?'

'Who else can I tell?'

'Tell Dolly.'

'I tried to. Last night. I saw her going into the garden and I doubled back after leaving you.'

'What did she say?'

'She was determined to be angry – just as she was at dinner. She found fault with everything I said. She told me to go back. She would not see me again. I stayed up all night, thinking what do I do next? In any other place, I would have had people to turn to: my friends would have learnt her mind from her friends. I would have asked someone to speak to her family. Then I would have gone myself to meet her father. We would have discussed money, settlements. Things like that. I would have had some help. People to speak for me.'

'Yes.' Uma nodded. 'There would have been intermediaries. Go-betweens. People who can explain us better than we can ourselves.'

He was right, she knew – that was how these things happened: someone carried word from one mouth to another and so it went, whispers travelling like tendrils along hothouse trellises. That was exactly how it had happened in her own case: one night, a gaari had come clattering into the paved courtyard of their family home in Calcutta – the house to which her father had given the name Lankasuka. There was a loud banging on the front door, downstairs. It was late, after dinner. Her father was in his study, busy working on his treatise on temple architecture. Her mother was preparing to go to bed. 'Someone must have died,' her mother had declared. 'There's only ever bad news at this time of night.'

Uma and her little brother had gone running to the veranda that overlooked the courtyard. One of their aunts was standing by the door downstairs. 'Has someone died?' Uma had shouted.

'Died?' Her aunt had burst into laughter. 'No, you silly girl. Let me in.'

Uma and her brother had listened at the door while their mother conferred with the visitor. They heard them mention the Collector's name and recognised it: they'd read about him recently, in newspapers and magazines. He was known to be a brilliant man. As a student, he'd done so well at Calcutta University that the well-to-do families of his neighbourhood had pooled their resources together to send him to Cambridge. He'd returned a minor hero, having been accepted into the grandest and most powerful imperial cadre, the Indian Civil Service.

It transpired that he had seen Uma at a *puja*: she'd been sixteen at the time, a schoolgirl. On his return from Cambridge, he'd made enquiries about her. His family was none too pleased: they'd had proposals from all over the city and thought they could do much better. But he persisted, insisting that he didn't want a conventional marriage. He'd be working with Europeans: it wouldn't do to have a conservative, housebound wife. He needed a girl who would be willing to step out into society; someone young, who wouldn't be resistant to learning modern ways.

'And he's asking about my Uma?'

Her mother's incredulous shriek had resounded through the house. Uma was by no means the best-looking or the most accomplished girl in her circle: she could neither sing nor sew; her hair wasn't quite straight and she was thought to be too tall to be graceful.

'My Uma?'

Her brother had backed away from her, his mouth falling open in disbelief. 'You!' To tease him she'd said: 'Well, he can hardly marry *you*.' He'd burst into tears, as though that were exactly what he'd been hoping for.

'Why me?' Uma had asked the question over and over again, of all the usual intermediaries and go-betweens. 'Why me?' The most that anyone had been able to tell her was: 'He thinks you'll be quick to learn.'

Their wedding was unlike any other. The Governor came, and many English civil servants and army officers. Instead of a *shehnai* there was a military band from Fort William.

When they were alone, in the flower-hung bedroom of the first night, they'd both sat a long while silent on the bed, held still by shyness, he no less than she. They'd listened to the voices of their friends and relatives, clustered round the closed door, laughing, making the usual ribald jokes. At last, to her relief, he'd begun to talk: he'd told her about Cambridge, about the cobbled streets and stone bridges, about concerts he'd attended. He'd hummed a tune: it was by his favourite composer, he said. She liked the liveliness of the tune and asked: what is it called? He was pleased that she'd asked.

'It's from "The Trout",' he explained, 'by Schubert.'

'It's nice. Hum it again.' She'd drifted off to sleep, waking hours later to his touch. The pain was not as terrible as she'd been told – not much worse than going to the doctor – and the room was very dark, which made it easier. When her mother asked the next day, she was embarrassed that she didn't have a fearsome story to tell, like everyone else.

'He was kind, gentle.'

'What more could anyone ask?' her mother had said. 'Treasure your good fortune, Uma. Don't let a day go by without being grateful for what you've got.'

A month later, in a train, the Collector had asked suddenly if she remembered the name of the tune he'd hummed that night. Her mind had gone empty. They were heading through the stark flatness of Western Rajputana and she was entranced by the landscape. 'I don't remember,' she'd said. He had turned abruptly away, his face lengthening into a downcurl of disappointment. She had felt a tremor of dismay creeping slowly through her body like palsy. There would be more of this, she knew: these small episodes of disappointment would follow quickly on each other, in a long leaden chain.

Rajkumar's voice startled her back to the present: 'Will you help me then, Madame? You are the only person through whom I can reach Dolly now. There is no one else I can turn to.'

She tried to picture Dolly through the eyes of the man who was sitting beside her, this virtual stranger. Suddenly she felt her heart brimming over with tenderness, with love. Whose was it, this love? Was it his? Or her own? Or perhaps both? What would she do if Dolly left? Such brightness as there was in her life came from Dolly, although by rights, it should have been the other way round. It was Dolly who was the prisoner, after all: she was the lucky one, Mrs Uma Dey, of whom everyone always said, what more could you ask? But now, thinking of what it would be like in Ratnagiri without Dolly, she felt tears flooding into her eyes. She reached for the edge of the earthen bench to steady herself and her hand brushed against his.

'Madame? Mrs Dey?' He was peering at her, frowning in concern. 'Mrs Dey, are you all right?'

'Yes, yes.' She snatched her hand away. 'Just a little dizzy. I don't know what the matter is.'

'Shall we go back inside?'

'Yes.' She rose to her feet. 'Mr Raha, you still haven't told me. What is it that you expect of me?'

'Perhaps you could speak to her.'

'You must speak to her yourself, Mr Raha. Things never turn out well when there are go-betweens.'

He looked at her closely and then, suddenly, taking her by surprise, he said: 'The Collector is a fine man, Mrs Dey, a good man. Men like him are worth many –'

'Yes, of course,' she interrupted him quickly. 'Yes. Come let us go in.'

The ayah led Dolly to the drawing room and showed her the open window. 'Madame went into the garden – just a few minutes ago.'

Dolly nodded: of course, at this time of the day Uma was always to be found under the peepul tree. She went hurrying down the lawn, past the salaaming malis, to the wicket gate. Just as she was fumbling with the latch, she heard voices. Before she could turn back, Uma and Rajkumar appeared before her, stepping suddenly out of the peepul's gnarled grey beard. They stood staring at each other, all three of them.

Uma was the first to speak. 'Mr Raha,' she said quietly, 'I hope you will not take it amiss if I ask you to leave us for a minute? I would like to talk to Dolly – just a few words. Perhaps you could wait for us here by the garden gate?'

'Of course.

Uma took Dolly's arm. 'Come, let's go and sit under the tree for a bit.'

As they were picking their way through the labyrinth of roots beneath the peepul tree, Dolly whispered: 'What was he doing here, Uma? What does he want?'

'He was talking. About you.'

'What did he say?'

'I think he was trying to tell me that he's in love with you.' Uma seated herself under the tree and pulled Dolly down beside her.

'Oh, Uma.' Dolly buried her face in her hands. 'Last night, in your garden, he said so many things to me. It was so strange, so upsetting. I couldn't sleep, I kept thinking of home – Mandalay, the palace, the walls of glass.'

'He said you had no memory of him.'

'I thought not.'

'Do you then?'

'I'm not sure Uma. I remember someone, a boy, very dark; I remember being given a little packet of food; I remember Evelyn saying, take it, take it. But nothing is clear. It was so long ago, and whenever I think of it, I am frightened.'

'I think he really is in love with you, Dolly.'

'He's in love with what he remembers. That isn't me.'

'What about you, Dolly? What do you feel?'

'I'm frightened, Uma. I've made such terrible mistakes in the past. I promised myself I would never allow myself to make another.'

'What mistakes?'

'I've never told you this Uma, but many years ago, I thought I was in love with Mohanbhai – our coachman. Then the Princess found out. She threatened us. I suppose she was already in love with him herself.'

'Did you want to marry him?'

'I don't know, Uma. I was very young, and I didn't really understand what was happening. During the day I would keep him out of my mind. But at night I would dream of him and then I would wake up and think: Why can't we run away? Why can't I just wrap my things in a bundle right now, and go down to him and wake him up and say: "Mohanbhai, let's go, there's nothing for us here at Outram House"? But where could we have gone? And what would we have done? His family is very poor and they depend on him. In my heart I knew that even if I had begged him he would not have left. And this was the worst part of it, the humiliation. I would think, to myself, have I too become a servant, in my heart, as he has?'

'Did you ever tell him?'

'No. We never spoke, except of everyday matters. And after a while the dreams stopped and I thought, I am free of him now, it's all right at last. But last night, when I was sleeping in that room of yours, I began to dream again. I was at Outram House, in my bed. There was a mango tree beside my window. I got out of my bed and tied my things together, in a bundle, and slung it over my back. I climbed down and went running through the compound to the gatehouse. The door was open and I went in. It was dark and all I could see of him was his white langot, knotted tightly between his legs, rising and falling with his breath. I put my hand on his body. My knuckle fitted perfectly into the hollow at the base of his throat. He woke up and he looked at me and touched my face. And then he said: Shall we go? We went outside, and when we were in the moonlight I saw that it was not Mohanbhai.'

'Who was it?'

'It was him.' She inclined her head in the direction of the gate, where they had left Rajkumar.

'And then?'

'I woke up. I was terrified. I was in your house, in that bedroom. I couldn't bear to stay another moment. I went and woke Kanhoji.'

'Dolly. I think you have to tell him.'

'Whom?'

'Mr Raha.'

'No.' Dolly began to sob with her head on Uma's shoulder. 'No. Uma, all I can think of now is the birth of my child. There is no space in my head for anything else.'

Gently, Uma ran her hand over Dolly's head. 'The child is not yours, Dolly.'

'But it could have been.'

'Dolly, listen to me.' Putting her hands on Dolly's shoulders, Uma propped her up so she could look into her face. 'Dolly, will you believe me if I tell you that I love you like I've never loved anyone before? I was just a girl before I met you. You've shown me what courage is, what human beings can endure. I can't bear to think of being without you. I don't think I could remain here a single day if you weren't here. But I know this too, Dolly: you must go if you can. You must go now. The birth of this child will drive you out of your mind if you stay on at Outram House.'

'Don't say that, Uma.'

'Dolly, listen to me. This man loves you. I am convinced of it. You must at least allow yourself to listen to him.'

'Uma, I can't. Not now. Not with the child coming. If it was last year . . .'

'Then you must tell him that yourself. You owe him that.'

'No. Uma, no.'

Uma rose to her feet. 'I'm going to send him here. It'll only take a minute.'

'Don't leave, Uma. Please.' She clutched at Uma's hands. 'Please don't.'

'This is something that has to be done, Dolly. There is no way round it. I'll send him here. Then I'll go to the house. I'll be waiting. Come and tell me what happens.'

Rajkumar spotted her as he was picking his way round the tree: Dolly was sitting erect on the earthen bench, her hands folded neatly in her lap. He threw away his dying cheroot and put another to his lips. His hand was shaking so hard that it took him several tries to light a match.

'Miss Dolly.'

'Mr Raha.'

'My name is Rajkumar. I would be glad if you would call me that.'

She mouthed the syllables hesitantly. 'Rajkumar . . .'

'Thank you.'

'Uma wanted me to speak to you.'

'Yes?'

'But the truth is I have nothing to say.'

'Then let me –'

She held up a hand to stop him. 'Please. Let me finish. You must understand. It's impossible.'

'Why is it impossible? I would like to know. I am a practical man. Tell me and I will try to do something about it.'

'There is a child.'

'A child?' Rajkumar removed the cheroot from his mouth. 'Whose child? Yours?'

'The First Princess is with child. The father works in Outram House. I too was once in love with him – the father of the Princess's child. You should know this. I am not the nine-year-old girl I was in Mandalay.'

'Are you in love with him now?'

'No.'

'Then the rest is immaterial to me.'

'Mr Raha, you must understand. There are things you cannot change no matter how much money you have. Things might have been different for us in another time, another place. But it's too late now. This is my home. I have lived all my life here. My place is here at Outram House.'

Now, at last, the hopes that had sustained him this far began slowly to leak away. He had said all he could. He could think of no other way to plead with her, and she silenced him before he could begin.

'Please. I beg you, do not say anything more. You will merely cause unnecessary pain. There are things in this world that cannot be, no matter how much we may want them.'

'But this can be . . . could be, if only you would allow yourself to think of it.'

'No. Please say no more. I've made up my mind. There is only one thing I want to ask of you now.'

'What is that?'

'I ask that you leave Ratnagiri as soon as you can.'

He flinched, then bowed his head.

'I can see no reason to refuse.' Without another word, he turned and walked away, into the shadows of the bearded peepul.

Fourteen

'Sawant.'

Removing his binoculars from his eyes, the King pointed in the direction of the bay. A boat stood moored at the jetty, a large country craft of a type known locally as a hori: a deep-hulled catamaran with a single outrigger.

'Sawant, he is leaving.'

'Min?' It was very early and Sawant had brought the King the cup of tea he liked to drink at daybreak.

'The man who arrived the other day on the Bombay steamer. He is leaving. They are loading his luggage at the jetty.'

'Min, there is no steamer today.'

'He's hired a boat.' At this time of year, soon after the departure of the monsoons, there was a change in the prevailing currents and the waters round the mouth of the bay became, for a short while, exceptionally hazardous. During these weeks horis were the only sailing craft that would brave the swirling undertow that swept the coast.

'Min.' Sawant placed the pot of tea beside the King's chair and backed quickly out of the room.

Apart from the King and Sawant himself, the house was still asleep. The anteroom where Dolly slept was just a couple of doors down the corridor. Dolly had the suite to herself now, for the First Princess rarely came upstairs any more, preferring mainly to stay in the gatehouse, with Sawant.

Pushing Dolly's door open, Sawant slipped inside. She was asleep, lying on the same narrow cot that she had used for the last twenty years. Her hair had come loose during the night and lay fanned across her pillow. In repose her skin looked almost translucent, and her face had the serene beauty of a temple carving. Standing over her bed, watching the slow rhythms of her breath, Sawant hesitated.

Yesterday, on his way to his village on the estuary, Sawant had met a goatherd who was returning from the direction of the Residency. They had talked for a while, about the peepul tree, about the Collector's memsahib, about the rich prince from Burma and how he was besotted with Dolly.

It was impossible to think of Outram House without Dolly; impossible to imagine Ratnagiri emptied of her presence. But better that than to see her waste away before his eyes. No, he owed her this. He kneeled beside her and raised his hand.

She was wearing a crumpled night-time sari. The cloth was white and it hung like a veil over her long slender limbs. He thought of the time when they'd sat together on his sagging rope bed, with his blood-stained langot draped over their interlocking limbs. Just as he was about to wake her, his hand froze. To think of being without Dolly: it was madness! He began to back away. But then again he stopped. No, he owed her this.

Suddenly she opened her eyes. 'You!' She sat upright, folding her arms over her chest.

He put a finger to his lips. 'Quiet. Everyone's asleep. Quick. Get dressed.'

'Why?'

'He's leaving. Your man.'

Her eyes widened, in dismay. 'So soon?'

'Yes.'

'But there's no steamer. And at this time of year, I didn't think he would be able to go.'

'He's hired a hori.'

'But isn't it too late now?'

'No. They won't be able to leave until the light's better. Quick. You have to stop him. Too much has gone wrong for you, Dolly. Not again. Come. Quick.'

'How?'

'I'll harness the trap and take you down to Mandvi. Quick.'

By the time she was dressed, the trap was outside, ready to go.

Sawant had harnessed it to his fastest horse, a grey mare. He held out a hand to help Dolly in and then flicked the tip of his whip over the mare's head. The trap lurched forward, and they went rattling down the hill, past the police lines, the gaol, the Cutchery. At the Jhinjhinaka bazaar, a pack of guard dogs ran howling after them as they went racing past. From a long way off they saw the hori, casting off its moorings and pulling away, under oar, into the bay.

'Mohanbhai!'

He cracked his whip. 'I can go no faster, Dolly.'

When they reached the jetty the boat was a long way gone, approaching the mouth of the bay. 'Run, Dolly, run!' Sawant leapt off and gripped the mare's bit. 'Run! Run!'

She ran down the jetty, waving: in the distance the boat was trying to manoeuvre its bows so that it would be able to slip through the shoals and currents ahead. Its stern bucked furiously as it approached the pounding waters of the open sea. In a few minutes it would be out of the bay. She waved again and just as she was about to give up the hori's bows began to turn, away from the bay's mouth. Circling all the way around the bay the heavy craft came back to the waterfront, pulling up at the end of the jetty. The hori sat high in the water and Rajkumar easily vaulted the distance between the boat and the jetty's outermost plank.

He walked up to her puffing on his cheroot. 'Yes?'

She could feel herself flushing, the blood rising to her face. 'Mr Raha,' she said, picking her words with care. 'The currents are dangerous at this time of year and the Dak Bungalow has been booked for a week. There is no reason to leave in such a hurry.'

'But it was you who said –'

'Yes, but there is sometimes a difference between what one says and what one means . . .'

Rajkumar took the cheroot from his mouth with a hand that was moving very slowly, as though in stunned disbelief. Then he uttered a shout of laughter and threw his cheroot high into the air. They stood looking at it, side by side, laughing, watching as it rose circling above them. Suddenly the glowing tip disintegrated and a shower of sparks came floating down. It was as though fireworks were raining down from the heavens.

The Collector gave the appearance of being delighted when Uma told him that Rajkumar and Dolly were to be married. 'Splendid!' he said. 'Splendid!'

Uma explained that Dolly wanted to have a very quiet ceremony: she was sure that the Queen would do her best to stop the marriage if she got to know of it.

In the spirit of the moment the Collector offered several suggestions. Why not have the ceremony at the Residency? He would issue the licence himself and preside over their marriage in person. Afterwards, perhaps champagne; just for the four of them – Uma must make sure to be careful in husbanding the last batch of ice from Bombay . . . The enthusiasm in his voice was such that Uma couldn't help feeling that her husband was delighted by the prospect of seeing the last of Dolly.

The day came and Uma provided two garlands, of marigolds and jasmine. She wove them herself, with flowers picked from the garden. At the end of the civil ceremony, in the Collector's 'camp office', Uma and Rajkumar garlanded each other, smiling like children.

The plan was for the couple to spend their wedding night at the Dak Bungalow where Rajkumar was staying. Dolly had smuggled a few belongings and a bagful of clothes out of Outram House with the help of the First and Second Princesses. The First Princess had given her a pair of earrings and the Second a jade bracelet. They were happy for her and they were sure the other girls would be too. But for the moment in order to keep the news a secret, they hadn't told the two younger Princesses. Later, when everything was safely signed and sealed, Dolly could go back to Outram House with her new husband to pay her respects.

Everything went as planned until it came time for Dolly and Rajkumar to sign the register. Uma was the only available witness and Dolly balked at asking the bearers. But just then, quite miraculously, Mrs Khambatta, a lady photographer from Bombay, drew up in a gaari, toting her bags and her camera. Rajkumar went running out to rope her in. She readily agreed to be a witness and afterwards they all went out to the garden. The Collector called for champagne. A gentle breeze was blowing in from the sea. The light was mellow and golden.

Mrs Khambatta's camera was an instrument of superb craftsmanship: a 1901 Graflex single-lens reflex, with a cube-like body, a bellows extension and a four-sided hood. It was fitted with a Globe wide-angle lens which proved perfect for the panorama deployed before the shutter. Before exposing her first plate, Mrs Khambatta spent a full half-hour working with a Hurter and Driffield Actinograph Exposure Calculator, peering at its slide rule and calibrating its rotary cylinder for the present time and latitude. Then, signalling her readiness with an upraised hand, she exposed several plates in quick succession, standing back from her camera to squint at the group before squeezing the bulb of her Guery Flap-Shutter.

At dusk Rajkumar and Dolly gathered up their belongings. Uma lent them Kanhoji's gaari. On the way to the Dak Bungalow Dolly changed her mind.

'Let's go to Outram House now,' she said to Rajkumar. 'Let's talk to the Queen. Let's get it over with.'

It was dark by the time they got there. A lamp was shining in the King's room and another in Sawant's by the gate. The Princesses would be downstairs, Dolly thought, sitting around a single light, to save oil. How surprised they would be!

The gates were locked, so she told Kanhoji to use the knocker. He banged hard for a full five minutes but there was no answer.

Dolly went to the gatehouse window and knocked on the wooden shutters. 'Mohanbhai,' she called out. 'Open the gates. It's me, Dolly. I've come to say goodbye. Open the gates.'

The lights in the room went out and a minute or two later, she heard Sawant's voice, whispering: 'Dolly?'

'Where are you Mohanbhai?'

'Here. By the gatepost.' He was peering through the crack between the wall and the gate. 'Dolly, Mebya knows. She's told me not to let you in, not to open the gates.'

Dolly gasped. How could she leave Ratnagiri without saying

goodbye to Min and Mebya, to the Princesses? 'But, Mohanbhai, it's me, Dolly. Let me in.'

'I can't, Dolly. You know I would if I could. But Mebya is in one of her rages. You know how angry she gets.'

There was a pause and then a cloth bundle appeared at the top of the gate.

'Mebya had us pack some of your things,' said Sawant. 'She told me to make sure you got this.'

Dolly let the bundle drop to the ground.

'Mohanbhai, let me in.' She was pleading now. 'Just for a few minutes. Just to say goodbye.'

'I can't, Dolly. I really can't. Mebya said she would sack me if I did; she said we couldn't ever say your name again in this house.'

Dolly began to sob, knocking her head against the gatepost.

'Don't cry, Dolly.' Sawant looked through the crack. 'We'll miss you, all of us. Look, the girls are waving to you from up there.'

The four Princesses were standing close together, at one of the windows upstairs. They waved and she tried to wave back too, but her legs buckled under her. She fell to her knees, sobbing. Rajkumar rushed to lift her off the ground. Holding her up with one arm, he picked up her bundled clothes with his free hand.

'Come, Dolly. Let's go. There's nothing to be done.' He had to lift her bodily off the ground to get her inside the gaari.

'*Chalo, chalo, jaldi chalo.*'

When they were trotting past the police-barracks, near the parade ground, some of the constables' wives and children came out to wave. They all seemed to know that Miss Dolly was going away.

She waved back, wiping the tears fiercely from her eyes. She would not allow herself to be robbed of this last glimpse of the lane: the leaning coconut palms, the Union Jack, flapping above the gaol on its crooked pole, the rickety teashop at the entrance to the lane. This was home, this narrow lane with its mossy walls of laterite. She knew she would never see it again.

She sat bent over in her seat, hugging her old clothes. A cloth bundle, once again: only this time she wasn't carrying it on her head.

* * *

With her hand raised to knock, Uma noticed that the door of the Collector's study was slightly ajar. She could see him through the crack. He was sitting upright in his straight-backed chair. His glasses were dangling around his neck and he was staring into space.

He turned with a start when she knocked. 'Come in.'

She seated herself opposite him, in a chair that had no arms. This was where his stenographer sat, she guessed, little Mr Ranade, with a pad on his knees, taking dictation. They looked at each other silently across the broad, leather-covered expanse of the desk. A letter lay open in front of him; she noted, in passing, that it was sealed with a florid rosette of red wax. She was the first to drop her eyes and it was only then that he spoke.

'You have come to tell me that you want to go home,' he said. 'Am I right?'

She nodded. 'Yes.'

'May I ask why?'

'I am useless here. There's nothing I can do for you that you cannot do better for yourself. And with Dolly gone . . .'

He cleared his throat, cutting her short. 'And may I ask when you will be coming back?'

She made no answer, looking silently down at her lap.

'Well?'

'You deserve better than me.'

He turned his face away abruptly, so that she could see only one side of his face.

'You can marry again,' she said quickly, 'take another wife. I will see that my family makes no objection.'

He raised a finger to silence her.

'Could you tell me,' he said in a coldly formal voice. 'What did I do wrong? Did I mistreat you? Behave badly?'

'No. Never.' The tears welled up in her eyes, blinding her. 'You have been nothing but kind and patient. I have nothing to complain of.'

'I used to dream about the kind of marriage I wanted.' He was speaking more to himself now than to her. 'To live with a woman as an equal, in spirit and intellect: this seemed to me the most wonderful thing life could offer. To discover together the world of literature, art: what could be richer, more fulfilling? But what I dreamt of is not yet possible, not here, in India, not for us.' He ran his fingers over the letter in front of him, picking idly at the the heavy wax seal.

'So you'll go back to live with your parents then?'

'Yes.'

'You've picked a good time.' He gave her his thin, ironic smile. 'You would have had to pack your things soon enough anyway.'

'Why?' She was suddenly alert. 'What are you talking about?'

He picked the letter off his desk and tapped it with his gold-rimmed glasses. 'This is from the Chief Secretary, in Bombay. It came today. A reprimand, as it were. The Princess's pregnancy has awoken our teachers suddenly to the enormity of what they have done to this family. All the letters that I and my predecessors wrote had no effect whatever. But the smell of miscegenation has alarmed them as nothing else could have: they are tolerant in many things, but not this. They like to keep their races tidily separate. The prospect of dealing with a half-caste bastard has set them rampaging among their desks. I am to be the scapegoat for twenty years of neglect. My tenure here is terminated and I am to return to Bombay.'

He brought his fingertips together and smiled across the desk in his thinly ironic way.

'As I said, you've chosen a good time to leave.'

In the Ratnagiri boathouse there was one craft that was rarely used. This was the double-oared racing scull that had once belonged to Mr Gibb, the rowing legend.

It was the Collector's practice to go down to the Ratnagiri boathouse a couple of times each week. He had done a little rowing at Cambridge and would have done more if he had not been so busy studying for the Civil Service examinations. He enjoyed the focused concentration of the sport, the sense of moving ahead at a regulated pace, quick but unhurried. Besides, he had an almost religious belief in the importance of exercise.

Today, as he was walking into the boathouse, the Collector's eyes fell on Mr Gibb's racing shell. The elderly *chowkidar* who looked after the boathouse talked often of Mr Gibb. He was a rowing blue, Mr Gibb, and a skilled sailor besides. In the history of the Ratnagiri Club he was the only person who was known to have taken the slim, fragile craft out into the open sea and come back to tell the tale.

On his departure Mr Gibb had donated his shell to the boathouse. Since that time the boat had turned into a monument of sorts, a reliquary of Mr Gibb. It lay at one end of the shed and was never used. The Collector said to the chowkidar: 'How about this one?'

'That was Mr Gibb's boat,' came the answer. 'It was in that boat that Gibb-sahib used to row out to sea.'

'Is it usable?'

'Yes, sahib. Of course.' The chowkidar was proud of his job and worked hard to keep his boats in good repair.

'Well then, perhaps I'll take it out today.'

'You, sahib?' The chowkidar gasped. 'But Mr Gibb was very experienced –'

The Collector bridled at his tone. 'I think I can manage it,' he said coldly.

'But, sahib –'

'Please do as you're told.'

The boat was carried out to the water and the Collector climbed in and picked up the oars. He rowed once across the bay and turned round. He felt oddly exhilarated. The gap between the two arms of the bay began to beckon.

For several weeks now, he'd been thinking of trying the sea channel. He'd watched the local fishermen when they were slipping out of the bay, marking in his mind the precise point of their exit, the route through which they led their crafts into the open sea.

One day, he'd told himself, one day . . . He would start with a short, experimental foray, to test the waters, as it were. One day. But there were no more days now. Next week he would be in Bombay, in a windowless office, dealing with municipal taxation.

He scarcely noticed that his craft had veered from its trajectory; that its nose had turned westwards, pointing towards the opening of the bay. It was as though the shell had been reclaimed by the spirit of some other, departed official, as though it were steering itself.

He felt strangely reassured, at peace. It was best to leave these things to men like Mr Gibb: you would always be safe with them, looked after, provided for.

There was no reason to hurry back to the Residency. No one was waiting for him there. The sea seemed warm and inviting and the scull seemed to know its own way.

High above the bay, in Outram House, the King was on his way to the balcony, with his father's gilded glasses clasped in one hand. He had lain awake much of the night and was up even earlier than usual. Dolly's departure had created an unquietness in the house. He was sensitive to these things; they upset him. It wasn't easy to cope with change at his age. He'd found it hard to sleep.

He lifted the glasses to his eyes. The light was not good. The fishermen of Karla village were not out of the estuary yet. Then he spotted the thin, long shape of a racing shell arrowing across the dark water. The oarsman was rowing in a strong, steady rhythm, almost touching his knees with his forehead before straightening out again.

He was taken aback. It was a long time since he had last seen the shell steering for the open sea – not since Mr Gibb, and that was a long time ago, more than ten years now. And even Mr Gibb had never ventured out on the sea during the monsoons: he wouldn't have thought of it, he knew about the cross-currents that swept the shore during the rains.

He watched in surprise as the streamlined craft shot forward in the direction of the foaming white line that separated the calm waters of the bay from the pounding monsoon sea. Suddenly the boat buckled and its nose shot out of the water. The oarsman flung up an arm, and then the undertow took hold of him and sucked him down, beneath the surface. The King started to his feet, in shock. Gripping the balcony's rails, he leant over the balustrade. He began to shout: 'Sawant! Sawant!'

It was early in the morning and his voice had grown prematurely feeble. Sawant was asleep in the gatehouse, on his string bed, with one arm thrown protectively over the First Princess.

'Sawant, Sawant!'

It was the Queen who heard his shouts. She too had been up all night – thinking of Dolly, remembering how she'd come to her as a child, of how she'd been the only person in the palace who could quiet the Second Princess; of how she had stayed on when the others left.

'Sawant.'

She climbed slowly out of bed and went over to see what the King wanted.

The King pointed to a few bits of wreckage, drifting in the distance, at the mouth of the bay. 'The Collector!'

She took a long look with his gilded binoculars.

'Is he dead?'

'I think so.'

If it were not for that man Dolly would still be at Outram House: Dolly, whom she'd adopted and brought up and loved like her own child. But Dolly was gone now, and it was right that he should pay. She leant over the balustrade and spat into the garden, in commemoration of her gaoler's death.

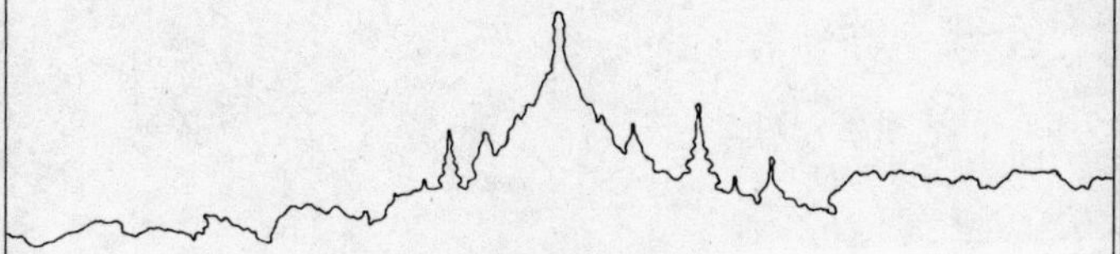

PART THREE

The Money Tree

Fifteen

Rangoon's Barr Street Passenger Jetty was something of a curiosity. It was built to resemble a floating pavilion, with fine woodwork and a peaked roof, like that of an Alpine cottage. Saya John held on to one of its carved posts as he leant over the jetty's side, scanning the river for the *Nuwara Eliya*, the steamer in which Rajkumar was returning to Rangoon with Dolly. When at last he spotted the ship, it was still a long way off, just approaching the mouth of the Pazundaung Creek, fighting the powerful currents that tore at the river's mud-brown surface.

It had been decided that Rajkumar and Dolly would stay initially with Saya John, at his spacious second-floor flat on Blackburn Lane – such accommodation as there was at Rajkumar's Kemendine compound was too rudimentary for the two of them to inhabit together. Saya John had sent a telegram to Rajkumar to let him know that he and Dolly were welcome to stay at Blackburn Lane until such time as they were able to build a habitable home.

The Pazundaung Creek was the wide inlet that marked the southern boundary of the city. Many of Rangoon's sawmills and rice mills were concentrated along the shores of this waterway – among them also the timberyard that was Rajkumar's principal place of business. When the steamer drew abreast of the creek, Rajkumar, watching from the *Nuwara Eliya*'s bows, caught a brief glimpse of the raised teakwood cabin that served as his office. Then the whole Rangoon waterfront opened up in front of him: the Botataung Pagoda, the stately buildings of the Strand, the golden finial of the Shwe Dagon in the distance.

Rajkumar turned impatiently away and headed for his cabin.

Since early that morning he had been trying to persuade Dolly to step outside: he was eager to show her this vista of Rangoon from the river; eager also to see whether she remembered any of it from her journey out, twenty-five years before. But over the last three days, as their ship approached Burma, Dolly had grown increasingly withdrawn. That morning she had refused to step out on deck; she'd said that she was seasick; that she would come out later, when she felt better; for the time being she wanted only to rest and collect herself.

But now there was no time at all. They would be at the jetty in a matter of minutes. Rajkumar burst into the cabin, his voice loudly exuberant: 'Dolly – we're home. Come on – outside . . .' When she didn't answer he broke off. She was sitting on the bed, curled up, with her forehead resting on her knees, dressed in the red, silk htamein that she'd changed into for the occasion.

'What's the matter Dolly?' He touched her shoulder to find that she was shivering. 'What's happened?'

'Nothing.' She shrugged his hand off. 'I'm all right. I'll come later; just let me sit here until everyone else is off the ship.'

He knew better than to make light of her apprehensions. 'All right,' he said. 'I'll come back for you in twenty minutes.'

'Yes. I'll be ready then.'

Dolly stayed as she was, with her head resting on her knees, trying to calm herself. She felt a jolt as the steamer docked and then she heard the voices of coolies and porters ringing through the gangways. Rippling patterns of opalescent light were dancing on the ceiling, shining in through a porthole, off the river's silt-dark surface. In a while, the cabin door squeaked open, and she heard Rajkumar's voice: 'Dolly . . .'

She looked up to see Rajkumar ushering someone into the cabin: a small, portly, owlish man, dressed in a grey suit and a felt hat. The visitor doffed his hat and smiled, so broadly that his eyes almost disappeared into the creases of his deeply lined face. This had to be Saya John, she knew, and the knowledge of this made her more apprehensive than ever. This was the meeting she had most dreaded: Rajkumar had talked of his mentor at such length that Saya John had become the equivalent of a father-in-law in her mind, to be either feared and propitiated, or else to be resisted and fought with – she had no idea how things would turn out between the two of them. Now, faced with him in person, she found herself folding her hands together, in the Indian way, unconsciously, through the force of long habit.

He laughed and came quickly across the cabin. Addressing her in Burmese, he said, 'Look, I have something for you.' She noticed that his accent was thickly foreign.

He reached into his pocket and took out a filigreed gold bracelet, wrapped in tissue paper. Taking hold of her wrist, he slipped the bracelet over her knuckles. 'It belonged to my wife,' he said. 'I put it aside for you.'

She spun the bracelet around her wrist. The polished gold facets gleamed in the dappled light that was shining in through the portholes. He put his arm around her and under the pressure of his hand, she felt her apprehensions seeping away. She glanced at him shyly and smiled. 'It's beautiful, Saya. I'll treasure it.'

Rajkumar, watching from the doorway, saw a lightening in the mists that had gathered around her over the last few days. 'Come,' he said quickly. 'Let's go. The gaari is waiting.'

On the way to Blackburn Lane, in the carriage, Saya John reached into his pocket once again. 'I have something for you too, Rajkumar.' He took out a small, spherical object, also wrapped in tissue paper. He handed it carefully to Rajkumar.

Undoing the tissue paper, Rajkumar found himself holding a spongy ball, made of whitish-grey strings that were tangled around each other, like wool. He raised the ball to his face, wrinkling his nose at the unfamiliar odour. 'What is it?'

'Rubber.' Saya John used the English word.

'Rubber?' Rajkumar recognised the word, but had only a dim awareness of what it referred to. He handed the ball to Dolly and she sniffed it, recoiling: its smell was more human than botanical, the scent of a bodily secretion, like sweat.

'Where did you get this, Saya?' Rajkumar said, in puzzlement.

'In my hometown – Malacca.'

Saya John had been travelling too, while Rajkumar was away in India: he had gone east, to Malaya, visiting friends and looking up his relatives by marriage. He'd stopped at Malacca, to visit his wife's grave. It was some years since he'd last been back, and he'd noticed immediately that something had changed in the interim, something new was afoot. For years, ever since he could remember, Malacca had been a town that was slowly dying, with its port silted up and its traders moving away, either northwards to Penang, or southwards to Singapore. But now, suddenly, Malacca was a changed place; there was a palpable quickening in the muddied veins of the sleepy old city. One day a friend took him to the outskirts of the town, to a place that he, John Martins, remembered from his childhood, an area that had once been home to dozens of small spice gardens, where pepper plants grew on vines. But the vines were all gone now, and in their place there were long straight rows of graceful, slender-trunked saplings.

Saya John had looked hard at the trees and had not been able to name them. 'What are they?'

'Rubber.'

Some nine years before, Mr Tan Chay Yan, scion of a well-known Peranakan Chinese family of Malacca, had converted his pepper garden into a rubber plantation. In 1897 this had seemed like a mad thing to do. Everyone had advised against it: rubber was known to be a risk. Mr Ridley, the curator of the Singapore Botanical Gardens, had been trying for years to interest British planters in giving rubber a try. The imperial authorities in London had spent a fortune in arranging to have seed stocks stolen from Brazil. But Mr Ridley was himself the first to admit that it might take as many as ten years for a rubber plantation to become productive. Malaya's European planters had backed away on learning this. But Mr Tan Chay Yan, persevering undeterred, had succeeded in milking rubber from his trees in three short years. Now everyone, even the most timid British corporation, was following his lead, planting rubber; money had been pouring into the city. The B. F. Goodrich company had sent representatives all the way from Akron, Ohio, urging the planters of Malaya to plant this new crop. This was the material of the coming age; the next generation of machines could not be made to work without this indispensable absorber of friction. The newest motor cars had dozens of rubber parts; the markets were potentially bottomless, the profits beyond imagining.

Saya John had made enquiries, asking a few knowledgeable

people about what was involved in planting rubber. The answers were always short: land and labour were what a planter needed most; seed and saplings were easily to be had. And of the two principal necessities, land was the easier to come by: of labour there was already a shortage. The British Colonial Government was looking to India to supply coolies and workers for the plantations.

Saya John had begun to toy with the idea of buying some land for Matthew, his son. He'd quickly discovered that land prices around Malacca had risen steeply; he was advised to travel north, in the direction of the Siam border. He'd set off, not quite convinced still. He was too old to start up a vast new project, this he knew; but there was Rajkumar to be counted on – he would know what to do about building a workforce – and of course there was always Matthew, who had been away in America many years. No one knew exactly what Matthew was doing there; the last he'd heard, the boy had travelled east, to New York. There had been a letter a while back; he'd said something about looking for a job – nothing at all about coming home. Perhaps this was exactly what was needed to bring the boy home: a huge new enterprise to which he could dedicate himself: something that would be his own; something that he could build up. He could see himself growing old, living with Matthew – the boy would have a family, children; they'd live together in a quiet place, surrounded by trees and greenery.

These ideas were still forming in his mind, when he glimpsed the perfect place, from the deck of a ferry boat: the south-facing slope of a mountain, an extinct volcano that reared out of the plain like the head of some fantastic beast. The place was a wilderness, a jungle; but at the same time, it was within easy distance of the island of Penang and the port of Butterworth.

'I've got land there now,' Saya John said to Rajkumar, 'and it's waiting for the day when Matthew comes back.'

Rajkumar, newly married and eager in his anticipation of the pleasures of domestic life, was not disposed to take his mentor seriously. 'But, Saya, what does Matthew know about rubber or plantations?'

'It doesn't matter. He'll find out. And of course, he'll have you to help him. We'll be partners, the three of us: you, me, Matthew.'

Rajkumar shrugged. 'Saya, I know even less about this than Matthew does. My business is timber.'

'Timber is a thing of the past, Rajkumar: you have to look to the future – and if there's any tree on which money could be said to grow then this it – rubber.'

Rajkumar felt Dolly's hand, pressing against his own, in anxious enquiry. He gave her a reassuring nudge as though to say: it's just one of the old man's fancies; there's no need to worry.

In the immediate aftermath of her widowhood, Uma returned to Lankasuka, her parents' house, in Calcutta. Hers was a small family: she had only one brother, who was much younger than herself. Their house was spacious and comfortable, although not grand: it had two storeys, with a semi-circular balcony on each. The rooms were airy and bright with high ceilings and stone floors that stayed cool even in the hottest of summers.

But Uma's homecoming was not a happy one. Her father was an archaeologist and a scholar: he was not the kind of man to insist on all the customary observances of a Hindu widowhood, but nor was he so enlightened as to be wholly impervious to the strictures of his neighbours. Within his lights he did what he could to mitigate the rigours of his daughter's situation. But as a widow living at home, Uma's life was still one of rigid constraints and deprivation: her hair was shaved off; she could eat no meat nor fish and she was allowed to wear nothing but white. She was twenty-eight and had a lifetime ahead of her. As the months dragged by it became clear that some other solution would have to be thought of.

Uma was now a woman of independent means, the beneficiary of a very substantial pension. During his lifetime the Collector had held one of the most lucrative jobs in the Empire, and on his death it was discovered that he had made many astute investments, several of them in Uma's name. With her livelihood assured, and no children to care for, there was nothing to hold her at home and every reason to leave. The matter was decided when she received a letter from Dolly, inviting her to visit Rangoon. It was evident that the best possible solution was for her to go abroad.

On the journey over, Uma kept her head covered, with a shawl to hide her shaven head. Dolly and Rajkumar met her at the Barr Street Jetty and the moment she stepped off, Dolly tore away her shawl.

'Why are you hiding your face?' she said. 'I think you look nice like that.'

Dolly and Rajkumar brought Uma directly to their new home in Kemendine: they had only recently moved in and the house was still under construction. Having been very rapidly erected, the house was a haphazard, old-fashioned structure – two floors of interconnected rooms, grouped around a square courtyard. The floors were of polished red stone and the courtyard was lined with corridor-like balconies. The balustrades were of spindly wrought-iron. Along the walls of the compound there were a number of small outhouses. These were inhabited by watchmen, gardeners and other household employees.

Rangoon was almost as much a foreign city to Dolly as it was to Uma, and the two of them began to explore it together: they climbed the steps of the Shwe Dagon pagoda; they visited Uma's uncle in kalaa-basti, the Indian quarter; they attended the pony races at the Kyaikasan racecourse; they went walking in the narrow streets of Syriam, across the river, they promenaded around the Royal Lakes and went for drives around the Cantonment. Everywhere they went, Dolly was courted, sought after, besieged by armies of acquaintances, asked endless questions about the King and Queen and their life abroad. This was a subject of universal interest in Burma, and Dolly's sharing of the Royal Family's exile made her something of a celebrity herself.

Uma's time passed very pleasantly. She was often invited out with Dolly and was never at a loss for things to do. But as the weeks passed she found herself growing ever more painfully aware of the distance between Dolly's ebullient happiness and her own circumstances. In the past, Uma had often wondered about Dolly's marriage: had she married Rajkumar in order to escape the imprisonment of Outram House? Or was it just that she had fallen in love – that and nothing else? Now, watching them together, Uma saw that these reasons were not exclusive of each other: that each of these motives had played a part in creating a wholeness, as in the fitting together of the misshapen pieces of a puzzle. She saw also that this was a completeness that she, who had always prided herself on knowing her own mind in all things, had never known and perhaps would never know, because it was not within her to yield to the moment, in Dolly's way.

Dolly and Rajkumar seemed to have little knowledge of one another's likes and dislikes, preferences and habits, yet the miracle was – and this too Uma could see clearly – that far from weakening their bond, their mutual incomprehension served rather to strengthen it. Between herself and the Collector, on the other hand, every eventuality had been governed by clearly defined rules and meanings. Whenever there was a question about what either of them might like or want, all they had to do was to refer implicitly to usage and etiquette. Now, thinking back, she saw that she herself had come to resemble the Collector more closely than she had ever thought to admit; that she too had become a creature of rules and method and dogged persistence, and was in this sense utterly unlike Dolly.

As the days passed, she became conscious of a gathering grief, an emotion more powerful than any she had ever known. In the light of hindsight, she realised that those words that people had always used of the Collector – *he's a good man* – were true; that he indeed had been a good man, an honest man – a man of great intelligence and ability who happened to have been born into a circumstance that could not offer him an appropriate avenue for the fulfilment of his talents. He had wielded immense power as a District Collector, yet paradoxically, the position had brought him nothing but unease and uncertainty; she recalled the nervous, ironic way in which he had played the part of Collector; she remembered how he'd watched over her at table, the intolerable minuteness of his supervision, the effort he had invested in moulding her into a reflection of what he himself aspired to be. There seemed never to be a moment when he was not haunted by the fear of being thought lacking by his British colleagues. And yet it seemed to be universally agreed that he was one of the most successful Indians of his generation; a model for his countrymen. Did this mean that one day all of India would become a shadow of what he had been? Millions of people trying to live their lives in conformity with incomprehensible rules? Better to be what Dolly had been: a woman who had no illusions about the nature of her condition; a prisoner who knew the exact dimensions of her cage and could look for contentment within those confines. But she was not Dolly and never would be; some part of her was irretrievably the Collector's creation, and if nothing was to be served by mourning this disfigurement, then it was her duty to turn her abilities to the task of seeking a remedy.

One day, Rajkumar said to her: 'Everything we have we owe to you. If there's anything you should ever need, we would want to be the first to be asked.'

She smiled. 'Anything?'

'Yes, of course.'

She took a deep breath. 'Well then, I am going to ask you to book me a passage, to Europe . . .'

As Uma's ship made its way westwards, a wake of letters and postcards came drifting back, to wash up at Dolly's door in Kemendine. From Colombo there was a picture of the sea at Mount Lavinia, with a note about how Uma had met a family friend on board her ship, a Mrs Kadambari Dutt – one of the famous Hatkhola Dutts of Calcutta, a cousin of Toru Dutt, the poetess and a relative of the distinguished Mr Romesh Dutt, the writer and scholar. Mrs Dutt was a good deal older than herself and had lived a while in England; she was very experienced and knowledgeable about things – the perfect person to have on board, a godsend really. They were enjoying themselves together.

From Aden there was a postcard with a picture of a narrow channel, flowing between two immense cliffs. Uma wrote that she'd been delighted to discover that this waterway – which formed the link between the Indian Ocean and the Red Sea – was known in Arabic as the *Bab al-Mandab*, 'the gateway of lamentation'. Could there possibly be a better-chosen name?

From Alexandria there was a picture of a fortress, with a few wry remarks about how much friendlier the Europeans on the ship had become once they were past the Suez Canal. She, Uma, had been taken aback, but Mrs Dutt had said that it was always like this: there was something about the air of the Mediterranean that seemed to turn even the most haughty colonialists into affable democrats.

From Marseilles, Uma sent her first long letter: she and her newfound friend, Mrs Dutt, had decided to spend a few days in that city. Mrs Dutt had changed into a European skirt before going ashore; she'd offered to lend Uma one, but Uma had felt awkward and had refused; she'd stepped off the ship in a sari. They hadn't gone far before Uma was mistaken – of all things! – for a Cambodian; dozens of people had gathered around her, asking if she was a dancer. It turned out that King Sisowath of Cambodia had recently visited the city, with a troupe of dancers from his palace. The dancers had enjoyed a great success; the whole city was mad for them; the great sculptor, Mr Rodin, had come down from Paris, just to draw their likenesses. Uma had almost wished that she did not have to disappoint everyone by explaining that she was an Indian, not Cambodian.

They'd had a wonderful time, the two of them, she and Mrs Dutt; they'd walked around town and gone sightseeing and even ventured into the countryside. It had been strange, heady, exhilarating – two women travelling alone, unmolested, drawing nothing more than the occasional curious stare. She'd asked herself why it was not possible to do the same at home – why women could not think of travelling like this in India, revelling in this sense of being at liberty. Yet it was troubling to think that this privilege – of being able to enjoy this sense of freedom, however momentary – had become possible only because of the circumstances of her marriage and because she now had the money to travel. She had talked of this at length with Kadambari – Mrs Dutt: Why should it not be possible for these freedoms to be universally available, for women everywhere? And Mrs Dutt had said that of course, this was one of the great benefits of British rule in India; that it had given women rights and protections that they'd never had before. At this, Uma had felt herself, for the first time, falling utterly out of sympathy with her new friend. She had known instinctively that this was a false argument, unfounded and illogical. How was it possible to imagine that one could grant freedom by imposing subjugation? that one could open a cage by pushing it inside a bigger cage? How could any section of a people hope to achieve freedom where the entirety of a populace was held in subjection? She'd had a long argument with Mrs Dutt and in the end she had succeeded in persuading her friend that hers was the correct view. She'd felt this to be a great triumph – for of course Mrs Dutt was much older (and a good deal better educated) and until then it was always she who was telling her, Uma, how she ought to think of things.

Dolly was in bed when she read this letter. She was drinking a pungent concoction prescribed by a midwife and trying to rest. Some weeks earlier she had begun to suspect that she was pregnant and this intuition had been recently confirmed. As a result she'd been put on a regimen that required many different medicinal infusions and much rest. But rest was not always easy to come by in a household as busy and chaotic as her own. Even as she sat reading Uma's letter, there were frequent interruptions – with the cook and U Ba Kyaw and the master-bricklayers bursting in to ask for instructions. In between trying to guess what was to be prepared for dinner and how much money U Ba Kyaw would have to be advanced for his next visit home, she tried to think of Uma, revelling in the freedom of being able to walk out alone, in Europe. She understood intuitively why Uma took such pleasure in this, even though she herself would not have cared for it at all. Her mind seemed to have no room for anything but the crowded eventlessness of her everyday life. It struck her that she rarely gave any thought to such questions as freedom or liberty or any other such matters.

When she picked up a pen to write back to Uma, she could think of nothing to say; there was something incommunicable about the quotidian contentments of her life. She could try, for instance, to write about how her friend Daw Thi had stopped by last Wednesday and how they'd gone to look at the new furniture at Rowe and Co.; or else she could describe her last visit to the Kyaikasan racecourse and how Rajkumar had won almost one thousand rupees and had joked about buying a pony. But none of this seemed worth putting down on paper – certainly not in response to such concerns as Uma had expressed. Or else she could write about her pregnancy, about Rajkumar's happiness, about how he'd immediately started to think of names (the child was to be a boy of course). But she was superstitious about these things: neither she nor Rajkumar was telling people yet and wouldn't do so until it was unavoidable. Nor did she want to write to Uma about this subject: it would be as though she were flaunting her domesticity in her friend's face; underscoring her childlessness.

Two months passed without any further communication from Uma. As the days went by Dolly found herself less and less able to sleep. Shooting abdominal pains made her double over in bed at night. She moved into a room of her own, so as not to disturb Rajkumar. The midwife told her that everything was proceeding normally, but Dolly was not persuaded: she was increasingly sure that something had gone wrong. Then, late one night, the now-familiar pains changed suddenly into convulsions that shook the whole of her lower body. She realised that she was miscarrying and shouted for Rajkumar. He roused the household and sent people off in every direction – to fetch doctors, nurses, midwives. But it was too late and Rajkumar was alone with Dolly when the stillborn foetus was ejected from her body.

Dolly was still convalescing when Uma's next letter arrived. The letter bore a London address and opened with profuse apologies and an implied reproach. Uma wrote that she was saddened to think that they had allowed so many months to pass without an exchange of letters. She herself had been very busy in London, she said. Mrs Dutt had helped her find accommodation – as the paying guest of an elderly missionary lady who'd spent much of her life in India. The arrangement had worked out well and Uma had not lacked for company. Shortly after her arrival, people had begun to seek her out: mainly former friends and colleagues of the Collector's, most of them English. Some of them had known her late husband at Cambridge, others had worked with him in India. They had all been very kind, showing her around the city, taking her to events of the sort the Collector had liked to attend – concerts, plays, lectures at the Royal Academy. After a while, Uma had begun to feel as though the Collector were with her again; she would hear his voice describing Drury Lane or Covent Garden, pointing to the notable features; telling her what was in good taste and what was not.

Fortunately, she'd also kept up her connection with her shipboard friend, Mrs Dutt. It turned out that Mrs Dutt knew every Indian living in London, or almost. Through her she'd met many interesting people, most notably a lady by the name of Madame Cama. A Parsee from Bombay, Madame Cama seemed, at first glance, more European than Indian – in clothes, manner and appearance. Yet she, Uma, had never known anyone who spoke more truthfully or forthrightly on matters concerning India. She'd been kind enough to introduce Uma into her circle. Uma had never met such people – so interesting and idealistic, men and women whose views and sentiments were so akin to her own. Through these people Uma had begun to understand that a woman like herself could contribute a great deal to India's struggle from overseas.

Lately Madame Cama had been urging her, Uma, to visit the United States. She had friends among the Irish in New York, many of whom, she said, were sympathetic to India's cause. She thought it important for Uma to meet these people and felt that she might like living in that city. Uma was thinking the matter over quite seriously. Of this she was certain at any rate: that she would not long remain in England. In London she was haunted by the notion that the whole city was conspiring to remind her of her late husband.

Exhausted by the effort of reading this letter, Dolly dropped it on her bedside table. Later that day, when Rajkumar came home, he saw it lying there and picked it up.

'From Uma?'

'Yes.'

'What does she say?'

'Read it.'

Rajkumar smoothed down the page and read the letter through, slowly, following Uma's cramped handwriting with his forefinger, asking for Dolly's help with such words as he could not follow. At the end, he folded the pages and put them back on Dolly's bedside table.

'She's talking of going to New York.'

'Yes.'

'That's where Matthew is.'

'Yes. I'd forgotten.'

'You should send her his address. If she goes there, Matthew could help her settle in.'

'That's true.'

'And if you write to her you could also say that Saya John is worried about Matthew. He's been writing to Matthew to come home – but Matthew hasn't answered. Sayagyi can't understand why he won't come back. Perhaps Uma will be able to solve the puzzle.'

Dolly nodded. 'All right,' she said. 'It'll give me something to write about.' She spent a week composing a letter, writing out the paragraphs one at a time. She made no mention of her condition. Having said nothing about her pregnancy, it seemed out of place to refer to a miscarriage. She wrote mostly about Saya John and Rajkumar and posted the letter to Uma's London address.

By the time Dolly heard back, Uma had already crossed the Atlantic; she was in New York, and had been there several weeks already. Again, she was full of apologies for not having written earlier – there was so much to write about that she did not know where to start. New York had proved to be all that she had hoped – a kind of haven for someone like herself, except that the shelter it afforded consisted not of peace and quiet but the opposite. It was the kind of place where one could lose oneself in the press of people. She had decided to remain here for the time being: even on the way over, she had known that this was a place that would be to her taste because so many of the other passengers were people who were tired of the ruthless hypocrisies of Europe, just as she was.

But she also had something important to report, on the very subject that Dolly had written to her about. She had met Matthew

Martins soon after her arrival in America; he had come to see her, at the Ramakrishna Mission in Manhattan, where she was staying temporarily. He was not at all the person she had expected; his resemblance to his father was very slight. He was athletic in build and very good-looking, extremely urbane in manner. She had quickly discovered that he had a great passion for motor cars; it had been instructive to walk down the streets with him, for he would point here and there and announce, like a magician: 'there goes a brand-new new 1908 Hutton'; or 'there's a Beeston Humber' or 'that's a Gaggenau . . .'

As for the 'mystery' of his reluctance to leave New York, that had been very quickly solved. It turned out that he had an American fiancée, a woman by the name of Elsa Hoffman. He'd introduced her to Elsa and Uma had thought her to be a very pleasant woman: her demeanour was briskly good-natured, in the American way, and she was fine-looking too, with a gentle, heart-shaped face and long black hair. They'd quickly become friends, she and Elsa, and one day Elsa had confided that she was secretly engaged to Matthew. She hadn't told her family because she knew they'd disapprove and was afraid that they might try to send her away. And Matthew too was uncertain of how his father would respond – what with Elsa being a foreigner and a Protestant as well. Uma's feeling was that this was all that prevented Matthew from returning. If only Saya John were to drop Matthew a hint, that he had nothing to fear on this score, then it was quite likely that he would change his mind about staying in America . . .

By the time this letter was delivered to her, Dolly was perfectly recovered. She was so excited by Uma's report that she decided to go immediately to Rajkumar's timberyard, to give him the news. A hired gaari took her rattling down the dusty, village-like roads of Kemendine, to the black macadam of the Strand, where cargo ships stood moored along the wharves, past the Botataung Pagoda, with its goldfish-filled pools, across the railway crossing, and through the narrow lanes of Pazundaung to the walled compound that marked the premises of Rajkumar's yard. Inside, a team of elephants was hard at work, stacking logs. Dolly spotted Rajkumar standing in the shade of the raised wooden cabin that served as his office. He was dressed in a longyi and vest, smoking a cheroot, his face and head powdered with sawdust.

'Dolly!' He was startled to see her at the yard.

'I have news.' She waved the letter at him.

They climbed the ladder that led up to Rajkumar's office. She stood over him while he read Uma's letter and when he reached the end, she said: 'What do you think, Rajkumar? Do you think Sayagyi would disapprove – about Matthew's fiancée not being Catholic, and all that?'

Rajkumar laughed out loud. 'Sayagyi's no missionary,' he said. 'He keeps his religion to himself. In all the years I worked for him he never once asked me to go to church.'

'But still,' said Dolly, 'you have to be careful when you tell him . . .'

'I will be. I'll go and see him today. I think he'll be relieved to know that this is all it is.'

Soon after this, Dolly learnt that she was pregnant again. She forgot about Matthew and Elsa and even Uma: all her energies went into making sure that nothing went wrong again. Seven months went quickly by and then, on the doctors' advice, she was moved to a mission hospital on Dufferin Road, not far from Kemendine.

One day, Saya John came to see her. He seated himself beside her bed and took her hand, pressing it between his. 'I've come to thank you,' he said.

'For what, Sayagyi?'

'For giving me back my son.'

'What do you mean, Sayagyi?'

'I had a letter from Matthew. He's coming home. He's already making the arrangements. I know it's you who's to be thanked. I haven't even told Rajkumar yet. I wanted you to be the first to know.'

'No, Sayagyi – it's Uma who's to be thanked. It's all because of her.'

'Because of the both of you.'

'And Matthew? Is he coming alone?'

Saya John smiled, his eyes shining. 'No. He's bringing home a bride. They're going to be married by special licence, just before they leave, so that they can travel together.'

'So what will this mean, Sayagyi?'

'It means that it's time for me to move too. I'm going to sell my properties here. Then I'm going to go to Malaya, to get things ready for them. But there's plenty of time yet. I'll be here for the birth of your child.'

Six weeks later Dolly was delivered of a healthy, eight-pound boy. To celebrate, Rajkumar shut down his yards and announced a bonus of a week's wages for his employees. An astrologer was called in to advise them on the child's names: he was to have two, as was the custom among Indians in Burma. After deliberations that lasted for several weeks, it was decided that the boy's Burmese name would be Sein Win; his Indian name was to be Neeladhri – Neel for short. The names were decided on just in time for Saya John to hear of them before leaving for Malaya.

Four years later, Dolly had a second child, another boy. Like Neel he was given two names, one Burmese and one Indian: they were, respectively, Tun Pe and Dinanath. The latter was quickly shortened to Dinu, and it was by this name that he was known at home.

Soon after Dolly's delivery Rajkumar had a letter from Saya John: by coincidence Elsa too had just had a baby, her first. The child was a girl and had been named Alison. What was more, Matthew and Elsa had decided to build a house for themselves, on the plantation: the land had already been cleared and a date fixed for the ground-breaking ceremony. Saya John was very keen that Rajkumar and Dolly attend the ceremony, along with their children.

In the years since Saya John's departure from Rangoon, Rajkumar had spent a great deal of his time travelling between Burma, Malaya and India. As a partner in the plantation he had been responsible for ensuring a steady supply of workers, most of them from the Madras Presidency, in southern India. Rajkumar had kept Dolly abreast of the plantation's progress, but despite his pleas, she had not accompanied him on any of his trips to Malaya. She was not a good traveller, she had said. It had been hard enough to leave Ratnagiri to come to Burma; she was not in a hurry to go anywhere else. As a result, Dolly had never met Matthew and Elsa.

Rajkumar showed Dolly Saya John's letter, with the comment: 'If you're ever going to go there then this is the time.'

After she'd read the letter Dolly agreed: 'All right; let us go.'

From Rangoon, it was a three day voyage to the island of Penang in northern Malaya. On their last day at sea, Rajkumar showed Dolly a distant blue blur on the horizon. This grew quickly into a craggy peak that rose like a pyramid out of the sea. It stood alone, with no other landfall in sight.

'That's Gunung Jerai,' Rajkumar said. 'That's where the plantation is.' In years past, he said, when the forest was being cleared, the mountain had seemed to come alive. Travelling to Penang, Rajkumar would see great black plumes of smoke rising skywards from the mountain. 'But that was a long time ago: the place is quite changed now.'

The steamer docked at Georgetown, the principal port on the island of Penang. From there it was a journey of several hours to the plantation: first they took a ferry to the road- and rail-head of Butterworth, across a narrow channel from Penang. Then they boarded a train that took them northwards through a landscape of lush green paddies and dense coconut groves. Looming ahead, always visible through the windows of the carriage, was the soaring mass of Gunung Jerai, its peak obscured by a cloudy haze. It rose steeply out of the plain, its western slopes descending directly into the sparkling blue waters of the Andaman Sea. Dolly, now habituated to the riverine landscapes of southern Burma, was struck by the lush beauty of the coastal plain. She was reminded of Ratnagiri, and for the first time in many years, she missed her sketchbook.

This leg of their journey ended at Sungei Pattani, a district town on the leeward side of the mountain. The rail-track was newly laid and the station consisted of not much more than a length of beaten earth and a tiled shed. Dolly spotted Saya John as their train was pulling in; he looked older and a little shrunken; he was peering shortsightedly at a newspaper as the train chugged into the station. Standing beside him were a tall, khaki-clothed man and a woman in an ankle-length black skirt. Even before Rajkumar pointed them out, Dolly knew that they were Matthew and Elsa.

Elsa came up to Dolly's window when the train stopped. The first thing she said was: 'I'd have known you anywhere; Uma described you perfectly.'

Dolly laughed. 'And you too – both of you.'

Outside the rudimentary little station, there was a large compound. In its centre stood a thin sapling, not much taller than Dolly herself.

'Why,' Dolly said, startled, 'that's a padauk tree, isn't it?'

'They call them angsana trees here,' Elsa said. 'Matthew planted it, soon after Alison was born. He says that in a few years it's going to grow into a huge umbrella, casting its shade over the whole station.'

Now Dolly's eyes were drawn to a startling new sight: a motorcar – a gleaming, flat-topped vehicle with a rounded bonnet and glittering, twelve-spoked wheels. It was the only car in the compound and a small crowd had gathered around to marvel at its brass lamps and shining black paint.

The car was Matthew's. 'It's an Oldsmobile Defender,' he announced. 'Quite a modest car really, but mint-new, this year's model, a genuine 1914. It rolled out of the factory in January and was delivered to me six months later.' He spoke like an American, Dolly noticed, and his voice bore no resemblance to his father's.

Theirs was a sizeable party: there was an ayah for Dinu and Neel as well as a man to help with the luggage. The car was not large enough for all of them. After Dolly, Elsa and the children had been seated there was room only for the ayah and Matthew, who was driving. The others were left behind to follow in a buggy.

They drove through Sungei Pattani, along wide streets that were lined with tiled 'shophouses' – storefronts whose facades were joined together to form long, graceful arcades. Then the town fell away and the car began to climb.

'When was the last time you heard from Uma?' Dolly said to Elsa.

'I saw her last year,' said Elsa. 'I went to the States for a holiday and we met in New York.' Uma had moved into an apartment of her own, Elsa said. She'd taken a job, as a publisher's proof-reader.

But she was doing other things too; she seemed to keep herself very busy.

'What else is she doing exactly?'

'Political things mainly, I think,' Elsa said. 'She talked about meetings and speeches and some magazine that she's writing for.'

'Oh?' Dolly was still thinking about this when Elsa pointed ahead. 'Look – the estate. That's where it starts.'

They were climbing steeply, driving along a dirt road that was flanked on both sides by dense forest. Looking ahead, Dolly saw a wide gateway, with a sign that arched across the road. There were three words inscribed on the sign, in enormous gold lettering; Dolly read them out aloud, rolling them over her tongue: 'Morningside Rubber Estate.'

'Elsa named it,' Matthew said.

'When I was a child,' Elsa explained, 'I used to live near a park called Morningside. I always liked the name.'

At the gate, there was a sudden rent in the tangled curtain of greenery that covered the mountainside: ahead, stretching away as far as the eye could see, there were orderly rows of saplings, all of them exactly alike, all of them spaced with precise, geometrical regularity. The car went over a low rise and a valley appeared ahead, a shallow basin, cupped in the palm of a curved ridge. The basin had been cleared of trees and there was an open space in the middle. Grouped around this space were two ramshackle tin-roofed buildings, little more than huts.

'These were meant to be the estate's offices,' Elsa said apologetically. 'But we're living in them for the time being. It's very basic I'm afraid – which is why we need to build ourselves a habitable place.'

They settled in and later in the day, Elsa took Dolly for a walk through the rubber trees. Each tree had a diagonal slash across its trunk, with a halved coconut shell cupped underneath. Elsa swirled her forefinger through one of these cups, and dug out a hardened crescent of latex. 'They call these cup-lumps,' Elsa said, handing the latex to Dolly. Dolly raised the spongy grey lump to her nose: the smell was sour and faintly rancid. She dropped it back into the coconut-shell cup.

'Tappers will come by to collect the lumps in the morning,' Elsa said. 'Not a drop of this stuff can be wasted.'

They headed through the rubber trees, walking uphill, facing the cloud-capped peak of Gunung Jerai. The ground underfoot had a soft, cushioned feel, because of the carpet of dead leaves shed by the trees. The slope ahead was scored with the shadows of thousands of trunks, all exactly parallel, like scratches scored by a machine. It was like being in a wilderness, but yet not. Dolly had visited Huay Zedi several times and had come to love the electric stillness of the jungle. But this was like neither city nor farm nor forest: there was something eerie about its uniformity; about the fact that such sameness could be imposed upon a landscape of such natural exuberance. She remembered how startled she'd been when the car crossed from the heady profusion of the jungle into the ordered geometry of the plantation. 'It's like stepping into a labyrinth,' she said to Elsa.

'Yes,' said Elsa. 'And you'd be amazed how easy it is to lose your way.'

They entered a large clearing and Elsa came to a stop. 'This,' she said, 'is where Morningside House is going to be.'

Turning around, Dolly saw that the spot offered spectacular views on every side. To the west the mountain sloped gently into the reddening sunset sea; to the north rose the forested peak of Gunung Jerai, looking directly down on them.

'It's a wonderful spot,' Dolly said. But even as she was saying the words it struck her that she would not have wanted to live there, under the scowling gaze of the mountain, in a house that was marooned in a tree-filled maze.

'It's beautiful, isn't it?' Elsa said. 'But you should have seen what it looked like before it was cleared.'

She'd been horrified, she said, when she first came out to Gunung Jerai. The place was beautiful beyond imagining, but it was jungle – dense, towering, tangled, impassable jungle. Matthew had led her a little way in, on foot, and it was like walking up a carpeted nave, with the tops of the trees meeting far above, forming an endless, fan-vaulted ceiling. It was hard, almost impossible, to imagine that these slopes could be laid bare, made habitable.

Once the clearing of the forest started, Matthew had moved out to the land and built himself a small cabin, where the estate office now stood. She had lived away from him in a rented house, in

Penang. She would have preferred to be with Matthew, but he wouldn't let her stay. It was too dangerous, he said, like a battle-field, with the jungle fighting back every inch of the way. For a while Saya John had stayed with Matthew too, but then he'd fallen ill, and had had to move to Penang. Even though the plantation was his own idea, he'd had no conception of what would be involved in laying it out.

Several months went by before Elsa had been allowed to visit the location again and she understood then why Matthew had tried to keep her away. The hillside looked as though it had been racked by a series of disasters: huge stretches of land were covered with ashes and blackened stumps. Matthew was thin and coughed incessantly. She caught a glimpse of the workers' shacks – tiny hovels, with roofs made of branches and leaves. They were all Indians, from the south: Matthew had learnt to speak their language – Tamil – but she couldn't understand a word they said. She'd looked into the mud-walled hut where they went to be treated when they fell ill: the squalor was unimaginable, the floors covered with filth. She'd wanted to stay and work as a nurse, but Matthew had refused to let her remain. She'd had to go back to Penang.

But when she next returned, the transformation was again so great as to appear miraculous. The last time around she had felt as though she were entering a plague site; now the sensation was of walking into a freshly-laid garden. The ashes had been washed away by the rain, the blackened tree-stumps had been removed and the first saplings of rubber had begun to grow.

For the first time, Matthew had allowed her to stay over, in his cabin. At daybreak she'd looked out of the window and seen the morning pouring down the side of the mountain, lying on their land like a sheet of gold.

'That was when I told Matthew,' Elsa said, 'that there could only ever be one name for this place: Morningside.'

Later, back where they were staying, Elsa showed Dolly her sketches for Morningside House. She wanted it to look like the grand Long Island houses of her memory; it was to have a turret-like tower, steep gables and a veranda that went all the way around, to take advantage of the spectacular views. The one Eastern touch was to be the roof, which would be red, with carved, upcurling eaves.

While the women were poring over the sketches, Saya John was going through the newspaper that he had bought at the railway station: it was the previous day's edition of the *Straits Times*, published from Singapore. Suddenly he glanced up and beckoned to Matthew and Rajkumar, from across the room.

'Look at this,' he said.

Folding the paper in half, he showed them a report about the assassination of the Grand Duke Ferdinand in Sarajevo. Rajkumar and Matthew read through the first couple of paragraphs and then looked at each other and shrugged.

'"Sarajevo"?' said Rajkumar. 'Where's that?'

'A long way away.' Matthew laughed.

No more than anyone else in the world, did either of them have any inkling that the killing in Sarajevo would spark a world war. Nor did they know that rubber would be a vital strategic material in this conflict: that in Germany the discarding of articles made of rubber would become an offence punishable by law; that submarines would be sent overseas to smuggle rubber; that the commodity would come to be valued more than ever before, increasing their wealth beyond their most extravagant dreams.

Sixteen

Even when Neel and Dinu were very young, it was evident that they each took after a single parent. Neel looked very much like Rajkumar: he was big and robust, more Indian than Burmese in build and colouring. Dinu, on the other hand, had his mother's delicate features as well as her ivory complexion and fine-boned slimness of build.

Every year, around December, Dolly and Rajkumar took the boys to Huay Zedi. Doh Say and Naw Da had returned to their old village some years before. The expansion of their business had made Doh Say a wealthy man, and he owned several houses in and around the village: one of these was earmarked for Dolly and Rajkumar's annual visits. It seemed to Dolly that the boys enjoyed these trips, especially Neel, who had been befriended by one of Doh Say's sons, a sturdy thoughtful boy by the name of Raymond. Dolly, too, looked forward to these annual visits: since her trip to Morningside she had begun sketching again, and would spend hours by Huay Zedi's stream, with her sketchbook open on her lap and Dinu playing nearby.

One year, while they were at Huay Zedi, Dinu fell suddenly ill. Dolly and Rajkumar were not particularly alarmed. Dinu was prone to bouts of sickness and it was a rare week when he was entirely free of colds, coughs and fevers. But Dinu was also gifted with an innate resilience that made him actively combat his ill health, and his fevers rarely lasted for more than a day or two at a time. Knowing how well he fought off his fevers, Dolly and Rajkumar were certain that he would recover quickly. They decided to remain at Huay Zedi.

The house they were staying in was very much like a teak camp's tai, standing some six feet off the ground on massive timber posts. It was set at a slight remove from the rest of the village, a little distance up the thickly forested slope that served as a backdrop for the village. The jungle rose like a cliff behind the tai, skirting it on three sides. Just visible from the balcony was Huay Zedi's pebbled stream and the soaring bamboo steeple of its church.

As in all tais, the rooms were arranged in a row, one leading into another. Because of Dinu's illness, Dolly decided to change their usual sleeping arrangements. She took the child into her bed for the night, and dispatched Rajkumar to one of the inner rooms. With Dinu sleeping beside her, Dolly drifted into a dream. She saw herself lifting up her mosquito net, climbing out of bed and going to sit in a chair on the balcony. The tai was in darkness but the night was alive with cicadas and fireflies. Two doors away she could hear Rajkumar breathing heavily in his sleep. She saw herself sitting awhile in the chair and then, after some time had passed, someone spoke, in a voice that was well known to her: it was Thebaw. He was saying something to her with great urgency. As so often in dreams, she could not tell the words apart, but she understood exactly what he was trying to communicate.

She screamed.

Rajkumar stumbled out with a candle and found her sitting in a chair, on the veranda, rocking back and forth, hugging herself with shaking arms.

'What's happened?'

'We have to leave,' she said. 'We have to get Dinu to a hospital in Rangoon.'

'Why?'

'Don't ask me now. I'll tell you later.'

They left Huay Zedi while it was still dark. Doh Say provided them with two ox-carts and escorted them personally to Pyinmana. They arrived in Rangoon late the next night. Dinu was taken immediately to hospital.

After a long examination, the doctors took Dolly and Rajkumar aside. The boy had polio, they said; but for Dolly's promptness in bringing him to hospital, they might well have lost the child.

'I knew I had to bring him,' said Dolly.

'How did you know?'

'I was told.'

'By whom?'

'It doesn't matter. What matters is that we came.'

Dolly stayed the night in hospital and next morning, a nurse brought her breakfast on a tray. 'Did you hear, ma'am?' the nurse said. 'The old King is dead. He died in India.'

The breakfast tray slipped from Dolly's lap. 'When did it happen?' she asked the nurse.

'Let's see . . .' The nurse counted off the dates on her fingers. 'I think it must have happened the night before you came.'

It was Dolly's old charge, the Second Princess, who took the blame for the King's death. One bright December day in 1916, she eloped with a Burmese commoner and hid herself in the Residency. This was the beginning of the end.

By this time much had changed in Ratnagiri. The First Princess had had her baby, a girl (this was an event that Dolly had missed by only a few weeks). The child was nicknamed Baisu, Fatty, and to everyone's surprise, she had quickly become a favourite of the Queen's.

Soon after the birth of the child, the District Administration had discovered itself to be in possession of monies sufficient to build the King his long promised palace. A mansion had appeared on the hillside that faced the Residency. It came complete with a durbar hall, a gallery, outhouses, running water and a garage to accommodate the two cars that had recently been provided for the King and Queen (one a Ford, the other a De Dion). All of Ratnagiri turned out to celebrate the move. Cheering crowds lined the roads as the Royal Family drove out of Outram House for the last time. But as with all moves, the new place was quickly discovered to possess certain drawbacks. Its upkeep was found to require a small army: twenty-seven gatekeepers, ten peons, six *hazurdaars* and innumerable other attendants, cleaners, sweepers and ayahs – a total of one hundred and sixty-one in all. In addition, there were now more visitors from Burma and many more hangers-on. How to feed them? How to provide for them? Without Dolly no one knew how to manage.

And then, one morning the Second Princess disappeared. Enquiries revealed she had run away with a young man and taken refuge in the Residency. The King gave Sawant a note to take to his daughter, asking her to return to the palace. Standing at a window, he trained his binoculars on the De Dion as it made its journey across the hill. When the car turned around to come back he saw that his daughter was not in it. The binoculars dropped from his hands. He fell to the floor, clutching his left arm. The doctor arrived within the hour and pronounced him to have suffered a heart attack. Ten days later the King died.

The Queen let it be known that the Second Princess would never again be permitted to enter her presence.

> And the funeral, Dolly, *the First Princess wrote in the first of several clandestine letters.* It was such a sad and miserable affair that Her Majesty flatly refused to attend. The Government was represented by a mere Deputy Collector! You would have wept to see it. No one could believe that this was the funeral of Burma's last King! We wanted the coffin stored in such a way that we could transport the remains to Burma some day. But when the authorities learnt of this they had the coffin forcibly removed from us. They are afraid that the King's body might become a rallying point in Burma! They built a monument on his grave, almost overnight, to make it impossible for us ever to take him back! You should have been here with us, Dolly. We all missed you, even Her Majesty, though of course she could not say so, since it was she who forbade us ever to utter your name.

Through the duration of Dinu's convalescence, Dolly never once left the premises of the hospital. She and Dinu had a room to themselves – large and sunny and filled with flowers. From the window they could see the majestic, shining hti of the Shwe Dagon. Rajkumar did everything in his power to ensure their comfort. U Ba Kyaw drove over at mealtimes, bringing fresh-cooked food in an enormous brass tiffin-carrier. The hospital was prevailed upon to relax its rules. Friends dropped by at all times of day and Rajkumar and Neel stayed late into the evenings, leaving only when it was time for Dinu to go to bed.

Dinu endured his month-long stay in hospital with exemplary stoicism, earning accolades from the staff. Although he had partially lost the use of his right leg, the doctors promised that he would recover to the point where a slight limp would be the only lasting trace of his illness.

On their return home, after Dinu's discharge, Dolly tried hard to revert to her normal domestic routines. She put Dinu into a room of his own, under the care of an ayah. For the first few days, he made no complaint. Then, late one night, Dolly woke suddenly, at the touch of his breath on her face. Her son was standing beside her, propped up on the edge of the bed. He had left his ayah snoring in his room, and crawled down the corridor, dragging his right leg behind him. Dolly took him into her bed, hugging his bony body to her chest, breathing in the soft, rain-washed smell of his hair. She slept better that night than she had at any time in the last several weeks.

During the day, as Dinu began trying to walk again, Dolly hovered over him, darting to move stools and tables out of his way. Watching him as he struggled to regain his mobility, Dolly began to marvel at her son's tenacity and resilience – at the strength of will that made him pick himself up, time and time again, until he was able to hobble just a step or two farther than before. But she could see also that this daily struggle was changing him. He was more withdrawn than she remembered, and seemed years older in maturity and self-possession. With his father and brother he was unresponsive and cold, as though he were self-consciously discouraging their attempts to include him in their exuberant games.

Dolly's absorption in Dinu's convalescence became so complete as to claim the entirety of her mind. She thought less and less about her circle of friends and the round of activities that had occupied her before – the gatherings, the tea-parties, the picnics. When occasionally a friend or an acquaintance dropped by, there were awkward silences: she would feign interest in their stories, without contributing a word of her own. When they asked what she did with her time, she found it hard to explain. So small was the span by which Dinu's successes were measured – an extra step or two at a time, a couple more inches – that it was impossible to communicate either the joy or the crestfallen emptiness that attended upon the passing of each day. Her friends would nod politely as they listened to her explanations and when they left she knew that it would be a long time before she saw them again. The odd thing was that far from feeling any regret, she was glad.

One weekend, Rajkumar said: 'You haven't been out in months.' He had a horse running for the Governor's Cup, at the Rangoon Turf Club: he insisted that she go with him to the races.

She went through the motions of dressing for the races as though she were performing a half-forgotten ritual. When she went down to the driveway, U Ba Kyaw bowed her into their car as though he were welcoming her home after a long absence. The car was a Pic-Pic – a Swiss-manufactured Piccard-Pictet – a commodious, durable machine with a glass pane separating the driver's seat from the interior cabin.

The Pic-Pic circled around the Royal Lake, driving past the Chinese burial grounds and passing within sight of the Rangoon Club. Now Dolly too began to feel that she'd been away a long time. All the familiar sights seemed new and startling – the reflection of the Shwe Dagon, shimmering on the lake; the long, low-slung building of the Boat Club, perched on the shore. She found herself leaning forward in her seat, with her face half out of the window, as though she were looking at the city for the first time. The roads around the racecourse had been sealed off by the police, but the Pic-Pic was recognised and they were waved through. The stands looked festive with pennants and flags fluttering above the terraces. On the way to Rajkumar's box, Dolly found herself waving to a great number of people whose names she had forgotten. Once they were seated, dozens of friends and acquaintances stopped by to welcome her back. She noticed, after a while, that

Rajkumar was whispering their names to her, under cover of his programme, to remind her who they were – 'U Tha Din Gyi, he's a Turf Club steward; U Ohn, the handicapper, Mr MacDonald, the totalizator . . .'

Everyone was kind. Old Mr Piperno, the bookmaker, sent one of his sons to ask if she wanted to place any bets. She was touched and chose a couple of horses at random, from her programme. The band of the Gloucestershire Regiment came marching out and played a serenade from Friedemann's *Lola*. Then they started on another piece, with a great flourish, and Rajkumar gave her arm a sudden tug.

'It's "God Save the King",' he hissed.

'I'm sorry,' she said, rising quickly to her feet. 'I wasn't paying attention.'

At last, to her relief, the races started. There was a long wait before the next race and another after it was over. Just as everyone around her was becoming more and more excited, Dolly's mind began to wander. It was weeks since she'd been away from Dinu for this long – but of course he probably hadn't even noticed that she was gone.

A sudden outburst of applause jolted her back to her surroundings. Sitting next to her was Daw Thi, the wife of Sir Lionel Ba Than, who was one of the stewards of the Turf Club. Daw Thi was wearing her famous ruby necklace, idly fingering the thumbnail-sized stones. Dolly saw that she was looking at her expectantly.

'What's happened?' said Dolly.

'Lochinvar has won.'

'Oh?' said Dolly.

Daw Thi gave her a long look, and burst into laughter. 'Dolly, you silly thing,' she said, 'have you forgotten? Lochinvar is your husband's horse!'

In the car, on the way back, Rajkumar was unusually quiet. When they were almost home, he leant over to slam shut the window that separated the driver's seat from the rear. Then he turned to look at her a little unsteadily. He'd been plied with champagne after his visit to the winner's paddock, and was slightly drunk.

'Dolly?' he said.

'Yes?'

'Something's happened to you.'

'No.' She shook her head. 'No. Nothing's happened.'

'You're changing . . . You're leaving us behind.'

'Who?'

'Me . . . Neel . . .'

She flinched. She knew it was true that she'd neglected her elder son lately. But Neel was filled with energy, boisterousness and loud-voiced goodwill and Rajkumar doted on him. With Dinu on the other hand, he was nervous and tentative; frailty and weakness worried him, puzzled him: he had never expected to encounter these in his own progeny.

'Neel doesn't need me,' Dolly said, 'in the way that Dinu does.'

He reached for her hand. 'Dolly, we all need you. You can't disappear into yourself. You can't leave us behind.'

'Of course not.' She laughed uneasily. 'Where would I go if I left you behind?'

He dropped her hand and turned away. 'Sometimes I can't help feeling that you've already gone away – shut yourself behind a glass wall.'

'What wall?' she cried. 'What are you talking about?' She looked up to see U Ba Kyaw watching her, in the Pic-Pic's rear-view mirror. She bit her lip and said nothing more.

This exchange came as a shock. She couldn't make sense of it at first. After a day or two she decided that Rajkumar was right, she ought to go out more, even if it was just to the Scott Market, to look round the shops. Dinu was already more self-sufficient; soon it would be time for him to start school. She would have to get used to being without him, and besides, it wasn't healthy to be always shut away behind the walls of the house.

She began to schedule little expeditions for herself. One morning she found herself stuck in one of the most crowded parts of the city, near Rangoon's Town Hall. Just ahead, at the intersection of Dalhousie Street and Sule Pagoda Street there lay a busy roundabout. An ox-cart had collided with a rickshaw; someone was hurt. A crowd had gathered and the air was full of noise and dust.

The Sule Pagoda was at the centre of this roundabout. It had been freshly whitewashed, and it rose above the busy streets like a rock rearing out of the sea. Dolly had driven past the pagoda countless times but had never been inside. She told U Ba Kyaw to wait nearby and stepped out of the car.

She made her way carefully across the crowded roundabout and climbed a flight of stairs. Removing her shoes, she found herself standing on a cool, marble-paved floor. The noise of the street had fallen away and the air seemed clean, free of dust. She spotted a group of saffron-robed monks, chanting in one of the small shrines that ringed the pagoda's circular nave. She stepped in and knelt behind them, on a mat. In a raised niche, directly ahead, there was a small gilded image of the Buddha, seated in the *bhumisparshamudra*, with the middle finger of his right hand touching the earth. Flowers lay heaped below – roses, jasmine, pink lotuses – and the air was heady with their scent.

Dolly closed her eyes, trying to listen to the monks, but instead it was Rajkumar's voice that echoed in her ears: 'You're changing. . . leaving us behind.' In the tranquillity of that place, those words had a different ring: she recognised that he was right, that the events of the recent past had changed her no less than they had Dinu.

In hospital, at night, lying in bed with Dinu, she'd found herself listening to voices that were inaudible during the day: the murmurs of anxious relatives; distant screams of pain; women keening in bereavement. It was as though the walls turned porous in the stillness of the night, flooding her room with an unseen tide of defeat and suffering. The more she listened to those voices, the more directly they spoke to her, sometimes in tones that seemed to recall the past, sometimes in notes of warning.

Late one night she'd heard an old woman crying for water. The voice had been feeble – a hoarse, rasping whisper – but it had filled the room. Although Dinu had been fast asleep, Dolly had clapped a hand over his head. For a while she'd lain rigid on her side, clutching her child, using his sleeping body to shut out the sound. Then she'd slipped out of bed and walked quickly down the corridor.

A white-capped Karen nurse had stopped her: 'What are you doing here?'

'There was a voice,' Dolly had said, 'someone crying for water . . .' She'd made the nurse listen.

'Oh yes,' the nurse had said, offhandedly, 'that's from the malaria ward below. Someone's delirious. Go back to your room.' The moans had stopped soon afterwards but Dolly had stayed up all night, haunted by the sound of the voice.

Another time she had stepped out of the room to find a stretcher in the corridor. A child's body had been lying on it, covered with a white hospital sheet. Although Dinu had been no more than a few feet away, sleeping peacefully, Dolly had not been able to quell the panic that surged through her at the sight of the shrouded stretcher. Falling to her knees in the corridor, she had torn away the sheet that covered the corpse. The child had been a boy, of Dinu's age, and not unlike him in build. Dolly had begun to cry, hysterically, overwhelmed as much by guilt as relief. A nurse and an orderly had had to lift her up to take her back to bed.

Again that night, she had not been able to sleep. She'd thought of the child's body; she'd thought of what her life would be like in Dinu's absence; she'd thought of the dead boy's mother. She'd begun to cry – it was as though her voice had merged with that of the unknown woman; as though an invisible link had arisen between all of them – her, Dinu, the dead child, his mother.

Now, kneeling on the floor of the Sule Pagoda, she recalled the voice of King Thebaw, in Ratnagiri. In his later years the King had seemed more and more to dwell on the precepts he had learnt as a novice, in the palace monastery. She remembered a word he'd often used, *karuna* – one of the Buddha's words, Pali for compassion, for the immanence of all living things in each other, for the attraction of life for its likeness. A time will come, he had said to the girls, when you too will discover what this word karuna means, and from that moment on, your lives will never again be the same.

Shortly after King Thebaw's funeral, the Queen wrote to her gaolers asking for permission to move back to Burma. Her request was denied, on grounds of security, because of the war in Europe: it was felt that her presence might prove inflammatory at a delicate moment for the Empire. It was only after the end of the war that the Queen and her daughters were allowed to return to their homeland.

The First Princess now occasioned a fresh crisis. Was she to leave Ratnagiri to go to Burma with her mother? Or was she to stay with Sawant?

The Princess made a promise to her husband: she told him that she would travel with her mother to Burma and then return once Her Majesty had been safely installed in her new home. Sawant took her at her word and made no objection. But it was with a heavy tread that he walked down to the jetty at Mandvi, on the day of the royal party's departure. For all he knew this was the last time that he or his children would ever see the Princess.

The Queen's party made its way slowly across the subcontinent, travelling eastwards from Bombay by rail. In Calcutta the Queen's entourage stayed at the Grand Hotel. It so happened that the Second Princess was now also living in Calcutta, with her husband: she could scarcely ignore the presence of her mother and sisters. One evening the disowned Princess gathered her resolve and went over to the Grand Hotel to call on her mother.

The Queen flatly refused to receive either her daughter or her son-in-law. The Princess, knowing her mother all too well, retreated in good grace – not so her husband, who summoned the temerity to venture uninvited into Her Majesty's presence. This assault was quickly repulsed: with a single enraged shout the Queen sent her errant son-in-law fleeing down the Grand's marble staircase. It was his misfortune to be shod in smooth-soled leather pumps. His feet slipped and sent him flying into the lobby, where a chamber ensemble was serenading an audience of assembled guests. He flopped into their midst like a leaping trout. A cello splintered and a viola twanged. Seated nearby was the Third Princess, whose nerves had been sadly strained by her recent travels. She broke into hysterics and could not be calmed. A doctor had to be sent for.

On April 16, 1919, the Queen and her party boarded the R.M.S. *Arankola*. They arrived in Rangoon four days later and were spirited quietly off to a bungalow on Churchill Road. A fortnight went by in a flurry of activity. Then the First Princess took everybody aback by announcing that she was ready to go back to Sawant. The family's advisors wrung their hands. It was suggested that the Princess, as the eldest daughter, had a duty to remain with her mother – promises were, after all, frequently allowed to lapse in the interests of good sense and decency. No one doubted that a means could be found for discreetly closing the door on Sawant.

It was now that the First Princess showed herself to be a true daughter of her dynasty, every inch a Konbaung – her love for her family's former coachman proved just as unshakable as her mother's devotion to the late King. Defying her family, she went back to Sawant and never left Ratnagiri again. She lived the rest of her life with her husband and her children in a small house on the outskirts of town. It was there that she died twenty-eight years later.

The Second Princess and her husband lived in Calcutta for several years before moving to the hill-station of Kalimpong, near Darjeeling. There the Princess and her husband opened a dairy business.

So it happened that of the four Princesses, the two who'd been born in Burma both chose to live on in India. Their younger sisters, on the other hand, both born in India, chose to settle in Burma: both married and had children. As for the Queen, she spent her last years in her house on Rangoon's Churchill Road. Such money as she could extract from the colonial authorities, she spent on religious charities and on feeding monks. She never wore anything but white, the Burmese colour of mourning.

After the Queen's arrival in Rangoon, Dolly wrote her several letters, entreating to be allowed to call at her residence. None was ever answered. The Queen died in 1925, six years after her return from Ratnagiri. Even though she'd been cloistered for so many years, there was a sudden surge of sentiment in the city and people poured out to mourn. She was buried near the Shwedagon Pagoda in Rangoon.

Seventeen

In 1929, after a gap of several years, Dolly received a letter from New York. It was from Uma and she was writing to say that she was leaving America. Uma was fifty now and had been away from India for more than twenty years. In her absence her parents had died, leaving her the ground floor of their house, Lankasuka (the upper floor had gone to her brother, who was now married and the father of three children). She had decided to go home, to Calcutta, to settle.

Because of various engagements in Tokyo, Shanghai and Singapore, Uma wrote, she would be sailing across the Pacific rather than the Atlantic. One of the advantages of this route was that it would also enable her to visit friends – Matthew and Elsa in Malaya, and of course, Dolly and Rajkumar in Rangoon. She was writing now to propose that she and Dolly meet at Morningside and spend a fortnight there: it would be a pleasant holiday and afterwards they could travel back to Burma together – after so many years, there was a lot of catching up to be done. What would be better still was if Dolly came with Neel and Dinu: it would give her an opportunity to get to know the boys.

Dolly was oddly shaken by this letter. Although happy to hear from her friend, she was more than a little apprehensive. To resume a friendship that had been so long dormant was no easy matter. She could not help admiring Uma for her forthrightness; she knew that she herself had drawn away from the world, become increasingly reclusive, unwilling to travel or even go out. She was content leading the life she did, but it worried her that the boys had seen very little of the world – of India or Malaya or any other country. It wasn't right that they should never know any place other than Burma: no one could predict what lay ahead. Even through the shuttered windows of her room she could feel an unquietness in the land.

Dolly had not been back to Morningside in fifteen years, ever since her first visit; nor had the boys. It was unlikely, she knew, that Rajkumar would consent to go. He was working harder than ever at his business and there were whole weeks when she hardly saw him. When she mooted the idea to him, he shook his head brusquely, just as she had known he would: no, he was too busy, he couldn't go.

But for her own part, Dolly found herself increasingly drawn to the idea of meeting Uma at Morningside. It would be interesting to see Matthew and Elsa again: the Martinses had come to stay with them once, in Burma, with their two children – after Alison, they'd had a boy, Timmy. The children were all very young then and had got on well together, even Dinu who was withdrawn by nature and very slow to make friends. But that was a long time ago: Dinu was fourteen now, a student at St James's School, one of the best-known in Rangoon. Neel was eighteen, brawny and outgoing, reluctantly engaged in pursuing a course of studies at Rangoon's Judson College: he was eager to get into the timber business but Rajkumar had said that he would not take him into the family firm until his studies were finished.

When Dolly sounded Neel out about going to Morningside, he was immediately enthusiastic, keen to be off. She was not really surprised; she knew that he was always on the lookout for ways of getting out of attending his classes. Dinu proved to be much less keen but said he was willing to strike a bargain: he would go, he said, if she bought him a Brownie camera from Rowe and Co. She agreed; she liked to encourage his interest in photography – partly because she believed it to have grown out of his childhood habit of looking over her shoulder while she sketched; and partly because she felt that she ought to encourage any activity that would draw him out of himself.

The arrangements were quickly set in motion, with letters shooting back and forth between Burma, Malaya and the United States (Rangoon had recently acquired an air mail service, and this made communications much quicker than before). In April the next year, Dolly boarded a Malaya-bound steamer with her two sons. Rajkumar came to see the family off, and after Dolly had boarded, she looked over the side to find that he was waving to her from the jetty, gesticulating wildly, trying to draw her attention to something. She looked at the vessel's bows and discovered that she was on the *Nuwara Eliya*, the same vessel that had brought her to Rangoon immediately after her marriage. It was an odd coincidence.

Matthew and his family were waiting at the Georgetown docks when the *Nuwara Eliya* pulled in. It was Dinu who spotted them first, through the viewfinder of his Brownie. 'There . . . over there . . . look.'

Dolly leant over the gunwale, shading her eyes. Matthew looked very distinguished, with a thick frosting of grey around his head. Elsa had grown a little matronly since their last meeting, but in a regal and quite imposing way. Timmy was standing beside her, tall for his age and as thin as a string bean. Alison was there too, wearing a schoolgirl's frock, her hair braided into long pigtails. She was an unusual-looking girl, Dolly thought, her face an arresting blend of elements taken from both her parents: she had Matthew's cheekbones and Elsa's eyes; his silky hair and her upright carriage. It was clear that she would grow into a real beauty one day.

Matthew came on board and escorted them off the ship. They were all to spend the night in Georgetown and he had booked rooms in a hotel. Uma was due to arrive the next day and they were to drive to Morningside together. Matthew had brought two cars and a chauffeur: they were waiting at Butterworth, on the mainland.

The next morning, after breakfast, they walked together to the port, all seven of them. At the pier, they found themselves caught in a noisy throng. A large number of people had already gathered there, most of them Indians. Many were armed with flowers and garlands. At the head of this crowd stood two flamboyant and colourful figures, one a saffron-robed sadhu and the other a Sikh Giani, with a flowing beard and bushy white eyebrows. Neel, burly and assertive beyond his twenty years, pushed his way into the crowd to find out what the fuss was about. He came back looking puzzled.

'I asked them what they were doing here and they said: we've come to greet Uma Dey.'

'Do you think they mean our own Uma?' Dolly said incredulously, to Elsa.

'Yes, of course. There can't be two Uma Deys on the same ship.'

Then the ship came into view and a cheer erupted from the crowd: *'Uma Dey zindabad, zindabad* – long live, long live, Uma Dey.' This was followed by other shouts and slogans, all in Hindustani: *'Inquilab zindabad'* and *'halla bol, halla bol!'* When the ship docked the crowd's leaders went swarming up the gangplank, with garlands and marigolds. Then Uma appeared, at the head of the gangplank, and was met by a wild outburst of cheering: *'Uma Dey zindabad, zindabad!'* For a while there was complete confusion.

Watching from the far end of the pier, Dolly could tell that Uma had been taken by surprise: she was evidently unprepared for the reception that had been accorded her and didn't quite know how to respond. She was scanning the crowd, as though she were looking for someone in particular. Dolly raised an arm and waved. The gesture caught Uma's eye and she waved back worriedly, sketching a gesture of helplessness. Dolly made a sign to reassure her – don't worry, we'll wait.

Then Uma was ushered down the gangplank and garlanded again. Several people made speeches while everyone stood sweating under the hot sun. Dolly tried hard to concentrate on what was being said, but her eyes kept straying back to her friend. She saw that Uma had grown gaunt and her eyes had retreated into deep hollows, as though in protest against a hectic and uncertain life. But at the same time, there was a new assurance about the way she carried herself. It was clear that she was accustomed to being listened to and when it was her turn to speak, Dolly noticed, with dawning awe, that Uma seemed to know exactly what to say and how to handle the crowd.

Then, abruptly, the speeches were over, and Uma was pushing her way through the crowd. Suddenly, she was standing in front of Dolly, her arms thrown open: such a long time! such a long time! They laughed and hugged and held on to each other while the children looked quizzically on, standing a little apart.

'How well you look, Elsa! And your daughter – she's a beauty!'

'You look well too, Uma.'

Uma laughed. 'You don't have to lie to me. I look twice my age . . .'

Dolly broke in, jogging her friend's arm: 'Who are these people, Uma? We were so surprised . . .'

'They belong to a group I've been working with,' Uma said quickly. 'A group called the Indian Independence League. I hadn't told them I was coming here, but I suppose the word got out . . .'

'But what do they want, Uma? Why were they here?'

'I'll tell you later.' Uma took hold of Dolly's hand and stuck an arm through Elsa's. 'There's so much to talk about and I don't want to run out of time . . .'

In the afternoon they took the ferry to Butterworth where Matthew's cars were waiting at the port, one of them longer than any that Dolly had ever seen, almost the size of a railway carriage. This was a Duesenberg Model J Tourster, Matthew explained. It had a hydraulic braking system and a 6.9 litre, straight-8 engine. It had chain-driven overhead camshafts and could do up to 90 m.p.h. in second gear. In top gear it could cruise at 116.

Matthew was keen to show the Duesenberg off to Neel and Dinu so they rode with him, along with Timmy and Alison. Dolly and Elsa followed more sedately, in the car that Matthew had given Elsa for her fiftieth birthday – a magnificent tan-and-gold Isotta-Fraschini Tipo 8A Berlina Transformabile with power-assisted brakes. The coachwork was by Castagna and the upholstery was of Florentine leather.

The Isotta-Fraschini headed north with the sun dipping low over the Andaman Sea and by the time they reached Sungei Pattani, it was almost dark. They began to climb the slopes of Gunung Jerai with the Isotta-Fraschini's headlights shining into a fog of dust. Passing under the estate's arched gateway they went speeding up a red, dirt track. Then the car turned a corner, and a mansion appeared ahead, springing dramatically out of the slope, with lamps blazing through its windows and doorways. A rounded turret formed the fulcrum of the house. Built around this were wide, sweeping verandas and a roof that curved gently upwards, in the Chinese style.

'Morningside House,' announced Elsa.

Dolly was dazzled. In the inky darkness, it looked as though an unreal brightness were pouring out of the house; that the light was welling up from some interior source of illumination, spilling out of the mountain on which it stood.

'It's magnificent, Elsa,' Uma said. 'There's no other word for it. I think it's possibly the most beautiful house I've ever seen . . .'

Inside, the house was aglow with the rich warmth of polished wood. On their way down to dinner, both Dolly and Uma went astray in the long corridors, distracted by the many fine details of the interior: the floor was of intricate parquetry, and the walls were panelled with rich, fine-grained woods. Elsa came up to look for them and found them tapping the banister of the great stairway that wound through the centre of the house.

'How beautiful this is.'

'Do you like it?' Elsa's face lit up with pleasure. 'When we were building Morningside, Matthew said one day: Everything I have, I owe to trees of one kind or another – teak, rubber. And I thought to myself, why that's it: Morningside will be a monument to wood! I made Rajkumar send me the best teak from Burma; I sent people to the Celebes and Sumatra. You'll notice that each room has wood of a different kind . . .'

Elsa led them downstairs and ushered them into the dining room, which was very large, with a long, polished hardwood table running down the middle. The walls were lined with knitted bamboo and the lights that hung from the ceiling were set inside glowing nests of rattan. As they stepped in, Saya John rose from the table and came up to Dolly and Uma, walking slowly, with the help of a cane: he seemed smaller than before, and more gnome-like as though his body had shrunk in proportion to his head.

'Welcome, welcome.'

At dinner, Uma and Dolly sat between Matthew and Saya John. The men worked hard at keeping their plates filled with food.

'That's gulai tumis, fish cooked with pink ginger buds, bunga kuntan.'

'And this?'

'Prawns roasted in pandanus leaves.'

'Peanut crumpets.'

'Nine-layered rice cakes.'

'Chicken with blue flowers – bunga telang.'

'Pickled fish with turmeric leaves and lime leaves and leaves of purple mint.'

'A salad of shredded squid and polygonum and duan kado, a creeper that smells like a spice-garden.'

With every morsel their mouths were filled with new tastes, flavours that were as unfamiliar as they were delicious. Uma cried: 'What is this food called? I thought I'd eaten everything in New York, but I've never tasted anything like this.'

Saya John smiled: 'So you like Nyonya cooking then?'

'I've never eaten anything so wonderful. Where is it from?'

'From Malacca and Penang,' Elsa said smiling. 'One of the world's last great secrets.'

Replete at last, Uma pushed her plate away and sat back. She turned to Dolly who was sitting beside her.

'So many years.'

'Twenty-three, almost to the day,' said Dolly, 'since I last saw you in Rangoon.'

After dinner Dolly accompanied Uma to her bedroom. She sat on the bed, cross-legged, while Uma combed her hair at the dressing table.

'Uma,' Dolly said shyly, 'you know I'm still wondering . . .'

'About what?'

'Your reception at the port today – all those people . . .'

'Oh, you mean the League?' Uma put her comb down and smiled at Dolly, in her mirror.

'Yes. Tell me about it.'

'It's such a long story, Dolly. I don't know where to begin.'

'Never mind. Just start.'

It went back to New York, Uma said. That was where she had first joined the League, inducted by friends, other Indians living in the city. The Indians there were few in number but closely connected; some had come to seek shelter from the surveillance of the Empire's intelligence services; others had been drawn there because of the relative affordability of the education. Almost without exception they were passionately political; it was impossible, in that circumstance of exile, to remain aloof. At Columbia there was the brilliant and intense Dadasaheb Ambedkar; there was Taraknath Das, gentle in manner but stubborn in spirit. Midtown, there was the Ramakrishna Mission, housed in a tiny, loft-like apartment and manned by a single, saffron-robed *sant* and scores of American sympathisers; downtown, in a tenement south of Houston Street, there was an eccentric Raja who believed himself to be India's Bolivar. It was not that America was hospitable, either to them or their enterprise: it was merely oblivious, uninterested, but indifference too provided shelter of a certain kind.

Soon Uma's apartment had became one of the nodes in this small but dense net of Indian connections. She and her compatriots were like explorers or castaways; watching, observing, picking apart the details of what they saw around them, trying to derive lessons for themselves and their country. Witnessing the nascency of the new century in America, they were able to watch at first hand the tides and currents of the new epoch. They went to visit mills and factories and the latest mechanised farms. They saw that new patterns of work were being invented, calling for new patterns of movement, new ways of thought. They saw that in the world ahead literacy would be crucial to survival; they saw that education had become a matter of such urgency as to prompt every modern nation to make it compulsory. From those of their peers who had travelled eastwards they learnt that Japan had moved quickly in this direction; in Siam too education had become a dynastic crusade for the royal family.

In India on the other hand, it was the military that devoured the bulk of public monies: although the army was small in number it consumed more than sixty per cent of the Government's revenues, more even than was the case in countries that were castigated as 'militaristic'. Lala Har Dayal, one of Uma's most brilliant contemporaries, never tired of pointing out that India was, in effect, a vast garrison and that it was the impoverished Indian peasant who paid both for the upkeep of the conquering army and for Britain's eastern campaigns.

What would become of India's population when the future

they had glimpsed in America had become the world's present condition? They could see that it was not they themselves, nor even their children who would pay the true price of this Empire: that the conditions being created in their homeland were such as to ensure that their descendants would enter the new epoch as cripples, lacking the most fundamental means of survival; that they would truly become in the future what they had never been in the past, a burden upon the world. They could see too that already time was running out, that it would soon become impossible to change the angle of their country's entry into the future; that a time was at hand, when even the fall of the Empire and the departure of their rulers would make little difference; that their homeland's trajectory was being set on an unbudgeable path that would thrust it inexorably in the direction of future catastrophe.

What they saw and thought, seared them, burned them: they were all to some degree mutilated by the knowledge of the evil that was their enemy. Some became a little unhinged, some went mad, others simply gave up. Some turned communist, some took to religion, searching the scriptures for imprecations and formulae, to apply on themselves, like balm.

Among Uma's Indian contemporaries in New York there were many who took their direction from a newsletter published from the University of California, in Berkeley, by Indian students. This publication was called *Ghadar*, after the Hindustani word for the uprising of 1857. The people who were involved with the magazine were known as the Ghadar Party. Much of their support came from the Indians who'd settled on the Pacific coast in the late nineteenth and early twentieth centuries. Many of these immigrants were Sikhs – former soldiers of the British Indian army. The experience of living in America and Canada served to turn many of these former loyalists into revolutionaries. Perceiving a link between their treatment abroad and India's subject status, they had become dedicated enemies of the Empire they had once served. Some of them concentrated their efforts on trying to convert such of their friends and relatives as were still serving in the British Indian army. Others looked for allies abroad, developing links with the Irish resistance in America.

The Indians were, comparatively, novices in the arts of sedition. It was the Irish who were their mentors and allies, schooling them in their methods of organisation, teaching them the tricks of shopping for arms to send back home; giving them instruction in the techniques of fomenting mutiny among those of their countrymen who served the Empire as soldiers. On St Patrick's Day in New York a small Indian contingent would sometimes march in the Irish parade, with their own banners, dressed in sherwanis and turbans, dhoties and kurtas, angarkhas and angavastrams.

After the start of the First World War, under pressure from the British intelligence services, the Ghadar Party had gone underground, metamorphosing slowly into a number of different groups. Of these the Indian Independence League was the most important, with thousands of partisans among overseas Indians: it was their offices that Uma had been visiting in eastern Asia.

Here, Dolly, who had been growing increasingly puzzled, broke in. 'But, Uma,' she said, 'if what you're telling me is true, then why have I never heard of the League? The papers are always full of Mahatma Gandhi, but no one ever speaks of your group.'

'The reason for that, Dolly,' said Uma, 'is that Mr Gandhi heads the loyal opposition. Like many other Indians he's chosen to deal with the Empire's velvet glove instead of striking at its iron fist. He cannot see that the Empire will always remain secure while its Indian soldiers remain loyal. The Indian army will always put down opposition wherever it occurs – not just in India, but also in Burma, Malaya, East Africa, no matter where. And of course, the Empire does everything possible to keep these soldiers in hand: only certain castes of men are recruited; they're completely shut off from politics and the wider society; they're given land and their children are assured jobs.'

'What do you hope to do then?' Dolly asked.

'To open the soldiers' eyes. It's not as difficult as you might think. Many of the League's leaders are old soldiers. Giani Amreek Singh for instance – do you remember him? He was the distinguished Sikh Giani who came to the pier today, remember?'

'Yes.'

'I'll tell you a story about him. I first met him in California, many years ago. He's an old military man himself: he'd risen to the rank of a junior NCO in the British Indian army before deserting. The first time I heard him speak, he talked about the necessity of opening the eyes of Indian soldiers. After a while I said to him: "But Gianiji, you served in this army yourself; why did it take you so long to understand that you were being used to conquer others like yourself?"'

'And what did he say?' Dolly asked.

'He said: "You don't understand. We never thought that we were being used to conquer people. Not at all: we thought the opposite. We were told that we were freeing those people. That is what they said – that we were going to set those people free from their bad kings or their evil customs or some such thing. We believed it because they believed it too. It took us a long time to understand that in their eyes freedom exists wherever *they* rule."'

Dolly acknowledged this with a smile and a nod. 'But what else, Uma? Did you ever meet anyone? A man? Did you never talk of anything but politics with your revolutionaries?'

Uma gave her a wan smile. 'I met many men, Dolly. But we were always like brothers and sisters – that's how we spoke to one another, *bhai* and *bahen*. As for me, because they knew that I was a widow, I think the men looked to me to be a kind of ideal woman, a symbol of purity – and to tell you the truth, I didn't much mind. That's the thing about politics – once you get involved in it, it pushes everything else out of your life.'

Eighteen

Uma woke the next morning to find that breakfast had been served on a veranda that looked down the slope of the mountain, towards the brilliant blue of the Andaman Sea. Neel and Timmy were leaning on the balcony's rail, talking about cars. Alison and Dinu were listening without joining in. Looking at them, it occurred to Uma that even until the day before, she would not have known them if she'd passed them in the street. Yet now, in their faces, she could see inscribed the history of her friendships and the lives of her friends – the stories and trajectories that had brought Elsa's life into conjuction with Matthew's, Dolly's with Rajkumar's, Malacca with New York, Burma with India.

'The children' – here they were, standing in front of her: a day had gone by and she had not said a single word to any of them. In San Francisco, before boarding, she'd gone into a shop to buy presents and had ended up wandering off in the direction of the baby clothes and rattles and silver cups. It was with a jolt that she'd recalled that 'the children' were almost adults now – that Neel was twenty or thereabouts, that Dinu and Alison were sixteen and Timmy just two years younger. It occurred to her that if she'd had children of her own, they would have been of the same age, they would all have been friends – the canvas of a lifetime's connections would have acquired the patina of another generation. But that was not to be, and now, listening to her friends' children as they bantered in the shorthand of their youth, Uma felt oddly shy: trying to think of things to say to them, she realised that she had no idea what they did with their time, the things they thought about, the books they read.

She felt herself slipping into a silence that would become, she knew, irremediable if it were allowed to persist. So, because she was the kind of person she was, she did exactly what she would have done at a political meeting: rising to her feet, she called them to order: 'I have something to say, so please listen. I feel I must talk to each of you on your own, or I'll never know what to say to any of you . . .'

Their eyes widened as they turned to look at her. She thought to herself: what have I done? I've scared them off; I've lost them for ever. But then, as the meaning of what she'd said dawned on them, they began to smile; she had the impression that no adult had ever spoken to them like this before; no grown-up had ever thought to seek them out for their company.

'All right then, Alison, let's go for a walk.'

From then on, it was easy: they seemed to want to show her round the estate, to go with her for walks. They called her 'Auntie' and this was oddly pleasing too. Soon they were not just 'the children' any more; each was someone she could recognise: Timmy was the confident one, who knew exactly what he intended to do: he wanted to go to America, to study, just as Matthew had, and then he wanted to go into business, on his own. Neel was a blunter and softer version of Rajkumar: she could see his father in him, quite clearly, but overlaid by a generation of wealth and comfort. Alison was a bit of an enigma, sometimes quiet and moody, but on occasion, wildly exuberant, full of laughter and sharp, intelligent conversation.

Dinu was the only one who left Uma feeling at a complete loss. Every time she tried to talk to him he seemed sullen, dour, and such observations as he occasionally had to offer were usually tart to the point of sourness. When he spoke, it was in odd staccato bursts, swallowing half his words and shooting out the rest: a manner of speech that made her afraid of saying anything, for fear that she might appear to be interrupting him. It was only when Dinu had a camera in his hands that he seemed to relax a little: but of course it was impossible to talk to someone who had no mind for anything but his viewfinder.

One morning, Alison said to Uma, 'There's something I want to show you. Can I take you for a drive?'

'By all means.'

Dinu was well within earshot and the invitation was extended in such a way as clearly to include him. But Alison's offer seemed to cast the boy into an agony of shyness. He began to back away, making a great show of dragging his right foot behind him.

'Dinu, won't you come with us?' Alison said.

'I don't know . . .' He went pale and began to mumble in confusion.

Uma was watching him closely and she knew suddenly that the boy was secretly infatuated with Alison. She was tempted to smile. Nothing would come of it, she could tell: they were as different as could be, he a creature of the shadows, she an animal that craved the spotlight. He would spend his life nurturing unuttered yearnings. Uma was tempted to grip him by the shoulders, to shake him awake.

'Come on, Dinu,' she ordered in a sharp, peremptory voice. 'Don't be a child.'

'Yes, do come,' Alison said brightly. 'I think you'll enjoy it.'

'Can I bring my camera?'

'Of course.'

They went down the sweeping, mahogany staircase, out into the gravelled driveway where a small, cherry-red roadster stood parked under the porch. The car was a 6-litre Paige Daytona, a three-seater, with a single rear seat that pulled out like a drawer, resting on the running board. Alison pulled the rear seat out for Dinu and then clicked open the passenger door for Uma.

'Alison!' Uma's voice rose in surprise. 'Does your father let you drive his cars?'

Alison grinned. 'Only this one,' she said. 'He won't hear of us driving the Duesie or the Isotta.' She gunned the engine and the car rocketed forward, shooting a shower of pebbles back into the porch.

'Alison!' Uma cried, clinging to her door. 'You're going far too fast.'

'This isn't half as fast as I'd like to go.' Alison laughed and tossed her head. The wind caught her hair and carried it out behind her, like a sail. Roaring through the gate at the bottom of the garden, they plunged abruptly into the hushed gloom of the plantation, with slender, long-leafed trees arching high above them on either side. The trees were ranged in lines that stretched as far as the eye could follow, dwindling into long, straight tunnels: the effect was giddying as they flashed past, thousands upon thousands of them. It was like staring at stripes on a fast-moving screen: Uma felt herself growing dizzy and had to lower her eyes.

Suddenly the trees ended and a small shantytown appeared, with rows of shacks lining the road – hutches of brick and mortar, sheltered under steepled sheets of tin. The shacks were exactly similar in design and yet each was defiantly distinctive in appearance: some were neat, with little curtains fluttering at their front windows, while other were hovels, with pyramids of filth piled at their doors.

'The coolie lines,' said Alison, slowing briefly. In a moment they were past and then the car picked up speed again. Once again, a tunnel of arched tree trunks closed around them, and they disappeared into a tube of kaleidoscopic lines.

The road ended at a stream. A ribbon of water was flowing down the face of a tilted sheet of rock, its surface braided with tiny ripples. On the far side, the mountain climbed steeply upwards, blanketed in a dense tangle of forest. Alison ran the car into a sheltered clearing and snapped her door open.

'The estate ends here,' she said. 'Now we have to walk.'

Taking Uma's hand, Alison helped her pick her way slowly over the stream. On the other side was a path that led directly into the jungle, heading up the slope of Gunung Jerai. The climb was steep and Uma soon ran out of breath.

'Do we have a long way to go?' she called ahead to Alison.

'No. We're almost there.'

'Where?'

Suddenly Dinu came up to stand beside her. 'Look.'

Following the direction of his pointing finger, Uma glanced up. Through a tangle of vines and bamboo, she caught a glimpse of a line of red masonry. 'Why,' she said, 'it appears to be a ruin of some kind.'

Dinu went ahead, hurrying in excitement after Alison. Uma caught up with them at a spot where the slope levelled out into a flat, rocky ledge. Directly ahead of her were two cenotaph-like structures, placed on square plinths: walled chambers of simple design, each with a doorway that led into a small enclosure. Their stone walls were mossy with age and their roofs had caved in.

'I was hoping you'd be able to tell us what they are, Auntie Uma.'

'Why me?'

'Well your father was an archaeologist, wasn't he?'

'Yes but . . .' Uma shook her head slowly. 'I didn't learn much from him . . .'

The sight was as evocative as any she'd ever seen: the crumbling red stone juxtaposed against the tangled greenery of the jungle, with the mountain rising serenely above, a halo of cloud around its peak. Dinu was absorbed in photographing the ruins, moving round the structures as fast as his foot would let him. Uma felt a sudden pang of envy: if I were his age, this would have taken hold of me too, it would have changed my life; I would have come back here again and again; I wouldn't rest until I'd had my fill of it; I'd want to dig them up and take them with me . . .

'Auntie Uma,' Dinu called to her, across the clearing, 'what are they – these ruins?'

She ran the edge of her thumb over the spongy stone. 'I think these were what my father used to call *chandis*,' she said softly. 'Shrines.'

'What sort of shrine?' said Dinu. 'Who built them?'

'I'd say they're either Hindu or Buddhist shrines.' She threw up her hands, in frustration at her own ignorance. 'I wish I could tell you more.'

'Do you think they're old?' Dinu said.

'Yes,' said Uma. 'I'm sure of that. Just look how weathered the stone is. I would say these chandis are very old indeed.'

'I knew they were old,' Alison said triumphantly. 'I knew it. Daddy doesn't believe me. He says nothing here can be old because there was only jungle when he first came.'

Dinu turned to Alison, in his abrupt way: 'And how did you find this place?'

'My father sometimes takes us shooting in the jungle,' Alison said. 'One day we stumbled upon this place.' She took Dinu's hand. 'Let me show you something,' she said. 'Come.'

She led him into the larger of the two structures. Stopping at the plinth, she pointed to an image on a pedestal, a weathered Ganesh, carved in moss-covered stone.

'We found the image lying on the floor,' said Alison, 'and we put it back – it seemed to belong there.'

Uma caught a glimpse of Dinu and Alison, standing framed in the ruined doorway, next to each other. They looked very young, more children than adolescents. 'Give me your camera,' she called out to Dinu. 'I'll take a picture of the two of you together.'

She took the Brownie from him and stepped back, with her eye to the viewfinder. It gave her a start to see them framed together. Suddenly she understood why people arranged marriages for their children: it was a way of shaping the future to the past, of cementing one's ties to one's memories and to one's friends. Dinu and Alison – if only they were better suited to each other; how wonderful it might be, the bringing together of so many stories. Then she recollected what she was supposed to be doing and was annoyed with herself for thinking about things that were none of her business. She clicked the shutter and handed the camera back to Dinu.

The day began very early at the plantation. Every morning, well before dawn, Uma was woken by Matthew's footsteps, going down the grand staircase and out to his car. From her window she would see his headlamps streaking down the slope, in the pre-dawn darkness, heading in the direction of the estate office.

One day she said to Matthew: 'Where do you go, so early in the morning?'

'To Muster.'

'What's that?'

'We have an assembly ground near the estate office. The tappers come there in the morning and the contractors give them their jobs for the day.'

She was intrigued by the jargon: muster, contractors, tappers. 'Can I come?'

'Certainly.'

The next morning Uma drove down to the office with Matthew, along shortcuts that went corkscrewing down the slope. Scores of tappers were converging in front of the plantation's tin-roofed offices by the light of blazing kerosene lamps: they were all Indians, mainly Tamils; the women were dressed in saris and the men in sarongs.

The ceremony that followed was part military parade and part school assembly. It was presided over by the estate's manager, Mr Trimble, a portly Eurasian. The tappers fell into straight lines, facing a tall flagpole that stood at the far corner of the assembly ground. Mr Trimble hoisted the Union Jack and then stood at attention beneath the flagpole, saluting stiffly, with two rows of Indian overseers lining up behind him – these were the 'conductors'.

Mr Trimble kept attentive watch as the conductors took attendance. His manner varied between that of a strict headmaster and a snappish sergeant. Occasionally he would dart into the ranks, with his rattan cane tucked under his arm. For some of the tappers he had a smile and a quick word of encouragement; with others, he made a great show of losing his temper, gesticulating and pouring out obscenities, in Tamil and English, singling out the object of his wrath with the tip of his pointing cane: 'You dog of a coolie, keep your black face up and look at me when I'm talking to you . . .'

Uma was disturbed by this spectacle: she had the feeling of watching something archaic, a manner of life that she had believed to be fortunately extinct. In the car Matthew asked what she had thought of 'Muster' and she had difficulty in keeping her voice under control.

'I don't know what to say, Matthew. It was like watching something that no longer existed: I was put in mind of the American South before the Civil War, of *Uncle Tom's Cabin*.'

'Oh, come on, aren't you exaggerating a bit? Our tappers are well fed and well looked after. And they're a lot better off than they would be if they were back where they came from.'

'Isn't that what masters have always said about slaves?'

Matthew raised his voice. 'They're not slaves, Uma.'

'No, of course not.' Uma reached out to touch his arm, in

apology. 'No. But did you see the terror on their faces when that man – the manager – shouted at them?'

'He's just doing his job, Uma. It's a very hard job and he does it very well. It's no easy thing to run a plantation you know. To look at, it's all very green and beautiful – sort of like a forest. But actually it's a vast machine, made of wood and flesh. And at every turn, every little piece of this machine is resisting you, fighting you, waiting for you to give in.'

He brought the car to a sudden halt. 'Let me show you something.' Opening his door, he led the way into a stand of rubber. 'Come. Over here.'

It was first light now and dawn was descending on the peak of Gunung Jerai. This was the one time of day when the mountain's heights were always visible, unclouded by the haze that rose later from the heated plain. On the slopes above them, the jungle was coming slowly to life, with flocks of birds rising from the forest canopy, and unseen troops of monkeys sailing through the treetops, leaving wakes of tossing leaves.

Under the rubber trees, there was a slow dripping of dew. Matthew leant against a tree trunk and pointed up. 'Look at this tree,' he said, 'and look at the others around it. Wouldn't you say they're all exactly the same?'

'Yes,' Uma nodded, 'it struck me the other day: even their limbs branch off at the same height, and in exactly the same way.'

'And so they should. An enormous amount of human ingenuity has been invested in making these trees exactly similar. They're called clones, you know, and scientists have been working on them for years. Most of our trees are of a clonal variety called Avros – developed by the Dutch in Sumatra in the twenties. We pay a lot of money to make sure that we get reliable clonal seed. But let me show you something.'

He pointed into a coconut-shell cup that was fastened in the tree's trunk, beneath a long, spiral slash in the bark. 'See how much latex this tree has produced overnight? The cup is half full, which is about right. If you walked down this row of trees, you'd find that most of them had yielded roughly the same amount of latex. But now look over here.'

He led the way to another tree. 'Look at this cup.'

Uma looked in and saw that the cup he was pointing to was almost empty. She asked: 'Is something wrong with this tree then?'

'Not that I can tell,' Matthew said. 'It looks all right – no different from the others. Think of all the human effort that has gone into making it the same as the rest. And yet . . .' – he pointed into the almost-empty cup, '. . . there you are.'

'So what do you think the matter is?'

'Botanists will tell you one thing and geologists will tell you another and soil specialists will tell you something else again. But if you ask me, the truth is quite simple.'

'What is it?'

'It's fighting back.'

Uma gave an astonished laugh. 'You can't really believe that.'

'I planted this tree, Uma. I've heard what all the experts say. But the tappers know better. They have a saying, you know – "every rubber tree in Malaya was paid for with an Indian life". They know that there are trees that won't do what the others do, and that's what they say – this one is fighting back.'

Through the surrounding tree trunks, the plantation's offices were visible in the distance, on the slope below. Matthew pointed to them, making a sweeping gesture with his hand.

'This is my little empire, Uma. I made it. I took it from the jungle and moulded it into what I wanted it to be. Now that it's mine I take good care of it. There's law, there's order, everything is well run. Looking at it, you would think everything here is tame, domesticated, that all the parts have been fitted carefully together. But it's when you try to make the whole machine work that you discover that every bit of it is fighting back. It has nothing to do with me or with rights and wrongs: I could make this the best-run little kingdom in the world and it would still fight back.'

'And what's the reason for that?'

'It's nature: the nature that made these trees and the nature that made us.'

'So are you saying then . . .' – Uma began to laugh, 'that some of your trees are rebels by instinct?'

'Not in so many words.'

'But, Matthew,' Uma laughed again, 'what on earth are you

going to do if your tappers decide to take a lesson from your trees?'

Now it was Matthew's turn to laugh. 'Let's hope it never comes to that.'

Unable to sleep past daybreak, Uma began to go for long walks in the rubber groves. It was years now since she had risen this early: dawn was a discovery. There were days when teams of rubber tappers would loom suddenly out of the golden early morning mist, with tendrils of fog clinging to their saris and sarongs. They would pass within inches of her, oblivious of her presence, utterly absorbed in keeping pace with each other, their scythe-like knives glinting in the half-light as they peeled slivers of bark from the tree trunks.

On one of these early morning walks, Uma became aware that she was being followed. She looked over her shoulder, and saw a figure slipping out of view: it was either a boy or a man, she couldn't tell. It was easy to lose sight of things in the rubber groves, especially in the half-light of dawn. The arrangement of the trees was such that things would slip away, from one line of sight into another, and you'd have no idea where they were in relation to yourself.

The next day, hearing the crackle of leaves behind her, it was she who hid herself. This time she was able to catch a glimpse of him in the distance: it was a boy, thin, lanky and dark. He was dressed in a shirt and checked sarong. She took him to be one of the worker's children.

'You, there . . .' she called out, her voice echoing through the tunnels of foliage. 'Who are you? Come here.' She caught a glimpse of the whites of his eyes, flaring suddenly in the darkness. Then he disappeared.

Back at the house, Uma described the boy to Alison. 'Do you know who he might be?'

'Yes.' Alison nodded. 'His name is Ilongo. He's from the coolie lines. Was he following you?'

'Yes.'

'He does that sometimes. Don't worry; he's completely harmless. We call him Morningside's village idiot.'

Uma decided to befriend the boy. She set about it carefully, taking little gifts with her each morning, usually fruit, rambutans, mangoes or mangosteens. On catching sight of him she'd stop and call out, 'Ilongo, Ilongo, come here.' Then she'd put her offering down on the ground and walk away. Soon, he became confident enough to approach her. The first few times, she made no attempt to talk. She set down her gifts and watched him retrieve them, from a distance. He was about ten, but tall for his age, and very thin. His eyes were large and very expressive: looking into them, she could not believe that he was a simpleton.

'Ilongo,' she said to him one day, in English, 'why do you follow me around?' When he didn't answer she switched to Hindustani, asking the same question again.

This produced an immediate effect: spitting out an orange seed, he suddenly began to speak.

'After my mother leaves for Muster, I don't like to stay in the house, all by myself.'

'Are you alone at home then?'

'Yes.'

'What about your father?'

'My father isn't here.'

'Why? Where is he?'

'I don't know.'

'Have you never met him?'

'No.'

'Do you know where he lives?'

'No. But my mother has a picture of him: he's an important man, my mother says.'

'Can I see the picture?'

'I'll have to ask my mother.' Then something startled him and he vanished into the trees.

A couple of days later, walking past a line of rubber tappers, Ilongo pointed to a woman with a strong, square face and a silver nose ring. 'That's my mother,' he said. Uma made as though to approach her and the boy panicked. 'No. She's working now. The conductor will fine her.'

'But I'd like to talk to her.'

'Later. At our house. Come here at five, and I'll take you.'

That evening, Uma walked with Ilongo to the line of shacks where he lived. Their dwelling was small but neat and bare. Ilongo's mother had changed into a bright, peacock-green sari in anticipation of Uma's visit. She sent the boy out to play and set a pot of water on the fire, for tea.

'Ilongo said you had a picture of his father.'

'Yes.' She handed over a piece of fading newsprint.

Uma recognised the face at first glance. She realised now that she'd known all along, without wanting to acknowledge it to herself. She shut her eyes and turned the picture over so that she wouldn't have to look at it. It was Rajkumar.

'Do you know who this man is?' she said at last.

'Yes.'

'Do you know that he's married?'

'Yes.'

'How did it happen? Between you and him?'

'They sent me to him. On the ship, when I was coming over. They called me out of the hold and took me up to his cabin. There was nothing I could do.'

'That was the only time?'

'No. For years afterwards, whenever he was here he'd send for me. He wasn't so bad, better than some others. One time, I saw a picture of his wife and I said to him, she's so beautiful, like a princess – what do you want with a woman like me?'

'What did he say?'

'He told me that his wife had turned away from the world; that she'd lost interest in her home and her family, in him . . .'

'And when was the last time you saw him?'

'Many years ago. He stopped coming after I told him I was pregnant.'

'Did he not want to have anything to do with the boy – with Ilongo?'

'No. But he sends money.'

'Why haven't you spoken to his wife? Or to Mr or Mrs Martins? They could do something. What he's done is very wrong: he can't be allowed to abandon you like this.'

Ilongo's mother glanced at her visitor and saw that her face was flushed with indignation on her behalf. Now a note of anxiety entered the matter-of-fact tone of her voice. 'Madame, you won't speak of this to anyone?'

'You can be sure that I will,' Uma retorted. 'This is a shameful business. I'll go to the police if I need to . . .'

At this the woman panicked. She came quickly across the room and sank to her knees at Uma's feet. 'No,' she said, shaking her head vehemently. 'No. No. Please understand. I know you mean to help me but you are an outsider. You do not know how things are here.'

'What do you want then?' Uma rose angrily to her feet. 'Do you want that I should just let this pass? That he should get away with it?'

'This is my business. You have no right to speak of this to anyone . . .'

Uma was breathing heavily, her chest heaving in anger. 'I don't understand,' she said. 'This man should be punished for what he has done to you – to you and to his own wife and family. Why do you want to keep this matter hidden?'

'Because it will not help me to see him punished: it will only make things worse for everyone. The money will stop; there'll be trouble. I am not a child: it is not for you to take this decision on my behalf . . .'

Tears of frustration welled up in Uma's eyes. She'd often railed against women who allowed themselves to be trapped within labyrinths of fear – but now, confronted with this circumstance she was helpless, herself a part of the maze.

'. . . Madame, I want you to give me your word that you will not speak of this: I will not let you leave until you have.'

There was nothing Uma could do but produce a forced nod of assent.

Nineteen

From that point on, Uma's journey began to acquire an involuntary, dream-like quality, with impressions and events following scattershot on each other, like hailstones battering against a netted screen.

At Morningside, on the last day of her stay, Uma had a conversation with Dinu that took her completely by surprise. She'd noticed that Dolly spent an inordinate amount of time on her own, staying in her room all morning and rarely making an appearance downstairs before noon.

Succumbing to curiosity, Uma asked Dinu: 'Why doesn't Dolly have breakfast with us? Why does she come down so late?'

Dinu gave her a glance of surprise: 'Don't you know? She does her *te-ya-tai* in the morning.'

'What's that?'

'I don't know how to explain . . . I suppose you could say she meditates.'

'Oh.' Uma paused to digest this. 'And when did this start?'

'I don't know. She's been doing it ever since I can remember . . . Was there a time when she didn't?'

'I don't remember . . .'

Uma changed the subject abruptly and didn't touch on it again.

The next stop on Uma's itinerary was none other than Rangoon. Her trip had been so planned as to allow her to make the journey over from Malaya in the company of Dolly, Neel and Dinu. She was to stay with Dolly and Rajkumar for one month, before sailing on to Calcutta. While planning the trip, it was this leg of the journey that Uma had most looked forward to: she had imagined herself and Dolly spending hours together during the voyage, talking as they once had. Now, the prospect filled her with dread.

But once they were on board, the constraints of the last few days disappeared almost magically. Gradually, the old intimacy returned, to the point where Uma could even bring herself to comment on Dolly's daily periods of seclusion.

One morning, when they were both out on deck, Uma said, 'You know, Dolly, after we talked that first night, at Morningside, I thought it would be just like the old days. Do you remember, Dolly, at Ratnagiri, how we would talk through the night, and then when we woke up, we would start again, as though falling asleep were just an interruption? At Morningside, every morning, I'd say to myself, today I'll go for a walk with Dolly and we'll sit under a tree and look at the sea. But you were never there; you were never even down for breakfast. So one morning, I asked Dinu and he told me why you stayed so late in your room . . .'

'I see.'

'I tried so hard to tell you about my life and you never said a word about yours; nothing about what's on your mind or what you do with your time.'

'What could I say, Uma? If I'd been better with words, perhaps I could have. But I didn't know what to say. And especially to you . . .'

'Why especially me?'

'With you I feel that I have to account for myself – provide an explanation.'

Uma saw that this was not untrue. 'Perhaps you're right, Dolly. Perhaps I would have found it hard to understand. It's true that I'm not religious myself – but I would have tried to understand, simply because of you. And I'll still try, Dolly, if you'll let me.'

Dolly was silent for a moment. 'It's hard to know where to start, Uma. You'll remember that I wrote to you about Dinu's illness? After it was over, I found that something had changed in me. I couldn't go back to the life I'd led before. It wasn't that I was unhappy with Rajkumar, or that I no longer felt anything for him: it was just that the things I did no longer filled my time or occupied my mind. It was the feeling that you get when your day is empty and there's nothing to do – except that it went on, day after day. Then I heard about an old friend – we used to call her Evelyn. I heard she was at Sagaing, near Mandalay, and that she had become the head of a *thi-la-shin-kyaung* – what do you call it? – a Buddhist nunnery. I went up to see her, and I knew at once that that was where I wanted to be – that this would be my life.'

'Your life!' Uma stared at her, in shock. 'But what about the boys?'

'It's because of them – and Rajkumar – that I haven't gone yet. I want to see them settled first – in India perhaps, somewhere away from Burma, at any rate. Once they're safe, I'll feel free to go to Sagaing . . .'

'Safe? But aren't they safe where they are?'

'Things have changed in Burma, Uma. I feel frightened now. There's a lot of anger, a lot of resentment, and much of it is aimed at Indians.'

'But why?'

'Money, politics –' Dolly paused – 'so many different things, who's to say? Indian moneylenders have taken over all the farmland; Indians run most of the shops; people say that the rich Indians live like colonialists, lording it over the Burmese. I don't know what the wrongs and rights of it are, but I know that I feel frightened for the boys – even for Rajkumar. Some time ago, Dinu was shouted at, on the streets: they called him *Zerbadi* – which is a swear word, for people who're half-Indian, half-Burmese. And the other day in Rangoon, a crowd surrounded the car and shook their fists at me. I said to them: "Why are you doing this? What have I done to you?" Instead of giving me an answer, they began to chant *Amyotha Kwe Ko Mayukya Pa Net* . . .'

'What does that mean?'

'It's a political song: the gist of it is that it's wrong for Burmese to marry foreigners – that women like me, who're married to Indians, are traitors to their own people.'

'Did you say anything to them?'

'Yes I did. I was very angry. I said: "Do you know that I spent twenty years of my life in exile, with Burma's last king? Over here you forgot all about us. What little joy we had came from Indians."'

'And what did they say to that?'

'They looked sheepish and went away. But another time – who knows what they would do?'

'Have you told Rajkumar – that you want the family to leave Burma?'

'Yes. But of course, he won't listen. He tells me: "You don't understand. The economy wouldn't work without Indian businessmen; the country would collapse. These protests about Indians are the work of agitators and troublemakers who're just trying to incite the public." I've tried to tell him that it's he who doesn't understand; that the Burma of today is not the Burma he came to when he was eleven. But of course he pays no attention . . .' She broke off. 'You'll see what it's like when we get there . . .'

The next day, they reached Rangoon. The steamer was manoeuvring itself into position beside the floating pavilion of the Barr Street Passenger Jetty, when Uma spotted Rajkumar standing in the shade of the ornamental eaves. He gave her a broad smile and waved. His hair was greying brightly at the temples and he seemed larger and bulkier than ever, with an immense, bellows-like chest. Uma gritted her teeth and forced a smile on to her face.

They drove to Kemendine in Rajkumar's new car, a grey 1929 Packard saloon. On the way Rajkumar pointed out the changes in their surroundings. The city seemed transformed beyond recognition to Uma. There were stately hotels, enormous banks, fashionable restaurants, arcaded department stores and even nightclubs. The one landmark that seemed to be proof against these changes was the Shwe Dagon Pagoda. It was exactly as Uma remembered, its graceful, gilded hti rising above the city like a benediction.

The Kemendine house had changed too: it still had its haphazard improvised look, but it was much larger now, with added-on floors above and sprawling wings at its side. Everywhere Uma looked there were caretakers, gardeners, chowkidars.

'How much your house has grown!' Uma said to Dolly. 'You could have an army in here if you wanted.'

'Rajkumar wants it to be large enough for the boys to live in,' Dolly said. 'They're each to have a floor of their own. He sees himself ruling over one of those vast joint families, growing larger with every generation . . .'

'It doesn't look,' said Uma, 'as if you're going to have a very easy time persuading him to leave.'

'No. It's going to be very hard . . .'

Later in the day, Dinu brought a Burmese school-friend to see her. His name was Maung Thiha Saw and he was a gawky, eager-looking boy with a great mass of shiny black hair and thick, smudged spectacles. He was as talkative as Dinu was reserved, and he peppered Uma with unexpected questions about America and the Depression.

The day was unnaturally still and airless and it was very hot inside the house. 'Come,' said Uma, 'let's talk outside – it may be a little cooler.'

They went downstairs and stepped out to walk round the compound. A tall electricity pole stood by the front gate and as they were approaching it, Uma noticed that it had begun to tilt. She came abruptly to a stop and ran a hand over her eyes. Then suddenly her feet grew unsteady. She felt as though her legs were going to pitch her forward.

'Dinu,' she cried, 'what's happening?'

'Earthquake!' Dinu put a hand on her shoulders and they huddled together with their arms round each other. It seemed like a very long time before the heaving in the earth came to a stop. Warily they let go of each other and looked around, taking stock. Suddenly Maung Thiha Saw shouted, his eyes fixed on the horizon.

'No!'

Uma spun round, just in time to see the great golden hti of the Shwe Dagon toppling over.

Soon after this, Uma made arrangements to travel round Burma with fellow-members of the Indian Independence League. From Rangoon she went eastwards to Moulmein and then turned north to go to Taunggyi, Toungoo, Meiktila and Mandalay. Everywhere she went she could see signs of a widening rift between Indians and their Burmese neighbours. Amongst students and nationalists an agitation was under way to separate Burma's administration from that of British India. Many Indians saw this as a cause for alarm, believing that their safety would be threatened by a separation.

Uma was riven by this controversy: she sympathized with the fears of the Indian minority and yet it troubled her that they believed their safety lay in what she saw as the root cause of the problem – the pattern of imperial rule and its policy of ensuring its necessity through the division of its subjects. On returning to Rangoon, Uma was quick to offer Dolly an apology: 'Dolly, I hope you'll forgive me for treating your fears so lightly. I can see now that there's a lot to worry about. Frankly I feel utterly confused . . .'

A few days before her departure for Calcutta, Uma went for an early morning drive with Dolly in the grey Packard. They went first to Rangoon's Churchill Road, to look at the house where Queen Supayalat had died, a few years before.

'Did you ever see her again, Dolly?' Uma asked.

'No.' Dolly slowly shook her head. 'As far as she was concerned, I was in the same boat as the Second Princess: banished for ever from her presence . . .'

On the way back, they drove past the Sule Pagoda and found the streets unusually quiet for that time of day. 'I wonder why there are no rickshaws, no hawkers . . .' Dolly paused to look around. 'How odd: I can't see a single Indian on the street.'

In the distance, at a street corner there was a long line of men. As the Packard rolled past, they saw that the men were queueing to have tattoo-like designs painted on their chests. Dolly's reaction was instantaneous. She leant over to shake U Ba Kyaw's shoulder.

'Dolly – what's the matter? What's happening?'

'We have to turn round. We have to go back – back to the house.'

'Because of those men? Why? Does it have something to do with those tattoos?'

'Those weren't tattoos, Uma. Those designs were for soldiers who're going to war . . .' Dolly began to drum her fist distractedly on her knees. 'I think there's going to be some kind of trouble.

We have to find out where the boys are – where Rajkumar is. If we're quick maybe we'll be able to stop them leaving the house.'

Some twenty yards ahead of the Packard, a man leapt off a footpath and ran into the street. Uma and Dolly noticed him when he appeared in one corner of the Packard's wide, curved windscreen. He was an Indian, a rickshaw-puller, dressed in a tattered vest and a longyi. He was running hard and beads of sweat were flying off his arms. One of his hands was clawing the air, and the other was holding up his longyi, keeping it from getting entangled in his legs. His face was dark and his eyes very white and bulbous. Two steps carried him from the edge of their windscreen to its middle; he turned to glance over his shoulder and his eyes started in his head. Now they saw that he was being closely pursued by a man who was just two steps behind him. This man was bare-bodied and a black design was painted over his chest. He was carrying something but they couldn't see what it was, because it was hidden beneath the edge of their windscreen. Then, all of a sudden, the pursuer swung his shoulders and drew his arms back, in the manner of a tennis player preparing to make a stroke. They saw now that the instrument in his hands was a da, a long, glinting blade with a short handle, part sword, part axe. They sat transfixed in their seats as the da scythed through the air in a circular motion. The rickshaw-puller had almost reached the far end of their windscreen when suddenly his head toppled over like a lopped-off branch, hanging down over his spine, held on by a thin flap of skin. But the body did not fall instantly to the ground: for a fraction of a second the decapitated trunk stayed upright. They saw it advance by one more step before crashing to the pavement.

Uma's first impulse was to reach for the door handle.

'What are you doing?' Dolly screamed. 'Stop.'

'We have to help, Dolly. We can't just leave him on the street . . .'

'Uma, have you gone mad?' Dolly hissed. 'If you get out of the car now, you'll be killed too.' She gave Uma a push, thrusting her on to the floor of the car. 'You have to hide, Uma. We can't run the risk of your being seen.' She made Uma lie flat and then ripped the cloth covers off the Packard's back seat. 'I'm going to cover you with these. Lie still and don't say a word.'

Uma put her head down on the floor-mat and closed her eyes. The rickshaw-puller's face appeared in front of her: she saw his head once again, toppling backwards. In that instant when the decapitated body had still been upright, still moving forward, she had caught a glimpse of those white eyes, hanging down over his spine: their gaze had appeared to be directed into the car, right at her. Uma felt her gorge rise and then vomit came pouring of her mouth and her nose, fouling the floor-mat.

'Dolly.' Just as she was beginning to raise her head, Dolly gave her a sharp nudge. The car came to a sudden stop and she froze, with her face inches from the vomit-covered mat. Somewhere above Dolly was talking to someone – a group of men – she was explaining something in Burmese. The conversation took just a minute or two, but an eternity seemed to pass before the car moved on again.

The riots lasted several days and the casualties numbered in the hundreds. The toll would have been higher still, if it had not been for the many Burmese who had rescued Indians from the mob and sheltered them in their homes. It was discovered later that the trouble had started with a clash between Indian and Burmese workers at the docks. Many Indian- and Chinese-owned businesses were attacked, among them one of Rajkumar's timberyards. Three of his workers were killed and dozens were injured.

Rajkumar was at home when the trouble broke out. Neither he nor anyone else in the family suffered any personal injury. Neel happened to be safely out of town when the riots started, and Dinu was taken home from school by his friend, Maung Thiha Saw.

Despite his losses Rajkumar was now more adamant than ever about remaining in Burma: 'I've lived here all my life; everything I have is here. I'm not such a coward as to give up everything I've worked for at the first sign of trouble. And anyway, what makes you think that we'll be any more welcome in India than we are here? There are riots in India all the time – how do you know that the same thing wouldn't happen to us there?'

Uma saw that Dolly was near collapse and she decided to stay on in Rangoon, to help her cope. A week became a month and then another. Every time she spoke of leaving Dolly asked her to stay on a little longer: 'It's not over yet – I can feel something in the air.'

As the weeks passed, there was a deepening of the sense of unease that had settled on the city. There were more strange events. There was talk of trouble at the Rangoon Lunatic Asylum, where several thousand homeless Indians had been accommodated after the riots. In the city gaol a mutiny erupted among the prisoners and was suppressed at the cost of many lives. There were whispers of an even greater upheaval in the offing.

One day a stranger stopped Dolly on the street: 'Is it true that you worked in the Mandalay palace, in the time of King Thebaw?' When Dolly answered in the affirmative the stranger gave her a smile. 'Prepare yourself: there is soon to be another coronation. A prince has been found who will liberate Burma . . .'

A few days later they learnt that there had indeed been a coronation of sorts, not far from Rangoon: a healer by the name of Saya San had had himself crowned King of Burma, with all the traditional observances. He'd gathered together a motley band of soldiers and told them to avenge the capture of King Thebaw.

These rumours reminded Uma of the events that preceded the outbreak of the Indian uprising of 1857. Then too, well before the firing of the first shot, signs of trouble had appeared on the north Indian plains. Chapatis – those most unremarkable of everyday foods – had begun to circulate from village to village, as though in warning. No one knew where they came from or who had put them in motion – but somehow people had known that a great convulsion was on its way.

Uma's premonition was proved right. The uprising started in the interior of Tharawaddy district, where a forest official and two village headmen were killed; the next day rebels stormed a railway station. A company of Indian troops was sent to hunt down the insurgents. But suddenly the rebels were everywhere: in Insein, Yamthin and Pyapon. They appeared like shadows from the forest, with magical designs painted on their bodies. They fought like men possessed, running bare-chested into gunfire, attacking aeroplanes with catapults and spears. Thousands of rural folk declared their allegiance to the King-in-waiting. The colonial authorities fought back by sending more Indian reinforcements to root out the rebellion. Villages were occupied, hundreds of Burmese were killed and thousands wounded.

For Uma, the uprising and the means of its suppression were the culmination of a month-long nightmare: it was as though she were witnessing the realisation of her worst fears; once again, Indian soldiers were being used to fortify the Empire. Nobody in India seemed to know of these events; no one seemed to care. It seemed imperative that someone should take on the task of letting the people of her country know.

It so happened that KLM, the Dutch airline, had recently started a plane service linking a chain of cities between Batavia and Amsterdam. There were now regular flights between Rangoon's new airstrip at Mingaladon and Calcutta's Dum Dum. The journey from Rangoon to Calcutta took some six hours – a fraction of the sailing time. Uma was by now too distraught to undertake the four-day steamship voyage: Rajkumar bought her a ticket on KLM.

In the Packard, on the way out to the airstrip at Mingaladon, Uma became tearful. 'I can't believe what I've seen here – the same old story, Indians being made to kill for the Empire, fighting people who should be their friends . . .'

She was interrupted by Rajkumar: 'Uma, you're talking nonsense.'

'What do you mean?'

'Uma, have you for one moment stopped to ask yourself what would happen if these soldiers weren't used? You were here during the riots: you saw what happened. What do you think these rebels would do to us – to me, to Dolly, to the boys? Don't you see that it's not just the Empire those soldiers are protecting, it's also Dolly and me?'

The anger that Uma had held contained since Morningside came welling up. 'Rajkumar, you're in no position to offer opinions. It's people like you who're responsible for this tragedy. Did you ever think of the consequences when you were transporting people here? What you and your kind have done is far worse than the worst deeds of the Europeans.'

As a rule Rajkumar never challenged Uma on political matters. But he was on edge too now, and something snapped. 'You have so many opinions, Uma – about things of which you know nothing. For weeks now I've heard you criticising everything you see: the state of Burma, the treatment of women, the condition of India, the atrocities of the Empire. But what have you yourself ever done that qualifies you to hold these opinions? Have you ever built anything? Given a single person a job? Improved anyone's life in any way? No. All you ever do is stand back, as though you were above all of us, and you criticise and criticise. Your husband was as fine a man as any I've ever met, and you hounded him to his death with your self-righteousness –'

'How dare you?' Uma cried. 'How dare you speak to me like that? You – an animal, with your greed, your determination to take whatever your can – at whatever cost. Do you think nobody knows about the things you've done to people in your power – to women and children who couldn't defend themselves? You're no better than a slaver and a rapist, Rajkumar. You may think that you will never have to answer for the things you've done, but you're wrong.'

Without a further word to Uma, Rajkumar leant over to U Ba Kyaw and told him to stop the car. Then he stepped out on the road and said to Dolly: 'I'll find my own way back to the city. You see her off. I don't want anything to do with her.'

At Mingaladon, Uma and Dolly found the plane waiting on the airstrip. It was a trimotor Fokker F-VIII, with a silver fuselage and wings that were held up by struts. Once they were out of the car, Dolly said in hushed voice: 'Uma, you're very angry with Rajkumar and I suspect I know why. But you should not judge him too harshly, you know; you must remember that I too bear some of the guilt . . .'

They were at the gates; Uma held Dolly fast.

'Dolly, will this change everything – for us, you and me?'

'No. Of course not. I'll come to see you in Calcutta, whenever I can. It'll be all right – you'll see?'

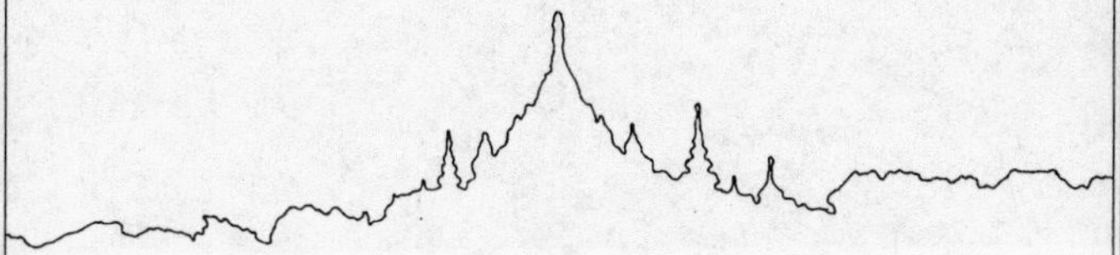

PART FOUR

The Wedding

Twenty

At the other end of the Bay of Bengal, in Calcutta, Uma's brother and his family were waiting to receive her at the Dum Dum airstrip.

Her brother was a quiet and somewhat colourless man who worked in the accounts department of a shipping company. His wife was a severe asthmatic who rarely left the house. Of their children, Bela, a girl, was the youngest, at six. Her siblings were twins and they were a full seven years older. The older twin was a boy, Arjun; the younger was a girl and she went by her family nickname, Manju. Her given name – marvellous to recount – was 'Brihannala', which proved obdurately resistant to everyday use.

For the twins, Uma's arrival in Calcutta was an event of unparalleled significance. This was not just because of who she was: it was at least partly because no one in the family had ever had occasion to go to Dum Dum before. It was just ten years since an aeroplane was first seen in Calcutta: in 1920, a Handley Page had been received at the racecourse by cheering crowds. Since then, planes belonging to Imperial Airways and Air France had also touched down in the city. But it was KLM that had started the first regular passenger service and the drama of its recently instituted comings and goings had held the city in thrall for months.

On the day of Uma's arrival the excitement in the house was such that the family went to the unprecedented step of hiring a car, a new 1930 Austin Chummy. But the twins' expectations were dashed on their arrival at the Dum Dum airstrip: there was nothing there but a stretch of tarmac, bordered by rice fields and coconut palms. This was too new a means of travel to have developed the trappings of ceremony. There was none of the pomp that accompanied an expedition to the docks: no uniformed sailors or peaked caps or beribboned harbourmasters. The terminal was a tin-roofed shed and the personnel consisted of foul-mouthed mechanics in grease-blackened overalls. What there was of a sense of occasion derived from the presence of the crowd of supporters who'd come to welcome Uma.

The waiting area consisted of a small, unroofed pen, fenced in with wire. The family, thoroughly intimidated, found itself pushed further and further back by Uma's exuberant well-wishers. They heard the Fokker F-VIII while it was still hidden by clouds. Arjun was the first to spot it when it broke through, its squat silver body glinting between its double wings. Its silver fuselage wobbled above the palm trees as it came in to land.

There was a long wait in the sun before Uma was cleared. When the people ahead began to cheer they knew Uma was through. And then, suddenly, there she was, in person, very simply dressed, in a white cotton sari.

To the twins Uma was a creature of legend: the firebrand aunt who had dedicated herself to a life of politics instead of accepting the usual lot of the Hindu widow. On finding themselves in her presence they were awed into silence: it seemed incredible that their heroine should be a frail-looking woman, with greying hair and a haggard face.

On the way back to Lankasuka, they sat crowded together in the Austin, exchanging news, catching up. Then Uma did something that took her relatives completely by surprise: unaccountably, for no reason that they could understand, she began to cry. They stared in horror as she sobbed into her sari. Intimidated by her legend, they could not bring themselves to reach out to her. They sat in silence, fidgeting, no one daring to say a word.

When the ride was almost over, Uma collected herself. 'I don't know what came over me,' she said, addressing no one in particular. 'These last few months have been very hard. I feel as if I'm waking from a terrible dream. In Rangoon, just before I left there was a terrible quarrel. I must try to forget some of these things . . .'

* * *

It was a while before the family saw anything of Uma again. In the following months, she devoted all her energies to bringing the Burmese rebellion to the knowledge of the Indian public. She sent articles to Calcutta's *Modern Review* and wrote letters to major newspapers; she made every effort to alert her compatriots to the part that Indian soldiers were being made to play in the suppression of the uprising. Her writings had no perceptible effect. The Indian public was consumed with the preoccupations of local politics and had little time to spare for Burma.

One day, opening a Bengali newspaper, she saw a grisly illustration of sixteen decapitated heads lined up on a table. The accompanying article said: *These are the heads of Burmese rebels who fell in an encounter with Imperial troops in Prome District in Burma. It was believed that they were displayed at the military headquarters at Prome for the purpose of striking terror into the hearts of those who might be rebelliously inclined.*

Uma tore the article out with shaking hands. She took it to her desk, intending to put it in the file where she kept her clippings. As she was putting it away, her eyes fell on the folder that held the remains of her KLM ticket: it had been lying forgotten on a corner of her desk ever since her arrival.

Looking at it now, she thought of the city she had flown out of in the silver Fokker; she thought of the businessmen – the timber merchants and oilmen – who were her fellow-passengers; she thought of how they had all congratulated themselves on being present at the dawn of a new era, an age when aviation would make the world so small that the divisions of the past would disappear. She too had joined in: looking down from above, on the foaming waves of the Bay of Bengal, it seemed impossible not to believe that the shrunken world that had built this aircraft was a better one than those that preceded it.

And now, a few months later, here was this picture – of sixteen severed heads, put on display by the ruling power – as starkly medieval an image as could be imagined. She recalled that Prome was the site of the Shwesandaw Pagoda, almost equal in veneration to Rangoon's Shwe Dagon: she remembered a story that one of her fellow-passengers, a big, swarthy oilman, had told her. On the day of the earthquake he'd been sitting in the English Club at Prome, right beside the Shwe Sandaw Pagoda. Right before his eyes, the pagoda had been rent by the movement of the earth. A great part of it had come crashing down in the grounds of the club.

Uma's eyes filled with remembered images: of the terrible sight she'd witnessed, framed in the windscreen of Dolly's Packard; of Rajkumar and his chain of betrayals; of the quarrel in the car on the way to the airport; and now of the deaths of those sixteen rebels and their gruesome decapitation.

That day marked the beginning of a change in Uma that was no less profound than the upheaval that had followed upon the death of the Collector. With the defeat of Burma's Saya San rebellion, she started to rethink her political ideas in their entirety. It was precisely on an uprising such as this that she and her political associates in the Ghadar Party had once pinned their hopes. But she saw now that a popular insurrection, inspired by legend and myth, stood no chance of prevailing against a force such as the Empire – so skilful and ruthless in its deployment of its overwhelming power; so expert in the management of opinion. In retrospect it became clear that disarmed, technologically backward populations such as those of India and Burma could not hope to defeat by force a well-organised and thoroughly modern military power; that even if such an effort were to succeed it would be at the cost of unimaginable bloodshed – a Saya San rebellion magnified many hundreds of times – that it would pit Indians against one another in such a way as to make victory just as undesirable as defeat.

In the past, she had been dismissive of Mahatma Gandhi's political thinking: non-violence, she had thought, was a philosophy of wish-fulfilment. She saw now that the Mahatma had been decades ahead of her in his thinking. It was rather the romantic ideas of rebellion that she had nurtured in New York that were pipe dreams. She remembered the words of the Mahatma, which she had often read and always disregarded: that the movement against colonialism was an uprising of unarmed Indians against those who bore arms – both Indians and British – and that its chosen instruments were the weapons of the weaponless, its very weakness its source of strength.

Once she had made up her mind, she was quick to act. She wrote to the Mahatma offering her services, and he, in return, invited her to his ashram at Wardha.

Twenty-one

Even when they were very young, Uma's nephew and older niece, the twins, were celebrated for their good looks. Manju and Arjun shared a feature that gave them an unusual charm: a dimple that appeared when they smiled, but only on one cheek, the left for Manju and the right for Arjun. When they were together it was as though a circuit had been completed, a symmetry restored.

The attention that her looks brought her made Manju self-conscious about her appearance from an early age. She grew up with a keen awareness of the impression she made on people. In this one regard Arjun was her opposite: he was easy-going to the point of slovenliness and liked nothing better than to lounge around the house in a threadbare vest, with a longyi knotted around his waist.

Arjun was the kind of boy of whom teachers complain that their performance is incorrigibly below their potential. Everybody knew that he had the intelligence and ability to do well in school but his interests appeared to be directed only towards ogling girls and reading novels. At mealtimes, long after everyone else was done, he would linger lazily over his plate, chewing on fish bones and sucking the last bits of dal-sodden rice from his fingers. As he grew older, Arjun became a cause of increasing concern to everyone in the family. People began to shake their heads, saying, 'Is that boy ever going to make anything of himself?'

Then one hot April day, Lankasuka's afternoon torpor was shattered by the sound of Arjun's voice uttering wild whoops and cries. Everyone in the house went running to the back balcony to look down into the courtyard.

'Arjun, what do you think you're doing?' his mother said.

'I've got in! I've got in!' Arjun was dancing around the courtyard, dressed in his usual dirty vest and torn longyi, waving a letter in one hand.

'Got into what?'

'The Indian Military Academy in Dehra Dun.'

'Idiot boy. What are you talking about?'

'Yes; it's true.' Arjun came running up the stairs, his face flushed, his hair falling over his eyes. 'They've accepted me as an officer cadet.'

'But how could this happen? How did they even know who you are?'

'I sat for an examination, Ma. I went with –' he named a school-friend – 'and I didn't tell you because I didn't think I'd get in.'

'But it's impossible.'

'Look.'

They passed the letter from hand to hand, marvelling at the fine stiff notepaper and the embossed emblem in the top right-hand corner. They could not have been more astonished if he'd announced that he'd sprouted wings or grown a tail. In Calcutta at that time, to join the army was almost unheard of. For generations, recruitment into the British Indian army had been ruled by racial policies that excluded most men in the country, including those from Bengal. Nor was it possible, until quite recently, for Indians to enter the army as commissioned officers. The founding of the Indian Military Academy in Dehra Dun dated back only five years and the fact that some of its seats were open to public examination had gone largely unnoticed.

'How could you do this, Arjun? And without saying anything to us?'

'I'm telling you, I never thought I'd get in. Besides, everyone's always saying that I'll never amount to anything – so I thought all right, let's see.'

'You wait till your father gets home.'

But Arjun's father was not at all displeased by the news: on the contrary, he was so glad that he immediately organised an expedition of thanksgiving to the temple at Kalighat.

'The boy's settled now and there's nothing more for us to worry about . . .' Relief was plainly visible on his face. 'This is a ready-made career: whether he does well or not he'll be pushed up the ladder. At the end, there'll be an excellent pension. So long as he makes it through the academy, he's taken care of for the rest of his life.'

'But he's just a boy, and what if he gets injured? Or worse still?'

'Nonsense. The chances are very slight. It's just a job like any other. Besides, think of the status, the prestige . . .'

Uma's response came as even more of a surprise. Since the time when she'd visited Mahatma Gandhi, at his ashram in Wardha, she had changed her political affiliations. She had joined the Congress Party and had started working with the women's wing. Arjun had expected that she would try to argue him out of signing up. But what she said instead was: 'The Mahatma thinks that the country can only benefit from having men of conscience in the army. India needs soldiers who won't blindly obey their superiors . . .'

Manju's career took a very different turn from her twin's. At the age of twenty-one she came to the attention of a prominent film personality – a director whose niece happened to be her classmate in college. A man of formidable reputation, the director was then engaged in a very public search for a lead actress. The story of his hunt had caused huge excitement in Calcutta.

Manju was spotted, unbeknownst to herself, while at college: the first she knew of it was when she was handed an invitation to a screen test. Manju's instinct was to refuse: she knew herself to be shy and self-conscious and it was hard for her to imagine that she could ever enjoy acting. But when she returned to Lankasuka that afternoon, she found that the invitation was not quite so easily disposed of as she had imagined. She began to have doubts.

Manju's bedroom had a large window: it was usually while sitting on the sill that she and Arjun had talked in the past. She'd never before had to decide on anything entirely on her own; she had always had Arjun to confer with. But Arjun was now many hundreds of miles away, at his battalion headquarters in Saharanpur, in northern India.

She sat on the sill alone, braiding and unbraiding her hair and watching the afternoon's bathers splashing in the nearby lake. Presently she rose and went to fetch the Huntley and Palmer's biscuit tin in which she kept Arjun's letters. The earliest ones dated back to his days as a 'gentleman-cadet' and the notepaper was embossed with the emblem of the Indian Military Academy The pages crackled between her fingers. How well he wrote – in proper sentences and paragraphs. When they were together they always spoke Bengali, but the letters were in English – an unfamiliar, idiomatic English, with words of slang that she didn't recognise and couldn't find in the dictionary. He'd gone to a restaurant 'in town' with another cadet, Hardayal Singh – known as 'Hardy' to his friends – and they'd eaten 'lashings' of sandwiches and drunk 'oodles' of beer.

His latest letter had arrived just a few days ago. The notepaper was different now and it bore the insignia of his new regiment, the 1st Jat Light Infantry.

> It's quiet here, because we're at our home station in Saharanpur. You probably think we spend all our time marching about in the sun. But it's nothing like that. The only difficult thing is getting up early to go to the parade ground for P.T. with the men. After that it's pretty quiet; we stroll around taking salutes and watching the NCOs as they put the men through their drills and their weapons training. But this takes only a couple of hours, and then we change for breakfast, which is at nine (stacks of eggs, bacon and ham). Then some of us go off to wait in the orderly room just in case any of the men are brought in. Once in a while the signals officers take us through the latest field codes, or else we get lessons in map-reading or double-entry book-keeping – that kind of thing. Then there's lunch – and beer and gin if you want it (but no whisky!) – and after that you're free to go off to your room. Later there's

usually time for a game of football with the men. At about 7.30 we drift off towards the mess lawn for a few whiskies before dinner. We call the mess the Nursery, as a joke, because potted plants die the moment they're brought in – no one knows why. Some of the chaps say it's because of the Dust of Colonels Past. We laugh about the Nursery but I tell you, sometimes halfway through dinner, or when we're drinking a toast, I look around and even now, after all these months here, I just can't believe my luck . . .

The last time Manju had had a long talk with Arjun was on this very windowsill. It was a little more than a year ago, just after he graduated from the academy. She'd kept wanting to call him Second Lieutenant Arjun – partly to tease him, but also because she'd liked the sound of the words. She'd been disappointed that he didn't wear his uniform more but he'd laughed at her when she told him this.

'Why can't you show me off to your friends as I am?'

The truth was that most of her friends at college were in love with him already. They'd badger her for news of him, and when they were over at the house they'd go to amazing lengths to ingratiate themselves with the family – hoping, of course, that someone would remember them when it came time to find a bride for Arjun.

Before he left for the academy, she'd never quite understood why her friends thought him so good-looking: to her he was just Arjun, his face a brother's. Then he came back for that visit and it was as though she were seeing him for the first time. She'd had to admit that he'd made quite an impression, with his moustache coming along nicely and his hair cut short. She'd been jealous, afraid that he wouldn't want to spend time with her. But he'd been quick to put her fears at rest. He'd sat on the sill every day, dressed in his usual vest and scruffy old longyi. They'd chatted for hours and she'd peeled him oranges or mangoes or lychees – he was just as hungry as he'd ever been.

He'd talked endlessly about the 1st Jat Light Infantry. He'd applied to half a dozen other regiments but right from the start there was only one that he really wanted – and that was the 1st Jats. Part of the reason was that his friend Hardy had applied to the 1st Jats too, and was almost certain to get in. He came from an old army family and his father and grandfather had both served in the regiment. But, of course, it was different for Arjun – he had no army connections – and he had prepared himself for a disappointment. As a result he was overjoyed when he heard that the regiment had accepted him:

> The night when I was formally dined into the regiment was probably the happiest of my life. Even as I'm writing this, I realize that this will probably seem strange to you, Manju. But the thing of it is that it's true: you have to remember that the regiment is going to be my home for the next fifteen to twenty years – perhaps even more, if things don't go too well with my career and I never get a staff appointment (God forbid!).
>
> What I'm really chuffed about, though, is my battalion. This'll probably surprise you, for civilians always think that the regiment is the most important thing about the army. But actually, in the Indian army, a regiment is just a collection of symbols – colours, flags, and so on. We're proud of our regiments of course, but they're not operational units and just about the only time when all the battalions of a regiment get together is when there's a Changing of the Colours – and it takes donkey's years for that to happen.
>
> The rest of the time you live and work with your battalion and that's what really matters: your life can be hell if you find yourself thrown in with the wrong sort of crowd. But once again I've been hellishly lucky – Hardy pulled a couple of his '*fauji*' strings and made sure we were both in the same battalion – the First. Officially, we're the 1/1 Jat Light Infantry, but everyone just calls us the 1/1 Jats – except that every now and again you'll come across some ancient Colonel Walrus who'll still use our old name, which was 'the Royal'. The story is that the battalion fought so well in the

Mahratta Wars that when Lord Lake reached the coast, he honoured us with a special title: *The Royal Battalion*.

Yesterday Hardy and I were looking at the battalion's battle honours, and I swear to you, Manju, the list was as long as my arm. During the Mutiny our troops stayed loyal – one of our companies was in the column that captured the old Emperor, Bahadur Shah Zafar, at his hidy-hole at Humayun's tomb. I noticed something that I bet would interest Dinu and Neel – the Royal was in Burma during General Prendergast's advance on Mandalay and it fought so well that it came to be known as *'Jarnail-sahib ki dyni haat ki paltan'* – the general's right-hand battalion.

To tell you the truth, Manju, it's just a little overwhelming even to think of all this. You should see the list of our medals: a Victoria Cross from the Somme; two Military Crosses for putting down the Arab rebellion in Mesopotamia in '18; a half-dozen DSOs and OBEs from when we fought the Boxer rebels in China. Sometimes when I wake up in the morning, I still find it hard to believe that I really belong with these men. It makes one so proud, but also humble, to think that one has all this to live up to. What makes me prouder still is the thought that Hardy and I are going to be the first Indian officers in the 1/1 Jats: it seems like such a huge responsibility – as though we're representing the whole of the country!

To top it all, we have an absolutely spiffing CO – Lieutenant-Colonel Buckland – whom everybody calls Bucky. To look at you'd think he's not a soldier at all, more like a professor. He came to lecture at the academy a couple of times: he was so good that he even managed to make Military History interesting. He's also an operations wizard and the men love him. His family's been with the 1/1 Jats since the time when we were called the Royal Battalion, and I don't think there's a man on the base whose name he doesn't know. And it's not just their names either – he knows which village they're from and who's married to whose daughter and how much dowry they paid. Of course, I'm so junior I can't be sure he even knows I exist.

It's Guest Night at the Nursery tonight, so I'd better go. My new batman is busy ironing my cummerbund, and I can tell from the way he's looking at me that it's time to get into my dinner jacket. His name is Kishan Singh and I just got him a few weeks ago. He's a weedy, earnest-looking fellow and at first I didn't think he'd do, but he's turned out quite well. Do you remember that book Uma-pishi sent me – the O. Henry stories? You'll never believe it, but I'd left it by my bed and one night I walked in and found him with his nose stuck in it. He had a puzzled frown on his face, like a bear clawing at a wireless set. He was scared half out of his mind at being found looking into my book – just stood there like a statue. So I told him the story about the lost necklace. You should have seen him, standing there as though he were at a court-martial, staring at the wall, while I went through the pages, translating into Hindustani. At the end of it, I barked at him, in my best parade-ground voice: 'Kishan Singh! What do you think of this *kahani*?'

And he said: 'Sahib, it's a very sad story . . .' I could have sworn there were tears in his eyes. They're very sentimental, these faujis, despite their moustaches and bloodshot eyes. It's true what the Britishers say: at heart they're very unspoilt; the salt of the earth – you can depend on them to be faithful. Just the kind of men you'd want by your side in a tight spot.

It was Arjun's letter that made Manju reconsider the idea of a screen test. There was her twin, hundreds of miles away, drinking whisky, eating at the officers' mess and getting his batman to iron his dinner jacket. And here she was in Calcutta, in the same room she'd been in all her life, braiding her hair into pigtails as she'd done since she was seven. The awful thing was that he hadn't even made a pretence of missing home.

She was on her own now, and she would have to think about what she was going to do with herself. So far as her mother was concerned, Manju knew, her future had already been decided: she would leave the house as someone's wife and not a day sooner. The mothers of two prospective grooms had already come calling to 'see' Manju. One of them had given her hair a discreet tug to make sure she wasn't wearing a wig; the other had made her bare her teeth as though she were a horse, pushing apart her lips with her fingers, and making faint clucking sounds. Her mother had been apologetic afterwards, but she'd made it clear that it wasn't in her power to ensure that these incidents would not be repeated: this was a part of the process. Manju knew that many more such ordeals probably lay ahead.

Manju looked again at the director's invitation. The studio was in Tollygunge, at the end of the number 4 tram line, which she took to college every day. All she'd have to do was head in the other direction. It wouldn't take long to get there. She decided to go – just to see what it was like.

But now a host of practical problems came suddenly to the surface. What was she to wear, for instance? Her 'good' Benarasi silk, the sari she wore to weddings, was locked in her mother's *almirah*. If she were to ask for it her mother would wring the truth out of her in a matter of minutes and that would be the end of the screen test. Besides, what would people say if she stepped out of the house bedecked in a crimson and gold Benarasi at eleven in the morning? Even if she succeeded in slipping past her mother, the whole neighbourhood would be in an uproar before she got to the end of the street.

She decided that the director wouldn't have gone looking for a college girl if he wanted a fancily dressed-up actress. She settled upon the best of her white cottons, the one with small green checks. But as soon as this was resolved, a dozen new dilemmas seemed to follow. What about make-up? Powder? Lipstick? Perfume?

The morning came and predictably everything went wrong. The sari she'd decided on wasn't back from the dhobi's; she had to choose another one, much older, with a sewn-over tear in the *anchal.* Her hair wouldn't stay in place, and no matter how hard she tucked in her sari, the hem kept creeping down and tripping her. On her way out, she stepped into the puja room to say a prayer – not because she so badly wanted to be chosen, but just so that she would be able to get through the next few hours without making a fool of herself.

Sure enough, her mother spotted her coming out of the puja room. 'Manju, is that you? What were you doing in the puja room? Are you in some kind of trouble?' She peered suspiciously into Manju's face: 'And why've you got powder all over you? Is that any way to dress when you're going to college?'

Manju slipped away under the pretence of going to the bathroom to wipe her face. She walked quickly down the road to the tram stop. Keeping her face down, she looped her sari over her head, hoping that the neighbours wouldn't notice that she was waiting for the wrong tram. Just when she thought she'd managed to get by without drawing attention to herself, old Nidhu-babu came running out of the Lake Road Pharmacy.

'Is that really you, Manju-*didmoni*?' He hitched up his dhoti and bent double so that he could look up into her sari-shrouded face. 'But why are you waiting on the wrong side of the street? This way you'll end up in Tollygunge.'

Quelling her panic, she managed to invent a story about going to visit an aunt.

'Oh?' said the pharmacist, scratching his head. 'But then, you must come and wait in the shop. You shouldn't be standing out in the sun.'

'I'm all right, really,' she pleaded. 'Don't worry about me. I'll be all right. You should go back to your shop.'

'As you say.' He wandered off, scratching his head, but minutes later, he was back again, with an assistant who was carrying a chair. 'If you must wait here,' the old pharmacist said, 'at least you should sit down.' His assistant placed the chair at the tram stop and wiped it clean with a flourish.

It seemed easier to give in than to resist. Manju allowed herself to be enthroned on the chair, right beside the dusty tram stop. But within minutes, her worst fears were realised: a crowd gathered round to stare at her.

'The Roys' daughter,' she heard the pharmacist explaining to the crowd. 'Lives down the road – in that house over there. Going to visit her aunt in Tollygunge. Skipping college.'

Then, to her relief, the tram finally arrived. The pharmacist and his assistant held the others back so that Manju could be the first to step in. 'I'll send a note to your mother,' the old man shouted after her, 'to let her know that you got off safely to Tollygunge.'

'No,' pleaded Manju, wringing her hands and leaning out of the window. 'There's really no need . . .'

'What's that?' The pharmacist raised a hand to his ear. 'Yes, I said I'll send someone to your mother with a note. No, it's no trouble, none at all . . .'

Already shaken by this inauspicious start, Manju was even more put out when she arrived at the studio. She had expected something glamorous – like the Grand Hotel or the Metro Cinema, or the restaurants on Park Street, with their bright lights and red awnings. But instead she found herself walking into a building that looked like a warehouse or a factory, a big shed, with a roof of tin. Carpenters and *mistries* were hard at work inside, hoisting canvas backdrops and erecting bamboo scaffolding.

A chowkidar led her to a make-up room, a small, windowless cabin, with wooden walls made from sawn-up tea chests. Two women were lounging inside, sprawled in tilted chairs, chewing paan, their gauzy saris shining in the brightly lit mirrors behind them. Their eyes narrowed as they looked Manju over, their jaws moving in perfect unison.

'Why's this one dressed like a nurse?' one of them muttered to the other.

'Maybe she thinks she's going into hospital.'

There were cackles of laughter and then a sari was thrust into Manju's hands, a length of deep purple chiffon with a bright pink border.

'Go on. Get changed.'

'Why this?' Manju ventured in protest.

'Suits your colour,' snapped one of the women, cryptically. 'Put it on.'

Manju glanced around the room, looking for a place to change. There was none.

'What are you waiting for?' the women scolded. 'Be quick. The director's got an important guest coming today. Can't be kept waiting.'

In all her adult life Manju had never undressed in front of anyone, not even her mother. When it dawned on her that she would have to strip under the appraising scrutiny of these two paan-chewing women, her legs went numb. The courage that had brought her thus far began to seep away.

'Go on,' the women hurried her. 'The director's bringing a businessman who's going to put up money for the film. He can't be kept waiting. Everything's got to be tip-top today.' One of them snatched the sari out of Manju's hands and set about changing her clothes. Somewhere nearby a car drew up. This was followed by a patter of welcoming voices. 'The guest's arrived,' someone shouted through the door. 'Quick, quick, the director will want her any minute now.'

The two women ran to the door to peek at the newly-arrived personage.

'Doesn't he look important, with that beard and all?'

'And look at his suit – all dressed up like that . . .'

The women came back giggling and thrust Manju into a chair. 'Just one look and you can tell how rich he is . . .'

'Oh, if he'd only marry me . . .'

'You? Why not me?'

Manju stared into the mirror in an uncomprehending daze. The faces of the two women seemed monstrously large, their smirking lips grotesque in their size and shape. A sharp fingernail scraped her scalp, and she cried out in protest: 'What are you doing?'

'Just checking for lice.'

'For lice?' Manju cried in outrage. 'I don't have lice.'

'The last one did. And not just on her head.' This was followed by peals of laughter.

'How do you know?' Manju challenged them.

'The sari was crawling after she'd worn it.'

'The sari!' With a shriek Manju leapt out of the chair, clawing at the sari they'd given her, trying to tear it off.

The two women were helpless with laughter. 'Just a joke.' They were almost choking on their giggles. 'It was a different sari. Not this one.'

Manju began to sob. 'I want to go home,' she said. 'Please let me go. Don't send me out in front of them.'

'Everyone who comes here says that,' the women reassured her. 'Then they stay for ever.'

They took hold of her arms and led her out on to the brilliantly lit studio floor. Manju was now completely distraught, her nerves frayed and on edge. To keep herself from crying, she kept her gaze fixed on the floor, with her sari slung over her head. Presently a pair of polished black shoes edged into her circle of vision. She heard herself being introduced to the director. She put her hands together and whispered a *nomoshkar* without looking up. Then she saw a second pair of shoes approaching her, across the floor.

'And this here is my good friend,' the director's voice intoned. 'Mr Neeladhri Raha of Rangoon . . .'

She looked up. If she hadn't heard the name she would not have known who it was. She'd met both Neel and Dinu many years ago. They were visiting with their mother, staying downstairs, in her aunt Uma's flat. But he looked completely different now, with his trimmed black beard and his suit.

'Neel?'

He was staring at her, his mouth agape, his tongue locked above an unuttered exclamation. It was not that he had recognised her: the reason he was unable to speak was because she was, without a doubt, the most beautiful woman he'd ever spoken to.

'Neel, is that you?' said Manju. 'Don't you remember me? I'm Manju – Uma Dey's niece.'

He nodded, in slow disbelief, as though he'd forgotten the sound of his own name.

She flew at him and threw her arms round his chest.

'Oh, Neel,' she said, wiping her eyes on his jacket. 'Take me home.'

The dressing room was a different place when Manju went back to reclaim her own clothes. The two make-up women were now almost worshipful in their attentiveness.

'So you know him then?'

'But why didn't you tell us?'

Manju wasted no time on explanations. She changed quickly and went hurrying to the door. Neel was outside, waiting beside the passenger-side door of a new 1938 Delage D8 Drophead. He opened the door for her and she stepped in. The car smelt of chrome and new leather. 'What a beautiful car,' she said. 'Is it yours?'

'No.' He laughed. 'The dealer offered to let me borrow it for a few days. I couldn't resist.'

Their eyes met for a moment and they both looked quickly away.

'Where would you like to go?' he said. He turned the ignition key and the Delage responded with a purr.

'Let's see . . .' Now that she was seated in the car, she no longer felt quite so pressed to get home.

He started to say something: 'Well . . .'

She could tell that they were both thinking along similar lines. 'Perhaps . . .' A sentence that had begun promisingly in her head died unfinished on her tongue.

'I see.'

'Yes.'

Somehow this terse exchange succeeded in conveying everything they wanted to communicate. Neel started the car and they drove out of the studio. They both knew that they were going nowhere in particular, just enjoying the sensory pleasure of sitting in a moving car.

'I was so surprised to see you in that studio,' Neel said with a laugh. 'Do you really want to be an actress?'

Manju felt herself changing colour. 'No,' she said. 'I just wanted to see what it was like. Things are so dull at home . . .'

Having said this much, she couldn't stop. She found herself telling him things she hadn't told anyone else: how much she missed Arjun; how his letters from the Military Academy had filled her with despair about her own future; about what a curse it was for a woman to live vicariously through a male twin. She even told him about the matches her mother had tried to arrange for her; about the mothers of the prospective grooms and how they had tugged her hair and inspected her teeth.

He didn't say much but she understood that his silence was

caused principally by a habitual lack of words. His face was hard to read behind the heavy black beard but she had a feeling that he was listening sympathetically, taking everything in.

'And what about you?' she said at last. 'Are you really a big film producer?'

'No!' The word burst out of his mouth with the force of an expletive. 'No. It wasn't my idea at all. It was Apé – my father – who suggested it . . .'

What he really wanted, he said, was to work in the timber trade. He'd asked to be allowed to join the family business – only to be turned down by his father. Rajkumar had suggested that he think of other lines of work: the timber business wasn't for everyone, he'd said, especially a city-bred boy like Neel. When Neel persisted, he'd given him a sum of money and told him that he should come back after he'd doubled his capital. But how? Neel had asked. Rajkumar's response was: Go and put it in films – anything. Neel had taken him at his word. He'd looked around for a film to invest in and hadn't been able to find one in Rangoon. He had decided to travel to India instead.

'How long have you been here then?' Manju said. 'And why didn't you come to see us? You could have stayed with Uma-pishi, downstairs.'

Neel scratched awkwardly at his beard. 'Yes,' he said, 'but you know, the trouble is . . .'

'What?'

'My father doesn't get along with your aunt.'

'That doesn't matter,' Manju said. 'Your mother often comes. I'm sure your father wouldn't mind if you did too.'

'Maybe not – but I wouldn't want to anyway.'

'Why not?'

'Well,' Neel scratched his beard again. 'It wouldn't be right . . .'

'What wouldn't be right?'

'I don't know if I can explain.' He gave her a bemused glance and she saw that he was struggling to find words for a thought that he'd never articulated before, even to himself.

'Go on.'

'You see,' he said, almost apologetically, 'it's just that I'm the only one who's on his side.'

Manju was startled. 'What do you mean?'

'That's just how I feel,' Neel said. 'That I'm the only one on his side. Take my brother Dinu, for example – I sometimes think he really hates Apé.'

'Why?'

'Maybe – because they're opposites.'

'And you're alike?'

'Yes,' he said. 'At least, that's what I would like to think.'

He turned his eyes away from the road to grin at her.

'I don't know why I'm telling you all this,' he said. 'I feel like an idiot.'

'You're not – I know what you're trying to say . . .'

They went on driving, more or less at random, down one street and another, backing out of blind alleys, and making U-turns on the wider avenues. It was almost dark by the time he dropped her off. They agreed that it would be better if he didn't come in.

They met again the next day and the day after that. He extended his stay and after a month had gone by he sent a telegram to Burma.

One day Dolly presented herself at Uma's office door.

'Dolly? You here?'

'Yes. And you'll never believe why . . .'

Twenty-two

The wedding was like a force of nature, changing everything it touched. In a matter of days Lankasuka was transformed into a huge, noisy fairground. Up on the roof a team of *pandal*-makers was at work, erecting an immense awning of coloured cloth and bamboo. In the tree-shaded yard at the back, a small army of hired cooks had pitched tents and dug pits for cooking fires. It was as though a carnival had moved in.

Bela was the youngest in the house: at fifteen, she was a thin, gawky girl, blossoming into a late and awkward adolescence. She was alternately apprehensive and exhilarated, unsure of whether to throw herself into the festivities or to hide in her bed.

As the wedding approached a whirlwind of telegrams – until then so rare and so dreaded – blew through Lankasuka, rattling its shuttered doors and windows. Not a day went by without Bela spotting a postman, running up the stairs with a pink envelope. Arjun was to arrive by rail, accompanied by his batman, Kishan Singh. Dolly, Dinu and Rajkumar were flying in two days before, on one of KLM's brand-new DC3s.

The excitement reached its pitch the day the Rangoon party was to arrive. Providentially, the family had just that year decided to buy a car, with the expenses shared equally between Uma and her brother. The car was delivered just as the arrangements were getting under way, a brand new 1939 model, a modest, 8 horse-power Jowett, with a long bonnet and beautiful oval grille. In addition to this, the wedding party also had the use of the Delage Drophead, which Neel had once again succeeded in borrowing from the dealer.

They arrived at Dum Dum airport to find it completely changed since the time of Uma's return to India. The old airstrip was now a fully-fledged airport, with customs facilities of its own. A hundred and fifty acres of land had been cleared and three new runways built. There was a fine three-storeyed administration building with a glass-paned control tower and radio room. The visitors' area had changed too: they found themselves entering a large, brightly lit gallery with fans whirring energetically overhead. At one end of the gallery there was a radio tuned in to the news; at the other there was a counter selling tea and snacks.

'Look!' Bela went running to the windows and pointed to a plane that was circling above. They watched the DC3 as it came into land. The first to come out was Dinu. He was wearing a longyi and a loose shirt, and his clothes flapped against his lean, compact frame as he stood on the tarmac, waiting for his parents.

Dolly and Rajkumar were among the last to emerge. Dolly was wearing a striped green longyi and as always there was a white flower in her hair. Rajkumar was walking very slowly, leaning on Dolly a little. His hair was covered with a thick frosting of white and the lines of his face had sagged into tired, drooping curves.

Rajkumar was now in his mid-sixties. He had recently suffered a minor stroke and had left his bed against his doctor's wishes. His business, wounded by the Depression, was no longer as profitable as it had once been. The teak industry had changed over the last decade, and old-fashioned timbermen like Rajkumar had become anachronisms. Rajkumar was saddled with huge debts and had been forced to sell off many of his properties.

But so far as the arrangements for Neel's wedding were concerned, Rajkumar was determined to put aside his financial difficulties. Everything that everybody else did he wanted to do on a larger and grander scale. Neel was his favourite and he was determined to make his boy's wedding an occasion to compensate for all the missed celebrations of his own life.

* * *

Dinu was a favourite of Bela's: she liked the way he looked, with his thin, bony cheeks and his wide forehead; she liked his seriousness and his manner of listening to people with an attentive frown, as though he were worrying about what they'd said; she even liked the way he talked, in explosive little bursts, as though his thoughts were spurting out of him in jets.

The day they went to Howrah station to get Arjun, Bela made sure that she was sitting next to Dinu. She noticed that he had a leather bag in his lap.

'What have you got in there?' she asked.

He opened the bag and showed her. It was a new camera, a kind she'd never seen before.

'It's a Rolleiflex,' he said. 'A twin-lens reflex . . .' He took it out of the bag and showed her how it worked; it opened like a hinged box, with its hood flipping back so that you had to look down on it from above.

'I've got a tripod for it,' he said. 'You can look through it . . . when I set it up . . .'

'Why're you taking it to the station?' she asked.

He shrugged vaguely. 'I saw some pictures recently,' he said. 'Railyard shots by Alfred Stieglitz . . . they made me wonder . . .'

The camera caused a stir when Dinu set it up at Howrah. The station was crowded and many people gathered round to stare. Dinu adjusted the tripod's height to suit Bela. 'Here, come . . . look.'

The platform was a long one, and it was topped with a steepled roof of corrugated steel. The late afternoon sunlight was filtering in from under the roof's scalloped skirt, creating a stark, back-lit effect. In the foreground there were great numbers of people: red-jacketed porters, hurrying tea-boys, and waiting passengers with mountains of luggage.

Dinu pointed out the details to Bela. 'I think this is even better than the pictures I had in mind,' he said, 'because of all the people . . . and the movement . . .'

Bela looked in again, and suddenly, as if by magic, Arjun appeared in the frame. He was hanging out of a carriage, holding on to the steel bar of the open doorway. He jumped off when he spotted them and the momentum of the still-moving train gave him a running start. He came racing out of the opaque white fog that was pouring from the engine's steaming smoke-stack, laughing as he dodged the vendors and porters who were swarming across the platform. The tunic of his khaki uniform was drawn tight around his waist and his cap was tilted back on his head. He swept down on them with his arms outspread, laughing, and lifted Manju off her feet and swung her round and round.

Bela stepped away from the camera, hoping to conceal herself until the first flush of Arjun's homecoming exuberance was spent. But just then he spotted her. 'Bela!' He swooped down to fling her up, over his head, ignoring her cries of protest. As she flew upwards, with the tumult of the station whirling around her head, her eyes fastened on a soldier who had approached unseen and was standing just a step behind Arjun. He looked younger than Arjun and was smaller in build; she noticed that he was carrying Arjun's luggage.

'Who is that?' she whispered into Arjun's ear.

He threw a glance over his shoulder, to see whom she was looking at. 'That's Kishan Singh,' he said, 'my batman.'

He put her down and went on ahead, with the others, talking excitedly. Bela followed behind, keeping pace with Kishan Singh. She stole a glance: he was nice-looking, she thought; his skin had a sheen like dark velvet, and although his hair was very short she could tell that it was fine and straight; she liked the way it made a pattern along the edges of his forehead. His eyes were fixed ahead of him, as though he were a moving statue.

It was only when they were about to get into the car that she knew without a doubt that he was aware of her presence. His eyes met hers for an instant and there was a fleeting change in his expression, a slight smile. Bela's head reeled: she had never known that a smile could have a physical impact – like a blow from a flying object.

As she was about to step into the car Bela heard Dinu say to Arjun: 'Have you heard? Hitler's signed a pact with Mussolini . . . there could be another war.'

But her brother's answer was lost to her. All the way home, she didn't hear a word that anybody said.

Twenty-three

Although Dinu and Arjun had known each other a long time they had never been friends. Dinu tended to think of Arjun on the analogy of a friendly and bumbling pet – a large dog perhaps, or a well-trained mule – a creature of unfailing, tail-wagging goodwill, but incurably indolent and barely capable of coherent utterance. But Dinu was not so arrogant as to be unwilling to correct himself. At Howrah station, on the day when he photographed Arjun running across the platform, he saw immediately that this was a significantly changed person from the boy he had known. Arjun had lost his somnolence, and his patterns of speech were no longer so garbled and indistinct as they had once been. This itself was an interesting paradox, for Arjun's vocabulary seemed now to consist mainly of jargon intermixed with assorted bits of English and Punjabi slang – everyone was now either a 'chap' or a '*yaar*'.

But on the way home from the station Arjun did something that astonished Dinu. In reminiscing about a tactical exercise, he launched into a description of a feature of topography – a hill. He listed its ridges and outcrops, the exact nature of its vegetation and the cover it afforded, he quoted the angle of the slope's incline and laughed about how his friend Hardy had got it wrong so that his results 'wouldn't play'.

Dinu understood words and images and the bridge of metaphor that linked the two – these were not languages with which he had ever thought to associate Arjun. Yet, by the end of Arjun's description, Dinu felt that he could see the hill, in his head. Of those who listened to Arjun's account, he alone was perhaps fully aware of the extreme difficulty of achieving such minuteness of recall and such vividness of description: he was awed, both by the precision of Arjun's narrative and by the off-handed lack of self-consciousness with which it was presented.

'Arjun,' he said, fixing him with his dour, unblinking stare. 'I'm amazed . . . you described that hill as though you'd remembered every little bit of it.'

'Of course,' said Arjun. 'My CO says that, under fire, you pay with a life for every missed detail.'

This too made Dinu take notice. He'd imagined that he knew the worth of observation, yet he'd never conceived that its value might be weighed in lives. There was something humbling about the thought of this. He'd regarded a soldier's training as being, in the first instance, physical, a matter of the body. It took just that one conversation to show him that he had been wrong. Dinu's friends were mainly writers and intellectuals: he had never met a serviceman in all his life. Now suddenly, in Calcutta, he found himself surrounded by soldiers. Within hours of his arrival, Arjun had filled the house with his friends. It turned out that he knew a couple of officers at the Fort William cantonment in Calcutta. Once he'd made contact, his friends began to turn up at all times of day, in jeeps and occasionally even in trucks, their arrival signalled by booming klaxons and noisy boots.

'This is how it always happens in the army, yaar,' one of them said, by way of apologetic explanation. 'Where one fauji goes, the whole *paltan* follows . . .'

In the past Dinu's attitude towards the army had varied between outright hostility and amused indifference. Now he found himself more puzzled than antagonistic, increasingly interested in the mechanisms that made them tick. He was astonished by the communal nature of their lives; by the pleasure that Arjun, for instance, took in 'mucking in' with the others. This was a way of thinking and working that was the antithesis of everything that Dinu stood for and believed in. He himself was always happiest when he was on his own, His friends were few and even with the best of them there was always a residue of unease, an analytic guardedness. This was one of the reasons why he derived so much pleasure from photography. There was no place more solitary than a dark room, with its murky light and fetid closeness.

Arjun, on the other hand, seemed to find immense satisfaction in working on the details of plans that had been dictated by others – not necessarily people either, but manuals of procedure. Once, speaking of his battalion's move from one cantonment to another, he described their 'entrainment' routines with as much pride as though he had personally guided every soldier into the station. But at the end it emerged that his part had consisted of nothing more than standing at the door of a carriage and filling in a roster. Dinu was astonished to note that it was precisely from this that his satisfaction derived: the slow accumulation of small tasks, a piling up of rosters that culminated in the movement of a platoon and then a battalion.

Arjun was often at pains to explain that in the army, it was a vital necessity for 'the chaps' to possess a thorough and exhaustive understanding of one another; to know exactly how each of them would respond in certain circumstances. Yet, there was a paradox here that did not escape Dinu: when Arjun and his friends spoke of one another, their assessments were so exaggerated that they seemed to be inventing versions of themselves for collective consumption. In the fantastic bestiary of their table-talk, Hardy was the Spit-and-Polish perfectionist, Arjun a Ladies' Man, another a Pukka Sahib and so on. These paper-thin portraits were a part of the collective lore of their camaraderie – a fellowship in which they took immense pride, investing it with metaphors that sometimes extended even beyond mere kinship. Usually they were just 'brothers' but at times they were also much more, even the 'First True Indians'. 'Look at us –' they would say, – 'Punjabis, Marathas, Bengalis, Sikhs, Hindus, Muslims. Where else in India would you come across a group such as ours – where region and religion don't matter – where we can all drink together and eat beef and pork and think nothing of it?'

Every meal at an officers' mess, Arjun said, was an adventure, a glorious infringement of taboos. They ate foods that none of them had ever touched at home: bacon, ham and sausages at breakfast; roast beef and pork chops for dinner. They drank whisky, beer and wine, smoked cigars, cigarettes and cigarillos. Nor was this just a matter of satisfying appetites: every mouthful had a meaning – each represented an advance towards the evolution of a new, more complete kind of Indian. All of them had stories to tell about how their stomachs had turned the first time they had chewed upon a piece of beef or pork; they had struggled to keep the morsels down, fighting their revulsion. Yet they had persisted, for these were small but essential battles and they tested not just their manhood, but also their fitness to enter the class of officers. They had to prove, to themselves as well as to their superiors, that they were eligible to be rulers, to qualify as members of an elite: that they had vision enough to rise above the ties of their soil, to overcome the responses instilled in them by their upbringing.

'Look at us!' Arjun would say, after a whisky or two, 'we're the first modern Indians; the first Indians to be truly free. We eat what we like, we drink what we like, we're the first Indians who're not weighed down by the past.'

To Dinu this was profoundly offensive. 'It's not what you eat and drink that make you modern: it's a way of looking at things . . .' He'd fetch reproductions that he'd cut out of magazines, of photographs by Stieglitz, Cunningham and Weston.

Arjun would shrug these off with a laughing retort: 'To you the modern world is just something you read about. What you know of it you get from books and newspapers. We're the ones who actually live with Westerners . . .'

Dinu understood that it was through their association with Europeans that Arjun and his fellow-officers saw themselves as pioneers. They knew that to most of their compatriots the West was a distant abstraction: even though they might know themselves to be ruled by England, very few Indians had ever actually set eyes on an Englishman and fewer still had had occasion to speak to one. The English lived in their own enclaves and followed their own pursuits: most of the day-to-day tasks of ruling were performed by Indians. In the army, on the other hand, Indian officers were a band of the elect; they lived in a proximity with Westerners that was all but unknown to their compatriots. They shared the same quarters, ate the same food, did the same work: in this their situation was unlike that of any of the Empire's other subjects.

'We understand the West better than any of you civilians,' Arjun liked to say. 'We know how the minds of Westerners work. Only when every Indian is like us will the country become truly modern.'

Meals with Arjun's friends were boisterous events, accompanied by 'lashings' of beer, loud laughter and a great deal of acerbic joke-making, mainly by the officers, at each other's expense. This they described as 'ragging' and most of it was good-natured. But there was an occasion once when the flow of the meal was ruptured by an odd little incident. Seeing a dish of hot, steam-puffed chapatis, one of the officers said, in a loud, derisory 'ragging' voice: 'Hardy should have been here: he's the one who really loves chapatis . . .' These words, apparently innocuous, had a startling effect; the noise died abruptly and the officers' faces turned suddenly grave. The lieutenant who'd spoken changed colour, as though in acknowledgement of a collective rebuke. Then, as if to remind his friends of the presence of outsiders – Dinu, Manju and Neel, in other words – Arjun loudly cleared his throat and the conversation turned instantly to another subject. The interruption lasted no longer than a moment and passed unnoticed by everyone but Dinu.

Later that night, Dinu stopped by Arjun's room and found him sitting in bed, with a book against his knees and a brandy in his hand. Dinu lingered.

'You want to tackle me, don't you?' Arjun said. 'About what happened this evening?'

'Yes.'

'It was nothing really.'

'All the more reason to tell me . . .'

Arjun sighed: 'It was about a good friend of mine, Hardy. Odd to think he wasn't even here.'

'What were they talking about?'

'It's a long story. You see Hardy was in a row last year. It'll sound idiotic to you . . .'

'What happened?'

'Are you sure you want to know?'

'Yes.'

'Hardy's a *sardar*,' Arjun said, 'a Sikh – from a family that's been in the army for generations. You'd be surprised how many of the chaps are from that kind of family. I call them the real faujis. Fellows like me, who have no army connections, are the exception . . .'

Hardy had grown up at the battalion's depot in Saharanpur, Arjun said. His father and grandfather had both served in the 1st Jats. They had joined as private soldiers and worked their way up to the rank of Viceroy's Commissioned Officer – which was the highest an Indian could rise in those days, somewhere between an NCO and an officer. Hardy was the first in his family to join the army as a commissioned officer, and he'd set his heart on getting into the 1/1 Jats. He used to joke that his dream was to be called 'Sahib' by his father's old colleagues.

But between the lives of officers and the other ranks there was a difference that Hardy had not reckoned with. The other ranks were served Indian food in their messes, prepared according to the precise dietary prescriptions of their various religions. The officers' mess, on the other hand, served 'English' food – and the trouble with Hardy was that he was one of those chaps who, no matter how hard they tried, simply could not get by without his daily dal-roti. He dutifully ate whatever was served in the mess but at least once a day, he'd find a pretext to leave the cantonment so that he could eat his fill somewhere in town. This was a commonplace enough occurrence among Indian officers, but Hardy crossed an unseen line: he started visiting the other ranks' messes. He enjoyed these little visits: he'd called some of the men 'uncle' as a child and he assumed that they would afford him the same indulgence and affection that he remembered from the past. They would keep his visits a secret, he thought. After all many of them were from the same village, the same extended family. Many had known his father.

It turned out that he could not have been more wrong. Far from being pleased at serving under Hardy, his father's old colleagues were deeply offended by his presence in the battalion. They were of the first generation of Indian soldiers to serve under Indian officers. Many of them were uneasy about this: their relationship with their British officers was the source of their pride and prestige. To serve under Indians was a dilution of this privilege.

A day came when the battalion's Commanding Officer, Lieutenant-Colonel 'Bucky' Buckland, recommended that Hardy be given command of C Company. So far as the company's NCOs were concerned, this was the last straw. Some of them knew Lieutenant-Colonel Buckland well; they had served with him for many years and it was part of their job to keep him informed about the happenings in the unit. They formed a delegation and went to see him. They told him: this boy, Hardayal Singh, to whom you've given charge of C Company, his father is known to us, his sisters are married to our brothers, his home is in the village next to ours. How can you expect us to treat this boy as an officer? Why, he cannot even stomach the food that officers eat. He steals secretly into our messes to eat chapatis.

Lieutenant-Colonel Buckland was deeply disturbed by these complaints: it was impossible not to be repelled by the murkiness of these sentiments. If there was an implicit self-hatred in trusting only your own, then how much deeper was the self-loathing that led a group of men to distrust someone for no reason other than that he was one of them?

Lieutenant-Colonel Buckland gave the NCOs a sharp reprimand: 'You are living in the past. The time has come when you will have to learn to take orders from Indians. This man is the son of your former colleague: do you really want to shame him in public?'

The NCOs held fast, despite this berating. In the end, it was the Lieutenant-Colonel who had had to yield. There had always been an unspoken compact between the men and their English officers: on certain matters it was understood that their wishes had to be taken into account. The Lieutenant-Colonel was left with no choice but to send for Hardy – to tell him that his appointment couldn't go through just yet. This proved to be the most difficult part of the whole affair. How were the charges to be explained to Hardy? How does a soldier defend himself against the accusation of being, as it were, a covert chapati-eater? What does this do to his self-respect?

Lieutenant-Colonel Buckland dealt with the situation as tactfully as anyone could have, and Hardy emerged from the interview without showing any visible signs of discomfiture. Only his closest friends knew how deeply he'd been wounded; how hard it had been for him to face those NCOs the next day. And, of course, the army being a small, tight institution, word always got around and from time to time even friends would say the wrong thing, just as they had that night.

'Do all of you face this then?' Dinu asked Arjun. 'Is it hard for you to be accepted as officers by your own men?'

'Yes and no,' Arjun replied. 'You always have the feeling that they're looking at you more closely than they would if you were a Britisher – especially me, I suppose, since I'm just about the only Bengali in sight. But you also have a sense that they're identifying with you – that some of them are urging you on, while others are just waiting to see you fall. When I'm facing them I can tell that they're putting themselves in my place, crossing a barrier that has become a great divide in their minds. The moment they imagine themselves past that line, something changes. It can't be as it was before.'

'What do you mean?'

'I'm not sure I can explain, Dinu. I'll tell you a story. Once, an old English colonel visited our mess. He was full of tales about the Good Old Days. After dinner I happened to hear him talking to Bucky – our CO. He was huffing and puffing and blowing through his whiskers. His view was that this business of making officers out of Indians would destroy the army; everyone would be at each other's throats and the whole thing would fall apart. Now Bucky's just about as fair and decent as a man can be and he wasn't going to put up with this. He defended us stoutly and said his Indian officers were doing a very good job and all the rest of it. But you know, the thing of it was that in my heart I knew that Bucky was wrong and the old codger was right.'

'Why?'

'It's simple. Every institution has its own logic, and the British Indian army has always functioned on the understanding that there was to be a separation between Indians and Britishers. It was a straightforward system: they stayed apart, and obviously both sides felt that this was to their benefit. It's no easy thing you know, to make men fight. The Britishers found a way of doing it, and they made it work. But now, with us being inside the officers' mess, I don't know that it can go on.'

'Why not?'

Arjun got up to pour himself another brandy. 'Because it's true what the old codger said: we're at each other's throats.'

'Who?'

'Indians and Britishers.'

'Really? Why? What about?'

'Most of it is just little things. In the mess for instance, if a Britisher turns the radio to a broadcast in English, you can be sure that minutes later an Indian will tune it to Hindi film songs. And then someone will turn it back, and so on until all you can do is hope that it gets switched off altogether. Things like that.'

'You sound like . . . squabbling schoolchildren.'

'Yes. But there's something important behind it, I think.'

'What?'

'You see we all do the same work, eat the same food and so on. But the chaps who're trained in England get paid a lot more than we do. For myself I don't mind so much, but chaps like Hardy care very much about these things. To them this is not just a job as it is for me. You see, they really believe in what they're doing; they believe that the British stand for freedom and equality. Most of us when we hear big words like that tend to take them with a pinch of salt. They don't. They're deadly serious about these things, and that's why it's so hard for them when they discover that this equality they've been told about is a carrot on a stick – something that's dangled in front of their noses to keep them going, but always kept just out of reach.'

'Why don't they complain?'

'They do sometimes. But usually there's nothing in particular to complain about. Take the case of Hardy's appointment: who was to blame? Hardy himself? The men? It certainly wasn't the CO. But that's how it always is. Whenever one of us doesn't get an appointment or a promotion, there's always a mist of regulations that makes things unclear. On the surface everything in the army appears to be ruled by manuals, regulations, procedures:

it seems very cut and dried. But actually, underneath there are all these murky shadows that you can never quite see: prejudice, distrust, suspicion.'

Arjun tossed his brandy back and paused to pour himself another. 'I'll tell you something,' he said, 'something that happened to me while I was at the academy. One day a group of us went into town – Hardy, me, a few others. It started to rain and we stepped into a shop. The shopkeeper offered to lend us umbrellas. Without thinking about it I said, yes, of course, that'll be a help. The others looked at me as though I'd gone mad. "What are you thinking of?" Hardy said to me. "You can't be seen with an umbrella." I was puzzled. I said: "But why not? Why can't I be seen with an umbrella?" Hardy's answer was: "Have you ever seen an Indian soldier using an umbrella?" I thought about it and realised I hadn't. I said: "No."

'"Do you know why not?"

'"No."

'"Because in the old days in the East, umbrellas were a sign of sovereignty. The British didn't want their sepoys to get over-ambitious. That's why you'll never see umbrellas at a cantonment."

'I was amazed. Could this possibly be true? I felt sure there were no regulations on the subject. Can you imagine a rule that said: "Indians are not to keep umbrellas in their barracks"? It's inconceivable. But at the same time, it was also true that you never saw anyone with an umbrella at a cantonment. One day I asked the adjutant, Captain Pearson. I said: "Sir, why do we never use umbrellas, even when it rains?" Captain Pearson is a short, tough, bull-necked fellow. He looked at me as though I were a worm. Nothing could have shut me up quicker than the answer he gave me. He said: "We don't use umbrellas, Lieutenant, because we're not *women*."'

Arjun began to laugh. 'And now,' he said, 'I would rather do anything than be seen with an umbrella – I'd rather drown in the rain.'

Twenty-four

That year it seemed as though the monsoons had broken over Lankasuka well before the first clouds had appeared in the skies. Manju's wedding was in late June, just before the coming of the rains. The days were very hot, and in the park in front of the house, the lake fell to a level where boats could no longer be taken out on the water. It was the time of year when even the rotation of the earth seem to slacken in speed, in anticipation of the coming deluge.

But within Lankasuka the wedding created the semblance of a strange climatic anomaly: it was as though the compound was awash in a flood, its inhabitants swirling hectically downriver, carried along by great tides of disparate things – people, gifts, anxiety, laughter, food. In the courtyard at the back, cooking fires burnt all day long and on the roof, under the bright tented awnings that had been erected for the wedding, there seemed never to be a moment when several dozen people were not sitting down to a meal.

The days went by in a storm of feasting and observances: the solemn familial commitments of the *paka-dekha* led inexorably to the yellowed turmeric-anointing of the *gaye-holud*. Slowly, much as the rising water of the monsoons overwhelms the chequerboard partitions of a paddy field, so did the steady progression of the wedding sweep away the embankments that divided the lives of the people in the house. Uma's white-saried political associates pitched in to help, as did a great many khaki-clad Congress workers; Arjun's friends at Fort William sent auxiliary detachments of cooks, mess-boys, waiters and even, on occasion, entire marching bands, complete with wrap-around brass and uniformed bandmasters; much of Manju's college came pouring in, and so did a colourful throng of Neel's acquaintances from the film studios of Tollygunge – directors, actors, students, playback singers, even the two terrifying make-up women who had dressed Manju on the day of her fateful audition.

Dolly too had a hand in stirring the mix. Through her years of visiting Uma in Calcutta, she had developed a close connection with the city's Burmese temple. Small though this temple was, its past was not without lustre. Many great Burmese luminaries had spent time there, including the famous activist monk, U Wisara. By way of Dolly's links, Manju's wedding came to be attended by a substantial part of the city's Burmese community – students, monks, lawyers and even a few hulking sergeants of Calcutta's police force (many of whom were Anglo-Burmese in origin).

Considering how oddly assorted these groups were, disagreements were relatively few. But in the end it proved impossible to shut out the powerful winds that were sweeping the world. On one occasion a friend of Uma's, an eminent Congressman, arrived dressed in the manner of Jawaharlal Nehru, in a khaki cap and a long black *sherwani*, with a rose in his buttonhole. The elegant politician found himself standing next to a friend of Arjun's, a lieutenant dressed in the uniform of the 14th Punjab Regiment. 'And how does it feel,' the politician said, turning to the soldier with a sneer, 'for an *Indian* to be wearing that uniform?'

'If you must know, sir,' Arjun's friend snapped back, matching sneer for sneer, 'this uniform feels rather warm – but I imagine the same could be said of yours?'

Another day, Arjun found himself facing off against a strangely assorted crowd of Buddhist monks, Burmese student-activists and Congress Party workers. The Congressmen had bitter memories of their confrontations with Indian soldiers and policemen. They began to berate Arjun for serving in an army of occupation.

Arjun recalled that it was his sister's wedding and he managed to keep his temper. 'We aren't occupying the country,' Arjun said, as lightly as he could. 'We are here to defend you.'

'From whom are you defending us? From ourselves? From other Indians? It's your masters from whom the country needs to be defended.'

'Look,' said Arjun, 'it's a job and I'm trying to do it as best I can . . .'

One of the Burmese students gave him a grim smile: 'Do you know what we say in Burma when we see Indian soldiers? We say: there goes the army of slaves – marching off to catch some more slaves for their masters.'

It was with a great effort that Arjun succeeded in keeping control of himself: instead of getting into a fight, he turned round and marched away. Later, he went to complain to Uma and found her wholly unsympathetic. 'They were just telling you what most people in the country think, Arjun,' Uma said bluntly. 'If you're strong enough to face enemy bullets, you should be strong enough to hear them out.'

For the duration of his stay in Lankasuka, Kishan Singh had been allotted a small room that was tucked away at the rear of the house. At other times this room was generally used for storage, mainly food. Along the walls stood great, stone martabans, packed with pickles; in the corners were piles of ripening mangoes and guavas; hanging from the rafters, beyond the reach of ants and cats, were the rope-slung earthen pots in which the household's butter and ghee were stored.

One afternoon, Bela was sent to the storeroom on an errand, to fetch some butter. The wooden door was slightly warped and could not be properly closed. Looking through the crack, Bela saw that Kishan Singh was inside, lying on a mat. He'd changed into a longyi for his siesta, and his khakis were hanging on a peg. He was sweating in the June heat, bare-bodied but for the ghostly shadow of the army singlet that was singed on to his chest.

From the pumping motion of his ribs Bela could tell that he was fast asleep. She slipped into the room and tiptoed around his mat. She was on her knees, undoing the strings of the earthen butter pot, when Kishan Singh suddenly woke up.

He jumped to his feet and pulled on his khaki tunic, his face turning red with embarrassment.

'My mother sent me . . .' she said quickly, 'to fetch this . . .' She pointed at the earthen pot.

With his tunic on, he seated himself cross-legged on the mat. He gave her a smile. Bela smiled shyly back. She felt no inclination to leave; she hadn't spoken to him till then and it occurred to her now that there were many things she wanted to ask him.

The first question she blurted out was the one that was uppermost in her mind. 'Kishan Singh,' she said, 'are you married?'

'Yes,' he said gravely. 'And I have a little son. Just one year old.'

'How old were you when you were married?'

'It was four years ago,' he said. 'So I must have been sixteen.'

'And your wife,' she said, 'what is she like?'

'She's from the village next to mine.'

'And where is your village?'

'It's up north – a long way from here. It's near Kurukshetra – where the great battle of the Mahabharata was fought. That is why the men of our district make good soldiers – that's what people say.'

'And did you always want to be a soldier?'

'No.' He laughed. 'Not at all – but I had no choice.'

The men in his family had always lived by soldiering, he explained. His father, his grandfather, his uncles – they had all served in the 1/1 Jats. His grandfather had died at Passchendaele, in the Great War. The day before his death he had dictated a letter that was to be sent to his family, filled with instructions about the crops in the fields and what was to be planted and when they were to sow and when to harvest. They next day he had gone over the top of his trench, to save his wounded *afsar*, an English captain whose batman he had been for five years and whom he honoured above all men. For this he had been awarded, posthumously, the Indian Distinguished Service Medal, which his family had kept, in their *haveli*, in a glass box.

'And to this day the afsar's family send us money – not because we ask, nor from charity, but out of love of my grandfather, and to honour what he did for their son . . .'

Bela hung upon his words, drinking in every movement of the muscles of his face. 'Go on.'

His father had served in the army too, he said. He had been wounded in Malaya, at the time of a rebellion. A stab wound had ripped open his side and pierced his colon. The army doctors had done what they could for him, but the wound had burdened him with chronic, crippling stomach pains. He'd travelled far afield, visiting experts in Ayurveda and other systems of medicine; the expense had forced him to barter away his share of the family land. He hadn't wanted a fate like that for his Kishan Singh; he'd wanted his son to go to college and understand things; he himself had travelled the world – Malaya, Burma, China, East Africa – and had understood nothing.

Kishan Singh too would have liked to go to college, but when he was fourteen his father died. After that the option of school was no longer open: the family had needed money. His relatives urged him to report to the local recruitment office; they said that he was lucky to have been born into a caste that was allowed to enroll in the English sarkar's army.

'That was why you joined?'

He nodded. 'Yes.'

'And the women in your village,' she said, 'what are they like?'

'Not like you.'

She was hurt by this. 'Why? What do you mean?'

'In a way,' he said, 'they are soldiers too. From the time they are little they begin to learn what it means to be widowed early; to bring up children without their men; to spend their lives with husbands who are maimed and crippled . . .'

Just then she heard her mother calling her name, and went running out of the room.

For the duration of the wedding, Rajkumar and his family were staying at the Great Eastern Hotel. (It was unthinkable, in light of their past hostilities, for Rajkumar to stay with Uma, as Dolly usually did.) It had been agreed upon, however, that Neel and

Manju would spend their wedding night – their last in Calcutta – in Lankasuka, in Uma's flat.

When the day came, Uma and Dolly prepared the bridal bedroom themselves. They went early to the flower market at Kalighat and came back with dozens of loaded baskets. They spent the morning draping the wedding bed with garlands of flowers – hundreds of them. While working, they reminisced about their own weddings and how very different they'd been. In the afternoon they were joined by the Second Princess, who'd made a special trip from Kalimpong: this completed the circle.

It was hot and they were quickly drenched in sweat. 'I've had enough,' said Dolly. 'My wedding was easier.'

'Remember Mrs Khambatta – with the camera?'

They sat on the floor, laughing at the memory.

As the day progressed, a hundred minor crises accumulated. Mainly they concerned odds and ends that someone had forgotten to buy: yet another dhoti for the purohit; a fresh handful of *durba* grass; a sari for a forgotten aunt – small but essential items. In the late afternoon Arjun was told to organise a quick shopping expedition in the family Jowett. Dinu, Uma and Bela were to go with him, each armed with a shopping list.

Arjun brought the Jowett into the courtyard and the others climbed in.

'Where exactly are we going?' Uma asked.

'To the market at Kalighat,' Arjun said.

'Well, you'll have to be quick then,' said Uma.

'Why?'

'There's a big demonstration today – we could get cut off.'

'A demonstration?' Arjun was taken by surprise. 'What on earth is it about this time?'

This annoyed Uma. 'Don't you ever read the papers, Arjun?' she said. 'It's an anti-war march. We in the Congress believe that in the event of another war Britain can't expect our support unless they're willing to provide a guarantee of Indian independence.'

'Oh I see.' Arjun shrugged. 'Well, we're safe then – it'll take them a long time to get through all of that . . .'

Dinu laughed.

It took just fifteen minutes to get to the market, and within half an hour their shopping was done. They were on their way back, when they turned into a wide avenue and spotted the first of the demonstrators, approaching from a distance.

'Nothing to worry about,' Arjun said calmly. 'We're a long way ahead. They won't box us in.' But even as he was speaking the Jowett's engine had begun to splutter. And then suddenly the car went dead.

'Do something, Arjun!' Uma snapped. 'We can't stop here.'

'The spark plug,' Arjun muttered incredulously. 'I knew I should have cleaned it this morning.'

'Can't you fix it?'

'It's going to take a few minutes.'

'A few minutes!' Uma said. 'But they'll be all around us. Arjun, how could you allow this?'

'These things happen . . .'

Dinu and Arjun went around to the front and propped the hood open. The Jowett had been idling a good while in the courtyard and the engine was very hot. By the time the plug was fixed, the demonstration had closed around them. Marchers were flowing past on every side, some of them breaking ranks to stare at the stalled car and the two men standing beside the open hood. Arjun and Dinu got back into the car: there was nothing to do but sit and wait until the last demonstrators were past.

A marcher dropped a pamphlet through the car window. Arjun picked it up and glanced down at the front page. There were quotations from Mahatma Gandhi and a passage that said: 'Why should India, in the name of freedom, come to the defence of this Satanic Empire which is itself the greatest menace to liberty that the world has ever known?'

Arjun was extremely irritated by this time and he made an angry, spitting noise. 'Idiots,' he said. 'I wish I could stuff this down their throats. You'd think they'd have better things to do than march about in the hot sun . . .'

'Watch what you say, Arjun,' Uma said sharply, from the back seat. 'I hope you know that I was meant to be in that march too. I don't think you should be calling them idiots. After all what do you know about these things?'

'Oh, well . . .' Arjun was about to shrug this off when Dinu spoke up, unexpectedly, in his defence.

'I think Arjun's right,' he said. 'Those people *are* idiots . . .'

'What?' said Uma. 'What are you talking about, Dinu?'

'I'm talking about Fascism,' Dinu said, 'and why the most important thing right now is to fight it. Because if war does break out, it won't be like any other war . . . Hitler and Mussolini are among the most tyrannical and destructive leaders in all of human history . . . They're grotesque, they're monsters . . . If they succeed in imposing their will on the world, we'll all be doomed. Look at what they believe in . . . their whole ideology is about the superiority of certain races and the inferiority of others . . . Look at what they're doing to Jews . . . And if they have their way they'll destroy the working-class movement everywhere in the world . . . Their rule will be the most violent and despotic you can imagine, with some races at the bottom and some at the top . . . And don't imagine for a moment that India and Burma will be better off if the British are defeated . . . The Germans' plan is simply to take over the Empire and rule in their place . . . And think of what'll happen in Asia . . . The Japanese are already aspiring to an Empire, like the Nazis and Fascists . . . Last year, in Nanking, they murdered hundreds of thousands of innocent people . . . The last we heard from Saya John, he said that many of his wife's relatives had been killed . . . Lined up against walls and shot . . . Men, women, children . . . Do you think that if the Japanese army reached India they wouldn't do the same thing here? If you do, you're wrong . . . They would . . . They're imperialists and racialists of the worst order . . . If they succeed, it'll be the worst catastrophe in all of human history.'

Uma responded calmly. 'Dinu,' she said, 'you must not think for one moment that I, or anyone in the Congress, has an iota of sympathy for the Nazis and Fascists. Absolutely not: they are exactly what you say – monstrous, grotesque. As Mahatma Gandhi has said, many times, they represent the exact opposite of everything we stand for. But as I see it, we are caught between two scourges: two sources of absolute evil. The question for us is, why should we pick one over the other? You say that Nazism will rule through violence and conquest, that it will institutionalise racialism, that it will commit unspeakable atrocities. All of this is true: I don't dispute it for a moment. But think of the evils you have listed: racialism, rule through aggression and conquest. Is the Empire not guilty of all of this? How many tens of millions of people have perished in the process of this Empire's conquest of the world – in its appropriation of entire continents? I don't think there could ever be an accounting of the numbers. Worse still, the Empire has become the ideal of national success – a model for all nations to aspire to. Think of the Belgians, racing off to seize the Congo – they killed ten or eleven million people there. And what was it they wanted, other than to create a version of this Empire? Isn't that what Japan and Germany want today – empires of their own?'

Bela leant over the seat, trying to break in. 'We have to get back,' she cried. 'We can't just sit here, arguing. It's Manju's wedding night.'

The last of the demonstrators were now past. Arjun started the car and turned it round. They went speeding down the road, towards Lankasuka.

But the argument was not over so far as Dinu was concerned. He turned round in his seat. 'Aunt Uma,' he said, 'you're always talking about the evils of Empire and what the British have done to India . . . But do you think that terrible things weren't happening here before they came? Look at the way women are treated even today, look at the caste system, untouchability, widow-burning . . . all these terrible, terrible things.'

Uma retorted sharply: 'Let me be the first to admit the horrors of our own society – as a woman I assure you that I am even more aware of them than you are. Mahatma Gandhi has always said that our struggle for independence cannot be separated from our struggle for reform. But having said this, let me add that we must *not* be deceived by the idea that imperialism is an enterprise of reform. Colonialists would like us to believe this, but there is a simple and clear refutation. It is true that India is riven with evils such as those you describe – caste, the mistreatment of women, ignorance, illiteracy. But take the example of your own country, Burma – they had no caste system there. On the contrary the Burmese were very egalitarian. Women had a high standing –

probably more so than in the West. There was universal literacy. But Burma was conquered too, and subjugated. In some ways they fared even worse than we did at the hands of the Empire. It is simply mistaken to imagine that colonialists sit down and ponder the rights and wrongs of the societies they want to conquer: that is not why empires are built.'

Dinu gave a hoarse laugh. 'Here you are, so full of indignation about the British. And yet you use the English language more often than not . . .'

'That's neither here nor there,' Uma shot back. 'Many great Jewish writers write in German. Do you think that prevents them from recognising the truth?'

From the driver's seat, Arjun gave a shout: 'Hold on!' He threw the car into a steep turn, taking it through the gates of Lankasuka. As they were getting out, they were met by the sound of ululations and the trumpeting of conch-shells. They went racing upstairs to find Neel and Manju walking around the fire, his dhoti joined to her sari by a knot.

From under the hood of her sari, Manju had been peering about the room, looking everywhere for Arjun. When she finally saw him walking in, dressed in his grease-blackened clothes, her head snapped up, throwing off the hood. Everyone in the room froze, astonished by the sight of an unveiled bride. Just then, a moment before Manju had pulled her sari back in place, Dinu's flash went off. Later, everyone was to agree that this was by far the best picture of the wedding.

The night was unbearably hot. Bela's bed was drenched with sweat, despite the whirring of the electric fan overhead. She couldn't sleep; she kept smelling the scent of flowers – the heady fragrances of the last, hottest nights before the breaking of the rains. She thought of Manju, in her flower-strewn bed downstairs, with Neel. It was strange how heat had the effect of heightening the scent of flowers.

Her throat was dry, as parched as sand. She got out of bed and went into the hall outside. The house was dark and for the first time in weeks, there was no one about. The silence seemed almost unnatural, especially after the tumult of the last few days. She tiptoed through the hall to the veranda at the back of the house. There was a full moon, and its light lay on the floor glinting like silver foil. She glanced at the door of the room where Kishan Singh slept. It was, as always, slightly ajar. She wondered if she should shut the door. Stepping across the veranda, she went up to the door and looked in. She could see him lying on his mat, with his longyi tucked between his legs. A gust of wind blew the door a little further open. It seemed cooler inside. She slipped through and seated herself in a corner, with her chin on her knees.

Suddenly he stirred and sat up. 'Who is it?'

'It's me – Bela.'

'Bela?'

She heard a note of apprehension in his voice and she understood that it had more to do with Arjun than with herself; that he was afraid of what might happen if she was found in his room – an officer's sister, a girl who'd just turned fifteen and was still unmarried. She didn't want him to be afraid. She pushed herself across the floor and touched his hand. 'It's all right, Kishan Singh.'

'And what if . . . ?'

'Everyone's asleep.'

'But still . . .'

She saw that he was still afraid, so she stretched out her legs and lay down beside him. 'Tell me Kishan Singh,' she said, 'when you were married – what was it like, your first night with your wife?'

He laughed softly. 'It was strange,' he said. 'I knew that my friends and relatives were at the door listening and laughing.'

'And your wife? Was she scared?'

'Yes, but I was too – even more than her in some ways. Later, when we talked of it with others, we learnt that that is how it always is . . .'

He could have made love to her then and she would have let him, but she understood that he wouldn't, not because he was afraid, but because of some kind of innate decency, and she was glad of this because it meant that it was all right to be there. She was happy just to be lying beside him, aware of his body, knowing that he was aware of hers. 'And when your son was born,' she said, 'were you there?'

'No. She was in the village and I was at the base.'

'What did you do when you heard the news?'

'I bought sweets from a *halwai* and I went to your brother and said: Sah'b, here is some *mithai*. He looked at me and asked: Why? So I said, Sah'b, I have a son.'

She tried to think of Arjun, in his uniform, talking to Kishan Singh. The picture wouldn't come to life. 'My brother – what is he like? As a soldier, I mean?'

'He's a good officer. The men, we like him.'

'Is he hard on you?'

'Sometimes. Of all the Indians in our battalion, he's the one who's the most English. We call him the "Angrez".'

She laughed: 'I must tell him.'

Suddenly he clapped a hand over her mouth. 'Shh.' There was a sound, of someone stirring downstairs. He sat up in alarm. 'They're flying to Rangoon today,' he said. 'They'll all be up early. You must go.'

'Just a little longer,' she pleaded. 'It's still night.'

'No.'

He pulled her to her feet and led her to the door. Just as she was about to slip out, he stopped her. 'Wait.' With a hand under her chin, he kissed her, very briefly, but full on the lips.

When Neel shook her awake, Manju could not believe that it was already time.

'Just a little longer,' she pleaded. 'Just a few more minutes.'

He put his chin against her cheek and tickled her with his beard. 'Manju, the plane leaves at 4 a.m.,' he said. 'We haven't got time . . .'

It was still dark when the chaos of departure got fully under way. Keyrings were found and forgotten; suitcases were sat upon and strapped with buckled belts; doors and windows were locked and checked and locked once again. A final round of tea was served and then, with the neighbourhood fast asleep, their luggage was loaded into a car. The family stood around the courtyard, waving: Uma, Bela, Arjun, their parents. Kishan Singh looked on from upstairs. Manju cried a little but there was no time for long goodbyes. Neel hurried her into the car and shut the door.

'We'll be back next year . . .'

It was so early that the roads were empty and it took just half an hour to drive to the Willingdon Air Base, on the banks of the Hooghly river. A few minutes later, Dolly, Rajkumar and Dinu arrived. At exactly 4 a.m. they were led to a jetty, where a sleek, grey motor-launch was waiting. The launch's engine started with a roar and they went shooting upriver, with the decks tilted backwards at a rakish angle. It was very dark, and all Manju could see of her surroundings was the muddy circle of water that was illuminated by the launch's powerful spotlight.

The launch slowed and the roar of its engine dwindled to a gentle whine. Its bows dropped back into the water and its spotlight roamed the waters ahead. Suddenly two immense white pontoons loomed out of the water and then the light climbed higher, illuminating the aircraft that was to take them to Rangoon. The plane was enormous, an eighteen-and-a-half-ton flying boat. The logo of the airline was painted on the plane's tail and a name was written in large letters across its nose – *Centaurus.*

'It's a Martin C-130 seaplane,' Neel whispered into Manju's ear. 'It's the kind that does the Pacific run for PanAm.'

'Like Humphrey Bogart's plane, in *China Clipper*?'

'Yes.' He laughed. 'And there was one in *Flying Down to Rio* too, remember, with Fred Astaire and Ginger Rogers?'

It was when she stepped through the hatch that the full extent of the plane's size became evident to Manju. The interior was as spacious as a ship's lounge, with deep, well-padded seats and glowing brass light fixtures. Manju pressed her nose to the window and saw the propellers starting to spin. Flecks of white froth appeared on the churning brown water below and then the shuddering fuselage began to advance, and the wake of its bow wave fanned out towards the invisible shore, rocking the little islands of water hyacinth that were floating downriver. A gurgling, sucking sound issued from the pontoons as the plane fought the water's grip, gathering speed. Suddenly the *Centaurus* shot forward, as though catapulted by the beat of wind upon water. Manju saw the wind-drummed waters of the Hooghly falling away as the aircraft rose slowly above the river's steep embankments. Soon the lights of the city were gone and there was only darkness below: they were now flying over the mangrove swamps of the Sunderbans, heading towards the Bay of Bengal.

Shortly afterwards a steward took Manju and Neel on a tour of the plane. They went straight through to the navigating bridge, where the captain and the first officer sat side by side, behind identical controls. The first officer explained that the Calcutta–Rangoon flight was only one leg of a fortnightly, eleven-thousand-mile round trip that took the *Centaurus* from Southampton to Sydney and back.

Behind the bridge lay the cabins of the main deck. There was an area for the stewards, a midship cabin, a smoking cabin and a promenade deck – an area that was kept free of seats, so that passengers could stretch their legs in mid-flight. Well appointed as everything was, it was the ingenious design of the kitchen and pantry that took Manju's breath away. In an area that was no larger than the average closet, space had somehow been found for all the amenities of a first-rate restaurant – crockery, linen, silverware and even fresh flowers.

With dawn approaching the steward advised Manju and Neel to go to the promenade deck to watch the sunrise. They stepped through the arched entrance just in time to see the dark expanse of the Sunderbans yielding to the metallic glint of the Bay of Bengal. In the distance a sliver of colour had appeared on the horizon, like light leaking through a doorway. The dark skies turned quickly mauve and then a shimmering translucent green, shot with streaks of crimson and yellow.

While Dinu was attempting to photograph the sunrise, Manju and Neel crossed the aisle to look in the other direction. Manju cried out loud: to the west lay a stupefying view. The horizon was obscured by a mass of darkness, a bank of cloud that was as vast as a mountain range. It was as though the Himalayas had been magically transported across the sea. So heavy were the cloudbanks that their flat bottoms seemed almost to touch the waves while their peaks towered far, far above the plane – great Everests of cloud reaching tens of thousands of feet into the sky.

'The monsoons,' Neel said incredulously. 'We've run straight into the incoming rains.'

'Is it going to be dangerous?' Manju asked.

'In some other aircraft perhaps,' Neel said confidently. 'But not in this one.'

They went back to their seats and soon sheets of rain were whiplashing against the windows with a force that made Manju flinch from the glass. Yet, the starkly visible violence of the weather had almost no effect upon the plane – the speedometer in the cabin showed the *Centaurus* to be flying at a steady 200 miles per hour. But a while later the captain announced that the *Centaurus* would make a change of altitude to ride out the storm. It would descend from its present cruising height of 3,000 feet to a few hundred feet above sea level.

Manju fell into a doze and was jolted awake only when a ripple of excitement ran through the plane. Land had been spotted on the starboard side: a picture-book island ringed with beaches. Huge waves were disintegrating into sheets of white foam on the sand. At the centre of the island there stood a striped black and white tower.

'Ladies and gentlemen,' the captain announced, 'what we have here is the lighthouse of Oyster Reef. You should have your first glimpse of Burma very shortly. Watch out for the Arakan coast . . .'

Then there it was – close enough to touch – a densely clotted carpet of mangrove, veined with thin creeks and silver rivulets. As Manju sat looking through the window, Neel whispered into her ear, telling her the story of how his grandmother – Rajkumar's mother – had died somewhere below, on a sampan that was moored in one of those branching inlets.

The town of Akyab, the capital of the Arakan, was their first stop. 'This,' said Neel proudly, 'was where my father was born.' The airline's base lay in a natural sea-lane, a good distance from the town. All they saw of Akyab as the *Centaurus* came down was a clock-tower in the far distance. After a quick refuelling the plane was in the air again. The rain stopped and in the bright daylight the waters of the coast were revealed to be lined with miles of reef and great floating forests of seaweed – all clearly visible from above, as stains on the sparkling sea. Rangoon now lay due east, and the *Centaurus* soon turned inland, flying over a stretch of uninhabited countryside. The steward came by, handing out voluminous leather-bound menus.

At the end of her breakfast, Manju found herself looking down on a vista of square paddy fields. Some were already green and others were in the process of becoming so, with lines of workers advancing through the mud, transplanting seedlings. The workers stood up as the plane flew over, throwing their heads back and waving huge conical hats.

Manju caught sight of a river, curving across the landscape. 'Is that the Irrawaddy?' she asked Neel.

'No,' said Neel. 'That's the Rangoon river – the Irrawaddy doesn't flow past the city.'

Then a glint of sunlight drew her eye to an immense structure, far in the distance – a gilded mountain that tapered into a spire of gold. 'What's that?'

'That's the Shwe Dagon Pagoda,' Neel whispered in her ear. 'We're home.'

Manju glanced at her watch and saw that the journey had lasted exactly five and a half hours. It seemed impossible that less than a day had passed since her wedding night, since the time when Neel had shut the door of their flower-bedecked bedroom. She thought of how frightened she'd been and she wanted to laugh. It was only now, circling above the city that was to be her home, that she acknowledged how completely she was in love. He was her present, her future, the entirety of her existence. Time and being held no meaning without him. She slipped her hand into his and looked down again on the great muddy river and the spire of gold. 'Yes,' she said. 'I'm home.'

was in the air [illegible] stopped and [illegible] the [illegible]
[illegible] of the [illegible] were [illegible]
[illegible] and [illegible] from
above, as [illegible] on the [illegible]
[illegible]
[illegible]
[illegible] feather [illegible].

At the end of [illegible] Mark [illegible]
down on [illegible]
green and [illegible] were [illegible]
[illegible] advancing [illegible]
[illegible] another over the [illegible]
[illegible].

[illegible] the [illegible] landscape
[illegible] she asked [illegible].

'No,' said [illegible]. 'That's the [illegible]
doesn't [illegible].'

[illegible]
in the distance [illegible] into a [illegible]
of [illegible]. 'What [illegible]?'

[illegible]
[illegible] homes.'

[illegible] said [illegible]
[illegible]
[illegible] the wedding night [illegible]
[illegible]
[illegible]
[illegible]
[illegible]
[illegible]
[illegible]
[illegible] she said. '[illegible]'

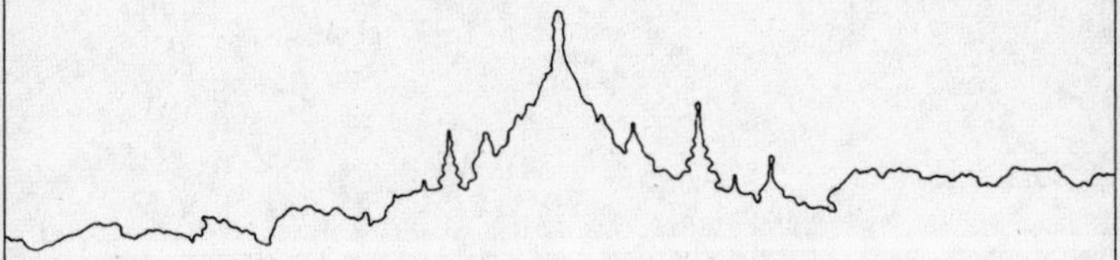

PART FIVE

Morningside

Twenty-five

Manju and Neel had not been married quite three months when the British Prime Minister, Neville Chamberlain, declared war on Germany, on behalf of Britain and her Empire. With the start of the war, an Air Raid Precautions scheme was prepared for Rangoon. The city was divided into sections and an ARP committee was formed for each. Medical officers were taught to deal with gas injuries; wardens were shown how to identify incendiary bombs; fire-fighting parties were formed and first-aid centres were set up. Rangoon's water table was too high to allow the building of underground shelters, but slit trenches were dug at strategic points around the city. Periodically there were 'blackouts'; trains entered and left the Rangoon railway station with darkened windows; wardens and civic guards stayed on duty through the night.

There was nothing unsatisfactory about the conduct of these exercises: the city's inhabitants followed their instructions good-humouredly and disturbances were few. But there was no denying the fact that a Rangoon blackout had more the feel of a performance than a drill: the public seemed to be going through the motions without being persuaded either of the imminence of war, or of its possible bearing on their lives. Certainly, in Burma, as in India, public opinion was deeply divided: in both places many important personages had expressed their support of the colonial Government. But many could also be heard to voice bitter condemnation of Britain's declaration of war on their behalf, without any binding guarantees of eventual independence. The mood among Burma's student activists was summed up in a slogan coined by a charismatic young student leader, Aung San:

Colonialism's difficulty, he said, was Freedom's opportunity. One day, Aung San disappeared: a rumour circulated that he was on his way to China to seek the support of the Communists. Later it came to be known that he had gone instead to Japan.

But these concerns were relatively distant from the life of the streets, where people seemed mainly to regard the ARP exercises as a species of entertainment, a mass diversion. Merrymakers strolled blithely through the darkened thoroughfares; young people flirted unseen in the parks; filmgoers flocked to see Ernst Lubitsch's *Ninotchka* at the Metro; *When Tomorrow Comes* had a long run at the Excelsior, and Irene Dunne was enshrined as one of the city's idols. At the Silver Grill on Fytche Square, cabarets and dancing continued as usual.

Dinu and his friend, Thiha Saw, were among the few who dedicated themselves wholeheartedly to the Air Raid Precautions scheme. At this time, both Dinu and Thiha Saw were deeply involved in student union politics. They were on the far left of the political spectrum and were involved in the publication of an anti-Fascist magazine. Participating in civil defences seemed a natural extension of their political work.

Dinu still lived at the Kemendine compound, in a couple of rooms at the top of the house. But at home, he made no mention of the work he was doing as an ARP warden – partly because he knew that Neel would tell him that he was wasting his time and needed to do some real work, and partly also because experience had led him to assume that his opinions would always be violently at odds with his father's. This was why he was taken completely by surprise at an ARP warden's meeting when he found himself suddenly face-to-face with none other than his father.

'You?'

'You!' There was no telling which of them was the more astonished.

After this encounter, there developed – for the first time ever – a brief bond between Rajkumar and Dinu. The outbreak of war had brought them through opposite routes to a shared position: Rajkumar had come to be convinced that in the absence of the British Empire, Burma's economy would collapse. Dinu's support for the Allied war effort was rooted in other kinds of soil: in his leftist sympathies; in his support for the resistance movements in China and Spain; in his admiration of Charlie Chaplin and Robert Capa. Unlike his father, he was not a believer in colonialism – indeed his antipathy to British rule was surpassed only by his loathing of European Fascism and Japanese militarism.

Whatever the reasons, this was an instance when father and son were in agreement – a situation that was without precedent in the memories of either. For the first time in their lives, they were working together – attending meetings, discussing such matters as the necessity of importing gas masks and the design of wartime posters. So novel was this experience that they both relished it in silence, speaking of it neither at home nor anywhere else.

One night an ARP blackout was accompanied by a thunderstorm. Despite the rain Rajkumar insisted on accompanying the wardens on their rounds. He was drenched when he got home. The next morning he woke up shivering. A doctor came and diagnosed pneumonia. Rajkumar was taken to hospital in an ambulance.

For the first few days, Rajkumar was barely conscious, unable to recognise Dolly, Dinu or Neel. His condition was judged to be serious enough for the doctors to bar all visitors. For several days he lay in a near-coma.

Then, slowly, the fever began to recede.

In his periods of lucidity Rajkumar took stock of his surroundings. It so happened that chance had brought him to a familiar place: the hospital room that Dolly and Dinu had occupied twenty-four years before. Looking around his bed, Rajkumar recognised the view from the window: the Shwe Dagon was framed exactly as he remembered. The blue and white curtains were slightly faded but still spotless and crisply starched; the tiled floors were, as ever, sparkling clean; and the dark, heavy furniture was recognisably the same, with inventory numbers stencilled on the varnished wood, in white paint.

When at last he was well enough to sit up, Rajkumar saw that the room had two additions. One was a Carrier air conditioner and the other a bedside radio – a 7-valve Paillard, with a 'magic eye', a metal cabinet, and chromium-plated mountings. The air conditioner Rajkumar had no use for, but the radio intrigued him. He flipped a switch and found himself listening to a station in Singapore: a newsreader's voice was recounting the latest developments in the war, describing the evacuation of British troops from Dunkirk.

After this, Rajkumar kept the radio on most of the time. Each night the nurse would turn it off when she was extinguishing the lights; Rajkumar would wait for her footsteps to die away before turning it on again. He would lie on his side and spin the knob, coasting from station to station. Twenty-four years before, at the time of Dolly's stay in that room, Europe had been convulsed by another war. Dolly too had stayed awake in this room, listening to the sounds of the night. But the whispers she'd heard had come from within the hospital: now, the room was filled with voices from around the world – London, New Delhi, Chungking, Tokyo, Moscow, Sydney. The voices spoke with such urgency and insistence that Rajkumar began to feel that he had lost touch with the flow of events; that he had become one of those men who sleepwalk their way to disaster by failing to note the significance of what was happening round them.

For the first time in many years, he allowed himself to think about the way he had been running his businesses. Day after day, month after month, he'd tried to handle every decision, review all the daily accounts, visit each location, every mill, every yard and outlet. He had been running his company as though it were a food-stall in a bazaar, and in the process he had blinded himself to the wider context.

Neel had long been pushing for a bigger role in the running of the business; Rajkumar had responded by trying to shut him out. He'd handed him money and told him to go and put it in films – as though he were buying off a child with packets of sweets. The ploy had worked, if only because Neel was too much in awe of him to challenge his authority. Now, the business was foundering. This was a fact that he'd refused to face. He'd suppressed hints from his accountants and managers, shouted at them when they tried to give him warning. And the stark fact was that he had no one to blame but himself: he had simply lost sight of what he was doing, and why.

As he lay listening to the radio's crackling voices, remorse settled on Rajkumar like a damp, stifling quilt. The doctors pronounced him to be well on the way to a complete recovery but his family could see no sign of an improvement, in either his manner or his appearance. He was in his mid-sixties at this time, but looked much older: his eyebrows had turned grey and bushy and his cheeks had begun to sag into overlapping dewlaps and jowls. He seemed scarcely to register the presence of the people who came to his room to see him; often when they tried to speak to him, he would silence them by turning up the radio.

One day Dolly unplugged the radio and shut the door. 'Rajkumar, what's on your mind? Tell me.'

At first he wouldn't speak but she prodded him until he answered.

'I've been thinking, Dolly.'

'What about? *Tell me.*'

'Do you remember how you and Dinu were in this room, that time . . .?'

'Yes. Of course.'

'That night, at Huay Zedi, when Dinu was ill and you said we had to get him to a hospital – I thought you were hysterical. I went along just for your sake . . .'

She smiled: 'Yes. I know.'

'But you were right.'

'It was just luck – a premonition.'

'That's what you say. But when I look back now, I can see that you often are right. Even though you live so quietly, shut away in the house, you seem to know more about what's happening in the world than I do.'

'What do you mean?'

'I've been thinking about what you've been saying these many years, Dolly.'

'What exactly?'

'That we should leave.'

With a long sigh of relief, Dolly reached for his hand. 'So you've been thinking of that at last?'

'Yes. But it's hard, Dolly – it's hard to think of leaving: Burma has given me everything I have. The boys have grown up here:

they've never known any other home. When I first came to Mandalay the nakhoda of my boat said: This is a golden land – no one ever starves here. That proved true for me, and despite everything that's happened recently, I don't think I could ever love another place in the same way. But if there's one thing I've learnt in my life, Dolly, it is that there is no certainty about these things. My father was from Chittagong and he ended up in the Arakan; I ended up in Rangoon; you went from Mandalay to Ratnagiri and now you're here too. Why should we expect that we're going to spend the rest of our lives here? There are people who have the luck to end their lives where they began them. But this is not something that is owed to us. On the contrary, we have to expect that a time will come when we'll have to move on again. Rather than be swept along by events, we should make plans and take control of our own fate.'

'What are you trying to say, Rajkumar?'

'Just that it doesn't matter whether I think of Burma as home or not. What matters is what people think of us. And it's plain enough that men like me are now seen as the enemy – on all sides. This is the reality and I have to acknowledge it. My job now is to find a way of making sure that Dinu and Neel are provided for.'

'Surely they're provided for already?'

Rajkumar paused before answering. 'Dolly, I think you're aware that the business hasn't been doing well lately. But you probably don't know the full extent of it.'

'And how bad is that?'

'It's not good, Dolly,' he said quietly. 'There are debts – many of them.'

'But, Rajkumar, if we sold the house, the yards, our share in Morningside – surely something would be left so that the boys could make a start somewhere else?'

Rajkumar began to cough. 'That wouldn't work, Dolly. As things stand at this minute, even if we sold everything it still wouldn't be enough. As for Morningside, Matthew has troubles of his own, you know. Rubber was very badly hit by the Depression. We can't rush into this, Dolly – that way we're sure to run into disaster. This has to be done very, very carefully. We have to give it time . . .'

'I don't know, Rajkumar.' Dolly began to pick worriedly at the end of her htamein. 'Things are happening so fast now – people say that the war may spread; that Japan may get into it; that they could even attack Burma.'

Rajkumar smiled. 'That's impossible, Dolly. You just have to look at a map. To get here the Japanese would have to come across Singapore and Malaya. Singapore is one of the most heavily defended places in the world. The British have tens of thousands of troops there. There are thirty-six-inch guns all along the shore. We can't be chasing after smoke, Dolly, we can't do things in a panic. If this is to work, we have to be realistic, we have to make careful plans.'

Dolly leant over him to fluff up the pillows on his bed. 'So do you have a plan then?'

'Not yet, but I've been thinking. Whatever we do, it'll take time – at least a year, maybe more. You have to prepare yourself. I want to make it possible for us to leave Burma with enough so that the boys can settle comfortably somewhere – in India, or wherever they want to go.'

'And after that?'

'The two of us will be free.'

'To do what?'

'Well, you've already decided – you want to live in Sagaing.'

'And what about you?'

'Perhaps I'll come back too, Dolly. I sometimes think of living quietly in Huay Zedi – I'm sure Doh Say would have a place for me – and it wouldn't be so far from you.'

Dolly laughed. 'So you're going to sell everything, uproot all of us, go through all this, just to come back and live quietly in Huay Zedi?'

'It's not for myself that I'm thinking of doing this, Dolly – it's for the boys.'

Rajkumar smiled and allowed his head to fall back against his pillows. Once before in his life, he had known himself to be at a crossroads – that was when he was trying to get his first contract, for the Chota-Nagpur Railway. He'd thought hard and come up with a plan that had worked, laying the foundations of his future success. This time too he would have to think of something, a plan that would work: this would be his last challenge, the last hill to cross. After that he would rest. There was no shame in growing old and seeking rest.

The first months of the war found Arjun and his battalion on the frontiers of Afghanistan. Arjun was on garrison duty, at a small outpost called Charbagh, near the Khyber Pass. The border was quiet – unusually so, the older officers said – and the conflict in Europe seemed very far away. Charbagh was manned by a single company of soldiers, Arjun being the sole officer. The surroundings were spectacularly beautiful: craggy, ochre mountains, streaked with great slashes of brilliantly coloured rock. There was little to do apart from daily drills, barracks inspections and occasional marches with training columns. Arjun spent long hours reading and soon ran out of books.

At regular fortnightly intervals, the battalion's Commanding Officer, Lieutenant-Colonel 'Bucky' Buckland, stopped by on tours of inspection. The CO was a tall, professorial-looking man with a ruff of wiry hair clinging to the base of his high-domed, balding head.

'And what do you do with your time, Lieutenant?' the CO asked offhandedly on one of his visits. 'Do you shoot at all? I've heard there's plenty of game to be had here.'

'Actually, sir,' Arjun said quietly, 'I read books . . .'

'Oh?' The CO turned to look at him with new interest. 'I didn't take you for a reader. And may I ask what you read?'

Their tastes proved to be complementary: the CO introduced Arjun to Robert Graves and Wilfred Owen. Arjun lent him his copies of H. G. Wells's *War of the Worlds* and Jules Verne's *Twenty Thousand Leagues Under the Sea*. These exchanges became a pleasurable part of Arjun's life at Charbagh and he began to look forward to the CO's visits. In between there were long days when nothing happened. There was little to do apart from talking to the occasional traveller.

Late in the summer, Arjun's friend Hardy stopped by on his way to his own post, atop the Khyber Pass. Hardy was a quiet, clear-eyed man of medium height and average build. Whether in or out of uniform he was always neatly dressed – with the folds of his turban layered in precise order and his beard combed tight against his chin. Despite his soldiering background, Hardy did not in any way resemble the Sikh warriors of military lore – he was soft-spoken and slow-moving, with an expression of habitual sleepiness. He had a good ear for a tune and was usually the first in the mess to learn the latest Hindi film songs. It was his habit – annoying to some and entertaining to others – to hum these melodies under his breath as he went about his work. These quirks sometimes brought him a little more than his fair share of 'ragging' – yet his friends knew that there were certain limits beyond which he could not be goaded: although generally slow to take offence, Hardy was inflexible when roused and had a long memory for grudges.

Hardy had just spent a period of leave in his village. On his first night at Charbagh he told Arjun about some odd rumours that he'd heard during his stay. Most of his neighbours had relatives in the army, and some of them had spoken of incidents of unrest: troops were said to be resisting transfer orders abroad. In Bombay, a Sikh unit – a squadron of the Central India horse – was said to have mutinied. They had lain down their weapons and refused to board the ship that was to take them to North Africa. Two men had been executed. A dozen others had been exiled to the prisons of the Andaman Islands. Some of these men were from Hardy's own village: there could be no doubt about the reliability of these reports.

Arjun was astonished to hear this. 'You should tell Bucky,' he said. 'He should know.'

'He must know already,' Hardy said. 'And if he hasn't said anything to us, it must be for a reason . . .' They looked at each other uneasily and dropped the subject: neither of them mentioned these stories to anyone else.

A few months later the 1/1 Jats moved back to their battalion's base at Saharanpur, near Delhi. With the descent into the plains the rhythms of their life underwent a dramatic change. The army was now expanding at a furious pace: regiments were raising new battalions and headquarters was looking everywhere for experienced personnel. Like every other battalion in the regiment, the 1/1 Jats were milked of several officers and NCOs. Suddenly they found themselves struggling to fill the gaps in their ranks. Newly recruited companies were sent up from the battalion's training centre and a fresh batch of officers arrived, as replacements for those who'd left. The new officers consisted mainly of expatriate British civilians with Emergency Commissions – men who had until recently held jobs as planters, businessmen and engineers. They had little experience of the Indian army and its intricate customs and procedures.

Arjun and Hardy were both full lieutenants now and they were among the few regular army officers left in the unit. Lieutenant-Colonel Buckland began to depend on them more and more for the day-to-day running of the battalion.

First he saddled them with the job of forming a new administrative platoon. Then, sooner than anyone had expected, the battalion's motorised transport was brought up to authorised strength. Three dozen fifteen-hundredweight trucks arrived, along with a dozen smaller lorries. It was discovered that the battalion had mule-trainers aplenty, but lacked drivers. Arjun was taken off the administrative platoon and appointed Motor Transport Officer. It fell to him to teach the new drivers the tricks of threading heavyweight trucks through Saharanpur's narrow alleys and bazaars.

Even as the battalion was adjusting to its new vehicles, a shipment of armaments was sent up from New Delhi: 3-inch mortars, tommy guns and Vickers-Berthier light machine guns. Then came three Bren guns, with their carriers, six medium machine guns and five Boye's anti-tank rifles, one for each company. Hardy was given the responsibility of running weapons training courses for the men.

Just as Hardy and Arjun were settling cheerfully into their new jobs, the CO turned everything upside down again. He pulled both Arjun and Hardy from their assignments and set them to work on preparing a unit mobilisation scheme.

By this time, most of Arjun and Hardy's classmates from the Military Academy had already been sent abroad. Some were serving in North Africa, some in Eritrea (where one had won a Victoria

Cross), and some in the East – Malaya, Hong Kong and Singapore. Arjun and Hardy assumed that they too would soon be going abroad to join other units of the Indian army. When the CO asked them to draft a mobilisation plan, they took it as a sign that their departure was imminent. But a month went by without any further news, and then another. On New Year's Eve, they saw 1941 in with a wan celebration. Despite the ban on shop talk at the mess, the conversation kept returning to the question of where they would be sent, east or west – to North Africa or towards Malaya.

Opinion was evenly divided.

Rajkumar was discharged from hospital with strict orders to remain in bed for at least a month. On returning home, he insisted on being moved up to a room at the top of the house. A bed was brought up and placed by a window. Neel bought a radio, a Paillard just like the one in the hospital, and placed it on a table, beside the bed. When everything was exactly as he wanted, Rajkumar lay down, with a wall of pillows against his back, positioning himself so that he'd be able to look across the city, towards the Shwe Dagon.

As the days passed the outlines of a plan began to take shape, very slowly, before his eyes. During the last war the price of timber had soared. The profits he had made then had sustained him for a decade afterwards. It was not too far-fetched to imagine that something similar might happen again. The British and the Dutch were reinforcing their defences throughout the East – in Malaya, Singapore, Hong Kong, Java, Sumatra. It stood to reason that they would need materials. If he could build up a stockpile of timber in his yards, it was possible that he'd be able to sell at a good price next year. The problem was liquidity: he would have to sell or mortgage all his assets to find cash – he would have to get rid of the yards, the mills, the timber concessions, even the Kemendine house. Perhaps he could persuade Matthew to buy him out of Morningside: there might be some cash there.

The more he thought of it, the more plausible the plan seemed.

The risks were huge of course, but they always were when anything important was at stake. But the rewards too could be very great; enough to clear his debts and finance a new beginning for Neel and Dinu. And there would be other advantages to arranging things in this way: all his assets would have been disposed of by the time he made his final move. After that he'd be free to leave – nothing to hold him back, nothing more to worry about.

One afternoon, when Dolly brought him his meal, he sketched his plan for her. 'I think it could work, Dolly,' he concluded. 'I think it's our best chance.'

Dolly had many objections.

'How is all this to be done, Rajkumar? In your state of health, you can't be up and about, travelling to Malaya and all that.'

'I've thought of that,' he said. 'Neel and Dinu will do the travelling – not me. I'll tell them what they have to do. One of them can go upcountry; the other can go over to dispose of our part of Morningside.'

Dolly shook her head. 'Dinu won't agree. He's never wanted to have anything to do with the business – you know that.'

'He doesn't really have a choice, Dolly. If I were to die today, he would find himself paying off my debts whether he liked it or not. All I'm asking is a few months of his time. After that he'll be free to follow his own interests.'

Dolly fell silent, and Rajkumar reached out to jog her arm. 'Say something, Dolly – tell me what you think.'

'Rajkumar,' Dolly said quietly, 'this plan of yours – you do know what they call this kind of thing?'

'What?'

'Hoarding – war-profiteering.'

Rajkumar scowled.

'Hoarding applies to essential commodities, Dolly. That's not what I'll be dealing in. There's nothing illegal about my plan.'

'I'm not talking about the law . . .'

Rajkumar's tone grew impatient. 'Dolly, there's nothing else to be done. We have to take this chance – don't you see?'

Dolly rose to her feet. 'Does it really matter what I think, Rajkumar? If this is what you're set upon, then this is what you'll do. It is not important what I think.'

Late that night, when the whole house was asleep, the telephone began to ring in a hallway downstairs. Dolly got out of bed and ran to pick it up before it woke Rajkumar. She heard an operator's voice, crackling down the line, telling her she had a trunk call. The instrument seemed to go dead for a moment, and then she heard Alison's voice; it was very faint as though she were shouting across a crowded room.

'Alison?' She heard a sound that was like a sob. She raised her voice. 'Alison, is that you?'

'Yes.'

'Alison – is everything all right?'

'No . . . there's bad news.'

'Is it Sayagyi?'

'No.' There was a sob again. 'My parents.'

'Alison. I'm so sorry. What happened?'

'They were on holiday. Driving. In the Cameron Highlands. The car went over an embankment . . .'

'Alison, Alison . . .' Dolly couldn't think of what she was going to say next. 'Alison, I'd come myself, if I could, but Rajkumar isn't well. I can't leave him. But I'll send someone – one of the boys, probably Dinu. It may take a few weeks but he'll be there. I promise you . . .' The line went dead before she could say anything else.

Twenty-six

The day before Arjun's twenty-third birthday he and Hardy borrowed a jeep and drove down to Delhi for the weekend. Walking through the arcades of Connaught Circus, they ran into an acquaintance, Kumar, a debonair and famously fun-loving contemporary of theirs from the academy.

Kumar belonged to the 14th Punjab Regiment and his battalion was currently stationed in Singapore. He was in India only briefly, attending a signals training course. Kumar appeared distracted and preoccupied, very different from his usual high-spirited self. They went out for lunch, and Kumar told them about a very strange incident – something that had caused a lot of unease at headquarters.

At Singapore's Tyersall Park Camp an Indian soldier had inexplicably shot an officer and then committed suicide. On investigation it was discovered that this was no simple murder-suicide: there were undercurrents of unrest within the battalion. Certain officers of this battalion had been heard to say that Indians should refuse to participate in this war: that this was a competition for supremacy among nations who believed it to be their shared destiny to enslave other peoples – England, France, Germany. There was much concern at headquarters: more than half the troops in Malaya were Indian and it was clear that the colony could become indefensible if unrest were to spread. Despite the incendiary nature of these rumours, the high command had decided on a judicious and measured response. All that was done by way of disciplinary action was to send one of the battalion's junior officers back to India.

It so happened that the officer who was singled out for censure was a Muslim. When news of his punishment reached his battalion, a company of Muslim soldiers proceeded to lay down their weapons, in a show of sympathy. The next day many of the battalion's Hindu soldiers also laid down their arms.

At this point the incident assumed a new gravity. For generations, the British Indian army had operated on the principle of maintaining a careful balance between the troops. Every battalion was constituted of companies drawn from different castes and religions – Hindus, Muslims, Sikhs, Jats, Brahmins. Each company had its own mess, run strictly according to the dietary rules of the group from which the troops had been recruited. As an additional safeguard, infantry divisions were so composed that Indian troops were always balanced by a certain number of Australian or British units.

That Hindu and Muslim troops could act together to support an Indian officer came as a shock to the High Command. No one needed to be reminded that nothing of this kind had happened since the Great Mutiny of 1857. At this point half-measures were dispensed with. A platoon of British soldiers from the Argyll and Sutherland Highlanders was sent in to surround the mutinous Indians.

Thus far into the story Kumar had told them neither the name of the battalion concerned nor that of the officer who was to be punished. When at last he mentioned these, it became clear that Kumar, like the good raconteur that he was, had been saving his punchline for the last. It turned out that the battalion in question was a brother unit of the 1/1 Jats – a part of a Hyderabad infantry regiment. The officer who was being sent home was someone they had all known well at the academy.

Kumar concluded the story with an offhand observation: 'Going overseas has disturbing effects on the troops,' he said, shrugging his shoulders. 'On officers too. You'll see.'

'Perhaps it won't happen to us,' Hardy said hopefully. 'There's no certainty that we'll be sent abroad. They'll need forces here too, after all . . .'

Arjun was quick to challenge this. 'And what would that do for us?' he said. 'For you and me? We'll sit out the war and our careers will be dead on their feet. I think I'd rather take my chances abroad.'

They walked away in silence, not knowing what to make of this conversation. There was something about Kumar's story that defied belief. They both knew the officer who'd been punished – he was a quiet kind of man, from a middle-class family. He needed his job if nothing else. What had made him do what he'd done? It was hard to understand.

And if the story was true – and they were by no means sure of this – then the incident had other implications too. It meant for example that the other ranks were now taking their cues from their Indian officers rather than the High Command. But this was worrying – to them no less than to the High Command – for if the men were to lose faith in the structure of command, then the Indian officers too would eventually be rendered redundant. Only by making common cause with their British counterparts could they hope to prevent this. What would happen if there really were to be a fissure? How would the men respond? There was no telling.

Disquieting as the subject was, Arjun felt oddly exhilarated: it was an uncommon responsibility to be faced with such questions at the age of twenty-three.

That night they changed into *kurtas* and *churidar* pyjamas and went to a dancer's *kotha* near Ajmeri Gate. The dancer was in her forties and her face was painted white, with eyebrows that were as thin as wires. At first glance she looked stony and unattractive, but when she stood up to dance the hardness in her face melted away: her body was supple and lithe and there was a marvellous lightness in her feet. As the tabla's tempo increased she began to spin, whirling in time to the beat. Her gauzy knee-length *angarkha* corkscrewed around her, in tight spirals. The aureoles of her breasts stood outlined against the thin, white cloth. Arjun's throat went dry. When the tabla sounded its climactic stroke, her index finger came to rest on Arjun's forehead. She beckoned to him to follow her.

Arjun turned to Hardy in astonishment and his friend smiled and gave him a nudge. 'Go, yaar, it's your birthday isn't it? Jaa.'

Arjun followed the dancer up a flight of narrow stairs. Her room was small, with a low ceiling. She undressed him slowly, picking at the drawstring of his cotton churidar pyjamas with her nails. When he reached for her she pushed his hand away with a laugh.

'Wait.'

She made him lie face down on the bed and massaged a handful of oil into his back, her fingertips tripping over the knuckles of his spine in imitation of the rhythms of a dancer's feet. When at last she lay down beside him she was still fully clothed. He reached for her breasts and she pushed his hand away: 'No, not that.' She undid her drawstring and guided him into her body, watching with a smile, as he lay on her. When he was done she slipped quickly away, and it was as though nothing at all happened: even her drawstring seemed instantly back in place.

She put a finger under his chin and tipped his head back, puckering her lips as though she were looking at a beautiful child.

'So young,' she said. 'Just a boy.'

'I'm twenty-three,' he said proudly.

She laughed. 'You look sixteen.'

When Alison first broke the news of her parents' deaths to Saya John, his response had consisted of nothing more than a slight smile. A series of questions had followed, asked almost playfully, as though the situation that was under discussion was at best a remote possibility – an imaginative hypothesis that Alison had propounded in order to explain her parents' prolonged absence from the dinner table.

Alison had been so afraid of the impact the news might have on her grandfather that she had gone to great lengths to compose herself, caking make-up over the discolourations of her face and tying a scarf over her disarranged hair. Every eventuality that she could think of she had tried to prepare herself for. But the sight of her grandfather's childlike smile proved beyond her bearing. She got up and ran out of the room.

Saya John was now in his late eighties. His lifelong regimen of early-morning exercise had served him well, and he was in relatively sound health. His hearing had not deteriorated greatly and although his eyesight had never been good, he was still able to see his way round the house and grounds. Before the accident his advancing age had occasionally betrayed itself in a tendency towards confusion. He would often forget things that had been said to him minutes before, while still being able to recall, in minute detail, events that had occurred forty or fifty years before. The accident greatly accelerated this tendency: Alison could see that contrary to his pretence, the news of her parents' deaths had indeed registered on her grandfather's mind. But his response was not unlike that of a child's reaction to unwelcome noise: he had figuratively stopped his ears with his fingers, in order to shut out what he did not wish to know. With each passing day he spoke less and less. He would come down to eat with Alison, but he'd sit at the hardwood table in blank silence. Such sentences as he addressed to Alison, would begin, almost invariably, with observations like: 'When Matthew comes back . . .' or, 'We must remember to tell Elsa . . .'

In the beginning Alison responded to these remarks with undisguised fury, slamming her hands on the polished table, and repeating several times over: 'Matthew is *not* coming back . . .' At the time nothing seemed more important than that he should make proper acknowledgement of what had happened. In this she envisaged, if not a lessening of her own grief, then at least a sharing of its burden. But he would smile through her outbursts, and at the end he would carry on where she had interrupted him: '. . . and when they come back . . .'

It seemed somehow indecent, even obscene – a profanation of parenthood – that he should respond so blandly to so great a loss. But she saw that her insistence and her banging of tables made no difference: that short of hitting him, she had no means of forcing a rupture in the protective blanket of confusion that he had drawn around himself. She forced herself to gain control of her anger, but this came at the cost of acknowledging a further loss – that of her grandfather. She and her Baba, as she called him, had always been very close. Now it was as though she were being forced to accept that he was no longer a sentient presence in her life; that the comforts of the companionship they had shared had ceased for ever; that he who had always been an unfailing source of support had now, in the hour of her greatest need, chosen to become a burden. Of all the betrayals he could have perpetrated, this seemed the most terrible – that he should become a child in this moment of her utter abandonment. She could never have imagined it.

These weeks would have been unendurable, but for a single fortuitous circumstance. Some years before, acting on a whim, Saya John had adopted one of the plantation workers' children – 'that boy who's always hanging around the house' – Ilongo. The boy had continued to live with his mother, but Saya John had paid for his schooling in the nearby town of Sungei Pattani. Later he had sent him to a technical institution in Penang and Ilongo had qualified as an electrician.

Ilongo was now twenty, a dark, curly-haired youth, slow-moving and soft-spoken, but of imposing height and build. On finishing his electrician's course, Ilongo had returned to the vicinity of Morningside – his mother now lived in a small, tin-roofed house on the outskirts of the estate.

In the aftermath of the accident, Ilongo came often to see Saya John at Morningside House. Gradually, and without an unduly intrusive display of concern, he took over many of the daily functions of caring for the old man. His was an unobtrusive yet quietly reliable presence, and Alison soon found herself looking to him for help in running the plantation's offices. Ilongo had grown up on Morningside and knew every worker on the estate. They in turn accorded him an authority unlike that of anyone else on the plantation. He had come of age on the estate, but he'd also stepped outside its boundaries, learnt to speak Malay and English, acquired an education. He had no need to raise his voice or utter threats in order to gain respect: they trusted him as one of their own.

Saya John too found reassurance in his company. Every Sunday Ilongo would borrow a truck from the estate and drive him down to the Church of Christ the King, in Sungei Pattani. On the way they would stop at the shaded arcades of the red-tiled shophouses that lined the town's main street. Saya John would go into a small restaurant and ask for the proprietor, Ah Fatt, a large man with bright gold incisors. Ah Fatt had political connections in southern China, and Saya John had been a generous contributor ever since

Japan's invasion of Manchuria. Each week he would hand Ah Fatt a sum of money, in an envelope, to be sent on.

On those days when he was at Morningside House, it was Ilongo who answered the telephone. One day he came cycling down from the house to see Alison at the estate office.

'There was a call . . .'

'From whom?'

'Mr Dinu Raha.'

'What?' Alison was sitting at her desk. She looked up with a frown. 'Dinu? Are you sure?'

'Yes. He was calling from Penang. He's just arrived from Rangoon. He's coming to Sungei Pattani by train.'

'Oh?' Alison thought back to the letters that Dolly had written her in the weeks after her parents' deaths: she recalled a reference to an impending visit – but the letter had said that it would be Neel who'd be coming, not Dinu.

'Are you sure it was Dinu?' she asked Ilongo again.

'Yes.'

She glanced at her watch. 'Perhaps I'll go to the station to meet him.'

'He said there was no need: he'd find a taxi.'

'Oh? Well, I'll see. There's still time.' Ilongo left and she sat back in her chair, turning to face a window that looked out over the plantation, towards the distant blue of the Andaman Sea. It was a long time since she'd last had a visitor. Immediately after her parents' death, the house had been full. Friends and relatives had come from Penang, Malacca, Singapore – there had been piles of telegrams. Timmy had come all the way from New York, flying across the Pacific on PanAm's *China Clipper*. In the overwhelming bewilderment of that time, Alison had found herself praying that Morningside would be filled for ever with people: it was inconceivable that she should have to face, on her own, those rooms and corridors – the stairway where every join in the wood was a reminder of her mother. But a week or two had gone by and then the house had emptied just as suddenly as it had filled up. Timmy had left to go back to New York. He had his own business now and couldn't be too long away. In departing he had as good as handed Morningside over to her – to sell or run as she chose. In time, her sense of abandonment had yielded to the understanding that she could not look to the past to fill the gaps in her present; that she could not hope for the lingering traces of her parents' lives to serve as a buffer between herself and the aching isolation of Morningside – the crushing monotony, the solitude that resulted from being always surrounded by the same faces, the same orderly rows of trees, the inescapable sight of the same clouds hanging upon the same mountain.

And now here was Dinu, on his way to Morningside – strange old Dinu – so incorrigibly serious, so awkward and unsure of himself. She looked at her watch and at the window. Far in the distance, she could see a train making its way across the plain. She reached for her handbag and found the keys to the Daytona roadster. It would be a relief to get away, even if just for a couple of hours.

Twenty-seven

It was because of the war that Dinu's arrival at Morningside was so long delayed. The threat of submarine activity in the Bay of Bengal had forced steamship companies to cease publishing their schedules. Departures were now announced only hours before the time of sailing. This meant, in effect, that a constant vigil had to be maintained at the companies' offices. Dinu had considered himself lucky to get a berth at all and had not given any thought to wiring ahead.

The station at Sungei Pattani was as pretty as a toy: there was a single platform shaded by a low red-tiled awning. Dinu spotted Alison as the train was drawing in: she was standing in the shade of the tin awning, wearing sunglasses and a long, black dress. She looked thin, limp, wilted – a candlewick on whom grief burnt like a flame.

The sight of her induced a momentary rush of panic. Emotion of any kind inspired fear in him, but none so much as grief: for several minutes after the train pulled in he was literally unable to rise from his seat. It was not till the station master brandished his green flag that he started for the door.

Stepping out of the train, Dinu tried to recall the phrases of condolence he had rehearsed in preparation for this moment. But now, with Alison approaching across the platform, the idea of consolation seemed like an impossible impertinence. It would be kinder, surely, to behave as though nothing had happened?

'You shouldn't have come,' he said gruffly, dropping his eyes. 'I would have found a taxi.'

'I was glad to come,' she said. 'It's nice to have a break from Morningside.'

'Still.' Hefting his leather camera cases on his shoulders, he handed his suitcase to a porter.

She smiled. 'Is your father better?'

'Yes,' Dinu said stiffly. 'He's fine now . . . and Manju and Neel are expecting a baby.'

'That's good news.' She gave him a smile and a nod.

They stepped out of the station into a compound that was shaded by an immense, dome-like tree. Dinu stopped to look up. From the tree's moss-wrapped branches there hung a colourful array of creepers and wildflowers.

'Why,' said Dinu, 'isn't that a padauk tree?'

'We call them angsana trees here,' Alison said. 'My father planted this one the year I was born.' She paused. 'The year we were born I should have said.'

'Why yes . . . of course . . . we were born the same year.' Dinu smiled, hesitantly, surprised both by the fact that she'd remembered and that she'd chosen to comment on it.

The Daytona was parked nearby, with its hood pulled up. Alison slipped into the driver's seat, while Dinu saw to the loading of his luggage in the back. They drove out of the station and past the main marketplace with its long arcades of tiled shophouses. On the outskirts of town they passed a field that was ringed with barbed-wire fencing. At the centre of the field there stood several orderly rows of *attap* huts, roofed with sheets of corrugated iron.

'What's this?' Dinu asked. 'I don't remember any of this . . .'

'It's our new miltary base,' said Alison. 'Sungei Pattani has a big army presence now, because of the war. There's an airstrip in there and it's guarded by Indian soldiers.'

The road began to climb and Gunung Jerai reared up ahead, its peak obscured by the usual daytime heat haze. Dinu sank back in his seat, framing the mountain in an imaginary lens. Alison's voice took him by surprise.

'Do you know what the hard part is?'

'No – what is it?'

'Nothing has any shape.

'What do you mean?'

'It's something you don't see until it's gone – the shapes that things have and the ways in which the people around you mould those shapes. I don't mean the big things – just the little ones. What you do when you get up in the morning – the hundreds of thoughts that run through your head while you're brushing your teeth: "I have to tell Mummy about the new flowerbed" – that sort of thing. Over the last few years I'd started to take over a lot of the little things that Daddy and Mummy used to do at Morningside. Now, when I wake up in the morning those things still come back to me in just that way – I have to do this or that, for Mummy or for Daddy. Then I remember, No, I don't have to do any of those things; there's no reason to. And in an odd way, what you feel at those moments is not exactly sadness but a kind of disappointment. And that's awful too, for you say to yourself – is this the best I can do? No: this isn't good enough. I should cry – everyone says it's good to cry. But the feeling inside doesn't have an easy name: it's not exactly pain or sorrow – not right then. It feels more like the sensation you have when you sit down very heavily in a chair: the breath rushes out of your body and you find yourself gagging. It's hard to make sense of it – any of it. You want the pain to be simple, straightforward – you don't want it to ambush you in these roundabout ways, each morning, when you're getting up to do something else – brush your teeth or eat your breakfast . . .'

The car veered suddenly towards the side of the road. Dinu snatched at the wheel to steady it. 'Alison! Slow down – careful.'

She ran the car on to the grassy verge that flanked the road and stopped under a tree. Raising her hands, she touched her cheeks in a gesture of disbelief. 'Look,' she said. 'I'm crying.'

'Alison.' He wanted to reach for her, touch her shoulder, but it was not like him to be demonstrative. She lowered her forehead to the wheel, sobbing, and then suddenly his hesitations evaporated.

'Alison.' He drew her head to his shoulder, and felt the warmth of her tears dampening the thin cotton of his shirt. Her hair was silky against his cheek and smelt faintly of grapes. 'Alison, it's all right . . .'

He was struck by a deep astonishment at what he had done. It was as though someone had reminded him that gestures of this kind did not come naturally to him. The arm that was holding her cradled against his shoulder grew heavy and wooden and he found himself mumbling awkwardly: 'Alison . . . I know it's been hard . . .'

He was cut short by the roar of a fifteen-hundredweight truck, rolling down the road. Alison pulled quickly away and sat upright. Dinu turned as the truck rumbled by. A squad of Indian soldiers was squatting in the back of the truck, dressed in turbans and khaki shorts.

The sound of the truck faded away and the moment passed. Alison wiped her face and cleared her throat. 'Time to go home,' she said, turning the ignition key. 'You must be tired.'

It was mid-February when the long-awaited mobilisation orders finally arrived. Hardy was one of the first to know and he came running to Arjun's room.

'Yaar – have you heard?

It was early evening and Hardy didn't bother to knock. He pushed the door open and looked in: 'Arjun, where are you?'

Arjun was inside the curtained dressing room that separated his bathroom from the living area. He had just finished washing off the dirt of a football match and his mud-caked shoes and shorts lay heaped on the floor. It was a Thursday – a night when, by tradition, dinner jackets were worn at the mess, this being the day of the week when the news of Queen Victoria's death had been received in India. Kishan Singh was at work in Arjun's bedroom, laying out his clothes for the evening – dinner jacket, dress trousers, silk cummerbund.

Hardy crossed the room quickly: 'Arjun? Did you hear? We've got the orders.'

Arjun pulled back the curtain, with a towel fastened around his waist.

'You're sure?'

'Yes. Heard from Adjutant-sah'b.

They looked at each other without knowing what else to say. Hardy seated himself on the edge of the bed and began to crack his knuckles. Arjun started to button his starched dress shirt, flexing his knees, so that he could see himself in the mirror. He caught a glimpse of Hardy behind him, staring morosely at the floor. Trying to sound jocular, he said: 'At least we'll get to see if those damned mobilisation plans that we drew up are any good or not . . .'

Hardy made no answer, and Arjun glanced over his shoulder. 'Aren't you glad the waiting's over? Hardy?'

Hardy's hands were clasped between his knees. He looked up suddenly. 'I keep thinking . . .'

'Of what?'

'Do you remember Chetwode Hall? At the Military Academy in Dehra Dun?'

'Of course.'

'There was an inscription which said: *The safety, honour and welfare of your country come first, always and every time. The honour, welfare and comfort of the men you command come next . . .'*

'. . . *And your own ease, comfort and safety come last, always and every time.'* Arjun laughed as he finished the quotation for Hardy. 'Of course I remember. It was inscribed on the podium – stared us in the face every time we entered Chetwode Hall.'

'Didn't it ever puzzle you – that inscription?'

'No. Why should it?'

'Well, didn't you ever think: this country whose safety, honour and welfare are to come first, always and every time – what is it? Where is this country? The fact is that you and I don't have a country – so where is this place whose safety, honour and welfare are to come first, always and every time? And why was it that when we took our oath it wasn't to a country but to the King Emperor – to defend the Empire?'

Arjun turned to face him. 'Hardy, what are you trying to get at?'

'Just this,' said Hardy. 'Yaar, if my country really comes first, why am I being sent abroad? There's no threat to my country right now – and if there were, it would be my duty to stay here and defend it.'

'Hardy,' Arjun said lightly, 'staying here wouldn't do much for your career . . .'

'Career, career.' Hardy clicked his tongue, in disgust. 'Yaar, don't you ever think of anything else?'

'Hardy.' Arjun gave him a look of warning, to remind him of Kishan Singh's presence.

Hardy shrugged and looked at his watch. 'All right, I'll shut up,' he said, standing up to go. 'I'd better change too. We'll talk later.'

Hardy left and Kishan Singh carried Arjun's trousers into the dressing room. Kneeling on the floor, he held them open, by the waistband. Arjun stepped into them gingerly, taking care not to shatter the fragile sharpness of their glassy creases. Rising to his feet, Kishan Singh began to circle around Arjun, tucking his shirt-tails into his trousers.

Kishan Singh's hand brushed against the small of Arjun's back and he stiffened: he was on the verge of snapping at his batman to hurry up, when he stopped himself. It annoyed him to think that after two years as a commissioned officer he had still not succeeded in training himself to be at ease with the enforced intimacies of military life. This was one of the many things, he knew, that set him apart from the real faujis, the born-and-bred army-wallahs like Hardy. He'd once watched Hardy going through this very process of dressing for Guest Night with his batman's help: he was oblivious of the man's presence in a way that he, Arjun, never was of Kishan Singh's.

Suddenly Kishan Singh spoke up, taking Arjun by surprise. 'Sah'b,' he said, 'do you know where the battalion is going?'

'No. Nobody does. We won't know till we're on the ship.'

Kishan Singh started wrapping Arjun's cummerbund around his waist. 'Sah'b,' he said, 'the NCOs have been saying that we'll be going east . . .'

'Why?'

'At first we were training for the desert and everyone said we would be going to North Africa. But the equipment we were sent recently was clearly meant for the rain . . .'

'Who's been telling you all this?' Arjun said in surprise.

'Everyone, sah'b. Even in the villages they know. My mother and my wife came to visit last week. They'd heard a rumour that we were about to leave.'

'What did they say?'

'My mother said, "Kishan Singh, when are you going to come back?"'

'And what did you tell her?'

Kishan Singh was kneeling in front of Arjun now, checking his fly buttons and smoothing down his trousers, pinching the creases to restore their edge. Arjun could see only the top of his head, and the whorled patterns of his close-cropped hair.

Suddenly, Kishan Singh looked up at him. 'Sah'b, I told her that you would make sure that I came back . . .'

Arjun, caught by surprise, felt the blood rushing to his face. There was something inexplicably moving about the sheer guilelessness of this expression of trust. He felt at a loss for words.

Once, during their conversations at Charbagh, Lieutenant-Colonel Buckland had said that the reward of serving in India, for Englishmen of his father's generation, lay in their bonds with 'the men'. This relationship, he had said, was of an utterly different kind from that of the regular British army, the mutual loyalties of Indian soldier and English officer being at once so powerful and so inexplicable that they could be understood only as a kind of love.

Arjun recalled how strange this word had sounded on the CO's reticent lips and how he had been tempted to scoff. It seemed that in these stories 'the men' figured only as abstractions, a faceless collectivity imprisoned in a permanent childhood – moody, unpredictable, fantastically brave, desperately loyal, prone to extraordinary excesses of emotion. Yet, he knew it to be true that even for himself there were times when it seemed as though the attributes of that faceless collectivity – 'the men' – had been conjured into reality by a single soldier, Kishan Singh: that the bond that had come into being between them really was a kind of love. It was impossible to know how far this was Kishan Singh's own doing and how far it was the product of the peculiar intimacy of their circumstances; or was it perhaps something else altogether, that Kishan Singh, in his very individuality, had become more than himself – a village, a country, a history, a mirror for Arjun to see refractions of himself?

For an eerie instant Arjun saw himself in Kishan Singh's place: as a batman, kneeling before a dinner-jacketed officer, buffing his shoes, reaching into his trousers to tuck in his shirt, checking his fly buttons, looking up from the shelter of his parted feet, asking for protection. He gritted his teeth.

Twenty-eight

The morning after his arrival, Dinu borrowed a bicycle and went to look for the ruined chandis of Gunung Jerai. Alison drew him a map and he followed it: the track ran uphill most of the way from Morningside House and he had to mount and dismount several times, wheeling his machine up the steeper inclines. He made a couple of wrong turns but eventually found his way to the very spot where Alison had parked her car the last time. The stream lay below and its surroundings were exactly as he remembered: there was a shallow ford, bridged by flat stones. A little lower down the slope, the stream widened into a pool, ringed by massive boulders. On the far side, a narrow path led into the jungle.

By this time his right leg was sore and aching. He hung his camera bags on a branch and stepped down to the pool. On the bank there was a boulder that was so shaped as to serve perfectly for a seat. Dinu kicked off his shoes, rolled his trousers up to his knees, and plunged his legs into the cool, rushing water.

He'd been hesitant about coming to Malaya, but now that he was here, he was glad to be away from Rangoon, glad to leave behind the tensions of the Kemedine house and all the constant worrying about the business. And it was a relief, too, to put a distance between himself and the political infighting that seemed to be consuming all his friends. He knew his father wanted Alison to sell Morningside – it would be too much for her to manage on her own, he'd said; the estate would lose money. But as far as he could tell Morningside was running smoothly enough and Alison seemed to be very much in control. He couldn't see that she had any need for his advice, but he was glad to be here anyway. It would give him a chance to think things over for himself: in Rangoon he was always too busy, with politics, with the magazine. He was twenty-eight now and this, if any, was the time to decide whether photography was going to be just a hobby or a career.

He lit a cigarette and smoked it down to the butt, before picking up his camera bag to cross the stream. The path was more overgrown than he remembered, and in places he had to beat down the undergrowth. When he came to the clearing, he was awed by the serene beauty of the place: the colours of the moss-covered chandis were even more vivid than he remembered; the vistas in the background even more sweeping. He wasted no time in setting up his tripod. He exposed two rolls and it was sunset by the time he got back to Morningside House.

He went back the next morning and the morning after that. The ride became a regular routine: he'd set off early, taking along a couple of rotis for lunch. When he got to the stream, he'd daydream for a while, sitting on his favourite rock, with his legs plunged deep in the water. Then he'd make his way to the clearing and set up his equipment. At lunchtime he'd take a long break and afterwards he'd have a nap, lying in the shade in one of the chandis.

One morning, instead of stopping at the chandis, he went a little further than usual. Pushing into the forest he spotted an overgrown mound a short distance ahead. He beat a path through the undergrowth and found himself confronted with yet another ruin, built of the same materials as the two chandis – laterite – but of a different design: this one was roughly octagonal and shaped like a stepped pyramid or ziggurat. Despite the monumental design, the structure was modest in size, not much taller than his head. He climbed gingerly up the mossy blocks and at the apex he found a massive square stone, with a rectangular opening carved in the centre. Looking down, he found a puddle of rainwater trapped inside. The pool had the even shape and metallic glint of an antique mirror. He took a picture – a snapshot – and then sat down to smoke a cigarette. What was the opening for? Had it once been a base for a monumental sculpture – some gigantic, smiling monolith? It didn't matter: it was just a hole now, colonised by a family of tiny green frogs. When he looked down on his rippling reflection the frogs croaked at him in deep affront.

That evening, back at the house, he said to Alison: 'Did you know that there was another ruin – a kind of pyramid – a little farther into the jungle?'

She nodded. 'Yes, and there are others too. You'll find them if you go deep enough.'

The next day proved her right. Pushing a little further up the slope Dinu stumbled, quite literally, on a ten-foot-square platform made of laterite blocks – apparently the foundation of a small shrine. The plan of the temple was clearly visible on the floor, laid out like an architect's sketch. with a line of square embrasures indicating the placement of a row of columns. A day or so later he found another, much stranger ruin: a structure that had the appearance of being suspended within an explosion, like a prop in a photographic illusion. A banyan had taken root within the temple, and in growing, had pushed the walls apart, carrying away adjoining blocks of masonry. A doorway had been split in two, as though a bomb had exploded on the threshold. One stone post had been knocked over, while another had been carried off, coiled in a tangle of greenery, to a distance of several feet off the ground.

Sometimes, stepping into the ruins, Dinu would hear a rustle or a prolonged hiss. Occasionally the surrounding treetops would stir as though they'd been hit by a gust of wind. Dinu would look up to see a troop of monkeys examining him warily from the branches. Once he heard a sawing cough that could have been a leopard.

As his intimacy with the ruins deepened, Dinu began to find that his eye would go directly to the place where the temple's principal image would once have stood: his hands would reach automatically for the niches where offerings of flowers would have been laid; he began to recognise the limits beyond which he could not step without removing his shoes. When he crossed the stream, after bicycling through the estate, it was no longer as though he were tiptoeing into a place that was strange and unfamiliar, where life and order yielded to darkness and shadow. It was when he crossed back into the monochrome orderliness of the plantation that he felt himself to be passing into a territory of ruin, a defilement much more profound than temporal decay.

Late one afternoon, while standing at his tripod, he was alerted to the sound of a car by a commotion among the jungle's birds. He made his way quickly down the path to a vantage point where a gap in the greenery permitted a view of the stream below. He spotted Alison's red Daytona approaching on the far side. He left his tripod standing where it was and went hurrying down the path.

Dinu had seen very little of Alison since the day of his arrival. She left the house before dawn, in order to be present at Muster, and when she came back, he was usually out on the mountainside taking pictures. They generally met only at dinnertime, when conversation was inevitably constrained by Saya John's vacant silences. She seemed not to know how to fit a visitor into the fixed routines of her life on the plantation, and Dinu, for his part, was burdened by the knowledge of the task with which he had been entrusted. He knew that he would have to find a way of telling her that his father wanted to dispose of his share of Morningside and this seemed impossible at a time when she was so preoccupied, both with the grief of her parents' death, and with the daily anxieties of keeping the plantation afloat.

By the time Dinu reached the end of the path Alison had crossed the stream. Finding himself face to face with her now, he couldn't think of what to say and began to fumble in his pockets for a cigarette.

'Going back to the house?' he said at last, through his teeth, while striking a match.

'I thought I'd come by and see how you were getting on.'

'I was just setting up my camera . . .' He walked with her to the clearing, where his tripod was placed in front of one of the chandis.

'Can I watch you take pictures?' she asked brightly.

He hesitated, raising the cigarette to his mouth, squinting into the smoke. As though sensing a reluctance, Alison said: 'Would you mind? Would I be bothering you?'

'No,' he said. 'It's not that ... you wouldn't be bothering me exactly ... It's just that when I'm shooting I have to concentrate very hard ... or it's a waste ... It's like any other kind of work, you know ... it's not easy to do if you're being watched.'

'I see.' The hollow sound of her voice indicated that she'd read this as a rebuff. 'Well, I'll go then.'

'No,' he said quickly, 'please stay ... but then, if you're going to be here, could I take a few pictures of you ... ?'

She was quick to deal out a rebuff of her own. 'No. I'm not really in the right frame of mind to become a part of your – your work.' She turned on her heel and headed down the path, towards the stream.

Dinu knew himself to be stranded unwittingly in a quarrel.

'Alison ... I didn't mean ...' He hurried after her, but she was walking fast and his leg put him at a disadvantage. 'Alison ... please stay.' He caught up with her at the edge of the stream. 'Alison ... I was just telling you what it's like ... when I make a picture ... I didn't mean to put you off ... won't you stay?'

'Not now,' she glanced at her watch. 'Not today.'

'Then you'll come back?'

She'd already started across the ford. In mid-stream, without turning round, she raised a hand to wave.

Just before the battalion's departure from Saharanpur, new war equipment tables arrived. This meant that Arjun and Hardy had to stay up all night, revising their carefully-prepared Unit Mobilisation Scheme. But in the end all was well: the CO was pleased and the battalion was able to go ahead with its entrainment as planned. The train left for Bombay on schedule.

At Ajmer there was a slight delay. The 1/1 Jats were shunted aside so that a trainload of Italian prisoners of war could pass by. The Italians and Indians stared at each other in silence across the platform, through the barred windows of their respective carriages. This was their first glimpse of the enemy.

Next morning, they arrived at Bombay's Victoria terminus. They were told that their troop ship, the H.M.T. *Nuwara Eliya,* was waiting at the harbour. They drove to the Sassoon docks to find that their embarkation orders had already been issued.

The docks proved to be unexpectedly congested. It turned out that a British battalion was boarding another ship at exactly the same time. Soon the two battalions' baggage and equipment were hopelessly entangled with each other. NCOs began to shout, spreading panic among the dockworkers. Hardy was thrown into the midst of the confusion: he was the baggage officer for the 1/1 Jats and it fell on him to try and restore order.

Looking in Hardy's roster, Arjun learnt that he had been allotted a cabin to himself. He had never been on a ship before and was barely able to contain his excitement. He went hurrying up the gangplank to look for his cabin, with Kishan Singh following close behind, carrying his luggage.

They were the first to board and the ship was empty, but for its crew. Everything seemed new and startling: the white gunwales and narrow catwalks, the yawning hatches and the rounded frames of the portholes.

As they were stepping on to the upper deck, Kishan Singh happened to glance over the side. 'Sah'b – look!' He pointed, drawing Arjun's attention to an altercation on the docks below. Arjun saw that Hardy had got himself into a shouting match with a hulking British sergeant. They were standing toe to toe, with Hardy shaking a sheaf of papers under the sergeant's nose.

'Stay here.'

Arjun went racing down the way he had come. He arrived on the scene just a moment too late. Another officer from their battalion had got there before him – Captain Pearson, the adjutant, a bluff, stocky Englishman, with a booming voice and a quick temper.

Watching from a few paces away, Arjun saw Hardy turning to Captain Pearson. It was clear that Hardy was relieved to see the adjutant, fully confident that his senior would back him up – out of loyalty to a fellow-member of the battalion, if nothing else. But Captain Pearson had never made a secret of his belief that Hardy was 'difficult' and 'overly sensitive'. Instead of supporting him, he let his annoyance show: 'Lieutenant, have you got yourself into a row again . . . ?'

Arjun saw the look on Hardy's face change from relief to seething outrage. It was painful to stand there as a silent witness to his friend's humiliation. He turned and slipped away.

Later that day, Hardy came to his cabin.

'We've got to teach that bastard Pearson a lesson,' he said. 'That bloody sergeant called me a stinking nigger in front of the men. Pearson let him get away with it. Yaar, would you believe it, the bugger blamed me! The only way we can stop this kind of thing is by sticking together.'

'What exactly do you mean?'

'I think we should boycott him.'

'He's the adjutant, Hardy,' Arjun said. 'How can we boycott him? Be reasonable.'

'There are ways of getting a message across,' Hardy said angrily. 'But that can happen only when you know which side you're on.' Rising abruptly to his feet, he left Arjun's cabin.

For two days the *Nuwara Eliya* waited offshore, while nine other ships assembled in the harbour. There was a rumour that a German submarine was lurking nearby and the ships were assigned an escort of two destroyers, an armed merchantman and a light cruiser. When the convoy finally departed, it was in a westerly direction, heading towards the setting sun. Their destination was still unknown; they had no idea whether they were to go east or west.

In Bombay, the CO had been handed a sealed envelope that was to be opened exactly twenty-four hours after their departure. When the time came, Arjun and the other officers gathered in a dining room on the *Nuwara Eliya*'s upper deck. The CO opened the envelope in his usual deliberate way, prising the seal off the paper with a knife. The officers waited in expectant silence. Arjun could feel a clammy dampness welling up in the palms of his hands.

Then at last, the CO looked up with a thin smile. He held the sheet of paper in front of him and read out aloud: 'This ship is headed for Singapore.'

Arjun stepped out on deck and found Hardy already there,

leaning over the gunwale, humming softly under his breath. Behind them the white ribbon of the ship's wake had already begun to describe a curve as the convoy slowly changed direction.

Twenty-nine

Manju had never been happier than she was in the first months of her pregnancy. She relished every reminder of her changing condition: the often imaginary twitches and movements; the pangs of hunger that could never be properly satisfied; even the nausea that woke her every morning and the acid tingling of her teeth.

The Kemendine house had changed greatly in the two years she'd been in Rangoon. Dinu was gone of course, and his apartment upstairs lay empty. Neel and Rajkumar were often away, arranging for the disposal of the family's properties or buying new stocks of teak. For much of the time Manju and Dolly had the house to themselves. The compound had grown unkempt; where there had once been a lawn the grass now stood knee-high. Many rooms and outhouses were locked up; much of the furniture had been sold. The dozens of employees who had once populated the place were gone – the servants, watchmen, gardeners and their families. Even U Ba Kyaw, the chauffeur, had gone back to his village. The Packard was one of the few disposable possessions that Rajkumar had retained, but it was now driven mainly by Neel.

Neither Manju nor Dolly regretted the emptying of the house. On the contrary, it was as though an enormous accumulation of cobwebs had been swept away, allowing them new and unaccustomed freedoms. In the past Dolly had often seemed remote and unapproachable to Manju, but now they became allies, colleagues, team-mates, working together for the family's renewal. Between the two of them they had little difficulty in managing the house.

On waking in the morning, Manju would find Dolly on her knees, dressed in a frayed old longyi, wiping the floors with tattered shreds of cloth. They would work together, going through a couple of rooms each day, breaking off when the monks came by for their daily visits.

For Manju these mid-morning breaks were the best-loved aspect of daily life in Rangoon. She'd always known that Buddhist monks lived by collecting alms, but it came as a surprise to observe the ways in which this tenet, more or less abstract, came to be translated into the mundane mechanics of everyday life – into the workaday reality of a tired-looking group of young men and boys, walking down a dusty street in saffron robes, with their baskets balanced on their hips. There was something magical about the fact that this interruption came always at a time of day when the tasks of the household were at their most pressing; when there was scarcely room in one's head but to think about what had to be done next. And in the midst of all that – to open the door and see the monks standing there, waiting patiently, with the sun beating down on their shaven heads: what better way could there be of unbalancing everyday reality?

Calcutta seemed very far away now. The flow of letters from India had suffered disruptions because of the threat of submarines in the Bay of Bengal. Steamer traffic between Calcutta and Rangoon had become so irregular that letters tended to arrive in bunches.

One such bunch brought news both of Arjun's impending departure and of his arrival in Malaya. Dolly was very glad to hear of this development: 'Perhaps Arjun could find out what's become of Dinu,' she said. 'It's a long time since we last heard from him.'

'Yes, of course. I'll write . . .'

Manju sent a letter to the address her father had provided – via army headquarters in Singapore. Many weeks went by without an answer.

'Don't worry,' Manju said to Dolly. 'I'm sure Dinu's fine. We'd have heard if anything was wrong.'

'You're probably right.' But a month passed and then another and Dolly seemed to become resigned to her son's continuing silence.

The baby was now kicking urgently against the walls of Manju's stomach and she had no attention to spare for anything other than her own condition. With the approach of the monsoons, the days grew hotter and the effort of carrying the child grew very much greater. Sooner than they had expected, the festival of Waso was upon them. Dolly took Manju on a drive into the countryside in a taxi rented for the day. They stopped in a wooded area off the Pegu road, and collected armloads of fragrant yellow padauk flowers. They were on their way back to Rangoon when Manju had a dizzy spell and fainted on the back seat.

After this episode the doctor confined Manju to bed. Dolly became her nurse, bringing her food, helping with her clothes, occasionally leading her around the compound. The days went by in a kind of trance; Manju would lie dreamily in bed, with a book beside her, open but unread. Hours would pass while she did nothing but listen to the sound of the pouring rain.

They were now well into Thadin – the annual three-month period of reflection and abstinence. Often Dolly would read to Manju, mainly from the scriptures – from such translations as she could find, since Manju knew neither Pali nor Burmese. One day Dolly chose a discourse by the Buddha, addressed to his son, Rahula.

She read: *Develop a state of mind like the earth, Rahula, for on the earth all manner of things are thrown, clean and unclean, dung and urine, spittle, pus and blood, and the earth is not troubled or repelled or disgusted . . .*

Manju watched her mother-in-law as she read: Dolly's long, black hair was slightly flecked with grey and her face was etched with a webbing of lines. Yet, there was a youthfulness in her expression that belied these signs of age: it was hard to believe that this was a woman in her mid-sixties.

. . . develop a state of mind like water, for in the water many things are thrown, clean and unclean, and the water is not troubled or repelled or disgusted. And so too with fire, which burns all things, clean and unclean, and with air, which blows upon them all, and with space, which is nowhere established . . .

Dolly's lips seemed hardly to move, and yet every word was perfectly enunciated: Manju had never before known anyone who could appear to be in repose when she was actually at her most intently wakeful, her most alert.

When Manju reached the eighth month of her pregnancy Dolly banned Neel from any further travels. He was at home when Manju's labour started. He helped her into the Packard and drove her to the hospital. They could no longer afford the private suite that Dolly and Rajkumar had taken before, and instead Manju went into the general maternity ward. The next evening she was delivered of her child – a healthy, sharp-voiced girl, who began to suckle the moment she was put to Manju's breast. The baby was given two names – Jaya was to be her Indian name and Tin May the Burmese.

Exhausted by her labour Manju fell asleep. It was dawn when she woke up. The baby was in her bed again, rooting hungrily for her feed.

Holding her daughter to her breast, Manju remembered a passage that Dolly had read to her just a few days before: it was from the Buddha's first sermon, delivered at Sarnath, two thousand and five hundred years before: *. . . birth is sorrow, age is sorrow, disease is sorrow, death is sorrow; contact with the unpleasant is sorrow, separation from the pleasant is sorrow, every wish unfulfilled is sorrow . . .*

The words had made a great impression on her at the time, but now, with her newborn daughter beside her, they seemed incomprehensible: the world had never seemed so bright, so replete with promise, so profligate in its rewards, so generous in its joys and fulfilments.

For their first few weeks in Singapore the 1/1 Jats were based at the Tyersall Park camp. This was the very place that Arjun's friend Kumar had talked about – where a soldier had shot an officer and then committed suicide. In New Delhi the story had sounded unlikely and far-fetched – an extreme situation – like a report of a mother lifting up a car to save her children. But now that they were in Singapore themselves, with India half a continent away, nothing seemed improbable any more – everything appeared to be turned on its head. It was as though they no longer knew who they were, no longer understood their place in the order of things. Whenever they ventured beyond the familiar certainties of the battalion, they seemed to lose themselves in a labyrinth of hidden meanings.

It so happened that Kumar was in Singapore when the 1/1 Jats first arrived. One afternoon he took Arjun and Hardy to an exclusive club, for a swim. The pool was very crowded, filled with European expatriates and their families. It was a hot sticky day and the water looked cool and inviting. Following Kumar's lead, Arjun and Hardy jumped in. Within a few minutes they found themselves alone: the pool had emptied as soon as they entered the water.

Kumar was the only one who was not taken aback. His battalion had been in Malaya more than a year and he had travelled all round the colony.

'I should have warned you about this,' Kumar said, with a mischievous smile. 'It's like this everywhere in Malaya. In smaller towns, the clubs actually put up signs on their doors saying, "No Asiatics allowed". In Singapore they let us use the pool – it's just that everyone leaves. Right now they've had to relax the colour bar a little because there are so many Indian army units here. But you may as well get used to it because you'll come across it all the time – in restaurants, clubs, beaches, trains.' He laughed. 'We're meant to die for this colony – but we can't use the pools.' Ruefully shaking his head he lit a cigarette.

Soon their battalion was sent north. The Malayan countryside was a revelation to the Indian officers. They had never seen such prosperity, such beautiful roads, such tidy, well-laid-out little towns. Often, when they stopped, the local Indian residents would invite them to their houses. These were usually middle-class people with modest jobs – provincial lawyers and doctors, clerks and shopkeepers. But the signs of affluence in their homes were such as to amaze Arjun and his fellow-soldiers. It seemed that in Malaya even ordinary people were able to afford cars and refrigerators: some even had air conditioners and telephones. In India only Europeans and the richest of rich Indians could afford such things.

Driving along rural roads, the officers discovered that in Malaya the only people who lived in abject, grinding poverty were plantation labourers – almost all of whom were Indian in origin. They were astonished at the difference between the plantations' ordered greenery and the squalor of their coolie lines. Hardy once remarked on the starkness of the contrast and Arjun responded by pointing out that in India, they would have taken such poverty for granted; that the only reason they happened to notice it now was because of its juxtaposition with Malaya's prosperous towns. This thought made them both cringe in shame. It was as though they were examining their own circumstances for the first time, in retrospect; as though the shock of travel had displaced an indifference that had been inculcated in them since their earliest childhood.

Other shocks awaited. Out of uniform, Arjun and his friends found that they were often mistaken for coolies. In markets and bazaars shopkeepers treated them offhandedly, as though they were of no account. At other times – and this was worse still – they would find themselves being looked upon with something akin to pity. Once, Arjun got into an argument with a shopkeeper and found himself being called *Klang* – to his puzzlement. Later, enquiring about the meaning of this word, he discovered that it was a derogatory reference to the sound of the chains worn by the earliest Indian workers who were brought to Malaya.

Soon it seemed as though there was not a man in the battalion who had not found himself embroiled in an unsettling encounter of one kind or another. One evening, Kishan Singh was oiling Arjun's revolver, squatting on the floor, when he looked up suddenly. 'Sah'b,' he said to Arjun, 'can I ask you the meaning of an English word?'

'Yes. What is it?'

'*Mercenary* – what does it mean?'

'*Mercenary?*' Arjun started in surprise. 'Where did you hear this word?'

Kishan Singh explained that during one of their recent moves, their convoy of trucks had stopped at a roadside tea-stall, near the town of Ipoh. There were some local Indians sitting in the tea-stall. They had announced themselves to be members of a political group – the Indian Independence League. Somehow an argument had started. The civilians had told them that they – the 1/1 Jats – weren't real soldiers; they were just hired killers, mercenaries. A fight would have broken out, if the convoy hadn't got under way again. But later, when they were back on the road, they had begun to argue again – with each other this time – about the word mercenary and what it meant.

Arjun's instinct was to bark an order at Kishan Singh, telling him to shut up and get on with what he was doing. But by now he knew his batman well enough to be aware that an order would not deter him from looking for an answer to his question. Thinking quickly Arjun embarked on an explanation: mercenaries were merely soldiers who were paid for their work, he said. In this sense all soldiers, in all modern armies, were mercenaries. Hundreds of years ago soldiers had fought out of religious belief, or because of allegiance to their tribes, or to defend their kings. But those days were long past: now soldiering was a job, a profession, a career. Every soldier was paid and there was none who was not a mercenary.

This seemed to satisfy Kishan Singh, and he asked no more questions. But it was Arjun himself who now came to be troubled by the answer he had given his batman. If it was true (and it undoubtedly was) that all contemporary soldiers were mercenaries, then why did the word have the sting of an insult? Why did he feel himself smarting at its use? Was it because soldiering was not just a job after all, as he had taught himself to believe? That to kill without conviction violated some deep and unalterable human impulse?

One night he and Hardy stayed up late, discussing this subject over a bottle of brandy. Hardy agreed that it was hard to explain why it was so shameful to be called a mercenary. But it was he who eventually put his finger on it: 'It's because a mercenary's hands obey someone else's head; those two parts of his body have no connection with each other.' He paused to smile at Arjun: 'Because, yaar, in other words, a mercenary is a *buddhu*, a fool.'

Arjun refused to be drawn into Hardy's jocularity. He said: 'So are we mercenaries, do you think?'

Hardy shrugged. 'All soldiers are mercenaries today,' he said.

'In fact, why just stop with soldiers? In one way or another we're all a little like that woman you went to in Delhi – dancing to someone else's tune, taking money. There's not that much difference.' He tipped back his glass, with a laugh.

Arjun found an opportunity to take his doubts to Lieutenant-Colonel Buckland. He told him about the incident at the tea-stall and recommended that the other ranks' contacts with the local Indian population be more closely supervised. Lieutenant-Colonel Buckland heard him out patiently, interrupting only to nod assent: 'Yes, you're right, Roy, something must be done.'

But Arjun came away from this conversation even more disturbed than before. He had a feeling that the lieutenant-colonel could not understand why he was so outraged at being described as a 'mercenary'; in his voice there had been an undertone of surprise that someone as intelligent as Arjun could take offence at something that was no more than a statement of fact. It was as though the lieutenant-colonel knew something about him, that he, Arjun, either did not know or was not willing to recognise. Arjun was embarrassed now to think that he'd allowed himself to go off at the deep end. It was as though he were a child who'd taken umbrage at the discovery that he'd spoken prose all his life.

These experiences were so peculiar, so provocative of awkward emotions, that Arjun and the other officers could rarely bring themselves to speak of them. They had always known their country to be poor, yet they had never imagined themselves to be part of that poverty: they were the privileged, the elite. The discovery that they were poor too came as a revelation. It was as though a grimy curtain of snobbery had prevented them from seeing what was plainly before their eyes – that although they had never been hungry, they too were impoverished by the circumstances of their country; that such impressions as they'd had of their own wellbeing were delusions, compounded out of the unimaginable extremity of their homeland's poverty.

The strange thing was that even more than Arjun, it was the real faujis – the second- and third-generation army-wallahs – on whom these experiences had the most powerful effect. 'But your father and grandfather were here,' Arjun said to Hardy. 'It was they who helped in the colonisation of these places. They must have seen some of the things that we've seen. Did they never speak of all this?'

'They didn't see things as we do,' Hardy said. 'They were illiterate yaar. You have to remember that we're the first generation of educated Indian soldiers.'

'But still, they had eyes, they had ears, they must occasionally have talked to local people?'

Hardy shrugged. 'The truth is yaar, they weren't interested; they didn't care; the only place that was real to them was their village.'

'How is that even possible . . . ?'

In the following weeks Arjun thought often of this: it was as though he and his peers had been singled out to pay the price of a monumental inwardness.

With every day that he spent on the mountainside Dinu could feel his pictures changing. It was as though his eyes were adjusting to unaccustomed lines of sight; as though his body were adapting to new temporal rhythms. His earliest pictures of the chandis were angular and densely packed, the frames filled with sweeping vistas. He saw the site as being replete with visual drama – the jungle, the mountain, the ruins, the thrusting vertical lines of the tree trunks juxtaposed against the sweeping horizontals of the distant sea – he laboured to cram all these elements into his frames. But the more time he spent on the mountain, the less the background seemed to matter. The vastness of the landscape had the effect of both shrinking and enlarging the forest-enclosed clearing in which the chandis stood: it became small and intimate, but saturated with a sense of time. Soon he could no longer see either the mountains or the forest or the sea. He found himself moving closer and closer to the chandis, following the grain of the laterite and the pattern of the moss that covered its surface; trying to find a way of framing the curiously voluptuous shapes of the toadstools that grew within the joins of the stone.

The rhythms of his work changed in ways that he could not fully control. Hours would go by before he made a single exposure; he would go back and forth dozens of times, between his camera and his subject; he began to stop his lens further and further down, experimenting with aperture settings that required exposures of several minutes at a time, even as much as half an hour. It was as though he were using his instrument to mimic the pinprick eyes of the lizards that sunned themselves on the chandis' floors.

Many times each day, inexplicable perturbations would sweep through the surrounding forests. Flocks of birds would rise screaming from the surrounding trees and go boomeranging through the skies, only to settle back in exactly the same spots from which they had risen. To Dinu each of these disturbances now seemed like an augury of Alison's arrival, and in listening for their causes – sometimes the backfiring of a truck on the estate, sometimes a plane coming in to land at the nearby airstrip – his senses came to achieve an uncannily close attunement to the sounds of the forest. Every time the trees were shaken alive, he would break away from his work, straining to catch the sound of the Daytona. Often he would go running down the path to the gap where he could look down on the ford. As the disappointments mounted, he grew steadily more impatient with himself: it was plain idiocy to imagine that she'd drive out this way again, considering the last time. And in any event, why come all the way here, when she would see him in the house at dinnertime?

But then one day there really was a glimmer of red on the far side of the stream and the Daytona really could be seen to be standing under a tree, half-obscured by a tangle of greenery. Dinu looked once more, incredulously, and spotted Alison. She was dressed in a dark-blue cotton frock, with a wide belt tied around her waist. But instead of making her way to the ford, she was heading downstream, to the very rock where he sat every morning, dangling his legs in the pool. He could tell from the practised way in which she seated herself – swinging her feet up and then pivoting around to plunge them into the water – that this was a familiar place, a spot where she often came to be alone.

As her feet slid beneath the water, her fingers picked at the hem of her skirt and pulled it back. The water rose past her ankles, to her knees, and with it her skirt rose too, slowly climbing the long line of her thigh. Now, to his surprise, he made the discovery that he was no longer looking at her directly, but through the ground glass of his viewfinder, so that the image was partitioned from its surroundings and endowed with a startling clarity and vividness. The lines were clean, pure, beautiful – the curve of her thigh crossing his viewfinder diagonally, describing a gentle ellipsis.

She heard the click and looked up, startled, her fingers instantly loosening their grip on her skirt so that the fabric dropped into the water and ballooned around her, swirling in the current.

'Dinu?' she called out. 'Is that you?'

He had only this one chance now, he knew that, and he was powerless to stop himself. He stepped away from the gap and began to walk down the path, moving with the slow deliberation of a sleepwalker, holding his camera immobile in front of him.

'Dinu?'

He didn't try to answer but kept on moving, concentrating on the placing of one foot in front of the other, until he was clear of the greenery. From the far side of the pool, she looked into his eyes and swallowed back the words of greeting she'd been about to utter.

Dinu kept on walking. He dropped his camera on the grass and walked straight down the sandy bank, into the pool, directly across from the spot from where she sat. The water rose to his knees as he waded in, then to his groin, his hips, almost to his chest. The current began to tug at his clothes and his thin canvas shoes filled with sand and grit. He slowed to keep his footing, and then he saw her feet, hanging in the water, rippling in the current. He kept his eyes fixed on the shimmering flow and when his hands made contact with her legs he felt a deep breath rising from his lungs. It was the water that made this possible, he was sure of that; it was the stream that had washed away the barriers of fear and hesitation that had chained his hands before. He began to move his fingers, up the curve of her ankle, along the fine edge of her shin bone. Then his hands began to move on their own, pulling him behind them, between her parted knees, until suddenly her thighs were level with his face. It seemed the most natural thing in the world to follow his hands with his mouth, to move his lips along the elliptical line of her thigh, all the way along its length until the line parted. There he came to a stop, his face buried in her, his arms raised to shoulder height, holding her around her waist.

'Alison.'

She slid off the rock and stood neck deep in the water beside him. Taking his hand, she led him back through the pool, exactly the way he had come, to the other bank. They walked hand in hand, fully clothed and dripping wet, up the path that led to the ruined chandis. She took him through the clearing, up to a stone floor where a bed of moss lay thick on the laterite.

Then she reached for his hand and pulled him down.

Thirty

Neither Arjun nor anyone else in the 1/1 Jats knew quite what to expect when they arrived at Sungei Pattani. Before their departure from Ipoh they had been briefed – sketchily – on the problems they might encounter there. They knew that a mutiny had been narrowly averted just a few months before, but they were still unprepared for the cloud of disquiet that shrouded the base.

The troops at the Sungei Pattani base belonged to the 1st Bahawalpur Regiment. There had been a lot of friction between the battalion's officers and their English CO. Their CO had taken no pains to disguise his low opinion of his Indian officers: he'd been known to call them 'coolies' and to threaten them with his swagger stick. On one infamous occasion he had even kicked an officer. Things had got so bad that the GOC of the 11th Division had had to intervene personally; the CO had been relieved of his command and a number of officers had been sent home to India.

At their briefing the 1/1 Jats had been given to understand that these measures had substantially altered the situation; that the difficulties of the past had been resolved. But within a day of their arrival at Sungei Pattani it was evident that the troubles of the Bahawalpurs were far from over. Through the whole two hours of their first meal at the Bahawalpurs' mess hardly a word was exchanged between their British and Indian officers. And if the tensions in the Bahawalpurs' mess were clearly visible to Hardy and Arjun, they were certainly no less so to Lieutenant-Colonel Buckland. Over the next two days the Lieutenant-Colonel made a point of speaking to his officers individually, to let them know that fraternisation with the 1st Bahawalpurs would not be encouraged. In a way Arjun was glad. He knew this to be the right approach under the circumstances, and was more than ever grateful to have a commanding officer of the calibre and good sense of Lieutenant-Colonel Buckland. But the knowledge of this did not ease any of the small difficulties that arose in trying to avoid the Bahawalpurs' officers – some of whom were acquaintances from the academy.

Arjun had a room to himself, like all the officers of the 1/1 Jats. Their quarters, men and officers alike, consisted of attap huts – wooden barracks with palm-thatched roofs. These structures were mounted on pilings that were designed to keep out termites and damp. Yet, both insects and moisture figured large in the experience of living inside these barracks. The beds were frequently preyed upon by swarms of ants; after nightfall mosquitoes were so numerous that to climb out of bed for even a minute meant having to restring the whole mosquito net; the roofs often dripped and at night the rustling palm thatch seemed to come alive with rats and snakes.

Lieutenant-Colonel Buckland wanted the 1/1 Jats to use their time at Sungei Pattani on combat training, but circumstances conspired to confute all his plans. When they ventured into the surrounding rubber plantations the planters protested. Their attempts to acquaint the men with the terrain had to be called off. Then the medical corps began to complain about rising rates of malaria. As a result their plans for night training had to be cancelled. Frustrated in his more imaginative schemes, the CO set the battalion to a monotonous regimen of constructing fortifications around the base and the airstrip.

The airfield at Sungei Pattani consisted of just a single concrete runway and a few hangars, but it was still one of the few bases in north-western Malaya that boasted an operational air-squadron. The airmen at the base could on occasion be persuaded to provide joy-rides in their heavy-bellied Blenheims and Brewster Buffaloes. Arjun went on several of these rides, circling above the slopes of Gunung Jerai, looking down on the rubber plantations, swooping low over the grand houses and villas. At the summit of the mountain there stood a small lodge that served as a popular destination for holiday-makers. The pilots would often buzz the lodge, passing so close that the joy-riders could wave to the diners sitting at the tables on the veranda.

Through his first few weeks at Sungei Pattani Arjun had no idea that Dinu was living nearby. He was dimly aware that the Rahas owned shares in a rubber estate in Malaya, but he had no idea of where this plantation was. The first he knew of it was when he received a letter from Manju, posted in Rangoon.

Manju was unaware of her twin's exact location and knew only that he was somewhere in Malaya. She wrote to say that she was well and that her pregnancy was proceeding smoothly enough. But Neel and his parents were worried about Dinu: he'd gone over to Malaya several months before and hadn't been heard from for a while. They would be glad if Arjun would look him up. He was probably staying at the Morningside Estate with Alison, who had recently lost her parents. She provided a postal address.

Later in the day Arjun borrowed an Alvis staff car and drove into Sungei Pattani. He went to a Chinese restaurant where he and Hardy had eaten a couple of times. He asked for Ah Fatt, the proprietor, and showed him the address.

The proprietor took him outside into the shaded arcade and pointed across the street to a red roadster. That was Alison's car, he told Arjun, everyone in town knew it by sight. She had gone to her hairdresser's and would be out in a few minutes.

'There she is.'

She was wearing a *cheongsam* of black silk, with a slit that ran from her instep to her knee. Her hair framed her face like a polished helmet, its deep black sheen contrasting brightly with the soft glow of her skin.

It was several weeks since Arjun had spoken to a woman, and a very long time since he had beheld such a strikingly attractive face. He removed his cap and began to turn it over in his hands. He was just about to cross over, to introduce himself, when the red car pulled away from the shop and disappeared down the road.

* * *

Now the periodic disturbances of the mountainside did indeed become auguries of Alison's arrival. The rising of the birds from the canopy was a sure sign for Dinu to go hurrying down to the gap to look below – and often enough it really was Alison, dressed in one of the sombre black dresses that she wore to the office. Knowing that he'd be there, she'd look up and wave, and even as she was crossing the stream she'd begin to unbutton her blouse and unfasten her belt. Her clothes would be gone by the time she stepped into the clearing and he would be waiting, with his shutter primed.

It seemed that the hours he had spent attuning his eye to the mountainside had been an unconscious preparation for this – for Alison. He would spend long stretches of time thinking of where to place her, against which wall, or which part of the plinth; he'd imagine her seated upright, leaning against a lintel, one leg stretched straight in front of her and another bent back at the knee. In the gap between her legs he would glimpse a striation in the pitted surface of the laterite, or a soft mound of moss, as visual echoes of her body's fissures and curves. But the materiality of her presence would quickly disarrange these carefully imagined schemes. Once her body was placed where he wanted it, something would prove to be not quite right; he would frown into his square canvas of ground glass and go back to kneel beside her, sinking his fingertips softly into the tensile firmness of her thighs, teasing out minute changes in the angles of her limbs. Coaxing her legs further apart – or closer together – he would run a finger through the triangular swell of her pubis, sometimes combing the curls down, sometimes raking them back. Framed within the unnatural clarity of his viewfinder, these details seemed to assume a monumental significance: kneeling between her legs, he would wet his forefinger to draw a thin trail of moisture, a glistening hairline.

She would laugh at the intent seriousness with which he executed these intimate caresses, only to go hurrying back to his camera. When the reel was done, she would stop him before he could load another. 'No. Enough. Come here now.'

She would tug impatiently at his clothes – the shirt that was tucked carefully into his waistband, the undershirt beneath it.

'Why don't you just take these off when you come here – as I do?'

He would turn gruff. 'I can't, Alison . . . it's not my way . . .'

She would make him sit on the stone plinth and then peel away his shirt. Pushing him back, she would make him lie prone upon the stone. He would shut his eyes and knot his fingers under his head while she knelt between his legs. When his head cleared he would see her smiling at him, like a lioness looking up from a kill, mouth glistening. The lines were as perfect as any that could be imagined, the horizontal planes of her forehead, her eyebrows and her mouth, perfectly balanced by the verticals of her black, straight hair, and the translucent filaments that hung suspended from her lips.

She would see, reflected in his eyes, exactly what he beheld. Laughing out loud, she would say: 'No. This is a picture you'll never see anywhere but in your own head.'

Then afterwards, quickly but methodically, he would dress himself again, tucking his shirt carefully into his trousers, fastening his belt, kneeling to tie the laces of his canvas shoes.

'Why bother?' she'd challenge him. 'You'll just have to take them off again.'

He'd answer seriously, unsmiling: 'I have to, Alison . . . I have to be dressed when I work.'

Sometimes she would grow bored with the length of sitting. Often she would talk to herself while he was adjusting his camera, throwing in words of Malay, Tamil and Chinese, reminiscing about her mother and father, thinking aloud about Timmy.

'Dinu,' she cried one day in exasperation, 'I feel I have more of your attention when you're looking into your camera than when you're lying here with me.'

'And what's wrong with that?'

'I'm not just a thing, for your camera to focus on. Sometimes it's as if you have no other interest in me but this.'

He saw that she was upset and he left his tripod to sit with her. 'I see more of you in this way than I would in any other,' he said. 'If I were to talk to you for hours I wouldn't know you better. I don't say this is better than talking . . . it's just my way – my way of understanding . . . You mustn't think this is easy for me . . . I never do portraits; they frighten me . . . the intimacy . . . being in someone's company that long – I've never wanted to do them . . . nudes even less. These are my first and it's not easy.'

'Should I be flattered?'

'I don't know . . . but I feel my pictures have helped me know you . . . I think I know you better than I've ever known anyone.'

She laughed. 'Just because you've taken some pictures?'

'Not just that.'

'Then?'

'Because this is the most intimate way that I can know anyone . . . or anything.'

'Are you saying you wouldn't have known me if it weren't for your camera?'

He looked down at his hands, frowning. 'I can tell you this. If I hadn't spent this time with you, here, taking pictures . . . I wouldn't be able to say, with such certainty . . .'

'What?'

'That I'm in love with you.'

She sat up, startled, but before she could speak, Dinu continued, '. . . And I also know . . .'

'What?'

'That I want you to marry me.'

'Marry you!' She rested her chin on her knees. 'What makes you think I'd want to marry someone who can only talk to me through a camera?'

'Don't you then?'

'I don't know, Dinu.' She shook her head impatiently. 'Why marriage? Isn't this good enough?'

'Marriage is what I want – not just this.'

'Why spoil everything, Dinu?'

'Because I want it . . .'

'You don't know me, Dinu.' She smiled at him, running a hand over the back of his head. 'I'm not like you. I'm wilful, I'm spoilt: Timmy used to call me wayward. You'd hate me in a week if you were married to me.'

'I think that's for me to judge.'

'And what would we be marrying for? Timmy isn't here

and nor are my parents. You've seen how unwell my grandfather is.'

'But what if . . . ?' He leant over to place a hand on her belly. 'What if there's a child?'

She shrugged. 'We'll see then. For now – let's just be content with what we have.'

Without a single word being said on the subject, Dinu understood, soon after the time of their first meeting, that between himself and Ilongo there existed some sort of connection – a link that was known to Ilongo but of which he himself was unaware. This understanding arose gradually, out of their conversations, nurtured by a pattern of questions and occasional oblique asides – by Ilongo's curiosity about the Raha house in Rangoon, by his interest in family photographs, by the manner in which his references to 'Your father' slowly metamorphosed so that the pronoun disappeared.

Dinu understood that he was being prepared, that when Ilongo judged it right he would let him know about whatever it was that lay between them. This awareness evoked strangely little curiosity in Dinu – and this was not merely because his attention was wholly claimed by Alison. It was also because of Ilongo himself – because there was something about him that was so transparently trustworthy that it caused Dinu no anxiety to concede to him his superior knowledge.

Except for Alison, Dinu saw more of Ilongo than of anyone else at Morningside: he was dependent on him for many small things – posting letters, cashing cheques, borrowing bicycles. When he decided to set up his own dark room, it was Ilongo who helped him find second-hand equipment in Penang.

One Sunday, Dinu accompanied Ilongo on his weekly trip to Sungei Pattani, with Saya John. They visited Ah Fatt's restaurant, where Saya John handed over an envelope, as always. 'I do it for my wife,' he told Dinu. 'She was Hakka you know, on both sides. She always said that I was Hakka too, except that no one could tell for sure, since I never knew my parents.'

Afterward Dinu and Ilongo drove Saya John to the Church of Christ the King, on the outskirts of town. The church was bright and cheerful-looking with a soaring white-washed steeple and a facade that was ornamented with polished wooden rails. Under the shade of a flowering tree, a colourfully-dressed congregation had gathered. A white-robed Irish priest led Saya John away, clapping him on the back: 'Mr Martins! And how are you today?'

Dinu and Ilongo went to the morning show at the cinema and saw Edward G. Robinson in *I am the Law*. On the way back, after collecting Saya John, they stopped at Ilongo's mother's house, for a bowl of noodles.

Ilongo's mother was near-sighted and prematurely bent. When Ilongo introduced him, Dinu could tell that she already knew exactly who he was. She asked him to come closer and touched his face with fingers that were cracked and callused. She said, in Hindustani, 'My Ilongo looks much more like your father than you do.'

In some region of his consciousness Dinu understood exactly what she was saying, but he responded to her words as though to a pleasantry. 'Yes, that's true. I can see the resemblance.'

Apart from this one charged moment, the visit went well. Saya John seemed unusually alert, almost his old self. They all ate several helpings of noodles and at the end of the meal, Ilongo's mother served thick, milky tea in glass tumblers. When they left, they were all aware – in a manner that was not in the least uncomfortable – that a visit that had begun as a meeting between strangers, had somehow changed, in tone and texture, to a family reunion.

On the way back to the house they sat three abreast in the truck, with Ilongo driving and Saya John in the middle. Ilongo looked visibly relieved, as though some sort of hurdle had been crossed. But Dinu found it hard to give shape to the thought that Ilongo might be his half-brother. A brother was what Neel was – a boundary to mark yourself off against. This was not what Ilongo was. If anything, Ilongo was an incarnation of his father – as he'd been in his youth, a far better man than the one whom he, Dinu, had known. There was some consolation in this.

It was on this night that Dinu mentioned his suspicions to Alison for the first time. She'd slipped into his room after dinner, as she sometimes did after settling her grandfather in his bed. At midnight she woke to see Dinu sitting by the window, smoking a cigarette. 'What's the matter, Dinu? I thought you were asleep.'

'Couldn't sleep.'

'Why not?'

Dinu told her about his visit to Ilongo's mother and what she had said. Then he looked straight into her eyes and asked: 'Tell me, Alison . . . am I just imagining all this – or is there something to it?'

She shrugged and took a puff of his cigarette, without answering the question. So he asked again, more insistently: 'Is there any truth to this, Alison? You should tell me if you know . . .'

She said: 'I don't know, Dinu. There were always rumours. But nobody's ever said anything directly – not to me anyway. You know how it is – people don't talk about these things.'

'And you? Do you believe these . . . these rumours?'

'I didn't used to. But then Grandfather said something that made me change my mind.'

'What?'

'That your mother had asked him to look after Ilongo.'

'So she knows – my mother?'

'I think so.'

He lit another cigarette, in silence. Alison knelt beside him and looked into his face: 'Are you upset? Angry?'

He smiled, stroking her naked back. 'No. I'm not upset . . . and no angrier than I've always been. That's the strange thing really – knowing the kind of man my father is, it comes as no surprise. It just makes me want never to go back home . . .'

A few days later Alison sent up a letter that had just arrived. Dinu was working in his dark room and he broke off to look at the envelope: it was from Rangoon, from his father. Without another thought, he tore it up and went back to work.

That evening, after dinner, Alison asked: 'Dinu, did you get the letter?'

He nodded.

'It was from your father, wasn't it?'

'I suppose so.'

'Didn't you read it?'

'No. I tore it up.'

'Didn't you want to know what he was writing about?'

'I know what he was writing about.'

'What?'

'He wants to sell his share of Morningside . . .'

She paused and pushed her plate away. 'Is that what you want too, Dinu?'

'No,' he said. 'As far as I'm concerned, I'm going to be here for ever . . . I'm going to set up a studio in Sungei Pattani, and make a living from my camera. It's what I've always wanted to do – and this is as good a place as any to do it.'

Thirty-one

The night Ilongo brought Arjun to Morningside House, Dinu, Alison and Saya John were in the dining room, sitting at the long mahogany table. On the walls glowed the bamboo-shelled sconces that Elsa had designed. The room was filled with a rich, warm light.

Ilongo was smiling broadly, in anticipation of Dinu's surprise. 'Look who I've brought with me.' Then Arjun walked through the door, dressed in uniform, with his cap in his hands. His Sam Browne glistened in the golden glow of the bamboo sconces.

'Arjun?'

'Hello.' Arjun walked around the table and patted Dinu on the shoulder. 'Nice to see you, old chap.'

'But, Arjun . . .' Dinu stood up. 'What are you doing here?'

'I'll tell you soon enough,' Arjun said. 'But won't you introduce me first?'

'Oh yes. Of course.' Dinu turned to Alison. 'This is Arjun. Neel's brother-in-law – Manju's twin.'

'I'm so glad you came.' Alison leant over to Saya John and spoke softly into his ear. 'Grandfather, this is Dinu's brother-in-law,' she said. 'He's posted at the army base in Sungei Pattani.'

Now it was Arjun's turn to be surprised. 'How did you know I was posted at Sungei Pattani?'

'I saw you in town the other day.'

'Really? I'm amazed that you noticed.'

'Of course I noticed.' She threw back her head to laugh. 'In Sungei Pattani a stranger stands out.'

Dinu broke in. 'You didn't say anything to me, Alison . . .'

'I just saw a man in a uniform.' Alison laughed. 'How was I to know he was your brother-in-law?'

'I knew,' Ilongo said. 'I knew the moment I saw him.'

'He did.' Arjun nodded. 'I walked into the estate office to ask for Dinu. And before I'd even opened my mouth he said: "Aren't you Mister Neel's brother-in-law?" You could have knocked me over with a feather. I said: "How did you know?" and he said: "Mr Dinu showed me a picture – from your sister's wedding."'

'So I did.'

Dinu recalled that it was two years since he and Arjun had last met – in Calcutta. Arjun seemed to have grown in the meanwhile – or was it just that he had filled out his uniform? Even though Arjun had always been tall, Dinu could not remember ever feeling dwarfed in his presence as he did now.

'Well,' said Alison brightly. 'You must have something to eat – both you and Ilongo.'

The table was spread with dozens of small, colourful china bowls. Most of them still had their contents intact.

Arjun eyed the food with longing. 'A real meal, at last . . .'

'Why?' said Alison. 'Don't they feed you at your base?'

'They do their best I suppose.'

'There's plenty here for both of you,' Alison said. 'So sit down – Ilongo, you too. The cook's always complaining that we send the food back untouched.'

Ilongo shook his head. 'I can't stay . . .'

'Are you sure?'

'Yes. My mother will be waiting.'

Ilongo left and another place was laid at the table, next to Alison's. Arjun seated himself and Alison began to pile his plate with food.

'We call this *ayam limau purut* – chicken with lime leaves and tamarind; and here's some prawn sambal with screwpine leaves; and these are belacan brinjals; and over there is some chinchalok with chillies – shrimps, pickled in lime juice; and this here is fish steamed with ginger buds . . .'

'What a feast! And this was just an everyday dinner?'

'My mother was always very proud of her table,' Alison said. 'And now it's become a habit of the house.'

Arjun ate with gusto. 'This food is wonderful!'

'Your aunt Uma loved it too. Do you remember, Dinu? That time?'

'Yes I do.' Dinu nodded. 'I think I even have pictures.'

'I've never eaten anything like this,' Arjun said. 'What is it called?'

'It's Nyonya food,' Alison said. 'One of the world's last great secrets, my mother used to say.'

Suddenly Saya John spoke up, catching them all by surprise.

'It's the flowers that make the difference.'

'The flowers, Grandfather?'

Saya John looked at Arjun with eyes that were fleetingly clear. 'Yes – the flowers in the food. Bunga kentan and bunga telang – ginger flowers and blue flowers. They're what give the food its taste. That's what Elsa always says.'

A shadow passed over his face and his eyes grew cloudy again. He turned to Alison. 'We must remember to send Matthew and Elsa a telegram,' he said. 'They should stop in Malacca on the way back.'

Alison rose quickly from her chair. 'You must excuse us,' she said to Arjun. 'My grandfather is tired. I should take him up to bed.'

'Of course.' Arjun stood up.

Alison helped Saya John to his feet and led him slowly across the room. At the door, she turned to look back at Arjun. 'It's nice to have a visitor who likes our food – the cook's always saying that Dinu doesn't eat at all. She'll be delighted you enjoyed her cooking. You must come again.'

'I will.' Arjun grinned. 'You can be sure of that.'

There was a warmth and lightness in Alison's voice that Dinu hadn't heard before. Watching her from his place at the table, he was conscious of a sudden rush of jealousy.

'Well old chap,' said Arjun, in a booming, hearty voice, 'did you know that you've got everyone worried at home?'

'No.' Dinu flinched. 'And there's really no need to shout.' It was a struggle to muster the self-control to go on talking to Arjun.

'I'm sorry.' Arjun laughed. 'Didn't mean to put you out . . .'

'I'm sure you didn't.'

'I had a letter from Manju, you see – that's how I knew where to find you.'

'I see.'

'She said they hadn't heard from you in a while.'

'Oh?'

'What would you like me to tell them?'

Dinu raised his head with great deliberation. 'Nothing,' he said flatly. 'I'd like you to tell them nothing . . .'

Arjun raised an eyebrow. 'Can I ask why?'

'It's not very complicated.' Dinu shrugged. 'You see . . . my father sent me here because he wants to sell our share of Morningside.'

'And?'

'Now that I'm here . . . I've decided it wouldn't be a good idea.'

'You've grown to like the place I suppose?'

'It's not just that.' Dinu looked Arjun straight in the eye. 'It's Alison really.'

'What do you mean?'

'Well, you've met her . . .'

'Yes.' Arjun nodded.

'You probably know what I mean.'

'I think you're trying to tell me something, Dinu.' Arjun pushed his chair back from the table. 'Let me guess: are you saying you've fallen for her?' He laughed.

'Something like that.'

'I see. And do you think she's keen on you too?'

'I think so.'

'Hasn't she told you so?'

'Not . . . in so many words.'

'Hope you're right then.' Arjun laughed again and the light sparkled on his perfect teeth. 'I have to say I don't know if she's right for a chap like you – a woman like that.'

'It doesn't really matter, Arjun . . .' Dinu tried to smile. 'In my case it's something I have to believe . . .'

'And why is that?'

'You see – I'm not like you, Arjun. It's never been easy for me to get on with people – especially women. If something went wrong . . . between me and Alison, that is . . . I don't know how I'd cope . . .'

'Dinu, am I right to think that you're warning me – telling me to stay away?'

'Perhaps I am.'

'I see.' Arjun pushed his plate away. 'There's really no need, you know.'

'Good.' Dinu felt a smile returning to his face. 'Well, that's out of the way then.'

Arjun looked at his watch and stood up. 'Well, you've certainly made yourself clear. So perhaps I should be off. You'll make my excuses to Alison?'

'Yes . . . of course.'

They went together to the front door. Arjun's Ford V8 staff car was parked outside, under the porch. Arjun opened the door and held out his hand. 'It was nice to see you, Dinu,' he said. 'Even if briefly.'

Dinu was suddenly ashamed of his lack of generosity. 'I don't mean to send you away, Arjun . . .' he said guiltily. 'Please don't think that you're not welcome. You must come back . . . Soon . . . I'm sure Alison would like that.'

'And you?'

'Yes. Me too.'

Arjun appraised this with a frown. 'Are you sure?'

'Yes, of course. You must . . . you must come back.'

'I will then, if you don't mind, Dinu. It would be nice to get away from the base every now and again.'

'Why? Is something wrong?'

'Not wrong exactly – but it's not always as pleasant as it might be . . .'

'Why?'

'I don't know how to explain, Dinu. Ever since we've got to Malaya nothing's been the same.'

Arjun's entry into their lives was like a turning of the seasons. He dropped by almost daily, often bringing Hardy or some other friends with him. Sungei Pattani had now become the headquarters of the 11th Division, and Arjun had linked up with many old acquaintances and friends. In the evenings he would gather them together and drive up from the base, in whatever vehicle was at hand – sometimes an Alvis staff car, sometimes a Ford V8, sometimes, even, a Harley-Davidson motorcycle. Usually they came after nightfall, driving up with their headlights blazing, sounding triumphal flurries on their horns.

'They're here!' Alison would run down to the kitchen to warn the cook.

It was evident that she enjoyed these visits; Dinu could tell that it delighted her to see the house filled with people again. She produced clothes that he did not know she possessed: until then he'd seen her only in the plain dresses she wore to the office, and an occasional silk cheongsam. Now richly coloured, beautifully tailored clothes poured out of her closets – elegant hats and gowns that her mother had ordered from Paris, in Morningside's heyday.

Almost every evening the house echoed to the sound of parade-ground voices and loud laughter. They seemed never to stop laughing, these young officers – the smallest joke would set them roaring, pounding each other on the back. They usually brought bottles of whisky, gin or rum from their mess. Sometimes Kishan Singh came with them to serve them their drinks. They would sit out on the veranda, sipping *stengahs* and gin slings. As if by magic, vast quantities of food would appear on the dining-room table. Alison would lead them in and then Arjun would take over, showing his friends round the table, explaining the dishes in minute detail: 'Look over here, this is duck – it's cooked in sugar-cane juice, you've never tasted anything like it. And here, see, these prawns? They're made with flowers – ginger buds – that's what gives them that amazing taste . . .'

Dinu would look on, like a spectator at a circus: he knew that the part of host should have been his own to play. But with each of these evenings he could feel his presence in the house diminishing, shrinking. It didn't seem to matter whether Arjun came alone or was accompanied by a troop of his friends. He seemed to have a way of filling the house, even when he was on his own. There was no denying that there was something magnetic about him – a self-confidence, a habit of command, an exuberant abundance of appetites. Dinu knew he could not hope to keep up with him.

At the end of each meal, Arjun would crank up the gramophone and clear the rugs off the hardwood floors. He and his friends would take turns dancing with Alison. It was a revelation to Dinu to discover how well she danced – better than anyone he'd ever known, just as well as dancers in the movies – with flair and rhythm and an energy that seemed inexhaustible. Amongst the men, Arjun was the best dancer by far. At the end of each night, he would put on his favourite record – Tommy Dorsey's band playing 'I'm Getting Sentimental Over You'. Everyone else would pull back to make space for them, and when the record came scratching to a stop the room would fill with applause. At the end of these evenings Alison seemed scarcely to remember that he, Dinu, still existed.

Once in a while Arjun would announce that he had succeeded in scrounging some extra petrol from the 'pilot chappies' at the airstrip. They would set out on an expedition, sometimes just the three of them, sometimes as a part of a much larger crowd. One such foray took them to the lodge that sat atop the summit of Gunung Jerai. A group of pilots had commandeered the place for a party; they were to be Arjun's guests.

They went in a Ford V8 staff car. To get to the summit they had to circle around the mountain driving past quiet *kampongs* with palm-shaded mosques. Children waved at them from ricefi-elds, standing on tiptoe to reach above the grain-heavy stalks. It was a cloudy late November day and there was a cool breeze blowing in from the sea.

The road that led to the summit was not much better than a dirt track. It tacked back and forth across the slope, rising steeply. The mountainside was thickly forested and the track wound through dense patches of jungle. It was several degrees cooler than in the plain, and the sun was blocked by a constant, quick-moving blanket of cloud. At the top the vegetation ended abruptly and the lodge appeared – it looked a little like an English cottage, except that it was surrounded by a balcony that provided dramatic views of the coast and the surrounding plains.

The balcony was crowded with servicemen in grey, blue, khaki and bottle-green. Scattered among the uniforms were a few women dressed in brightly printed cottons. Somewhere inside the lodge a band was playing.

Arjun and Alison went off into the lodge to dance and Dinu was left to himself. He walked round the balcony, past tables that were draped in flapping white cloths. The view of the plain was hindered by a mantle of clouds blowing in from the sea. But every so often the wind would tear the cloud-cover apart, providing spectacular glimpses of the plain: he caught sight of Sungei Pattani, at the foot of the mountain, with hundreds of acres of rubber stretching away from it in all directions. In the distance, he spotted the craggy peaks of the island of Penang and the finger-like wharfs of the port of Butterworth. The north–south highway ran like a great stripe across the landscape, approaching from the southern end of the plain and disappearing towards the north, where the border lay. Along the west lay the Andaman Sea, alight with the bright colours of the sunset.

On the next clear day, Dinu promised himself, he would bring his cameras to the lodge. For the first time in his life, he regretted never having learned to drive: for this view alone, the effort would have been worthwhile.

The next day Arjun was back at Morningside again, at an unusual hour – at eleven in the morning. He was driving a motorcycle, a wasp-waisted, pigeon-breasted Harley-Davidson, painted a dull, military green. It had a sidecar attached. Arjun drove up to the house from the plantation office with Alison sitting in the sidecar.

Dinu was in his dark room when Arjun shouted up from the porch: 'Dinu! Come down here. I've got some news.'

Dinu went running downstairs. 'Well . . . ?'

Arjun laughed, punching his shoulder. 'You're an uncle, Dinu – and so am I. Manju's had a baby – a girl.'

'Oh . . . I'm glad . . .'

'We're going to celebrate. Come with us.'

'Where are you going?'

'Down to the sea,' said Arjun. 'Jump on. Behind me.'

Dinu glanced at Alison, who looked away. He felt his feet growing leaden. Over the last many days he had struggled to keep pace with the two of them, but he could not be what he was not. He did not want to be with her just so that his presence would weigh on her as a reminder – anything but that.

'I don't think you really want me with you,' Dinu said quietly.

They sounded a chorus of protests.

'Oh, Dinu. Rubbish!'

'Oh, come on, Dinu. Don't be an ass.'

Dinu turned on his heel. 'I have work to finish in the dark room. You go ahead. You can tell me about it when you get back.' He went back into the house and ran upstairs. He heard the coughing sound of the motorcycle's kick-starter and could not keep himself from looking down, from a window. The Harley-Davidson was speeding down the drive, heading into the estate. He caught a glimpse of Alison's scarf, fluttering like a pennant.

He went back into his dark room and found that his eyes were smarting. In the past he'd always been able to count on the ambience of the dark room for reassurance; its dim red glow had been an unfailing source of comfort. But now the light seemed too bright, unbearably so. He switched it off and sat crouched on the floor, hugging his knees.

His instincts had been true from the start. He'd known that Arjun could not be trusted – nor Alison, not with him. Yet what could he have done? They were adults, and he had no real claim on either of them.

In a while he touched his face and found that it was wet. He grew angry with himself: if there was any tenet on which he'd wanted to build his life, it was that of never giving in to self-pity – that was a road that would not end, he knew, once he had started down it.

He rose to his feet and walked around the room in the darkness, trying to recall its exact size and layout as well as the placement of every bit of furniture and every object. He counted his paces and every time he touched a wall or bumped against something, he started over again.

He came to a decision. He would leave. It was clear that Alison had lost interest in him and there was nothing to be gained from remaining at Morningside. He would pack his things and spend the night at Ilongo's mother's house. Tomorrow he would go to Penang, to wait for a steamer that would take him back to Rangoon.

The motorcycle headed due west, down a road that dwindled into a fraying ribbon of tarmac, fringed by dust and sand. They drove through a small town with a blue-domed mosque and then the sea appeared in front of them, sparkling blue. Waves were climbing gently up a long shelf of sand. The road turned left and they stayed on it, driving parallel to the beach. They came to a small hamlet and the road ended. The marketplace smelt of salt water and drying fish.

Alison asked: 'Should we leave the motorcycle here?'

'No.' Arjun laughed. 'We don't have to. We can take it with us. This Harley can go anywhere.'

The villagers gathered to stare as they drove through the marketplace, slipping through the gaps between the shacks. The motorcycle whined as it climbed over the dune that separated the hamlet from the sea. The sand was blindingly white in the noonday sun. Arjun kept to the edge of the beach, where the ground was held together by a thin carpet of weeds. He drove slowly, dodging between the windblown trunks of coconut palms.

They left the village far behind and came to a cove that was sheltered by screwpines. The beach consisted of a thin, white fingernail of sand. At the mouth of the cove, no more than a hundred yards from the shore, there was a tiny island. It was thickly wooded, with green bushes and dwarf pines.

'Let's stop here,' said Alison.

Arjun wheeled the motorcycle into a patch of shade and pulled it on to its kickstand. They took off their shoes and left them on the sand. Arjun rolled up his trouser cuffs and they ran across the burning sliver of beach, straight into the water. It was low tide and the sea was very calm, with gentle waves lapping at the shore. The water was so clear that it magnified the shifting patterns of the sea floor, giving them the appearance of coloured mosaics.

'Let's swim,' said Arjun.

'I didn't bring anything.'

'It doesn't matter.' Arjun began to unbutton his khaki shirt. 'There's no one here.'

Alison was wearing a workaday cotton dress. She'd been holding it up, keeping the hem above the water. Now she let it drop. The water soaked quickly into the cotton, rising towards her waist.

'Come on, Alison. We have the whole place to ourselves.' Arjun's shirt-tails were hanging loose, the buttons undone.

'No.' She laughed. 'It's December. You have to respect our winter.'

'It's not cold. Come on.' He reached for her hand, his tongue flicking over the sparkling line of his teeth.

She dug her toes into the sand. Through the clear water, she spotted the curved edge of a seashell, buried between her feet. Reaching into the water she dug it out. The shell was unexpectedly heavy, large enough to fill both her hands.

'What is it?' said Arjun, looking over her shoulder. His khaki trousers were wet almost to the waist.

'It's a nautilus,' she said.

The shell had an elliptical opening at one end, like a horn: the colour inside was a rich mother of pearl, tinged with silver highlights. Its body was coiled into an almost perfectly circular mound. A spiral line ran along the mound, ending in a tiny protrusion, not unlike a nipple.

'How do you know what it's called?' Arjun asked. She could sense his presence behind her. He was looking over her at the shell, his chin resting lightly on her head.

'Dinu showed me a photograph of a shell like this one,' she said. 'He thinks it's one of the greatest pictures ever made.'

His arms reached round her shoulders, encircling her body. His hands closed on the shell, his fingers dwarfing hers, his palms wet against the back of her hands. He ran his thumb along the edge of the mother of pearl mouth, over the line that encircled the swelling body, to the tiny nipple-like point that topped the mound.

'We should . . .' She felt the touch of his breath blowing through her hair. 'We should take this back for Dinu,' he said. His voice had gone hoarse.

He let his arms drop and stepped away from her. 'Let's go and explore,' he said, pointing in the direction of the island that lay at the mouth of the cove. 'I bet we could walk over. The water's very low.'

'I don't want to get my dress wet.' She laughed.

'You won't,' he promised. 'If the water gets too high I'll carry you on my back.'

He took hold of her hand and pulled her deeper into the water. The ground dipped until the water was at waist-level. Then the sandy floor began to rise again, sloping up towards the island. Arjun began to move faster, pulling her with him. They were running when they reached the shore. They raced across the sun-baked fringe of sand, into the shaded interior of the island. Alison fell on her back, on the soft, sandy earth, and looked up at the sky. They were encircled by bushy screwpines, screened from the shore.

Arjun threw himself down beside her, on his stomach. She was still holding the shell and he prised it free of her grip. He laid it on her chest, and ran his finger along the shell's spiral edge, cupping its body with his palm.

'It's so beautiful,' he said.

She saw how badly he wanted her; there was something irresistible about the insistency of his desire. When his hand slipped off the shell, on to her body, she made no effort to stop him. From that moment on, when it was already too late, everything changed. It was as though he wasn't really there and nor was she; as though their bodies had been impelled more by a sense of inevitability than by conscious volition; by an inebriation of images and suggestion – memories of pictures and songs and dances; it was as though they were both absent, two strangers, whose bodies were discharging a function. She thought of what it was like with Dinu; the intensity of his focus on the moment; the sense of time holding still. It was only against the contrast of this cohabiting of absences that she could apprehend the meaning of what it meant to be fully present – eye, mind and touch united in absolute oneness, each beheld by the other, each beholding.

When Arjun rolled off her she began to cry, pulling her dress down over her body, clasping her knees. He sat up, in consternation. 'Alison – what's the matter? Why're you crying?'

She shook her head, her face buried between her knees.

He persisted. 'Alison, I didn't mean ... I thought you wanted . . .'

'It's not your fault. I'm not blaming you. Only myself.'

'For what, Alison?'

'For what?' She looked at him in disbelief. 'How can you look at me after this and ask me a question like that? What about Dinu?'

'Alison.' He laughed, reaching for her arm. 'Dinu doesn't need to know. Why tell him about this?'

She pushed his hand away. 'Please,' she said. 'Please. Don't touch me.'

Then they heard a voice, calling in the distance, just loud enough to carry over the lapping of the water.

'Sah'b.'

Arjun pulled on his wet uniform and stood up. He saw Kishan Singh standing on the beach; behind him was a helmeted motor-cyclist, on a Harley-Davidson just like the one Arjun had driven up from the base.

Kishan Singh was waving a piece of paper, snapping it urgently through the air.

'Sah'b.'

'Alison,' Arjun said, 'something's up. They've sent a messenger from the base.'

'You go ahead,' Alison said. All she could think of at that moment was of throwing herself into the water, to wash off the feel of his touch. 'I'll follow in a minute.'

Arjun walked into the water and waded over to the beach. Kishan Singh was waiting at the water's edge; his eyes held Arjun's for an instant. There was something in them that made Arjun check his pace and look again. But now Kishan Singh had snapped to attention, his hand raised in a salute, his eyes fixed in an unseeing gaze.

'What is it, Kishan Singh?'

Kishan Singh handed him an envelope. 'Hardy-sah'b sent this.'

Arjun tore the envelope open and unfolded Hardy's note. He was still frowning at it when Alison stepped out of the water and walked up to him.

'What is it?' she said.

'I have to get back,' Arjun said. 'Right now. It looks as if something big is under way. We're leaving Sungei Pattani – my battalion, that is.'

'You're going away?' Alison stared at him, as though she couldn't believe what she'd heard.

'Yes.' He glanced at her. 'And you're glad – aren't you?'

She walked off without answering and he followed her. When they were over the crest of the dune, out of Kishan Singh's sight, he turned her around with a sudden violence.

'Alison,' he said sharply, 'you didn't answer me.'

She narrowed her eyes. 'Don't take that tone with me, Arjun. I'm not your batman.'

'I asked you a question.'

'What was it?'

'Are you glad that I'm leaving?'

'If you really want to know,' she said flatly, 'the answer is yes.'

'Why?' His voice was halting and confused. 'You came here because you wanted to. I don't understand this: why are you so angry with me?'

'I'm not.' She shook her head. 'I'm not angry at all – you're wrong about that. It wouldn't make sense to be angry with you, Arjun.'

'What the hell are you talking about?'

'Arjun – you're not in charge of what you do; you're a toy, a manufactured thing, a weapon in someone else's hands. Your mind doesn't inhabit your body.'

'That's crap . . .' He cut himself short. 'The only reason you can get away with that,' he said, 'is because you're a woman . . .'

She saw that he was a hair's-breadth away from hitting her and this had the odd effect of making her suddenly sorry for him. And then she realised that she had always felt sorry for him, a little, and that was why she had come with him that morning to the beach. She saw that despite the largeness and authority of his presence, he was a man without resources, a man whose awareness of himself was very slight and very fragile; she saw that Dinu was much stronger and more resourceful, and she understood that that was why she'd been tempted to be cruel to him; that that was why she had had to take the risk of losing him. The thought of this made her suddenly apprehensive.

She walked quickly to the Harley-Davidson. 'Come on,' she said to Arjun. 'Take me back to Morningside.'

PART SIX

The Front

Thirty-two

It was early evening by the time the 1/1 Jats left Sungei Pattani. They drove out of their base in a convoy of trucks, heading northwards, on the north–south highway. On reaching the town of Alor Star, they were deposited at the railway station and told to await further instructions. The men settled down at one end of the platform, the officers commandeered the other.

The station was the smallest and prettiest that Arjun had ever seen: it looked like a dolls' house version of the railway stations he'd known in India. There was a single, narrow platform, under a low, red-tiled awning. Potted palms hung in clusters from the beams and the wooden columns that lined the platform were wrapped in brightly-coloured bougainvillea bushes.

Lieutenant-Colonel Buckland had stayed on at divisional headquarters and he arrived late. At midnight he called his officers together to brief them on the latest sitrep. There was to be a drastic change in tactics, he said. There were indications that the Japanese were about to enter the war: their forces were believed to be preparing to attack Malaya from the north. In order to forestall this a strike force was to thrust deep into Siam, to secure the eastern seaboard: this was intended to be a pre-emptive attack to deny a Japanese invasion force the potential landing grounds of the coast. The 1/1 Jats were to play a key part in this operation. The battalion's orders were to hold itself in readiness to entrain at a half-hour's notice. At dawn they would move northwards with the objective of occupying a beach-head near the coastal town of Singora. 'Jot these down.' Lieutenant-Colonel Buckland read out a string of map references while the officers took notes.

After the briefing Arjun spread a map on the station floor, under a naked lightbulb, brushing away the insects and moths that came to settle on the surface. He could feel his index finger shaking in excitement as he followed the thin red line of the road that led to the beach-head. This was it then: the proof of all these years of training; the waiting was over at last. Arjun glanced at the flower-bedecked platform: it struck him that this was a very unlikely place from which to launch a major operation.

It was hard to sleep. At about 3 a.m. Kishan Singh brought him a cup of tea in an enamel mug. Arjun took it gratefully, without asking where it had come from. Beside him Hardy was dozing peacefully in a long-armed chair, with his turban tipped back. Arjun stood up and strolled down the platform, picking his way past the huddled figures of the men. He noticed a light in the station master's office, and stepped in.

The station master was a Goan Christian. He was fast asleep, lying sprawled at his desk. There was a radio on a shelf. Arjun stepped round the desk and turned on the radio. He began to fiddle idly with the knobs. Presently, the crackling airwaves yielded a newsreader's voice: '. . . heavy fighting near Kota Baharu . . .'

Kota Baharu was in eastern Malaya: Arjun knew of it because of a friend who was stationed there. It was a small, out-of-the-way coastal town. Arjun turned up the volume and listened again: now the newsreader was talking of massive Japanese landings along the seaboard – he heard him mention Singora, the town they were meant to occupy the next day. Arjun turned and went sprinting down the platform to the waiting room where he had left the CO.

'Sir.'

The CO and Captain Pearson were dozing in armchairs.

'The balloon's up, sir: the Japs have landed.'

'Impossible, Lieutenant.' The CO sat up.

'It's on the radio, sir.'

'Where?'

Arjun led them to the station master's room. Along the platform the men were stirring now, aware that something was under way. Arjun pushed the station master's door open. The man was awake, groggily rubbing his fists in his eyes. Arjun stepped round him and turned up the volume. The newsreader's voice filled the room.

This was how they learnt that their pre-emptive strike had itself been pre-empted by an operation of unprecedented scale, involving synchronised attacks on targets thousands of miles apart – an air attack on Pearl Harbor and amphibious landings along the Malay peninsula. Singora, the town that was to have been their objective, was one of the first to have been occupied.

'Gentlemen.' Lieutenant-Colonel Buckland gave his officers a polite smile. 'If my knowledge of the army is any guide, I would suggest that you make yourselves comfortable here. It may be a while before we hear anything from HQ . . .'

There was something very comforting about the note of irony in his voice: listening to him, Arjun found it hard to imagine that anything could go seriously wrong.

There was a large airfield at Alor Star, and at first light a squadron of Blenheims took to the air. The 1/1 Jats cheered as the planes buzzed over the station. A couple of hours later, the Blenheims came circling back with empty fuel tanks. Within minutes of their return a flight of Japanese planes came humming over the horizon. They attacked the airport in close formation, at the precise moment when the refuelling Blenheims were at their most vulnerable. In a matter of minutes the planes were in flames. The timing of the raid was uncannily precise. There could be no doubt that the enemy had been tipped off by a spy or a local informer.

Later in the day Lieutenant-Colonel Buckland drove over to the airfield with a few of his officers. A medical centre had been hit and there was a powerful smell of chemicals. On the apron, the tar had liquefied around the Blenheims. In the distance there was a row of attap huts. These served as barracks for the Malay auxiliaries who guarded the airfield. The men were nowhere to be seen and Arjun was sent to look for them. He found their barracks in perfect order. The beds were all made and each had a kitbag hanging beside it. Rifles stood leaning against the wall, in neat rows, exactly as regulations demanded. But the men were gone. It was evident that after going through all the daily motions of tidying their quarters, the troops had quietly deserted.

* * *

Dinu had spent the night on a cot on the veranda of Ilongo's mother's house. He woke up early. Both Ilongo and his mother were still asleep. He looked at his watch. The train to Penang wasn't till midday; many long hours lay ahead.

He stepped outside and looked up at the mountain. The light had begun to change; the forest seemed to be coming alive. It struck him that he had never photographed the chandis at this time of morning. He spotted Ilongo's bicycle, standing inside a doorway. He decided to cycle up to the mountain with his cameras.

He put his equipment together quickly and cycled faster than usual. When he got to the stream he dispensed with his usual rituals: instead he went straight up to the clearing and set up his tripod. He was changing a roll when the first raiders flew over Gunung Jerai. At first he paid no attention, assuming that the planes were landing at the Sungei Pattani airbase. But minutes later, when the forest began to reverberate to the sound of explosions, he knew that something was wrong. When the next flight of bombers came by he looked more closely. The planes were flying quite low and there was no mistaking their markings. They were Japanese.

Dinu's first thought was for Alison. He hadn't seen her since she'd left for the beach, with Arjun, but he remembered that she had planned to go to Sungei Pattani that day – she had told him this the day before. She had errands to run.

It struck Dinu that she was probably still in town. He left his tripod standing where it was and hurried down to the bicycle. He went first to Morningside House where the cook confirmed that Alison had left the house very early that morning, in the Daytona. On his way out Dinu stopped to check on Saya John. He found him dozing peacefully in an armchair, on the veranda.

Cycling down to the office, Dinu noticed that a large number of people had collected on the parade ground. On approaching he saw that Ilongo was addressing the assembly, standing on a chair, speaking in Tamil. Dinu caught his eye and signalled to him to step aside for a quick word.

'What's happening, Ilongo?'

'Haven't you been listening to the radio?'

'No . . .'

'Japan's entered the war. The airstrip at Sungei Pattani has been bombed.'

Dinu took a moment to absorb this. 'Alison went to Sungei Pattani this morning . . .' he said. 'We have to go down there and see if she's all right . . .'

'I can't go right now.' Ilongo gestured at the people assembled on the parade ground. 'They're waiting . . .'

'Why – what do they want?'

'The managers of some of the neighbouring estates have abandoned their offices and driven off to Singapore. Our people here are worried. They want to make sure they'll get paid . . .' Breaking off to reach into his pocket Ilongo pulled out a set of keys. 'Here – you go yourself. Take the truck.'

Dinu pushed the keys back. 'I don't drive.'

'Then wait – I'll be done soon.'

Dinu watched from the balcony of the estate office while Ilongo addressed the assembly. The meeting seemed to last for ever: it was noon by the time the crowd began to disperse. Shortly afterwards Ilongo started up the truck, and they drove off in the direction of Sungei Pattani.

They soon ran into another crowd. The air raids had ended a good few hours before, but people were pouring down the road, heading away from town. Many were on foot; several families had their belongings slung over their shoulders, tied up in sheets; a boy was pushing a bicycle with a huge radio strapped to the carrier; two men were pulling an elderly woman behind them in a makeshift trolley. Nearer town the roads were clogged with honking cars. Sitting stalled in the truck, Ilongo began to ask questions, leaning out of the driver's window: he learnt that the air raid had taken the town by surprise; there had been no alarms, no warning. Now, everyone who had the option was heading into the countryside, to wait out the trouble.

They parked the truck behind a shop and walked into town. They checked all the places where Alison might conceivably have gone – the banks were empty and most of the shops had their shutters down. Alison's hairdresser was gone.

'Where could she be?'

'She'll be all right – don't worry.'

On the way back to the estate, they took a road that led them past the perimeter of the airstrip. The apron was littered with smoking heaps of metal but the runways were untouched. They came across an Indian – a caretaker who told them that there was a rumour that the Japanese bombers had been guided in by a spy, a traitor from the British forces.

'An Indian?' Dinu asked apprehensively.

'No – an Englishman. We saw him being led away, under arrest.'

Dinu was both shocked and relieved.

It was only when they were back at Ilongo's house that Dinu remembered that he'd been planning to leave for Penang. He decided to put off his departure for the time being: he couldn't leave without making sure that Alison was all right. He went up to Morningside and sat down to wait.

By the time Alison's car came up the driveway it was almost sunset. Dinu was at the door, waiting. The relief of seeing her unharmed had the effect of uncorking all the anxieties of the day. He began to shout as she stepped out of the roadster. 'Alison . . . where the hell have you been? You've been gone the whole damned day . . .'

She snapped back at him: 'And what about you? Where were you last night?'

'I was at Ilongo's,' he said defiantly. 'I'm going to leave . . . for Rangoon.'

She gave a hard little laugh. 'Good luck to you then. Let's see how far you get.'

'What do you mean?'

'I was in Butterworth this morning. There's chaos on the roads. I don't think you're going to get very far. '

'Butterworth? What were you doing in Butterworth?'

She raised an eyebrow and her voice went cold. 'It's none of your business.' She brushed past him and went up the stairs to her bedroom.

Dinu stood fuming in the porch for a few minutes and then followed her up the stairs. 'Alison . . .' He knocked at the door, his voice contrite. 'I'm sorry . . . I was just worried.'

She opened the door, wearing a white satin slip. Before he could say any more, she threw her arms around him. 'Oh, Dinu.'

'Alison . . . I was frantic . . . you being gone all day, with the bombing . . .'

'You shouldn't have worried. I was fine – nowhere near the bombs. They were hitting the port and I was on the other side of town.'

'But why did you go there anyway . . . ? All the way to Butterworth? What for?'

She took his face between her hands and kissed him. 'I'll tell you later,' she said. 'Let's not talk about it now. Let's just be glad we're together and we're both all right.'

Thirty-three

Several hours passed without the 1/1 Jats receiving any word from divisional headquarters. Just after nightfall, a convoy of trucks arrived to move them to another location. They could tell they were travelling north but it was very dark and they could see nothing of the countryside.

At dawn Arjun discovered that they were encamped inside a rubber plantation. Beyond a few hundred yards the greenery seemed to solidify into a circular, bark-striped wall. Between the canopy of green leaves above and the carpet of dead foliage underfoot there seemed to be no direct light and no shadows. Sound appeared to travel and linger without revealing its point of origin. It was as though he had woken up to find himself inside an immense maze where the roof and the floor had been padded with cotton wool.

At the morning's briefing they learnt that the battalion was now positioned near the township of Jitra, very close to the northernmost tip of the Federated Malay States. Here the peninsula narrowed to a thin neck, forming a bridge between Malaya and Siam: any army advancing from the north would have to squeeze through this gullet and it was here that a southerly advance could best be throttled. The 1/1 Jats, along with several other battalions, had been concentrated along the north–south highway. It was along this road that the Japanese were expected to make their advance. Chance had thus thrust the 1/1 Jats into the first line of defence.

Arjun was commanding his battalion's C Company: they were positioned a few hundred yards to the left of the north–south highway. Hardy was with D Company, on the far side of the road.

They were flanked by the Leicestershire Regiment on one side and the 14th Punjab on the other.

The first job was to dig trenches, but here again the terrain proved deceptive. The soft loamy soil was easy to dig into, but hard to shore up. Ground water leaked in at unpredictable depths. The wireless sets began to malfunction and the problem was traced to the environment: the placement of the trees was found to interfere with the reception of radio waves. Even runners could not be relied upon. Disoriented by the geometrical maze of the plantation, they kept losing their way.

Then the rains broke. It dripped constantly and this too reinforced the impression of being locked inside a padded cage. Looking up, the soldiers would see rain pouring down from the sky. But by the time the water reached them, the showers had slowed to a steady drizzle. The dripping would continue long after the rain had stopped. They would look up to find that the skies had cleared; yet down where they were the rain kept falling, hour after weary hour. It was as though the leafy canopy were a wet mattress, emptying slowly under its own weight.

With the soil turning to mud, their jeeps and lorries began to slide out of control. The vehicles were found to have been equipped with sand-grip tyres, intended for use in the deserts of North Africa. Orders were issued banning them from entering the plantation: supplies now had to be carried in on foot.

On the afternoon of the second day, Hardy came running over and dropped into the trench. Arjun could tell from his face that he was ripe with news.

'What's happened?'

'Just heard a rumour.'

'What?'

'There was trouble with the 1st Hyderabads, at Kota Baharu.'

'What kind of trouble?'

'After the first Jap attack there was a panic at the airstrip. The airmen were Australians and apparently they left in a hurry. The Hyderabads' NCOs wanted to pull out too but the CO wouldn't let them. They mutinied, shooting a couple of officers. They've been disarmed and arrested. They're being sent to Penang, as a labour force.'

Arjun surveyed his trench, looking uneasily at the faces of his men. 'Better keep that to yourself, Hardy.'

'Just thought I'd let you know.'

The battalion's headquarters were deep inside the plantation, well to the rear of Arjun's company. Late on the second day, signals engineers laid a telephone line. The first call was from Captain Pearson.

'Contact?'

'Nothing yet,' said Arjun. The day had faded almost imperceptibly away, the gloom deepening slowly into a dripping, clammy darkness. At that very moment, the dark wall ahead was pierced by a red flash.

'Sniper!' said the *havildar*. 'Down, sah'b, down.' Arjun lunged face forward into the ankle-deep water at the bottom of the trench. There was another shot and then another. Arjun fumbled for the phone only to find that the line had gone dead.

Now the flashes of gunfire began to range through the surrounding darkness. The shots sounded at irregular intervals, punctuated by the dull thud of mortars and the spitting of light machine guns. To the right, from the direction of Hardy's emplacement, there came the sound of a Bren gun. This brought only a moment's relief, for Arjun noted suddenly, with an odd sinking feeling in his belly, that the Bren was rattling on too long: it was as though the men were too panicked to remember the ordered bursts that Hardy had tried to drill into them during weapons training.

Now the enemy snipers appeared to be on the move, pivoting freely around their position. As the hours passed the trench began to seem more a trap than a shelter: there was a peculiar defencelessness about being pinned into a stationary position by a mobile adversary. When they returned fire, it was as though they were letting fly randomly, in the way that a chained animal circles at the end of its leash, snapping at an unseen tormentor.

The dripping of the trees continued without interruption through the night. Soon after daybreak, they saw a Japanese spotter plane, circling overhead. A half-hour later another plane flew by, dipping low over their lines. It left behind a trail of paper that fluttered slowly down from the sky, like a great flight of butterflies.

Most of these sheets settled on the canopy above, but a few trickled through to the ground. Kishan Singh fetched some, handing one to Arjun and keeping a couple for himself.

Arjun saw that it was a pamphlet, written in Hindustani and printed in both Devanagari and Arabic script. It was an appeal directed to Indian soldiers, signed by one Amreek Singh of the Indian Independence League. The text began: *Brothers, ask yourselves what you are fighting for and why you are here: do you really wish to sacrifice your lives for an Empire that has kept your country in slavery for two hundred years?*

Arjun heard Kishan Singh reading the pamphlet aloud to the others and the blood rushed to his head. He shouted: 'Hand those to me.' Crumpling the pamphlets, he buried them deep under his heel, in the mud. 'Anyone who's found with these,' he said crisply, 'will be up for court martial.'

Minutes later, with a blast that was like a moving wall of sound, the Japanese heavy artillery opened up. The first shells went skimming over the tops of the trees, sending down showers of leaves and small branches. But then, slowly, the explosions began to move in their direction. The earth shook so violently as to send the water at the bottom of the trench shooting into their faces. Arjun saw a fifty-foot rubber tree rising gracefully from the earth and jumping several feet into the air before somersaulting towards them. They flattened themselves at the bottom of the trench just in time to get out of its way.

The bombardment continued without a break for hours.

Manju was in a deep sleep when Neel shook her awake. She rolled over, in a daze. It seemed as though weeks had gone by since she had last slept. Jaya was a colicky baby and often cried for hours. Nothing would stop her once she started. Even Woodward's Gripe Water had little effect: a tablespoonful would send her into a light doze but an hour or two later she'd be up again, crying harder than ever.

Manju glanced at Jaya's crib and saw that she was still asleep. She rubbed her eyes and turned away from Neel. She could not disguise her annoyance at being disturbed. 'What is it?' she said. 'Why did you wake me up?'

'I thought you'd want to know . . .'

'What?'

'The Japanese have entered the war.'

'Oh?' She still could not understand what this had to do with her being roused from her sleep.

'They've invaded Malaya.'

'Malaya?' Now everything was suddenly clear. She sat up. 'Arjun? Dinu? Is there any news?'

'No.' Neel shook his head. 'Nothing directly. But the radio said something about the 11th Division being involved in the fighting. Isn't that Arjun's division?'

She'd had a letter from Arjun just last week. He hadn't said very much about himself – just that he was well and thinking of her. Mostly, he'd asked about Jaya and her own health. He'd also mentioned that he'd met Dinu and he was fine – Dolly had been glad to hear that.

'Do you still have Arjun's letter?' Neel asked.

'Yes.' Manju jumped out of bed and went to fetch the letter.

'Does it say anything about his division?' Neel said.

The numeral 11 leapt at her almost at once, from the folds of the page. 'Yes,' she said. 'That's his division.' She looked at her husband and her eyes filled with tears.

Neel put his arm round her shoulders and held her tight. 'There's no reason to worry,' he said. 'As far as I can make out the 11th Division is headquartered very close to Morningside. Dinu will let us know what's going on.'

Then the baby woke up. Now, for the first time, Manju was grateful for Jaya's cantankerousness. Her ceaseless crying left her with no time to think of anything else.

Later that evening they were paid a visit by an eminent member of the Indian community in Rangoon – a lawyer by the name of Sahibzada Badruddin Khan. It so happened that the whole family was at home when the visitor dropped by.

Mr Khan was worried and he had come to give them some news. He had attended a meeting of some of the city's most prominent Indians. They had decided to form a Refugee Evacuation

Committee. It was felt that in the event of a Japanese advance into Burma the Indian population would be vulnerable on two fronts – they would be defenceless against hostile sections of the Burmese public and, what was more, as subjects of the British Empire, they would be treated as enemy aliens by the Japanese. Many members of the community had expressed fears of a coming catastrophe: the committee's intentions were to get as many Indians out of Burma as possible.

Rajkumar was amazed to learn of these measures. He was in an optimistic mood, despite the recent news. He had just discovered that a friend of his had secured a contract for a long stretch of the Burma–China road. He was now absolutely confident that he would be able to sell his stocks of timber at exactly the kind of price he had been hoping for.

'What?' Rajkumar broke into a disbelieving laugh. 'You mean you people are going to run away from Burma – because the Japanese have invaded Malaya?'

'Well, yes. People feel . . .'

'Nonsense, Khan.' Rajkumar slapped his friend on the back. 'You shouldn't be taken in by these scaremongers. Malaya's a long way from here.'

'Still,' said Mr Khan, 'there's nothing wrong with being prepared – especially where there are women and children involved . . .'

Rajkumar shrugged. 'Well, Khan, you must do what you think best. But as for myself I think this is a great opportunity –'

'Opportunity!' Mr Khan raised an eyebrow. 'How so?'

'There's no mystery to it, Khan. With America in the war, there'll be more money for defence preparations. Burma is crucial to the survival of the Chinese Government in Chungking: the north–south road will be their main supply line. I'm willing to bet that the road is going to be built faster than anyone ever expected.'

'And if there's an attack?'

Rajkumar shrugged. 'It's a question of nerve, Khan. I can understand why you'd want to leave. But for us it would be too soon. I've spent a long time preparing for this and I am not going to leave now.'

Manju was hugely reassured by Rajkumar's words. It was a great comfort to know that she did not have to think about going anywhere right now. Coping with Jaya was hard enough at home: she could not begin to imagine what it would be like in less favourable circumstances.

In the morning, a runner brought a message to Arjun's trench. It was from battalion headquarters: they were to fall back on the Asoon line – a string of defensive fortifications along a river, a few miles down the road. When Arjun gave the order to move there was a muted cheer. He felt like joining in himself – anything would be better than staying pinned in that trench.

They made their way through the plantation in good order but when they reached the road it became clear that the withdrawal was turning quickly into a headlong retreat. The men began to show signs of apprehension as truck after truck passed them by, packed with troops from other units. Arjun stayed with them long enough to see them into a truck and then he jumped into a jeep with Hardy.

'Yaar, did you hear?' Hardy said under his breath.

'What?'

'The Japs have sunk the *Prince of Wales* and the *Repulse*.'

'Impossible.' Arjun looked at him in disbelief. These were two of the most powerful battleships ever made, the pride of the British navy. 'It can't be true.'

'It *is* true – I ran into Kumar; he told me.' Suddenly a gleeful grin lit up his face. 'I can't wait to tell Pearson: I want to see the look on that bastard's face . . .'

'Hardy,' Arjun shouted, 'have you gone mad?'

'Why?'

'Have you forgotten that those ships were here to defend us? We're all on the same side, Hardy. A Jap bullet can't pick between you and Pearson . . .'

Hardy gave him a startled glance, and for a moment they looked at each other in mutual bewilderment. 'You're right,' said Hardy. 'Of course. But you know . . .'

'Let's drop it,' Arjun said quickly.

When they reached the Asoon river, the Japanese artillery fell unaccountably silent. Grateful for the respite, the 1/1 Jats took up positions beside the road, with their backs to the river. At this point, the north–south highway ran along a raised embankment, with thick stands of rubber on either side, leading as far as the eye could see. The whole battalion was now concentrated in one place, positioned to defend the approaches to the river. Their vehicles were lined up off the road, along the slopes of the embankment.

Arjun saw Hardy stepping out on the road and went to join him. Lieutenant-Colonel Buckland was just a few paces away, at the battalion's temporary command post. He was with Captain Pearson, who was fumbling with a map case.

Arjun stopped in the middle of the road to confer with Hardy. 'Why do you think they've stopped shelling?' he said.

'They seem to hold back at times,' Hardy said. 'It's hard to say why.'

'You don't think it's because their own armour is moving up, do you?'

Hardy scoffed at this. 'What armour? None of us has any tanks – neither them nor us. This isn't tank country.'

'That's what we were told. But . . .' Somewhere in the distance there was a rumbling sound. They both spun about on their heels to look down the road. It was now almost sunset. The clouds had cleared briefly and the sky had turned bright scarlet. The highway ran straight for a couple of hundred yards before disappearing around a bend: rubber trees rose above it on either side, almost coming together at the top to form an arch. The road was empty: there was nothing ahead.

Hardy breathed a sigh of relief. 'That gave me a fright . . .' He raised his sleeve to his forehead. 'I told you – this isn't tank country: that's the one thing we can be sure of, thank God.'

A moment later, with a great grinding of its metal treads, a tank turned the corner. On top of the turret, silhouetted against the sky, was a gunner's helmeted head. The turret swivelled in their direction until its gun became a single circular eye. Then the tank shuddered and its hollow eye turned a blazing red. At the bottom of the embankment, a petrol tank exploded and a half-ton truck did a little hop and burst into flames.

For an instant Arjun stood his ground. Nothing in his training had prepared him for this. A dim recollection of unfinished business urged him to turn and run back down the road, to his company, to rally them into throwing up the wall of fire that the CO had talked about at the last briefing. But the CO had said categorically that there would be no tanks – and anyway, the CO was gone now, rolling down the side of the embankment, along with Captain Pearson. On both sides of the highway, men were scattering into the plantation, running for cover.

'Run, Arjun!' The voice was Hardy's, and it jolted him awake. 'Run, run.'

He was stranded in the middle of the road, like a startled deer, and the first tank was almost upon him, so close that he could see the eyes of the man in the turret, darkened by a thick pair of goggles. He jumped, throwing himself over the side of the embankment, lunging sidewise to clear the CO's burning jeep. Then he picked himself up and ran for the trees: suddenly he was inside a long tunnel of greenery, his feet cushioned by a carpet of fallen leaves.

The lucidity that had possessed him momentarily as he was standing in the middle of the road had vanished now. Its place was taken by a blind, unseeing urgency. It was quite possible that he was heading straight towards a nest of Japanese guns. But even if he had known that to be so he would not have been able to stop himself. It was as though his breath and his blood had fused together to pound at his brain in unison, urging him on, pushing him to run in this direction.

He ran several yards without stopping. Then, leaning against a tree trunk, he turned, panting, to look back: the trees fell into a sightline at the end of which a small stretch of road was clearly visible, enclosed in a circular frame, as though he were looking through a telescope. He saw tank after tank rolling down the highway. By the sides of the embankment lay the vehicles of the 1/1 Jats. Some were upturned and some were on fire.

The sight was beyond comprehension. He could find no way of explaining what had happened, even to himself. Was this what was meant by the phrase 'put to rout' – this welter of fear and urgency and shame; this chaotic sensation of collapse in one's head, as though the scaffolding of responses implanted by years of training had buckled and fallen in?

Arjun had a sudden aching vision of their battalion's headquarters in Saharanpur: he recalled the building they called 'the Nursery' – the long, low bungalow in which the officers' mess was housed. He thought of the heavy, gilt-framed paintings that hung on its walls, along with the mounted heads of buffalo and nilgai; the assegais, scimitars and feathered spears that his predecessors had brought back as trophies from Africa, Mesopotamia and Burma. He had learnt to think of this as home, and the battalion as his extended family – a clan that tied a thousand men together in a pyramid of platoons and companies. How was it possible that this centuries-old structure could break like an eggshell, at one sharp blow – and that too, in this unlikeliest of battlefields, a forest planted by businessmen? Was the fault his own? Was it true then, what the older Englishmen said, that Indians would destroy the army if they became officers? This at least was beyond doubt: as a fighting unit the 1/1 Jats no longer existed. Every man in the battalion would now have to fend for himself.

He'd left his pack in the jeep, on the river: it hadn't occurred to him that he'd be running for his life within minutes of climbing out. All he had on him now was his .45 Webley, his water bottle and his belt with its small pack of odds and ends.

He looked around. Where was Hardy? Where were the CO and Captain Pearson? He'd caught glimpses of them earlier, as he was running into the plantation. But now in the gathering gloom it was hard to tell what lay ahead.

The Japanese infantry would almost certainly be mopping up behind their tanks, combing the plantations. It was possible that he was being watched even as he stood there, through any one of the hundreds of sightlines that converged on the precise spot on which he was standing.

What was he to do now?

Thirty-four

To drive to Gunung Jerai was Alison's idea. She and Dinu left the house well before sunset, in the Daytona, taking the road that circled around the mountain. The kampongs seemed deserted now, the daytime panic having yielded to a watchful quiet. In the markets there were hardly any people in sight. Alison was able to drive through at high speed.

They made good time and turned on to the summit road while there was still plenty of light. When they began to climb, the sound of the car rose to a shrill, steady whine. It was twilight on the slopes, because of the thick forest cover. Alison had to switch on her headlamps.

The turns on the road were very sharp. They came to a bend that switched back on itself, rising upwards at a steep angle. Alison had to stop and reverse the car in order to make the turn. As they were coming out of the corner, they both looked up at the same time. The sky above the northern horizon seemed to be darkened by a stain – a cloud of tiny, horizontal brushstrokes. Alison stopped dead, and they stared – several moments passed before they realised that they were looking at a flight of planes, heading directly towards them, from the north. They were facing the aircraft head-on and in profile the planes seemed stationary, their advance signalled only by a gradual thickening of their outlines.

Alison started the car again, and they went speeding up the road. The lodge loomed ahead, in the gathering darkness. It was empty, deserted. They parked under the porch and walked up to the veranda that ran around the building. Tables were placed along its length, draped in white cloth, weighted down with heavy ashtrays. Plates had been laid out, as though in expectation of a crowd of diners.

They could feel the roar of the approaching bombers under their feet, in the vibrating planks of the wood floor. The planes were very close now, flying at low altitudes. As they stood watching, the flight suddenly separated into two, parting round the mountain, like a stream flowing past a boulder. Banking steeply one wing veered off towards the seaward slope of the mountain, on a flight path set for Butterworth and Penang. The other wing headed for Sungei Pattani, on the landward side.

Alison reached for Dinu's hand and they began to walk along the balcony, making their way between the dining tables. The tablecloths were flapping in the breeze and the plates were covered with a thin film of dust.

There were no clouds today. Far below, in the dimming twilight, the island of Penang appeared as a dark shoal afloat on the sea; to the south-east lay Sungei Pattani, a small raft of habitation, marooned in an ocean of rubber trees. They could see roads and rail-lines, glimmering in the last flicker of daylight. The landscape was like a map, lying unfurled at their feet.

The planes were losing height in preparation for their bombing runs. Sungei Pattani was the nearest of the targets and it was the first to be hit. Bursts of flame appeared on the dark landscape, strung closely together in straight lines, like rows of bright stitches on an inky fabric.

They went around the veranda, picking at the tablecloths and running their fingers over the dust-filmed plates. They saw yet another cloud of planes approaching; on the seaward side, the bombers were diving low over the port of Fort Butterworth. Suddenly a great tower of orange flame shot up from the coast reaching hundreds of feet into the sky; the blast that followed was of such magnitude as to make itself felt all the way up the mountain.

'Oh my God!' Alison threw herself on Dinu. 'They've hit the oil-tanks at Butterworth.'

She buried her face in Dinu's chest, snatching at his shirt, bunching up the cloth in her fists. 'I drove past them, just that day.'

Dinu held her fast. 'Alison, you still haven't told me why you went . . .'

She wiped her face on his shirt and pulled away from him. 'Give me a cigarette.'

Dinu lit a cigarette and put it between her lips. 'Well?'

'I went to see a doctor, Dinu – a doctor who doesn't know me.'

'Why?'

'I thought I might be pregnant.'

'And?'

'I'm not.'

'And what if you had been pregnant, Alison,' Dinu said quietly. 'Would you have wanted the child to be Arjun's?'

'No.' She threw her arms round him, and he could feel her sobbing into his shirt.

'Dinu, I'm sorry. I'm so, so sorry.'

'About what?'

'About everything, Dinu. About going away that day – with Arjun. It was a mistake – a terrible, terrible mistake. If you only knew, Dinu . . .'

He silenced her by putting a finger over her lips. 'I don't want to know . . . Whatever happened . . . I don't want to know. It'll be better that way . . . for both of us. We don't need to talk about Arjun again.'

He was cut short by a flash of light, an explosion that illuminated the whole town of Sungei Pattani. A series of lesser explosions followed, one after the other, like a string of fireworks.

'The armoury,' Alison said. She lowered herself to her knees and stuck her head into a gap between the veranda's rails, holding on to the wooden bars with her fists. 'They must have hit the armoury.'

Dinu knelt beside her. 'Alison,' he said urgently, gripping her shoulders. 'One thing's for sure . . . You have to go away. With Japan and America at war, you're in danger here. Your mother was American . . . Your brother still lives there . . . There's no telling what would happen if the Japanese managed to push through. You've got to get away.'

'But where to?'

'To Singapore; you'll be safe there. It's very well defended.

We're too close to the border here . . . and you have to take your grandfather with you. You've got to leave.'

She shook her head, violently. 'I don't want to. I don't want to go.'

'Alison, you can't just think about yourself.'

'You don't understand, Dinu – I'm a territorial animal. I'd rather take a few of them with me than give up what's mine.'

'Alison, listen to me.' Dinu gripped her hands and shook them. 'You have to do it . . . For your grandfather's sake, if not your own.'

'And what about the estate?'

'Ilongo will run it while you're away . . . You'll see . . . You can trust him, you know that.'

'And you – you'll come with us, of course. Won't you?'

'Alison, I should go back, to Burma . . . My family . . . They might need me now.'

'But you could come to Singapore with us first; you could probably get a ship there. It might even be easier.'

Dinu paused to think. 'You may be right. Yes . . . I'll come.'

She reached for his hands. 'I don't think I could bear to go without you. Especially now.'

'Why now?'

She dug into his chest with her forehead. 'Because I think I'm in love with you, Dinu – or something like that at any rate. I didn't know it before, but I know it now.'

He pulled her closer. He did not care what had happened between her and Arjun; nothing mattered but this – that she loved him and he loved her. Nothing else was of any account, not the planes, not the bombs, nothing but this. This was what happiness was – he'd never known it before; this melting away, this exaltation, your guts spilling into your head, filling your eyes – your mind transformed into your body, your body instinct with the joy in your mind; this sensation of reality having met its end.

Although the sunset was still a few minutes away, under the rubber trees it was already dusk. Arjun had heard many complaints about the terrain over the last few days, but it was only now that he became fully aware of the peculiar deceptiveness of his surroundings. He had a strange sense of having stepped into a picture that had been created with the express purpose of tricking the eye. At times the tunnels of foliage around him seemed still and empty, but moments later they appeared to be alive with movement. With every step, figures and shapes seemed to appear and disappear, as rows of trees fell into and out of alignment. Every gracefully arched tree held the promise of cover, yet there was no point that did not intersect with a perfect line of fire.

Arjun knew that many others had taken shelter in the plantation; at times he could sense their presence around him. Every now and again he'd hear whispers, or the sound of footsteps, echoing down the long, straight corridors that stretched away from him in every direction. Sometimes he'd hear a sound, somewhere close at hand. He'd spin around only to find that he'd stepped on a branch that was hidden under the carpet of dead leaves on the ground. It was impossible to distinguish form from shadow, movement from stillness – the real and the illusory seemed to have merged without seam.

Just as twilight was turning to darkness, he heard the click of a safety catch. A whisper followed, from somewhere nearby. '*Kaun hai?* Who is it?'

The voice sounded familiar, but Arjun waited until he heard the whisper again: '*Kaun?*'

This time he was certain. 'Kishan Singh?'

'Sah'b.'

Arjun took a couple of steps to his right and found himself face to face with his batman. 'How did you find me?' He acknowledged Kishan Singh's salute gravely, trying not reveal the full extent of his relief.

'Buckland-sah'b sent me,' Kishan Singh said.

'Where is he?'

'Over there.'

It turned out that Kishan Singh had escaped into the plantation with a dozen others from the battalion. They'd succeeded in keeping together through the confusion that had followed the Japanese tank attack. Eventually they'd met up with Hardy as well as

Lieutenant-Colonel Buckland. Captain Pearson was still missing. They were now keeping watch to see if they could intercept anyone else.

Lieutenant-Colonel Buckland was sitting with his back against a tree trunk, his right arm cradled in an improvised sling. He acknowledged Arjun's salute with a nod and a slight gesture of his left hand.

'Glad to have you back with us, Lieutenant.'

Arjun was elated to hear his wry voice again. He grinned. 'Glad to see you too, sir. How bad's your arm?'

'Just a graze – and it's been seen to. Fortunately we have a medical chap with us.' Lieutenant-Colonel Buckland gave Arjun a stiff-lipped smile. 'Do sit down, Roy. No need to stand on ceremony now.'

'Thank you, sir.' Arjun cleared a place for himself on the carpet of dead leaves.

'You'll be glad to know that Hardy made it too,' Lieutenant-Colonel Buckland said. 'I've sent him off to forage for water. We're very short.'

'It happened so fast, sir.'

'Yes, it did rather, didn't it?' Lieutenant-Colonel Buckland's voice faded away. When he spoke again, his voice was hoarse, rasping, almost unrecognisable.

'Tell me, Lieutenant,' he said, 'do you think I let the side down?'

There was something about his tone that moved Arjun. 'No, sir,' he said vehemently. 'There was nothing you could have done, sir.'

'There's always something one could have done.'

'But what could you have done, sir? We didn't have any air support. We didn't know about the tanks. It's not our fault, sir.'

'If you're in command it's always your fault.'

They were quiet again for a while. Presently the lieutenant-colonel said: 'Do you know what I've been thinking of, Roy?'

'Sir?'

'The Nursery – in Saharanpur. I remember when it was built. My father was CO at the time, you know – and the 1/1 Jats were still called the Royal Battalion. We were away in Simla for the summer and when we came back there it was – the building that would come to be known as the Nursery. There was a ceremony and a *burra khana* for the men. My mother cut a ribbon. I remember how proud I was to see our colours hanging there – moth-holes and all. This was what got me started on military history. By the age of ten I knew our battle honours by heart. I could have told you exactly how Jemadar Abdul Qadir got his Victoria Cross. I was in my last year at school when the Royal Battalion went to the Somme. I came across something that Field Marshal Sir John French said in a speech and I cut it out.'

'What did he say, sir?'

'Something to the effect of: "The Jats will never be forgotten on the Western Front."'

'I see, sir.'

The lieutenant-colonel's voice dropped to a whisper. 'And what do you think they'll say about what happened to us today, Roy?'

Arjun replied quietly: 'I think they'll say we did what we could under the circumstances.'

'Will they? I can't help wondering. This was one of the finest units in one of the finest armies in the world. But today we were dispersed without being able to return fire. I will have to live with the knowledge of that for the rest of my life.'

'You can't blame yourself, sir.'

'Really?' Lieutenant-Colonel Buckland was quiet again. In the silence that followed Arjun became aware that it was raining and the canopy had begun to release its usual slow, unvarying drip.

'Sir.' Hardy stepped suddenly out of the darkness, taking them by surprise. He handed the CO a green bottle. 'Water, sir.'

'Where did you get it?'

'There was a small pond sir. We strained the water and used a few chlorine tablets. I think it's safe, sir.'

'All right then.' Lieutenant-Colonel Buckland's voice was businesslike again. 'You two had better get some rest. Tomorrow we'll head south-east. With any luck we'll be able to circle back towards our own lines.'

The rain continued without interruption, the moisture descending with the steady insistence they had all come to dread. Hardy commandeered a bedroll from one of the men, and he and Arjun sat leaning against a tree trunk, sitting at right-angles to each other, keeping watch in the darkness. Mosquitoes buzzed incessantly and for once Arjun was grateful for his puttees. But there was little he could do about his unprotected neck and face. He slapped at the insects and thought with longing of the mosquito cream he'd left behind at the Asoon river, tucked deep inside his pack.

'Sah'b.' Arjun was startled by the sound of Kishan Singh's voice.

'Kishan Singh?'

'Sah'b.'

Kishan Singh slipped something into his hand and was gone before Arjun could say anything else.

'What is it?' Hardy said.

Arjun held his hand up to his nose. 'Why,' he said, 'I do believe it's mosquito cream. He must have given me his own . . .'

'Lucky bloody *chootiya*,' Hardy said mournfully. 'My batman would happily see me eaten alive before he parted with his. Let me have some – there's a good chap.'

Sleep was impossible: there was nothing to do but to wait out the night. At times Hardy hummed, under his breath, with Arjun trying to guess the tunes. Intermittently they talked, in muted voices, catching up on the events of the last few hours.

In a low whisper Hardy asked: 'What was Bucky saying to you back there?'

'We were talking about what happened . . .'

'What did he say?'

'He was blaming himself.'

'But there was nothing he could have done.'

'That's not how he sees it. It was strange to listen to him – to hear him talking about it in such a personal way, as though he was responsible. I just hadn't thought of it like that.'

'Well, how could you?'

'Why couldn't I?'

'To us it makes no difference really, does it?'

'Of course it does. If it didn't we wouldn't be sitting here in the rain.'

'Yes, but think about it, yaar Arjun – for example, what would have happened if we'd held our position on the Asoon? Do you think we – us Indians – do you think we would have been given the credit?'

'Why not?'

'Think of those newspapers in Singapore – the ones that were writing about all the brave young soldiers who'd come to defend their colony. Do you remember?'

'Of course.'

'Remember how all those brave young soldiers were always Australian or Canadian or British?'

Arjun nodded. 'Yes.'

'It's as if we never existed. That's why what happened at Asoon doesn't matter – not to us, anyway. Whether we'd held our position or not, it would have been the same. Yaar, I sometimes think of all the wars my father and grandfather fought in – in France, Africa, Burma. Does anyone ever say – the Indians won this war or that one? It would have been the same here. If there had been a victory the credit for it would not have been ours. By the same logic the blame for the defeat can't be ours either.'

'It may not matter to others, Hardy,' Arjun said, 'but it matters to us.'

'Does it really, Arjun? I'll tell you what I felt when I was running into the plantation. Frankly I was relieved – I was glad that it was over. And the men, I'll bet most of them felt exactly as I did. It was as if some kind of charade had come to an end.'

'What charade, Hardy? There was nothing make-believe about those tanks.'

Hardy slapped at the mosquitoes that were buzzing around them. 'You know, yaar Arjun, over these last few days, in the trenches at Jitra – I had an eerie feeling. It was strange to be sitting on one side of a battle line, knowing that you had to fight and knowing at the same time that it wasn't really your fight – knowing that whether you won or lost, neither the blame nor the credit would be yours. Knowing that you're risking everything to defend a way of life that pushes you to the sidelines. It's almost as if you're fighting against yourself. It's strange to be sitting in a trench, holding a gun and asking yourself: who is this weapon really aimed at? Am I being tricked into pointing it at myself?'

'I can't say I felt the same way, Hardy.'

'But ask yourself, Arjun: what does it mean for you and me to be in this army? You're always talking about soldiering as being just a job. But you know, yaar, it isn't just a job – it's when you're sitting in a trench that you realise that there's something very primitive about what we do. In the everyday world when would you ever stand up and say – "I'm going to risk my life for this"? As a human being it's something you can only do if you know why you're doing it. But when I was sitting in that trench, it was as if my heart and my hand had no connection – each seemed to belong to a different person. It was as if I wasn't really a human being – just a tool, an instrument. This is what I ask myself, Arjun: in what way do I become human again? How do I connect what I do with what I want, in my heart?'

'Hardy – it doesn't do any good to think like that . . .'

They heard Lieutenant-Colonel Buckland's voice, somewhere nearby: 'Not so much talk, please . . .'

Arjun cut himself short.

Thirty-five

The offer, when it finally came, was so good, so much in excess of Rajkumar's highest hopes, that he made the messenger repeat it twice, just to make sure that he had got it right. On hearing confirmation, he looked down at his hands and saw that they had begun to shake. He could not trust himself to rise to his feet. He smiled at the messenger and said something that his pride would not otherwise have allowed him to say.

'Could you help me up?'

Leaning on the messenger's arm he went to the open window of his office and looked down into his timberyard to see if he could spot Neel. The yard was now stacked high with the stocks of timber he had accumulated over the last year. His son's bearded face was half-hidden behind an eight-foot pile of freshly milled planks.

'Neel.' Rajkumar's voice erupted from his chest in a joyful bellow. He shouted again. 'Neel.'

There was no reason to disguise his gladness: if ever in all his life he had had a moment of triumph, it was this.

'Neel!'

'Apé?' Neel turned his face up to his father, in surprise.

'Come up, Neel – there's good news.'

His legs were steadier now. Standing upright, he clapped the messenger on the back and handed him a coin. 'Just some tea money . . .'

'Yes, sir.'

The messenger smiled at the openness of Rajkumar's delight. He was a young clerk, sent to Rangoon by Rajkumar's contractor friend – the one who was working on the Burma–China road, up in the far north. Just as Rajkumar had foreseen, the building of the road had assumed a new strategic urgency with America's entry into the war. It was to be the principal supply line for the Government of Generalissimo Chiang Kai-Shek. New funds had become available and work was proceeding apace. The contractor now found himself in need of a very substantial amount of timber – hence the offer to Rajkumar.

The deal was not without its drawbacks. There was no advance of the kind that Rajkumar would have liked, and the exact date of payment was not guaranteed. But this was wartime after all, and every businessman in Rangoon had learnt to adapt. Rajkumar had no hesitation in accepting the offer.

'Neel!'

'Apé?'

Rajkumar observed his son's face closely as he told him the news. He was delighted when he saw Neel's eyes lighting up; he knew that Neel was glad not merely because of the concluding of a long-hoped-for deal but also because this would be a vindication of his almost childlike belief in his father. Looking into his son's shining eyes, Rajkumar could feel his voice going hoarse. He drew Neel to his chest and hugged him, holding him tight, squeezing the breath from his body, so that his son gasped and cried out aloud. Between the two of them there had always been a special bond, a particular closeness. There were no other eyes in the world that looked into Rajkumar's without reservation, without judgement, without criticism – not Dolly's, not Saya John's, Dinu's least of all. Nothing about this triumph was sweeter than the redemption of his boy's trust.

'And now, Neel –' Rajkumar gave his son's shoulder an affectionate punch – 'and now there's a lot to be done. You're going to have to work harder than you ever have.'

'Apé,' Neel nodded.

Thinking of all the arrangements that had to be made, Rajkumar's mind returned quickly to the matter at hand. 'Come on,' he said, starting down the ladder, 'let's try to get an idea of what we have to do and how much time we have.'

Rajkumar had sold off all his properties except for the

timberyard on the Pazundaung Creek. The creek's mouth lay at the intersection of the Rangoon and Pegu rivers and it provided quick access to the riverport. Many of the city's sawmills, warehouses, petroleum tanks and rice-mills were concentrated along the banks of this waterway. The yard itself consisted of not much more than an open space, crammed with timber and perpetually wreathed in a fog of sawdust. It was surrounded by a high perimeter wall and at its centre there stood a small cabin, elevated on stilts – a structure that vaguely resembled the tais of upcountry forests, except that it was built on a much smaller scale. The cabin served as an office for Rajkumar.

As he walked around the yard Rajkumar could not help congratulating himself on his foresight in concentrating all his stocks in one place – he'd known all along that the order, when it came, would have to be quickly executed: events had proved him right. But even then the job ahead would not be an easy one. Rajkumar saw that he would require large teams of oo-sis and elephants, coolies and trucks. His own elephants had long since been sold off and, with the exception of a couple of caretakers, all his regular employees had been dismissed. He had accustomed himself to managing with hired workforces.

There was a lot to be done and he wished he had more help. Rajkumar could tell that Neel was trying hard, but he was a town-boy, inexperienced in the timber business. Rajkumar knew that Neel was not to blame for this: it was his own fault for never having encouraged him to work in the timber business.

'I don't want to be working with strangers,' Rajkumar confided to Neel. 'I'd prefer to have Doh Say. He'd know exactly how to go about this.'

'But how are we to reach him in Huay Zedi?'

'We can reach him through Raymond.' This was Neel's old friend, Doh Say's son. He was now a student at Rangoon's Judson College. Rajkumar thought the matter over and nodded to himself. 'Yes, Raymond will be able to send him word. We must make sure to go and look for him this evening.'

When Rajkumar and Neel got back to Kemendine, the glow of victory was still bright on their faces. Dolly guessed at once that something was up. 'What is it? Tell me.'

Both Rajkumar and Neel began to talk at once, in voices that were loud enough to bring Manju running down the stairs, with the baby in her arms.

'Tell me too. Start again . . .'

Now for the first time in many weeks there was a lightening in the atmosphere of the house. Neither Arjun nor Dinu had yet been heard from – but this was an occasion when the anxieties of the war could legitimately be forgotten. Even Dolly, so long the sceptic, finally began to believe that Rajkumar's plans were about to pay off; as for Manju, she was overjoyed. The whole family piled into the Packard, with Manju holding the baby and Neel in the driver's seat. Laughing like children, they set off for Judson College, to find Doh Say's son, Raymond.

It was not long before Christmas now, and the central part of Rangoon was being readied for the festivities. This was the area that housed the big department stores, the fashionable restaurants, the clubs, bars and hotels. It was here too – within range of a few blocks of gabled, red-brick buildings – that most of the city's churches, schools and other missionary institutions were located. In December this quarter became one of the city's great seasonal attractions. People flocked in from other neighbourhoods – Kemendine, Kokine, Botataung, Kalaa Bustee – to promenade through the streets and admire the Christmas decorations.

This year the customary bright lights had been forbidden by the air-raid wardens. But otherwise the war had not greatly affected the spirits of the neighbourhood; on the contrary, the news from abroad had had the effect of heightening the usual Christmastime excitement. Among many of the city's British residents, the war had occasioned a renewed determination to carry on as usual. As a result the big shops and restaurants were just as brightly decorated as ever before. Rowe and Co. – the big department store – had put up its usual Christmas tree, a real pine, sent down, as always, from the Maymyo hills. The tree's base was surrounded by drifts of cottonwool and its branches were whitened with a frosting of Cuticura talcum powder. At Whiteway, Laidlaw – another large department store – the tree was even larger, with trimmings imported from England.

They stopped at the Scott Market and went to the Sun Cafe, to sample the famous chocolate-covered Yule logs. On the way they passed a Muslim butcher who was tending a flock of live turkeys and geese. Many of the birds bore little wire tags – they had been reserved months in advance, by European families. The butcher was fattening them for Christmas.

Judson College was customarily one of the centres of Rangoon's Christmas festivities. The college was run by American Baptists and it was one of the best-known educational institutions in Burma.

Raymond was in the college's red-brick chapel. He was rehearsing Handel's *Messiah* with the choir. They sat down to wait, at the back of the chapel, and listened to the massed voices, surging through the arched rafters. The music was glorious and even the baby was lulled into silence.

At the end of the rehearsal Neel intercepted Raymond and brought him over. Raymond was a good-looking, sturdily-built young man with sleepy eyes and a doleful smile. He had been studying in Rangoon for three years, and was thinking of a legal career.

Raymond was delighted to see them and immediately undertook to send word to his father. He was confident that he would be able to get word to Huay Zedi within a few days, by means of a complicated network of telegrams and forwarders.

Rajkumar did not doubt for a moment that Doh Say would come immediately to Rangoon to help him out.

Next morning, Lieutenant-Colonel Buckland sent Arjun ahead with Kishan Singh and two other men. The men were armed with their usual Lee Enfield .303 rifles, while Arjun was issued their only Tommy gun.

Shortly before noon, Arjun came upon the plantation manager's house. It was a squat, two-storeyed bungalow with a tiled roof. It stood in the centre of a clearing that was almost perfectly square. The clearing was surrounded on all sides, by straight, orderly stands of rubber trees. A gravelled driveway snaked across a well-mowed lawn, leading to the front door. The garden was dotted with bursts of colour: the flowers were mostly English varieties – hollyhocks, snapdragons, hydrangeas. At the back there was a tall jacaranda tree with a wooden swing suspended from a branch. Beside it stood an elevated water storage tank. There were beds planted with vegetables – tomatoes, carrots, cauliflowers. A paved path led through the vegetable patch, to the back door. A cat was clawing at the door, crying to be let in.

Arjun circled around the clearing, keeping well within the shelter of the rubber trees. He followed the driveway a little distance down the slope: it could be seen winding through the plantation to join a tarred road, a half-mile or so away. No one was in sight.

Arjun put one of his men on watch and sent another to report back to Lieutenant-Colonel Buckland. Then, with Kishan Singh following close behind, he skirted round the house until he was facing the back door. He crossed the back garden at a run, taking care to keep his head down. The door was latched but gave way easily when he and Kishan Singh put their shoulders to it. The cat that was waiting outside went streaking into the house, through Arjun's feet.

Arjun stepped across the threshold and found himself standing in a large kitchen of European design. There was a wood-burning oven, made of iron, and windows that were draped with white lace curtains. Porcelain plates and bowls stood in rows in the wooden cabinets that lined the walls; the ceramic sink was scrubbed clean and the tin drainer beside it was stacked with glass tumblers and a row of freshly cleaned baby bottles. On the floor, there was a dog's feeding bowl. Where a refrigerator had once stood there was a rectangular discolouration, outlined against the whitewashed wall. On the kitchen table there lay heaps of eggs and bread, and a couple of half-used tins of Australian butter and processed cheese. It was evident that the refrigerator had been emptied in great haste before being carried away.

Although Arjun was now certain that there was no one in the house, he was careful to have Kishan Singh back him up as he went through the other rooms. The bungalow was littered with signs of a hasty departure. In the bedroom, drawers lay upturned, and brassieres and women's underclothing were strewn across the floor. In the living room, a piano stool stood forlornly by the wall. Half-hidden behind a door Arjun found a stack of framed photographs. He glanced at the pictures – a church wedding; children, a car and a dog – the photographs had been piled into a box, as though ready to be transported. Arjun had a sudden vision of the woman of the house making a last frantic run through the bungalow, looking for the box while her husband and family sat outside in a lorry that was piled high with strapped-down luggage; he imagined her rummaging in the cupboards while her husband gunned the engine and the dog barked and the children cried. He was glad that they'd got away when they had; annoyed, on their behalf, with whoever it was that had argued them out of leaving earlier.

He went back to the kitchen and switched on the overhead fan. To his astonishment it worked. On the table there stood a couple of bottles of water, still awash in the puddles of sweat that had formed around them when they were emptied from the refrigerator. He handed one to Kishan Singh and drained the other himself, almost at a gulp. The water had a dull, metallic taste as it coursed down his throat: it was only now that he remembered that it was a long time since he had last eaten.

Minutes later the others arrived.

'Plenty of food here, sir,' Arjun said.

Lieutenant-Colonel Buckland nodded. 'Good. Heaven knows, we need it. And I imagine we can clean up a bit as well.'

Upstairs there were two bathrooms, with fresh towels waiting in the racks. Lieutenant-Colonel Buckland used one bathroom while Arjun and Hardy took turns with the other. The water came from the shaded tank outdoors and was pleasantly cool. Before undressing Arjun stood his Tommy gun against the door. Then he filled a bucket and poured the cool water over his head. On the sink there lay a curled tube of toothpaste: he couldn't resist squeezing some on to his forefinger. With his mouth foaming he glanced out of the bathroom window. Kishan Singh and a couple of the other men were standing under the water tank, bare-bodied, sluicing water over their heads. Another man was keeping watch, smoking a cigarette, his hand resting loosely on his rifle.

They went back to the dining room and found it neatly laid, with plates and silverware. A meal had been prepared by a lance-

naik who had some experience of the officers' mess. There was a salad of tomatoes and carrots; eggs scrambled in butter and hot toast. Canned goods of many kinds had been found in the kitchen cupboards: there was duck-liver pâté, a plate of pickled herrings, thick slices of Dutch ham – all laid out nicely on porcelain plates.

In the sideboard that stood beside the dining table Arjun discovered a few bottles of beer. 'Do you think they would mind, sir?'

'Don't see why they should.' Lieutenant-Colonel Buckland smiled. 'I'm sure if we'd met them at the club they'd have told us to help ourselves.'

There was an interjection from Hardy. 'If *you* had met them at the club, sir,' he said quietly, offering a politely worded correction. 'The two of us wouldn't have been allowed in.'

Lieutenant-Colonel Buckland paused, with a tilted beer bottle in his grasp. Then he raised his glass and gave Hardy an ironic smile. 'To the clubs that won't have us, gentlemen,' he said. 'May they be for ever legion.'

Arjun raised a half-hearted cheer. 'Hear, hear.' He put his glass down and reached for the plate of ham.

Just as they were helping themselves, new cooking smells came wafting out of the kitchen: the fragrance of freshly rolled parathas and chapatis, of frying onions and chopped tomatoes. Hardy glanced down at his plate and its piles of ham and herring. Suddenly he stood up.

'Sir, may I be excused for a minute?'

'By all means, Lieutenant.'

He went into the kitchen and returned with a tray of chapatis and *ande-ka-bhujia* – eggs fried with tomatoes and onions. Glancing at his plate, Arjun found himself growing hungry all over again: to look away was an effort.

'It's all right, yaar.' Hardy was watching him with a smile. 'You can have some too. A chapati won't turn you into a savage, you know.'

Arjun sank back in his seat as Hardy shovelled chapatis and bhujia on to his plate: he lowered his gaze, in the sullen way of a child who is caught between warring parents. The weariness of the night before came on him again and he could barely bring himself to touch his food.

When they were done with eating Lieutenant-Colonel Buckland told Hardy to go outside, to check on the men who were guarding the bungalow's approach road.

Hardy saluted. 'Yes, sir.'

Arjun would have risen from the table too, but Lieutenant-Colonel Buckland stopped him. 'No hurry, Roy.' He reached for a beer bottle. 'Some more?'

'I don't see why not, sir.'

Lieutenant-Colonel Buckland poured beer into Arjun's glass and then filled his own.

'Tell me, Lieutenant,' he said presently, lighting a cigarette. 'How would you rate our morale at this moment?'

'After a lunch like this one, sir,' Arjun said brightly, 'I would say it couldn't be better.'

'It was a different story last night, eh, Lieutenant?' Lieutenant-Colonel Buckland smiled through a cloud of cigarette smoke.

'I don't know if I would say that, sir.'

'Well, you know I have ears of my own, Lieutenant. And while my Hindustani may not be as good as yours, I can assure you it's perfectly adequate.'

Arjun shot him a startled glance. 'I'm not sure I know what you're getting at, sir.'

'Well, none of us could sleep much last night, could we, Lieutenant? And whispers can carry a long way.'

'I don't quite take your meaning, sir.' Arjun felt his face growing hot. 'Are you referring to something I said?'

'It doesn't really matter, Lieutenant. Let's just say that there was a certain similarity of tone in all the voices around me.'

'I see, sir.'

'Lieutenant – I think you probably know that I – we – are not unaware of some of the tensions in our Indianised battalions. It's quite plain that many of our Indian officers feel strongly about public issues – particularly the question of independence.'

'Yes, sir.'

'I don't know what your own feelings are, Roy, but you should know that as far as the thrust of British public opinion goes, independence for India is just a matter of time. Everyone knows that the days of Empire are over – we're not fools, you know.

The last thing an ambitious young Englishman wants to do today is to go out to a backwater. The Americans have been telling us for years that we're going about this the wrong way. One doesn't have to keep up an Empire with all the paraphernalia of an administration and an army. There are easier and more efficient ways to keep a grip on things – it can be done at less expense, and with much less bother. We've all come to accept this now – even chaps like me who've spent our lives out east. The truth is that there's only one reason why England holds on any more – and that is out of a sense of obligation. I know this may be hard for you to believe but it's true. There's a feeling that we can't go under duress and we can't leave a mess behind. And you know as well as I do that if we were to pack our bags now, then you chaps would be at each other's throats in no time – even you and your friend Hardy, what with him being a Sikh and you a Hindu, a Punjabi and a Bengali . . .'

'I see, sir.'

'I'm telling you this, Lieutenant, only to alert you to some of the dangers of the situation in which we now find ourselves. I think we both know that our morale is not what it might be. But this is, of all times, the last in which anybody should waver in their loyalties. The reverses we've suffered are temporary – in a way they are a blessing in disguise. America's entry into the war makes it absolutely certain that we shall prevail, in time. In the meanwhile perhaps we should remind ourselves that the army has a very long memory when it comes to questions of allegiance and loyalty.'

The lieutenant-colonel paused to extinguish his cigarette. Arjun sat staring silently into his glass.

'You know, Roy,' Lieutenant-Colonel Buckland said quietly, 'my grandfather lived through the Mutiny of 1857. I remember that he bore very little rancour towards the civilians who'd got mixed up in the troubles. But as for the soldiers – the sepoys who'd led the Mutiny – that was another matter altogether. Those men had broken an oath: they were traitors, not rebels, and there is no traitor so contemptible as a soldier who reverses his allegiances. And if such a thing were to happen at a dodgy time, I think you would agree with me, wouldn't you, Roy, that it would be hard to conceive of anything quite so unspeakable?'

Arjun was about to answer when he was interrupted by the sound of racing footsteps. He turned to a window to see Hardy running across the front lawn.

'Sir,' Hardy came panting to the windowsill. 'Got to move, sir . . . Jap convoy heading up the road.'

'How many? Could we take them on?'

'No, sir . . . There're at least two platoons – maybe a company.'

Lieutenant-Colonel Buckland pushed his chair calmly back, dabbing his lips with a napkin. 'The main thing, gentlemen,' he said quietly, 'is not to panic. Take a moment to listen to me: this is what I want you to do . . .'

They left the house by the rear entrance with Arjun in the lead and Hardy and Lieutenant-Colonel Buckland bringing up the rear. On reaching the shelter of the first row of trees Arjun fell into a defensive position. With him was a detail composed of Kishan Singh and two other men. Their orders were to cover the others until everyone was clear of the grounds.

The first Japanese truck pulled into the compound just as Hardy and Lieutenant-Colonel Buckland were running across the back garden. For a moment Arjun allowed himself to believe that they had managed to escape unseen. Then a volley of gunfire erupted out of the back of the truck and Arjun heard a chorus of whistles shooting past, well over his head.

Lieutenant-Colonel Buckland and Hardy were almost abreast of him now. Arjun waited till they were clear before giving the order to return fire. *'Chalao goli.'* They fired indiscriminately, in the general direction of the bungalow. The only result was the immediate shattering of the kitchen's windows. In the meantime, the Japanese truck had swung round to take shelter on the far side of the house.

'Piche. Chalo.'

Arjun gave the order to fall back while staying in position himself, firing randomly, hoping to give Kishan Singh and the others time to regroup. He saw that the newly arrived Japanese soldiers were slipping into the trees one by one. He rose to his feet and began to run, holding his Tommy gun under his arm. Glancing over his shoulder, he encountered the now familiar sight of dozens of long files of trees, telescoping towards him – but with the difference that now, each tunnel offered a glimpse of a tiny grey-uniformed figure, somewhere in the far distance, running in pursuit.

Arjun began to run faster, breathing hard, watching out for the branches that lay hidden underneath the fallen leaves. A hundred feet or so ahead, the land fell away steeply. If he could get as far as that he might be able to lose the pursuing soldiers. He sprinted, shortening his steps as he neared the lip of the declivity. Just as he was going over the top he felt his right leg shooting out from beneath him. He fell, tumbling face first down the slope. The shock of the fall was compounded by confusion: he could not understand why he had fallen. He hadn't tripped and he hadn't lost his footing – he was sure of that. Grasping at the undergrowth he managed to bring himself to a halt. He tried to get back on his feet and found that he couldn't. He looked down and saw that his trouser leg was covered in blood. He could feel the wetness of the cloth against his skin yet he was not conscious of any pain. His pursuers' footsteps were closer now, and he glanced around himself quickly, looking at the carpet of dead leaves that stretched away in every direction.

Just then he heard a sound, a familiar whisper. 'Sah'b.'

He rolled over to find himself looking at Kishan Singh: his batman was lying prone, hidden inside a dark opening – a culvert or drainage pipe of some kind. The opening was blanketed by leaves and undergrowth. It was very well-hidden, almost invisible. The only reason that Arjun could see it at all was because he was lying flat on the ground.

Kishan Singh extended a hand and dragged him into the culvert. Then he crawled out to scatter leaves over the traces of Arjun's blood. Minutes later they heard the sound of footsteps racing past overhead.

The culvert was just wide enough for the two of them to lie side by side. Now, suddenly, Arjun's wound began to make itself felt, the pain welling out of his leg in waves. He tried to stifle a groan, not quite successfully. Kishan Singh threw a hand over his mouth and wrestled him into silence. Arjun realised that he was about to black out and he was glad: at that moment there was nothing he wanted more than oblivion.

Thirty-six

Even though he was following the news closely on the radio, Dinu had trouble understanding exactly what was under way in northern Malaya. The bulletins mentioned a major engagement in the region of Jitra but the reports were inconclusive and confusing. In the meantime, there were other indications of the way the war was going, all of them ominous. One of these was an official newspaper announcement, listing the closing of certain post offices in the north. Another was the increasing volume of southbound traffic: a stream of evacuees was pouring down the north–south highway in the direction of Singapore.

One day, on a visit to Sungei Pattani, Dinu had a glimpse of this exodus. The evacuees seemed to consist mainly of the families of planters and mining engineers. Their cars and trucks were filled with household objects – furniture, trunks, suitcases. He came across a truck that was loaded with a refrigerator, a dog and an upright piano. He spoke to the man who was driving the truck: he was a Dutchman, the manager of a rubber plantation near Jitra. His family were sitting crowded in the truck's cab: his wife, a newborn baby and two girls. The Dutchman said he'd managed to get out just ahead of the Japanese. His advice to Dinu was to leave as soon as possible – not to make the mistake of waiting until the last minute.

That night, at Morningside, Dinu told Alison exactly what the Dutchman had said. They looked at each other in silence: they had been over the subject several times before. They knew they had very few choices. If they went by road one of them would have to stay behind – the estate's truck was in no shape to make the long journey to Singapore and the Daytona would not be able to carry more than two passengers over that kind of distance. The only alternative was to go by train – but rail services had been temporarily suspended.

'What are we going to do, Alison?' Dinu said.

'Let's wait and see,' Alison said hopefully. 'Who knows? Perhaps we won't have to leave after all.'

Late that night they were woken by the crunch of bicycle wheels, rolling up the gravelled drive of Morningside House. A voice called out from below: 'Miss Martins . . .'

Alison got up and went to the window. It was still dark. Parting the curtains, she leaned out, peering down into the drive. Dinu glanced at a bedside clock and saw that it was four in the morning. He sat up: 'Alison? Who is it?'

'It's Ilongo,' Alison said. 'He has Ah Fatt with him – from the restaurant, in town.'

'At this time of night?'

'I think they want to tell me something.' Alison let the curtain drop. 'I'm going downstairs.' She pulled on a dressing gown and ran out of the room. A few minutes later, Dinu followed. He found Alison sitting in a huddle with the visitors. Ah Fatt was talking urgently, in rapid Malay, stabbing a finger in the air. Alison was biting her lip, nodding: Dinu could see a deepening anxiety in the crimped lines of her face.

In a while Dinu jogged her elbow. 'What are you talking about? Tell me.'

Alison stood up and took him aside.

'Ah Fatt says that Grandfather and I have to leave – for Singapore. He says it's going badly on the front. The Japanese may be able to push through in a day or two. He thinks the Kempeitai – their secret police – have information about us . . .'

Dinu nodded. 'He's right. It won't do to wait any longer. You've got to go.'

Tears started into Alison's eyes. 'I don't want to go, Dinu. Not without you. I really don't.'

'You have to, Alison. Think of your grandfather . . .'

'Miss Martins,' Ah Fatt interrupted, to let them know that he'd heard that a special evacuation train would be leaving from

Butterworth that morning. He wasn't sure that they'd be able to get on it – but it was worth trying.

Dinu and Alison exchanged smiles. 'We'll never get another chance like this,' Alison said.

'Let's wake your grandfather,' Dinu said. 'Let's not waste any time.'

They left early the next day in one of the estate's trucks. Ilongo drove and Dinu rode in the back with the luggage. Alison sat in front, with Saya John. There was little traffic, because of the time of day, and they arrived in Sungei Pattani in half the usual time. The town was silent: many of the shops and houses were locked or boarded up. Some had notices hanging outside.

A short way from town they picked up the main highway. The road's embankment was dotted with parked vehicles. Families could be seen to be sleeping in their cars, snatching a little rest before daylight. At intervals one-and-a-half-ton military trucks came barrelling down the highway, heading south. They would bear down very suddenly, pushing other traffic off the road, headlights blazing, sounding their horns. Dinu caught occasional glimpses of soldiers, squatting in the trucks' tarpaulin-covered beds.

Approaching Butterworth, the road was jammed with cars and trucks. The railway station was right next to the ferry terminus that connected the mainland to the island of Penang. This area had taken several hits during the recent bombing raids and there was a great deal of confusion in the rubble-strewn streets. People could be seen heading towards the station on foot, carrying bags and suitcases.

Ilongo parked in a side street and left Alison, Dinu and Saya John in the truck while he went ahead to make inquiries. He came back an hour later to report that they had a long wait ahead. There were rumours that the train would not leave until after midnight. Penang was being evacuated too and a fleet of ferries was to be dispatched under cover of darkness. The train would not depart until the ferries had returned to Butterworth with the Penang evacuees.

Alison took a room in a hotel so that Saya John could rest. They spent the day taking it in turns to go out to make inquiries.

Night fell and at ten o'clock there was still no news. Then, a little after midnight, Ilongo came running into the hotel with the information that the ferries had been sighted, returning from Penang. Shortly afterwards a train was shunted into the platform of the railway station.

Alison woke Saya John and Dinu paid for the hotel room. They stepped out into the darkened street and joined the crowd that was hurrying toward the station. The entrance had been cordoned off and could only be approached through a defile that was packed with people and luggage.

A few yards from the entrance Ilongo decided to turn back. He put an arm around Saya John and gave him a big hug. 'Goodbye, Saya.'

Saya John gave him a blankly affectionate smile. 'Be careful how you drive, Ilongo.'

'Yes, Saya.' Ilongo laughed. He turned to Alison and Dinu but before he could say goodbye they were pushed ahead by the press of bodies. He shouted after them: 'I'm going to spend the night in the truck. You can find me there – just in case. Good luck.'

Dinu answered with a wave. 'And to you too . . . good luck.'

The entrance to the platform was manned by two guards, both Indian. They were dressed in green uniforms and had rifles slung over their shoulders. There were no tickets to be checked: the guards were looking the evacuees over and ushering them through.

They got to the gate with Saya John leaning heavily on Alison. Dinu was directly behind them, carrying their suitcases. Just as they were about to go through the entrance, a guard stopped Alison with an outstretched arm. There followed a hurried consultation between the two guards. Then the guards gestured to Dinu, Alison and Saya John to step aside. 'Please . . . Move away from the gate.'

'What's the matter?' Alison said to Dinu. 'What's happening?'

Dinu stepped up to face the guards. '*Kya hua*?' he said, addressing them in Hindustani. 'Why've you stopped us?'

'You can't go through.'

'Why not?'

'Don't you have eyes?' a guard said to him brusquely. 'Can't you see that this train's only for Europeans?'

'What?'

'You heard – it's only for Europeans.'

Dinu swallowed, trying to keep his composure. 'Listen,' he said carefully, 'that can't be true . . . This is wartime. We were told that this was an evacuation train. How can it be only for Europeans? There must be some mistake.'

The guard looked him in the eye, and gestured at the train with his thumb. 'You've got eyes of your own,' he said. '*Dekh lo* – take a look.'

Craning over the guard's shoulder, he looked up and down the platform, at the train's windows: he could not see a single face that looked Malay or Chinese or Indian.

'This is impossible . . . it's madness.'

'What? What's impossible?' Alison tugged at his arm. 'Dinu, tell me, what's going on?'

'The guards say this train is only for whites . . .'

Alison nodded. 'Yes. I had a feeling that it would be – that's how things are . . .'

'How can you say that, Alison?' Dinu was frantic now and sweat was pouring down his face. 'You can't put up with this stuff . . . Not now. Not when there's a war . . .'

Dinu spotted a uniformed Englishman, walking along the platform, checking a roster. Dinu began to plead with the guards: 'Listen – let me through – just for a minute . . . just to have a word with that officer over there . . . I'll explain to him; I'm sure he'll understand.'

'Not possible.'

Dinu lost his temper. He shouted into the guard's face. 'How can you stop me? Who's given you the right?'

Suddenly a third man appeared. He was dressed in a railway uniform and he too appeared to be Indian. He herded them away from the entrance, towards a flight of stairs that led back to the street. 'Yes please?' he said to Dinu. 'I am the station master – please tell me: what is the problem?'

'Sir . . .' Dinu made an effort to keep his voice even. 'They are not letting us through . . . They say the train is only for Europeans.'

The station master smiled apologetically. 'Yes – that is what we have been given to understand.'

'But how can that be? . . . This is wartime . . . This is an evacuation train.'

'What can I say? Why, in Penang, Mr Lim, the magistrate, was turned back even though he had an official evacuation letter. The Europeans would not let him board the ferries becuse of his being Chinese.'

'You don't understand . . .' Dinu began to plead. 'It's not just Europeans who are in danger . . . You can't do this . . . It's wrong . . .'

The station master pulled a face, shrugging dismissively. 'I do not see what is so wrong with it. After all it is common sense. They are the rulers; they are the ones who stand to lose.'

Dinu's voice rose. 'That's nonsense,' he shouted. 'If that's the way you look at it, then the war's already lost. Don't you see? You've conceded everything worth fighting for . . .'

'Sir,' the station master glared at him, 'there is no reason to shout. I am just doing my job.'

Dinu raised his hands and grabbed hold of the station master's collar. 'You bastard,' he said, shaking him. 'You bastard . . . it's you who're the enemy. People like you – just doing their jobs . . . you're the enemy.'

'Dinu,' Alison screamed. 'Look out!'

Dinu felt a hand closing on the back of his neck, wrenching him away from the station master. A fist slammed into his face, knocking him to the floor. His nostrils filled with the metallic smell of blood. He looked up to see the two guards glaring angrily down at him. Alison and Saya John were holding them off. 'Let him be. Let him be!'

Alison reached down and helped Dinu to his feet. 'Come on, Dinu – let's go.' She picked up their luggage and ushered Dinu and Saya John down the stairs. When they were back on the street, Dinu steadied himself against a lamp-post and put his hands on Alison's shoulders. 'Alison,' he said, 'Alison – maybe they'll let you on, by yourself. You're half-white. You have to try, Alison.'

'Shh.' She put a hand over his mouth. 'Don't say that, Dinu. I wouldn't think of it.'

Dinu wiped the blood from his nose. 'But you have to leave,

Alison . . . With your grandfather – you heard what Ah Fatt said. One way or another you have to go . . . You can't stay at Morningside any more . . .'

From inside the station there was a piercing whistle. All around them, people began to run, crowding into the station's entrance, pushing at the gates. Dinu, Alison and Saya John held on to each other's arms', anchoring themselves to the lamp-post.

At last they heard the train pulling away. 'It's gone,' said Saya John.

'Yes, Baba,' Alison said quietly. 'It's gone.'

Dinu stepped back and picked up a suitcase. 'Let's go and find Ilongo,' he said.

'Tomorrow morning we'll go back to Morningside.'

'To stay?'

Dinu shook his head. 'I'll stay there, Alison,' he said. 'They won't harm me – I don't have anything particular to be afraid of. But you and your grandfather – with your connections – American and Chinese . . . There's just no telling what they would do to you. You have to go . . .'

'But how, Dinu?'

At last Dinu said the words they'd both been dreading: 'The Daytona . . . It's the only way, Alison.'

'No.' She threw herself on him. 'Not without you.'

'It'll be all right, Alison.' He was careful to speak quietly, feigning a confidence that he was far from feeling. 'I'll join you soon . . . in Singapore, you'll see. We won't be long apart.'

It was dark when Arjun returned to consciousness. The sensation in his leg had subsided to a raw, throbbing pain. As his mind cleared Arjun realised that a stream of water was flowing past him and the culvert was resounding to a dull, drumming noise. It took him several minutes to understand that it was raining.

Just as he was beginning to stir, Arjun felt Kishan Singh's hand tightening on his shoulder, in warning. 'They're still around, sah'b,' Kishan Singh whispered. 'They've posted pickets in the plantation. They're waiting.'

'How close are they? Within earshot?'

'No. They can't hear us in the rain.'

'How long was I out?'

'More than an hour, sah'b. I bandaged your wound. The bullet passed cleanly through your hamstring. It'll be all right.'

Arjun touched his thigh gingerly. Kishan Singh had unwrapped his puttees, rolled up his trousers and applied a field dressing. He'd also made a kind of cradle to keep his leg out of the water, by propping two sticks against the sides of the culvert.

'What shall we do now, sah'b?'

The question confounded Arjun. He tried to look ahead but his mind was still clouded by pain and he could think of no clear plan. 'We'll have to wait them out, Kishan Singh. Tomorrow morning we'll see.'

'*Han*, sah'b.' Kishan Singh seemed relieved.

Lying motionless in the inches-deep water, Arjun became acutely aware of his surroundings: of the wet folds of cloth that were carving furrows into his skin, of the pressure of Kishan Singh's body, stretched out beside him. The culvert was filled with the smell of their bodies: the mildewed, rain-soaked, sweat-stained odour of their uniforms, the metallic smell of his own blood.

His mind strayed, disordered by the pain in his leg. He remembered suddenly the look that Kishan Singh had given him on the beach that day, when he came back from the island with Alison. Was it scorn that he'd seen in his eyes – a judgement of some kind?

Would Kishan Singh have done what he had? Allowed himself to make love to Alison; to prey upon her; to betray Dinu, who was both a friend and something more? He didn't know himself why he'd been driven to do it; why he'd wanted her so much. He'd heard some of the chaps saying that these things came on you in wartime – on the front. But Kishan Singh was on the front too – and it was hard to think of him doing anything like that. Was that part of the difference between being an officer and a *jawan* – having to impose yourself, enforce your will?

It occurred to him that he would have liked to talk about this. He remembered that Kishan Singh had once told him that he'd been married off at the age of sixteen. He would have liked to ask Kishan Singh: what was it like when you were married? Had you known your wife before? On the night of your wedding how did you touch her? Did she look you in the face?

He tried to form the sentences in his head and found that he did not know the right words in Hindustani; did not even know the tone of voice in which such questions could be asked. These were things he did not know how to say. There was so much that he did not know how to say, in any language. There was something awkward, unmanly even, about wanting to know what was inside one's head. What was it that Hardy had said the night before? Something about connecting his hand and his heart. He'd been taken aback when he said that; it wasn't on for a chap to say that kind of thing. But at the same time, it was interesting to think that Hardy – or anyone for that matter, even he himself – might want something without knowing it. How was that possible? Was it because no one had taught them the words? The right language? Perhaps because it might be too dangerous? Or because they weren't old enough to know? It was strangely crippling to think that he did not possess the simplest tools of self-consciousness – had no window through which to know that he possessed a within. Was this what Alison had meant, about being a weapon in someone else's hands? Odd that Hardy had said the same thing too.

Waiting for the minutes to pass he could feel his mind fixing on his wounded leg. The pain grew steadily, mounting in intensity until it saturated his consciousness, erasing all other sensation. He began to breathe in gasps, through gritted teeth. Then, through the fog of pain in his head, he became aware of Kishan Singh's hand, gripping his forearm, shaking his shoulder, in encouragement.

'*Sabar karo, sah'b*; it'll pass.'

He heard himself say: 'I don't know how long I can last, Kishan Singh.'

'You can last, sah'b. Just hold on. Be patient.'

Arjun had a sudden premonition of blacking out again, sinking face first into the rainwater, drowning where he lay. In panic he clutched at Kishan Singh, holding on to his arm as though it were a life raft.

'Kishan Singh, say something. Talk. Don't let me pass out again.'

'Talk about what, sah'b?'

'I don't care. Just talk, Kishan Singh – about anything. Tell me about your village.'

Hesitantly Kishan Singh began to speak.

'The name of our village is Kotana, sah'b, and it's near Kurukshetra – not far from Delhi . It's as simple a village as any, but there is one thing we always say of Kotana . . .'

'What is that?'

'That in every house in Kotana you will find a piece of the world. In one there is a hookah from Egypt; in another a box from China . . .'

Speaking through a wall of pain, Arjun said: 'Why is that, Kishan Singh?'

'Sah'b, for generations every Jat family in Kotana has sent its sons to serve in the army of the English sarkar.'

'Since when?'

'Since the time of my great-grandfather, sah'b – since the Mutiny.'

'The Mutiny?' Arjun recalled Lieutenant-Colonel Buckland's voice, speaking of the same thing. 'What does the Mutiny have to do with it?'

'Sah'b, when I was a boy, the old men of the village used to tell us a story. It was about the Mutiny. When the uprising ended and the British re-entered Delhi it came to be known that a great spectacle was to be held in the city. From Kotana a group of elders was deputed to go. They set off at dawn and walked, with hundreds of others, towards the southern postern of the old capital. When they were still far away they saw that the sky above the city was black with birds. The wind carried an odour that grew stronger as they approached the city. The road was straight, the ground level and they could see a long way into the distance. A puzzling sight lay ahead. The road seemed to be lined by troops of very tall men. It was as though an army of giants had turned out to stand guard over the crowd. On approaching closer, they saw that these were not giants, but men – rebel soldiers whose bodies had been impaled on sharpened stakes. The stakes were arranged in straight lines and led all the way to the city. The stench was terrible. When they returned to Kotana the elders gathered the villagers together. They said, "Today we have seen the face of defeat and it shall never be ours." From that day on, the families of Kotana decided that they would send their sons to the army of the English sarkar. This is what our fathers told us. I do not know whether this story is true or false, sah'b, but it is what I heard when I was a boy.'

In the confusion of his pain, Arjun had trouble following this. 'What are you saying then, Kishan Singh? Are you saying that the villagers joined the army out of fear? But that can't be: no one forced them – or you for that matter. What was there to be afraid of?'

'Sah'b,' Kishan Singh said softly, 'all fear is not the same. What is the fear that keeps us hiding here, for instance? Is it a fear of the Japanese, or is it a fear of the British? Or is it a fear of ourselves, because we do not know who to fear more? Sah'b, a man may fear the shadow of a gun just as much as the gun itself – and who is to say which is the more real?'

For a moment, it seemed to Arjun that Kishan Singh was talking about something very exotic, a creature of fantasy: a terror that made you remould yourself, that made you change your idea of your place in the world – to the point where you lost your awareness of the fear that had formed you. The idea of such a magnitude of terror seemed absurd – like reports of the finding of creatures that were known to be extinct. This was the difference, he thought, between the other ranks and officers: common soldiers had no access to the instincts that made them act; no vocabulary with which to shape their self-awareness. They were destined, like Kishan Singh, to be strangers to themselves, to be directed always by others.

But no sooner did this thought take shape in his mind than it was transformed by the delirium of his pain. He had a sudden, hallucinatory vision. Both he and Kishan Singh were in it, but transfigured: they were both lumps of clay, whirling on potters' wheels. He, Arjun, was the first to have been touched by the unseen potter; a hand had come down on him, touched him, passed over to another; he had been formed, shaped – he had become a thing unto itself – no longer aware of the pressure of the potter's hand, unconscious even that it had come his way. Elsewhere, Kishan Singh was still turning on the wheel, still unformed, damp, malleable mud. It was this formlessness that was the core of his defence against the potter and his shaping touch.

Arjun could not blot this image from his mind: how was it possible that Kishan Singh – uneducated, unconscious of his motives – should be more aware of the weight of the past than he, Arjun?

'Kishan Singh,' he said hoarsely, 'give me some water.'

Kishan Singh handed him a green bottle and he drank, hoping that the water would dissipate the hallucinatory brilliance of the images that were passing before his eyes. But it had exactly the opposite effect. His mind was inflamed with visions, queries. Was it possible – even hypothetically – that his life, his choices, had always been moulded by fears of which he himself was unaware? He thought back to the past: Lankasuka, Manju, Bela , the hours he had spent sitting on the windowsill, the ecstatic sense of liberation that had come over him on learning that he had been accepted into the Military Academy. Fear had played no part in any of this. He had never thought of his life as different from any other; he had never experienced the slightest doubt about his personal sovereignty; never imagined himself to be dealing with anything other than the full range of human choice. But if it were true that his life had somehow been moulded by acts of power of which he was unaware – then it would follow that he had never acted of his own volition; never had a moment of true self-consciousness. Everything he had ever assumed about himself was a lie, an illusion. And if this were so, how was he to find himself now?

Thirty-seven

When they left for Morningside, the next day, the roads were even busier than on the way out. But theirs seemed to be the only vehicle going north: everyone else was heading in the opposite direction – towards Kuala Lumpur and Singapore. Heads turned to stare as they drove by; they were flagged down several times by helpful people who wanted to make sure they knew where they were going.

They passed dozens of army trucks, many of them travelling two abreast, with their klaxons blaring, crowding them off the road. Over long stretches they were forced to drive on the grassy verge, crawling along at speeds of fifteen to twenty miles an hour.

It was late afternoon when they came into Sungei Pattani: it was just a day since they'd last driven through, but the town already seemed a changed place. In the morning, they'd found it empty and ghostlike: most of its inhabitants had scattered into the countryside; its shops had been boarded and locked. Now Sungei Pattani was empty no longer: everywhere they looked there were soldiers – Australians, Canadians, Indians, British. But these were not the orderly detachments they had grown accustomed to seeing; these were listless, weary-looking men, bunched together in small groups and ragged little clusters. Some were ambling through the streets with their guns slung over their shoulders, like fishing rods; some were lounging in the shade of the shophouse arcades, eating out of cans and packets, scooping out the food with their fingers. Their uniforms were sweat-stained and dirty, their faces streaked with mud. In the town's parks and roundabouts – where children usually played – they saw groups of exhausted men, lying asleep, with their weapons cradled in their arms.

They began to notice signs of looting: broken windows, gates that had been wrenched open, shops with battered shutters. They saw looters stepping in and out of the breaches – soldiers and locals were milling about together, tearing shops apart. There were no policemen anywhere in sight. It was clear that the civil administration had departed.

'Faster, Ilongo.' Dinu rapped on the truck's window. 'Let's get through . . .'

They came to a road that was blocked by a group of soldiers. One of them was pointing a gun at the truck, trying to wave it down. Dinu noticed that he was swaying on his feet. He shouted to Ilongo. 'Keep going; they're drunk . . .' Ilongo swerved suddenly, taking the truck over the median, into the other lane. Dinu looked back to see the soldiers staring after them, cursing: 'Fuckin' monkeys . . .'

Ilongo turned into an alley, then took the truck speeding down a side road, out of town. A few miles further on, he spotted an acquaintance standing by the roadside. He stopped to ask what was going on.

The man was a contractor on a rubber plantation not far from Morningside. He told them they were lucky that they were still in possession of their truck: on his estate, every single vehicle had been commandeered. An English officer had come through with a detachment of soldiers earlier in the day: they'd driven their trucks away.

They exchanged glances, all of them thinking immediately of the Daytona, back at its Morningside garage.

Dinu began to chew on his knuckles: 'Come on, let's not waste time . . .'

A few minutes later they drove past Morningside's arched gateway. It was as though they had entered another country; here there was no sign of anything untoward. The estate was tranquil and quiet; children waved at them as they drove up the unpaved road. Then the house appeared, far ahead on the slope: it looked majestic, serene.

Ilongo took the truck directly to the garage. He jumped down and pulled the door open. The Daytona was still inside.

Dinu and Alison stood looking at the car. Dinu took hold of her arm and nudged her into the garage: 'Alison . . . you should set off right now . . . there's so little time.'

'No.' Alison pulled her arm free and slammed shut the garage door. 'I'll leave later – at night. Who knows how long it'll be before we see each other again? I want to spend a few hours with you before I go.'

In the morning Kishan Singh went to investigate and found that the Japanese had withdrawn from the plantation, under cover of night. He helped Arjun crawl out of the culvert and propped him upright, on the leaf-carpeted ground. Then he eased off Arjun's wet clothes, wrung them out, and spread them in a sunlit spot.

Arjun's chest and stomach were puckered from their long immersion, but the pain in his leg had eased. He was relieved to see that the bandage on his thigh had done its work, stopping the flow of blood.

Kishan Singh found a branch that could be used as a crutch and they started off slowly with Arjun stopping every few paces to adjust his grip. Presently they arrived at a gravelled track. Keeping to the shelter of the treeline they followed the direction of the track. In a while they began to notice signs of approaching habitation – shreds of clothing, footprints, discarded eggshells that had been carried away by birds. Soon they saw curls of woodsmoke rising above the trees. They caught the familiar smells of rice and scorched mustard seeds. Then they spotted the plantation's coolie lines: twins rows of shacks, facing each other across the track. Large numbers of people were milling about in the open and it was clear, even from a distance, that something unusual was under way.

The shacks lay in a gentle depression, a basin, surrounded by higher land on all sides. With Kishan Singh's help Arjun climbed up a low ridge. Lying flat on their stomachs, they looked down into the basin below.

There were some fifty dwellings in the lines, arranged in parallel rows. At one end there was a small Hindu temple – a tin-roofed shed surrounded by a wall that was painted red and white. Next to the temple there was a clearing with an open-sided shed, also roofed in tin. This was evidently a communal meeting place. It was this shed that was the focus of the excitement. Everyone in the hamlet was heading in its direction.

'Sah'b. Look.' Kishan Singh pointed to a black car standing half hidden beside the shed. There was a flag on the bonnet, affixed to an upright rod. The flag seemed very small from that distance and Arjun failed to recognise it at first glance. It was both familiar and unfamiliar; of a design that he knew well, but had not seen in a long time. He turned to Kishan Singh and found his batman watching him warily.

'Do you know that *jhanda*, Kishan Singh?'

'Sah'b, it is the *tiranga* . . .'

Of course – how could he have failed to recognise it? It was the flag of the Indian national movement: a spinning wheel, set against a background of saffron, white and green. He was still puzzling over the flag when there followed a second surprise. A familiar khaki-turbaned figure came out of the shed, walking towards the car. It was Hardy and he was deep in conversation with another man, a stranger – a white-bearded Sikh, dressed in the long, white tunic of a learned man, a Giani.

There was no reason to wait any longer. Arjun struggled to his feet. 'Kishan Singh, *chalo* . . .' Leaning heavily on his crutch he began to walk down the slope towards the shed.

'Hardy! *Oye*, Hardy!'

Hardy broke off his conversation and looked up. 'Yaar? Arjun?'

He came running up the slope, a grin spreading across his face. 'Yaar – we thought for sure the bastards had got you.'

'Kishan Singh came back for me,' Arjun said. 'I wouldn't be here now if it wasn't for him.'

Hardy clapped Kishan Singh on the shoulder. '*Shabash!*'

'Now tell me –' Arjun jogged Hardy's elbow – 'what's going on here?'

'No hurry, yaar,' Hardy said. 'I'll tell you, but we should get you cleaned up first. Where exactly were you hit?'

'Hamstring, I think.'

'Is it bad?'

'Better today.'

'Let's go somewhere where we can sit down. We'll get your wound dressed.'

Hardy beckoned to a soldier. *'Jaldi – M.O. ko bhejo.'* He led Arjun into one of the shacks and held the door open. 'Our HQ,' he said with a grin.

It was dark inside, the narrow windows being draped in ragged bits of cloth. The walls were of wood, covered with layers of soot, and there was a powerful smell of smoke. Beside one wall there stood a narrow string *charpoy*: Hardy led Arjun to the bed and helped him sit down.

There was a knock at the door and the medical orderly entered. He subjected Arjun's bandage to a careful examination and then ripped it off, in one quick movement. Arjun grimaced and Hardy handed him a glass of water.

'Drink up. You need it.'

Arjun drained the glass and handed it back. 'Hardy?' he said. 'Where's Bucky?'

'He's resting,' said Hardy. 'There's a vacant shed down the road. It was the only suitable place for him. His arm's been troubling him. We had to give him painkillers. He's been out all morning.'

The orderly began to swab Arjun's wound and he braced himself by gripping the edge of the bed.

'So tell me, Hardy,' he said, through gritted teeth. 'What's going on here?'

'I'll make it as short as possible,' said Hardy. 'It happened like this: last night, not long after we lost you, we came across a couple of rubber tappers. They were Indian and when we spoke to them they said we would be safe in the coolie lines. They brought us here. They were very welcoming: gave us food, beds. Showed us the shed where we put Bucky. We didn't know this then, but it turned out that some of them were members of the Indian Independence League. They sent word to their office and this morning Gianiji arrived, in a car – flying the flag. You can imagine how amazed we were. Turns out he's Giani Amreek Singh – recognise the name? His signature was on the pamphlets the Japs dropped on us at Jitra.'

'Yes,' said Arjun, drily. 'I know that name. What does he want?'

Hardy paused, humming a tune under his breath. Arjun knew that he was thinking carefully about what he was going to say next.

'Arjun, do you remember Captain Mohun Singh?'

'Yes. 1/14 Punjab, right? Wasn't he at Jitra too? I thought I saw him on the way to the Asoon line.'

'Yes. They took cover in the plantation and headed eastwards just as we did.'

'So what about Captain Mohun Singh?'

'Gianiji told me that he'd made contact with the Indian Independence League.'

'Go on.'

'Wait.' The orderly had finished dressing Arjun's wound. Hardy saw him out and then shut the door. He paused, running a finger through his beard. 'Look, Arjun,' he said, 'I don't know how you'll take this. I'm just telling you what I know . . .'

'Go on, Hardy.'

'Captain Mohun Singh has taken a big step.'

'What step?'

'He's decided to break with the Britishers.'

'What?'

'Yes,' said Hardy in a flat, even voice. 'He's going to form an independent unit – the Indian National Army. All the 14th Punjab officers are with him – the Indians I mean. Kumar, Masood, many others too. They've invited all of us to join . . .'

'So?' Arjun said. 'Are you thinking of doing it?'

'What can I say, Arjun?' Hardy smiled. 'You know how I feel. I've never made a secret of my views – unlike some of you chaps.'

'Hardy, wait.' Arjun stabbed a finger at him. 'Just think a minute. Don't be in a hurry. How do you know who this Giani is? How do you even know he's telling the truth about Captain Mohun Singh? How do you know he's not just a Japanese stooge?'

'Amreek Singh was in the army too,' Hardy said. 'He knew my father – his village isn't far from ours. If he is a Japanese stooge then there must be some reason why he became one. In any case, who are we to call him a stooge?' Hardy laughed. 'After all, aren't we the biggest stooges of all?'

'Wait.' Arjun tried to marshal his thoughts. It was a huge relief to be able to speak out at last, to bring into the open the long arguments that he had conducted with himself in the secrecy of his mind.

'So what does this mean?' Arjun said. 'That Mohun Singh and his lot will be fighting on the Japanese side?'

'Yes. Of course. For the time being – until the British are out of India.'

'But Hardy – let's think this thing through. What do the Japanese want with us? Do they care about us and our independence? All they want is to push the Britishers out so they can step in and take their place. They just want to use us: don't you see that?'

'Of course they do, Arjun,' Hardy shrugged his acquiescence. 'If it wasn't them it would be someone else. There'll always be someone trying to use us. That's why this is so hard, don't you see? This is the first time in our lives that we're trying to make up our own minds – not taking orders.'

'Hardy, look.' Arjun made an effort to keep his voice calm. 'That's how it may look to you right now, but just ask yourself: what are the chances that we'll be able to do anything for ourselves? Most likely we'll just end up helping the Japs to get into India. And what would be the point of exchanging the Britishers for the Japanese? As colonial masters go the British aren't that bad – better than most. Certainly a lot better than the Japanese would be.'

Hardy gave a full-throated laugh, his eyes shining. 'Yaar Arjun, think of where we've fallen when we start talking of good masters and bad masters. What are we? Dogs? Sheep? There are no good masters and bad masters, Arjun – in a way the better the master, the worse the condition of the slave, because it makes him forget what he is . . .'

They were glaring at each other, their faces no more than inches apart. Hardy's eyelid was twitching and Arjun could feel the heat of his breath. He was the first to pull away.

'Hardy, it won't help for us to fight each other.'

'No.'

Arjun began to chew his knuckles. 'Listen, Hardy,' he said. 'Don't think that I disagree with what you're saying. I don't. I think for the most part you're right on the mark. But I'm just trying to think about us – about men like you and me – about our place in the world.'

'I don't follow.'

'Just look at us, Hardy – just look at us. What are we? We've learnt to dance the tango and we know how to eat roast beef with a knife and fork. The truth is that except for the colour of our skin, most people in India wouldn't even recognise us as Indians. When we joined up we didn't have India on our minds: we wanted to be sahibs and that's what we've become. Do you think we can undo all of that just by putting up a new flag?'

Hardy shrugged dismissively. 'Look,' he said, 'I'm a simple soldier, yaar. I don't know what you're trying to get at. To me, it's a question of right and wrong – what's worth fighting for and what's not. That's all.'

There was a knock on the door. Hardy opened it to see Giani Amreek Singh standing outside.

'Everyone's waiting . . .'

'Gianiji, *ek minit* . . .' Hardy turned back to Arjun. 'Look, Arjun –' his voice was tired after the effort of the argument – 'I'll tell you what I'm going to do. Gianiji has offered to take us through the Jap lines, to Mohun Singh. For myself I've made up my mind already. I'm going to explain this to the men; I'm going to tell them why I think this is the right thing to do. They can decide for themselves. Do you want to come and listen?'

Arjun nodded. 'Yes.'

Hardy handed Arjun his crutch and they went together to the communal shed, walking slowly down the gravel track. The shed was full: the soldiers were at the front, squatting in orderly rows. Behind them were the inhabitants of the coolie lines: the men were in sarongs, the women in saris. Many of the tappers had children in their arms. At one end of the shed there stood a table and a couple of chairs. Hardy took his place behind the table while Arjun and Giani Amreek Singh seated themselves on the chairs. There was a lot of noise: people were whispering, talking, some of the children were giggling at the novelty of the occasion. Hardy had to shout to make himself heard.

Once Hardy began, Arjun realised, with some surprise, that he was a talented speaker, almost a practised orator. His voice filled the shed, his words echoing off the tin roof – *duty, country, freedom.* Arjun was listening intently when he became aware that a film of sweat was running down his face. He looked down and realised that he was dripping – sweat was pouring off his elbows and off his legs. He felt himself growing feverish as he had the night before.

Suddenly the shed rang to the sound of massed voices. The noise was deafening. Arjun heard Hardy bellowing into the crowd: 'Are you with me?'

There was another eruption; a huge burst of sound welled up to the roof and came echoing back. The soldiers were on their feet. A couple of them linked arms and began to dance the *bhangra*, shaking their shoulders and stamping their feet. Behind them the workers were shouting too – men, women, children – throwing things in the air, clapping, waving. Arjun looked at Kishan Singh and saw that his face was flushed, joyful, his eyes alight.

Arjun noted, in a detached and almost disinterested way, that since the time he'd entered the shed, everything seemed to have altered. It was as though the whole world had suddenly changed colour, assumed a different guise. The realities of a few minutes before now seemed like an incomprehensible dream: had he really been surprised to look over the bluff and see an Indian flag in the coolie lines? But where else would such a flag be? Was it really true that Kishan Singh's grandfather had won a decoration at Flanders? Was it true that Kishan Singh was the same man that he had always taken him to be – the most of loyal of soldiers, descended from generations of loyal soldiers? He looked at the dancing men: how was it possible that he had served with those men for so long and never had an inkling that their acquiescence was not what it seemed to be? And how was it possible that he had never known this even of himself?

Was this how a mutiny was sparked? In a moment of heedlessness, so that one became a stranger to the person one had been a moment before? Or was it the other way round? That this was when one recognised the stranger that one had always been to oneself; that all one's loyalties and beliefs had been misplaced?

But where would his loyalties go now that they were unmoored? He was a military man and he knew that nothing –

nothing important – was possible without loyalty, without faith. But who would claim his loyalty now? The old loyalties of India, the ancient ones – they'd been destroyed long ago; the British had built their Empire by effacing them. But the Empire was dead now – he knew this because he had felt it die within himself, where it had held its strongest dominion – and with whom was he now to keep faith? Loyalty, commonalty, faith – these things were as essential and as fragile as the muscles of the human heart; easy to destroy, impossible to rebuild. How would one begin the work of re-creating the tissues that bound people to each other? This was beyond the abilities of someone such as himself; someone trained to destroy. It was a labour that would last not one year, not ten, not fifty – it was the work of centuries.

'So, Arjun?' Suddenly Hardy was kneeling in front of him, looking into his face. He was beaming, glowing with triumph.

'Arjun? What are you going to do then? Are you with us or against us?'

Arjun reached for his crutch and pushed himself to his feet. 'Listen, Hardy. Before we think of anything else – there's something we have to do.'

'What?'

'Bucky, the CO – we have to let him go.'

Hardy stared at him, without uttering a sound.

'We have to do it,' Arjun continued. 'We can't be responsible for his being taken prisoner by the Japs. He's a very fair man, Hardy, and he's been good to serve under – you know that. We have to let him go. We owe him that.'

Hardy scratched his chin. 'I can't allow it, Arjun. He'd give away our position, our movements . . .'

Arjun interrupted him. 'It's not a question of what you'll allow, Hardy,' he said tiredly. 'You're not my senior, and I'm not yours. I'm not asking you. I'm letting you know that I'm going to give the CO some food and some water and then I'm going to let him find his way back across the lines. If you want to stop me you'll have a fight on your hands. I think some of the men would take my side. You decide.'

A thin smile crossed Hardy's face. 'Look at you, yaar.' His voice was acid with sarcasm. 'Even at a time like this you're a *chaploos*

– still thinking of sucking up. What are you hoping for? That he'll speak up for you if things don't turn out right? Take out a little insurance against the future?'

'You bastard.' Arjun lurched towards Hardy, reaching for his collar, swinging his crutch.

Hardy stepped away easily. 'I'm sorry,' he said gruffly. 'I shouldn't have said that. *Theek hai.* Do what you want. I'll send someone along to show you where Bucky is. Just be quick – that's all I ask.'

Thirty-eight

Alison and Dinu spent an hour clearing out the dark room. There was no electricity and they had to work by candlelight. They took down his enlarger, stacked his trays, packed away his prints and his negatives, wrapping them in old cloth and laying them in boxes. When they were done, Dinu snuffed out the candle. They stood still in the airless warmth of the cupboard-like room, listening to the night-time buzz of cicadas and the croaking of wet-weather frogs. Intermittently they could hear a distant, staccato sound, a kind of barking, as though a pack of dogs had been disturbed in a sleeping village.

'Guns,' she whispered.

Dinu reached for her in the darkness, pulling her towards him. 'They're very far away.'

He held her, his arms tightening round her body. He opened the palms of his hands and ran them over her hair, her shoulders, along the concave curve of her back. His fingers snagged in the strap of her dress and he peeled the fabric slowly away, picking it off her shoulders, tugging it back. Sinking to his knees, he ran his face down the length of her body, touching her with his cheek, his nose, his tongue.

They lay on the cramped floor, pushed up close, legs intertwined, thigh on thigh, arms extended, the flatness of their bellies imprinted on each other. Membranes of sweat hung cobwebbed between their bodies, joining them, pulling them together.

'Alison . . . what am I going to do? Without you?'

'And me, Dinu? What about me? What will I do?'

Afterwards, they lay still, pillowing each other's heads on their arms. He lit a cigarette and held it to her lips.

'One day,' he said, 'one day, when we're back here together, I'll show you the true magic of a dark room . . .'

'And what's that?'

'When you print by contact . . . when you lay the negative on the paper and watch them come to life . . . the darkness of the one becomes the light of the other. The first time I saw it happen I thought, what must it be like to touch like this? . . . with such utter absorption? . . . For one thing to become irradiated with the shadows of another?'

'Dinu.' She ran her fingertips over his face.

'If only I could hold you in that way . . . so that you were imprinted on me . . . every part of me . . .'

'Dinu, there'll be time.' She took his face between her hands and kissed him. 'We'll have the rest of our lives . . .' Rising to her knees she lit the candle again. Holding the flame in front of his face, she looked fiercely into his eyes, as though she were trying to bore into his head.

'It won't be long, Dinu?' she said. 'Will it?'

'No . . . not long.'

'Do you really believe that? Or are you lying – for my sake? Tell me the truth, Dinu: I'd rather know.'

He gripped her shoulders. 'Yes, Alison.' He spoke with all the conviction he could muster. 'Yes. We'll be back here before long . . . We'll be back at Morningside . . . Everything will be the same, except . . .'

'Except?' She bit her lip, as though she were afraid of hearing what he was going to say.

'Except that we'll be married.'

'Yes.' She burst into delighted laughter. 'Yes,' she said, tossing her head. 'We'll be married. We've left it too long. It was a mistake.'

She picked up the candle and ran out of the room. He lay still, listening to her footsteps: the house was quieter than he'd ever known it to be. Downstairs, Saya John was in bed, exhausted and asleep.

He got up and followed her through the dark corridors to her bedroom. Alison was unlocking closets, rummaging through drawers. Suddenly she turned to him, holding out her hand. 'Look.' Two gold rings glinted in the candlelight.

'They belonged to my parents,' she said. She reached for his hand and pushed one of the rings over the knuckle of his ring finger. '*With this ring I thee wed.*'

She laughed, placing the other ring in his palm. Then she extended a finger, holding her hand in front of her.

'Go on,' she challenged him. 'Do it. I dare you.'

He turned the ring over in his hands and then slipped it into place, on her finger.

'Are we married now?'

She tossed her head, laughing, and held her finger up to the candlelight. 'Yes,' she said. 'In a way. In our own eyes. When you're away you'll still be mine because of the ring.'

She shook free the mosquito net that hung down from the ceiling, draping it over the sides of her bed. 'Come.' She blew out the candle and drew him into the net.

An hour later, Dinu woke to the sound of approaching planes. He reached for her hand and found that she was already awake, sitting up with her back against the headboard. 'Alison . . .'

'Don't say it's time. Not yet.'

They held each other and listened. The planes were directly overhead, flying low. The windows rattled as they went past.

'When I was little,' Dinu said, 'my father once told me a story about Mandalay. When the king was sent into exile, the palace girls had to walk through the city, to the river . . . My mother was with them and my father followed, keeping to the shadows. It was a long walk and the girls were tired and miserable . . . My father put together all his money and bought some sweets . . . to lift their spirits. The girls were guarded by soldiers – foreigners, Englishmen . . . Somehow he – my father – managed to slip through the cordon . . . He gave my mother the packet of sweets. Then he ran back into the shadows . . . He watched her open the packet . . . He was amazed . . . The first thing she did was to offer some to the soldiers who were marching beside her. At first he was angry; he felt betrayed . . . Why was she giving them away . . . especially to these men, her captors? But then, slowly he understood what she was doing and he was glad . . . He saw that this was the right thing to do – a way to stay alive. To shout defiance would have served no purpose . . .'

'I think you're trying to tell me something, Dinu,' she said quietly. 'What is it?'

'I just want you to be careful, Alison . . . not to be headstrong . . . not to be the woman you are, just for a while . . . to be cautious, quiet . . .'

'I'll try, Dinu.' She squeezed his hand. 'I promise. And you too: you have to be careful as well.'

'I will – it's in my nature. We're not the same in that way . . . That's why I worry about you.'

Another flight of planes went by. It was impossible to keep still any longer, with the windows rattling as though they would break. Alison swung her legs off the bed. She picked up the handbag in which she carried the Daytona's keys. It was unexpectedly heavy. She opened the clasp, looked inside and raised an eyebrow at Dinu.

'It's your father's revolver. I found it in a drawer.'

'Is it loaded?'

'Yes. I checked.'

She shut the clasp and slung the bag over her shoulder. 'It's time.'

They went down to find Saya John sitting on the veranda, in his favourite wing-chair. Alison dropped to her knees beside him and put an arm around his waist.

'I want your blessings, Grandfather.'

'Why?'

'Dinu and I are going to be married.'

His face broke into a smile. She saw to her delight that he had understood; that his eyes were clear and unclouded. He motioned to both of them to come closer and put his arms round their shoulders.

'Rajkumar's son and Matthew's daughter.' He swayed gently from side to side, holding their heads like trophies, under his arms. 'What could be better? The two of you have joined the families. Your parents will be delighted.'

They went outside and found that it had begun to rain. Dinu buckled down the Daytona's hood and held the door open for

Saya John. The old man gave him a pat on the back as he stepped in.

'Tell Rajkumar that it'll have to be a big wedding,' he said. 'I shall insist on having the Archbishop.'

'Yes.' Dinu tried to smile. 'Of course.'

Then Dinu went to Alison's side and knelt beside the window. She would not look at him.

'We won't say goodbye.'

'No.'

She started the car and he stepped back. At the bottom of the drive, the Daytona came to a stop. He saw her leaning out, her head silhouetted against the car's rain-haloed lights. She raised an arm to wave and he waved back. Then he ran up the stairs, racing from window to window. He watched the Daytona's lights until they disappeared.

The shed in which Lieutenant-Colonel Buckland had spent the night was a small red-brick structure, surrounded by trees. It was about a quarter of a mile from the coolie lines. Arjun was led there by a fast-talking young 'contractor', dressed in khaki shorts: it was he who carried the water bottle and the cloth bundle of food that had been prepared for the lieutenant-colonel.

The contractor showed Arjun a track that led southwards through a range of low hills. 'There's a town a couple of miles away,' he said. 'The last we heard it was still held by the British.' They came up to the steps that led into the building. The contractor handed over the water bottle and the bundle of food that he had been carrying.

'The colonel will be safe if he keeps to this track. It won't take him more than an hour or two to the town, even if he walks very slowly.'

Arjun went gingerly up the steps to the door. He knocked and when there was no answer, he used the tip of his crutch to push the door open. He found Lieutenant-Colonel Buckland lying on the cement floor, on a mattress.

'Sir.'

Lieutenant-Colonel Buckland sat up suddenly, peering around him. He said sharply: 'Who is it?'

'Lieutenant Roy. Sir.' Arjun saluted, leaning on his crutch.

'Oh, Roy.' Lieutenant-Colonel Buckland's voice warmed. 'I'm glad to see you.'

'I'm glad to see you too, sir.'

'You're wounded – what happened?'

'Bullet through the hamstring, sir. It'll be all right. And how's your arm?'

'Been acting up a bit.'

'Do you think you're well enough to walk, sir?'

Lieutenant-Colonel Buckland raised an eyebrow. 'Why?' He glanced sharply at the cloth bundle and the water bottle that Arjun was carrying in his hands. 'What have you got there, Roy?'

'Some food and water, sir. The Japanese are advancing down the north–south highway. If you head in the other direction you should be able to get across the lines.'

'Get across the lines?' Lieutenant-Colonel Buckland repeated this slowly to himself. 'Am I going alone then? What about you? And the others?'

'We're staying here, sir. For the moment.'

'I see.' Lieutenant-Colonel Buckland rose to his feet, holding his right arm stiffly across his chest. He took the water bottle from Arjun and examined it, turning it over in his hands. 'So you're going over, are you – to the Japs?'

'That's not how I would put it, sir.'

'I'm sure you wouldn't.' Lieutenant-Colonel Buckland looked at Arjun closely, frowning.

'You know, Roy,' he said at last. 'You, I never took for a turncoat. Some of the others, yes – you could see where the possibility might lie. But you: you don't have the look of a traitor.'

'Some would say that I've been a traitor all along, sir.'

'You don't really believe that, do you?' Lieutenant-Colonel Buckland shook his head. 'In fact you don't believe any of it.'

'Sir?'

'You don't. Or else you wouldn't be here, bringing me food and water. Only an incompetent soldier would help an enemy escape. Or a fool.'

'I felt I had to, sir.'

'Why?'

'Because,' said Arjun, 'it's not your fault, sir. You've always been fair to us. You were the best CO we could have hoped for – under the circumstances.'

'I suppose you expect me to thank you for saying that?'

'I don't expect anything, sir.' Arjun held the door open. 'But if you don't mind, sir, there's not much time. I'll show you the way.'

Lieutenant-Colonel Buckland stepped out and Arjun followed him. They went down the steps and into the trees. When they were a little distance away, Lieutenant-Colonel Buckland cleared his throat. 'Look, Roy,' he said. 'It's not too late. You can still change your mind. Come away with me. We can give them the slip. We'll forget about this . . . this incident.'

A moment passed before Arjun answered. 'Sir, may I say something?'

'Go ahead.'

'Sir, do you remember when you were teaching at the academy – you once quoted someone in one of your lectures. An English general – Munro, I think his name was. You quoted something he'd said over a hundred years ago about the Indian army: *The spirit of independence will spring up in this army long before it is even thought of among the people . . .*'

Lieutenant-Colonel Buckland nodded: 'Yes. I remember that. Very well.'

'All of us in the class were Indians and we were a little shocked that you'd chosen to quote something like this to us. We insisted that Munro had been talking nonsense. But you disagreed . . .'

'Did I?'

'Yes. At the time I thought you were playing devil's advocate; that you were just trying to provoke us. But that wasn't true, was it, sir? The truth is you knew all along: you knew what we'd do – you knew it before we did. You knew because you made us. If I were to come away with you now no one would be more surprised than you. I think, in your heart, you would despise me a little.'

'That's rubbish, Roy. Don't be a fool, man. There's still time.'

'No, sir.' Arjun brought himself to a halt and held out his hand. 'I think this is it, sir. This is where I'm going to turn round.'

Lieutenant-Colonel Buckland looked at his hand and then at him. 'I'm not going to shake your hand, Roy,' he said quietly, in an even, emotionless voice. 'You can justify what you're doing to yourself in a thousand different ways, but you should make no mistake about the truth, Roy. You're a traitor. You're a disgrace to the regiment and to your country. You're scum. When the time comes you'll be hunted down, Roy. When you're sitting in front of a court-martial I'll be there. I'll see you hang, Roy. I will. You should have not a moment's doubt of that.'

Arjun dropped his hand. For the first time in many days he felt completely certain of his mind. He smiled.

'There's one thing you can be sure of, sir,' he said. 'On that day, if it comes, you'll have done your duty, sir, and I'll have done mine. We'll look at each other as honest men – for the first time. For that alone this will have been worthwhile.'

He saluted, balancing on his crutch. For an instant, Lieutenant-Colonel Buckland hesitated and then, involuntarily, his hand rose to acknowledge the salute. He turned on his heel and walked into the trees.

Arjun watched him leave and then he swung himself round on his crutch and went hobbling back to the coolie lines.

Alison had been driving for about an hour when she noticed that the Daytona's pedals were growing hot under her feet. She began to watch the bonnet and caught sight of leaking wisps of steam. She pulled off the road, and when her grandfather turned to look at her, she flashed him a reassuring smile. 'It's all right, Baba,' she said, 'don't worry. It'll just take a minute.' She left him sitting inside and climbed out.

With the car at a standstill, she could see steam leaking through the grille. The bonnet was too hot to touch. She wrapped her scarf around her hand and felt under the hood for the catch. A geyser of steam gushed into her face and she sprang back, coughing.

It was very dark. She reached through the window on the driver's side and turned the headlights on. She spotted a branch, lying on the ground, near her feet. She used it to lever up the hood and a cloud of steam welled out. She propped the bonnet open and went back to the driver's window to turn the headlights off.

'It won't be long, Baba,' she said. 'We'll just wait a while.'

To the north, she could see flashes of light. On the highway the flow of traffic had dwindled to an occasional speeding car. She had the feeling that she was among the last on the road; those who'd planned to leave were long gone and everyone else was waiting to see what would happen next.

The night was cool and it wasn't long before the steam from the radiator dissipated. She wrapped her hand in the scarf again and unscrewed the cap. Then she fetched a bottle and poured in some water: it boiled up almost immediately, frothing over the top. She splashed some water over the radiator and waited a while longer before pouring the rest in. Slamming the hood shut, she went back to the driver's seat.

She gave her grandfather a smile. 'It's all right now,' she said. 'We'll be fine.'

She turned the key and was hugely relieved when the engine responded. Switching on the headlamps she pulled on to the road again. No other cars had passed them in a while. With the road to herself, she was tempted to drive at high speed. She had to remind herself that she had to go slowly if the car was not to overheat.

They'd gone only a few miles when the engine started to knock. She knew now that there was no point trying to go any further. At the next turn she pulled off the main road. She was on a dusty side road, little more than a gravelled track. On both sides, there were stands of rubber: she felt obscurely grateful for this, glad to be in a familiar environment.

The best thing to do, she decided, was to stay close to the road: perhaps she'd be able to flag down some help in the morning. She took the car a short distance down the track and then turned into the trees, pulling up at a spot that was sheltered by a bush. She turned the engine off and opened her door.

'We'll stay here for a while, Baba,' she said. 'We can go on when the light's better.' She prised the bonnet open again and came back to the driver's seat. 'Go to sleep, Baba,' she said. 'There's no point staying awake. There's nothing we can do right now.'

She climbed out and walked around the car. With the headlights turned off, it was very dark: she could see no lights and no sign of habitation. She went back to the driver's seat and sat down again. Saya John was sitting up, looking intently at his hand. His fingers were spread out in front of him, as though he were counting something.

'Tell me, Alison,' he said. 'Today is Saturday – isn't it?'

'Is it?' She tried to think what day it was but she'd lost track. 'I don't know. Why do you ask?'

'I think it's Sunday tomorrow. I hope Ilongo remembers that I have to go to church.'

She stared at him. 'I'm sorry, Baba,' she said sharply. 'I'm afraid you're going to have to miss church tomorrow.'

He glanced at her like a disappointed child and she was suddenly contrite for having snapped at him. She reached for his hand. 'Just this once, Baba. We'll go to Mass in Singapore, next week.'

He gave her a smile and leaned back, resting his head against his seat. She looked at her watch. It was four in the morning. It would be dawn soon. Once it was light she'd go back to the highway and see if she could flag down a truck or a car: something was sure to come along. She let her head fall back against the seat: she was tired – not afraid, just tired. She could hear her grandfather, drifting off to sleep, breathing slowly and deeply. She shut her eyes.

She was woken by a shaft of sunlight, shining through the feathery canopy above. She stirred and her hand fell on the seat beside her. It was empty. She sat up, startled, rubbing her eyes. When she looked at the seat she saw that her grandfather was gone.

She opened the door and stepped out. 'Baba?' He'd probably gone into the trees to relieve himself. She raised her voice. 'Baba – are you there?' Shading her eyes, she turned all the way around, peering into the dim tunnels of rubber around her. He was nowhere to be seen.

Stepping around the car, she stumbled on his brown leather

suitcase. It was lying open on the ground, with clothes spilling out, scattered among the leaves. He'd been looking for something – but what? Glancing around, she spotted some clothes, lying on the ground, a few feet away. She went to investigate and found a pair of trousers and a shirt, the clothes her grandfather had been wearing the night before.

A thought struck her. She darted back to his suitcase and rummaged quickly through the rest of his clothes, looking for the dark suit that he liked to wear to church. It wasn't there: she was sure that he'd had it with him when they set out. It wasn't like him to go anywhere without it. That was what he'd changed in to; she was sure of it. He'd probably wandered off, along the highway, thinking that it would lead him to his church. She would have to hurry if she was to find him before he got into trouble.

She reached into the car and snatched her handbag off the seat. It occurred to her that she could try and follow in the car but she decided against it. There was no telling how much time she'd waste trying to start it. It would probably be quicker on foot. Slinging her handbag over her shoulder, she began to run towards the highway.

She could tell, even when she was a good distance away, that there was no traffic. The highway was very quiet. But when she was some twenty yards from the road she heard some distant voices. She stopped to look, glacing sidewise along a corridor of tree trunks. She spotted a group of bicyclists, in the distance: there were some half-dozen of them and they were cycling in her direction.

Her first reaction was relief; she knew that if she ran hard, she'd be able to reach the road just as the cyclists were going past. Maybe they'd be able to help. She took a couple of steps and then she stopped and looked again, sheltering behind the trunk of a tree. She realised now that the bicyclists were all wearing caps and that their clothes were all of exactly the same colour. Grateful for the shelter of the plantation, she slipped a little closer to the road, being careful to stay out of view.

When the cyclists were some twenty yards away, she saw that they were Japanese soldiers. They were unshaven and their grey uniforms were spattered with dust and mud, their tunics drenched in sweat. Some had caps with long neckcloths while others wore helmets, covered with nets. They were wearing tightly bound puttees and canvas shoes. The man who was in the lead had a sword attached to his belt: the scabbard was clattering rhythmically against his bicycle's mudguard. The others were carrying rifles, fitted with bayonets. Their bicycles creaked and squealed as they went past. She could hear them panting as they pedalled.

A short distance ahead, there was a corner where the highway described a sharp turn. The cyclists were still in view as they went around the bend: she heard one of them shout, raising his hand to point down the road. Suddenly she was seized by a sharp sense of misgiving. She'd thought that she'd find her grandfather heading back, in the direction of Sungei Pattani: but what if, instead, he'd headed in the other direction?

She glanced in both directions and saw that the highway was empty. Sprinting across the road, she slipped into the stands of rubber on the far side. Heading diagonally through the trees, she caught sight of the highway again: she saw the backs of the cyclists, pedalling along, pointing at a diminutive figure a long way ahead. It was a man, wearing a hat and a suit, ambling along by the side of the road. Alison knew that it was her grandfather. The soldiers were closing on him, pedalling hard.

She began to run, fast, dodging between the trees. She was still several hundred yards away when the soldiers caught up with Saya John. She saw them dismounting, letting their bicycles drop on the grass. They surrounded him and the sound of a voice came floating back to her: one of the soldiers was shouting, saying something she couldn't follow. She began to mumble to herself as she ran, 'Please, please . . .'

She could tell that her grandfather hadn't understood what the soldiers were saying. He touched his hat and turned away, trying to push past them. One of the soldiers put out a hand to stop him and he waved it aside. All the soldiers were shouting at him now, but he seemed not to hear anything. He was flicking his hand at them, as though trying to brush off street-corner loiterers. Then one of the soldiers struck him, slapping him hard across his face, knocking him off his feet. He fell heavily to the ground.

Alison came to a stop, panting, leaning her weight against a tree trunk, holding it with both hands. If only he would keep still, they would go away, she was sure of that. She began to mumble to herself, praying that he'd been knocked unconscious. They wouldn't bother with him: surely they'd see that he was just a confused old man; that he meant no harm.

But then her grandfather's prone body began to move again. He stirred and sat up with his legs spread out in front of him, like a child waking in the morning. He reached for his hat, put it on his head and pushed himself to his feet again. He looked at the soldiers with a bewildered frown, rubbing his face. And then he turned his back on them and began to walk away.

She saw one of the soldiers pulling his rifle off his back. He shouted something and cocked the gun so that the bayonet was pointing directly at the old man's back.

Almost without thinking, Alison reached for her handbag. She pulled out the revolver and dropped to one knee. Crossing her left arm in front of her, she steadied her wrist against her forearm, just as her father had taught her. She took aim at the man with the bayonet, hoping to drop him. But at exactly that moment, another soldier stepped across her line of fire; the bullet hit him in the ribs and he fell screaming to the ground. The man with the bayonet froze for an instant, but then, suddenly, as though triggered by a reflex, his arm moved, driving the blade in and out of Saya John's body, in one quick motion. Saya John toppled over, falling face first on the road.

She was perfectly calm now, breathing evenly. She took aim carefully, and fired again. This time she hit the man with the bayonet. He screamed and dropped his rifle, falling face first on the ground. Her third shot went wide, ploughing up a divot of grass on the roadside. The soldiers were flat on their stomachs now, and a couple of them were sheltering behind Saya John's inert body. Her targets were smaller now, and her fourth shot went wide. But with her fifth, she hit another soldier, sending him spinning on his side.

Then, suddenly, something slammed into her with great force, throwing her on her back. She could feel no pain, but she knew she'd been hit. She lay still, looking up at the arched branches of the rubber trees around her. They were swaying in the breeze, like fans.

She was glad that it would end like this; with her eyes resting on something familiar. She remembered what Dinu had said about his mother and the sweets she had shared with her captors. The memory made her smile; that wouldn't have suited her at all. She was glad that she'd made them pay; that she hadn't gone without striking back.

She could hear their footsteps now and knew that they were running towards her. She raised the gun to her temple and shut her eyes.

Thirty-nine

Doh Say, ever the loyal friend, forswore his family's Christmas celebrations in order to be of help to Rajkumar. He arrived in Rangoon on December 22. Just as Rajkumar had expected, he quickly took matters in hand, arranging for the hiring of a team of elephants and some half-dozen oo-sis. Neel had already organised the rental of two lorries. It was decided that the clearing of the Pazundaung timberyard would start the next day.

They left the house early in the morning – Doh Say, Raymond, Neel and Rajkumar. They went in the Packard, with Neel driving. Dolly and Manju waved them off. They got to the yard to find that the oo-sis had already arrived, along with their elephants. The rented lorries were there too. Rajkumar was relieved: he'd been hoping to get an early start. He'd worried that the teams might turn up late.

But then, an unexpected hitch arose. 'We would like to talk to you,' one of the lorry drivers said. A delegation came up to the small cabin that served as an office; it turned out that the oo-sis and lorry drivers wanted a part-payment at midday.

It was not uncommon, of course, for hired crews to make demands just as the day's work was getting started: that was exactly when they were in the best position to bargain. Rajkumar's original plan had been to go to the bank in the early afternoon, when the work was almost done. With the Christmas holidays beginning tomorrow, this was the last day in the week when the banks would be open. He'd taken the precaution of visiting the bank the day before to make sure that the money was ready and available. He could have taken it with him right then, but had thought better of it. It wasn't safe – especially now that they were alone at home, with no gatekeepers to keep watch. He'd decided to come back when the work was near completion.

This new development meant that Rajkumar would have to change his plans. He persuaded the men to start work, promising to have the money ready at midday. He went to the window of his office to watch them get started.

He smiled as he looked down on the yard, with its huge, neat stacks of timber. It was unnerving to think that this was the sum total of everything he possessed. He knew he ought to be on his way, but he couldn't help dawdling. Even now, after all these years, he could not resist the spectacle of watching elephants at work: once again he found himself marvelling at the sure-footedness with which they made their way through the narrow aisles, threading their great bodies between the timber stacks. There was something almost preternatural about the dexterity with which they curled their trunks around the logs.

He spotted Neel, darting between the elephants. It made Rajkumar nervous to see his son down there, with the animals.

'Neel,' Rajkumar called out. 'Be careful.'

Neel turned round, a wide smile on his bearded face. He waved. 'I'll be fine, apé. You should be on your way to the bank now. Don't leave it too late.'

Rajkumar looked at his watch. 'There's still time. The bank's not even open yet.'

Doh Say added his voice to Neel's. 'Yes, go now, Rajkumar. The sooner you get there, the sooner you'll be back. I'll take care of everything here – it'll be all right.'

Rajkumar walked out into the street and found a cycle-rickshaw. The driver pedalled hard and they soon found themselves nearing the centre of the city. The traffic was heavy and Rajkumar was afraid that he'd be held up. But the driver threaded deftly through the streets and brought him to the bank in good time.

Rajkumar paid off the driver and climbed a wide flight of stairs. The bank's main doors were closed: it was still a quarter of an hour to opening time. Some half-dozen men were already waiting at the door. Rajkumar joined the line. The morning was exceptionally clear with scarcely a cloud in the sky. It was an unusually cool day for Rangoon and many passers-by were swathed in woollen shawls and cardigans.

The bank was situated at a busy intersection. The surrounding streets were jammed with the usual start-of-the-day rush-hour traffic. Buses were inching along the road, belching smoke; under looped awnings of wire, trams were rumbling by, their bells tinkling.

Suddenly, an air-raid siren started up, somewhere in the distance. Neither Rajkumar nor the people around him paid much attention. Air-raid warnings had sounded several times over the last few weeks – they had all proved to be false alarms. At the bottom of the bank's steps, a footpath hawker was frying bayagyaw in a large, soot-blackened pot. She grimaced in irritation and went on with what she was doing. Rajkumar's response was much the same as hers: he was annoyed to think of the delays the sirens would cause.

The sirens sounded a second time and now people paid more attention. It was unusual to have two alarms going off in such quick succession. Heads appeared in the windows of the buses and trams; eyes turned towards the sky as though in search of rain.

Rajkumar spotted an air-raid warden in a tin hat. He was walking down the street, waving his arms at pedestrians. Rajkumar knew the warden: he was an Anglo-Burmese bookmaker, an acquaintance from his own racing days. He went hurrying down the steps to accost him.

The warden wasted no time on civilities. 'Better find a safe place, Mr Raha,' he said brusquely. 'The balloon is definitely up. They've passed the second warning system.' Cupping his hands around his mouth the warden began to shout at the passers-by: 'Get out of here; get to your shelters, go home . . .'

A few people stared but otherwise no one paid attention. The warden fumed, with his hands on his hips. 'Look at them; they think it's a bloody circus . . .'

There was a small patch of garden in front of the bank. Months before, slit trenches had been dug between the ornamental palms. But in the meantime evil-smelling pools of moisture had accumulated in the trenches, along with white-haired mango-pits and other bits of refuse. People balked at jumping in.

Rajkumar went back up the steps to see if the bank had opened. Just then the air-raid sirens went off, for the third time. Now everyone took notice. The traffic on the streets came to an abrupt halt. There was no panic and no running for shelter. Instead people climbed out of their trams and buses and stood on the streets in a half-disbelieving daze, looking skywards, shading their eyes against the light. Several men came up the stairs to stand beside Rajkumar: the bank's threshold commanded an excellent view of the surroundings.

'Listen.' A low steady droning became audible in the distance.

The sound lent a sudden and ominous credibility to the idea of an imminent air raid. There was a moment of uncertainty and then panic swept like a gale down the streets. People began to run. Some darted indoors, others hurried away, dodging through the stalled traffic. The foul-smelling trenches at the corner were filled in seconds.

Somewhere nearby, a woman let out a howl of pain. Spinning round, Rajkumar saw that the baya-gyaw cart had been upended at the bottom of the steps; the vendor's pot had tipped over, spattering her with boiling oil. She was running down the road, shrieking, clawing at her clothes with both hands.

Rajkumar decided not to brave the panicked crowd. Instead he braced himself against the bank's heavy doors. The distant drone changed into a loud rhythmic noise. Then the first planes came into view: tiny specks, approaching from the east. The city's anti-aircraft guns opened up with a dull, thudding sound. The guns were few and they were concentrated mainly in the vicinity of Mingaladon airport and the military cantonment. But there was something reassuring about the thought that the city's defences were operational. Even in the midst of the panic, many people could be heard to cheer.

The bombers changed formation as they approached the eastern peripheries of the city, dipping lower in the sky. Their fuselages opened and their cargo of bombs began to descend, trailing behind the craft like glinting, tinsel ribbons. It was as though an immense silver curtain had suddenly appeared over the eastern horizon.

The first bombs fell several miles away, the explosions following in evenly spaced rhythmic succession. Suddenly there was a booming sound, several times louder than all the preceding blasts. From somewhere in the eastern reaches of the city, a huge cloud of black smoke mushroomed up towards the sky, almost engulfing the bombers.

'They've hit the oil tanks,' someone said, 'on the Pazundaung Creek.'

Rajkumar knew at once that this was right. His stomach lurched. The city's main oil reservoirs were on the far side of the creek, well within sight of his timberyard. He looked up at the bombers and saw that they were making another run over the same area. He realised now that they were not bombing blindly: they were targeting the city's long waterfront, aiming for its mills, warehouses, tanks and railway lines.

Suddenly Rajkumar thought of the elephants, working in his yard. He recalled how unpredictable these animals were in their response to noise. It sometimes took just a single sharp sound to stampede a herd. Once, in the old days, at a teak camp, he had witnessed such a stampede; the echo of a gunshot had startled an old cow elephant into producing a distinctive trumpeting note; this had triggered an instinctive response in the herd. There had been a lot of damage and it had taken the oo-sis hours to regain control of their animals.

What would happen if a team of elephants were to panic inside the log-jammed confines of a timberyard? It was unthinkable.

Rajkumar could no longer bear to remain where he was. He set off on foot, in the direction of Pazundaung. The bombs were coming closer now, falling in curtains, floating towards the city's centre. Suddenly a bullock-cart appeared directly ahead, racing at him down the footpath. The runaway bullocks were foaming at the mouth, showing the whites of their eyes. The driver was screaming, holding on to the sides of the cart. Rajkumar jumped aside just in time to let it pass by.

A flight of planes was passing directly overhead. Rajkumar looked up into the bright, clear December sky. They swooped downwards and their bays opened. Strings of bombs appeared, falling sidewise, catching the light, sparkling like diamonds.

There were no trenches nearby. Rajkumar crouched in a doorway, holding his hands over his head. The air shook and he was aware of the sound of shattering glass.

He lost track of how long he stayed there. He stirred only when he felt a warmth at his back. Turning around he saw a dog, pushing against him, whimpering in fear. He thrust the dog aside and stood up. Columns of smoke were climbing into the sky from all around him. He thought of Dolly, Manju and Jaya, his grandchild. He glanced in the direction of Kemendine and was relieved to see that that part of the city was relatively unaffected. He started to walk in the other direction, towards his timberyard, in Pazundaung.

On Merchant Street a marketplace had been hit. Fruit and vegetables lay scattered along the sides of the road. Already beggars and ragpickers were scratching through the debris. He noticed the burnt-out remains of a shop and recalled, almost with a sense of nostalgia, that this was his favourite place to buy tandoori chicken. A blast had driven a set of skewers through the clay walls of the oven, breaking it in half, like an eggshell. He heard a man's voice calling for help. He hurried on. He had no time: he had to get to his yard in Pazundaung.

He passed the storefront of Rowe and Co. The windows were shattered and there were gaping holes in the walls. Looters were climbing in through the gaps. He could see the store's Christmas tree lying aslant on the floor. There was an old woman working busily beside it, her face white with talcum powder. She was picking cottonwool off the floor, stuffing it into a sack.

In front of the telegraph office a water main had been hit. A ten-foot-high jet was spraying into the sky. There was water everywhere, gathering in puddles, flowing down the road. A whirlpool was swirling around the mouth of the shattered main.

People had been crouching along the walls of the telegraph office when the water source was hit. Many had died. Dismembered limbs could be seen in the pool that was spinning around the main: there was a child's arm, a leg. Rajkumar averted his eyes and walked on.

Approaching Pazundaung, he saw that both sides of the creek

were blanketed in flames. While still a good distance away he spotted the perimeter walls of his yard. They were shrouded in clouds of smoke.

Everything he owned was in that place, all that he had ever worked for; a lifetime's accumulation of labour stored as a single cache of wood. He thought of the elephants and the bombs falling around them; the flames leaping from the well-stacked wood; the explosions, the trumpeting.

It was he who had concentrated all his holdings in this one place – that too was a part of the plan – and now the bombs had claimed it all. But it didn't matter; nothing mattered so long as Neel was unharmed. The rest were just things, possessions. But Neel . . .

He turned into the alley that led to his yard and saw that it was filled with swirling clouds of smoke. On the skin of his face, he could feel the scorching heat of the fire that was raging through his yard. He shouted into the smoke: 'Neel.'

He saw a figure taking shape in the distance. He began to run.

'Neel? Neel?'

It was Doh Say. His lined, wrinkled face was blackened with smoke. He was weeping.

'Rajkumar . . .'

'Where's Neel?'

'Forgive me, Rajkumar.' Doh Say covered his face.'There was nothing I could do. The elephants ran wild. I tried to send your boy away but he wouldn't listen. The logs got loose and he fell under.'

Now Rajkumar saw that Doh Say had been dragging a body through the alley, pulling it away from the fire. He ran over to it and fell on his knees.

The body was almost unrecognisable, crushed by an immense weight. But despite the terrible disfigurement Rajkumar knew that this was his son and that he was dead.

Once, when she was still a girl, Manju had observed the shaving of a widow's head. This was at a neighbour's house in Calcutta:

a barber had been paid to do it and the women of the family had been round to help.

In her sewing box Manju came upon a pair of scissors. Seating herself at her dresser she looked into the mirror and tried the scissors on her hair. The blades were dull with use and her hair was strong, thick and black – a young woman's hair. The scissors were useless. She dropped them back into her sewing box.

The baby began to cry, so Manju shut the door on her. She went down the stairs to the kitchen – a dark, sooty, airless room, at the back of the house. She found a knife, a long, straight-bladed knife with a serrated edge and a wooden handle. She tried it on her hair but found that it was no more use than the scissors.

Casting around for a better instrument, Manju recalled the scythes that had once been used to cut the compound's grass. These scythes were very sharp: she remembered how the hissing of their blades had echoed through the house. The malis who'd tended the grounds were long gone, but the scythes remained. She knew where they were to be found: in an outhouse by the front gate.

She opened the front door and ran across the compound to the outhouse. The scythes were exactly where she had thought, piled in a heap with the other gardening implements. She stood in the knee-deep grass of the compound and held up her hair, drawing it away from her head. She raised the scythe and hacked at it, blindly, because her hand was behind her head. She saw a lock of hair falling on to the grass and this gave her encouragement. She sawed at another handful and then another. She could see the pile of hair growing in the grass around her feet. The one thing she could not understand was the pain: why should it hurt so much to cut one's hair?

She heard a voice, speaking softly, somewhere nearby. She turned around and saw that it was Raymond, standing beside her. He put out a hand, reaching for the scythe. She took a step away: 'You don't understand . . .' she said. She tried to smile, to let him know that she knew what she was doing and that it could not be done any other way. But suddenly his hands were on her wrist. He twisted her arm and the scythe fell from her grasp. He kicked it, sending it flying aside.

Manju was astonished at the strength of Raymond's grip; at the way he was restraining her with a wrestler's armlock. No one had ever held her in this way – as though she were a madwoman.

'What do you think you're doing, Raymond?'

He twisted her hands around so that they were in front of her face. She saw that her fingers were smeared with blood.

'You've cut yourself,' he said quietly. 'You've cut your scalp.'

'I didn't know.' She tried to jerk her arms free but this only made him tighten his hold. He led her into the house and made her sit in a chair. He found some cottonwool and swabbed her scalp. The baby began to cry: they could hear her downstairs. Raymond led her to the stairs and gave her a nudge.

'Go. The child needs you.'

She went up a few steps, and then she couldn't go any more. She couldn't bear to think of going into that room and picking up the child. It was pointless. Her breasts had run dry. There was nothing she could do. She buried her face in her hands.

Raymond came up the stairs and pulled her head back, gripping it by the remains of her hair. She saw him drawing his arm back and then his hand hit her across the cheek. She clutched her stinging face and looked at him. His gaze was steady and not unkind.

'You are the mother,' he said. 'You must go to the child. A child's hunger doesn't stop, no matter what . . .' He followed her to the room and kept watch until she picked the baby up and held her to her breast.

The next day it was Christmas and in the evening Doh Say and Raymond left the house to go to church. Shortly afterwards the sirens sounded and the bombers came back. The baby had been sleeping but the sirens woke her. She began to cry.

The day of the first raid, Manju and Dolly had known exactly what to do: they'd gone to a windowless room on the ground floor and waited until the sirens sounded the all clear. There had been such a sense of urgency then: but now none of it remained. It was as though the house were already empty

Manju stayed in bed with the baby while the bombs fell. That night the infant's voice seemed louder than ever: louder than the sirens, the bombs, the distant explosions. After a while Manju could no longer bear the sound of the child's crying. She climbed out of bed and went down the stairs. She opened the front door and stepped into the compound. It was very dark except for distant flames and flashes of light shooting through the sky.

She saw another figure ahead of her and somehow, even in the darkness, she knew that it was Rajkumar. This was the first time that she'd seen him since Neel's death. He was still dressed in the clothes that he'd been wearing that morning: a pair of trousers and a shirt that was now blackened with soot. His head was thrown back and he was staring into the sky. She knew what he was looking for and she went to stand beside him.

The planes were far up in the sky, barely visible, like the shadows of moths. She longed for them to come closer; close enough to see a face. She longed to know what kind of being this was that felt free to unleash this destruction: what was it for? What sort of creature could think of waging war upon herself, her husband, her child – a family such as hers – for what reason? Who were these people who took it upon themselves to remake the history of the world?

If only she could find some meaning in this, she knew she would be able to restore order to her mind; she would be able to reason in accustomed ways; she would know when and why it was time to feed the baby; she would be able to understand why it was necessary to take shelter, to care for one's children, to think of the past and the future and one's place in the world. She stood with Rajkumar and looked into the sky. There was nothing to be seen but shadows far above and nearer at hand, flames, explosions and noise.

Doh Say and Raymond returned the next morning, after sheltering in a church through the night. The streets were mostly empty now, they said. The workers who serviced the city were mainly Indians and many of them had fled or gone into hiding. In some areas there was already a stench of uncleared nightsoil. At the port, ships were going up in flames, with their cargoes still intact in their holds. There were no stevedores left to do the unloading: they too were mainly Indian. The administration had opened the gates of the Rangoon lunatic asylum and the inmates were now wandering about trying to find food and shelter. There were looters everywhere, breaking into abandoned houses and apartments, carrying their trophies triumphantly through the streets.

Doh Say said that it was no longer safe to remain in Rangoon. The Packard had miraculously survived the bombing. Raymond had retrieved it and brought it to back to Kemendine. Dolly loaded the car with a few necessities – some rice, dal, milk powder, vegetables, water. Then Raymond took the wheel and they drove out of the house: the plan was that they would all go to Huay Zedi and remain there until conditions changed.

They took the Pegu road, heading northwards. The central areas of the city were eerily empty, yet many major thoroughfares were impassable and they had to circle round and round to find their way out of the city. Buses lay abandoned at intersections; trams had jumped off their tracks and ploughed into the tar; rickshaws lay sidewise across the road; electric cables and tramlines lay knotted across the footpaths.

They began to notice other people – a few scattered handfuls at first, then more and more and still more, until the roads became so thickly thronged that they could barely move. Everyone was heading in the same direction: towards the northern, landward passage to India – a distance of more than a thousand miles. They had their possessions bundled on their heads; they were carrying children on their backs; wheeling elderly people in carts and barrows. Their feet had stirred up a long, snaking cloud of dust that hung above the road like a ribbon, pointing the way to the northern horizon. They were almost all Indians.

There were cars and buses too, along with taxis, rickshaws, bicycles and ox-carts. There were open trucks, with dozens of people squatting in their beds. The larger vehicles kept mainly to the centre of the road, following each other slowly in a straight line. Cars went leapfrogging along this line, passing the buses and trucks with a great trumpeting of their horns. But the press of traffic was such that even they made very slow progress.

At the end of the first day the Packard had not quite left Rangoon behind. By the second day, they had worked their way towards the head of the column of refugees, and now they made better time. Two days later they found themselves looking across the river, towards Huay Zedi.

They made the crossing and stayed in Huay Zedi several weeks. But then it became clear that the Japanese advance was accelerating. Doh Say decided to evacuate the village and move its inhabitants deeper into the jungle. By this time Manju's behaviour had become very erratic: Dolly and Rajkumar decided that she had to be taken home. They elected to make one last effort to reach India.

An ox-cart took them to the river – Manju, Dolly, Rajkumar and the baby. They found a boat that took them upriver, through Meiktila, past Mandalay to the tiny town of Mawlaik, on the Chindwin river. There they were confronted by a stupefying spectacle: some thirty thousand refugees were squatting along the river-bank, waiting to move on towards the densely forested mountain ranges that lay ahead. Ahead there were no roads, only tracks, rivers of mud, flowing through green tunnels of jungle. Since the start of the Indian exodus, the territory had been mapped by a network of officially recognised evacuation trails: there were 'white' routes and 'black' routes, the former being shorter and less heavily used. Several hundred thousand people had already tramped through this wilderness. Great numbers of refugees were still arriving, every day. To the south the Japanese army was still advancing and there was no turning back.

They carried the baby in a shawl that was slung hammock-like over their shoulders. Every few hundred yards they would stop and switch loads, taking turns, all three of them, Manju, Dolly and Rajkumar. They would switch between the baby and the tarpaulin-wrapped packages in which they kept their clothes and their bundle of firewood.

Dolly was using a stick, limping heavily. On the instep of her right foot there was a sore that had first showed itself as an innocuous-looking blister. In three days it had grown into a huge inflammation, almost as wide as her foot. It leaked a foul-smelling pus and ate steadily through skin, muscle and flesh. They met a nurse who said that it was a 'Naga sore'; she said that Dolly was lucky that hers had not been invaded by maggots. She had heard of a case when a boy had developed such a sore in his scalp: when it was treated with kerosene, no fewer than three hundred and fifty maggots were taken out, each the size of a small worm. And yet the boy had lived.

Despite the pain Dolly called herself lucky. They met people whose feet had almost entirely rotted away, eaten by these inflammations: hers was not nearly so badly affected. It made Manju wince to watch her: not because of her obvious pain, but because of her willed imperviousness to it. They were so strong, the two of them, Dolly and Rajkumar, so tenacious – they clung so closely together, even now, despite their age, despite everything. There was something about them that repelled her, filled her with revulsion: Dolly even more than Rajkumar, with her maddening detachment, as though all of this were a nightmare of someone else's imagining.

There were times when she could see pity in Dolly's eyes, a sort of compassion – as though she, Manju, were somehow a sadder creature than she herself; as though it was she who had lost her hold on her mind and her reason. That look made her seethe. She wanted to hit Dolly, slap her, shout in her face: 'This is reality, this is the world, look at it, look at the evil that surrounds us; to pretend that it is an illusion will not make it go away.' It was she who was sane, not they. What could be better proof of their insanity than that they should refuse to acknowledge the magnitude of their defeat; the absoluteness of their failure, as parents, as human beings?

Their firewood was wrapped in big, furry, teak leaves, to keep the rain out. It was tied with a rope that Rajkumar had rolled, from a length of vine. Sometimes the rope would come loose and a stick or a bit of wood would fall out. Every piece that fell out disappeared instantly – being either snatched up by the people behind, or else trampled into the mud, too deep to retrieve.

The mud had a strange consistency, more like quicksand than

clay. It would suck you in, very suddenly, so that before you knew it, you were in thigh-deep. All you could do was keep still and wait, until somebody came to your help. It was worst when you stumbled, or fell on your face; it would cling to you like a hungry animal, fastening upon your clothes, your limbs, your hair. It would hold you so tight that you could not move; it would immobilise your legs and arms, sucking them tightly in place, in the way that glue holds insects.

Somewhere they'd passed a woman. She was a Nepali and she'd been carrying a child in the same way that they were, slung in a folded cloth. She'd fallen face-first in the mud and been unable to move; it was her bad fortune that this happened on an unfrequented trail. There was no one around to help; she'd died where she lay, held fast by the mud with her child tied to her back. The baby had starved to death.

Rajkumar would get very angry if they lost any part of their trove of firewood. It was he who collected most of it. He'd keep watch as they walked and every now and again he'd spot a branch or some twigs that had escaped the notice of the tens of thousands of people who had gone ahead of them, passed the same way, tramping the sodden earth into a river of mud. In the evenings, when they stopped he would walk into the jungle and come back carrying armloads of firewood. Most of the refugees were afraid of leaving the trail; there were persistent rumours of thieves and dacoits, keeping watch and picking off stragglers. Rajkumar went anyway; he said that they could not afford for him to do otherwise. The firewood was their capital, their only asset. At the end of each day it was this wood that Rajkumar bartered for food – there were always people who needed wood; rice and dal were no use without fires to cook them on. Wood bought food more easily than money or valuables. Money cost nothing here. There were people – rich Rangoon merchants – who would give away fistfuls of notes in exchange for a few packets of medicine. And as for valuables, they were just an extra weight. The trails were littered with discarded goods – radios, bicycle frames, books, a craftsman's tools. No one even stopped to look.

They came across a lady one day, dressed in a beautiful silk sari, a peacock-green Kanjeevaram. She looked to be from a wealthy family but she too had run out of food. She was trying to bargain with a group of people who were sitting by a fire. Suddenly she began to undress and when she'd stripped off her sari they saw that she had others on underneath, beautiful, rich silks, worth hundreds of rupees. She offered up one of these, hoping to exchange it for a handful of food. But no one had any use for it; they asked instead for kindling and wood. They saw her arguing vainly with them – and then, perhaps recognising finally the worthlessness of her treasured possession, she rolled the sari into a ball and put it on their fire: the silk burnt with a crackling sound, sending up leaping flames.

The firewood had splinters, which would work their way into your flesh, but Manju preferred carrying the wood to carrying her daughter. The baby cried whenever it came near her. 'She's just hungry,' Dolly would say. 'Give her your breast.' They would stop and she would sit, in the rain, with the baby in her arms. Rajkumar would rig a shelter above them, with leaves and branches.

A little bit further, they said. India isn't far now. Just a little bit more.

There was nothing in her body – Manju was certain of this – but somehow the baby would find a way of squeezing a few drops from her sore, chafing breasts. Then, when the trickle ran dry, she would begin to cry again – in an angry, vengeful way, as though she wanted nothing more than to see her mother dead. At times she would try to feed the baby other things – she would work a bit of rice into a paste and tuck it into a corner of the child's mouth. She seemed to relish the taste: she was a hungry girl, greedy for life; more her grandparents' child than her own.

One day Manju fell asleep sitting up with the baby in her arms. She woke to find Dolly standing over her, looking worriedly into her face. She could hear the buzz of insects, flying around her head. They were the shimmer-winged bluebottles that Rajkumar called 'vulture-flies' because they were always to be seen on people who were too weak to go on – or who were near death.

Manju heard the baby screaming in her lap, but for once the sound did not bother her. There was a restful numbness in her body: she wanted nothing more than to sit there as long she could, relishing the absence of sensation. But as always her tormentors were bearing down on her; Dolly was shouting at her: 'Get up, Manju, get up.'

'No,' she said. 'Please let me be. Just a little longer.'

'You've been sitting there since yesterday,' Dolly shouted. 'You have to get up, Manju, or you'll stay there for ever. Think of the baby; get up.'

'The baby's happy here,' Manju said. 'Let us be. Tomorrow we'll walk again. Not now.'

But Dolly wouldn't listen. 'We won't let you die, Manju. You're young; you have the baby to think of . . .' Dolly took the child out of her arms and Rajkumar pulled her to her feet. He shook her hard, so that her teeth rattled.

'You have to go on, Manju; you can't give up.'

She stood staring at him in the pouring rain, in her white widow's sari, her hair shorn. He was dressed in a tattered longyi, shod in mud-caked slippers. His belly was gone and his frame was wasted with hunger; his face was mottled with white stubble, his eyes blood-shot and red-rimmed.

'Why, old man, why?' she shouted at him. She called him *buro* in contempt; she no longer cared that he was Neel's father and that she'd always been in awe of him: now he was just her tormentor, who would not let her enjoy the rest that she had earned. 'Why do I have to go on? Look at you: you've gone on – and on and on and on. And what has it brought you?'

Then, to her surprise, tears welled up in his eyes and rolled down the cracks and fissures of his face. He seemed like a stricken child: helpless, unable to move. She thought for a moment she'd won at last, but then Dolly stepped in. She took his arm and turned him round so that he was looking ahead, to the next range of mountains. He stood where he was, his shoulders sagging, as though the truth of their condition had finally dawned on him.

Dolly pushed him on. 'You can't stop now, Rajkumar – you have to go on.' At the sound of her voice, some inner instinct seemed to take hold of him. He slung the bundle of firewood over his shoulders and walked on.

There were places where the trails converged and became bottlenecks. Usually these were on the banks of streams and rivers. At each of these crossings there would be thousands and thousands of people gathered together, sitting, waiting – moving through the mud with tiny, exhausted steps.

They came to a river that seemed very broad. It flowed with the speed of a mountain stream and its water was as cold as ice. Here, on a stretch of sandy bank, surrounded by steep jungle, there was the largest gathering of people they had yet come across: tens of thousands – a sea of heads and faces.

They joined this great mass of people and sat squatting, on the river's sandy bank. They waited, and in time, a raft arrived. It was unwieldy-looking and not very large. Manju watched it as it bobbed on the swollen river: it was the most beautiful craft that she had ever seen and she could tell that it was her saviour. It filled up in minutes and went away upstream, chugging slowly round a great bend. She did not lose faith; she was certain that it would return. And sure enough, in a while, the raft came back again. And again and again, filling up in minutes each time.

At last it was their turn and they climbed in. Manju handed the baby to Dolly and found herself a place by the raft's edge, where she could sit by the water. The raft started off and she watched the river rushing past; she could see its whirlpools and its swirling currents – the patterns of its flow and movement were etched on its surface. She touched the water and found that it was very cold.

Somewhere in the distance, she could hear the baby crying. No matter how loud the noise around her, no matter how many people she was surrounded by, she always knew her daughter's voice. She knew that Dolly would soon seek her out and bring the baby to her; that she would stand over her, watching, to make sure that the child was fed. She let her hand fall over the raft's edge and thrilled to the water's touch. It seemed to be pulling at her, urging her to come in. She let her arm trail a little, and then dipped her foot in. She felt her sari growing heavier, unfurling in the water, pulling away from her, tugging at her body, urging her to follow. She heard the sound of crying and she was glad that her daughter was in Dolly's arms. With Dolly and Rajkumar the child would be safe; they would see her home. It was better this way: better that they, who knew what they were living for, should have her in their care. She heard Dolly's voice, calling to her –

'Manju, Manju stop – be careful . . .' – and she knew the time had come. It was no effort at all to slip over, from the raft into the river. The water was fast, dark and numbingly cold.

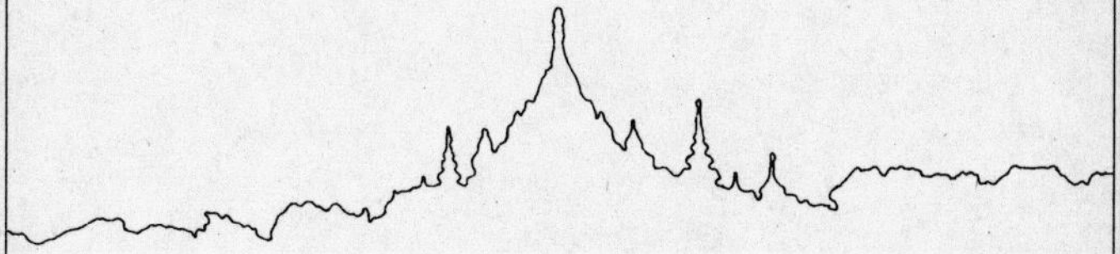

PART SEVEN

The Glass Palace

Forty

Bela was eighteen when Dolly and Rajkumar crossed the mountains. The day when they arrived in Lankasuka was to live in her mind for ever.

This was in 1942, which was as terrible a year as any that Bengal had ever known. At the time, little was known in India about conditions in Burma and Malaya. Because of wartime security, news was sketchy and all the usual channels of communication had broken down. The year before, when the first evacuation ship from Rangoon arrived in Calcutta, Bela and her parents had gone to meet it at the docks. They had hoped to see Manju among the disembarking passengers. Instead they learnt that Rajkumar and his family had decided to stay on in Burma.

Then came the bombing of Rangoon and the great northwards exodus of the Indian population. When the first refugees arrived in Calcutta, Bela sought them out, asking for information, citing names, addresses. She learnt nothing.

It was also in 1942 that Mahatma Gandhi launched the Quit India movement. Uma was one of the many thousands of Congress workers who were imprisoned. Some were gaoled until the end of the war. Uma's stay was relatively short; she fell ill with typhoid and was allowed to return home.

Uma had been home a couple of months when, one afternoon, her elderly gatekeeper came to tell her that there were some destitutes outside, asking for her. This was only too common at the time; Bengal was in the throes of a famine, one of the worst in history. The city was full of starving migrants from the countryside; people were stripping the parks of grass and leaves, sifting through the sewers for grains of rice.

At Lankasuka, such spare food as there was was distributed to the poor once a day. On that particular day, the morning's food distribution was long over. Uma was busy at her desk when the chowkidar walked in to tell her about the destitutes. She said: 'Tell them to come back tomorrow, at the right time.'

The chowkidar went away, only to return shortly afterwards. 'They won't leave.'

Bela happened to be at hand. Uma said: 'Bela, go and see what the matter is.'

Bela stepped out into the courtyard and began to walk towards the gate. She saw a man and a woman holding the metal bars. Then she heard a voice, saying her name, in a hoarse whisper – 'Bela' – and she looked closely at their faces.

Uma heard a scream and ran out into the courtyard. She snatched the keys from the chowkidar's hands. She went running to the gate and threw it open.

'Look.'

Rajkumar was kneeling on the pavement. He held out his arms and they saw that he was holding a child, a baby – Jaya. Suddenly the baby's face turned a bright, dark red and she began to cry at the top of her voice. At that moment the world held no more beautiful sound than this utterance of rage: this primeval sound of life proclaiming its determination to defend itself.

It was not till the latter months of the next year, 1943, that the first rumours of the Indian National Army began to reach India – but this was not the same force that Arjun had joined, in northern Malaya. The first Indian National Army had not lasted long. About a year after its founding, its leader, Captain Mohun Singh, had disbanded it, fearing that the Japanese were trying to take it over. The army was resurrected by Subhas Chandra Bose, the Indian nationalist politician, who reached Singapore in 1943 by way of Afghanistan and Germany. Bose reinvigorated the Indian National Army, drawing tens of thousands of new recruits from the Indian populations of South East Asia: Arjun, Hardy, Kishan Singh, Ilongo and many others joined.

At the end of the war thousands of members of the Indian National Army were brought back to India as prisoners of war. To the British they were JIFs – Japanese Inspired Fifth Columnists. They were regarded as traitors – both to the Empire, and to the Indian army, the bulk of which had continued to fight for the Allies, in North Africa, southern Europe, and finally in the British counter-invasion of Burma. The Indian public, however, saw the matter quite differently. To them imperialism and Fascism were twin evils, one being a derivative of the other. It was the defeated prisoners of the Indian National Army that they received as heroes – not the returning victors.

In December 1945 the colonial government chose to bring charges against three members of the Indian National Army – the famous 'Red Fort Three': Shah Nawaz Khan, Gurbakhsh Singh Dhillon and Prem Sahgal. The country erupted with protests and demonstrations; support committees were formed all over India, despite an official ban. General strikes shut down entire states; students held huge public meetings defying curfew orders. In the southern city of Madurai two people died after the police opened fire on a demonstration. In Calcutta tens of thousands of people poured into the streets. They took over the city for several days. Dozens were shot by the police. In Bombay, naval ratings mutinied. For the Congress Party the trial was a windfall. The party had lost the momentum it had gained in the pre-war years and it badly needed an issue that would serve to mobilise the country. The trial provided just such a cause.

Once the trial got under way, the prosecution quickly ran into problems. It was not able to produce any evidence to link the Indian National Army either with Japanese atrocities in South East Asia, or with the mistreatment of British and Australian prisoners of war. While it did prove that some Indian prisoners had indeed been mistreated, none of these cases had any link with the three defendants.

On December 1, 1945, Bhulabhai Desai, the chief defence lawyer, rose to make his concluding address. 'What is now on trial before this court,' he said, 'is the right to wage war with immunity on the part of a subject race.'

There was essentially only one charge against his clients, he argued, that of waging war against the King. All the other charges, he claimed, were derived from the first. It fell to Desai to demonstrate that international law recognised the right of subject peoples to wage war for their freedom and this he did by citing a series of precedents. He showed that the British Government had itself recognised this right, when expedient, in cases that dated back to the nineteenth century. They had, for example, supported the Greeks and a number of other nationalities in rebellions against the Ottoman Empire; more recently, they had supported the Polish National Army and Czechoslovak rebels; they had similarly insisted on the right of the French maquis to be treated as belligerents even though the Government of Marshal Pétain was at that time the *de jure* and *de facto* Government of France. The trial ended with all three defendants being found guilty of 'waging war against the King'. They were sentenced to transportation for life, but all three had their sentences commuted. They were set free and were received by tumultuous crowds.

Hardy was by this time a national figure (he was later to become an ambassador and a high-ranking official of the Indian Government). He came to see Jaya's grandparents in Calcutta in 1946. It was from him that they learnt that Arjun had died fighting in one the INA's last engagements – fought in central Burma, in the final days of the war.

At this point in the conflict, the Japanese were in retreat and the Allied Fourteenth Army, under the command of General Slim, was advancing rapidly southwards. The Indian units in central Burma were among the last to continue resisting. Their numbers were tiny and they were armed with obsolete weaponry, dating back to the early days of the war. The forces they were fighting against were often mirror-images of what they themselves had been at the start of the war: most were Indians, often from the same regiments, often recruited from the same villages and districts. It was not usual for them to be fighting their younger brothers and nephews.

The Indian National Army's resistance at this stage was largely symbolic, undertaken in the hope of inspiring a revolt in the Indian army. Although they were never a serious threat to the victorious Fourteenth Army they were more than a minor irritant. Many fought and died with great courage, providing heros and martyrs for the movement. Arjun was among those who had died a hero, Hardy said. And so had Kishan Singh. That was all they knew about Arjun's death and they were content that it should be so.

For the next six years Dolly and Rajkumar stayed with Uma, in her flat. The legacy of Rajkumar's quarrel with Uma was forgotten and the baby, Jaya, became a bond linking every member of the household.

Dolly took a job with an army publications unit, translating wartime pamphlets into Burmese. Rajkumar did occasional supervisory work at sawmills and timberyards. In January 1948 Burma gained her independence. Soon after this Dolly decided that she and Rajkumar would return to Rangoon, at least for a while. In the meantime, Jaya was to be left in Calcutta, with her aunt Bela and her other grandparents.

Dolly's eagerness to go back to Burma was due largely to the fact that Dinu had not been heard from in seven years. Dolly believed that he was still alive and she was keen to find him. Rajkumar expressed his willingness to go with her and she booked passages for both of them.

But as the day approached, it became clear that Rajkumar was very far from being certain of his own mind. Over the last six years, he had grown very attached to his orphaned grandchild. More than anyone else in the house, it was he who undertook the responsibilities of her everyday care: he sat with her through her meals, walked with her in the park, told her stories at bedtime. Dolly began to wonder whether he would be able to sustain the pain of wrenching himself away from the child.

The question was settled when Rajkumar disappeared, two days before they were due to depart for Burma. He came back after the ship had sailed. He was contrite and full of apologies; he said he had no memory of where he had been or why he'd gone. He urged Dolly to make another booking; he promised it would not happen again. In the meanwhile, Dolly had decided that it would be better to leave Rajkumar where he was – both for his own sake and Jaya's. Uma for her part made no objection; she was content to have him stay on: he was very little trouble and often made himself useful round the house.

Dolly went back to the steamship company's office and booked a single, one-way passage to Rangoon. She knew that Rajkumar would feel obliged to accompany her if he learnt of her plans. She decided not to tell him. She went about her daily business as usual. On the morning of her departure she cooked *mohingya* noodles, Rajkumar's favourite dish. They went for a walk around the lake and afterwards Rajkumar fell asleep.

It had been arranged that Uma would go with Dolly to the Khidderpore docks. Neither of them said much on the way; there was a finality about this departure that they could not bring themselves to acknowledge. At the end, when Dolly was about to board her ship, she said to Uma: 'I know Jaya will be fine. There are many of you to care for her. It's Rajkumar that I'm worried about.'

'He'll be all right, Dolly.'

'Will you look after him, Uma? For my sake?'

'I will; I promise.'

At Lankasuka, Rajkumar woke to find a note on his pillow: it was written in Dolly's careful hand. He picked up the note and smoothed it down. It said: *Rajkumar – in my heart I know that Dinu is still alive and that I shall find him. After that I shall go to Sagaing as I have so long wanted to do. Know that nothing in this world will be harder to renounce than you and the memory of our love. Dolly.*

He never saw her again.

Forty-one

As the only child in the house, Jaya had the run of Lankasuka when she was growing up. Her aunt Bela lived upstairs, inheriting the flat after her parents' death. She never married and the everyday tasks of looking after Jaya fell mainly to her: it was in her flat that Jaya usually slept and ate.

But Rajkumar was never more than one flight of stairs away: after Dolly's departure, he continued to live on the ground floor, in Uma's flat. He had a small room of his own, next to the kitchen, furnished sparsely, with a narrow bed and a couple of bookshelves.

The only inessential object in Rajkumar's room was a radio – an old-fashioned Paillard with a wooden cabinet, and a textile-covered grille. Rajkumar always took his afternoon siesta with the radio on – it was Jaya who usually turned it off, after coming home from school. The silencing of the radio would often rouse Rajkumar from his nap. He would sit up, leaning back against his pillow, settling his granddaughter beside him. When he put his arm around Jaya's shoulders she would disappear into the crook of his elbow; his hands were huge, the skin very dark, marbled with lighter-coloured veins. The white hairs on his knuckles stood out in startling contrast. He would shut his eyes and the hollows of his face would fill with leathery creases. And then he would begin to talk; stories would come pouring out of him – of places that Jaya had never been to and never seen; of images and scenes that were so vivid as to brim over from the measuring cup of reality into an ocean of dreams. She lived in his stories.

Rajkumar's favourite haunt was a small Buddhist temple in the centre of the city, a place that Dolly had liked to visit too, in the past. This was where Calcutta's Burmese community forgathered, and on special occasions Rajkumar would take Jaya there with him. The temple was on the fourth floor of a tumble-down old building, in an area where the streets were clogged with traffic and the air was dense with diesel smoke. They would make their way across town on a bus and get off at the stop for the Eden Hospital. They'd climb up the grimy marble stairs and when they reached the top, they would step into a hall that seemed a world away from its surroundings: full of light, perfumed with the scent of fresh flowers, its floors shining clean. On the floor there would be rush mats, woven in distinctive patterns: different from Indian mats, although at the same time, not dissimilar.

The temple was always at its liveliest during the great Burmese festivals – Thingyan, the water festival that inaugurated the Burmese New Year; Waso, which marked the beginning of Thadin, the annual three-month period of fasting and abstinence, and Thadingyut, the festival of light, which celebrated its end.

Once, when Jaya was ten, Rajkumar took her to the temple for Thadingyut. The temple was filled with people; women were bustling about in their longyis, preparing a feast; the walls glowed with the shimmering light of hundreds of lamps and candles. Suddenly, in the midst of the noise and the bustle, there was a hush. Whispers ran around the room: 'The Princess . . . the Second Princess, she's coming up the stairs . . .'

The Princess stepped in and there was a quickening of breath, a nudging of elbows; those who knew how performed the shiko. The Princess was wearing a scarlet *htamein* and a kind of sash; she was in her late sixties, with her greying hair tied at the back of her head in a severe little bun. She was tiny, with a kindly face and black, twinkling eyes. She too was living in India then, in the hill-station of Kalimpong. Her circumstances were known to be extremely straitened.

The Princess exchanged a few gracious pleasantries with the people around her. Then her eyes fell on Rajkumar and her face creased into a fond, warm smile. She broke off her conversations; the crowd parted and she made her way slowly across the room. Every eye in the temple was now on Rajkumar. Jaya could feel herself swelling with pride on her grandfather's behalf.

The Princess greeted Rajkumar warmly, in Burmese; Jaya couldn't understand a word of their conversation, but she watched both their faces carefully, studying their changing expressions, smiling when they smiled, frowning when they were grave. Then Rajkumar introduced her: 'And this is my granddaughter . . .'

Jaya had never met a princess before and didn't know what to do. But she was not without a certain resourcefulness; she recalled a movie she had recently seen – was it *Sleeping Beauty* or *Cinderella*? – and sketched the beginning of a curtsey, holding the edge of her dress pinched between finger and thumb. She was rewarded with a hug from the Princess.

Later, people gathered around Rajkumar, wondering why she had singled him out. 'What did Her Highness say?' they asked. 'How did she know you?'

'Oh, I've known her most of my life,' Rajkumar said offhandedly.

'Really?'

'Yes. The first time I saw her was in Mandalay and she was just six months old.'

'Oh? And how did that come about?'

And then Rajkumar would start at the beginning, going back to that day more than sixty years before, when he had heard the sound of English cannon rolling in across the plain to the walls of Mandalay's fort.

In a quiet corner of Lankasuka, there was a niche that served as a shrine to Jaya's parents and her uncle, Arjun. Two framed photographs stood in the niche: one of these was a picture of Manju and Neel, taken at their wedding – they'd been caught glancing up from the sacramental fire, in surprise. The hooded veil of Manju's sari had slipped momentarily from her head. They were smiling, their faces shining and radiant. The photograph of Arjun was taken at Howrah Station: he was in uniform, laughing. A second face was clearlv discernible, over his shoulder: Bela told her niece that this was her uncle's batman, Kishan Singh.

Three times each year, Bela and Jaya would perform a small ceremony at their shrine. They'd garland the photographs and light incense. Bela would hand Jaya flowers, directing her to pay her respects to her mother, her father and Arjun, the uncle she had never known. But when Bela lit the *dhoop* sticks, there were always four bunches, not three. Without ever being told, Jaya knew that the extra one was for Kishan Singh: he too was among their dead.

It was only when Jaya was ten years old, already conscious of a growing interest in cameras and photographs, that it occurred to her to ask her aunt about the pictures and who had taken them.

Bela was surprised.' I thought you knew,' she said in puzzlement. 'They were taken by your uncle Dinu.'

'And who was that?' said Jaya.

This was how Jaya learnt that she had a second uncle, on her father's side – an uncle who had not been memorialised because his fate was unknown. In Lankasuka no one ever spoke of Dinu – neither Rajkumar, nor Uma nor Bela. No one knew what had become of him. He was known to have stayed on at Morningside until the last weeks of 1942. At some point after that he'd left for Burma. Nothing had been heard from him since. Privately everyone suspected that he had become yet another casualty of the war, but no one wished to be the first to voice this fear and, as a result, Dinu's name was never mentioned in the house.

Through the late 1940s, the shadows of the Second World war deepened over Burma. First there were protracted civil conflicts and a large-scale Communist uprising. Then, in 1962, General Ne Win seized power in a coup and the country became subject to the bizarre, maniacal whimsies of its dictator: Burma, 'the golden', became synonymous with poverty, tyranny and misgovernment. Dinu was among the many millions who had vanished into the darkness.

Until the day of her marriage Jaya lived in Lankasuka, with Bela, Uma and Rajkumar. She married young, at the age of seventeen. Her husband was a doctor, ten years older. They were very much in love and a year after the wedding, they had a son.

But when the boy was two years old, tragedy struck: his father was killed in a train accident.

Soon after this Jaya moved back to Lankasuka. With her aunt Bela's support, she enrolled at Calcutta University, took a degree and found a job as a college teacher. She worked hard to give her son a good education. He went to the city's best schools and colleges and at the age of twenty-two he won a scholarship and went abroad.

Now for the first time in years, Jaya had time on her hands. She resumed work on a long-delayed PhD thesis, on the history of photography in India.

In 1996 Jaya's college sent her to an art history conference at the University of Goa. On the way, while changing planes at Bombay airport, she was ambushed by one of the worst of all possible airport experiences: on arriving at the check-in counter she was told that her plane had been overbooked. If she wanted to be sure of a seat she would have to wait at least a couple of days; alternatively the airline would pay for a bus or a train.

Jaya went to another counter, brandishing her ticket. She found herself at the end of a long line of angry people; they were all shouting the same refrain at the desk-clerk: 'But we had reservations . . .'

Jaya was slightly built and of medium height. Her hair was wispy and grey and she looked very much what she was – an unassuming and rather withdrawn college professor who often had difficulty keeping order in class. She knew that there was no point in adding her voice to the chorus of indignation at the counter: where the others had been foiled, no one was less likely to prevail than someone such as herself. She decided to take the train.

Bombay was not a city that Jaya knew well. She collected a voucher and went to Shivaji station on a bus provided by the airline. She bought a railway timetable and learnt that the earliest train was not till several hours later. She got her ticket and then decided to go for a walk. She checked her suitcase into the left-luggage facility and stepped out of the station. It was late afternoon, the start of the rush hour; she allowed herself to be swept along by the surging crowds.

After a while she found herself standing beside the tinted doors of an air-conditioned art gallery. Her breath created a misty halo on the chilled green glass. There was a flyer on the door, announcing an exhibit of newly-discovered work by a pioneering photographer from the early years of the century, a hitherto unknown Parsee woman. At the top of the flyer there was a small graphic, a computer-shrunken reproduction of one of the photographs in the exhibition – a group portrait of four seated figures. There was something about the picture that caught Jaya's eye. She pushed the door open. The gallery was very cold and almost empty. There was the usual surly chowkidar perched on a stool, and behind a desk, a bored-looking woman in a silk sari and diamond nose-ring.

'Could you please show me the picture that's on this flyer?'

The woman must have heard a note of excitement in Jaya's voice for she rose quickly to her feet and led her to the far corner of the gallery. 'That one?'

Jaya nodded. The image was blown up to a great size, larger than a poster, whereas the version she remembered was no bigger than a postcard. She had known the picture all her life, but she was looking at it now as though for the first time. The picture was taken in the garden of the Collector's residence. Four chairs were placed in a semicircular arrangement on a finely trimmed lawn. Uma and her husband were at the centre of the group, and seated beside them, on either side, were Dolly and Rajkumar.

Behind them was a terraced garden, descending steeply down the side of a hill. A number of people were visible in shadowy outline in the middle distance, in carefully arranged postures – servants, grooms and gardeners, all equipped with the instruments of their various trades: sickles, hoes, whips. In the background, stretched across the top of the frame, was a landscape – so sweeping and dramatic that it looked like a painted backdrop: a river curled round a hill and broadened into an estuary, a line of cliffs jutted out into a frothing sea, a palm-fringed beach slid gently into a sun-washed bay.

The Collector was in the foreground, thin and dapper, dressed in a three-button linen suit. He was sitting perched on the edge of his chair like an alert bird, with his head cocked at a stiff and slightly distrustful angle. Uma, on the other hand, seemed very much at ease. There was a certain poise and self-assurance about her demeanour, about the way her hand rested lightly on her knees. She was wearing a plain, light-coloured sari, with an embroidered border; the end was draped shawl-like over her head. Her eyes were large and long-lashed, her face generous but also strong: Jaya remembered it well from her childhood. It was strange, in retrospect, to think how little Uma's appearance had changed over the course of her life.

The gallery owner interrupted these reflections. 'I take it you know this picture?' she said.

'Yes. The woman in the middle was my great-aunt. Her name was Uma Dey.'

And then Jaya noticed a detail. 'Look,' she said, 'look how she's wearing her sari.'

The gallery owner leaned over to examine the print. 'I don't see anything unusual in it. That's how everyone wears it.'

'Actually,' said Jaya, 'Uma Dey was one of the first women in India to wear a sari in this particular way.'

'Which way?'

'The way I'm wearing mine, for example – or you yours.'

The woman frowned. 'This is how saris have always been worn,' she said matter-of-factly. 'Saris are a very ancient garment.'

'Yes, they are,' Jaya said quietly, 'but not the ways of wearing them. The contemporary style of wearing a sari with a blouse and petticoat is not very old at all. It was invented by a man, in the days of the British Raj.'

Suddenly, across the years, she heard Uma's voice, explaining the evolution of sari-wearing. It gave Jaya a thrill, even after all those years, to recall how astonished she'd been when she'd first heard the story. She'd always imagined saris to be a part of the natural order of the Indian universe, handed down from immemorial antiquity. It had come as a shock to discover that the garment had a history, created by real people, through human volition.

On her way out of the gallery, Jaya stopped to buy a postcard reproduction of the picture. On the back there was a brief explanatory note: it said that Ratnagiri lay between Bombay and Goa. On an impulse, Jaya pulled her railway timetable out of her bag: she saw that her train was scheduled to stop at Ratnagiri on its way to Goa. It occurred to her that she could easily stop there for a night or two: the conference wasn't due to start until two days later.

Jaya walked out of the gallery and wandered into an Irani restaurant. She ordered some tea and sat down to think. She was suddenly possessed with the idea of going to Ratnagiri: she'd often thought of going and had always found reasons for putting it off. But perhaps the time was now: the photograph in the gallery seemed to be an indication of some kind – almost a sign. Ratnagiri was the place where her own, very particular, history had had its origins – but the thought of going there unsettled her, stirring up forgotten sediments of anxiety and disquiet.

She felt the need to talk to someone. She paid her bill and went outside. Bracing herself against the crowd, she walked up the street to a long-distance telephone booth. Stepping in, she dialled her own Calcutta number. After two rings her aunt answered. 'Jaya? Where are you?'

'Bombay . . .' Jaya explained what had happened. As she talked, she pictured her aunt, standing over the chipped black phone in her bedroom, frowning anxiously, her gold-rimmed reading glasses slipping down her long thin nose.

'I'm thinking of spending a couple of nights in Ratnagiri,' Jaya said. 'My train stops there, on the way to Goa.'

There was a silence. Then she heard Bela's voice, speaking quietly into the phone. 'Yes – of course you must go; you should have gone years ago . . .'

Ratnagiri's setting was every bit as spectacular as Jaya had imagined. But she quickly discovered that very little remained of the places that she had heard about as a child. The jetty at Mandvi was a crumbling ruin; the Bhagavati temple, once just a spire and a shrine, was now a soaring mass of whitewashed concrete; Outram

House, where King Thebaw and his entourage had lived for some twenty-five years, had been torn down and rebuilt. Ratnagiri itself was no longer the small, provincial town of Thebaw's time. It was a thriving city, with industries clustered thickly around it on all sides.

But the strange thing was that through all of this, the town had somehow succeeded in keeping King Thebaw and his memory vibrantly alive. *Thiba-Raja* was omnipresent in Ratnagiri: his name was emblazoned on signs and billboards, on street-corners, restaurants, hotels. The King had been dead more than eighty years, but in the bazaars people spoke of him as though they'd known him at first hand. Jaya found this touching at first, and then deeply moving – that a man such as Thebaw, so profoundly untransportable, should be still so richly loved in the land of his exile.

Jaya's first real find was the site of the Collector's residence – the place where Uma had lived. It turned out that it was right around the corner from her hotel, on the crest of a hill that overlooked the bay and the town. The compound was government property and it was surrounded by a massive, forbidding wall. The hillside – thickly forested in Uma's time – had since been cleared, with the result that the view was even more dramatic than before, a vast panorama of river, sea and sky. Ratnagiri lay spread out below, the perfect model of a colonial district town, with an invisible line separating its huddled bazaars from the 'Cutchery' – the red-brick Victorian compound that housed the district courts and offices.

Impatient for a glimpse of the Collector's residence, Jaya piled a few bricks against the compound's walls and climbed up to look inside. She found another disappointment lying in wait: the old bungalow was gone, with its Grecian portico and its sloping lawn and terraced gardens. The grounds had been split up to accommodate several smaller houses.

Jaya was about to jump down when she was accosted by an armed guard. 'Hey you,' he shouted. 'What are you doing? Get down from there.'

He came running up and fired off a volley of questions: Who was she? Where was she from? What was she doing there?

To distract him, she produced the postcard she had bought at the gallery in Bombay. It had exactly the effect she had hoped for. The guard stared at the picture and then led her down the road to a lookout point, on a tongue of land that hung poised above the valley.

'There's the Kajali river,' he said, pointing, 'and that over there's the Bhate beach.'

Then he began to ask questions about the people in the photograph – the Collector, Uma. When his finger came to Rajkumar, he laughed.

'And look at this fellow,' he said, 'he looks as though he owns the place.'

Jaya looked more closely at the picture. She saw that there was indeed a jaunty tilt to Rajkumar's head, although he looked otherwise quite solemn. His face was massive and heavy-jawed, his eyes grave; he appeared gigantic beside the slim, diminutive form of the Collector. He was dressed in dark trousers, a linen jacket and a round-collared shirt. His clothes were neither as elegant nor as finely cut as the Collector's, but he looked much more at ease; his legs were negligently crossed, and he had a slim silver cigarette case in one hand. He was holding it up as though it were an ace of trumps, pinched between finger and thumb.

'That was my grandfather,' Jaya said, by way of explanation.

The guard had already lost interest in Rajkumar. Through all this his eyes had kept straying to Dolly, seated in her corner beside Uma, her body half turned against the camera as though to defend herself from its gaze.

Dolly was dressed in a green silk longyi and a white blouse. Her face was long and slender, with a scaffolding of finely moulded bones standing outlined beneath her skin. Her hair was tied back, but a single strand had escaped, curling down from her temple. She was wearing no jewellery, but she had a spray of flowers, white-petalled frangipani, pinned above one of her ears. In her hands she was holding a garland of white jasmine.

'She's very beautiful,' said the guard.

'Yes,' said Jaya. 'Everybody said so . . .'

The next day was Jaya's last in Ratnagiri. In the late afternoon she hired a scooter-rickshaw and asked the driver to take her to the

Bhate beach. The scooter drove through the town, past the red-brick buildings of the high school and college, over the bridge that crossed the estuary, to a beach on the southern side of the bay. In the distance, the sun had swelled to fill the mouth of the bay, growing ever larger as it dipped towards the horizon. The sand was copper-coloured and it slipped beneath the water at a gentle incline. Coconut palms grew thick along the edge of the beach, their trunks leaning thirstily into the wind. Along the line where the sand changed into soil there was a densely tangled accumulation of grass and shells and dried seaweed.

It was there, hidden in the undergrowth, that Jaya found what she was looking for – a small stone memorial to her great-uncle, the Collector. The engraved lettering was worn thin by the combined action of wind, water and sand. There was just enough light to read the inscription. It said: 'To the memory of Beni Prasad Dey Esq., District Collector, 1905–1906.' Jaya stood up to look at the windswept beach, sloping gently down to the waves. The red sand had turned grey with the setting of the sun. Uma had told her, long ago, that if she were to walk from the memorial stone to the water, in a straight line, she would cross the very spot where the Collector's body had been found, along with the wreckage of his capsized boat.

Forty-two

On her return to Calcutta, Jaya began to look through the huge collection of documents and papers that Uma had left her, in her will. Jaya had occasionally toyed with the idea of writing a biography of her great-aunt; an important publisher had even offered her a contract once. Jaya knew that there had been a great revival of interest in Uma recently, as a pioneering political figure. There was bound to be a biography soon – she was loath to think that it would appear under someone else's name.

It took Jaya several days to sort through Uma's papers, many of which had been eaten into by insects. The strange thing was that the more she read, the more she found herself thinking of Rajkumar. It was as though in this one regard, childhood habits of associative reasoning had remained with her. Through all the years that she'd known him, her grandfather had lived downstairs, in a small anteroom in Uma's flat. There was no inference of conjugality in these living arrangements: Rajkumar's status in the household was understood to fall somewhere between that of poor relative and employee. But the geography of the house being what it was, it meant that for Jaya, to think of the one was to think of the other: to go down to see her grandfather meant also seeing her great-aunt.

Recollections came flooding back to Jaya. She remembered the particular tone of voice in which Rajkumar would say, several times each day: 'Ah, Burma – now Burma was a golden land . . .' She remembered how he'd liked to smoke Burmese-style cheroots – longer and thicker than bidis but not as dark nor as big as cigars. Cheroots of this kind were not easily to be had in India, but there were certain substitutes that Rajkumar deemed acceptable. Not far from Lankasuka there was a paan shop that stocked these cheroots. Jaya would sometimes walk to this shop with her grandfather. She remembered how he'd narrow his eyes when he was lighting a cheroot. Then he would blow out a huge cloud of grey smoke and begin: 'Ah, Burma – now . . .'

The paan-wallah who owned this shop was more irascible than most. She remembered an occasion when she'd heard him snap at Rajkumar: 'Yes, yes, no need to tell us again. Your Burma is so golden you can pluck nuggets out of people's farts . . .'

She remembered how she'd go with Rajkumar to visit the Burmese temple in north Calcutta. She remembered the people who'd gather there – many of them Indians, people who'd left Burma in 1942, just like Rajkumar. There were Gujaratis, Bengalis, Tamils, Sikhs, Eurasians. In the temple they would all speak Burmese. Some had done well after their departure. They'd built new businesses, made new homes for themselves; others had dedicated themselves to their children and grandchildren – in much the same way that Rajkumar had built his new life around Jaya. Not all the people who came to the temple were Buddhists, by birth or conviction. They came because this was the one place where they could be sure of meeting others like themselves; people to whom they could say, 'Burma is a golden land' knowing that their listeners would be able to filter these words through the sieves of exile, sifting through their very specific nuances. She recalled how they had thirsted for news of Burma – longed to hear word of those who had been left behind. She remembered the stir that greeted new arrivals; how they would be besieged with questions: 'And what about . . . ?' '. . . and did you hear about so-and-so?'

Rajkumar was always the noisiest of the questioners, taking advantage of his booming voice to shout questions – questions about someone with a Burmese name; someone whom she had not known to be her uncle until Bela told her at the age of ten – her uncle Dinu, whom she'd never met.

These memories provoked a new chain of thought. Jaya put away Uma's papers and pulled out a file of her own – of old clippings that she had compiled over the last nine years. She'd started the file in 1987, on reading about the birth of a democracy movement in Rangoon. These events had rekindled a dormant interest in the land of her birth. She had tracked the emergence of the movement's leader, Aung San Suu Kyi, and had cut out many magazine and newspaper articles. In August 1988 when the military junta struck back, imprisoning Aung San Suu Kyi and unleashing a savage campaign of repression, Jaya had sat up nights, listening to the BBC. She had bought pamphlets that described the bloodshed that followed: the mass shootings, the imprisonments, the scattering of the activists.

Now, as she looked through the yellowing contents of her file, Jaya's attention was caught by a magazine photograph: a picture of Aung San Suu Kyi. It struck her that there was something different about the photograph; it had a quality that set it apart from most magazine illustrations. The photographer had caught Aung San Suu Kyi's fine-boned face in a moment of quiet reflection; there was something in the framing of the picture that reminded her of the silver-framed photographs that stood on Bela's dresser.

Jaya glanced at the line of fine print on the top edge of the picture. The photograph had been credited to one U Tun Pe. She said the name out loud and something stirred, deep within the settled sediments of her memory. She got up and went to Bela's room. 'Do you remember Dinu-kaka's Burmese name?'

'Let me see . . .' Bela paused, running her fingers through her short-clipped white hair. 'It was Tun – something. Of course, in Burma the prefix changes as you grow older. If you're a woman it goes from Ma to Daw and if you're a man, you're Maung and then Ko and then U. So if he were alive today, he would be U Tun . . . Something like that anyway.'

Jaya produced the picture and pointed to the credit line. 'Could it be this?'

Wrinkling her nose, Bela squinted through her gold-rimmed glasses. 'U Tun Pe? Let me see . . .' She mumbled under her breath: 'Ko Tun Pe . . . U Tun Pe . . . Why yes! That sounds right . . .' She turned the cutting over. 'But when was this picture taken?'

'Nineteen-eighty-eight.'

Bela pursed her lips. 'I know what you're thinking, Jaya. But don't get carried away. It could be someone else. In Burma thousands of people have the same name. And in any case, Dinu would have been seventy-four in 1988. That is to say, he'd be eighty-two if he were still alive. And he was never robust, what with his leg. It's very unlikely . . .'

'You're probably right,' Jaya said, taking the picture back. 'But I still have to find out. I have to know for sure.'

It was Bela who provided Jaya with her next lead. She gave her a name: Ilongo Alagappan. 'Try to find him – if anyone knows about Dinu it will be him.'

Over the last two years, in order to keep in touch with her son, Jaya had familiarised herself with e-mail and the Internet. She had an account at a commercial computer centre and the next time she went by, she bought herself a half-hour on the Web. First, she keyed in a search under the words: 'U Tun Pe'. Nothing turned up. She rested her fingers on the keyboard and took a deep breath. Then she typed in the words 'Ilongo Alagappan' and hit 'enter'.

The search engine quivered, like a hound that had sniffed a hot trail. For a long, nerve-racking minute, an icon winked on the monitor. Suddenly the screen quivered again and a message appeared: the list of entries under 'Ilongo Alagappan' ran to five hundred and sixty items. Jaya got up from her chair and went to the manager's desk. 'I think I'm going to need an extra hour. Maybe two . . .'

She went back to her seat and started with item number one. She began to copy paragraphs into a separate file. She discovered that Ilongo was a prominent figure in Malaysian politics; he'd been a minister in the Government and had been honoured with a title – 'Dato'. His career had started after the war, when plantation workers had begun to form trade unions. Many had become active in politics and Ilongo was one such; in a few short years he had become one of the most important trade-unionists in the country – something of a legend in the plantations. He had founded a co-operative and had raised enough money to buy the Morningside plantation. This was at a time when rubber prices had slumped and thousands of workers were losing their jobs. He had been responsible for transforming Morningside into one of the flagship enterprises of the co-operative movement. The plantation workers' unions had grown into an extraordinary success story: there were health-care systems, pensions, educational programme, worker-retraining projects.

One of the items on the screen listed a web page for the 'Morningside Co-operative'. Jaya decided to take a chance. She logged in and left a message for Ilongo. She introduced herself and said that she was gathering material for a book – on her great-aunt Uma and her grandfather, Rajkumar. She very much wanted to interview him, she wrote; she would be grateful for the favour of a response.

The next day she got a phone call from the manager of the computer centre. He was very excited. 'Good news, didi! Message for you! From Malaysia! We are all so happy! Someone is sending you a plane ticket . . .'

So striking was Ilongo's resemblance to Rajkumar that when Jaya first set eyes on him, at the Sungei Pattani railway station, the hairs rose on the back of her neck. Like Rajkumar, Ilongo was built on a generous scale: he was tall, wide-shouldered, very dark, and he too had a substantial belly, of the kind that is produced not by lethargy but rather by an excess of energy – his stomach was like an extra fuel tank, strapped to the outside of a truck. His hair was white and rumpled and he had a great deal of it, all over him – his arms, his chest, his knuckles: its lightness was a startling contrast to the colour of his skin. His face, like Rajkumar's, was deeply creased, with heavy dewlaps and jowls; it was enormous, thorny, and it seemed to be constructed mainly of armature, as though nature had equipped it for survival in the deep seas.

Only his speaking voice came as a true surprise. He sounded nothing like Rajkumar, in either English or Hindustani. His English was distinctively Malaysian – soft, peppered with floating interrogatives – *la?* – a very engaging, congenial manner of speech.

They stepped out of the station and Ilongo led her to a boxy, four-wheel-drive Toyota Land Cruiser. The vehicle's doors bore the logo of the co-operative that owned Morningside. They climbed in and Ilongo took out a flat tin box and lit a cheroot. This added to the eerie resemblance to Rajkumar.

'So tell me about your book,' he said. 'What is it going to be about?'

'I'm not sure yet,' she said. 'Maybe after I've interviewed you, I'll have a better idea.'

On the way to Morningside, Ilongo told her a little about his career and about the making of the Morningside co-operative. Timothy Martins, Alison's brother, had served in the US army during the war, as an interpreter. He'd been in the Pacific Theatre and at the end of the war, he'd come to Sungei Pattani for a brief visit. Ilongo had gone to see him. 'Aren't you going to visit Morningside?' he'd asked. Timothy had answered with a flat 'No'. He had no wish to return; the estate was a living reminder of everything that he wished to erase from his memory – the death of his parents, his sister, his grandfather; he wanted nothing so much as to be rid of it. Besides he had no interest in running a plantation. It was clear that the future of rubber, as a commodity, was none too bright. The war had stimulated research; substitutes were on their way. 'I'm going to put Morningside up for sale,' Timothy had told Ilongo. 'You should let everyone know.'

The estate was on the market for almost two years. There were no buyers. Timothy was not the only businessman who could see that the demand for rubber had run its course. All over Malaya, thousands of plantation workers were out of work; investors were buying up estates and selling off the land in parcels. In the end Ilongo had decided to make matters into his own hands: it was either that, or seeing everyone thrown out. He'd gone around with a begging bowl – quite literally – and in the end the money had been found.

'There it is,' Ilongo said proudly, pointing ahead. 'Morningside.'

They drove under an arched sign. The legend *Morningside Estate* was emblazoned across it in fine but faded Gothic characters. Underneath, in brighter, but more simple lettering there appeared the words: *A property of the Malaysian Plantation Workers'*

Co-operative. Gunung Jerai lay directly ahead, its peak veiled by a dense curtain of cloud.

The road headed uphill, snaking through alternating tracts of rubber and a crop of another kind – a short, stubby palm. These were oil palms, Ilongo explained, currently a more profitable investment than rubber: the plantation was increasing the acreage of the one at the expense of the other.

Jaya was fascinated by the oil palms: clusters of yellowish-orange fruit hung from the stub-like trunks, each as big as a lamb. The air was very still and it seemed to have the texture of grease. Between the palms there were bird-houses elevated on poles. These were for owls, Ilongo explained: the oil-rich fruit attracted great quantities of rodents; the birds helped keep their numbers under control.

Then Morningside House appeared ahead. It was freshly painted and had a bright cheerful look: its roof and shutters were red, while the rest of the house was a pale lime-green. There were trucks and cars parked in front – under the porch and all along the driveway. People were bustling about all over the grounds.

'The house seems very busy,' Jaya said.

'It is,' said Ilongo. 'I like to feel that it's being put to good use. I and my family occupy just one part of it: the rest of it serves as the co-op's office. I didn't want the house to become a monument. It's better this way: it serves a useful function.'

They drove round the house to the rear entrance. Mrs Alagappan, Ilongo's wife was waiting for them. She was tall and grey-haired, dressed in a green silk sari. The two of them lived alone in their part of the house: their children were grown up, all of them 'well settled and doing fine'. One of their daughters was in the civil service; another was a doctor; their son was a businessman, based in Singapore.

'It's just the two of us now.'

Every year, in the winter, they took a holiday on a cruise ship. The house was filled with mementoes of visits to South Africa, Mauritius, Fiji, Australia; there was a picture of the two of them dancing in a ship's ballroom. She was in a silk sari; he in a grey safari suit.

Mrs Alagappan had prepared *idlis* and *dosas* in anticipation of

Jaya's arrival. After lunch she was shown up to the guest room. She walked through the door and found herself facing the mountain through an open window. The clouds had cleared from the peak. On a wall beside the window there hung a photograph of the same view.

Jaya came to a dead stop, looking from the picture to the mountain and back. Ilongo was standing behind her. She turned to him. 'Dato?' she said. 'Who took that picture?'

He smiled. 'Who do you think?'

'Who?'

'Your uncle – Dinu.'

'And do you have other photographs of his?'

'Yes – many. He left a huge collection here, with me. That's why I wanted you to come. I thought he would have wanted you to have them. I'm getting old now, and I don't want them to be forgotten. I wrote to Dinu to ask what I should do but I never heard back . . .'

'So you're in touch with him then?'

'I wouldn't put it like that – but I had news of him once.'

'When?'

'Oh, it was a while ago now . . .'

Some five years earlier, Ilongo said, the co-operative had decided to start a programme for migrant workers. Malaysia's increasing prosperity had begun to draw many migrants from all over the region. Some of these workers were from Burma (or Myanmar as it was now called). It was not very difficult to cross clandestinely from Myanmar to Malaysia: the borders of the two countries were separated only by a few hundred miles of coastline. Among the Myanmarese migrants, there were some who'd been active in the democracy movement. They'd been driven underground after the crackdown of 1988 and had later decided to flee across the border. Quite by chance, Ilongo had met an activist of Indian origin – a young student who'd known Dinu well. He'd said that when he'd last heard of him, Dinu was living alone in Rangoon – Yangon as it was now called.

For over thirty years, Ilongo learnt, Dinu had been married to a well-known Burmese writer. His wife, Daw Thin Thin Aye, had been closely involved with the democracy movement. After the crackdown, both she and Dinu had been gaoled. They'd been let out after serving three years. But Daw Thin Thin Aye had contracted tuberculosis in prison and had died within a year of her release. That was four years ago, in 1992.

'I asked if there was any way I could contact him,' Ilongo said. 'The boy told me it wouldn't be easy – the junta has barred Dinu from having a phone or a fax. Even letters aren't safe, but that was the only way, he said. So I wrote, but I never heard back. I suppose someone kept the letter . . .'

'But you have an address for him then?' Jaya said.

'Yes.' Ilongo reached into his pocket and took out a sheet of paper. 'He has a small photo studio. Does portraits, wedding pictures, group photographs. That sort of thing. The address is for his studio: he lives right above it.'

He held the paper out to her and she took it. The sheet was smudged and crumpled. She peered at it closely, deciphering the letters. The first words that met her eyes were: *'The Glass Palace: Photo Studio.'*

Forty-three

A few months later, Jaya found herself walking down a quiet and relatively uncrowded street in one of the older parts of Yangon. The flagstones on the footpaths were buckled and broken and weeds were growing out of the cracks. The houses along the road had plaster walls, most of them patched and discoloured. She caught glimpses of courtyards with trees growing over the doors. It was mid-December, a clear, cool day. There was very little traffic; children were back from school, playing football on the road. Barred windows looked down on the street from either side: it occurred to Jaya that she was the only person in sight who was dressed in anything other than a longyi; women in saris were few, and trousers seemed to be worn almost exclusively by policemen, soldiers and men in uniform. She had the feeling that she was being observed by a great many eyes.

Jaya's visa allowed her just one week in Myanmar. This seemed a very short time in which to find someone. What if Dinu were away, visiting friends, travelling? She had nightmare visions of waiting in a dingy hotel, in a place where she knew no one.

Earlier, at the airport in Calcutta, she had found herself exchanging glances with her fellow-passengers. They'd all been trying to sum each other up: why was he or she going to Yangon? What sort of business would take a person to Myanmar? All the passengers were Indians, people like herself; she could tell at a glance that they were going for exactly the same reason that she was: to look for relatives and to explore old family connections.

Jaya had gone to some trouble to get a window seat on the plane. She had been looking forward to comparing her experiences of the journey to Yangon with all the accounts she had heard over the years. But once she was seated, a sense of panic set in. If she were to find Dinu, what was the surety that he would be willing to talk to her? The more she thought of it the more the imponderables seemed to mount.

Now here she was, on a street that bore the same name as the one on the address. The numbering of the houses was very confusing. There were numerals and fractions and complicated alphabetical demarcations. Small doorways led into courtyards that proved to be alleys. She stopped to ask directions at a pharmacy. The man behind the counter looked at her piece of paper and pointed her to the adjoining house. She stepped out to find herself looking at a pair of street-level doors that led to the outer room of a large old-style house. Then she noticed a small, hand-painted sign, hanging above the doorway. Most of the lettering was in Burmese, but at the bottom, almost as an afterthought, there were a few words in English: *The Glass Palace: Photo Studio.*

Clearly she was in the right place, but the door was locked and it was evident that the place was closed. She was about to turn away, in disappointment, when she saw that the man in the pharmacy was gesturing in the direction of an alley, right next to the Glass Palace. She looked round the corner and saw a door that seemed to be fastened from the inside. Beyond lay a courtyard and the threshold of an old warren of a house. Glancing over her shoulder, she saw that the pharmacist was signalling vigorously, apparently urging her to step through. She knocked and when there was no answer, she banged hard, thumping the wood with the heel of her palm. Suddenly the doors flew apart. She stepped through and found herself in a walled courtyard. A couple of women were squatting in a corner, tending a cooking fire. She went up to them and asked: 'U Tun Pe?' They nodded, smiling, and pointed to a spiral staircase that led to the second floor: evidently Dinu lived in an apartment that was situated directly above his studio.

Climbing the stairs, Jaya became aware of a voice speaking in Burmese. It was the voice of an old man, quavering and feeble: the speaker appeared to be delivering some kind of discourse – a lecture or a speech. He was speaking in staccato bursts, the sentences punctuated by coughs and pauses. She came to the landing that led to the apartment: dozens of pairs of slippers and rubber sandals lay on the floor. The doors of the apartment stood open, but the entrance was angled in such a way that she could not see in. It was clear, however, that large numbers of people were gathered inside and it occurred to her that she might have stumbled upon a political meeting, even a clandestine one; she began to wonder whether her presence would constitute an unwelcome intrusion. Then she had a surprise: she heard the speaker uttering some words that were not Burmese; they were names that were familiar to her from the history of photography – Edward Weston, Eugène Atget, Brassaï. At this point, curiosity triumphed over discretion. She kicked off her slippers and stepped up to the door.

Beyond lay a large room with a high ceiling: it was crammed full of people. A few were sitting on chairs but most were seated on mats, on the floor. The crowd was larger than the room could comfortably hold and despite the presence of several whirring table fans, the air was hot and close. At the far end of the room there were two tall windows with white shutters. The walls were a dank, patchy blue and parts of the ceiling were blackened with soot.

The speaker was sitting in a rattan armchair that was draped with a green antimacassar. His chair was so positioned that he was facing most of his listeners: she found herself looking at him directly, from across the room. His hair was neatly cropped and parted, grey only at the temples. He was wearing a dark purple longyi and a blue knit T-shirt, with some kind of logo embroidered on the chest. He was rail-thin and his forehead and cheeks were deeply scored, with creases and fissures that seemed to move with the fluidity of ripples on water. It was a very fine face, suffused with the enrichment of age: the mobility of its lines created the impression of a range of perception and feeling that exceeded the ordinary by several extra registers.

It struck Jaya for the first time that she had never seen a picture of her uncle Dinu: he'd always been behind the camera, never in front of it. Could this be he? Jaya saw no resemblance to Rajkumar: to her he looked completely Burmese – but then this was true of many people of Indian, or part-Indian parentage. Either way, she could not be sure.

Jaya noticed now that the speaker was holding something in his hands – a large poster. He appeared to be using it to illustrate his lecture. She saw that the picture was of a shell, closely photographed. Its voluptuously rounded tail curled into a trunk that seemed almost to rise out of the print's surface. She recognised it as a reproduction of a monumental Weston nautilus.

Jaya had been standing at the door a couple of minutes without being noticed. All of a sudden every eye in the room turned in her direction. There was a silence and the place seemed to fill, almost instantaneously, with a fog of fear. The speaker put away the poster and rose slowly to his feet. He alone seemed calm, unafraid. He reached for a cane and came limping up, dragging his right foot behind him. He looked into her face and said something in Burmese. Jaya shook her head and tried to smile. He saw that she was a foreigner and she could almost hear him breathing a sigh of relief.

'Yes?' he said quietly in English. 'May I help you?'

Jaya was about to ask for U Tun Pe when she changed her mind. She said: 'I'm looking for Mr Dinanath Raha . . .'

The creases of his face seemed to shimmer, as though a gust of wind had blown suddenly across a lake. 'How did you know that name?' he said. 'It's many, many years since I last heard it used.'

'I'm your niece,' she said. 'Jaya – your brother's daughter . . .'

'Jaya!'

Jaya realised that they had somehow switched languages and he was now speaking to her in Bengali. Letting his cane drop, he put a hand on her shoulder and looked at her closely, as though searching for a confirmation of her identity. 'Come and sit beside me,' he said, his voice falling to a whisper. 'I'll just be a few more minutes.'

Jaya helped him back to his chair and sat cross-legged on the floor while he resumed his lecture. She was facing Dinu's audience now and she saw that it consisted of a motley mix of people, old and young, girls and boys, men and women. They were all Burmese but some looked to be of Indian origin, some Chinese. Some were smartly dressed while others were wearing cast-offs.

There was a student in a black cap that said *Giorgio Armani*, and in one corner there sat a group of three monks in saffron robes. They were all listening to Dinu with intent attention; some were taking notes.

Rows of glass-fronted bookcases ringed the floor. On the walls there were dozens, perhaps hundreds of photographic reproductions that looked as though they had been cut out of books and magazines. Some were in wooden frames; some were pasted on cardboard. She recognised several of them; they were all reproductions of well-known photographs: there was a famous Weston image of a sea-shell; a print of Cartier-Bresson's veiled women, standing grouped on a Kashmir hilltop; there was a Raghubir Singh picture of an old house in Calcutta.

In one corner of the room there stood a brightly decorated table. A hand-painted banner hung above: it said: 'Happy Birthday'. On the table there were paper cups, snacks, presents wrapped in paper . . .

She wished she knew what was going on.

Dinu's talk ended in a wild outburst of cheering and laughter. He smiled and turned to her with apologies for keeping her waiting. 'You found me in the middle of my weekly session . . . I call it my *glass palace* day.'

'It was not a long wait,' she said. 'What were you talking about?'

'Pictures . . . photography . . . anything that comes to mind. I just start them off – then it's everyone else's turn. Listen.' He smiled, looking round the room: it was filled with the noise of a dozen different conversations. At the back, a handful of people were blowing up balloons.

'Is it a class?' she asked. 'A lecture course?'

'No!' He laughed. 'They just come . . . every week . . . some are new, some have been here before. Some are students, some are artists, some have aspirations to becoming photographers . . . Of course most of them cannot afford a camera – you know how poor we are in our *Myanmar*' – he laughed satirically as he said the word '– and even if they could, they would not be able to pay for film or printing or developing . . . But some of them have money – perhaps their parents are smugglers or contractors or colonels . . . I don't ask . . . It's better not to know. They take pictures and bring them here . . . We pass them around and discuss them . . . Or else I show them copies of old photographs and we talk about why they are good or why they are not. The Glass Palace is the only place in Yangon where you can see things like this . . . works of contemporary art . . .' He lifted his cane and pointed to his bookcases. 'Books, magazines . . . these are very hard, almost impossible to find here, because of the censors. This is one of the few places where they are to be found. People know, so they come . . .'

'How did you acquire these books?' she asked.

'It was hard . . .' He laughed. 'I made friends with ragpickers and the people who sort through refuse. I told them what I wanted and they saved them for me. The foreigners who live in Yangon – the diplomats and aid-workers and so on – they tend to read a lot . . . there's not much else for them to do, you see . . . they're watched all the time . . . They bring books and magazines with them and from time to time they throw them away . . . Fortunately the military does not have the imagination to control their trash . . . These things find their way to us. All these bookcases – their contents were gathered one at a time, by ragpickers. I sometimes think how astonished the original owners would be if they knew . . . It took me a long time . . . Then word got around and people began to come . . . they came, they looked and often they couldn't understand what they saw, so they would ask me and I would give them my opinion. First it was just a few people, then there were more . . . and more. Now they come every week . . . Even when I'm away they come . . . someone else talks . . . they look at pictures . . . Those who can afford it make a contribution – for tea, sweets, snacks. Those who can't don't . . . no one's ever been turned away. Today it's someone's birthday . . .' He pointed across the room to a young man. 'His friends are having the party here. That happens often . . . here they feel free to enjoy themselves . . . I encourage them to say whatever they like . . . to speak freely, even of simple things – for them this is an adventure, a discovery . . .'

'What do you mean?'

'You have to understand,' he said, 'that all their lives they've been trained to obey . . . their parents, their teachers, the military . . . this is what their education teaches: the habit of obedience . . .'

He laughed, his eyes twinkling. 'When they come here . . . they find that no one will scold them for what they say . . . they can criticise even their parents if they wish . . . this is a very shocking idea for many of them . . . some of them never come back . . . but many do, again and again . . .'

'Do they talk about politics too?'

'Yes. All the time. It is impossible not to, in Myanmar . . .'

'Doesn't the military do anything? Don't they try to stop you? Send spies?'

'Yes, of course. They send spies . . . There are probably a few here right now – in Myanmar there are always spies, everywhere. But no one ever discusses organisational matters here; we talk only of ideas and they know, also, that I'm not directly involved in the movement any more . . . my body won't allow me . . . They look at me and they see a tired old cripple . . . in a way my body protects me . . . You have to understand that their brutality is of a strangely medieval ilk . . . they are not so advanced as to be able to perceive a threat in what we do in this room. They would never be able to understand the attraction that brings people here, even though some of them are their own children . . . nothing that interests them is here – no booze, no drugs, no conspiracy . . . that is what protects us. And when we talk of politics it is in such ways that they cannot follow . . . we don't say things they can pin down . . . in Myanmar nothing that is worth saying can be spoken in ordinary language . . . everyone learns other means of communication, secret languages. Today for example, I was talking about Edward Weston's theory of pre-visualisation . . . that you must see the truth of your subject in your mind . . . after that the camera is incidental, unimportant . . . If you know the truth of what you see, the rest is mere execution. Nothing can come between you and your imagined desire . . . No camera, no lens . . .' He shrugged, smiling. 'To that list I could have added: No band of criminals like this regime . . . But I did not have to tell them that in so many words . . . They understood what I was saying . . . they knew . . . you saw how they laughed and clapped . . . Here in the Glass Palace photography too is a secret language.'

At the other end of the room, the birthday party was getting under way. A clamour arose for Dinu's presence at the table. He got to his feet and went over, leaning heavily on his stick. There were dishes of fried savouries, a cake, and a couple of large plastic bottles of Coca-Cola. A large can of Canadian beer stood at the centre of the table, untouched and immaculate, like an ornamental epergne. Dinu explained that one of the Glass Palace regulars was the son of a top general. He attended in secret, without his family's knowledge. From time to time he brought along a few items that were otherwise available only to smugglers and the junta's top brass. The beer can had stood on the table for more than a year.

Someone began to strum a guitar. A chorus started up and the cake was cut. Dinu presided over the celebration with benevolent good humour and there was a great deal of joking and lightheartedness. Jaya remembered one of Rajkumar's favourite sayings: 'Nowhere do they have such a gift for laughter as they do in Burma . . .' Yet it was evident that the laughter here had a special edge, honed upon fears that were never quite absent. It was a greedy kind of merriment, as though everyone wanted to have their fill while they could.

In other parts of the room a number of arguments and discussions were under way. Occasionally Dinu would be appealed to by one group or another. After one such intervention he turned to Jaya, in explanation: 'They're arguing about the picture that I was talking about – Weston's nautilus . . . some of them see themselves as revolutionaries . . . they insist that aesthetic matters have no relevance to our situation . . .'

'And what was your answer?'

'I quoted Weston . . . Weston reflecting on Trotsky . . . that new and revolutionary art forms may awaken a people or disturb their complacency or challenge old ideals with constructive prophecies of change . . . It doesn't matter . . . every week this comes up . . . every week I say the same thing.'

Presently a couple of young men took up a collection and went out to get biryani from a nearby shop. They were back in a few minutes, loaded down with paper packets. Dinu filled a plate and handed it to Jaya: she was surprised by how good the biryani was.

Slowly, as the evening neared its end, everyone grew quieter. A subdued resignation seemed to set in, as though darkness were knocking at the windows, providing a reminder of the constancy of its vigil.

Shortly before nine, Dinu said to Jaya: 'Where are you staying?'

She told him: it was a small hotel, picked at random.

'I would ask you to stay here,' he said. 'I live alone and you could look after yourself . . . It would be easy . . . But unfortunately the procedure takes a long time.'

'Procedure for what?' She was startled.

'For guests,' he said apologetically. 'Don't forget that you are in Myanmar. Nothing is simple here . . . Every household has a registered list of members . . . Nobody else can spend the night there without permission. I know a woman who after three years of marriage has to apply every week to be included in her husband's family's "guest list" . . .'

'And where does this permission come from?'

'The Chairman of the Ward Council . . . there's one in each neighbourhood . . . they can make your life hell . . . everyone hates them . . . mine is especially bad. So, you see, I would ask you to stay, but . . . The police make regular checks, especially at night. You never know when they're coming . . .'

Dinu gave Jaya a pat on the back: 'You'd better go now . . . the others will walk you back to your hotel . . . you will have been seen coming here, you may be sure of that . . . Was there a man in the pharmacy next door? There you are . . . If he isn't there by any chance, wait till he's seen you going . . . If he doesn't see you leaving you can be sure that there will soon be a knock on my door. Come back tomorrow . . . early . . . I'll get some pictures ready. We'll talk for as long as you want . . . We'll do nothing but talk . . . Every day that you're here . . .'

Forty-four

Dinu left Malaya shortly after Alison's death. Following the Japanese occupation, there was turmoil on the rubber estates. Many hundreds of workers left Morningside to join the Indian Independence League and the Indian National Army. Ilongo was one of them, and it was through him that Dinu came to know that Arjun had been one of the first to join Captain Mohun Singh's INA. The movement gathered such force that Dinu was powerless against it. His own views on the war remained unchanged, however, and after the news of Alison's death reached Morningside, he decided to cross over clandestinely into Burma.

Dinu eventually left Malaya in a fishing boat. Sailing mainly by night, hopping from island to island, he managed to make his way along the Isthmus of Kra. The boat left him on a beach, a few miles short of Mergui, the southernmost town in Burma. Dinu had hoped to make his way to Rangoon by land, but the Japanese invasion of Burma was now fully under way. The routes to the north were cut off.

Accompanying the Japanese ground forces was a small group of Burmese volunteers – the Burma Independence Army. This group was led by an acquaintance of Dinu's from Rangoon, the student leader, Aung San. As the Japanese army advanced, there were bloody clashes between the student-led group and some of the peoples of the border area – especially the indigenous Christians, many of whom remained loyal to the British. The border region was thrown into turmoil and there was no question of travelling north. Dinu remained in Mergui for several months.

By the time Dinu made his way to Rangoon, it was June 1942

and the city was under Japanese occupation. Dinu went to Kemendine and found the house gutted: the compound had suffered a direct hit. Dinu went to look for Thiha Saw, his old friend. He learnt that Thiha Saw, along with many other leftists, had escaped to India; his family had dispersed into the countryside. Only Thiha Saw's grandmother was still in Rangoon: she was being looked after by a young relative, a girl by the name of Ma Thin Thin Aye. Thiha Saw's relatives took Dinu in and gave him shelter; it was from them that Dinu learnt of Neel's death and of his family's subsequent departure for Huay Zedi.

North of Rangoon there was still fierce fighting between the Japanese forces and the retreating British army. To travel through the countryside at this time was very nearly an impossibility: all road and rail traffic was strictly controlled, through an elaborate regimen of cards and permits. The Japanese had installed a new government in Rangoon, under the leadership of a Burmese politician, Dr Ba Maw. Aung San and many others from the Burma Independence Army were members of this government – among them several former friends and acquaintances of Dinu's from Rangoon University.One of them helped him procure a pass that allowed him to travel north.

Dinu arrived at Huay Zedi only to find his family gone and the village almost deserted. He discovered that the sympathies of the people of this region were firmly with the Allies: Raymond was one of many men from Huay Zedi who had been recruited into an Allied partisan group – Force 136.

On receiving word of Dinu's arrival, Raymond materialised suddenly, to welcome him back. Raymond was no longer the sleepy-eyed student of Dinu's memory: he was wearing a khaki tunic and carrying a gun. He explained that his father, Doh Say, had urged Rajkumar and Dolly to stay on and had promised to do everything he could to ensure their comfort and safety. But after Neel's death Manju had become increasingly erratic in her behaviour and, in the end, fearing for her sanity, Rajkumar and Dolly had decided to take her back to India. They had left several months before Dinu's arrival; he had no hope of catching up with them now. Dinu decided to remain with Doh Say and Raymond, in their camp deep inside the jungle.

In 1944, the Allies launched a counter-invasion of Burma, spearheaded by the Fourteenth Army, under the command of General Slim. Within a few months the Japanese were pushed back from the Indian frontier and by early 1945 they were in headlong retreat. They were dealt a final blow by General Aung San who dramatically reversed his allegiances: although the Burma Independence Army had entered the country with the aid of the Japanese, they had never been more than reluctant allies for the occupiers. In 1945 General Aung San issued a secret order to his followers to join the drive to push the Japanese out of Burma. After this it was clear that the Japanese occupation was almost at an end.

But the fighting was not over yet. One day in March 1945, Doh Say sent for Dinu; he explained that he had received some worrying news. There had been a great battle at the town of Meiktila, some hundred miles to the north. The Fourteenth Army had won a decisive victory and the Japanese were in precipitate retreat. But a few last diehards from the Indian National Army were still battling on in central Burma, harrassing the advancing Allied army. One of these units had strayed across the Sittang and was believed to be advancing in the direction of their camp. Doh Say was concerned that the soldiers might cause trouble for the villagers; he wanted Dinu to seek them out and intercede with them. His hope was that by virtue of his Indian connections, Dinu would be able to persuade them to stay away from their village.

Dinu set off the next morning. Raymond went with him, as a guide.

After a few days' wait, a meeting was arranged, through the headman of a village. It was held at an abandoned teak camp, deep in the jungle. The camp was an old one, of the kind that Dinu had heard his father describe – with a teakwood tai standing at the centre of a large clearing. This camp had been abandoned for many years, since long before the war. Much of it had been reclaimed by the jungle; the clearing was covered in four-foot-high grass, and many of the oo-sis' huts had been blown over by wind and rain.

Only the tai was still standing, though its ladder was entwined with vines and parts of its roof had fallen in.

Dinu's instructions were to wait alone. Raymond led him to the edge of the clearing and then slipped back into the forest. Dinu stood in front of the tai, in a position where he could be observed from a distance. He was dressed in a brown longyi and a homespun, black-and-white Karen tunic. He had stopped shaving after his arrival at Huay Zedi and his beard had greatly altered his appearance. He had a red-and-white cloth tied around his neck and he was carrying a woven shoulder bag, with some food, water and tobacco.

There was a tree-stump directly in front of the tai, and Dinu seated himself on it. A gentle breeze started up, rustling the tall grass in the camp clearing. Beyond, wisps of mist were rising from the tops of the hundred-foot trees that surrounded the camp. The greenery was a dense, blank wall: Dinu knew that the Indian soldiers were somewhere beyond, watching him.

In his cloth shoulder bag Dinu had some packets of boiled rice, wrapped in banana leaves. He opened one, and began to eat. While eating he listened to the sounds of the forest: a commotion among a flock of parrots told him that the soldiers were approaching. He sat still and went on eating.

Presently, from the corner of his eye, he saw an Indian soldier stepping into the clearing. He rolled his banana leaf into a ball and tossed it away. The soldier's head was just visible: he was wading through the grass with a high-stepping motion, using his gun to sweep aside the undergrowth.

Dinu watched the man approach. His face was so gaunt that he looked almost wizened – although Dinu guessed, from his carriage and his build, that he was in his early twenties. His uniform was in tatters and his shoes were so badly worn that his toes were visible; the soles were tied to his foot with bits of string. The soldier stopped a couple of feet from Dinu and made a gesture with the tip of his rifle. Dinu stood up.

'I have no weapons,' he said in Hindustani.

The soldier ignored him. 'Show me what's in your bag,' he said.

Dinu opened the mouth of his cloth bag.

'What's inside?'

Dinu reached in and took out his water-container and a leaf-wrapped packet of boiled rice. There was a look in the soldier's eyes that gave him pause. He undid the strings of the packet and handed it to him.

'Here,' he said. 'Take it. Eat.'

The soldier held the packet to his mouth and wolfed the rice down. Dinu saw that his condition was even worse than he'd first thought: the whites of his eyes had a jaundiced tinge and he looked malnourished, with discolourations on his skin and blisters at the corners of his mouth. After watching him for a minute, it seemed to Dinu that there was something about the soldier that looked familiar. Suddenly he knew who it was. In a disbelieving voice he said, 'Kishan Singh?' The soldier looked at him uncomprehendingly, narrowing his yellow-flecked eyes. 'Kishan Singh – don't you remember me?'

The soldier nodded, still holding the rice to his mouth. His expression changed hardly at all: it was as though, by this time, he were too fatigued to make the effort of recognition.

'Kishan Singh,' Dinu said, 'is Arjun with you?'

Kishan Singh nodded again. Then he turned on his heel, tossed the leaf wrapper aside and went back into the trees.

Dinu reached into his cloth bag. He took out a cheroot and lit it with a shaking hand. He seated himself again on the tree-stump. In the distance, another figure had stepped into the clearing, followed by a group of some thirty men. Dinu stood up. For some reason he couldn't understand, his palms had begun to sweat, dampening his cheroot.

Arjun stopped a few paces away. He and Dinu stood facing each other across the tree-stump. Neither of them said a word. At length Arjun gestured at the tai. 'Let's go up there.'

Dinu nodded his agreement. Arjun set his men on guard round the tai, and he and Dinu climbed up the ladder, seating themselves on the rotting floor planks. Close up, Arjun looked to be in an even worse way that Kishan Singh. A part of his scalp had been eaten away by a sore; the wound extended from above his right ear, almost as far as his eye. His face was covered in lacerations and insect bites. His cap was gone and so were the buttons of his uniform; his tunic was missing a sleeve.

Dinu would not have come if he'd known that he would be

meeting Arjun. It was now more than three years since they had last met and so far as Dinu was concerned Arjun was guilty, by association, for much of the horror and devastation of those years. Yet now that they were face to face, Dinu felt neither anger nor revulsion. It was as though he were looking not at Arjun, but at his pounded remains, the husk of the man that he had once been. Dinu opened his cloth bag and took out his remaining packets of rice.

'Here,' he said. 'You look as if you need something to eat.'

'What is it?'

'Just some rice . . .'

Arjun raised the packets to his nose and sniffed them. 'That's good of you,' he said. 'The men will be grateful . . .'

He got up and went to the ladder. Dinu heard him telling his men to distribute the rice among themselves. When he came back, Dinu saw that he had given away all the packets. He understood that pride would not allow Arjun to accept food from him.

'What about a cheroot?' Dinu said. 'Can I give you one of those?'

'Yes.'

Dinu handed him a cheroot and struck a match. 'Why are you here?' Arjun said.

'I was asked to come,' Dinu said. 'I've been living in a village . . . not far from here. They heard that your men were heading in their direction . . . They were worried.'

'They have nothing to worry about,' Arjun said. 'We try to stay away from local people. We have no dispute with them. You can tell them they're safe – from us at any rate.'

'They'll be glad.'

Arjun drew on his cheroot, and blew the smoke out through his nose. 'I heard about Neel,' he said. 'I'm sorry – for you, for Manju . . .'

Dinu acknowledged this with a gesture.

'And what about your family?' Arjun said. 'Have you had any news – of Manju? The baby?'

'I haven't heard anything for the last three years,' Dinu said. 'They were here for a while . . . after Neel died . . . they were in the same place that I am now . . . with old family friends. Then they went to Mawlaik, to try to cross over . . . They haven't been heard from since . . . my mother, my father . . . None of them . . .'

Dinu chewed on his thumbnail and cleared his throat. 'And did you hear about Alison . . . and her grandfather?'

'No.' Arjun's voice was a whisper. 'What happened?'

'They were heading south from Morningside . . . the car broke down and they ran into some Japanese soldiers . . . they were both killed . . . but she fought back . . .'

Arjun covered his face with his hands. Dinu could tell from the rhythmic tremor in his shoulders that he was sobbing. Dinu felt only pity for Arjun now. He reached across the floor and put an arm around his shoulders.

'Arjun . . . Stop . . . It won't help . . .'

Arjun shook his head, violently, as though he were trying to wake himself from a nightmare. 'Sometimes I wonder if it'll ever end.'

'But, Arjun . . .' Dinu was surprised by the gentleness in his own voice. 'Arjun . . . it was you . . . you who joined them . . . of your own free will. And you're still fighting on – now . . . even after the Japanese . . . Why? What for?'

Arjun's looked up, his eyes snapping. 'You see, Dinu – you don't understand. Not even now. You think I joined *them*. I didn't. I joined an Indian army that was fighting for an Indian cause. The war may be over for the Japanese – it isn't for us.'

'But, Arjun . . .' Dinu's voice was still gentle. 'You must see that you don't have a hope . . .'

At this, Arjun laughed.

'Did we ever have a hope?' he said. 'We rebelled against an Empire that has shaped everything in our lives; coloured everything in the world as we know it. It is a huge, indelible stain which has tainted all of us. We cannot destroy it without destroying ourselves. And that, I suppose, is where I am . . .

Dinu put his arms round Arjun again. He could feel tears welling up in his eyes, yet there was nothing he could say; there was nothing to be said.

This is the greatest danger, he thought, this point at which Arjun has arrived – where, in resisting the powers that form us, we allow them to gain control of all meaning; this is their moment of victory: it is in this way that they inflict their final and most terrible defeat. For Arjun, now, he felt not pity but compassion: what must it be like to visualise defeat so accurately, so completely? There was a sort of triumph in this – a courage – the value of which he did not wish to diminish by arguing.

'I should go now,' Dinu said.

'Yes.'

They climbed down the vine-swathed ladder. At the bottom, they embraced again.

'Be careful, Arjun . . . be careful.'

'I'll be all right.' Arjun smiled. 'One day we'll laugh about this.' He waved and walked away into the shoulder-high grass.

Dinu leant against the tai's ladder and watched him go. Long after the soldiers were gone, he remained where he was. When Raymond appeared, out of the darkness, Dinu said: 'Let's stay here tonight.'

'Why?'

'I don't feel well enough to go.'

This encounter with Arjun left Dinu profoundly shaken: now, for the first time, he began to understand the irreducible reality of the decision that Arjun had made; he saw why so many others whom he'd known – men such as Aung San – had made the same choices. He began to doubt his own absolute condemnation of them. How does one judge a person who claims to act on behalf of a subordinated people, a country? On what grounds can the truth of such a claim be established or refuted? Who can judge a person's patriotism except those in whose name he claims to act – his compatriots? If the people of India chose to regard Arjun as a hero; if Burma saw Aung San as her saviour – was it possible for someone such as him, Dinu, to assume that there was a greater reality, a sweep of history, that could be invoked to refute these beliefs? He could no longer be confident that this was so.

Forty-five

Arjun's unit had initially numbered about fifty men: only twenty-eight now remained. Very few of these had been lost to hostile fire: most of the losses were due to desertion.

At the outset, the unit was evenly split between professional soldiers and volunteers. The professionals were those who'd been recruited in India, men like Kishan Singh, and Arjun himself. When Singapore fell, there were some fifty-five thousand Indian troops on the island. Of these more than half joined the Indian National Army. The volunteers were recruits from the Indian population in Malaya and most of them were Tamil plantation workers.

In the beginning some of Arjun's fellow-officers had been sceptical about the abilities and endurance of the new recruits. The army that had trained them, the British Indian army, had not recruited Tamils: they were counted as one of the many Indian groups that were racially unfit for soldiering. Being professional soldiers, Arjun's fellow-officers were steeped in the racial mythologies of the old mercenary army. Even though they knew those theories to be without foundation, they found it hard to rid themselves entirely of the old imperial notions about the kinds of men who made good soldiers and those who didn't. It was only under fire that they'd come to recognise how false those myths were: experience had demonstrated the plantation recruits to be, if anything, much hardier and more dedicated than the professionals.

In his own unit, Arjun found that there was a clear pattern to desertions: the men who'd melted away were almost all professionals; not a single plantation recruit had left. He'd been puzzled by this until Kishan Singh explained the reasons behind it. The professionals knew the men on the other side; the men they were fighting against were their relatives and neighbours; they knew that if they went over, they wouldn't be badly treated.

Arjun could tell that the plantation workers understood this too. They knew who the professional soldiers were and what class they came from; they knew exactly how their minds worked and why they deserted. Every time a few more 'professionals' went missing, Arjun would see a deepening contempt in their eyes; he knew that in private the plantation men laughed about the pampered lives the soldiers had been used to, about the way they'd been fed and fattened by their colonial masters. They – the plantation recruits – seemed to have recognised that in the end, theirs wasn't the same struggle as that of the professionals; in a way, they weren't even fighting the same war.

Not all the plantation recruits spoke Hindustani: Arjun often had difficulty in communicating with them. There was only one man with whom Arjun could converse fluently: his name was Rajan. He was a lean, wiry man, all muscle and bone, with red-flecked eyes and a thick moustache. Arjun had recruited him himself, at Sungei Pattani. He'd wondered at the time whether Rajan was suitable material. But after his recruitment, Rajan had become another person altogether: training had transformed him. He seemed to have developed an aptitude for soldiering and had emerged as the most forceful personality among the plantation recruits.

Once, going over a ridge, Rajan had asked Arjun to point in the direction of India. Arjun had shown him: it was to the west. Rajan stood a long time staring into the distance; so did many of the other men.

'Have you ever been to India?' Arjun asked.

'No, sir.' Rajan shook his head.

'What do you think you'll find there?'

Rajan shrugged: he didn't know and in a way, he didn't seem to care. It was enough that it was India.

Arjun discovered later that Rajan had been born in Malaya; his knowledge of India came solely from stories told by his parents. The same was true of all the plantation recruits: they were fighting for a country they had never seen; a country that had extruded their parents and cut them off. This made their fervour all the more remarkable. Why? What were their motivations? There was so much about their lives that he, Arjun, didn't know and could not fathom – the way they talked about 'slavery' for instance, always using the English word. At first Arjun had thought that they were using the term loosely, as a kind of metaphor – for after all, it wasn't true technically that they were slaves; Rajan knew that as well as Arjun did. What did he mean then? What was it to be a slave? When Arjun asked this question Rajan would always answer indirectly. He would begin to talk about the kind of work they'd done, on the plantation – every action constantly policed, watched, supervised; exactly so many ounces of fertiliser, pushed exactly so, in holes that were exactly so many inches wide. It wasn't that you were made into an animal, Rajan said – no, for even animals had the autonomy of their instincts. It was being made into a machine: having your mind taken away and replaced by a clockwork mechanism. Anything was better than that.

And India – what was India to them? This land whose freedom they were fighting for, this land they'd never seen, but for which they were willing to die? Did they know of the poverty, of the hunger their parents and grandparents had left behind? Did they know about the customs that would prevent them from drinking at high-caste wells? None of that was real to them; they had never experienced it and could not imagine it. India was the shining mountain beyond the horizon, a sacrament of redemption – a metaphor for freedom in the same way that slavery was a metaphor for the plantation. What would they find, Arjun wondered, when they crossed the horizon?

And it was in the act of posing this question that Arjun began to see himself through their eyes – a professional, a mercenary, who would never be able to slough off the taint of his past and the cynicism that came with it, the nihilism. He saw why they might think of him with contempt – as an enemy even – for it was true in the end, that he was not fighting their war; that he did not believe as they believed; that he did not dream their dreams.

* * *

It was Rajan who brought Kishan Singh back, with his hands tied, stumbling through the undergrowth. Kishan Singh's condition was such that he hadn't been able to get very far. Rajan had found him holed up under an overhang, hiding, shivering, praying.

Rajan gave Kishan Singh a push, and he fell on his knees.

'Get up,' Arjun said. He couldn't stand to look at Kishan Singh like this. '*Utho* – get up, Kishan Singh.'

Rajan took hold of Kishan Singh's collar and pulled him to his feet. Kishan Singh's frame was so wasted that he was like a stick-figure, a broken puppet.

Rajan had only contempt for Kishan Singh. He spoke to Arjun directly, looking him in the eyes: 'And what will you do with him now?'

There was no 'sir', no 'sahib', and the question wasn't 'what has to be done?' but, 'what will *you* do?' Arjun could see the challenge in Rajan's eyes; he knew what was in Rajan's mind – that the professionals would stick together, that he would find a way of letting Kishan Singh off. Time. He had to make time.

'We have to hold a court-martial,' Arjun said.

'Here?'

Arjun nodded. 'Yes. There's a procedure. We have to try and keep to it.'

'Procedures? Here?' The sarcasm was audible in Rajan's voice.

Arjun could tell that Rajan was trying to show him up in front of the other men. Using the advantage of his height, he went up to him and stared into his eyes,

'Yes,' said Arjun. 'Procedures. And we have to respect them. That's how armies are run – that's what make them different from street gangs.'

Rajan shrugged and ran his tongue over his lips. 'But where?' he said. 'Where are you going to find a place for a court-martial?'

'We'll go back to that teak camp,' Arjun said. 'It'll be easier there.'

'The camp? But what if we were followed?'

'Not yet. We'll go.' The camp was an hour away: it would buy a little time.

'Fall in.' Arjun took the lead. He didn't want to watch Kishan Singh being pushed along, with his hands tied behind his back.

It began to rain and they were drenched by the time they got to the camp. Arjun led the way across the clearing, to the tai. The area under the stilts was dry, sheltered from the rain by the structure above. Rajan let Kishan Singh go and he sank to the ground, squatting on his haunches, shivering.

'Here,' said Arjun. 'We'll hold the hearings here.'

Rajan fetched a chair from the tai and placed it in front of Arjun. 'For you, sir,' he said, with a mocking excess of politeness. 'Since you are the judge.'

Arjun ignored him. 'Let's begin.'

Arjun tried to prolong the ritual, asking questions, going over the details. But the facts were clear: there was no disputing them. When he asked Kishan Singh to speak in his own defence, all he could do was beg, clasping his hands together. 'Sah'b – my wife, my family . . .'

Rajan was watching Arjun, smiling. 'Any other procedures? Sir?'

'No.' Arjun saw that Rajan and the other men had formed a circle: he and Kishan Singh were at its centre. Arjun stood up. 'I've made my decision.' He turned to Rajan. 'I'm putting you in charge of the firing squad,' he said. 'Ask for volunteers. Do it quickly.'

Rajan looked straight back at him, shaking his head. 'No,' he said. 'None of us will volunteer. He's one of yours – one of your men. You will have to deal with him yourself.'

Arjun looked at the circle of men around him. They were all watching him; their faces were expressionless, their eyes unblinking. Arjun turned away; shreds of memory floated through his mind . . . this is how mutiny looks from the other end; you're alone, and the only thing you can fall back on is the authority of a distant chain of command; on threats of the army's justice, of eventual retribution once victory is won. But what do you do when you know that there will be no victory, when defeat is certain? How do you claim the validation of the future, knowing that it will not be yours?

'Come, Kishan Singh.' Arjun helped his former batman to his feet. His body was very light, almost weightless. Arjun could feel his hands growing gentle, as he took hold of Kishan Singh's arm.

It was strange to be touching him in this way, knowing what lay ahead.

'Come. Kishan Singh.'

'Sah'b.'

Kishan Singh stood up and Arjun took hold of his arm, pushing him forward, past the others, out of the tai's shelter, into the rain. They waded into the tall grass and Kishan Singh stumbled. Arjun put his arm round him and held him up. Kishan Singh was so weak that he could barely walk; he rested his head on Arjun's shoulder.

'Keep going, Kishan Singh.' His voice was soft, as though he were whispering to a lover. '*Sabar karo*, Kishan Singh – it'll be over soon.'

'Sah'b.'

When they came to the edge of the clearing, Arjun let him go. Kishan Singh dropped to his knees, holding himself upright by clinging to Arjun's leg.

'Sah'b.'

'Why did you do it, Kishan Singh?'

'Sah'b, I was afraid . . .'

Arjun unbuttoned his leather holster with one hand and took out his sidearm – the Webley that Kishan Singh had always polished and oiled for him.

'Why did you do it, Kishan Singh?'

'Sah'b – I couldn't go on . . .'

He looked down at the welts and jungle sores on Kishan Singh's head. He thought of another time when Kishan Singh had knelt between his feet, asking for his protection; he thought of his guilelessness and trust and innocence, of how he had been moved by the histories that lay behind them – the goodness and strength he had seen in him; all the qualities that he himself had lost and betrayed – qualities that had never been his to start with, he who had sprung from the potter's wheel, fully made, deformed. He knew he could not allow Kishan Singh to betray himself, to become something other than he was – to become a creature like himself, grotesque, misshapen. It was this thought that gave him the strength to put his gun to Kishan Singh's head.

At the touch of the cold metal, Kishan Singh raised his eyes, looking up at him. 'Sah'b – remember my mother, my home, my child . . .'

Arjun took hold of Kishan Singh's head, curling his fingers through his matted hair. 'It's because I remember that I must do this, Kishan Singh. So that you cannot forget all that you are – to protect you from betraying yourself.'

He heard the shot and then he staggered away, towards a clump of trees. He reached for a branch to steady himself, and he saw, suspended in the branches, a dripping shred of flesh and bone. He could not tear his eyes from it: it was a part of Kishan Singh, of the head he'd just held in his hands. He took another step and fell to his knees. When he looked up Rajan and the other men were standing around him, watching. In their eyes there was a kind of pity.

There was rejoicing at the camp when Doh Say decided to move back to Huay Zedi. The march down the slope was a triumphal, joyful parade, complete with drums, flutes and elephants.

Doh Say gave Dinu a small place of his own, at the edge of the village. Dinu was just settling in when Raymond sought him out.

'Come with me,' Raymond said. 'I have something to tell you.'

They went down to the stream, and watched the village children shooting for fish in the shallows of Huay Zedi's stream, with their crossbows and bamboo darts.

'I have some news.'

'What?'

Arjun was dead, Raymond said. He'd been tracked down by a unit from Force 136; they'd caught up with him at the old teak camp.

'Was it you who led them there?' Dinu asked.

'No. A deserter. One of his own men – an old soldier.'

'But you were there?' Dinu said. 'At the end . . .?'

'Yes.'

'What happened?'

'They'd called me in – the people who were hunting him. They'd heard that many of his men had left –'

'So was Arjun alone then?'

'Yes. Completely alone – he was back at the abandoned teak camp. The rest of his men had left, they were all gone – they'd taken off their uniforms, put on longyis and disappeared into the forest. I tried to track them – but it was impossible. They knew the jungle, those men – they'd vanished.'

'And Arjun?'

'There was an Indian colonel there. He tried to get Arjun to surrender, told him that it was over, he would be all right. But Arjun shouted back, calling them slaves and mercenaries. And then he stepped out, on the tai's veranda, shooting . . .'

Raymond stopped to toss a pebble into the stream.

'It was clear,' he said, 'that he did not want to live.'

Forty-six

In 1946, when it became apparent that Burma would soon become independent, Doh Say decided to leave Huay Zedi and move eastwards, into the mountainous regions of the Burma–Thailand border. The war had pitted the peripheries of the country against its centre: Doh Say was one of many who had deep misgivings about what the future held for Burma's minorities.

Most of Huay Zedi's population took Doh Say's advice, Dinu among them. The village was abandoned and its inhabitants settled in Loikaw, a small frontier town, deep in the Karenni hills, not far from the border of Thailand. For Dinu, there was one great advantage to being in Loikaw: he was once again able to find photographic materials – many of them smuggled across the Thai border. He set up a studio and became the only professional photographer within hundreds of miles. Even in difficult times, people married, had children – they needed records and were willing to pay, sometimes in cash but more often in kind.

In 1947, in preparation for the British departure, Burma's first national elections were held. They were won by General Aung San. It was widely believed that he alone would be able to ensure the country's unity and stability. But on 19 July, shortly before he was to assume office, Aung San was assassinated, along with several of his would-be colleagues. Within months of the assassination, a Communist-led insurgency broke out in central Burma. Some of the army's Karen units mutinied. The Karen were the country's largest ethnic group after the Burmans; a major Karen organisation took up arms against the Rangoon Government.

Other groups followed suit. In a short time, there were sixteen insurgencies raging in Burma.

One day, in Loikaw, a boy came running to Dinu's door. 'Ko Tun Pe – someone come looking for you.' Another child followed and then another. They stood in his doorway panting, watching in bright-eyed expectation. They all said the same thing. 'Ko Tun Pe – you have a visitor; she's walking up from the bus station.'

He ignored them; he stayed inside his studio, doing nothing, trying not to look out of the window. Then he heard more voices approaching – a procession appeared to be making its way towards his shack. He could hear people calling out: 'Ko Tun Pe – look who's here!' He saw a shadow on his threshold and looked up. It was Dolly.

It had taken Dolly several months to track Dinu to Loikaw. She had arrived in Burma late in 1948, just as the insurgencies were getting under way. On coming to Rangoon, she'd discovered that the authority of the elected Government did not extend far beyond the capital's municipal limits. Even the areas that bordered Mingaladon airport were in rebel hands. Much of Rangoon was in ruins, bombed to ashes by successive air campaigns. With the Kemendine house burnt to the ground, she had nowhere to stay; a friend gave her refuge.

One day Dolly heard that Dinu's old friend, Thiha Saw, was back in Rangoon, working for a newspaper. She went to see him to ask if he had any news of Dinu. It so happened that U Thiha Saw had recently attended a political conference where Raymond had also been present. U Thiha Saw told Dolly that Dinu was safe, living in Loikaw. Dolly had left Rangoon by boat the next day. After a journey of several weeks she had boarded a rattling old bus that was on its way to Loikaw.

Dolly and Dinu spent days talking. She told him about Neel's death and Manju's death; about the march across the mountains and how she and Rajkumar had made the journey from the Indian border, through Assam, to Calcutta; she explained why she had come back to Burma alone.

He took pictures of her. Dolly was very thin and the bones of her face could be seen as clearly as the ridges of a fluted cup. Her hair was tied tightly back at the nape of her neck: it was still dark and glossy, with only a few white streaks at the temple.

She urged him to write to his father: 'You should go and find him; you would not have the trouble with him that you had before. He is changed, a different man, almost a child. You should go to him; he needs you – he is alone.'

Dinu would make no promises. 'Maybe. Some day.'

He knew, without her telling him, that she had not come to stay. He was not surprised when she said: 'Next week I shall leave for Sagaing.'

He went with her. This was the first time he'd ventured into the plains since the end of the war. He was stupefied by the devastation. They travelled through territories that had been scorched not once but twice by retreating armies. River channels were blocked and railway lines lay mangled on their sleepers. From village to village a different group or party was in charge. Farmers ploughed round bomb-craters; children pointed out the places where mines lay unexploded. They took roundabout routes, skirting round those districts which were said to be particularly dangerous. They walked and hired ox-carts, and took an occasional bus or a river boat. At Mandalay they stopped a night. Much of the fort was in ruins; the palace had been destroyed by artillery fire; the pavilions that Dolly had known had burnt to the ground.

They walked the last few miles to Sagaing and took a ferry across the Irrawaddy. To their intense relief Sagaing was unchanged. The hills were tranquil and beautiful, dotted with thousands of white pagodas. Dolly began to walk faster as they approached the nunnery. At the entrance she held Dinu fast and then Evelyn led her in. The next day, when Dinu went to see her, her head was shaved and she was wearing a saffron robe. She looked radiant.

It was arranged that he would come back to see her again the next year. The time came and he went back, from Loikaw to Sagaing, making the long journey again. At the gates of the nunnery there was a long wait. At length Evelyn came down. She gave him a gentle smile.

'Your mother passed away a month ago,' she said. 'We could

not inform you because of the troubles. You'll be happy to know that it was very quick and she suffered no pain.'

In 1955 Doh Say died, in Loikaw. By this time, he had become a great patriarch and an influential leader. He was mourned by thousands. To Dinu, Doh Say had been almost as much a parent as a mentor: his death was a great blow. Shortly afterwards, Dinu decided to move to Rangoon.

The mid-1950s were a relatively quiet time in Burma. There was a stand-off in the insurgencies and the Government was a functioning democracy. U Thiha Saw had become the editor of one of the country's leading Burmese-language newspapers and wielded considerable influence in Rangoon.

On arriving in Rangoon, Dinu went to see his old friend: he had grown from a thin, tall boy into a portly, authoritative-looking man. He wore colourful longyis and floppy bush shirts, and almost invariably had a pipe in his hands. He gave Dinu a job as a photographer at his newspaper. Later, when Dinu found a suitable place for a studio, it was U Thiha Saw who loaned him the money to buy it.

Some of the best-known photographers of pre-war Rangoon had been Japanese. After the war many had closed down their studios and disposed cheaply of their equipment. In his years in Loikaw, Dinu had made himself an expert in repairing and restoring old and discarded photographic equipment: he was able to set up his studio at very little cost.

U Thiha Saw was one of the first visitors to Dinu's studio. He looked round it with approval. 'Very nice, very nice.' He stopped to puff on his pipe. 'But haven't you forgotten something?'

'What?'

'A signboard. Your studio has to have a name, after all.'

'I haven't thought of a name . . .' Dinu glanced around. Everywhere he looked, his eyes met glass: framed photographs, countertops, camera lenses.

'The Glass Palace,' he said suddenly. 'That's what I'll call it . . .'

'Why?'

'It was a favourite phrase of my mother's,' he said. 'Just something she used to say . . .'

The name stuck and Dinu's work quickly gained a reputation. The Fourth Princess was now living in Rangoon. Her husband was an artist. They were both regular visitors to the Glass Palace. Soon Dinu had more work than he could handle. He asked around for an assistant and U Thiha Saw recommended a relative, a young woman who was in need of a part-time job. This proved to be none other than Ma Thin Thin Aye – the young girl who'd helped to shelter Dinu when he'd passed through Rangoon in 1942. She was now in her mid-twenties, a student at Rangoon University. She was doing research in Burmese literature, writing a dissertation on *The Glass Palace Chronicles* – a famous nineteenth-century history, written in the reign of King Bodawpaya, an ancestor of King Thebaw's. The name of Dinu's studio struck Ma Thin Thin Aye as a happy coincidence. She took the job.

Ma Thin Thin Aye was slim, petite and neat in her movements. Every day, at four in the afternoon, she walked down the street, past the pharmacy, to the wooden door that led to the Glass Palace. Standing outside, she would sing out Dinu's name – 'U Tun Pe!' – to let him know that she'd come. At seven-thirty she and Dinu would close the studio: she'd walk away down the street and Dinu would lock up and go round the corner to climb the stairs to his room.

After a few weeks, Dinu discovered that Ma Thin Thin Aye's mornings were not spent solely on research. She was also a writer. Rangoon had a thriving culture of small literary magazines. One of these had published a couple of her short stories.

Dinu tracked down her stories. They took him by surprise. Her work was innovative and experimental; she was using the Burmese language in new ways, marrying classicism with folk usage. He was astonished by the wealth of allusion, by her use of dialect, by the intensity of her focus on her characters. It seemed to him that she had achieved much that he'd once aspired to himself – ambitions that he'd long abandoned.

Dinu was a little awed, and this made it hard for him to tell Ma Thin Thin Aye of his admiration for her work. Instead, he began to tease her, in his earnest, staccato way. 'That story of yours,' he said, 'the one about the street where you live . . . You say the people on the street are from many different places . . . from the coasts and the hills . . . Yet in your story they all speak Burmese. How is that possible?'

She was not at all put out.

'Where I live,' she said softly, 'every house on the street speaks a different language. I have no choice but to trust my reader to imagine the sound of each house. Or else I would not be able to write at all about my street – and to trust your reader is not a bad thing.'

'But look at Burma,' Dinu went on, still teasing. 'We are a universe on our own . . . Look at all our people . . . Karen, Kayah, Kachin, Shan, Rakhine, Wa, Pa-O, Chin, Mon . . . Wouldn't it be wonderful if your stories could contain each language, each dialect? If your reader could hear the vastness of the music? the surprise?'

'But they do,' she said. 'Why do you think they don't? A word on the page is like a string on an instrument. My readers sound the music in their heads, and for each it sounds different.'

At this point in his life, photography was no longer a passion for Dinu. He did only commercial work, making studio portraits and printing other people's negatives. He bestowed a great deal of care and attention on what he did, but took no particular pleasure in it: mainly he was grateful for possessing a skill that could be parlayed into a livelihood. When people asked him why he no longer photographed outside his studio, he told them that his eyes had lost the habit of looking; his vision had withered for lack of practice.

The photographs that he thought of as his real work, he rarely showed. These pictures were in, any case, very few in number. His early prints and negatives had been destroyed when the Kemendine house went up in flames; the work he'd done in Malaya was still at Morningside. All he possessed of his own work were a few pictures taken in Loikaw – of his mother, of Doh Say and Raymond and their families. Some of these he'd framed and hung on the walls of his apartment. He fought shy of inviting Ma Thin Thin Aye upstairs to see them. She was so young – more than ten years his junior. It mattered very much that she not think badly of him.

A year went by and every day Ma Thin Thin Aye left and entered the studio by the door that led to the street. One day she said: 'U Tun Pe, do you know what I find hardest in my writing?'

'What?'

'The moment when I have to step off the street and go into a house.'

He frowned. 'Why . . . ? Why that?'

She wrung her hands together in her lap, looking exactly like the serious student that she was. 'It is very hard,' she said. 'And to you it may seem like a small thing. But I do believe that it is this moment that marks the difference between classical and modern writing.'

'Of all things . . . ! How so?'

'You see, in classical writing, everything happens outside – on streets, in public squares and battlefields, in palaces and gardens – in places that everyone can imagine.'

'But that is not how you write?'

'No.' She laughed. 'And to this day, even though I do it only in my mind, nothing is more difficult for me than this – going into a house, intruding, violating. Even though it's only in my head, I feel afraid – I feel a kind of terror – and that's when I know I must keep going, step in, past the threshold, into the house.'

He nodded but made no comment. He gave himself a little time to think about what she'd said. One afternoon he bought biryani from Mughal Street and invited her up.

A few months later, they were married. The ceremony was a quiet one and they invited very few people. Afterwards, Ma Thin Thin Aye moved into Dinu's two rooms. She marked off a corner for herself and set up a desk. She began to teach literature at the university. In the afternoons, she still helped at the studio. They were happy, content with the smallness and privacy of their world. Their childlessness did not seem a great lack. Her work began to gain notice, even beyond literary circles. She became one of the select group of Burmese writers whose presence was regularly sought at festivals in the countryside.

One morning, Daw Thin Thin Aye was tutoring a promising young student at the university, when she heard a burst of gunfire close at hand. She went to the window and saw hundreds of young men and women running by, some covered in blood.

Her student pulled her away from the window. They hid under a desk. After a couple of hours they were found by one of Daw Thin Thin Aye's colleagues. There had been a coup, they learnt. General Ne Win had seized power. Dozens of students had been shot down, right inside the university.

Neither Dinu nor Daw Thin Thin Aye had ever been directly involved in politics. After the coup, they kept to themselves and waited for the winds to change. It was not until many years had passed that they realised that this was a storm that had come to stay.

U Thiha Saw was arrested and his newspaper was shut down. General Ne Win, the new dictator, began to juggle with the currency. Notes of certain denominations were declared to be valueless; overnight, millions of kyats became waste paper. Thousands of the country's brightest young people fled into the countryside. Rebellions multiplied and flourished. Raymond went underground with several hundred followers. In the east, on the Thai border, the insurgents gave a name to the territories under their control: they became a Karen Free State – Kwathoolei, with its capital at the riverbank town of Manerplaw.

With each year the generals seemed to grow more powerful while the rest of the country grew ever feebler: the military was like an incubus, sucking the life from its host. U Thiha Saw died at Insein gaol, in circumstances that were not explained. His body was brought home bearing marks of torture and the family was not permitted a public funeral. A new censorship regime developed, growing out of the foundations of the system that had been left behind by the old Imperial Government. Every book and magazine had to be presented to the Press Scrutiny Board, for the perusal of a small army of captains and majors.

One day Daw Thin Thin Aye was ordered to report to the

Scrutiny Board's office. The building was plain and functional, like a school, and its long corridors smelt of toilets and disinfectant. She went to an office with a plywood door and sat for several hours on a bench. When at last she was shown in, she found herself facing an officer who looked to be in his late twenties. He was sitting at a desk and the manuscript of one of her stories was lying in front of him. His hands were in his lap and he seemed to be toying with something – she could not tell what it was.

She stood at the desk, fidgeting with the hem of her blouse. He did not ask her to sit. He stared, looking her up and down. Then he jabbed a finger at the manuscript. 'Why have you sent this here?'

'I was told,' she said quietly, 'that that is the law.'

'The law is for writers,' he said. 'Not for people like you.'

'What do you mean?'

'You do not know how to write Burmese. Look at all these mistakes.'

She glanced at her manuscript and saw that it was covered with red pencil marks, like a badly filled schoolbook.

'I've wasted a lot of time correcting this,' he said. 'It's not my job to teach you people how to write.'

He got up from his chair and she saw that he was holding a golf club in his hands. It struck her now that the room was full of golfing paraphernalia – caps, balls, clubs. He reached for her manuscript and crumpled it into a ball, with one hand. Then he put it on the ground between his feet. He took many little steps, swinging the head of his club back and forth. He swung, and the ball of paper went sailing across the room. He held the pose for a moment, admiring his swing – the bent knee, the flexed leg. He turned to her. 'Pick it up,' he said. 'Take it home and study it. Don't send anything to this office again until you've learnt to write proper Burmese.'

In the bus, on the way home, she smoothed out the pages, one by one. His vocabulary, she realised, was that of a child; he was barely literate. He had run his pencil through everything he hadn't understood – puns, allusions, archaisms.

She stopped writing. Nothing could be published unless it had undergone the board's scrutiny. Writing was hard enough, even with nothing to deal with except yourself. The thought of another such encounter made those hours at the desk seem unendurable.

The newspapers were full of strident denunciations of imperialism. It was because of the imperialists that Burma had to be shut off from the world; the country had to be defended against neo-colonialism and foreign aggression.

These tirades sickened Dinu. One day he said to his wife: 'Look at the way in which these thugs use the past to justify the present. And they themselves are much worse than the colonialists; at least in the old days, you could read and write.'

Daw Thin Thin Aye smiled and shook her head in reproof. She said: 'To use the past to justify the present is bad enough – but it's just as bad to use the present to justify the past. And you can be sure that there are plenty of people to do that too: it's just that we don't have to put up with them.'

Their lives became very quiet and stunted: they were like plants whose roots had been trimmed to contain them inside tiny pots. They mixed with very few people, and were always careful about what they said, even with friends. They grew gnarled with age, inside and outside: they moved round their rooms with slow deliberation, like people who are afraid of knocking things over.

But all was not quiet around them. There were changes under way that they did not know about. Their lives were so quiet, so shut off that they didn't feel the first rumbles under the volcano. The eruption, when it came, took them by surprise.

It started with another of the general's crazed whims – another juggling of the currency. But this time people were not content to see their life's savings turned into waste paper. There were protests, quiet and hesitant at first. One day, in the university, there was a brawl in a teashop – a small, apparently innocuous event. But suddenly classrooms emptied, students came pouring out into the streets; leaders emerged and with astonishing speed, organisations developed.

One day Daw Thin Thin Aye was taken to a meeting. She went unwillingly, pushed on by her students. Afterwards, she helped write a pamphlet. When she picked up the pen her hand was shaking – she saw herself in the censor's office again. But as she began to write, a strange thing happened. With every sentence she saw her crumpled pages coming alive, rising off the floor and hitting back at the golf club, knocking it out of the major's hands.

She began to go to meetings all over town. She tried to get Dinu to come but he resisted. Then one day there was news of a new speaker: she was to address a huge gathering, near the Shwe Dagon – her name was Aung San Suu Kyi and she was the daughter of Dinu's old acquaintance from the university, General Aung San.

Dinu was seventy-four at the time; with age his right leg had grown stiffer and he walked with difficulty, but this new name had an energising effect on him. He went to the meeting and after that he was not able to stay at home again. He began to take pictures; he travelled with his camera, putting together a pictorial record of the movement in its headiest and most joyful days.

On August 8, 1988 Dinu woke up with a mild fever. Daw Thin Thin Aye made him a meal and told him to stay in bed. There was to be an important march in the city that day: she left early in the morning. Some three or four hours later, Dinu heard repeated volleys of gunfire in the distance. He was too ill to go out; he lay in bed and waited for his wife to come home. In the late afternoon there was a knock on the door. He dragged himself out of bed and threw the door open.

There were three or four uniformed policeman standing on the stairs. Behind them were several longyi-clad plain-clothes men.

'Yes?' said Dinu. 'What do you want?'

They pushed past him without a word. He looked on helplessly as they went through the flat, opening cupboards and closets, rifling through their possessions. Then a plain-clothes man pointed to a framed picture of Raymond. The others gathered around, whispering.

One of the policemen came over to Dinu, with the framed photograph in his hand. 'Do you know this man?' he said to Dinu.

'Yes.' Dinu nodded.

'Do you know who he is?'

Dinu picked his words carefully. 'I know his name.'

'Do you know that he's the leader of an insurgency? Did you know that he's one of the most wanted terrorists in the country?'

'No.' Dinu's answer was non-committal.

'Anyway – you will have to come with us.'

'Not right now,' said Dinu. 'I can't. I'm ill and I'm waiting for my wife.'

'Don't worry about her,' said the man in the uniform. 'She's already been taken to a place where she will be safe.'

Forty-seven

On Jaya's last day in Yangon, Dinu promised to take her to 38 University Avenue, to attend a public meeting at Aung San Suu Kyi's house.

The year 1996 marked the sixth of Aung San Suu Kyi's house arrest. Despite her confinement, Aung San Suu Kyi's compound was still the centre of the city's political life. Twice every week, on Saturdays and Sundays, she held a meeting at her house: people gathered outside and she addressed them from the gate. These meetings had become pilgrimages. A hush fell on Rangoon on weekend afternoons and thousands poured into the city from all round the country.

Dinu came to Jaya's hotel to pick her up. A friend of his had driven him there in car – a 1954 Czech-built Skoda. The car was making loud coughing noises as it idled on the street. As she was stepping in, Jaya noticed that the car's doors were all of different colours, all oddly misshapen, as though they'd been banged into shape with sledgehammers.

'What a strange-looking car,' she said.

Dinu laughed. 'Yes . . . this is a car that has been put together entirely from bits of other cars . . . The bonnet is from an old Japanese Ohta . . . one of the doors is from a Volga . . . It's a miracle that it runs at all . . .'

The backfiring of the Skoda's engine echoed through the streets as they drove away. The centre of the city was almost eerily quiet, emptier than Jaya had ever seen it before. But as they went northwards the traffic increased: there were cars, buses, small trucks. They came to a wide, tree-shaded avenue lined with large villas.

They parked a good distance away, and joined the many hundreds of people who were walking down the avenue.

They came to a house with a green and yellow fence. There was a large crowd outside. Not much was visible of the interior of the compound: the house was set well back from the road, surrounded by stands of tall bamboo. The gates were of metal, with spikes along the top. There were some ten thousand people gathered round them, most sitting patiently on the grassy verge that lined the avenue on both sides. The road was kept clear by volunteers and policemen, and traffic was flowing through, right past the gates, at a slow but steady pace.

The volunteers were wearing saffron tunics and green longyis: Jaya learnt that these were the colours of the democracy movement. Dinu was recognised by many of the volunteers. They waved him through to a vantage point that was quite close to the gates. The view was good and Jaya spent a long time looking at the people around her: there were many students and a fair sprinkling of Buddhist nuns and monks, but most of the people there seemed like ordinary folk. There were plenty of women, a large number being accompanied by children. The atmosphere was expectant but not tense; there were many food vendors making their way through the crowd, selling drinks and snacks.

Dinu nudged Jaya's elbow and pointed to a photographer and a couple of men in wire-rimmed sunglasses. 'M.I.,' he said with a chuckle. 'Military intelligence. They will film it all and take it back to their headquarters. Their bosses will watch it tomorrow.'

Jaya noticed that there were many Indians in the crowd. She commented on this to Dinu and he said, 'Yes, you can be sure this fact hasn't escaped the regime ... the official papers often describe these meetings as gatherings of evil Indians.' He laughed.

Suddenly there was a great uproar. 'There she is,' Dinu said. 'Aung San Suu Kyi.'

A slim, fine-featured woman stepped up. Her head was just visible above the gate. Her hair was dark black, and gathered at the neck. She was wearing white flowers above her hair. She was beautiful almost beyond belief.

Aung San Suu Kyi waved at the crowd and began to speak. She was using Burmese and Jaya could not understand what she was saying. But the delivery was completely unlike anything she'd ever heard. She laughed constantly and there was an electric brightness to her manner.

The laughter is her charisma, Jaya thought. She could hear echoes of Aung San Suu Kyi's laughter everywhere around her, in the crowd. Despite the swarming intelligence agents, the atmosphere was not heavy or fear-filled. There was a good-humouredness that seemed very much at odds with the deadened city beyond. Jaya understood why so many people had pinned their hopes on Aung San Suu Kyi; she knew that she herself would have been willing to do anything that was asked of her at that moment: it was impossible to behold this woman and not be half in love.

Both she and Dinu were silent as they walked back to the old Skoda. They got back inside, and presently Dinu said: 'It's strange . . . I knew her father . . . I knew many others who were in politics . . . many men who are regarded as heroes now . . . But she is the only leader I've ever been able to believe in.'

'Why?'

'Because she's the only one who seems to understand what the place of politics is . . . what it ought to be . . . that while misrule and tyranny must be resisted, so too must politics itself . . . that it cannot be allowed to cannibalise all of life, all of existence. To me this is the most terrible indignity of our condition – not just in Burma, but in many other places too . . . that politics has invaded everything, spared nothing . . . religion, art, family . . . it has taken over everything . . . there is no escape from it . . . and yet, what could be more trivial, in the end? She understands this . . . only she . . . and this is what makes her much greater than a politician . . .'

'But if that's true,' Jaya said hesitantly, 'doesn't it make it much harder for her to succeed – as a politician?'

Dinu laughed. 'But she has already succeeded . . . don't you see? She has torn the masks from the generals' faces . . . She has shown them the limits of what she is willing to do . . . and these limits have imprisoned them too . . . she haunts them unceasingly, every moment . . . She has robbed them of words, of discourse.

They have no defence against her but to call her an imperialist . . . which is laughable . . . when in fact, it is they who invoke the old imperial laws and statutes to keep themselves in power. The truth is that they've lost and they know this . . . this is what makes them so desparate . . . the knowledge that soon they will have nowhere to hide . . . that it is just a matter of time before they are made to answer for all that they have done.'

Forty-eight

Dinu came to Jaya's hotel to take her to the airport. On the way, as they were driving through the city in the Skoda, Dinu said: 'You've been here seven days and we've never once spoken of my father.'

'That is true,' Jaya said guiltily.

'Tell me about his last days,' Dinu said. 'Were you with him?'

'Yes, I remember it very well. My great-aunt Uma had died just a few days before, you see. They were almost ninety, both of them . . .'

They died within a few weeks of each other. Uma was the first to go: she died in her sleep and it was Rajkumar who found her. The news caused a stir: she was given a state funeral and the Governor came. The family was pushed quietly to the background.

Rajkumar died of a heart attack, a month later. His funeral was as modest as Uma's had been grand. A few of his friends from the Burmese temple carried his body to the crematorium. Afterwards Jaya and Bela took his ashes to the river. Jaya scattered them in the water.

'I remembered how he'd always said that for him, the Ganges could never be the same as the Irrawaddy.'

Jaya glanced at Dinu and saw that he was crying, tears running down the creases of his face. She reached for his hand.

'You asked me about his last days,' she said, 'and the truth is that what I told you is quite different from what I remember.'

'What do you remember?'

'I remember a story my son told me.'

'Your son? I didn't know you had a son.'

'Yes, I do. He's grown up now. He's been living in America these last few years.'

'And what was his story?'

I was very young, maybe four or five. Lankasuka was my home too; I lived upstairs with my mother and my great-aunt, Bela. Rajkumar lived downstairs, in Uma's flat, in a small room next to the kitchen. In the morning, on waking up, the first thing I would do was to go down to look for him.

That morning I went to Rajkumar's room and found that his bed had not been slept in. I was alarmed. I went running across the flat to Uma's bedroom, to tell her that my great-grandfather was missing.

Although Rajkumar had lived in Uma's flat for some twenty years, there was never any ambiguity about their living arrangements or the nature of their relationship. It was understood by everyone that their connection was one of charity, founded on Uma's affection for Dolly. Uma was a benevolent benefactress; he a near-destitute refugee. His presence in the household did not in any way compromise Uma's reputation as a woman of icy self-containment, a widow who had mourned her dead husband for more than half a century.

The geography of Uma's flat mirrored their relationship. Uma slept in the master-bedroom, overlooking the park; Rajkumar's room was a converted pantry, near the kitchen. It was only in the afternoons that he was allowed into Uma's room and he always sat in the same place – a large divan that was ringed with cotton-stuffed bolsters. They had lived thus for twenty years.

But that morning when I ran into Uma's room, I found, to my surprise, that Rajkumar was in her bed. They were fast asleep, their bodies covered by a thin, cotton sheet. They looked peaceful and very tired, as though they were resting after some great exertion. Their heads were thrown back on a bank of piled pillows and their mouths were open. This was the very pose that we children used in games that required the figuring of death: head bent back, mouth open, tongue protruding between the lips. That I should be confused was only natural.

I shouted: 'Are you dead?'

They woke up, blinking short-sightedly. They were both extremely short-sighted and there ensued a flurry of bed-slapping and pillow-turning as they fumbled for their eyeglasses. In the process, their covers slipped off and their bodies were revealed to be naked. Uma's skin looked very soft and was covered with a delicate tracery of tiny cracks; every single hair on Rajkumar's body had turned white, creating a startlingly elegant effect against his dark complexion.

'Why,' I said stupidly, 'your clothes are off . . .'

They found their glasses and snatched the covers back. Uma produced a loud gargling sound, a kind of volcanic mumble. Her mouth was strangely puckered, and on looking more closely I realised that both she and Rajkumar were without their teeth.

I was fascinated by dentures, as all children are, and I knew exactly where Uma put hers when she retired at night: to prevent them from being knocked over, they were placed out of reach of the bed, immersed in water, in a large glass tumbler.

In an effort to be helpful, I approached the tumbler, so that I could spare them the trouble and embarrassment of getting out of bed naked. But when I looked at the tumbler, I discovered that there was not one, but two sets of dentures inside. What was more, they had somehow become entangled, so that their jaws were interlocked, each reaching deep into the mouth of the other, each biting down on the other's teeth.

In a further effort to be helpful, I tried to pry the dentures apart. But Rajkumar had grown impatient and he snatched the tumbler from me. It was only after he had thrust his teeth into his mouth that he discovered that Uma's dentures were clamped within his. And then, as he was sitting there, staring in round-eyed befuddlement at the pink jaws that were protruding out of his own, an astonishing thing happened – Uma leant forward and fastened her mouth on her own teeth. Their mouths clung to each other and they shut their eyes.

I had never seen a kiss before. In India, in those days, such things were excised from sight by unseen censors, in real life as in film. Even though I did not know that this embrace had a name, I did realise that to remain in that room would be to violate something that was beyond my understanding. I slipped away.

What I saw that morning in my great-great-aunt Uma's bedroom remains to this day the most tender, the most moving sight I have ever seen, and from the day when I sat down to write this book – the book my mother never wrote – I knew that it was this that it would end.

Author's Notes

The seed of this book was brought to India long before my own lifetime by my father and my uncle, the late Jagat Chandra Datta of Rangoon and Moulmein – 'The Prince' as he was known to his relatives. But neither my father nor my uncle would have recognised the crop that I have harvested. By the time I started work on this book, the memories they had handed on to me had lost their outlines, surviving often only as patterns of words, moods, textures. In attempting to write about places and times that I knew only at second- and third-hand, I found myself forced to create a parallel, wholly fictional world. *The Glass Palace* is thus unqualifiedly a novel and I can state without reservation that except for King Thebaw, Queen Supayalat and their daughters, none of its principal characters bear any resemblance to real people, living or deceased.

Perhaps it was the very elusiveness of what I was trying to remember that engendered in me a near-obsessive urge to render the backgrounds of my characters' lives as closely as I could. In the five years it took me to write *The Glass Palace* I read hundreds of books, memoirs, travelogues, gazetteers, articles and notebooks, published and unpublished; I travelled thousands of miles, visiting and re-visiting, so far as possible, all the settings and locations that figure in this novel; I sought out scores of people in India, Malaysia, Myanmar and Thailand. In the process I amassed vast arrears in debts of gratitude – the one kind of insolvency that one may justly consider a form of riches – a roster so large indeed that I can, at best, hope only to make a few gestures of acknowledgement towards the most pressing of these debts.

Of the people who took the time to speak to me during my travels in 1995, 1996, 1997 and 1999, I would particularly like to record my gratitude to the following. In Malaysia: Janaki Bai Devadasan, G. Anthony Samy, E. R. Samikannu, Anjali Suppiah, A. V. Pillai, A. Ponnusamy, R. Chinamma Rangaswamy, S. P. Velusamy; Lt. K. R. Das, Abraham Muttiah, F. R. Bhupalan, M. Y. B. Abbas, M. Gandhinathan, Eva Jenny Jothi, Nepal Mukherjee, N. G. Choudhury, V. Irulandy, S. P. Narayanswamy, S. Natarajan and Y. B. Tan Sri Dato K. R. Somasundaram of the National Land Finance Co-operative Society Ltd. I would also like to thank D. Narain Samy and other members of the staff of the Bukit Sidim Estate for their hospitality during my stay. But I am beholden most of all to the storied Puan Sri Janaki Athinagappan of Kuala Lumpur, who introduced me to many of the above, and who has, over the years, taken me and my family into her own. In Singapore, my thanks go to Elizabeth Choy, Ranjit Das, Bala Chandran, Dr. N. C. Sengupta and particularly my friend Dr. Shirley Chew who opened many doors for me in that city. In Thailand, for their kindness in taking the time to talk to me, I would like to record my gratitude to: Pippa Curwen, U Aye Saung, Khun Kya Oo, Khun Kya Noo, Lyndell Barry, Sam Kalyani, Nyi Nyi Lwin, Abel Tweed, Aung Than Lay, Ma Thet Thet Lwin, Than Kyaw Htay, Oo Reh, Tony Khoon, David Saw Wah, Raymond Htoo, David Abel, Teddy Buri, and particularly Ko Sunny (Mahinder Singh). U Tin Htun (E. C. Nanabawa) also went out of his way to help me during my travels and I owe him many thanks.

In India I would like to thank: Aruna Chatterjee, Col. Chatterjee, Dr. Sugato Bose, Capt. Lakshmi Sahgal, Lt-Gen N. S. Bhagat, Capt. Khazan Singh, Capt. Shobha Ram Tokas, Shiv Singh, Hari Ram, Major Devinder Nath Mohan, Capt. A. Yadav, Barin Das, Tarit Datta, Arabinda Datta and Derek Munro. Mrs Ahona Ghosh kindly allowed me to consult her father's handwritten notes of the 1942 trek; I owe her many thanks. I am also deeply grateful to Nellie Casyab, of Calcutta, a survivor of that great trek which the historian Hugh Tinker calls the 'Forgotten Long March' of 1941. It was she who introduced me to the Burmese and Anglo-Burmese worlds of Calcutta and put me in touch with the few other remaining survivors of that terrible ordeal. I would also like to thank Albert Piperno, another survivor of the trek, for his efforts in recalling the bombing of Rangoon on December 23, 1941. I owe a very special debt to Lieutenant-Colonel Gurubakhsh Singh Dhillon, the last of the 'Red Fort Three', who met with me for several days and spent many hours recounting the events of December 1941.

I greatly regret that, for fear of reprisals against those concerned, I am unable to thank either my friends in Myanmar or those of their compatriots who went out of their way to speak to me, often at no little risk to themselves. I trust that, should any of them ever happen to read this, they will know who they are and understand the depth of my gratitude to each of them.

Sadly, circumstances permit me to acknowledge only one of my most salient debts in Yangon: to the late writer Mya Than Tint, who has been removed by his untimely death from the reach of the regime whose oppressions he had so long and so heroically endured. Mya Than Tint was, for me, a living symbol of the inextinguishable fortitude of the human spirit: although I knew him only briefly, I felt myself to be profoundly changed and deeply instructed by his vision of literature. Everyone who knew him will recognise at once the pervasiveness of his influence on this book.

In the course of writing this book I lost a close friend: Raghubir Singh, the photographer, who was my mentor and teacher in all things relating to photography. It is my great regret that I was unable to acknowledge the depth of my gratitude to him in his lifetime: if I do so now, it is not in the hope of making amends, but rather, in order to record an unrepayable debt. Naturally, neither he nor anyone else named above bears any responsibility for any aspect of the contents of this book, the onus of which rests on me alone.

Amongst published sources my greatest debt is to the monograph *Deposed King Thebaw of Burma in India, 1885–1916* (Bharatiya Vidya Series, Vol. 25, Bharatiya Vidya Bhavan, Bombay 1967) by Walter A. Desai. In his memoir, *The Changing of Kings* (Peter Owen, London, 1985), Philip Glass describes Desai as "a quiet old Indian historian from (Rangoon) University". I like to think of the 'quiet old Indian' living in India in his retirement, sifting through the archives of New Delhi and Bombay as an act of homage and restitution to the country he had lost. Desai's attempt to recover traces of this erased life is to me, in its slow careful unemphatic accumulation of detail, a deeply moving work; an affirmation that every life leaves behind an echo that is audible to those who take the trouble to listen.

Much of the travel and research for this book was supported by *The New Yorker*. I am grateful to many members of the staff of that magazine for their consistent support, and would like to thank, in particular, Tina Brown, Bill Buford, Alice Quinn, Peter Canby and Liesl Schillinger. Thanks also to Laura McPhee, for her help and advice, and to my old friend James Simpson, who has enriched this book immensely by his reading of the manuscript. I am deeply grateful to my editors Susan Watt, Ravi Dayal, Kate Medina and Rukun Advani. To Barney Karpfinger, my agent, who found me the time I needed to write this book and was a pillar of strength through its most difficult moments, my gratitude is beyond measure. To Debbie, my wife, for her unfailing support; and my children, Lila and Nayan, for their forbearance, I am, as ever, deeply beholden.

In the end my greatest debt is to my father, Lieutenant-Colonel Shailendra Chandra Ghosh. He fought in the Second World War as an officer of the 12th Frontier Force Regiment, a unit of the then British-Indian Army. He was in General Slim's Fourteenth Army during the Burma campaign of 1945 and was twice mentioned in dispatches: he was thus among those 'loyal' Indians who found themselves across the lines from the 'traitors' of the Indian National Army. He died in February 1998 and never saw any part of my manuscript. Only in his absence did I come to understand how deeply my book was rooted in his experience, his reflections on the war and his self-questioning: it is to his memory that I dedicate *The Glass Palace*.